The Chronicles of Heaven's War

Sisters of the BloodWind

Ava D. Dohn

ISBN 978-0-9748001-2-7

Published in the United States

This book is dedicated to the silent sentinels who have sacrificed everything for us, the unknowing and uncaring, so that we may have a hope of a better future. Without their assistance and protection, I doubt any freedom would still exist for mankind to enjoy.

೫   ೫   ೫

Table of Contents

Prologue

y children, you have asked me why your mother walks in the shadows of your world, seeking dark, quiet places. You say she prefers songs of lament to cries of mirth and joy. You wonder at her silence, her quiet moods and her distant stare. Be patient, for her days of mourning have yet to pass. Though the century comets have returned a thousand times, she has not come to forget the suffering. And should they return a thousand times more, she will still be haunted by ghosts from long ago. So, do learn from my story and come to understand.

To the days of long ago I will take you -
Before Shadow-walkers roamed the forests and hills,
Before the daughters of Tolohe danced beside the firelight,
Yes, before your people took a breath.
That is where I will transport you -
Into an age without light, filled with despair,
To a time when hope was little more than bitter faith.
You shall see things and you will become afraid.
Then you will comprehend,
And insight will grow in your minds.
Your mother you will gain empathy for,
Your mother you will begin to understand.
Your mother you will start to know.

So journey with me, my children of innocence. I will teach you the way it was then. And if my children should fail to learn, the Darkening Age may well come again. So be silent and listen. Gain wisdom and live.

 ఠు   ఠు   ఠు

Section One

Destiny's Road

'To reach the beginning, you must start in the middle,
And to attain the finish, you must comprehend all things.
Time goes ever forward,
But knowledge learns always from the past.' - ZoeStethos

'The child has arrived and is hurrying on to an uncertain destiny. Today will prove to be the beginning or ending of all things...'

The person sat back, eyes aching from haunting visions of twisted destinies, head pounding because of a distorted musical uncertainty playing its disenchanting melodies, along with a heart being overwhelmed with dread concerning future days.

All life hung upon a thread - the choice of a moment, the beat of a troubled heart... and little could the Maker of Worlds do than trust it to the wisdom of a very impetuous child who drew now ever closer to this uncertain destiny.

Chimes of the great clock sounded in the person's ears. How many times had it called out to the distress of nations? How many children could no longer hear the beautiful music it made? Was it ten million, a hundred million, maybe more? This one, sitting back waiting for the arrival of a treasured, precious child, did not recall. What the person did know was that the belly of Hell was not yet satisfied.

With head shaking from side to side, tears began. Should the Empire win this coming conflagration, even though the child may prove wise, many times those who had already gone to their deaths would fall to Wrath's coming storms. Should they lose? Well, that could not be allowed, even if it cost the lives of all the children of the Empire...the universe.

The person stood, walking onto a balcony, looking down on a jungle of greenery seen nowhere else but here, the lone remaining peaceful bastion in this tempestuous universe.

Sighing quiet remorse that no others were allowed to sense, a musical cry of dismay went out to the breeze, a cry of bitter lament from a 'wanton heart that sought only selfish cravings to never feel alone'.

"Lo, foolish dreamer, your wish come true,
To sense the world with heart imbued.

Doth now the vial of bitter brew,
Its caustic taste your heart renew?

And now Rhiannon in oath does take,
To bind her children to an evil fate.
For should the world be made anew,
It first must pass through this witch's brew."

The person looked off toward the sound of the great clock as it chimed its last refrain. Then, with head bent down in sadness, this Maker of Worlds turned and slowly retreated into the darkness of hidden rooms to await the evils of the coming Fates.

ꙮ   ꙮ   ꙮ

The speeder eased to a stop outside the opened entrance of an ancient blue marble wall. This pearl-white auto-car sat motionless, hovering just above the pavement, a subdued humming noise coming from its motor, opaque windows keeping secret any mysteries hidden within.

From a cloudless sky, the heat of the morning sun pressed upon the day. Steam from a late-night shower rose from pavement bricks and surrounding stones, vanishing as a mist in the summer air. Shrubs and trees in surrounding gardens dripped with a welcome deluge of the night, while little harvester ants scurried about, busy at their duties, as sunlight reflected off glistening water droplets, creating an illusion of a world filled with sparkling diamonds.

A loud *click!* followed by the low whir of servos disturbed the silence. As if rudely awakened from a pleasant slumber, a covey of mourning doves rose from secluded perches. As they noisily flew overhead, a door opened in the side of the auto-car, slowly sliding back along an inner rail, revealing a shadowy figure hiding in the cool darkness of the idling machine.

Slowly, a hand reached out, grabbing the roof rail, followed by a foot coming to rest on the pavement. Laboriously, like someone ancient, weighed down with burdens beyond their years, a woman emerged from the shadowy depths. With a grunt, she stood. How strange it would have been for an observer, for this woman did not look ancient. She was young and stunningly beautiful.

Squinting, the woman shaded her eyes to view the surrounding landscape, the silent grandeur of these sights vividly impressive. Giant leaved gates made from exotic, shimmering metal, delicately engraved with intriguing designs and runes stretched outward like two great arms, beckoning one to come forward and receive their ever-opened embrace. Massive pivots, buried deep within the walls' two opposing circular guard towers supported them.

These imposing gates paled next to the fortress towers and walled battlements whose marbled heights rose well over eighty cubits before reaching the open roadway traversing the wall. From there it was another sixty cubits to the roofed battlements of the towers. Black, polished onyx inset with chrysolite and other precious jewels,crowned both the towers and imposing ramparts.

The woman sighed, unmoved. She merely turned toward the machine and muttered a command, its door swiftly closing. The auto-car's motor sprang to life and, speeding away, soon disappeared down the road, leaving the solitary figure standing there, staring into the distance.

Again, she turned her attention to the battlements. Looking up, the woman could see the massive guard towers with their flags fluttering on poles far atop peaked roofs, recalling to her mind the grandiose beauty viewed from their ramparts. From these towers, on countless occasions, the breathtaking panorama of the surrounding countryside had unfolded before her eyes.

To the east were gently rolling hills and valleys covered with orchards, vineyards and pastures. Patches of woodland dividing fields of grain grew along the streams and brooks that descended to a broad plain below. These waters gathered together in force to produce a wide, serpentine river sluggishly laboring northward, fading from sight.

Beyond rose a wall of blue-green hills, dipping and swelling as though an army of shadowy giants were on the move, marching off into the distant haze, hiding the roots of rock-hewn mountains jutting above the clouds in snow-covered peaks. In the morning blackness, the sun would fill the sky behind these mountains with a dark glow as if orange fire were ascending from the depths below. As it struggled its way up the mountains, colors brightened until a vivid red sun would suddenly erupt over the peaks, flooding the countryside with its yellow brilliance.

The fortress walls stretched north and south for better than two leagues. Long ago, tall forests had grown up around these fortifications, shading the blue river of marble with their wide evergreen boughs. Old growths of giant cedar, hemlock and redwood trees towered high above the greatest battlements, dwarfing the heights with their three hundred cubit spires.

Nor was beauty lost on the secrets hidden behind the marble walls. Ornate patchworks of courtyards, orchards and gardens nestled along the trails and broadways, a rainbow hue of bright, scented flowers scattered throughout the dark green mats of shrubs and bushes, exciting one's emotions with its kaleidoscopic display. Flagstone roads of red, blue and green crisscrossed this expanse of luscious growth, sweeping in like a sea around the base of the walls.

"Enough of that!" The woman sputtered, shaking her head to clear it of seemingly useless memories. She started toward the gates along the jasmine-lined roadway leading into Palace City.

Glancing west, the woman took little note of the dazzling imagery and beauty of the city's center, nearly a league away. Had she bothered to look up while passing through the gates, she would have seen the splendor of this jewel of the Universe…had she bothered.

This inspiration for poems and songs went unnoticed by the woman, her mind caught up with other pressing matters. Whether she chose to observe it or not was of little concern to the artists who created it.

The 'Eternal City', as the architects had named it, would always shine with breathtaking delight, for they had willed it to be that way. The gilded palace towers of jade, inset with gold and precious stones, and the palace proper, crowned in onyx and domed in diamond crystal, gold, and chrysolite made it appear as though the sun had descended from its home in the heavens and settled here. The Old Palace had sat its weathered butte long before this woman's kind was born, and would continue to shine from it even if her kind should fail.

The woman smiled. She had chosen wisely this morning. As she expected, the streets were empty. And the guard towers? They never saw a guard… only occasional lovers seeking seclusion after a night's merry-making. This did not mean that her presence had gone unnoticed. Even now someone watched her, following her every move. But such knowledge was more reassuring than discomforting.

At Candletoe, a distant outpost, the woman first noticed this voice calling to her, beseeching her to journey here. She regretted abandoning the fleet at such a perilous time, but what else could be done? There was a tone of urgency in the request, a pleading on the part of the one making it. And to be called here, to the Royal Palace, could only mean the summons was of greatest importance.

Sounding of hurried footsteps descending a hidden staircase in the North Guard Tower startled the woman. Reaching for the dagger at her side, she crouched in battle preparedness. Then, eyeing the tower's opening, she listened and waited. Footfalls echoed from the passageway and off the metal gates, confusing her ears as to the number of feet on the stairs. An instant more and she would know if the approaching feet were that of friend or foe.

Laughter erupted from the doorway. In a sudden rush, a couple holding hands, eyes fixed on each other, sprang from the blackness. Paying no heed to their surroundings, they nearly bowled the woman over. At the last instant the man saw her and, pulling hard on the girl's arm, twirled her around and into his.

Not having noticed the stranger in their midst, the girl flirtingly cooed, "Why Zadar, has your hunger overcome you so quickly? Do you wish to revisit the tower lounge before we return to the others?"

A handsome man with thick dark hair, deep-set hazel eyes, bushy eyebrows, and a neatly trimmed beard pretended to clear his throat and pointed past the girl. "We…we have a visitor."

The girl's eyes followed Zadar's hand, her shining black hair dancing on the air as she spun her head around. She stared, the flirting smile still on her face, and then, when she recognized the woman standing there, cried out in surprise, "Mihai! My sister! What a thrill to see you safe and well! Oh, how I've missed you! Come! Share the wine and good times with me again!" Releasing Zadar's hand, the girl lunged for Mihai, locking her in an iron embrace.

Mihai wheezed, "I… I've missed you, too, my darling Darla. Please… allow me a breath."

Darla released Mihai, holding her at arm's length and the two stared into each other's eyes. Mihai pondered the wonders of her sister. 'How beautiful she is, and still with the seeming innocence of a carefree little girl. Seeing her here, who would ever guess an evil madness lurks, hiding in her mind. She covers it well, with her finery of silk and gold, makeup and twinkling eyes. But I know…I know that this child has not seen even one day of peace in her troubled life.'

A spark of hope ignited in Mihai's own troubled heart as she watched Darla's placid face. She lowered her head, speaking wistfully. "This place has the ability to lift the darkness from the mind. May it also do the same for me..."

Zadar stepped forward, arms spread wide. "M'lady! It is so good to see you after such a long absence!" He gently pushed Darla aside and hugged Mihai.

"Harrumph!" Darla snorted, placing her fists on her hips. "He just wants you in the tower with him, that's all!"

Mihai stepped back in mock surprise, grasping her dagger. "If I'd known that, I'd defended myself against your advances!"

Grinning, Zadar asked suspiciously, "Just like the way you did the night before you parted company for the fleet?" Not waiting for a reply, he snapped, "If I had known M'lady was gonna come sneakin' around the back door of this place, I would have brought some brandy to welcome her and possibly offered her an invitation to visit a spell."

Mihai retorted, "I wasn't *sneakin'!* I wanted some time to myself to clear the air in my head. Leave it to someone like you to spoil it for me. And stop calling me 'M'lady'!"

Zadar wrinkled up his face in fake apology. "Oh, excuse me, your Lordship, but I didn't give you that title. You did it to yourself. I've already heard rumors of a big change coming. I'm just getting a jump on the others, that's all." Sarcastically, he asked, "What name do you want me to call you by, 'Mihai' or 'Michael'?"

Mihai soured. "You know few call me by that *other* name. 'Mihai' will suit me just fine." Sadness grew on her face. "'Mihai' helps me forget things I wish not to remember." She took hold of Zadar's hands. "Please, my dear little brother, allow me, please, to leave certain memories in the clouds for now. They cover the things I don't want to see."

Zadar squeezed Mihai's hands, grinning, "Mihai it is, then."

Mihai's dark feelings quickly faded and her eyes began to twinkle. "I would have been grateful if you had brought that brandy with you."

Darla pretended to clear her throat. Getting their attention, she asked, "So, am I just an abandoned soul now? Tossed by the wayside like a discarded toy?"

Mihai laughed. "Oh yes, we could cast you aside as easily as one does a winter tempest." She looked into Darla's emerald-green eyes, pondering, 'A person could become lost in those fathomless pools and never want to return.'

Letting go Zadar's hands, she reached out and held the girl in another embrace. "Oh, my dear Darla, I have missed your company for so long!"

They stood, locked together as one, sharing inner thoughts, memories from some long-forgotten time. There were few people Mihai loved and trusted more than Darla. In fact, she owed her very life to her.

Mihai kissed Darla on her lips and then asked, "How is it we chance to meet at this time? I thought you were doing sentry duty on Stargaton."

Darla blinked in surprise. "The summons, of course! You are the last one to get here. Zadar and I, along with the others, have been here for several days. We were beginning to think you might choose to ignore it, like you have done in times past."

Mihai denied that was so. "You know I have never ignored a summons. But there have been times when I could not possibly abandon my duties to come. This time is different. I could feel the urgency."

Zadar piped in. "Well! If you'd let us know the time of your arrival, we'd come to the depot and gotten you."

"That I don't believe!" Mihai poked an accusing finger toward Zadar. "You?! Miss out on a sweet interlude with our most beautiful of flowers just to keep company with me? Please, don't make me laugh."

"That's not so! That's not so!" Zadar cried.

Pretending offence, Darla grumped, "What's not so...that I'm the most beautiful of flowers? You weren't shy about lavishing your attention on me last night in your attempts to lure me out here! Was it out of obligation you delivered your innocent sister to the tower, saying 'Let us watch the sunrise over the mountains'? And did you keep my glass filled with wine only fearing I might become thirsty?"

Zadar was shocked. "*Lure* you?! As I recall, you dragged me under the first mulberry tree we passed after leaving the others. And for the wine, you treated yourself to many more than I dispensed, including mine."

Mihai stopped the teasing. "Enough of this! You're both incorrigible! Should all the children be as passionate, there would be no time for strife or war."

She spread her arms wide, drawing both her companions close, speaking in little more than a whisper, confiding, "I told no one I was coming. This council meeting is secret, at least it is to be for the moment. I believe my lieutenants are trustworthy, but…let's just say not all secrets remain secrets. I didn't dare trust the enemy finding out about my absence."

Mihai changed the subject. Looking at Zadar and Darla's attire, she commented, "It must have been some fancy gathering you two were at last night." She was justified in the statement, as the couple was dressed in sheer, silky, ankle-length garments.

Darla's attire was more feminine in cut, gathered at the waist, accented by a diamond-studded belt. It also had an open bodice, with golden lace sweeping down from her shoulders and around her exposed breasts, which refused to be hidden under her knee-length cape of woven silk, gold and silver. A pair of white, laced sandals finished the woman's apparel. Her braided locks, although disheveled, were festooned with rings of diamond-studded gold. With her dangly ear-fobs, three bejeweled gold necklaces and jingling anklets, she was quite an alluring sight.

Zadar's garment was more like a long robe, and his ornaments simple, consisting of a finely braided gold chain necklace and a black onyx ring on his right hand. He also sported a finely crafted timepiece on his waist-belt, while a jade brooch tied the two ends of his long, flowing cape together.

Zadar explained the party had been a reunion of sorts. Some close acquaintances recently returned from a long sojourn in the Outer Ranges were celebrating the successes of their expedition. Mihai then asked if the party was last evening, why were they still dressed in such garb so late the following morning?

Zadar leaned close, nuzzling against Mihai in a sensual embrace, and whispered romantically, "Because they make me feel *sexy*…"

Mihai pushed him away and laughed. "Feel *sexy*?! Zadar, you have never felt anything but sexy! From the day of your coming of age, you have chased the ewe. Your first lover surrendered you up to her sisters before your days with her were to end, worn out and in need of rest. She said of you, 'But for necessity of food and drink, we would have grown to the bed!'"

Zadar looked abashed, then grinned. "That aside, these clothes can still make you feel…well…*special*." He put his arm around Mihai. "The council isn't going to assemble until evening. Do you want to come with us to the Winter Gardens? That's where we are to join up with the others. I'm sure we could find some *brandy* there…"

Merriment disappeared from Mihai's face. "It would be my greatest pleasure, but I must decline." She took Zadar's hand. "I have some business to conclude this morning, having need to change out of this stodgy uniform and freshen up first. May I walk with you to the palace? We can talk along the way."

Darla wrapped her hands around Mihai's arm, while Zadar did the same with her other. Darla made her 'little girl face', grinning in satisfaction. "How sweet a walk it will be, too."

Mihai thanked them both for their kindness and love, then glanced over at Darla's dress and asked, "I know it's such short notice, but can you manage to find me some clothes like yours for my morning's business? It would make me feel…feel like a woman again."

Darla giggled with pleasure. "For you, my sister, anything…anything at all."

ဢ   ဢ   ဢ

Mihai lingered with her companions until they reached the Winter Gardens, located at the convergence of four wide concourses. The gardens were a grand expanse of exotic flowers, shrubs and trees, crisscrossed by dozens of walking trails. A bubbling stream with its own waterfall completed the scene. Of course, there were many hidden, secluded corners where benches and tables had been conveniently placed for the wanderer's benefit.

Indulging herself in the fresh, mist-filled air, Mihai sucked in a long, deep breath and exclaimed, "It's always early summer here, like the after-breath of a late day shower." Looking up at the high, domed ceiling, watching the cool white of day shimmer through the translucent stone, she happily sighed, "In this place, time forgets itself. We are standing below the very center of Palace City, the North Concourse running directly under the Old Palace that was constructed upon a butte of solid diorite."

Darla and Zadar shot knowing glances at each other. Here it came, another 'you're so young, you won't know this'.

Mihai's eyes scanned their surroundings as she explained, "It is this part of Palace City that was said to have existed long before my kind were born. The remainder of the city, including the Winter Gardens and long concourses, with their hundreds of eateries, cafés, pubs and shops, was designed and built by the children of the First Age, countless millennia before my birth. How wel…"

Shouts echoed across the nearly empty building. Zadar waved his arm, calling back to the new arrivals. He excused himself and hurried away. Darla promised to find Mihai a sensual outfit and offered to walk her to the tramwaiter.

Mihai thanked her. Glancing in different directions, she said with a shudder, "It's such a long time since I've been here. Where are all the people?"

"Pay no mind to it, Sister." Darla casually replied, taking Mihai's hand. "This is still early morning, by business standards, anyway. Things will wake up around here by the lunch hour, and the dinner crowd will be pretty good. It's always quiet this time of day, remember?"

Mihai nodded. She remembered all right! Long before Darla was born, long before the Rebellion tore her people apart, long before all the wars, when she was a youngster, still in her teens, this place was off-handedly called, 'the world that never sleeps'. There was always a crowd here.

Mihai thought back to those long millennia passed. She could see the concourses packed with partiers and merrymakers, elbow to elbow, making their way from one festive event to another. There were the pools, spas, theaters, and gymnasiums that entertained the body and the mind. If food was to your liking, you could lose yourself in the hundreds of eateries, serving the palate anything from frozen chocolate crêpe to spicy, baked halibut smothered in clam sauce and onions.

And one must not forget the Palace Coliseum! Sometime during the First Age, architects hollowed out a cavern in the butte, directly under the Old Palace. Every technical innovation of that age was built into its design and construction, enabling artists to recreate their wildest imaginings in three dimensional sights and sounds, for audiences of over two hundred thousand. The Coliseum's doors closed many centuries ago, its vaulted chambers now filled with silent darkness.

The intoxicating excitement of that day was gone. This day, Mihai only heard the quiet echo of a few footsteps on the polished marble floors, mixing with the lonely splashing of the garden's waterfall. She sadly smiled. "Yes, my dear one, I remember..."

Darla walked with Mihai down the South Concourse until they came to the tramwaiter. In a few moments, there was heard the whirring of powerful gyro-motors, announcing the machine's rapid approach. The whirring stopped, followed by a *click!* and a hum. Double doors slid open, revealing the coach's opulent interior.

A woman stepped out, offering salutation, hurrying off, leaving the two alone. Mihai glanced into the empty car. "When the world was innocent, these things were always filled. It would be nothing to see several dozen riders queued along this wall, waiting for the next tramwaiter, and that was at this same time of day."

Darla said nothing. She believed her older sister, but could not comprehend such numbers. Her memory of large crowds had been watching great armies on the march or slaughtering one another on the battlefield.

Mihai had seen that look in Darla's face before. She smiled and squeezed her sister's hand. "The hour is coming, or so I've been told, that another great celebration is to take place here. It has even been said that the Palace

Coliseum's doors shall again be spread open. Then you will see for yourself what a wonderful world this place really is."

Darla's eyes filled with wonder and then question. "I have heard others speak of this 'marriage of the lamb'. Are you revealing secrets to me about mysteries hidden, or am I being the fool, wishing for shadows and dreams?"

Shaking her head, Mihai answered, "You are no fool. Trust me, *you are no fool*. If it has been promised to us, then it will happen, but when and how, I don't yet know. My dear one, wishing for shadows and dreams is not a bad thing. At times, it may be all we have to hold on to. As for the celebration that I speak of, it is something far grander than any of which you have been informed. It is part of the greatest mystery of all."

"What is it, my lovely one? If you know what it is, please tell your sister." Darla was nearly dancing with excitement.

Mihai tipped her head back in laughter. "You already know almost as much as I. For now, we must both place it in our shadows and dreams, trusting in the One who has promised it."

Stepping through the door and into the tramwaiter, Mihai turned and asked, "You will find me a lovely dress? I will have need of it soon."

Darla assured her sister that she would deliver it shortly, said goodbye and started for her waiting company.

The doors closed and the droning whir started. Mihai sat down on one of the ornate, overstuffed chairs as the machine whisked her away, relaxing to pleasant music as the tramwaiter snaked its way along hidden passageways toward her destination. Built by artisans of the First Age to complement the growing expanse of Palace City, the coach line traversed its length and breadth, except for the Old Palace.

In short order, the woman found herself standing in an open courtyard, untended and overgrown with summer greenery. A tiny apartment just across the way was her home during the early years of her youth. She inhaled the pleasant wisp of memories passed. This place was the 'keeper of her innocence', from its latticed balconies to its cool, shadowed walkways…the 'protector of her heart and soul'. It was for that very reason she returned to this childhood residence, to forget for a moment the dark days of despair and the evil that almost destroyed her.

The sun was still blocked entry by surrounding buildings as Mihai rambled across the deserted courtyard. There was something special about this shadow-world, full of life but still shaded in morning's mysteries. Reaching the apartment door, she paused to watch ghosts of happier times dancing on the multi-colored flagstone. She lingered to capture the fleeting vision, lest her mind might forget it completely.

A robin's song broke Mihai's dreamy spell. She sighed, turning back to the door, opening it. Glancing over her shoulder, she wistfully hoped to catch another glimpse of those bygone days, but the sun peeked over the roofline, flooding the courtyard with its yellow splendor, chasing away any hint of the past. Mihai frowned, slipped inside, silently closing the door.

                                        ॐ   ॐ   ॐ

True to her promise, Darla delivered a splendid-looking gown to her sister. Mihai grinned with delight, striking different poses for the mirror. Each movement caused the sky-blue silky cloth to dance this way and that. She stopped in a pose, standing at an angle, hands gracefully outstretched and curtsied. "Hello, my Lord PalaHar. It is such a pleasure to have your acquaintance this evening." She laughed and turned, repeating her action. "Well, well, my Lord Ardon, does our wise councilor approve of my attire?"

Pretending she was arrived at the coming council meeting, Mihai offered her gracious salutations to several others she expected to meet there. The tingling sensation of the fabric on her skin and the way it floated up like a billowing cloud as she turned made the woman laugh. As her feeling of sensuality grew, she began to slowly dance to a tune in her head.

A young, flirting maiden suddenly appeared in the mirror. "Why certainly you may not kiss me, you cad! When my lover hears of this, he will thrash you with his scolding tongue!" She bowed again. "Yes! Yes, the dinner has been so fine. Never have I tasted truffles prepared so splendidly."

Closing her eyes, the girl flung her arms out and head back as she gracefully twirled on one foot. She did not see the mesmerizing beauty in the mirror, or the feminine charms she revealed. Firm, toned muscles, accented by the woman's full, round features and milky-white skin enhanced her appeal. Her breasts bounced in rhythm to her moves as her buttocks rippled in tight little waves as she shifted her weight from one long sinewy leg to the other. What a sight! Oh, what a sight!

Spinning around one final time, Mihai stopped and, with a lissome move, bowed before the admiring audience. She peered into the mirror, examining the face staring back. Most pronounced were the piercing blue eyes, accented by golden eyebrows crowning a strong forehead. The face was misleading for, at first glance, one could see the semblance of a child not yet out of her teens. A closer look revealed a sharpness like hewn stone, weathered by the ages.

High cheekbones, a long, straight-bridged nose and a determined jaw gave Mihai a hardened, proud appearance of a noble leader, while her full-bodied, rose-colored lips and compassionate countenance suggested a guileless maiden. Whichever way a person chose to view her, there was no denying the breathtakingly handsome beauty this woman possessed.

Satisfied, Mihai stood upright and did a half turn, striking another pose.

Laughing, she snapped her head around to observe her stance, making her golden tresses float high in the air, revealing hidden secrets. The laughter died from her lips when what she saw resurrected painful memories.

Slowly, she reached behind her back to pull the golden tresses aside for another look. A jagged scar started at the base of her neck and trailed to the right, across the shoulder blade, and down her rib cage. And what had she accomplished from the near fatal experience? Nothing! Her kidnapped sister was still not free, and now her traitorous brother was making a big, diplomatic 'to-do' about it.

The Stasis Pirates' ion trail had been easy to follow…too easy, now that Mihai thought about it. She followed it along the Outer Corridor, past the Trizentine and into the Frontier. Nearing hostile territory, she disembarked from the battle cruiser in her fighter, telling its captain to remain there on patrol. The fighter stealthily passed the Frontier, following the pirates' trail far into forbidden territory.

The Stasis had made directly for ZemiaKone, meaning 'Lost Rabbit', the enemy's westernmost territory bordering on the Frontier. It was believed to be little more than an outpost - at least that is what was agreed upon at the armistice. As Mihai drifted toward its surface, dodging radar and sonic detection, she felt there was way too much chatter on the communication channels to be coming from a few lonely outposts.

Her ship settled down in a desert canyon a few miles from where the fighter's instruments indicated the pirates landed. Following the gullies and ravines, she gingerly made her way in the direction of a distant space terminal. About a mile away, she found a narrow draw, leading down to the plain far below. Soon the rocky walls stretched high above her head.

A sudden chill raced up the woman's spine. Something was wrong. Instinctively she twisted away from some unknown assailant. Mihai's prescience saved her from death, but not from injury. A plunging, razor-sharp claw from a guard droid caught her as she spun around, driving her toward the ground. She could feel its icy-cold blade tearing through the flight suit and into her flesh. Then came a sickening sound of cracking bones and snapping tendons as the beast ripped a deep gash down across her back, slamming her, facedown into the dirt.

Mihai rolled away to her left in a choking cloud of dust just in time to escape a second blow, the blade making a 'swooshing' noise as it passed her face. Still tumbling, she triggered her lanner, holstered on her left hip. There was no time to pull the weapon free. The raised arms of the droid were already dropping for the final thrust that would skewer her through.

In one violent kick, Mihai managed to roll right, reefing the gun barrel toward the metallic monster. She pulled the trigger, energy exploding from the muzzle, shredding the holster and sending a searing wall of fire down along the length of her leg into her attacker. After blasting a hole in the droid's armor, she quickly pulled the gun from its holster and fired a second charge into its open rupture. The infernal machine belched acrid smoke and crashed into the dirt.

Mihai's head spun in pain, but there was no time to take account of the injury. The guard droid undoubtedly sent a signal to the outpost. Soon the place would be swarming with others, and not droids this time.

She staggered to her feet, struggling to stand, fighting a numbing ache in her back, her right arm hanging limp and in pain. She could feel warm, sticky blood oozing down her back, and there were already large red stains in the dirt. Taking a step, the woman cried out in agony. She glanced down to see pieces of her flight-suit flaking away from her left leg, leaving gaping holes in the silver material. The air stunk with the smell of charred flesh. Fighting back a dizzying sickness trying to overtake her, she shook her head. 'They'll know who's been here when the blood's tested. No time to worry about that now.' She needed to get away.

Whirring of servos alerted Mihai to the fact there was more than one guard droid. She didn't even have the strength to lift her head and look in the monster's direction. There was nothing to do now but wait to die. Mihai remembered little else. The sound of metal smashing into metal filled her ears, and then silence, no servos, nothing.

Mihai dreamed she was falling, only to be caught up in strong arms and carried aloft on wings, or so it felt. After an eternity of silent flight, the woman came to her fighter, floated through the open cockpit and into the seat. Just before the canopy snapped shut, a voice fell on her ears. "Be well, my Lord."

The rest was just a painful blur in Mihai's mind. When she woke in the stillness of the darkened room, she was looking into the distraught face of a woman with smoky-grey eyes and platinum-colored hair.

"Ga… my G…" Gentle fingers rested on Mihai's lips.

"You're safe, my darling. Your soul has returned to us once more." The gentle voice continued to sing little songs of love in Mihai's ears.

> *"When the summer grass turns to brown and the leaves die from
> the tree,*
> *I shall call to you, my love, crying, 'come back, come back to me'.*
> *The river ever flows and the glade will never tell,*
> *The depth of care our hearts do share and the pain of a fallen
> dove."*

For some time, Mihai drifted in and out of strange and bewildering dreams. When she finally waked enough to fully comprehend her surroundings, the woman crooning the sweet tunes frowned and scolded, "It should be a blessing remembered and thankful you should be that the Grave-maker happened to cross your path. If not for her, you would be hanging from a pike, drying in the breeze."

The woman shook her finger in Mihai's face. "If you ever attempt another stunt like that again, you may find me less forgiving than that droid!" She quickly turned away and left the room.

Mihai was saddened to think her actions hurt the woman so. For six thousand years she had acted like a mother to her... indeed... a mother to thousands, many who never returned from such adventures. And only once had she allowed anyone see her weep.

Other than a nuisance pain when moving her arm, the scar was the only evidence of the droid's attack, but the lanner blast was different. Skin was now covering the burns that had eaten into her leg muscles, but the rejuvenating nerves itched and ached. She was well aware the pain would exist long after the red blotches disappeared. Even with the use of healing machines, nerves took a long time to heal.

Mihai considered herself very fortunate. The weapon she carried that day - her design - was an energy gun. It activated a chemical compound ignited by an electrical discharge passing across the gun's chamber, decomposing a portion of a stable agent suspending the very unstable mendelevium. The greater the voltage across the pellet, the faster the breakdown of the stable agent, thus the greater the energy delivered to the target. The power released could easily be controlled by adjusting the voltage capacitor. This lanner had a thumb lever for quick adjustment, giving its user the choice of stunning someone with a heat blast to instantly dissolving flesh from the bone.

Mihai shuddered. Had her leg been bent at the knee and received a more direct blast, surgeons would have been forced to amputate her lifeless leg. To regrow the bone, tendons, nerves and flesh could take years, even with healing machines.

She sadly walked from the mirror, the little girl having been chased away by the gloomy memories and sat on the edge of her bed, staring down at her hands. The woman became introspective, searching inside herself for answers to questions unasked... unasked out of fear... fear of what might be revealed. The time was now passed for such self-indulgence, for remaining in the world of pleasant indecision. Choices had to be made. To keep her sanity, changes were necessary.

She had been field marshal for too long. For over a thousand years, she ruled the army as 'lord dictator'. Her decisions were final. The greater the slaughter, the more willing the people were to follow her. They had obeyed her commands without hesitation...never once a complaint. The long war never really ended. The armistices only gave pause to it, allowing the enemy time to rebuild his forces. And what of the last war, the Great War? What had it accomplished?

Stargaton…twenty thousand lost in one hour…friends and lovers. And what had they achieved? A miserable little rock floating in a forgotten part of the galaxy! Memphis…two corps destroyed because she had calculated the enemy incorrectly. Through four years of bloody conflict, she had sentenced over three million of her people to pour out their blood for this holy war. How much closer to the end were they now? Had the price been worth it?

Those battles were over fifty years ago and the dying was still going on. Oh yes, there was an armistice, but the enemy still found excuse for the occasional bloodletting. How much longer would death keep devouring those she loved so much? How many more would be butchered because she thought it necessary? Mihai closed her eyes and shook her head in despair.

What else could have been done? They followed her because she was their leader. Her people would have fought without one. At least they didn't die for her or some imagined reward. Everyone was aware of what was at stake. Billions of innocent lives depended upon their success. The destiny of generations gone, present, and even those coming hinged upon the outcome of events.

But had the people not already paid the ultimate price? Was death really the supreme sacrifice? She thought not. The age of innocence was gone for them, destroyed forever on the fields of blood and betrayal. It mattered little the outcome. Her people would never be able to completely forget the death and suffering. 'Like a maiden violated by her guardian and protector…' Mihai nodded her head. 'except he has raped both the flesh and spirit.'

Mihai no longer feared her own death. In fact, there were times when death appealed, ending the guilt plaguing her mind. She could manage the daylight hours, but…but in the quiet of the night, when the rest of the world slept, accusing voices of all the slain would sing out in her head, their scolding faces passing in visions before her eyes. No matter how she made excuse or sought absolution, she could still see their blood dripping off her hands.

Mihai's thoughts conjured up visions creeping from dark corners of her mind into this waking moment. There suddenly appeared heaps of bodies, torn and mangled. In horror, she watched while her fingers went probing open wounds, seeking bloody flesh to satisfy an insatiable hunger. While Mihai's stomach churned in sickness, her lips smacked with anticipation, squealing, *"Is this all there is?! Are these tiny morsels all you have delivered?! How are we to survive on such paltry rations?! We are hungry! We are hungry!"*

Mihai shook her head violently to drive the ugly dream away. With many curses and outcries, the demon slowly crawled back to its hiding place, threatening a return. It would come again. It had promised. She dropped her head in dismay. How much longer could this continue on before the mist of insanity would completely envelop her? Did she have a day…a year…an hour?

A bitter chill swept the room, raising an army of goose bumps marching across Mihai's sweaty skin. She involuntarily shivered, more from the encounter with her monster within than from the cold. There was no more wondering which of Destiny's roads she was to take. One and only one path lay open. It was no longer a matter of choice. The time had come for her to speak of this while a small piece of innocence still resided within her heart, while she still retained mastery of her own mind.

It was time to leave. No longer did this room…this little world of her youth… have the power to drive away the evil. *She* was the evil. It was a part of her living being. Until it was driven away or destroyed, it would be part of her. There was no longer any need to hide from it. No place could protect her. Mihai gritted her teeth. She was determined to become whatever she must in order to defeat this enemy.

Standing, Mihai reached for her officer's cape and cloaked the beauty of the dress. She faced the door, willing to endure any storm that might come. Lifting her head high and throwing her shoulders back, the woman marched into the courtyard. No longer was she going to seek shelter from her fate. What tomorrow would bring, what battles there were to confront, no matter the results, they were going to be faced head on!

৪০   ৪০   ৪০

Fearing a reuniting of friends if she returned to the Winter Gardens, a direct route to the Old Palace, Mihai rode the tramwaiter to a more distant exit, to the north and east of her destination. From there it was a mile's walk to the Eastern Portal, the grand public entrance to the Old Palace, better known as the 'Upper Palace'.

The path traversed a labyrinth of narrow streets and broadways, snaking through the artfully created mountains of tall, ornate buildings. Constructed during the Second Age, this new palace city, better known as the 'Lower Palace', eclipsed the Upper Palace from view, except for its central domed spire and the four guard towers at the corners of upper battlements. Few were the feet on the street this morning, the echo of Mihai's footsteps often the only sound to be heard.

At the end of her walk through the city's streets, Mihai entered a narrow, deep, tapering recess in the face of a high cliff. At a juncture where the two walls converged, she arrived at the Majestic - a wide, winding staircase inlaid in the diorite butte, crisscrossing its way up hundreds of feet to the palace proper. Each flight of hewn stairs ended in an immense grotto that spread out into a beautiful, enclosed balcony carved into the mountain itself. Giant windows had been cut from the outer wall, providing a breathtaking view for a pilgrim journeying to the palace.

Said to have been built by the Ones Who Came Before as a gift to the children of the First Age, these stairs, like the rest of the Upper Palace, never needed repair nor did they weather with the passage of time. The Ancients, many of the oldest children of the First Age, called this place 'the Home of the Living Stones'.

A person needed to see this marvel of engineering to grasp the grandeur and beauty of the 'Road to Heaven', as it was often called. There were no visible construction marks, added building blocks or reinforcements, just one solid piece of finely polished obsidian, carved with intricate designs.

(Author's note: I believe it worthy to mention here that the Upper Palace was named 'Heaven' by the oldest of the Ancients who first sojourned into the unknown beyond the outer walls. Out there, in the 'Eres', translated 'Earth' in our tongue, travelers had to fend for themselves or carry supplies enough with them for their journeys. The paved highway, beginning at the east wall and leading west toward what would later be called the 'Majestic', became known as the 'road to Samayim', translated 'Heaven' or 'Heights' in our tongue.

Both words, Eres and Samayim, are said to be phonetic pronunciations from the language of the Ones Who Came Before, as the oldest of the Ancients recalled from hearing the words spoken. Eres literally means 'to go away from', as in 'going away from what is known'. Samayim has the understanding of 'becoming satisfied', as in 'filled up with every good pleasure'.

So it was, when the first children of the First Age ventured into the wilderness, they spoke of going into the Eres. After a long and exhausting journey, often filled with sacrifice and privations, the Eastern Gate, where the paved highway began, meant they were close to the luxuries of home. Being on the road to Heaven symbolized being near one's reward for having succeeded in accomplishing the return journey. Now the riches of home were no longer a dream or hope, but a reality.

As the children reached further into the wilderness, eventually leaving EdenEsonbar, the home planet, they carried the name 'Eres' with them to symbolize their going into the unknown. When the Second Realm or Second Universe was revealed to them as a place they would one day go, the name 'Eres' was given to it. Later, the sons of men on Earth were given that name for their home planet and, by the time of the Great Flood, were calling the land of the children's dwelling place 'Heaven'.)

Mihai remembered little more about this morning's journey up the Majestic than the day so long ago when her companions carried her up these same steps. Those six millennia passed had not changed the sights, but she believed they would never impress her like they once did. Now these stairs were merely a conveyance used on her road to destiny, a means to an end. So little remained of the joy this world once basked in.

About one hundred fifty cubits above the Majestic's threshold, the stairs made a sharp turn, tunneling into the butte as it rose toward the Upper Palace. It finally opened into a towering, vaulted chamber called 'Raven's End'. The chamber, like the Majestic, was built of polished obsidian, its finely chiseled pillars reaching thirty cubits to the shimmering black ceiling. Openings in the east wall allowed observers a panoramic view of the Lower Palace from twenty stories above the courtyard far below.

The sound of surging blood filled Mihai's ears as she staggered up the last set of stairs before reaching the chamber. Her lungs ached, her heart pounding against her chest. Three times she had stopped on her ascent, a climb often jogged in her more carefree days. Wheezing, she stumbled forward, seeking a bench near one of the pillars.

After sitting, Mihai rested her head in her hands. A smell of hot, sticky sweat filled her nostrils, making her stomach churn even worse than her headache had managed to do. She needed to take her mind off her personal concerns. 'Think girl, think!'

Looking around the empty expanse, she began to ponder its name. 'Raven's End? Raven's End? Oh, yes! Now I remember. It was told me that when the world was new, when the Ancients were still little more than children, sojourners beyond the distant walls would take birds along with them to send messages back to the palace.'

She stared at the windows. All around them were hundreds of tiny nooks. 'Pigeonholes! That's what they are. They say that at one time this chamber harbored thousands of birds of all kinds.'

Mihai could see and hear the excitement of that time, multitudes of birds cooing and crying while others swooped to and fro through the air. What a sight it must have been!

Gentle footfall echoing across the empty expanse interrupted Mihai's recollections of this place. She squinted, peering into the shadows. "Now who should be wandering out here at this time of day?" She muttered to herself.

Raven's End was cavernous and dark, its only light during the day coming from the windows and open exits. The Majestic's final staircase spiraled its way up the last sixty cubits to the Upper Palace's outer courtyard from the far end of the vaulted chamber, it offering little light for Mihai to observe who was coming.

The one approaching spoke first. "Mihai! What a wonderful surprise! I had no idea I would be seeing you before tonight." A woman of slight stature, medium build and delightful appearance materialized from the shadows, hurrying over, taking Mihai's hands, leaning down, giving her a gentle kiss.

Mihai grinned, asking, "Trisha?!" Then glancing at the woman's light blue uniform, puzzled aloud, "*General* Trisha?! I thought you were commanding Hunter's Brigade on Pilneser. What brings you here, I mean, so far away from your duties?"

Still gripping Mihai's hands, Trisha smiled. "Oh, my Lord, I have been a busy, busy person. I was called away from my duties on Pilneser some months ago, being given a temporary assignment in the Second Realm. Then, just three weeks ago, I was summoned to Palace City. Been here ever since, waiting for tonight's council…"

Mihai puzzled. "Who ordered you away from your post? I saw no request come across my desk."

Trisha's answer was upbeat and cheerful, but revealed little, as did her facial expressions. Her eyes, though, could not lie, twinkling in a way a child's does when hiding a secret. "My Lord, the day is young, and many a breeze must blow before its end. Rest assured, the powers that brought me here have also delivered my Lord to this same destination. The journey is long and may be dark, but the wind ever blows us home."

Mihai attempted to pry more information from Trisha, but the woman said nothing, which was very much part of her nature. If she chose to speak, all well and good, but no known force existed that could make her confess a word if that was her disposition. Mihai surrendered to what little she had been told, marveling at the woman's solid constitution, finally shaking her head. "You're hopeless. Just plain hopeless."

"Thank you!" Trisha replied, grinning. "I'll take that as a compliment. Better to look like a fool, I say, than to open one's mouth and remove all doubt."

Mihai returned a toothy smile, nodding. "There's a lot to you, General. Your youth confuses and intrigues me. I see eyes filled with wonder and excitement, but you speak with the wisdom of our councilors. The powers that delivered you to my world are wise and discerning." Her statement stirred memories of this woman in her mind.

Trisha was not a child of this realm. She had grown up during an age of violence, when old ways and beliefs were being challenged, and new religions were forcing themselves into the lives of people around her. She had refused to compromise her values and beliefs, making the woman an outcast among her people. But that was all gone now. By the time she awoke from the Field of the Minds, her memories were all that remained of the world of that day.

Mihai marveled at this woman's strength and lasting integrity, when suddenly recalling that this was the woman she had observed from her secret realms during those long-ago years. Trisha had suffered much back then, from the death of children to abandonment by her husband, and so much more. Those experiences had hardened her. Her years here had not removed that hardness. How could it? Mere months after her arrival found Trisha at CoblinPort, helping in its defense against Stasis Pirates.

Standing and gripping Trisha's upper arms, Mihai commented, "The storm-winds have swept your world all too often. Many people would have become bitter over their fate had they suffered such grief. How is it that you still carry such love and tenderness within you as I have many times seen displayed? You are always doing for others."

There was little change in Trisha's expressionas she softly replied, "My Lord, I am but a servant girl. You have lived from before the founding of my world. I have seen fewer than eighty summers, all filled with grief and despair. I think a starving man appreciates a dry crust of bread more than a king with a banquet of exotic dainties." She shook her head. "I do not have pity for my life. Hours of grief have taught me to cherish moments of pleasure. My heart reaches out to your kind, for the children of this world have not yet learned to find delight in one lonely star on a dark stormy night. Your kind cannot yet see that these times of distress will become a treasure of great worth. In future days, you will pity the children born in times of peace."

Trisha lowered her head, speaking as if to the floor. "I am but a babe newly birthed, surrounded by souls older than the oceans, yet I feel as ancient as the distant mountains." Staring into Mihai's eyes, she quietly pleaded, "Forgive me, my Lord, for I do what must be done. I have little more choice in the matter than a worm growing into a winter moth. What must come shall come."

"What are you talking about?!" Mihai was disturbed over Trisha's riddling comment. This woman did not speak idly. Few who knew her dared question her insight, which was equal to most and better than many, even some of the Ancients.

Sadness grew in Trisha's eyes as she took Mihai's hand. "You have not climbed heaven's stairs for no reason, my Lord. There are those who see beyond your secrets who have also ascended them with you this morning. Listen, if you can, to their voices. Remember, please, within the walls of this fortress no harm can come to you…" Her voice became grave, "unless you permit it." She added nothing more.

Pulling on Mihai's hand, Trisha offered to walk with her. "Come, my Lord, allow me the honor to accompany you for a little while. Ysuah's Ladder is best appreciated when a person walks it with a companion. I have heard it said that those who climb this stairway together share a vision as they walk. Will you permit me the pleasure of seeing if it is so?"

If a vision occurred as they climbed the stairs, neither woman could tell for a certainty, but Mihai spoke of a deep sense of peace she felt, and that her gloom dropped away as they rose toward the courtyard. She thanked Trisha for her company. "If there truly is a vision's song in those stones, I shall save it for debate at a later time, but I do believe your presence has lifted my spirits. Thank you for accompanying me here."

Trisha did a curtsy bow while lifting Mihai's hand and softly kissing it. She smiled sadly. "My Lady of the Court and lord of this land, the pleasure has been mine. Should you ask for my companionship to the edge of eternity, my heart would cry out with gladness. May we always remember this passing morning as one recalls the joy of first love."

There was no doubt in Mihai's mind that Trisha was, and had been speaking in cryptic riddles. Her lilting words were beautiful, but their hidden message was one of pleading, singing out in her heart:

"Forgive please the pain I bring.
Remember my love and praise that I sing.
The hour soon comes, when the night I shall bring.
Remember please, this love song I sing."

This woman hinted about things to come. Mihai believed the riddles came, not because Trisha wanted to hide things from her, but that the Maker of Riddles was busy about, doing things. Smiling, she nodded, "Your feet did not find me by chance. I detect the dabbling of One whose powers I do not understand. May I remember the wisdom hidden in your words. Thank you for being here to assist me."

Again Trisha bowed. "May gentle winds deliver you to safe harbor. I will take my leave now, my Lord." She looked around, observing, "A leisurely stroll through such beauty is medicine for the heart." The two kissed softly on the lips, after which Trisha turned and hurried back down the stairs, disappearing into the shadows.

Mihai listened to the tap of Trisha's feet echoing off the obsidian walls until the sounds drifted away. She drew in an intoxicating breath of the fresh morning air and stepped from the landing onto the rainbow-agate flagstone of the Palace's terrace. Even though the shade of the tall eastern buildings still cast their shadow here, there was no mistaking the elegant design and exquisite beauty of this place. And this was only what the children called the 'Outer Courtyard'.

As Mihai soaked in her surroundings of colossal jasper-marble walls and columns with finely engraved pictures and runes inlaid with precious metals and jewels, her thoughts returned to the days when she was a little girl, running naked over these very stones.

Mihai blinked in surprise as she suddenly found herself staring through the eyes of a wondering maiden, as a joyous world of long ago rose in greeting. There she stood, the carefree child, alone in a jungle of thousands of happy, partying adults reveling in merriment and celebration.

This way and that she ran, poking her face into this group of merry-makers and then another. Often, she would be scooped up by some burly giant who might toss her high above his head or wrap his arms around her and rub his curly beard on her naked belly. She'd squeal in laughter and cry to be let down. Off she'd run to assault another group lost in noisy conversation, hoping for more of the same.

Round and round the terrace the child would run, halting at the base of each corner battlement, planning her next assault. She would crouch behind the tower and, pressing her body against its blue marble surface, cautiously peek out in search of coming victims of her attacks. Spying a hapless foe, off she'd charge. One after another, they fell before her aggressive intrusions until she reached the far tower, a furlong's distance away. There she would repeat her offensive, first spying out the land in search of other hapless targets.

Off she'd go, popping under the cool of the slate-roofed breezeways and then into the open, under the bright blue sky. The ruckus and cries her intrusions created made the girl giggle with delight. After covering that section of terrace, the girl would begin anew. Round and round the child would go until, tired and satisfied, she would curl up in some giant's arms and drift off to sleep.

Mihai blinked. The vision was gone, yet the silent grandeur of this place was still unchanged. Indeed, all was still the same as it had been those many days before, all except...except for the people, always crowds of people. Before the darkness of the Third Age, the Upper Palace was the center of the universe for socialites. There was always something going on. Winter, summer, day or night, *this* was the place to be.

As a young woman, newly come of age, Mihai remembered one of the Ancients, PalaHar, comment, "My dear one, should you stand near these stairs long enough, every soul in the universe will pass your way."

Mihai waxed melancholy, smiling sadly. She wondered if PalaHar might be at the evening's council. After all, he was one of the great councilors, ranked among the twelve older men. It would be so good to see him again, considering the many years since their last meeting. The woman turned to take a fleeting glance back toward Ysuah's Ladder, half expecting to see PalaHar's shadow dancing up them. But, no, only the echo of memories passed greeted her.

Glancing up at Gradian's Laqah'Et, Mihai sighed. She had hurried to get here, not wishing to be late for her appointment, only to see the hour was still early. Staring again at the giant clock, the woman pondered her own insignificance. It was said by the Ancients that a great Cherub, Gradian, built this colossus of a timepiece in honor of the first child born in this realm.

Floating high above the southern battlement, observers saw a miniature of the fourteen planets of this star system as they whirled about in their orbits. As the instrument zipped along, spinning at the rate of a day for a year, in comparison to real time, the hour and minutes would magically chime in the peoples' ears.

When Mihai was but a child, she had asked her mother why the clock was called 'Laqah'Et'. Bending low, her mother picked up a handful of sand from one of the many rock gardens gracing the Upper Palace, smiling, letting the sand sift through her fingers. 'Time, my Dear, is fleeting at best, even for those with never-ending life. The word 'Laqah'Et' tells us to 'take hold of time so it is not wasted'.' She poked Mihai's button nose. 'There is never enough time for a person with a purpose…even for an immortal.'

Mihai recalled her mother sweeping her arm through the air as she explained time in words a child might understand. 'We are forever chasing the seasons… that is, unless we forget time. Then the seasons are always chasing us. Forever we run to stay ahead, or to catch up. The sun blinds our eyes at its morning's rise, shouting at us to 'Wake, foolish one! Do not squander the hour.' But all too quickly the moon creeps above the hills, calling, 'To bed! To bed! Sleep for the morn.''

Her mother's final words struck a chord deep within Mihai's heart as she stared upward at the clock. 'Time goes ever forward. Like a leopard on the chase, it will not falter or become distracted. You must remember that once you have given an act or a word to time, it shall brutally betray you for all the ages to come. What a person speaks in secret, time will broadcast to the universe. How will time judge you? Only you can decide that fate.'

Sighing in disappointment, Mihai cast her gaze down, shaking her head, muttering, "I've chosen the Road to Heaven to escape a duty I wish not to bear. Shall time call me wise, or will it declare me a shirker and coward for not living up to what was expected of me?"

Mihai's face reddened with anger and she snorted, "*Time be damned!* You are no friend of mine! To me, you chide, 'Oh, foolish one, how long do you dream of your innocence? And yet, I have stolen it away and there is no returning to it. Long will you wish for what you cannot have and your tears will mean nothing to me. Go! Be off from me, for you deserve nothing at all!'"

No wine can make merry a bitter heart, nor lilting songs bring joy to a maiden betrayed. Also, with Mihai, no amount of splendor could lift her gloom. And in this place, constructed by legend's Immortals, in an age before ages, splendor was bountiful. Still shaking her head, Mihai began to wander the outer courtyard, contemplating the coming hour.

To the woman's left rose a high battlement that separated the inner and outer courtyards. Where these walls adjoined, a slender tower, inlaid with onyx and chrysolite, reached hundreds of cubits into the sky. From the tops of these towers one could see over seventy leagues, as far as the giant snow-covered peaks of the Kaissal Mountain Range.

Just below the towers' crowns, doors opened onto causeways that connected to each of the four towers. Like spidery webs, they grew from the spires' sides, reaching ever outward, until gracefully gathering their wings to a like-searching web. Mihai had only once traversed those causeways, in the days of her servitude, after her coming of age. The man to whom she was given had allowed her entry there, to show her *his* kingdom.

Mihai glanced up at the walkway, so high above the courtyard. She could not help but remember the grand, spectacular view as seen through the eyes of a thirteen-year-old girl. It had been a day anxiously awaited, to be walking with the most ancient of her people, a man whose very birth began the First Age. Try as she might to ignore that day of innocence, now so long ago, her *master's* tales of the palace's history echoed in the woman's mind. How well she remembered the things he told her.

Standing proud and majestic, Chrusion began, waving his arm to and fro as he revealed history's past. 'This is the oldest of all known structures in our universe. The Cherubs, themselves, revealed to me the hour of its very creation. All alone, upon this butte it sat, with only the sound of a dry, lifeless wind to keep it company.'

Chrusion stared down, beyond Lower Palace City, and out toward the distant wall that enclosed the district. 'Eventually, for many leagues in every direction, the hills were flattened, preparing for the construction of the impressive marbled wall.' He paused to reflect. 'When I was a child, there existed six other enclosures beyond the wall, similar in design but smaller in stature. These were later removed when I felt need to have more farmland for my growing brotherhood.'

Sweeping his hand high above his head, Mihai's mentor went on. 'When finished with the wall, the Cherubs covered the entire district with a colossal dome that could become as transparent as clear crystal or as opaque as the black obsidian inlays in the courtyard towers. Inside the confines of this secluded world, monumental experiments were carried on in which every concept of life form was toyed with. From the tiniest of ants to the largest of sea monsters, all first saw life here.'

Chrusion drew Mihai close and began tenderly caressing her body, exciting new and still strange emotions within the child. He kissed her on the forehead, patting her long golden locks like one does a handsome dog. When he tired, he again took up his account. 'Ocean-like waves once crashed upon what we now call the 'Outer Courtyard' and, after the waters dried up, arid deserts took over the lands between the palace and the walls.'

Chrusion nodded. 'Yes, my mint of spicy delight, from jungles to swamps, to deserts and forest, even to the tundra of the frozen northlands, it has been told me by the Cherubs that all such things existed here first.'

Long did Chrusion stand there, telling Mihai tales of ages past. As they walked along what he called his 'crown', the man went on about his many deeds, from first exploring the then wild lands beyond the wall to the days he and his brothers first took to flight beyond the home planet, EdenEsonbar.

Mihai well remembered the man's sensuous kisses as they hid in the shadows of the southwest tower. Just when her passions were crying out for love, a voice fell upon the child's ears, calling for Chrusion. Anna innocently stepped from the landing, seeking an audience concerning a very important matter. She was an Ancient, 'Consort Divine' and 'Maiden of Song' at the festivals.

Going to her, Chrusion and Anna spent several minutes in quiet conversation, it concluding with Chrusion excusing himself and leaving Mihai to find her own way down through the tower to the courtyard below. It would be many lonely nights before her owner would find the time for escape, so that her desires might become satisfied.

Mihai snorted in disgust. She drove away those memories by concentrating on the wonders of the Outer Courtyard itself. It was a place she usually found both peculiarly strange as well as fascinating. The walkway was some forty long cubits in width, filled with a scattering of rock gardens, ornamental pools, and raised terraces. Their very lack of symmetry betrayed them as an afterthought, suggesting a more utilitarian purpose in the Outer Courtyard's design.

In a dark and cruel world, it becomes such a strong desire to return to more pleasant days. For Mihai, her childhood hours were enjoyable. It was so easy for her to escape these current times and wander yesterday's paths. Mihai closed her eyes, trying to remember this place when she was still a maiden.

Soon her mind heard the soft pat of bare feet on the cool stones. They were those of Terey, one of her mentors. As the two walked together, Terey took Mihai's hand and, pointing with her other, directed the girl's attention toward some of the courtyard's wonders.

She went on to tell Mihai, 'When I was a little girl, this was not a safe place for a child to play. Giant machines in various states of disrepair littered what is now the courtyard, and long cables lay curled up, or hung limply from tall derricks into deep caverns below. It wasn't pretty here, like it is now." She winked, "I wasn't a good little girl. Since this was such a dangerous place to be, it was also the most fun place for a naughty child to play."

Mihai nodded, smiling, as she recalled that interchange so long ago. While still a youngster she, too, had been a naughty child, extensively exploring the still hidden and abandoned lower chambers in the palace complex. She had discovered viaducts plunging deep into the bowels of the earth. Huge hewn halls, hidden in the lower cellars, once housed large machines, maybe pumps or bellows, which were now little more than unrecognizable piles of rust and corrosion.

She discovered other cathedral-sized chambers that appeared to have once been used as corrals or aquariums. Openings in some of these rooms tunneled back and down for miles. Mihai recalled struggling her way for many hours along one tunnel that was some four cubits high and three wide. The child eventually came to a fathomless, black abyss when, after pitching a stone into the darkness, she had counted to twelve before hearing a distant splash.

The woman smiled to herself as she recalled the sound tongue-lashing given her by one of the older children, Medeba, warning her never to go a wandering off alone again, 'or else!' Then, after sending the child off to bed early, she came in to ask the girl about her adventure. With twinkling eyes, she listened to Mihai's adventure unfold. Thinking about it now, Mihai concluded that there must have been many, many naughty children throughout the ages of this realm.

Chimes echoed from the peaks of the four battlements as Gradian's Clock drummed out the eleventh hour. Mihai cursed under her breath, "Does the *old sorcerer* wish the raise the dead before their day?! Or is his dream only to make all living souls deaf?!" Off she went in a huff, seeing that she would now be late for her appointment.

Shaking her head in disgust, Mihai hurried toward a set of double doors hidden deep in the shadows of the outer wall, holding up her left hand, pointing it toward the sealed opening. The ring on her finger sent a tingling wave of heat up her arm and into her head as words that she did not even understand rushed from the woman's mouth. "*Karak Contie Kontendee*!"

The doors groaned as if now fighting against ages of neglected use. '*Crack!*' Springing outward, their sudden opening stirred up a cloud of ancient dust rushing out to greet Mihai. Waving her hand in a futile attempt to fan away the choking cloud, she lowered her head and entered the musty blackness. The woman hurried away, paying no heed to the doors silently closing behind her, but the hot pulsing on her finger she could not ignore.

It troubled Mihai to think that she wore the one very special ring that could open this gate as well as other certain entrances sequestered within the Upper Palace. She mumbled, quoting her mother, "Only the Smaragdos, (*lit. – emerald, translated:' Son of God' or 'Firstborn'*) can reveal the secrets hidden within these walls. And only has one person ever been given it as a possession."

Mihai looked down at her hand, the pulsing glow fading in the darkness, sourly sputtering, *"And now I am only the second to carry this dreadful thing!"*

A wistful sadness swept the woman as she recalled the first ring her finger claimed. It was made of shiny black onyx and simply designed, with no markings. 'Teknion, the little child', was its name, and she had received it the day of her coming of age. Her mother had told her that very day, 'No longer does my little girl run without restraint upon this temple mount, for she has become a woman this day. To you it is granted the secrets Teknion allows.'

She kissed her daughter on the forehead and then went on to describe the many other kinds of rings, including the one previously mentioned. 'Many are the rings my children have been gifted with and more varied still are the powers they give to each wearer. Yours is simple, to teach you the secret of the rings. One day, when you have grown in wisdom, you shall be gifted another, and still others will come to you… if you become truly wise.'

She took her daughter's hand. 'There are brown, red, gray, and even green onyx rings. And then there are rings of gold, silver, and ruby-jade, to name a few. Each has its own living power, that can guide your paths to success, but only if you listen to its music. These rings are my personal gift to my children, so that they may never be found truly alone…' She paused in thought before finishing, sadness filling her eyes. '…and become lonely.'

Mihai was much older before she learned the *true* magic of the rings. The child's curiosity and insatiable thirst for knowledge, even at risk to life and limb, did not wane after her years blurred into ages. Along with many of her kindred, she eventually became absorbed with what was known at that time as the study of EbenCeruboam, literally meaning, 'The Cherubs' Greatest Stone'. It was an amalgam of the sciences of what we today call physics, mathematics, mechanics, and harmonics, in conjunction with psycho-anatomy.

Through experimentation, mentoring, and extensive research, Mihai gradually came to a limited understanding of the basic building blocks or stones of the physical universe and their connection with all living bodies. The keys to life and sense were simple in number, but beyond comprehension in scope.

Her quest for wisdom eventually delivered her to the doorsteps of one JabethHull, a true eccentric, still unchanged from the beginning days of the First Age. Named after one of the mythical sorcerers, the Cherubs, he was wild and controversial, a loner with the patience of a thunderstorm, but one of the most knowledgeable scientists of that day regarding EbenCeruboam. Why he ever put up with a chatty, spoiled and often very opinionated know-it-all, Mihai never was able to understand.

For six hundred years, she journeyed with JabethHull and his 'one true companion' – his reference to NhosetHebel - beyond the edges of the universe, the uncharted territories of that day. Needless to say, Mihai learned patience while in company with Jabeth. His moods would range all the way from casually ignoring her existence to outright resentment for permitting this creature's invasion into his private world. It took Mihai many years to understand that Jabeth and Nhoset talked mostly through their minds. Mihai's constant gabbing was often an intrusion into the couple's conversations.

But Jabeth's rare moments of genuine cordiality were worth all the waiting as far as Mihai was concerned. He could also be very affectionate, caring for all of Mihai's needs on their long sojourn through the lonely voids of space. But it was Nhoset who could put succinctly the lengthy explanations of her companion, Jabeth. That woman's simple interpretations of EbenCeruboam law stuck in Mihai's mind to this day.

So typical of her teaching style was an evening on some unknown planet where they had surfaced to make needed repairs to their ship. Nhoset and Mihai were gathering wood to make a fire when she took the girl's hand and sat down by a bubbling stream. The woman began to play with Mihai's opened palm, gently rubbing it with her fingers.

Staring off into the gathering darkness, Nhoset started to softly croon, 'My little darling of sweet repose, do you feel love when the southern wind blows soft, and does your soul become lonely on a dark winter night? Have you ever wondered why you turn to spy the tree just before the limb falls from it? Or have you pondered the reason your lover is able to finish the sentence you have started?'

She turned to search Mihai's face. 'You see me only after the reflected light from my face has reached your eyes and you hear my voice only after the disturbed air has reached your ears, but all these things are mere effects created by unseen causes. I speak because I think. You hear because you think. We think because we are alive. We live because the hidden universe surrounding us does not rest.'

'You see the moon above us and say it hangs upon nothing, and you are correct to say it is so. Yet it does not hang upon nothing, but is cradled within the swaddling bands of a very powerful living force that dictates its destiny. It is this force that gives us life and breath, for without it there would be nothing mortal at all. For one must be immortal to reach beyond the web that swaddles us all, and it belongs to the Immortals to keep it safe.'

Mihai spoke openly her confusion of the discussion.

Smiling, Nhoset continued, 'The Web of the Universe is made up of countless harmonic particles, each with an intelligence of sorts, that think and react. Into them has been planted all the building blocks that keep our universe alive. We have come to call those building blocks 'laws' or 'Cherubs' Stones'.'

Nhoset looked down at the leaves fallen to the ground. 'Left to themselves, these… these particles…' Glancing into the night breeze as she searched for a word to define the particles, the woman noticed a cluster of tiny insects tumbling about in their never-ending search for a moist home to lay fertile eggs. 'These *midges*, you might say, would all come to rest and nothing would ever again move.' She lifted a hand and snapped her fingers. 'But the Immortals do not permit that happening.'

'Energy, my dear one, energy! That is the secret of the universe that is so little understood. It is so common, we think, yet it is so elusive. Energy is the catalyst of heat and light, and movement requires energy, but,' She made a fist. 'if I could squeeze out the space from the energy found in this entire universe, I would be able to hold all the energy within my hand.'

'Midges are cold by nature. They are lazy, sleepy little fellows who would rather snooze the time away. They become very upset when energy touches them and desperately try to push it away. One very small speck of energy can ignite a flurry of activity amongst the midges, which effects can be felt for long distances away. The heat you feel on your skin on a bright summer day does not come from the sun. It is the result of the midges angrily reacting to energy welling up within the star.'

'Unlike a star that discharges energy through nuclear-chemical processes that yet remain hidden in secrecy, living matter such as plants, animals, and even we, ourselves, gathers energy. All the time, the midges are resisting living organisms. That is why plants and animals die. And we would, too, if Mother had not placed in us an undying mind. But that is information worthy of another discussion.'

Nhoset went on at length explaining how all matter is stored up energy and that the midges were constantly at work, attempting to escape from it by passing it on to other midges. 'The crumbling of a granite boulder is the reaction of the midges and energy. The boulder can gather very little energy, so it loses it at a faster rate than it can gather it. As the rock turns to dust, the midges begin to quiet, for the closer to its basic atomic structure that matter becomes, the less energy it possesses. A piece of dust can store very little energy within itself.'

Laughing, Nhoset added, 'It is the very desire of the midges to chase away energy from themselves that gives us gravity. The stronger ones push energy onto the weaker who are already burdened down with too much of it, weakening them still further. As the number of energy-laden midges increases, they become a repository for even more energy that the other midges are throwing off. This process continues until the weakened midges become powerless to resist the continual onslaught. At this stage, we say the midges are now in a dormant state.'

'The process where the midges seek to throw off energy now reverses. In an effort to dispel that ever-growing field of energy, they reach out to gather even more, attempting to create an overload where this energy, itself, will become unstable and dissipate, usually in a very violent, reactionary way.'

She smiled, pointing in the direction of the ship. 'Our ability to understand this principle helped the children develop the powerful engines that drive us across the universe.'

'It is this dormancy within the midges, when they are no longer fighting with the energy, that creates what we call gravity. So, as you have already come to learn that magnetism is caused by a reaction between energy and the Web of the Universe, you can now see that gravity is just another reaction between these same two elements.'

Lifting the child's hand, Nhoset toyed with NithStar, the ring Mihai possessed at that time of her life. "Sweet Lilly, golden flower of mist imbued, the heart of a woman-child is filled with passion, but it is the power of the midges that makes it explode in one's lovemaking. Your mind is who you truly are. It is your soul and all that is in it. But you cannot feel a thing in *this* world without the midges, for the midges move the energy that creates your feelings.'

'The thought processes of your mind trigger energy reactions in your brain, troubling the midges within their sphere of influence. Your thinking processes create various angles of energy. These various angles cause the midges to react in different ways. Some of their reactions feel good to us, while others feel bad. Through personality development, you have learned to adapt and change the angles of energy released from your brain, changing the way the midges cause you to feel.'

Nhoset softly caressed Mihai's lower thigh, her fingers ever so lightly touching the tiny hairs on the girl's skin. Mihai groaned in delight.

'There!' Nhoset slapped Mihai's leg. 'Your brain is sending a signal to the midges that makes them react in a way that brings you pleasure. But if you had thought a spider was creating those very same sensations, what would you have felt? The same pleasure…?'

Mihai frowned. Just the idea of a spider crawling along her leg troubled her, she having long remembered the nasty bite from one when she was little more than a babe.

'See!' Nhoset wagged her finger. 'The angle of energy you send to the midges is very important as to how they will make you feel.'

Then Nhoset gave warning to Mihai, a warning she regretted not giving greater heed to. 'Do not be seduced by sweet words that you hear come from the mouth, and do not become beguiled over an entrancing eye or sensuous touch. These are but the reactions of the midges upon your heart as you wish to interpret them. Learn to use your powers of reasoning that can see beyond the reactive creations of this universe and into the very depth of the mind as it drives the brain to speak.'

Again drawing Mihai's attention to NithStar, Nhoset cautioned, 'This ring will never lie, but you must learn to read it properly and must come to trust it. It may well speak bad to you when your heart seeks to hear only good. You see, NithStar enhances your ability to feel and even see the harmonics - the angles of energy - around you. It will help you peer into the mind of those drawing close to you. This ring will give you insight and wisdom, but you must choose to use that insight.'

(*For a lengthy, in-depth explanation of the rings given to the children, the book, The Ostrich Never Flies, by NhosetHebel is a must- read.*)

Leaning over, Nhoset kissed Mihai every so softly on the lips as her fingers wandered across the woman's skin. She finally sat back and then stood. 'Let us deliver our wood and then I shall prepare the meal. Tonight I will teach you about other matters that press upon your heart.'

Recalling that night, and many others while in the company of these two Ancients brought a smile to Mihai's face.

In an instant, her smile vanished. JabethHull and NhosetHebel died in the First Megiddo War, innocent victims of the confusion of battle. Their smoky-gray ship, Aeriona, was mistaken for the enemy as it glided through what are now called the 'Kalahnit Straits'. It was only later, when the crew of the howker, GyHook, explored the debris field, the sad truth was realized.

Mihai shook her head. "At least they didn't suffer!" She pushed the memory from her mind and hurried on toward her own hidden destiny.

Making her way along a labyrinth of dimly lit corridors interrupted by dark tunnels opening into voids long silent from disuse, Mihai finally came to another set of hewn stone steps leading up to a musty antechamber, exiting onto a great hall. With a loud *'clack!'* and some effort, she pushed back the rusted tumblers, releasing the locked door.

Stale air rushed in as the door finally yielded to Mihai's determined push, the breeze whipping up a cloud of ancient dust from the great hall's floor. Sunlight streamed in from hidden windows high above illuminated tiny particles swirling in the air, limiting her view, but Mihai remembered well the majesty veiled. Few had been the steps upon these marble floors during this current age. Little had changed in this room since the hour of violence had been heralded here.

Mihai exited the anteroom, seeking the double doors at the far end of the hall. She quietly walked past banquet dishes filled with ashes of the last feast held here. Breads and pastries not eaten or carried off by hungry mice littered tables abandoned by the merrymakers when news of the Rebellion reached their ears. Everything remained as it was that day, some six millennia ago. No one had ever returned long enough to exorcise the anguished memories still haunting this place.

Looking to her left, Mihai spied the clear obsidian ballroom floor. Long ago there were lights buried deep within the stone. When lit, those standing there would appear to be floating in a multicolored sky of brilliant hues, their feet suspended as though upon nothing. It was said that Mother stood on it when the children heard her scream in pain, clutch her head and collapse to the floor. For days she did not stir from the bed she was carried to, not even giving forth a breath.

Mihai hurried on, trying to fill her mind with more pleasant thoughts, but it was a futile attempt. Her steps brought the woman past the head table, a place of honor set up by the host of hosts for special guests. It was Mihai's place of honor that day, her decaying shawl still draped across a chair where she had cast it when her kingly host whisked her away to share with her his *special* gift prepared for *her* on *her very special day*.

Mihai spewed a torrent of foul oaths better left to the imagination, storming off toward the exit. Before the Rebellion, expletives were rarely if ever used, but now it was quite common. Like some kind of a pressure valve, the very fragrance of coloured language seemed to ease the stress a person was under. Although used by her only on occasion, Mihai was willing to unleash her share when conditions were ripe for it.

After bursting through doors that screeched as if in agony, Mihai stormed along a darkened corridor and then another, kicking up clouds of dust that swirled around behind her. At long last she came to a spiral staircase, its steps descending deep into the bowels of the palace, and also ascending all the way to the most secluded of all enclaves, the Inner Chambers. Without hesitating, she bounded up the stairs.

The air seemed to freshen as Mihai climbed, leaving the world of darkness behind her. She now carried the ring representing the palatine powers granted her, but this was the first time she had journeyed uninvited into that realm belonging to the Firstborn. Indeed, it appeared to her that she was the only one who had braved the evil that had long remained hidden there.

"It is my right!" She cried. "My right...! I will decide the fate of this place from now on!"

The mouth may shout brave words while the heart quails in trepidation. So with Mihai... She felt sick to her stomach, secretly wishing to never visit herself upon that sanctum again. But it was now her right. In reality, it was her obligation, she believed, one that she had put off for close to two millennia. Destiny would no longer be denied. Every step she climbed brought Mihai closer to its ending hour.

The realm of the Firstborn encompassed a large portion of the Upper Palace. Originally this area consisted of a few rooms that overlooked an immense garden courtyard hidden from all eyes outside the Inner Chamber. Over time, Chrusion expanded his domain to include a much larger portion of the Upper Palace. When he had managed to obtain all the space Mother permitted of the Inner Chamber, he reached out and down within the old palace, eventually mining huge excavations in the diorite butte.

Banquet halls, guest rooms, studies, laboratories, game rooms and more were multiplied seemingly beyond number. If the fancy struck him, Chrusion might build a second or even third or fourth chamber for the same purpose, each more extravagant than the one before. Few of the children, including Mihai, had ever seen his entire lair, it being a labyrinth of countless rooms and passages. No one entered his world without his permission. Even Mother kept her distance, unless invited. And Chrusion protected his domain with a jealous passion.

Mihai cringed at the thought of exploring this inner sanctum of despair, but there was nothing else for it. The world that Chrusion created before the Rebellion was now as much a part of the universe as those creations of Mihai's mother. As she had once told her, 'One turning evil does not negate all the work done before the evil arrives. Indeed, many evil men have created great works that I will not bring to ruin just because the ones building them were wicked.'

As she neared the top landing of the staircase, Mihai pondered the reason she had chosen this trail of despair. Not to save time, as she had excused earlier. If anything, it might well have consumed more of it but, then, why?

At that moment she felt it, the nagging in her heart. It was as if something - or someone - put it in her to search out the past. Was it important in helping her define her future? Destiny was calling her ever forward, yet coming decisions - she knew not which - would force the woman to stare into the past, for wisdom is a gift earned, not given.

Passing up the final section of the staircase, Mihai entered another ante-chamber. Stepping onto the landing, she looked around the brightly lit room.

To this side and that were several doors, all secured with Cherub locks. There were no rings made with the power to open these doors. It was said that to each is the ability given or denied. Most of the doors had remained ever locked, Mihai knowing of no child using them.

She remembered, as a little girl, being caught in the attempt of struggling to pry one open. With twinkling emerald green eyes and a loving grin, Mother had picked up the curious child, shaking her head. 'Not today, little one, not today... someday... yes... maybe someday.'

To her left, Mihai spied another door. Above it were inscribed the words, 'CherbadrecDieukEdon' – Eden's Path. This was a once secret door known only to a few of Mother's children. Mihai had known, for sure, of only two people who had ever taken it. It now led nowhere, Tolohe having destroyed the passage on her return. Mihai shook her head, wishing to drive the memories of that day from her mind.

Directly in front of the landing was a locked doorway that opened to the main corridor leading to the EhpriemEtSamayim – 'Heaven's Door', 'Journey's End', 'The Lord's Manor' - at least those were the different interpretations for the word given to Mihai over the ages. There were probably more. Which if any were correct, the woman did not know. For her, this day, it was the end of her journey… or was it the beginning?

Calling out, again using the power of the ring, Mihai ordered the door open. She stepped into the cool serenity of the long corridor.

To call this place a corridor was the same as calling the Majestic a staircase. The vaulted sky-blue ceiling was some thirty long cubits high and its width some forty. Furniture of emerald and jade, inlaid with gold, sapphires and chrysolite complemented a holographic menagerie covering the walls. As one walked along, it appeared as if an entire jungle full of strange and exotic creatures journeyed with them toward their final destiny. Mihai never tired of this adventure.

Opened were the doors exiting the corridor. Mihai was expected. She passed beyond the reception hall and along a passageway that led to an opened portico, giving her a glimpse of the hidden courtyard and gardens within. She stood on tiptoes to get a better view.

Here was the one place in the universe unaffected by the Rebellion. The breathtaking plants and creatures cloistered within those walls cared not for the world outside. Not only were they beautiful beyond description, pleasing the eye and lifting the heart, the garden had the power to hold back the ever-present darkness that covered this universe. In some way, Mother had created a world of living harmonics that no form of evil discord could penetrate. Truly, this was the most tranquil place in the universe.

Suddenly, with a rush, a cool, refreshing storm raced through Mihai's back. It surrounded her heart in a spinning vortex of energy that pulled away all trepidation and fear. Mihai's nauseous sickness faded away while an overpowering sense of peace filled her chest. For but a breath, her head spun into a fuzzy darkness of glowing tingles. When she had returned to the waking world, all her previous unease had vanished.

Realizing the lateness of the hour, Mihai hurried from the portico, down a narrow hallway to a white marble alcove. To her left was a huge oaken door, a giant golden knocker affixed to its face. Reaching up, she took hold of the hinged weight, lifted and let it drop.

As she was reaching for it a second time, a voice some distance beyond the door called out, "Please enter…"

಄   ಐ   ಐ

Two women stared out the window to the quiet street far below. Some time earlier, they had watched Mihai pass under that very window as she made her way toward the Majestic. One of them finally let go the curtain and turned away, retracing her steps to the small bed in the corner of the room.

Stretching in a yawn, she turned back to the other and cooed, "Come, my love, I have not yet been given my fill of your love songs promised. This day is so fleeting and, when it has passed, I will have to wait so long to feel your breath upon my neck again."

The second woman looked away from the window, her face displaying a flirting frown, veiling her secret disdain for this urchin of latter days. Masking her feelings, she sang a sweet, hushed refrain:

> *"Oh, how I love the scent of your skin,*
> *The joy of your heart pressed close to mine.*
> *But we to labors must not delay,*
> *For the 'morrow must whisk us far away."*

Releasing the other side of the curtain, casting the room back into dark shadow, she shook her head. "My pet, please, do not arouse my desires until business has been concluded. Then, if you are a good child, I will fill you up to bursting."

Wrapping herself in a quilted, floor-length shawl, the woman sat at a small table. Calling her companion over, after requesting she cover herself also, the two took up their former discussion. Reaching into a small drawer hidden in the table, she withdrew some papers with scribbles and drawings. After laying them out so her companion could see, she explained, "These first two papers contain what appears to be little more than nonsensical poetry. Do not be fooled! Each word in each stanza and the way in which it is positioned is most important! You must memorize these pages as you see them. It is vital that you do just so."

She pulled the page with a drawing out from under the other papers, pointing, "Here you see Hall of Assembly, the auditorium where Mother's council will gather this night. Wait for me under the main stadium. The shadows are long, and the light sparse there. If you're careful, no one will notice you. I will come to you before the meeting, as soon as may be and give you whatever else you will need for your return journey."

The woman shuddered nervously. "My Queen, your slave begs your pardon for her open brashness, but I fear Lord PalaHar will be there this eve. He is a great councilor to Mother and I doubt he will miss this meeting. He will feel my scent for a certainty, after our many years together on Mu…"

"Enough of your drivel!" scolded the woman. The hurt on the other woman's face was quickly assuaged with gentle words. "Oh please, my darling, my darling!" She put her hand over her brow, moaning, "My head aches from the stresses of the hour and my mouth speaks the lies of that stress. Please forgive me for my outburst." Smiling, she took the woman's hand. "I promise! I will make it up to you. I will make it up to you."

"Don't concern yourself with PalaHar." She swallowed hard, trying to push down a sour taste growing in her mouth. "Your scent will be a forgotten dream for him this night. I will make sure his mind thinks only of my charms." Oh, how she wanted to vomit at the thought of *romancing* that man.

Drawing attention back to the moment, the woman opened a locket hanging from her neck and removed a tiny key from it. "Here, take this. It will provide entrance to a storage closet under the stadium. There you can remain hidden until I come to you. We will meet there instead of the pillars…sooner, if time plays in our favor."

Standing, she tenderly drew the woman up, softly kissing her on the lips, then whispered, "You must see to our business tonight. Eliseah, if you swear your oath to me, then we can be about other more delightful pleasantries."

The woman promised with an oath, her eyes shining with desire, adding, "My Queen, no man has bequeathed me as great a gift as you can provide. My heart will long swoon over the affection you are showing it this very day!"

As they embraced, a sour look crossed the face of the one being called 'queen'. Oh what sacrifices she made for the only love she desired! Oh, how she wanted him and yearned for his love! A smile grew on her lips at the thought of their soon being together again. Three millennia she had been away, clandestinely doing his will. The evening's council meeting would bring her one step closer to his embrace.

She disrobed her companion and began her sensuous caresses, fantasizing about being with the man she so loved. Each touch, each kiss was for *him*, with *him*. When the thought of his passion for his fellow kind entered her mind, she pushed it away, contending, 'I will change him! He longs for me! For me! My breasts, alone, will make him forget the love songs of his *androgyne*!'

ဆ   ဆ   ဆ

Mihai slowly opened the door onto a porch of rainbow onyx and glittering diamonds, entrance to the most sacred of all chambers in the universe, ZoeStethos - literally, *'The Breasts of Life Absolute'*. Legend attributed the origin of the name to the Ones Who Came Before, otherwise known as the Cherubs. Indeed, Mihai had been told long ago that the Chief Cherub, RosMismar, oldest of all his race, gifted that name upon this place, and that the words ZoeStethos were but a poor rendition of the original phonetic pronunciation.

No one, not even the Firstborn, was allowed entrance into these chambers without permission of the One who dwelt within. This was the first visit Mihai had made here since taking up the staff of steward and field marshal over Mother's armies. She wondered at the reason her mother requested they meet in this sanctuary, something so rarely done. It could only be for a very special reason, but what?

Surprisingly, the ZoeStethos was not as impressive as a visitor might imagine when compared with the remainder of the palace. True beauty abounded here… but it was of a humble nature. It was subdued, as if restrained, fearing for a person's approval. One had to search for the beauty, from intricately carved, spindly pillars supporting the marble ceilings to ornate paintings and tapestries hanging from the walls, but it was well worth the effort.

If one studied these surroundings long enough, a plethora of exciting emotions would begin bubbling up in the person's soul, filling his or her being with a rhapsodic rush, flooding their senses with sounds and sights of overwhelming proportions. But Mihai was in no mood to search and had no desire to experience such delights. She remained content to see these sights through simple eyes.

Glancing around, she spied one of the sparse furnishings, a red onyx bench affixed to a wall. With her simple eye, everything appeared cold and distant. Even the elegant octagonal sapphire table in the nearby room with its accompanying golden divan held no warmth. Shaking her head, Mihai quietly strode from the porch and toward an opened wall facing the courtyard with its enchanting gardens.

As she approached, a light breeze lifted silky curtains that hid the outer balcony from view. Beyond the billowing sheets, embroidered with mystical horses prancing in fields of gilded flowers, Mihai glimpsed green treetops reaching high above the garden hidden far below. The sunlight betrayed such astounding delights upon the woman's senses that Mihai's spirits were forced to rise.

Stopping to straighten her gown, she brushed back her hair while eyeing herself in a mirror on a distant wall. Satisfied, she stood erect, pushed her shoulders back and called out to her mother. There was no answer. After waiting a moment, Mihai cautiously stepped from the room through the curtains and onto the white marble balcony.

Off to her right, she spied the person she was seeking, slumped forward, hands on the balcony rail, gazing down on the garden far below. Before Mihai could speak again, a voice, sharp and accusing, disturbed her mind. "So… *it* has chosen your path today? And *you* permitted it? Little one, do you not yet understand? It is *always* seeking its master… always will… until you *kill* it. You must *destroy it!*"

At first stunned by her mother's harshness, Mihai countered in telepathic response. "The hour was late and I needed to make haste. I chose to…"

Mother interrupted. "*It* chose your path today! I have felt its orgasmic excitement growing ever since you parted company with your Trisha companion. Do not enter the Dragon's Lair again until Shiloh has cleansed that place of the evil lurking within! There are reasons it remains sealed down to this day. You put yourself at great risk taking that forbidden path."

Mihai's mother turned, her emerald green eyes piercing the sky blue oceans of her daughter and spoke aloud. "No other mortal has ascended to the glory of Chrusion. Even my children raised from the lower abyss are not yet a match for him. Child, the madness he abandoned to those caves beneath has greater power than you possess! I, alone, saved you this day. Do not trust to my loving kindness should you attempt that path again."

Mihai stood silent as a mouse. Crestfallen, she cried out, "Your daughter is supposed to rule as Firstborn, but her very throne lies beyond her reach! Shall my demon always rule my flesh? Will it also take away my waking hours and deliver me up to the ever-madness that haunts the lost souls of the Jahouk? My power slips away as we speak…" She bowed her head, sobbing, "Oh, Ma-we, I don't think I can…!" and fell into uncontrolled weeping.

The one Mihai called 'Ma-we' reached out to her daughter, as Mihai did for her mother. They embraced, Ma-we letting her daughter's tears fall onto her shoulder and run down her ankle-length golden hair to the floor. Soon she stood in a puddle of tears that splashed upon her bare feet.

A groan came up from Ma-we's heart. Here she stood with a child of the latter years, yet the most precious of all her sons and daughters, helpless to dispossess her of the monster growing within. Never was there a more beautiful person than this immortal of immortals but, for the moment, she felt tired, weak, bitter… and old. 'What good is the Mother of Life if she cannot save one innocent child?!'

Ma-we kept her feelings secret, though. Everyone looked to her for rescue. She dared not let them know that she could not see the future clearly at this moment. Life and all that went with it dangled by the thread of uncertainty. The future was not guaranteed. How could she know the final outcome when this day was still cast in doubt? Should Mihai fail this day, there would be no future… and she could not even see the destiny of this coming hour.

Starting a little melody, Ma-we sang a soft and gentle lullaby to Mihai. Since the wars had begun, the tears of Ma-we's daughters had run rivers on this balcony while, at the same time, the healing powers of Mother's songs and the surrounding harmonics helped to draw out the poisons building within her children's hearts. Today she sang for Mihai. Who would the 'morrow bring to her doorstep?

(*Author's note:* The name 'Ma-we' was secret, known to only Mihai, she having named her that when a young child, and it is used throughout these Chronicles to assist the present-day reader in maintaining continuity. Names given the Maker of Worlds are many, the ages having bestowed them upon her. Ma-we's other names: Yehowah, Lowenah, Erithia and others help add flavor of understanding to my account. Authors may, at times, take poetic license with their works, as I have chosen to do here. The oldest of her names was given to her by the Ones Who Came Before, the first of her children. It was long kept a secret, being only divulged to the common children, the children of flesh, at the end of the last age. It was not until long after the King's War that Mihai revealed her name for the Maker of Worlds, 'Ma-we', to her own children in her relating to them tales of her own life.

The author has chosen to include this name, Ma-we, to identify the Maker of Worlds throughout these Chronicles because it will continually draw the reader back to the person to whom all time and history owe their existence. Although told through the eyes of so many participants of these profound events, the account itself rises from the heart of but one person, Mihai. Had this child not presented herself upon the altar of love so many countless millennia ago – long before any rebellion – the worlds we take so for granted might not exist, the contrast between the evil of the oldest child and the self-sacrificing love of an innocent child never having been realized. Asotos likely would have become king over the universe, he taking up the scepter prepared for him. By the time his evil nature would have become fully manifest, it might well have been too late for anyone living, thus sending the entire universe into chaotic oblivion.

These Chronicles are about but one heart, one soul, and one mind. The strengths and weaknesses, successes and failures, joys and sorrows of this one woman must be judged as a mosaic of her life, one rich in emotion and love. Indeed, it was her love that lifted her to life's pinnacle of achievements, but also sent her to depths of deepest despair. She risked all and sacrificed all for love, her name becoming synonymous with the very word. So easy can it be to see the flesh, and Mihai was a child of flesh - foolish, careless, impetuous to the point of arrogance, and often a victim of her own loyal mis-conceptions. Yet, I say these very weaknesses are what made so many fall in love with this woman. Few were the soldiers of these oft-forgotten wars who would hesitate to take up their sword and follow their beloved leader into certain death, even if that death might lead to no redemption.)

ಬ   ಬ   ಬ

Inhaling the fragrant bouquet rising from one of Mother's magic teacups lifted Mihai's spirits. Indeed, this was a most wonderful place, filled with mystery and magic. Things appeared from nowhere, like the hot tea and sweet treats on the table near the divan. All a person had to do when he or she had emptied a cup was to wish for more and... *poof!* there appeared a steaming drink swirling inside the bowl.

A very long time ago, Mihai had asked Ma-we about the magical mysteries found in her dwelling. Mother laughed, answering, 'Magic does not exist by itself. It is only magic when you cannot see or do not understand the tools used to make that magic. My servants and tools are many and varied. They do my bidding.'

She had then taken her daughter's hand. 'Your body is a tool used by your mind, something you cannot see. It lets you know that you are alive for, without it, you would feel nothing at all. Honey, most of my world is invisible to you. You can only see and touch what I want you to.'

Looking around the room, Ma-we smiled. "It gets so cluttered in here at times, like it is right now. Tomorrow I must rearrange things and tidy up a bit."

Mihai had begged her mother for a peek at the wonderful things hiding in the nearly empty room. Ma-we stroked her daughter's hand. "My secrets are not shared with those requesting them. They are much too precious for that." She reached out and touched Mihai's face. "Someday, I believe, I will find reason to give up my treasures to another. Yes, my heart believes that someone, someday, will deliver up the key that will unlock all my secrets to them." Lowering her head, Ma-we let out a sigh. Looking back into wondering eyes, she grinned. "Maybe you will find the key… maybe you."

Leaning back, Mihai closed her eyes. As she allowed her mind to drift, she could see ghostly objects dance and flit around the room. Her ears could hear sounds as if people were speaking and her eyes could see shadowy figures move about. Then there came a sudden jolt and something brushed her arm. Bolting upright, Mihai's eyes popped open in surprise.

"Oh! Sorry, dear one! I should have announced myself before sitting." Ma-we grinned mischievously. Oh yes, Mihai had found the key that would open Ma-we's world of secrets. Ma-we frowned. But at what cost? The universe now hung in the balance, and Mihai? Mihai's eventuality was still in question. More than one war must be won if the girl was to survive to enjoy the revealing of Mother's secrets.

Ma-we settled back against the divan, resting one hand on Mihai's knee while holding a mug of steaming drink in the other. Cool, fresh air drifted across the room, carrying wonderful scents from the garden far below. The evil found in the outside world seemed so far away here, it was easy to forget that it existed at all. She could feel Mihai's muscles relax. It was a good sign, for the hour of uncertainty was about to begin.

Closing her eyes, Ma-we imagined the many possibilities of this day's outcome. A wrong word or inflection and all might be lost. But, maybe, just maybe, everything would go perfectly. She frowned. 'No, not with this child, nothing ever goes perfectly with this child.' A sad smile grew on her face. Isn't that what she liked most about this child? The girl was full of unpredictable energy to the point of being impetuous, always looking in new directions, seeking answers to questions not asked.

"Thinking sideways..." The words slipped out before Ma-we realized she was speaking aloud.

"What, Mother?" Mihai stared at Ma-we. "What..."

Ma-we grinned. "Oh, I was just thinking about that new friend of yours. He is so full of witty remarks and observations. Yep, I believe that Mr. Garlock fellow is good medicine for a weary heart." She nodded. "Glad you wanted him here."

Mihai heartily agreed. The two chatted about him and other new arrivals for a little while. Ma-we felt it helped ease the moment, besides providing an opening for her to move on to more important matters.

Gently caressing Mihai's hand with her fingers, she began, "You have come a great distance because I summoned you for an important meeting, yet you have chosen to pay me a personal visit beforehand."

Ma-we wiggled close, until her leg was touching her child's. "The sun goes ever forward, waiting not for man or beast. My daughter has many things pressing on her heart, and her mother has many other things pressing on hers. We must not dally any longer or the shadows of evening will find our business still lingering. Please, my dear one, speak to me of what weighs upon your heart."

Mihai peered into her mother's emerald green eyes. She was so small of stature and soft, dainty and soft. 'How deceptive...' She reached out, covering her mother's hand with hers. "Mother, even the sun would obey your voice should you only wish it, but you have surrendered all to us, your children, to give us freedom... something I doubt we deserve... or use wisely. The power you hide behind your heart is only matched by the majesty you cloak with gentle words."

Ma-we, who had never flaunted her personal qualities or abilities, blushed, glancing away from Mihai's stare. She thought herself ordinary, no one special, at least by her own making. Who was this person? She had not created herself. She had always been, always would be, she believed. It was true, she was the 'Maker of all things', but wouldn't any one of her children do the same if they possessed identical powers?

Shaking her head, Ma-we gently dismissed Mihai's remarks and returned to the subject. "This hour is yours. Do not waste it, for I will demand my time as well... and it will come. Before the sun flees the hidden garden, my time will come." She sat back, patting Mihai's knee. "So, now, tell me the reason for your heart's journey here this day."

Mihai's greatest wish, to resign her position as field marshal, was the hardest of subjects to broach. She felt like a quitter, having been given the post by her mother at the personal request of Gabrielle, who willingly relinquished it after Mihai's victorious return from the Lower Realms some two millennia ago. It was an honor to have this greatest of titles. Mihai felt ashamed to even be thinking of giving it up.

Being field marshal was far more than having charge of the armies. It had a direct link to the rule of the Firstborn… at least that is how the children viewed it. When the Rebellion first started and after Chrusion was driven from the Palace, Gabrielle took over the headship of the children, standing the throne of the empire Chrusion had built.

For over four thousand years, Gabrielle ruled as archon robustus - pontifex maximus, meaning 'the greatest bridge builder'. As such, she stood before the other children as chief councilor and leader of the festivals. Her words became as powerful as Chrusion's once were. She spoke as the mouth of God. It was well into the fifth millennia before 'field marshal' replaced 'archon robustus' as the title for the highest office in the Empire. 'Such as war does to all things more peaceful…'

Mihai let out a groaning sigh. She could not make that request, at least not quite yet, and there were other pressing issues. "The insurgents are making deeper intrusions into the neutral territories near the Frontier. The Zephath was attacked. Although the crew was able to scuttle the ship, they were taken hostage."

Ma-we sat silent, eyes closed.

Seeing no response, Mihai added, "Sirion was among them."

Still nothing…

"I tracked them as far as the outpost on ZemiaKone. There I was confronted by a battle droid and got a good thrashing and couldn't go on." She looked down at the floor. "Was told the Gravemaker saved me from certain death..." Again, Mihai sighed. "I lost their trail after that."

Mihai turned toward Ma-we, asking, "Mother, who's the Gravemaker?"

Time pressed on. Still Ma-we said nothing.

This moment was becoming awkward for Mihai. She began to explain, "The Zephath was an imperial class heavy cutter, with a crew of over thirty. It was reconnoitering the Frontier beyond the Trizentine when it was attacked. I do not believe the Stasis Pirates would take on a ship of that size without additional support. The trail led us away from the Trizentine area, the Stasis home base, into enemy terr…"

"My dear!" Ma-we interrupted. "You have been too long away when you think tales of your misadventures are news for my ears." She stood and stepped a few paces away before turning to make further comment.

With feet together and hands clasped at her waist, she leaned forward and stared into Mihai's eyes. "After the Great War ended, as part of the armistice, my children established a neutral zone along the Frontier or Outer Corridor on which the Trizentine borders. At that time, if you do recall, it was suggested at the council to remove all inhabitants from that area including the district capital, Exothepobole. Also, if you remember, no one other than, say, myself deemed it necessary or even prudent."

"PalaHar, Tizrela, Ardon, Gabrielle, and..." She squinted. "and, I believe, even *you* 'pooh–poohed' my concerns. The atrocities inflicted upon that desolate place, including the senseless raids on distant settlements these recent months, need not have happened if my counsel had been held in reasonable account."

Although Ma-we's tone was gentle, the words spoken stung Mihai, but she remained silent.

Ma-we went on. "The news of the Zephath was troubling to my heart, but it was not unexpected. You have been forced to keep several military garrisons out there to protect the foolish people unwilling to leave. It was only going to be a matter of time before trouble would brew in those wild lands. The Stasis are bad enough, with their warped and twisted minds having turned them to little more than animals. But any of my children should have seen that Chrusion would not stay away from there long... especially if he could do something to get at you."

Standing straight, Ma-we turned toward the balcony. "Sirion... Sirion... let's see. She is one of my youngest." Ma-we glanced over her shoulder at Mihai. "What was she, just come of age a little before the bad happened, right?"

Mihai sadly nodded. "Fourteen she was at the time. Her birthday was the same as my coming of age anniversary."

Ma-we nodded back, then returning to look out over the balcony, added, "You were my wet nurse for her, too, weren't you? Your first child, as I recall, the first of your life's milk you gave to that girl." She smiled, remembering, "Oh, how my heart danced the day you gave your breasts to that child, the surprised look on your face as you felt, for the first time, the elixir of life being drawn from your body to nourish the soul of another." She closed her eyes. "I watched you fall in love with my girl that very hour."

"I handed my child over to you to raise, because I saw how close the two of you became. But I wasn't the only one who knew just how deep the bond was between you two. Remember the look of displeasure in Chrusion's eyes when Sirion ran to your arms after her coming of age, and how he chastised the child for her actions? He was jealous of you even then, before I gave the world of men as a gift to you."

Mihai silently pondered, thinking about those happier days before the bad came.

Ma-we walked back to the divan and sat, leaning back, looking toward the ceiling while rubbing Mihai's leg. "Had I been consulted on the matter, I would have cautioned you about sending Sirion away on the Zephath.

How you could have believed that sending a child of your blood out to the Dragon's Hearth would keep her safe from his fire is beyond me." She stared at Mihai. "But to go there, yourself, by yourself?!" She shivered. "I have no words for that."

She squeezed Mihai's leg. "Your foolishness almost got you captured… captured! Oh, I know your intentions were honorable, but the risk you took was far too great. Have you so little sense as to forget the oath Chrusion swore the day he was driven from this land? *You!* You, my dear…his entire passion is to bring to a finish what he attempted those many days ago, to hurt me by torturing you to death. Look how many of your sisters have already been destroyed by his madness!"

Ma-we shook her head. "There would have been no prisoner exchange for you. Chrusion would have denied your capture, forcing me to eventually move against him in war. How many of my children would the rescue of your flesh cost me? And what would it have proved? Chrusion would only claim the attack unjustified, that I used my powers for selfish reasons. He would have found cause to draw out this Rebellion until, maybe, the hope of all living things might fade away."

Mihai shuddered at the thought of Chrusion's touch. His last had left her broken in mind and body for endless days. Indeed, her mind still suffered his intrusions. As she thought of that long ago hour, the demon within snickered with quiet delight, feeling the woman's growing fear. Mihai hurriedly pushed those memories from her mind.

A wry smile broke on Ma-we's face. "But you were not alone, no thanks to you. And this should answer your question…or at least as well as I'm going to answer it. The Gravemaker walks in the shadows of mist and darkness. From the depths below I have raised it, only to hand it over to the Ones Who Came Before. Among your kind it walks, but cannot be seen or heard, for it fogs the mind of simple folk with thoughts of foolish prattle. My bidding does the Gravemaker do. Until the day of its revealing, secret it shall remain."

Although still troubled, Mihai thanked her mother for what information she was willing to share with her. The thoughts of Chrusion and his tortures hurried along a growing nauseous sickness that had troubled the woman for most of the morning. Seeing this, Ma-we offered her some soothing mint tea, taking a cup also. The two sat for a little while, relaxing in its healing powers.

When finished, Ma-we set her cup on the table. They both watched the dish begin to vibrate and shimmer, like heat on hot pavement, until it faded from sight. Mihai never tired of watching the magic of Mother's house, this just one small example.

Ma-we leaned back and looked into Mihai's eyes, asking, "Do you think the attack on the Zephath was a random coincidence?"

Surprised, Mihai asked, "You think it wasn't?!"

Shaking her head, Ma-we softly answered, "Chrusion was baiting you. He knew full well you would personally take up the search and attempt rescue of Sirion." She sat forward, eyes excited. "He failed to capture you! His primary plan has been foiled!"

Mihai countered, "That may be all well and good, but Sirion still remains in his clutches. I ache to think what ordeals he must be putting her through."

Ma-we patted Mihai's arm reassuringly. "He will try to break her. He will attempt it with the entire crew of the Zephath…already has. Some will die, some will falter, but…"

"But what, Mother? But what?"

Looking at the floor, Ma-we continued, "Sirion is made of a metal that is rarely found in this land. There is nothing they can do to that girl that can break her and there are powers greater than hers that will not allow death to pass her door, and…"

"And what, Mother? Mother, what?" Mihai's eyes brimmed with curiosity.

"And…" Ma-we looked away. "And it was not your Sirion that Chrusion was after, only the icing on the cake. Your heart is not the only one he wishes to destroy."

"What do you mean by what you say?!" Mihai asked, dread filling her heart.

Twisting her head around, fixing her gaze on Mihai, Ma-we answered, "What I have said is sufficient. Knowledge belongs to those deserving and at the time appropriate. You deserve to know, but not at this time. Let this suffice: your child, given over to your care, will return to you soon, but not as you wish. What I do see in my mind you will see with your eyes, and you will begin to understand what rulership is all about."

There were so many questions Mihai wanted to answers to. Ma-we allowed no time for them, hurrying on. "Your brother has been in contact with me. He feigns innocence concerning the capture of the Zephath's crew, claiming to have rescued them from the hands of the Stasis Pirates."

"The bastard! Insolent bastard!" Mihai went into a tirade, spewing curses and oaths regarding how evil and wicked Chrusion was. Ma-we finally silenced her after she cried out accusatively, "Asotos deserves only a butcher's skewer and a baker's furnace! Why do let him live?!"

"That is enough of you!" Ma-we scolded, glaring in anger. "Life is not as you know it! And death is not always the answer! When the forest becomes diseased, it must be swept with fire, first to bring to ruin the evil living there, second, to wake the seed that must suffer the holocaust to gain life."

Pausing long enough to regain her composure, Ma-we took hold of Mihai's hand, squeezing it. "Child! Who do you think I am, some weak-minded, emotional twit who's afraid of making decisions?!" She shook her head. "You don't know me, then!"

Ma-we stood, waving her arms as she paced. "I have swallowed up worlds in my rage, consigned women and children to the fire, leveled mountains when they have opposed me, and dried up the seas as if they were mere drops of water! Why have I allowed Chrusion to live down to this day? Why have I allowed *you* to live to this day? Neither of you has paid me the price of your blood. You both deserve the same reward, if I so choose."

She thumped her chest. "*I* made these universes... and *I* can take them away! How can you stop me? *No one can!* Life is a gift that *I, alone,* have given! To *me* it belongs! *With it, I will do as I please!*"

Mihai was ashamed of her actions. With downcast eyes, she stared at her folded hands resting in her lap. "Mother, the Maker of Worlds, the Beginning of the beginning and the End of all things, your name we children gave to you – 'Yehowah' – 'I shall choose to be whomever I so choose' – it is a beautiful name that gives us hope. Your servant girl has become impetuous and overstepped her position. I am so sorry."

Ma-we came forward and stooped in front of her daughter, resting her hands on the girl's knees. She looked up into teary eyes and smiled, slowly shaking her head. "No, my dear one, no, you have not *become* impetuous. You have never stopped!! From the time your brothers pulled you from the palace cistern because you believed there were diamonds hidden under the sparkling frigid waters, you have shown your impetuousness."

Mihai whimpered, "What good am I, then? As Firstborn, I have repeatedly led your children to slaughter. Has my foolishness brought them to ruin?"

"Now child..." Ma-we gently berated her daughter for acting so self-deprecatingly. "You have been an outstanding military leader. Why, even the most ancient of the Ancients willingly follow under your banner."

She stood and began to pace anew. "'Terror of the Skies'... I was informed that you earned that name from the enemy at the Battle of Mordem Heights, after your squadron of fighters faced off against an enemy force ten times your number. And, as I have also been told, your own sword cut down MitlockeDorzandee, the Tyrant of Ancepities. I ask you, how many lives did you preserve on that day?"

Mihai moaned, slowly shaking her head. "You speak of *minor* successes. I have failed miserably when the hour was most pressing."

She stared up at her mother who was patiently listening. "What about Memphis? For three months we laid siege to the Castle. It was ours for the taking, or at least I thought so. I ordered three full corps, *a quarter of a million soldiers,* into the 'valley of death' – the Battle of Bauglow, as you might recall."

Hanging her head in remorse, Mihai finished. "One hundred thousand never returned. We watched from the eastern hills, helpless, as they raped and tortured the wounded to death. It was *all my fault*. I misread the enemy, not reckoning on hidden reinforcements. All I could see was the capture of Memphis and the death of Legion."

"Memphis…" Ma-we sighed, closing her eyes. "Ah, yes… Memphis."

"Yehowah!" Mihai groaned, "Your servant girl was… is… too impetuous as you, yourself, have pointed out. How does such a reckless person ever wash away the blood of guilt from their own hands?"

Ma-we frowned, scolding, "Do not seek pity from me, and do not attempt your own demeaning. Full well I know that my agents stood your side that day, approving your decision to attack Castle Memphis. PalaHar, Gabrielle, Planetee, and Euroaquilo all agreed the hour for taking the city was ripe. Even Anna added her support. You acted with what knowledge you had." She turned away, bitter. "The serpents hidden in your camp betrayed your people – my children. Had all been honest with you, the Battle of Bauglow would not have been a defeat."

Excited, Mihai asked, "Tell me, tell me, please! Who are the spies among us?"

Shaking her head, Ma-we answered, "No! I will not say. For then you will ask me for proof. Remember your own law: 'At the voice of two or more, let the matter be settled'. I am but one voice, though I know for a fact who slinks around in dark corners."

She wagged her finger. "You and your people would know, too, if you did not blind your hearts with feelings of selfish love and mindless devotion. No! You must use your wisdom to discover the traitors in your midst."

It did Mihai no good to beg her mother. Ma-we refused to speak further about it, changing the subject. "I have other business that I must return to. As I said, your brother has been in contact with me and, as you will learn in greater detail tonight, wishes to offer another exchange of prisoners, but…"

"But what, Mother… er… Yehowah?!" Mihai asked, eager to hear more.

Ma-we's heart fluttered with joy. 'My daughter remembers who I have become in the eyes of my children. There is hope, then, that she will not forget me when my coming storm washes over her.'

Stepping forward, she again sat beside Mihai and started playing with the woman's fingers. "But your brother has demanded that I stand aside in the negotiations. Oh yes, I can be there, but must remain silent. He… he has demanded your soul as archon in standing before him or there will be no exchange at all."

Mihai's face paled as she coughed down rising bile from a churning stomach. She waved her hand, rejecting the thought of facing such evil.

Ma-we hugged her child. "Don't say no! Not yet! Think about it… Your brother, who has attempted to humiliate you so many times has lifted you up to the throne of God. By his own mouth, he has declared a woman to be his equal… a woman to stand as king over all the universe, a gift I was at one time preparing to give him. Can you believe it, a *woman* sitting the *throne* of the *King* of the *universe*? Even your *brother* has thought it possible."

Swallowing hard first, Mihai exclaimed, "But I'm too impetuous!"

Grinning, Ma-we nodded. "You are impetuous, yes, but not *too* impetuous. Chrusion is baiting you, yes, and he will use this prisoner exchange to create more of his mischief. And, I believe, he will attempt to destroy you to hurt me."

She hugged her daughter again, resting her head on Mihai's shoulder. "But I know my Michael better than he. If you say 'yes', I can prepare some *mischief* of my own that will both *humiliate* him and rescue Sirion and the others."

She looked into Mihai's face, begging, "Please say you'll come. Please say you'll stand before your brother."

Frowning, Mihai nodded she would go. Later, she would wonder if Mother's pleadings made the difference, or if the thought of having Sirion back in her arms was the true motivating force behind her accepting Ma-we's request. Whatever… Mihai was now going to have to confront her most feared protagonist again. This time it would be face to face without Gabrielle standing by her side.

"Good! Good!" Ma-we sang, her eyes lighting up with excitement. "Tonight I will make final arrangements for the trip. There will be some surprises for your brother that he will not have considered."

She wagged her finger in front of Mihai's face, cautioning, "Now, you must remember, his intention is to goad you into doing something out of line with his accepted form of diplomacy, providing him with excuse for a little blood-letting… yours and probably the prisoners, including Sirion. That must not be allowed to happen!"

Mihai moaned, "How is a *good old impetuous person* like me going to stop from doing something *stupid* and not get us all killed?!"

Smiling, Ma-we patted her daughter's arm. "You will do the best you can. That's all I expect. The rest? The rest… well, I'm sure it'll work out."

Mihai's head whirled, thinking of the many ways she could deliver tragedy and death upon the innocent at the coming prisoner exchange. Ma-we's gentle love strokes helped soothe the woman, releasing her fears to the day. Why should one trouble over coming moments when the Maker of Worlds cradles that person in her arms?

Resting her head against the back of the divan, Mihai whispered, "Yehowah, I love you..."

Ma-we broke out with a silly, cooing song, a little ditty she has sung to so many of her children.

"When the birds of summer come home to roost,
will you still play the fridderler dee?

Or will you say 'I am all grown up!'
and no more will come 'round for tea?

Will you dance in my garden to the leafy leaf's tune,
or cry out, 'I'm too big for those kinds of toys!'?

Oh, stay with me child,
until I can grow up.

Oh, stay with me...
and make my heart smile."

She repeated the tune over and over, changing the musical tones ever so slightly each time. To the ear of the listener, the altered tune would change the meaning of the song, creating new and different emotions from the stanza before. It was not long before Mihai was humming along with Mother's singing.

Mihai's thoughts drifted to and fro as she thought of her mother. 'Yehowah' was a name given her by the children, reminding them of promises to be kept. It was a reassuring name. Then there was 'Lowenah', a name Mother had given herself so long ago, long before Mihai was born.

'Ma-we'? That was Mihai's secret name given to Mother many long years ago, when she was but a child. 'Now, what was its meaning? Why, this day, should I ponder its existence?'

She was interrupted when Ma-we softly asked, "You have journeyed far this day to gain my ear. Tell me please, child, what business presses your soul to distraction?"

All Mihai's earlier trepidation and fear reawakened to do battle with her mind. Mother appeared confident for her daughter to continue to lead the armies of the Children's Empire. Mihai felt differently, but she did not want to hurt her mother, at least any further than she believed she already had.

Lifting her hand to her forehead, Mihai closed her eyes and groaned, "Mother... my sweet, dear Mother, I do not wish harm upon you because of my childish actions, but listen, please, to what I have need of argument for. There exist others in this land who can carry the torch of battle in a more qualified manner. Gabrielle, herself, has set such a stalwart example, being far better at it than myself."

She began to plead, "Mother...today, this very hour, your daughter has shown her weakness of command. There comes a time when other hands must gather the banners of war and another soldier must share in the responsibility of slaughter."

With tears, Mihai concluded, "I have come to request your acceptance of my resignation as field marshal over the armies of the Children's Empire."

Ma-we softly stroked Mihai's leg, asking, "My daughter, who among the children of this world is as qualified as you to lead this great host? Ah, but for Gabrielle? Little do you know about her, not enough to judge her worthiness of again leading my armies. Qualified? Yes! But I shall not have her ruin be at my hand. Who among my children besides her has the qualities needed to bring us victory?"

As a feeling of hopelessness grew in Mihai's heart, she could feel the demon within slowly crawling into her waking mind, and blurted out, "Mother, there is a beast inside me that grows in power from day to day! I fear it shall soon overtake my mental abilities!" Tears began anew. "I have carried the commander's staff for too long. I hear the laughter of the beast when I issue the sentence of death on my followers… your children. Now when I stand the admiral's bridge, I feel the monster's excitement, wishing me to send more people to the slaughter. It cries out to me in the voices of all who have fallen under my sword. It uses the songs of friends and lovers to mock me and discredit my motives. It throws my mind into a raging river of blood where the slain, both the evil and the good, cry out to me, cursing me for their death."

The demon was fully awake now, ignoring the harmonic peace found in this protected place. It began to hiss in disgust, chiding Mihai over her desire to remove herself from command. *'What is it that it hates? Power? No! It loves power, but is stupid in how it uses it. Listen to me and I will show you the true glory of power. I will make you great with it! Then I will let you rest…then…'*

Mihai cried aloud. "Leave me go, or I shall burn us both in Hell's fire!"

The monster yelped in fear, but refused to leave.

Mihai now cried out to her mother. "I fear that the day will arrive when this beast will overcome my reasoning! Should that happen in an hour of need, oh, the many souls I might bring down to nothing for, if I am taken over by this madness within, the whole world will dissolve into destruction as I turn on the innocent! And I shall bring evil upon the land, flooding over all good things, crushing and destroying all goodness, until nothing but the dust of memories remains!"

The demon clawed its way further into Mihai's consciousness, attempting to wrest control from the woman. Mihai groaned, sighing, her voice trailing off. "I am tired… oh, so tired. What is this day that I should rejoice for? I call out to friends who cannot call back. Then comes smoke of ages passed and I crawl through it only to find pain and suffering."

Suddenly, Mihai, eyes wild with fear, screamed, *"The beasts! The beasts! They are tearing me apart! Oh, god! My belly is burning up with fire! His laughter! His stinking, black breath... his wild laughter is shredding my mind! I am falling, falling! The stench of my own bowels fills my nostrils!"*

Desperate words frought with hysteria rent the air. *"I am choking on my own vomit, and his laughter, his ugly laughter!"* The woman raged on and on, her words more and more incoherent, mumbling strange, disjointed phrases as she babbled on about nothing and everything.

In her head, the demon laughed its little ditty as it clawed away at Mihai's sanity, seeking escape from its prison:

"A moment more!
A moment more!
And I shall rip apart this door,
That binds me to this horrid place...
And through these bars,
I'll make escape...
But not alone will be my fate.
For your mind and soul I'll also take!"

Out of the frantic, wild throes of a growing seizure, Mihai bolted upright, screaming angry curses and defiant oaths. As her eyes locked in a glassy stare and fingernails tore through skin and flesh, she suddenly froze like a haunted statue.

Focusing all her power inward, Mihai went on a hunt for the demon. Upon seeing the madness in her heart, the monster screeched in fear and anger, *"Let me go! Let me leave this horrid place! Curse your filth...your stink...your heart! Putrid thing! Putrid thing! Let me go! Let me leave!"*

With a banshee's fury, Mihai struck, catching the demon and throwing it down. As they struggled with one another, she hurled threats and curses. "Shall you find me so kind on the 'morrow, I will tear you asunder and feed your soul to all good things! Seek me and I will imprison you for all eternity until all life ceases its existence!"

Thrashing about to gain release, the monster finally got a grip on Mihai's arm, sinking its fangs deep into her flesh. Mihai cried out in pain, releasing the beast. Off it ran, chiding her with threats and oaths.

As the curses faded away, Mihai found herself drifting further into a fathomless darkness, floating aimlessly in a black fog, seeing and feeling nothing. Eventually the woman began to sense a gentle rocking motion and then a quiet voice calling her name. "Michael... my darling little Michael... Little child, come back to me..."

Mihai's eyes slowly fluttered open, gradually regaining their focus.

Ma-we sat close, arms wrapped around her baby-child, humming a silly tune that stirred Mihai's memory into recalling happier times, when the world was a friendlier place to be. Soon the recent ordeal with the demon was little more than an unpleasant dream.

Recalling her earlier request to be relieved of command, Mihai fitfully whispered, "You see what the blackness does when it overtakes me? What would be our fate should I be overcome at a critical moment? Mother, I dare not take such a chan…"

Ma-we stopped her daughter. "Now, Michael, that's not the case at all and you know it! My dear child, this this creature of darkness dares not enter your world until you have relaxed your hold on its barred door. Indeed, I saw that you were nearly free of it this day. That was at least my hope."

"Your hope?!" Mihai was disturbed and perplexed. "How could you *hope* such a thing?! The monster would have stolen my very being, clear to my hidden mind if I had permitted it leave!"

Ma-we's smile was sweet but sad as she shook her head. "This place is not like your world, for the laws of the universe do not hold dominion here. I, alone, can dictate good and bad in this place."

She returned to stroking her child's arm. "For reasons that you are not privy to at this time, had you surrendered to this beast within and given up your glory to it, it would now be only a bitter memory. No longer could your brother's creation trouble you."

Mihai stared at her mother in disbelief.

Ma-we sighed. "Even the most loving among my children has little faith. Faith is what you lack, the same as your brothers and sisters. Indeed! Had faith the size of a mustard seed been found among your kind on that first day of darkness, this world would not have been consumed with evil."

The feeling of being insulted rolled with the words off Mihai's tongue. "What is faith if I and my kind have not displayed it? Have we not given all that is ours to you, trusting that you will deliver us in the ending hour?"

Ignoring the tone, Ma-we replied, "Faith is not what your think it to be." She pointed first to her head and then her heart. "Faith is born not here, but here. It is not the blind acceptance that someone will make it right…save you, so to speak. It is the wisdom of harmonic feeling, the knowledge in your heart that the entire universe has been designed in my image. It has my soul living within it."

She took Mihai's hand. "Truth be told, if my children – the leaders of your kind – if they had demonstrated, en mass, the faith they should have possessed, the harmonic power they could have produced would have withered the very evil lurking in your brother's heart. He and his co-conspirators would have turned to dust that very day."

Turning away, Ma-we sighed. "Now the very future of all living things rests in doubt. Faith is but a fleeting hope in a strange and wild people, that they can gain understanding to harness the power of the harmonics and bring to nothing the discord before it destroys the universe."

Patting Mihai's hand, she looked into her daughter's face. "You have proved your mettle this day. You chide yourself, preaching your weaknesses, yet you stand a pillar of strength. Where among my children is there another like you to lead and direct my children?"

Not allowing her daughter to reply, she added, "This day I will provide you a helper to slow the demon's advance. It shall not trouble your waking hours for many days to come. Do be careful, though, for it will still attempt to swage your thoughts into doing its will."

Ma-we went on to console Mihai, finishing with a word of hope. "Although my powers to destroy your monster shall no longer be available - for I see your will is so strong - should I succeed at the demon's destruction, I would also destroy my daughter in the process. I see a man who is yet to prove to be a man, come in power and glory to bring to nothing what was created so long ago."

"My dearest one, most cherished of all my birthlings, when my daughters delivered you to this room, this very divan, I was helpless to assist you. When my strength returned, I saw the damage done to your body and hurried to rescue you from death. I also looked into your mind, searching for mental trauma, not perceiving your brother's inventions. He having kept them secret from me, I failed to find the seed of darkness he implanted in you. Only when your little sister revealed her monster within did I explore your mind. By then, the beast had become so entwined with your soul, like with your sister, I could not destroy it without damaging or killing your very being."

"So, my dear child, my hope was for this day, here in this very place, that I could bring to nothing what has become so strong. I have waited so long for this hour. Alas, your rescue now lies in the hands of your Shiloh to do what I can no longer accomplish. You must learn to trust this boy and have faith that his wisdom is greater than yours."

Pushing down a growing fear, Mihai promised, "I will listen to his voice! I will! I will!" She closed her eyes, softly crying.

Still patting Mihai's hand, Ma-we spoke, more to herself than to Mihai. "There remains yet hope hanging upon a thread, but hope it is. The 'morrow brings a new sun, and with it glory renewed."

Taking Mihai's face in her hands, Ma-we kissed her daughter, comforting her. "My Love, do not think your road too long or your adventure so harsh. Remember, it is the most perilous journey that is fondly remembered, the adventure most often retold. The more chilling the wind, the warmer the blazing hearth. You must remember that you do not walk through your valley of death alone. I would never abandon your heart."

"Now, my lovely one, you have time to gain needed rest here before your journey begins. Take advantage of that rest and enjoy some time with your family and acquaintances. You stay alone with your thoughts way too much. First we will finish our business!" She rubbed her stomach. "But not until we have gained some nourishment."

Taking Mihai's hands, she pulled her daughter up from the divan. "Come, please, we shall conjure something up together."

೮೦   ೮೦   ೮೦

The luncheon was a delight, taking Mihai's mind completely off any earlier unpleasantries. With Mother's help, she conjured up hot biscuits, sweet jams, a stick of salted, herbed cheese, two goblets of Medeba mint-cherry wine, and all sorts of little goodies that make a meal just right.

Although a few of the oldest children could master some control over the elements, as such mind manipulation was often called, only Ma-we had ever demonstrated it this powerfully. Sharing her ability by channeling her energy through Mihai's mind, but letting the girl choose what appeared for the feast, was appreciated and enjoyed, making the meal taste so much better.

After watching dishes and leftovers vanish from sight, Ma-we suggested they retire to the balcony. "The breeze drifts up from below, carrying with it the fragrance of so many summer flowers. Come, take my ivory chair and recline. The golden willow one I shall have."

The two strolled out to the balcony, chatting about unimportant matters. Mihai sat, patting her flowing dress to smooth it. Ma-we stopped behind her chair, gazing over the handrail at the garden below. Her clothing, other than a necklace of diamonds and rubies, and an anklet of sapphires, was but her long, golden hair dancing and floating on the breeze. When asked once by a newcomer to her world why the children so often went naked, she answered, surprised, 'Why, I have clothed them already! See how all that is private to each is hidden by downy fluff?' She laughed. 'And it is so easy to wash...'

Ma-we remained silent for some time, pondering the hours – past, present and future. The sun had long waxed high past the noon hour before she spoke. Time was such a fleeting thing. Today...today Ma-we had long ago chosen to be a pivotal point in fate's history...if Chance smiled on her. Faith was the only gift she had to curry Chance's favor – faith that her daughter could comprehend the meaning of true wisdom. Well, she would do her best to ignite that wisdom, starting at this moment.

Mihai patiently waited for her mother to speak. The morning had belonged to her. Now was Lowenah's turn. She did not know if Ma-we would approve her resignation... but Mother had not rejected it either. If the issue was to be addressed today, it was not to be done by her mouth. Ma-we knew her daughter's desires. She also knew her daughter's heart better than Mihai.

How to start? Ma-we puzzled. The future of all life in the realms above and below might well depend on decisions made this day. She thought of counsel she once offered to Tolohe, 'The wise often do not act wisely because they attempt to see wisdom through the eyes of another wise one. Wisdom is to make decisions based not on the knowledge of others, but on your own. If you ignore the *emotional* wisdom of your heart, seeing it as mere foolishness, and choose to follow only the *enlightened* wisdom of your mind, then you will surely fail.'

Today Mihai must decide the fate of worlds. There was nothing else for it. Mother had surrendered her sovereign powers up to her children when she endowed them with freedom... freedom to choose for themselves fate's course. Mihai must have the same freedom today and her mother must be careful in word and action not to violate that right. Should she fail, by robbing her daughter of this most precious gift, then all would be lost anyway.

Ma-we smiled. There was hope. Mihai was *very* emotional.

Her eyes still fixed on the garden below, Ma-we softly asked, "My child of the Golden Age, Mistress of the Emerald Sea, and heir of all things good in my heart, do you love me?"

What a simple question. In the world of men, it is carelessly bantered about whenever the heart flutters in disquiet. But, for Mihai, it was like the edge of a blazing sword, piercing flesh and spirit. What great failure on her daughter's part had driven Lowenah, the mother of love – indeed, the very *essence* of love – to question the motives of this most loyal of children? What evil did she see in her child?

Troubled to the point of being distraught, Mihai faltered, fearing the response from her reply. "Mother, the light of all my life, my heart knows no other like that of the love in my heart for you. If your little child has failed in her love, please, show her where she must correct her understanding."

Ma-we remained silent, seemingly absorbed in the visual delights of the garden. After what was an agonizing eternity for Mihai, Ma-we responded with another question. "Michael, daughter of the dawn, swaddled in moonbeams, serenaded by the swans, child of my flesh... do you trust me?"

Mother's words were filled with endearments, but Mihai could tell they were only a candy coating for a very bitter pill. It was obvious that Lowenah was probing the woman's very being, searching her to her kidneys, but for what? In what way was Mihai lacking? How had she injured her mother's heart so as to be receiving such punishment? Was she going in the way of her evil brother, just not arrived there yet?

No! Mihai could not believe her soul was so corrupted as that. Yet in some way she had failed... or was failing. In agony of heart, Mihai cried out, "How has the child of your dreams come to despise the Giver of life?! I cannot see the darkness of betrayal you impute I carry. Please! My Lord! My God! How do I lack trust in you?!"

Unmoved, Ma-we asked yet a third question. "My precious love, child of the free days, ruler as if Firstborn, to whom all things have been given, to whom do my children belong? Who is their God?"

To Mihai's already aching heart, this question added bewilderment and confusion. Mihai was not god over the souls of this place. Never had she contemplated such a thing. Asotos did! Was Mother implying that her daughter had, in some way, also sought godship for herself?

With tears, Mihai pleaded with Ma-we. "Mother! Oh, Mother! Creator of all things! Where have I failed you and how have I stolen your crown from off you? Please! Your child begs you. Do not torment her soul any longer! What wickedness is she guilty of?"

Ma-we did not reply swiftly. She was waiting for her daughter to absorb the full impact of the lesson being taught. Oh, yes! Mother was there for the present, to assist in time of need. She frowned at the thought, because off in the distance she could see a darkness ever growing. There were days coming when her wise counsel might well be far out of reach of her children. Mihai would then have to depend on her own heart to guide her across jagged skies.

"Tell me, oh king over all living things…" Ma-we paused for effect.

It worked very well. In only seconds, Mihai was sobbing in near uncontrolled tears. Mother's tone of voice had carried with it an accuser's tongue, implying a usurper in her company. Ma-we smiled to herself. Her child was not arrogant, proud or boastful, that she could tell. It is most interesting what a few well-placed questions can reveal.

Ma-we patiently waited for her daughter's tears to subside and then began to quiz Mihai on lessons past. "Tell me, please, when you long ago walked among men of clay, did you not see the evil of men over-lording men?"

Mihai nodded.

Turning to face her, Ma-we continued, "And did you not see how men would honor me with their lips, yet despise me with their actions?"

"Yes."

"And yet, those very men who so openly praised me rejected my power to bring a rebirth to those who had come before them. Am I not right?"

"Yes, Mother! You are so right." Mihai nodded.

Leaning forward, Ma-we squinted, eyeing her daughter. "If I recall correctly, when confronted by those *same* wicked men, you confessed openly that I was the 'God of the living', expressing your full confidence in my abilities to renew life. Is that not what you, yourself, said?"

Mihai's heart beat in trepidation, knowing that, in some way, her actions had stirred this conversation. But, as Mother was so skilled at doing, the girl's curiosity had been roused. No matter how painful the lesson, she must hear it out.

She answered, "Yes, Mother, those were my words to them."

Standing back, Ma-we asked, "Indeed! What ability did I pass along to you while your feet tread the fields of that land?"

With eyes not yet understanding, Mihai responded, "You handed over to me the gift of life renewed in order to prove to the wicked that you were a God to be reckoned with."

Ma-we wagged her finger. "And…after you, yourself, had been cut off from life among the people and your spirit had returned to the Field of the Minds, what did I do for you by my own hands?"

Mihai lowered her eyes, beginning to comprehend. Her reply was subdued, "You returned my spirit from the Field of the Minds, placing me in a body even more glorious than the one I earlier possessed. You returned me to the living."

Turning her back on Mihai, Ma-we walked to the balcony's rail and peered up toward the cloudless sky. "Tell me, Michael, daughter of eternity, the light of all lights… *to whom do the children belong?*"

"To you, Mother… to you!"

Ma-we's head snapped around, her eyes aflame, "Tell me, then, daughter of foolish and ignorant thought, why do you *steal* them from me, gathering them to your own bosom, when you can do nothing for them at all?!"

Mihai was caught up speechless.

Ma-we pointed a finger at her chest. "*My* milk was the first fruits for all my children! To suckle first at *my* breasts was the gift I gave to living things. *My* name that is yet secret to all my children is a name given me by the Ones Who Came Before to give glory to the Maker of life. Into *my* bosom do all the children, the wicked and the just, come!"

"Michael, into your hands have I placed the authority to bring death upon my children, the wicked and the righteous. But you cannot give one moment of glory to what is mine, alone, to give. To me does life belong and to me…" She thumped her chest again, *"my children yet live!"*

Ma-we added an explanation. "You have led my children into battle, fighting great wars in my name. You have ordered their death, but forgotten who they are willing to die for. Your have taken personal responsibility for the death of each one, forgetting they are a free people, making free choices, choosing a course they feel is best for all."

"You have cursed yourself for foolish actions, when my children… many far wiser than you… silently obey your commands. They do it not out of fear of you, for my children do not fear you, but it is out of love for *me*, because I placed you in such a relative position. They do what is right because they see it as the *right* thing to do."

She pointed down toward her garden. "Michael! My children would follow that turnip if I ask them to. They follow *me*!"

Ma-we gestured, waving her hands to and fro. "Michael, one who is field marshal is but a tool of mine, a *living, breathing, thinking tool*. I wield it as I see fit. Should I say to it, 'go forth and slaughter the world,' it will do as I command. The one who is my field marshal has thus surrendered up their freedom to follow my whim. They have become a slave to me, the *true* master of the sword."

"Do you not understand, Michael? When you place guilt upon your soul for the needless slaughter of my children, you are implying that I am no better than the Wicked One, sending my children to the death in an unholy war. If the ax cannot cut down the tree because it is not sharpened, do you hold guilty the ax or the woodsman? Michael, you are declaring me, the woodsman, guilty, because you accuse me of using a *dull* ax!"

"My child!" Ma-we was pleading for her daughter to understand. "You make my war with your brother invalid, because you take away its righteousness! You carry in your soul the memories of lost loved ones as if you'll never see them again! You become a false prophet, crying out with your mouth my praises, while with your actions you say that I am impudent - or worse, a *liar*! How is that showing love to me, if you declare me the one acting with falsehood?"

Ma-we did not leave Mihai time to rest in thought. "If your heart believes this war is unnecessary, thus the needless slaughter of righteous souls, you are saying to me that I have made a hasty decision and trod the way of the stupid one. Your words of self-deprecation imply that I…I am little better than a *fool! Who can trust a fool?!*"

"And…!" Ma-we repeatedly poked a finger into her opened palm. "And if your soul fears never seeing your loved ones again so that you must somehow protect *my* little lambs, you have committed thievery against me, stealing my children from my bosom!"

Abruptly turning away, Ma-we walked to the far end of the balcony and spun around, resting her hands on the ornate rail behind her. With majestic power, she demanded, "Michael, my trusted lieutenant, address me, please, regarding my words! As my chief steward, speak to me! Are my words not legitimate in their context and truth?!"

The blood had long since drained from Mihai's face, her pallor reflecting remorse and sadness, her heart aching with a desire for death. Yet, as Ma-we well knew, Mihai was made of good stuff. The woman would not allow her emotions to rule the day. There was a lesson in Mother's words – words, mind you, that she had so carefully conjured. Mihai pushed away the pain, seeking the prize of understanding, for understanding might just bring her wisdom, and wisdom might save her from disaster.

At long last, Mihai answered with halting reply, "Yehowah...the Maker of promises and Fulfiller of dreams, your servant - the tool you have put faith in - your servant girl does not have a reply for you. Should she live a million more moons, would there be found wisdom at her feet? Or if she suckled a million sons, how would it compare to the lives of your children? A prattler of empty thoughts and purveyor of mindless sayings is your daughter. Why does your wisdom allow her continued breath?"

She sat silent in thought as Ma-we ambled back, reclining in her willow chair. Gradually her color returned. After a long, remorseful sigh, Ma-we's child mourned, "Naked I came into this world, knowing nothing and caring even less. It appears that I have learned little since. I have acted so foolishly because I saw you through my heart, not accepting your wisdom could be far greater than mine, and your viewpoint far different. My little world of desire, wishing for things that lie in the ashes of the past, made me forget the reason I still live, why my brothers and sisters live. We are your agents, for good or for bad. Who are we to question you?"

Looking into Ma-we's eyes she asked, "Please forgive..."

"*Listen, then, and become wise!*" Ma-we went on with her lesson, not wanting to hear the confessions of a troubled heart. "People act foolishly. Why, if you include foreknowledge as part of the margin of wisdom, chiding someone for the lack of prescience, then I guess you could say that no one is exempted from foolishness...*no one*...which means we - including *me* - are deficient in wisdom."

She leaned forward, staring at a very surprised Mihai. "That's right! I have acted without wisdom, and on more than one occasion! Remember I said that I had failed to consider that a monster might be living in your mind? And what of the Rebellion? My heart refused to listen to the wisdom of my hidden council, warning me that such a thing would happen."

"Wisdom is based on knowledge, reasoning and understanding. If any one is lacking, then wisdom can never be achieved. Should a ship's captain reason, 'if a strong wind drives the vessel faster than a breeze, then a tempest should hurry us even more quickly to our destination', the only destination achieved will be one of disaster. Was the captain's knowledge of the wind in the sails wrong?"

She waved her hand, shaking her head. "No! But he lacked reasoning or understanding. I have no need to explain to you why such a viewpoint would be foolish, but you do need to see that, to the captain, his conclusions drawn were reasonable and possibly wise, not foolish."

"What of the proverb 'let the inexperienced one become wise'? To become wise, you must first accept your own limitations concerning a matter, whether it be from lack of knowledge, insight, experience or...or for any other reason. Don't try to out-think yourself... your personal abilities, I mean. If you would not make unattainable promises just to soothe someone's soul, don't do the same because you believe it is the right thing to do. In either case, you will fail in the end."

Mihai argued, "I grasp your words…at least I would like to think I do, but there have been times I did seek wisdom, not only my own, but that of my greatest councilors." She shook her head. "We still met with disaster. Memphis…"

"Let go of Memphis!" Ma-we sputtered. "Do you know for a certainty that you might not have averted an even greater disaster? I will tell you, Legion was preparing a massive counterattack that could well have swept your lead forces from their works and possibly been able to drive you to surrender. The Spider's Lair is an impossible place to hold without proper ground support. Had he succeeded in his plan, your losses would have been double and… and you could never have forced an armistice on your brother."

Mihai was shocked with surprise. "How…"

"Oh, stop it, Dear." Ma-we gently scolded. "I do not live in a cave. Few are the things that escape my attention."

A butterfly settled down on Ma-we's hand. She paused to examine it, stroking it with her finger. Eventually she returned to giving Mihai advice. "Learn from disaster. At times a person must make a decision, the outcome being *insignificant*. At Memphis, you had to attack. I knew it and put it in my children's hearts to do so. If you had refused to order, I would have found another to do it. *My* tool, remember? *My* will."

With a *poof!* Ma-we tossed the butterfly into the air, it spreading its wings onto the breeze and drifting into the sky. She smiled. "There! I have given it freedom. If my little friend lives to plant its eggs under a leaf or if it becomes a meal for a hungry bird, little is the matter. Freedom does not guarantee success. It only guarantees *freedom*!"

"And there is the difference between my children and the positions of power they attain to." Ma-we pulled her chair close so she could touch her daughter. After reaching out and taking Mihai's hand, she continued, "I have given to all my children freedom… freedom to choose good and bad… freedom to be wise or foolish… freedom to disagree, even with me. That is what freedom is all about."

She shook her head. "Even your brother I refuse to bring to nothing. Freedom means that I…even I…will not bring the wicked to eternal emptiness. No. Does this mean they will not come to an end? Not at all!" She pointed toward the distant butterfly. "Remember, when one refuses to act shrewdly, a hungry bird will devour it. The wicked no longer act shrewdly. They have entered a world filled with righteous birds who hunger to bring wickedness to nothing."

"Now, if your Mother will not bring down the wicked, because of the freedom I have endowed them with, do you think I will force my loyal children to bend to my will?" She shook her head. "With my *servants*, I demand they do my will, as I demand with my field marshal. The field marshal shall accomplish whatever I wish. But my children... well..."

Ma-we played with Mihai's fingers, her voice becoming chatty. "My children have freedom to choose what they wish to do. I never force them to do my will... never. You must understand. To take away a person's freedom is the greatest of all thefts. Far better it is to send the universe to damnation than to steal freedom from the least of my children."

She stared up into Mihai's eyes. "And *you* are far from the least..." Then shrugging, added, "Besides, if I did steal that freedom, directly or indirectly, the universe might fall into damnation eventually anyway, for I could not live with myself over such a theft. I very might well bring the universe to nothing because of my own grief!"

Curious, Mihai asked, "How, then, does one tell the difference between selfishness of the heart, the desire to satisfy one's flesh, and honest freedom, the need to do what is right for the soul?"

Ma-we grinned. "Need I remind you of your education? I will not waste our day explaining the basics of your EbenCeruboam, for you have studied it well. What I will say is this..." She began waving her hand as she went on. "Having all knowledge of something is not necessary when reasoning is added. The reasoning person will close up the barn, considering a storm might arrive late in the night. And a wise person will reason that a sword's blade is as sharp as a knife's. It is the principle of the matter. Principle is based on the harmonic law 'if the falling boulder will crush you, a crashing meteor will do no less'."

"So, if you reach out to the harmonics using a little reasoning, you will comprehend what is selfishness of the heart or flesh and what is necessary food for the soul. It is not the mind dictating through its logic, and it is not the heart, alone, feeling its way along. It is the balance of mind and heart. If you carefully use them both, you will gain success. Even if the decision should cause you pain, it will not bring you doom."

She slapped Mihai's hand. "My dear one, if you listen to the harmonic music surrounding you... and, may I add, enhanced by the ring you wear yet despise, you will not falter...ever!"

Mihai's face belied her confusion.

Ma-we sputtered, "I do not have all day to put a fire in your brain. Child, have you ever told me an untruth?"

Mihai groaned. "Yes, once long ago when I was little more than a babe. I tried to hide from you the beautiful stone I stole from your garden."

Ma-we peered into Mihai's eyes. "But you *confessed* your bad deed to me, without my asking. Why?"

"Because…" Mihai thought a moment. "Because it felt *wrong*. Something inside me said I had acted inappropriately. I was a *bad* girl."

Ma-we smiled again. "There! Enough said. When you listen to the harmonics, you will never falter. Never!"

               ဒ   ဒ   ဒ

*(**Author's note:** I feel it necessary to insert what was held in common knowledge by all of Ma-we's children of that day: the relationship between that of the fabric of the minds, the harmonics, and the living soul. The following excerpt is taken from a lecture given me by the Maker of Worlds on a sojourn with her into the secret lands of the North.*

"Every living cell has a minute amount of this fabric sticking to the tiny ladder-like structures found within it. When two reproductive cells come together, the fabric of the two bonds as one, but yet each remembers its own individuality. As the cells grow and divide, a little part of this bonded fabric is transferred to the new cells because the cells form around part of the tiny ladders, to which the fabric is clinging. As the new cells grow, this fabric attracts random pieces of the same fabric to it, and then changes them into exact copies of itself. The gathering continues until it has regained its full size again. This process of replication ensures that every fiber of the living organism will have a copy of the original fabric within it."

"Now, because cells from two parents produce one cell, the fabrics of the two parents mix together. As with the rest of the body, the offspring now has parts of both personalities or minds of the parents. The best part is yet to come! At a certain stage of growth, super-collector cells start to develop. The fabric within them gathers a much greater amount of the random pieces around itself. The tiny ladders become coated with this fabric. The concentration becomes so great that the cells start to take on independent thought. As the number of these cells multiplies, they start to cooperate and communicate with each other, forming separate communities within the growing body. Eventually, a brain and nervous system come into existence."

"All living things, regardless of which universe they are in, possess the same fabric and it reacts the same way with them. All I needed to do was transfer your fabric from one body to the next, even if it was just one cell. In that way your personality was transferred from one realm to another. Now, your mind is a slightly different story."

"For now I will add only this: The fabric in the cells is all woven in with the music of the universe. That is how you are able to feel the harmonics. Those trained to listen to the interrelationship between the music and the other fabric can often discern if a decision made is in harmony with the

music. If it is not, a feeling of discord flows through them.")

೮ ೮ ೮

Who of Ma-we's children could not recite verbatim all of Mother's words concerning life and harmonics? Why, the essence of harmonic life and conscience were the first major lessons taught to the children, beginning from infancy. Any child instructed at the feet of this wisest of all people knows far more concerning this science than those of you schooled in the greatest of institutions and taught by the ablest of educators. Mihai understood full well the real meaning of Mother's teaching.

What Mihai could not comprehend was the gravity of her soon to be made choices. For a person of humble heart, as was Mihai, it would be difficult to believe that one person could affect the future of the universe. Oh, yes, Ma-we knew, and all too well. Her little *butterfly* had been given its freedom, and how it chose to use that freedom might well judge for all living things the past, present and future. How very well Ma-we knew this.

This was not to say that Mihai did not understand she was to make important decisions this day. Ma-we did not waste words at times like this. With this in mind, she asked with all seriousness, "Mother, Maker of Worlds, the one who knows what good exists in dark places and can see the finish before something is begun, what must your child do to clear her mind and heart of empty matters so that she is able to hear clearly the music of harmonious songs?"

Ma-we reached out and firmly gripping Mihai's hands in hers, lowered her head as she pondered such a question. At length, she lifted her eyes and smiled, asking, "Does one smell the storm with their mind or heart? And if it is with the mind, how does the heart affect the decision one makes concerning that storm?"

Mihai puzzled, saying not a word.

Answering it herself, Ma-we replied, "It is the heart that considers the storm's potential, stirring with memories past of tempests endured. The heart recommends the mind to prepare for whatever may be delivered upon person and property."

She let go a hand, waving it. "The beast does not recall a thing with its heart. It waits until thunder rolls across the plain or a downpour brings the raging flood. Then its heart sends it into a panic or sends it into deep forgetfulness. Either way, the beast does not warn its mind to prepare, so invites the Fates to choose for it life or death."

"Do you not see the cattle flee for the trees when the lightning rules the sky, and the buffalo rush madly toward the cliffs at the crashing of the thunder? Why, even the horse will abandon all common sense and return to a burning barn for safety. See, the heart of a beast recalls no past and cannot discern the future. It does only what impassions it at the moment. It attempts no conference nor seeks any council with the mind."

She patted Mihai's hand. "My darling daughter, born of my flesh, created in my very image, you must not allow your mind to suppress your heart. Your kind have invented many machines with minds that can think and even reason. But they must have their power harnessed by the hearts of men, for they care not for friend or foe and feel no shame in crushing the innocent along with the guilty."

"Also!" She shook her finger. "You must not allow your heart to rule your mind. Many are the wise who have fallen into darkness because they listened to wicked reasonings and prattle that soothed and comforted the heart when, at the very same moment, their minds could see the utter folly of such reasonings."

"Do not forget my prophet and seer, AsreHalom! He stood among the greatest of my chief councilors, dispensing wisdom that even I marveled at. Like the Cherubs in understanding he was, showing greater insight than PalaHar, Tolohe, and even Ardon. Yet he fell away to the dark persuasions of Legion and Godenn, becoming worse than either in cruelty and evil."

Ma-we looked into the sky, speaking as though to herself. "He was not deceived like so many others were, for he, through his own insight, saw from afar the calamity of rebellion and the eternal ruin it could bring." She looked back at Mihai. "It was AsreHalom who penned the words of the book, PolutelesHuperephania: the Great Price of Pride. He knew from his own self-induced visions the future, but surrendered it all up to a fickle heart."

Wiping a tear from her eye, Ma-we went on. "So, my dear one, you can see that both the mind and the heart will think and reason on matters. Each will produce its own counsel. What you must do is force them to sit down together as allies – not opponents – and work out a battle strategy that will bring you, their ward, safely through whatever storm that may crash upon your shore."

She warned, "AsreHalom fell victim to his own unrestrained emotions, those emotions given to my children for the dream-share. Such emotion moves two lovers to share an ecstasy that only immortals can enjoy in reality. This ecstasy is so great, I had to design my children's minds to make a disconnect from their bodies of flesh when experiencing this dream-share in order to preserve the flesh alive. But that you already know."

"The point is this: unrestrained emotion was a gift given by me to my children when the world was innocent and carefree. In these troubled times, one must carefully control it…" She lowered her voice. "or it can gain rulership over the thinking of the heart and even the mind and bring the soul and all that belongs to it to ruin."

"Please, my dear, understand this." Ma-we's voice fell to little more than a hush. "You must never allow this form of emotion to gain mastery over your mind and heart. It ever seeks its own selfish reward, lying to your soul the reasons for its deceptive passions, haunting your thoughts and flooding them with doubt concerning future rewards and hopes... telling your heart, 'never will you see such joy unless you satisfy my desires'."

"Child, it cries out to your soul, confessing a lasting loneliness if it sees not its wishes fulfilled. Lost love, bad times, hope delayed, postponed dreams, anything that can make your heart ache, this *monster* will use to induce you to do its will. It listens not to the music... not now... not anymore." Ma-we bowed her head in sadness. "Its songs of love have stolen so many of my children away and journeyed them into the darkness beyond all hope. There it slowly eats away any goodness remaining until only its evil passions remain."

She shook her head. "Until this age of evil passes far from view, I fear the gift of the dream-share will remain a two-edged sword. Until your Shiloh can fully effect the cure...and that will be far into the next age...some of my children shall remain slaves to their own emotional demons."

Ma-we's sadness showed clearly in her eyes as she peered into Mihai's face. "One so precious to my flesh, you opened your heart up to a man you trusted beyond trust. He, for his part, murdered you that day so long ago, overloading an opened, innocent mind that was yearning the gift of the dream-share with a malice which had never been experienced before or since in our universe."

"I returned your power and strength to mind and flesh, but I could not repair your torn and tortured heart. My child, do not trust it for it has not yet fully healed. If you are not careful, it will gladly listen to your emotions, believing a cure is imminent or that you have the power to restrain all feeling."

Patting Mihai's leg, Ma-we concluded her counsel. "Anger, hatred, lust, greed and jealousy and other such feelings are the progeny of the dream-share emotion run amuck. They are the warped and twisted siblings of love, joy, peace, and contentment. They resist the harmony found in the universe, even creating a distorted music which produces the discord that threatens the very fabric of all living things."

She warned, "No matter how troubling or complex your journey is, no matter the turmoil and disquiet your heart and mind must endure, if you can feel the sweet harmony of peace, love, or contentment, well..." She nodded her head. "Then you have found the music. It will never betray you in the end. Your journey will always find success."

Mihai leaned forward, asking, "Mother...the music...does sadness or fear create the wrong music, too?"

Ma-we slowly shook her head. "No, my child, but either can distract your reasoning abilities to the point of blinding your senses to the musical harmonics. If you should become distracted by such things, you may misread the music, which may prove as dangerous as ignoring it."

Seeing a growing concern on Mihai's face, Ma-we quickly added, "A smart woman like you need not always depend on the sweet music, for it is only one of your many powers. Do not forget that your own mind has the ability to see the resulting future from acts committed. It is a very capable tool, full of reasoning abilities and logic. A wise child learns to depend on all her gifts possessed - even an old stodgy ring that she might despise. You must become skilled with all your weaponry."

Ma-we so much wanted to warn her daughter of her greatest weakness, but feared it would compromise the child's freedom of choice. She knew that Mihai's fathomless love and devotion for her mother fueled her overpowering desire to please Ma-we as well. This devotion could easily blind the girl of the need to have her own heart satisfied. Still, Ma-we remained silent. 'The child must choose for herself.'

Sitting back, Ma-we slapped her knees and exclaimed, "Enough of that! On with business!"

Relaxing, with folded hands in her lap, she continued. "This morning you requested to be relieved of your command as field marshal." She squinted, asking, "Is that still how you feel?"

Taken aback, Mihai hesitated before replying. "Why…why, why, yes, I believe it will be best for all parties. I…"

Ma-we jauntily interrupted. "I *accept* your resignation! Long before you entered my domain, I perceived this moment and have already given consideration to this matter, having already chosen your replacement!"

To say that Mihai was shocked would be an understatement. Not allowing time for her reply, Ma-we quickly moved to assuage any possible hurt feelings. "Michael, god of the armies and all the northern mountains, there has never been, nor will there ever be a better commander and chief over the armies than you have been. Yet I have seen the stress in your soul for many long days and some time ago set the wheels of fate in motion to relieve you of this *most worrisome* of responsibilities."

Mihai felt herself slow of wit on occasion, but she could clearly see that the timing of her return to EdenEsonbar had been well orchestrated to coincide with this very minute. This was no random meeting, nor was it contrived by Mihai. She had been set up big-time, and by her own mother! Her accusing question reflected her sense of betrayal. "Soooo…who did my *innocent* Mother happen upon so quickly to fill such an important position in her government?"

A dancing, winged beetle suddenly caught Ma-we's undivided attention.

For the longest time, she chattered on about its strange and wonderful qualities.

At length, Mihai put an end to her mother's charade. "Mother! It is not an uncommon insect and you know it full well! Why do you play with me?! You have chosen my successor. That's enough. Just tell me who it is! Er... please..."

Sweet innocence was reflected on Ma-we's face as her lilting voice softly answered, "My dear one, I intended to seek your permission." She nodded. "Yes, I did. But... er... well, you know... things came up... intruded, you might say. By the time you arrived... late, as I had predicted... the choice had been made, with the council's approval, of course."

"Who, Mother? *Who?!*" Mihai's patience was wearing thin.

As Ma-we became absorbed in the antics of another of her little creatures, she so casually replied, "TrishaQaShaibJal..."

Mihai almost jumped from her seat, her face reddening with anger and astonishment. "*Trisha* from the lost city of *nowhere*?! A land forgotten in the mist of time?! Why an urchin of an unknown sire, whose bloodline is unsure and strength unproven? My own people do not know this creature. How could you allow them to trust to her kind and of such untested stature? At least we have a record of life for others like AlbaMagadan, Tabitha Copeland, or... or even Symeon. *But not for her!*"

Ma-we did not take her eyes off the little bug as she calmly commanded, "Sit down, Peter. Hurrying feet in the darkness see not the tree roots that will cause calamity. Please sit down."

Grumbling, Mihai sat, staring into her lap.

Allowing moments to pass, Ma-we studied her daughter, finally asking, "Why do you hate the one who gave you breath this very day, the one I sent to you as comforter? I watched to see your love and passion rise for her on this very morn, and your parting words revealed only endearment. How has this woman suddenly become an abomination in your eyes? Tell me, please, why have you accosted an innocent heart?"

Feeling shame for her outburst against a close friend, but still showing resentment for her mother's decision, Mihai quietly answered, "It is true, I love this woman, but as a companion dear, not some warrior to lead my... er...*your* people. She is untested in so many ways and...and I have not found her that impressive in her leadership role, which you requested of me to give."

Finally, Mihai's real reason was revealed. "Mother, there are many warriors from *this* world who have proven themselves valiant beyond valiant. They deserve such a great gift be granted them. They deserve to be recognized for their whole-souled devotion to our cause."

Stopping her daughter, Ma-we asked, "If this position of field marshal is such a grand gift, why have you thrown it into the dirt, counting your years of wearing its crest as evil and forlorn? Why do you wish this upon your closest companions when you abhor it, yourself?"

Wagging a finger, Ma-we offered her kindly chastisement. "Unproved and untested in your eyes, maybe… and unknown, yes… but not only to you. Your enemy knows not of the tempest rising in the east. My Daughters of the Blade do live, some even walking among us as I speak! Tonight you shall confess my Swords…and one you will reveal as master over my people."

Mihai gasped, "Trisha is…?!"

"Yes!" Ma-we snapped. "And as for untrained, let me tell you, my Swords did not sleep while in the Field of the Minds! There were other forces working with them that have not yet touched your mind, teaching and training them in all the arts of war. Why, even Gabrielle cannot match them for knowledge gained. Now they walk among us, honing their skills for latter days. Your soul shall one day bless this lost creature, for she will deliver it and many others from a calamity you, yourself, will have created."

She poked her finger in Mihai's face. "Now tell me, why do you chafe at me giving to the kind from the Realms Below this gift of field marshal, instead of blessing one of *your* kind with it?"

Mihai lowered her head in thought. Her answer came with some effort. "I felt no discord, Mother, but my heart felt jealousy for long-time companions. It deceived me into thinking they were being slighted over honor given. Trisha is my friend… and I do love and trust her, but… but my heart feels her a threat to our world… like this gift bestowed upon her is a form of usurpation of my people's glory."

Ma-we shook her head, again wagging her finger. "The glory of your kind must fade. You, yourself, prophesied this very day long ago, reinforcing it through visions given to your trusting companion, John. You must take the lead in passing it along to these strangers from distant worlds if you wish to see victory in the end. Already I detect subtle jealousy growing among the children. You must put an end to it, *tonight!*"

Mihai's face lit up with surprise. "How am I to do such a thing?! Tonight belongs to you and your new field marshal. I shall be standing in the shadows as one of the observers."

A sly twinkle grew in Ma-we's eyes. "The breeze does not always drift in from the west. Flowers do not always open in the morning. We must not conclude our fate based upon the past, nor should we discount the sun when the rains shower upon us."

She sat back. "Tonight has not yet been decided. Whether you hide in the shadows or stand above the others is yet to be determined. Do not hurry the future, but learn that your heart is treacherous and deceitful. Wait upon the moment, seeing not to a distant hour."

"Now, I again ask you..." Ma-we stood, walked around her chair and rested her hands on its back. "Respectfully I ask you, do you approve of my choice of Trisha as our new field marshal?"

Mihai stood and walked to the balcony railing, staring into the jungle growth below. At length, she replied, "The news you bring to my ears is good, but surprising. Long have I yearned to see one of Shiloh's living Swords, often wondering if they should come from these worlds. Had I not known that Trisha was one selected to be a Sword, I would still decline my acceptance of her in such a role, feeling her under-qualified for the position."

With eyes seeking acceptance of her feelings, Mihai turned toward her mother. "Please do not hate me for my lack of faith in your choices, but I still cannot see what shines so clearly in your mind. My training as a soldier warns me not to fully trust others' suggestions and conclusions if I cannot discern matters myself." She nodded approvingly. "You're wise... so wise. I'm sure our Trisha will be a good commander."

Grinning, Ma-we thanked her daughter for accepting her choice, adding, "Do not think your old soldiering out of line. More often than not it will preserve you and others alive. It is well that you have remembered it."

Walking over to Mihai, Ma-we slipped an arm through hers. She could see the trouble hiding behind the woman's eyes and sought to expunge it. "My Love, how I love you and those who are like you. There are many truly great leaders among your siblings. I can see that, in the coming maelstrom, a grand crowd of them will surrender everything to accomplish the removal of evil from this land. From among your own kind, new and powerful leaders will rise, and shall become more renowned than those who have come before."

"Child, there is still to come a man-child who shall become greater in stature and power than even you have become. You will bend your knee to him before he even arrives, for you will see his future glory with your own insight. My Love, this Trisha from forgotten lands is no less capable a leader than this coming Shiloh. That is why she is to take up the sword in his stead, so that my children will gain a glimpse of the Whirlwind."

"The hour is soon coming on which the history of the entire universe will hinge. It will not determine who is fit to rule. If it were only that, I would have surrendered the world to your brother long ago and left for unreachable places to begin anew a race of children to comfort me. But it is much more than that, so much more."

"What, Mother?" Mihai quietly asked. "If we do not fight for you and what is righteous and good, what do my brothers and sister die for?"

Ma-we patted her daughter's arm. "You do fight and die for what is righteous and good, but that good is far grander than to decide who stands as chief over what is mere dust and stone. Your cause transcends the mundane and erstwhile things of this universe. You fight for the very souls of all the living, dead, and those yet to come. My dear one, you fight for *life itself*."

A dark cloud swept Ma-we's face as she squeezed Mihai's arm. "Please, Dear, listen to me and let the prattle of a troubled soul fill your ears with long-known words."

"Ages ago, when the worlds of men were little more than a dream, the wise of that day gathered to a great council, searching for answers to the question, 'How shall the universe of material things be constructed?' By the measurements of time, reckoned by your kind, a lifetime of star-systems came and passed, again and again, before the council was concluded, but for those present it was as if only a moment."

"There was finally a consensus come among us as to the construction, it being primarily made of three strata. We called them 'elements', each independent of the other, but also combined in an amalgam so that the fate of one would become the fate of all. The first stratum or element was what is commonly called the 'Web of the Universe'. Upon it, or into it, all the universes hang. Its power of artificial intelligence is what binds a universe together, never permitting its chaotic destruction."

"The second stratum has commonly come to be called 'the Web of the Minds'. Into it all the essences of lasting life were placed. It is this web that is the actual reality of all living things, for it contains the true materials that make up the mind, made up of the pure, immortal essence of life. The material comprising this element can not be destroyed, for it is a singular form of energy, taken directly from the soul of the Giver of life…not invented by her."

Ma-we shook her head. "Although the fabric making up the Web of the Minds cannot be destroyed, it can dissipate. Indeed, it is part of its very design. You see, all living flesh gathers this fabric to itself, but without the interweaving effect created by the third element or strata, at the death of the flesh, the fabric scatters like the snow on a driving wind. Only to my manly, human creatures is the gift of eternal bonding between all the strata given. And by their very design, with knowledge, my children would one day gain the ability to tap into the power of this third element, as some already have."

"Allow me, please, to digress." She swept her hand in a wide arc. "The council concluded that all life other than the children of my worlds needed to be temporary in order to produce the ultimate of harmony and balance with the laws of the new universes. Life, then, could be ever-changing, evolving, you might say, within a series of genetic laws implemented to rein in catastrophic diversity, something that could threaten life. Ever-changing life would contribute to an ever-changing universe."

She gently poked her daughter's arm. "Variety, ever-changing variety - it's the spice of life, my Dear! You never get bored when there's always something new and unexpected to look forward to."

Squeezing Mihai's arm, Ma-we added, "The council decided that freedom such as I had in mind for my children could lead to their demise through possible accident, because their flesh would be made from the very dust of the universe, instead of my immortal being. I accepted the council's recommendations, at least part of them so, that by giving each of my children an undying mind, I would never lose one to an accident brought on by my gift of freedom."

Ma-we now returned to the explanation of the three strata. "As I have said, the third element upon which your worlds hang and survive is the most precious because it bonds all the parts of the universe together. Although all intelligence, real and artificial, depends on this element for its cohesive existence, its power resides only within my children here and in the Lower Realms. And they, alone, can tap into its energy or decide its fate."

The way Ma-we was explaining the fabric of the universe was peculiarly strange and familiar all at the same time, especially this third constructive strata. The study of EbenCeruboam concerned itself primarily with the first two elements of the universal web, the third being explained by conflicting psychological theory and mathematical calculations relating to the actions of the harmonics, based upon the personal opinion of the individual educator.

Mihai excitedly interrupted. "You tell me of hidden secrets when you say, 'we alone can tap into this strata and decide its fate'. Still, what does it have to do with our long wars and the destiny of worlds?"

Ma-we slowed her daughter down with kindly counsel. "Now child, one does not make the wine before harvesting the grapes. Be patient and allow me to finish the harvest of information I have for you. Then you may make the wine to your liking."

"Hidden there are many secrets from you, but not all my children. There are those - often not the wisest nor most renown - who have deeper understanding than some of my greatest councilors. JabethHull, your one-time mentor, was such a man, but to himself he kept all things secret, as he should have."

She wagged her finger. "It was at my personal request that he allowed you passage with him, he being a recluse, finding only Nhoset to his liking. You were so very blessed by his company. Recall your dream-shares with him and wisdom will abound in your heart."

"Mother...?!"

Ma-we put a finger to Mihai's lips, shushing her. "The day will ever march forward and tomorrow eternally remains an elusive dream. Catch the wind when it gathers from the west and waste not the hour before the calm. You and I have so little time. It is my turn to speak and your turn to listen."

Mihai nodded, keeping silent.

"Good!" Ma-we grinned. "Now allow the breeze to catch your sails and

I will tingle your ears with secrets that few have come to know and even fewer understand." She reached up and cradled Mihai's chin in her hand. "The hour has come for the revealing of hidden things. You must now begin to understand them." Taking each other's hand, the two started to slowly pace the long balcony.

With eyes watching the floor, Ma-we began, "The third element is a product of the ultimate formula of what you children call 'mathematics'. It is the *absolute* equation, the very reason for the invention of your EbenCeruboam. Long have my children searched for this, believing it holds key to the secrets of the universe and beyond. Truth be said, it does, but not as my children think it should be."

"Child, my dearest one of my flesh, there are others I love as much as you, but none I love more. You, child, you yourself are the closest living product, in purity, of this absolute equation. Its energy surrounds you in swaddling bands that binds you to its fate. That is why just like me, those filled with discord hate you, while the ones in harmony with the universe love you."

"Please do not misunderstand, my sweet lover, you are not made up of this element, but are bound up with it. There is a difference, which I will attempt to explain later. Your birthing and early life were not noticeably different from that of my other children, other say, your fondness for snooping and inordinate need for reassurance of acceptance, the latter being most perplexing for me. Otherwise you were only ordinary... sorry."

"Life went on, and after your coming of age, I got on to other matters more pressing, including the birthing of many more sons and daughters, among them your next sibling, Euroaquilo. It was not until your first sojourn beyond EdenEsonbar's star system, and your returning... your sixtieth year, if I recall correctly... that I noticed a peculiar change within you. Indeed, it was after this time that Chrusion began to distance himself from you, as he later did with me."

"You were not yet in your two-hundredth year, only beginning your formal education, when I handed you over to JabethHull. He, I decided, should tutor you in the ways of EbenCeruboam, the emerging study of universal law, because he had greater understanding of it than any of my other children. At his feet you were taught not theory but divine secrets I had shared with him. This also gave me opportunity to make a close study of you," She grinned, "my captive specimen, to see just what was going on with you."

"Many were the things I discovered about my daughter. Oh, how intriguing you were, still are! This third element had entwined itself around your very being. Every fiber of every cell was alive with its energy, something I'd never seen to such an extent in *any* of my other children. Curiosity overwhelmed me, forcing me to search every part of your soul, seen and unseen, for a clue to what made you so different."

"What I found was profound beyond my wildest imaginings, for it renewed a hope within me that I had all but abandoned. My joy soared to new heights, so much so, I ignored a growing gloom that was slowly creeping into your world."

Ma-we paused a moment in thought, asking herself, 'Or was it that my daughter was now providing such a shining contrast, I could finally see what had always been there?'

She shrugged. "Whatever... I could find nothing physically, mentally or emotionally different between you and your fellow siblings. There was nothing about you that was special except... let me think, how do I explain this? Except the way your mind interacted with this third elemental building block. It was as if your mind – the invisible part made up of the Web of the Minds – the real you...it was as if your mind was calling out to the third element, drawing it in to itself."

"You, my child! *You* had become the *living equation* to revealing of the very secrets of the universe! And what was so profound to me was that you... your heart and mind... had formulated its composition and structure, nurturing it until you had mastered it flawlessly. Somehow you discovered then crafted the perfect harmonic music, creating a near true image of my heart within yourself." Ma-we laughed. "And you never knew it!"

"This was most important! You see, not by my hand had my most precious creation come into existence, but by yours did it take place. What a gift to me, to have one of my own give back to me what I so much needed but could not create for myself!"

Mihai could no longer contain herself. "Tell me, please, Mother! Tell me please what this *magic* formula is that I created!"

Ma-we laughed. "Oh child, do you not understand?! On your own - in your heart and mind - you made the near perfect magic of harmonic music, tapping your soul into the wonders of universe, the foundation of which is made of my perfect essence. It is this essence that built the third element, strata, and it is what binds all things together. I made it that way. It is also what makes my heart rejoice the most."

"What does?! Ma-we...Lowenah... My sweet Mother, what does?!"

Again Ma-we laughed. "Why, the perfect equation, my Cherished One. It is what I have encourage all men to search for, but until you unlocked its coded secrets, it had remained a mystery to the others." Loneliness grew in her voice. "And I was beginning to believe that no one ever would...or could..."

Ma-we perked up, squeezing Mihai's hand and smiling. "Now I knew that the others, all the others could attain to the same level, evolve to the new heights of awareness that have no bounds or hold any secrets. I also had a mentor to teach the others, if only by example, how to attain the near perfect concept, maybe even *perfect* concept of what you call 'mathematics'."

Placing her hand on her chest, Mihai gasped, "Me…?! A Mentor…?! How…?! I knew nothing of what you were doing and I taught no one a thing other than how to speak at the wrong time and impute the wrong understanding while doing it."

Ma-we grinned. "Oh, yes, my impetuous chatterbox! So true it was that you tried the patience of many of the older children. But you were the key to their unlocking the secrets of EbenCeruboam, the secrets of the universe. I needed to pass you among them, no matter how painful and trying it was for them." She winked. "You were their only hope."

There was a twinkle of satisfaction in her eyes as she peered into Mihai's. "Many were the ones you educated. Oh yes, most did not - still don't realize what they were learning. You changed them, brought them closer to the pure music, which drew the essence of the third element in to them…their hearts. A few others like Tolohe grew to consciously understand it in their hearts and became silent mentors, themselves."

"But it was you, child, that I gave my heart away to. Your music was sweetest of all. Oh, how my heart sang in rapturous song over you!" She squinted, eyeing her daughter. "Did you have no sense about you to wonder at my constant attention upon my treasure after your departure from Jabeth and Nhoset? Did you not see my fingers at work when, suddenly, so many of my older children began paying such a young, foolish, sibling so much *undue* attention?"

"After you had mastered your education and been put through many trials to test your mettle, and after you had reached an age acceptable to my other children, I brought you into my court along with Euroaquilo, your next younger sibling, thus keeping your heart humble. You became my emissary." Ma-we shook her head. "All right, you were one of my messengers, but very much like an emissary. Anyway, my children got to know you."

She shook her finger. "And you did rub off on them, subtly, mind you, but rub off, none the less."

Ma-we stopped her pacing. "You thought yourself so unimportant and insignificant, you could not see the effect you had on others. Oh, true, you were not honored like my princes and wise councilors, but you did not go unnoticed. Long before I lifted you up to grandeur, by giving into your hand the lower realms of men, my caring children adored you and what you were."

She stared at the floor. "Your brother grew angry with me when I gave you the Lower Realms. He did not understand, could not, for he had already grown beyond your kind, or should I say he had never grown up to it, but remained as a babe to selflessness, seeking only his own wanton desires."

Now lifting her eyes to Mihai's, she explained, "You see, my Lovely One, it was not you who my son came to hate and murder, but what was inside you. He realized that the world of earthly men, being taught by you, would become like you in this quality. They would learn to sing this alluring song and draw the third element to themselves, thus sing their music to me and not to him. His objective was to destroy your music, ruin the key that unlocks the secret universe of the heart and twist it so that it could only produce unimagined ugliness."

"You mean he intended not my death?!" Mihai cried. "He only wanted to hurt me?"

Ma-we stroked her daughter's hand. "Your brother accomplished just what he desired and I, in my foolish innocence, did not see it until... until it was nearly too late... and even then it was only by accident, as you know so well how Darla saved us all a most awful fate. Because of that discovery, we have been given time...time to perfect a healing while holding to the laws of the universe."

"Yes, to answer your question, your brother sought not your death, though making it appear to be such, so that his real purpose would remain hidden until it came to its fatal fruition. Then it would be too late to alter the Fates of history and then he, he supposed, could force me to abandon this universe to him, allowing him forever to satisfy his selfish desires to the limit."

She shook her head. "He is stupid...so *selfish stupid*! Little does he know or wants to know the final results should he find success to his evil plans."

Ma-we began anew, stroking Mihai's arm. "And that is why you must know what is at stake here and that the music played into this third element can either bond all living things together or rent them asunder, turning the universe - if there still is one - into a lifeless mass of stone and dust."

The two again took up strolling the balcony, Ma-we continuing. "There is so much I could explain, but the hours are not long enough in this age to tell you all I could. I will tell you this: Your brother understood that you were the key to my success at helping the others learn the secrets to this last element, both here and in the Realms Below. He also knew that once fully unlocked or understood, there would be nothing impossible for my children to do, so to speak. There would no longer be any need for *his* rulership, at least as a leader over the people."

"Chrusion feared his loss of glory, place among the people as 'Chief Host, God Personified', as he pictured himself. If he could warp the key so that it sang discord, it, better than all other children, could inflict damage to this third element, corrupting it to his liking or crushing forever its furtive power. Either way, he saw himself as the winner, becoming the Eternal Father over all the universe."

"Your brother also knew he must act quickly to stop your musical harmonics from infecting the world of men, something that would be so easy to do with young minds thirsting for knowledge. That is why he pushed the hour of your torment. I had unwittingly forced his hand the day I gave to you complete governance over the world of men. If permitted, you'd contaminate those creatures all too soon, they looking up to you as the god of Wisdom, and they would not consider him as of any worth."

"But he deceived himself into thinking you weak of mind, having little if any inner strength. The monster he planted in your mind was expected to overtake your soul long ago. What he could not understand was the inner strength you had and that, combined with the fibers your music gathered from the third element, made you nearly invincible to the demon's attacks. Notice I said *nearly...*"

She stopped strolling again. "Eventually, if you do not successfully remove it from your mind, your brother will attain success in what he has attempted. If you are in your mortal self, then you will die. If you have become immortal, it will drive away your sanity, delivering you into a world of damnable abomination, never to regain your senses again. Either way, it will lead to the eventual demise of everything mortal, my heart breaking, thus bringing an end to all that is held together by it."

Taking hold of the hand of a very astonished Mihai, Ma-we opened it and began playing her finger across her palm. "The hope of your mortal cleansing has passed on. Its hour ended this very morn. Now you must wait until your immortal flesh is delivered upon you. Until then, I will provide a helper to keep your demon in check. And, at an hour of need I will provide another, a man-child, who already sings the music that unlocks the elements. He will accomplish what I have not."

Hushing Mihai, Ma-we explained, "I sent my child to the world of men for this very reason. To save men? Do your really think your sacrifice in death on some lonely desert mount could save men? By law it did, but it was the power of your music that saved men and you, yourself. For while you lived upon the land, all the time you sang your song into receptive hearts that to this day drives men to act in strange and wonderful ways."

"Indeed, the power your music played on the hearts of men was far greater than even I expected. So great it was and still is, that it bonds their world together with surpassing strength, so much so, that the discord of evil produced is almost negated, thus slowing down the destructive forces attempting to rip that world apart. But it cannot hold things together forever."

"Even now there are signs of discord's destructive forces at work, like here. The increasingly strange weather conditions and mass die-off of certain species of flesh are sure signs that the Web of the Universe is beginning to fray faster than it can repair itself. The hour soon comes when all men in the realms above and below must be tested to fitness. You, my Love, bought us time, but not eternity."

Mihai's eyes belied her lack of understanding. What music had she played as she walked, as a man, among people filled with the discord given them by their wicked-minded father? So great was their lack of harmony, their bodies could not survive a hundred years before surrendering to the evil.

Seeing her bewilderment, Ma-we chided, "Must I explain everything to one so dense? Have my clues, so simple, not opened your thoughts up to what I have been talking about?" She shook her head in mock amazement. "So! I guess I must spell it out. Oh dear…oh dear…"

"Many men and women listening to your song succumb to it, surrendering up all things to search for me. At least they think it is me and, in a way, they are right. It is really the power of the elements they search for and many find but, upon finding it, they can not personify it or well-define it, it being something they have never felt so strongly before."

"One man in particular, the one your heart developed such a yearning for that you pulled him from the corrupted darkness of discord into your musical light by directly singing your song to him while you basked in angelic glory, he penned best what the power of this element really is, for he likened it to the only known feeling it held semblance to. He called it 'love'."

"This man, by his own reasonings… for I allowed him to write his letters by his own volition… this man could see that the love he spoke of was no mere feeling like the romantic and brotherly love of his day. He saw that the love - power he spoke of - bonded the universe together, giving life to all things. He influenced his friend, John, to later write that I don't *have* love, but I *am* love."

"So eloquently did this same man explain the effective contrasts between your harmonic music and your brother's discord, he summed it thusly:

'The works against the Spirit are evident to all men of insight as belonging to the lower nature of beastliness, they being wanton and set free of goodness and right. Among them are envy, indecency, fits of rage, selfish ambitions, dissensions, evil intrigues and jealousies. I warn you as I did before, those who surrender to such filth shall never see the face of God.'

'Those who have harvested the Spirit live a life flowing with love, joy when the world is dark, kindness when the power is to do ill, patience toward the secret person of another, fidelity toward a sworn oath or promise, self-control over the evil that lurks in all men, goodness when wickedness stands at the door, and gentleness when the foolish hurt the heart.'

'For the Spirit is our life and breath and without it we are nothing but unreasoning beasts, fit for little more than Gahanna. But the fruitage of the Spirit holds no bounds upon men, nor can any law be set up against it.'"

"This man could see the three elements of the universe with his heart and he attempted to live by the very harmonics you revealed to him through your love songs. Why do you think your heart fell so deeply fond of him? And why do you think I so quickly granted your wish to have him stand beside you in this realm?"

"The Spirit this man writes about is what I call the third element, '*Hascho-Binie*', from an ancient tongue meaning, 'all that must return to me'." Ma-we hugged her daughter. "And you fulfilled a prophecy I had given myself in the Beginning Hope, when your worlds were still little more than dust."

Ma-we released Mihai, sighed, and continued. "You asked me, 'what reasons are there for the long wars?' There are many, but these are the ones related to EbenCeruboam:

First: My children are the ones who must bring to a finish what has been started by the Evil One. They stand responsible because they knew long ago that the freedom I had granted them afforded me no avenue to use my powers to stop the Rebellion. They were free to choose who they would follow, whom they would worship. From their hand, by their blood, would the die be cast. For the one who ruled, they would decide.

Second: While it has been sad for me to see my children suffer and die for my cause, the very trials endured by my loyal ones have accelerated the infusion of this third element among my children. This has strengthened the fabric within the First Realm, buying time for me to accomplish my purpose and bring my genetic experiments in the Second Realm to a successful conclusion.

Third: The men and women in the Second Realm have been very fast learners regarding this EbenCeruboam. Though they know not of its existence - so many, in fact - I will be able to bring a large host of them into this realm if need be, to strengthen the web here. They will also hurry the end of wickedness much faster than my older children can."

Ma-we nodded, eyes twinkling. "Wait and see. What few hundred I have delivered here will make this universe shake in the nearing cataclysm coming upon your kind! When you witness what they will do, your mind will reel, thinking what an army of countless thousands will accomplish."

"And…" Ma-we squeezed Mihai's hand. "I think I have answered your other question as well about the destiny of worlds. We must not allow the elements to falter."

"Now, child," Ma-we began their pace anew, "let us return to our new field marshal. As you are well aware, so many of my children are faltering either by surrendering to the privations of war or failing to heed the cry to it. While it is true I can foresee coming events that will re-energize them, I dare not chance a return to conditions as they exist now. Why, the army is currently in such a pitiable state, if Chrusion attacked this moment, his battle fleets would soon be on our doorstep."

"Ah, but for the children of the Lower Realms! They are so much like

Darla and Zadar, the youngest of my children. They have no memory of peace and carefree days. Death and war are their birthing rings, the toys of their youth. They are both callous and brutal in the way they wage war, especially your little sister, Darla. It sometimes disturbs others the way they revel in destruction, but their energy is so very, very contagious!"

"Do you recall the Battle of the Tower Gate, where General DinChizki ordered a daring attack against Legion's forces, pushing them back, thus enabling a large part of your army to escape his deadly trap?"

Mihai nodded.

"But were you ever told of the heroic deeds of a lone cavalry officer and her remaining company?"

"No." Mihai answered. "Please tell me."

Ma-we nodded. "To the northwest, above the plain of shadow and death, a junior officer gathered the remainder of her badly mauled company to the rocky outcroppings overlooking the plain. To her front advanced the vanguard of Legion's best division, led by the most feared regiment in all his army. The officer did not waver, but held her banner high, calling out to any who would listen, 'To me! To me! We shall bring the Dragon down!'"

"With horn blasts and cursing shouts, the officer and her little band, three times, charged the advancing host, three times stalling their advance. In their final thrust, she personally struck down Colonel WsesTfoll, the regimental commander, felling him with a lance through his throat. His regiment fell into momentary confusion, giving time for General Din's troopers to gain the valley's position and hold the gap."

"Your valiant officer was felled by a missile as she drew her surviving soldiers back. It was only by chance that someone came upon her, still clutching a dead companion, and pulled the officer to safety."

Mihai was amazed at hearing of such valor. "This woman should be lauded among the bravest of the heroes honored among my people! Why did this report not fall upon my ears before this day?"

Ma-we shrugged. "It is the fate of war. For so many deserving honors, no honor is given. Your officer languished among the wounded for many months, while your army sought to reconcile its losses and weep over the slain at Memphis. No one remembered the soldier who held a battle line against thousands with a ragtag cavalry of less than eighty, of which only ten lived to tell the tale."

"To honor this woman is not the reason I have told you her account, and truth be told, you will shame her if you attempt to honor her for it now. Let it go, but remember this: Your officer has not rested from war these many long years. She has faithfully served from the beginning of the Megiddo Wars up through the Great War, and still stands the bulwarks today, sending her steel against the Stasis Pirates in the Trizentine. She has not faltered to this day."

"My dear daughter, it is her hatred for the Evil One and all that he has created that has preserved this child's sanity down to this day. Yes, your love has saved you, but her anger and contempt have saved her. And that is also the way with the children from the Realms Below."

"You speak of *Darla*?!" Mihai cried. "Why has she kept this secret from her sister?!"

"Enough, Michael. Let it go." Ma-we waved her hand. "Some think Darla insane, sick of mind, 'cracked' some say. My child does what she does to survive her demon. She tells others only what she believes they need to know. In isolation, the girl grieves over loss and in secret places she searches for her soul. Her cure is not your concern. Do not attempt to effect it."

"And..." Ma-we poked Mihai's arm. "honor and glory will come to your sister in their due time. The Fates cannot hold back an unstoppable storm. Let me assure you, as wondrous as are the deeds your sister has done, they pale to nothing as to the ones she will foment before the winds of fury have swept the evil from this land."

Looking again into Mihai's eyes, Ma-we confided, "My child, who can capture time and lead it about as a slave? Not even I have the authority to do such a thing. So it is with the coming hour. Already there rides upon restless skies the new guard, the coming kings and queens of majesty and glory. In my mind, it is as if their deeds have already been accomplished. There is nothing else for it. I cannot alter it any more than you. What is to be shall come to be. It will not be changed."

Gazing into the sky, Ma-we measured the hour as if searching for some coming moment. "My child, my lovely child..." She looked into Mihai's face, smiling. "A secret I shall tell you, though your wisdom should have already revealed it to you. The anger and rage my daughter displays does not harm the elements of the universe. In fact, they are nourished and strengthened by it, in much the same way your love does."

"You see, righteous wrath sings to the harmonics a sweet and terrible song, making it tough and resistant to any discord, while your songs of gentle refrain heal and nurture the web. Together, they have held back the destructive forces of the Darkness down to this day."

"Why, if all my children should fall in battle, driving themselves forward on to the spears of the enemy, I believe that, by their very death, they could bring to a finish all that is evil. I do think that their collective battle cry would bond the cords of the universe into a filament so strong the Immortals, themselves, could never rip it asunder."

She shuddered at the thought. "But I wish that only as a last resort. My hope still lies elsewhere, with a much less damnable battle plan."

"And that is why I have delivered into your hand certain men and women from the Realms Below. They have carried with them the desire to bring to a finish all that is wicked. They will be brutal, harsh, showing no concern for the enemy, but their wrath will be as holy as your love is. They, I do believe, will effect the cure that will save all mortal life."

"My child…oh, sweet, lovely child, please come to trust Trisha. You do not yet know her. She is not as she appears to be. The woman suppresses her feelings in order to maintain a clear mind. Really, she is a brilliant strategist. Few have I witnessed to be better, and she is a cold and calculating warrior. Feelings will never get in her way when making war. As you have taught my children to love, Trisha will instruct them in the ways of hatred and rage."

Ma-we glanced toward the sky. Her sensitive ears could hear Gradian's Clock chiming the third hour past the noon high. 'It has almost come.'

She turned to Mihai. "My lover of innocence, I will permit you a question… one and only one. Make it good, filled with the wisdom of this moment."

'How strange.' Mihai thought. Why was she to ask a question of Lowenah now, at this very moment? Wisdom? What question would be showing wisdom? She had so many. Funny, there was a rumbling in her heart of a nagging question troubling her for so many years, but she had felt it none of her business to ask. Should that be the question? It was not even related to this day's discussion.

She thought a while, choosing to ask it anyway. "Ma-we… Lowenah… Yehowah… who you are I really do not yet know. So tell me, please. This one question has troubled my soul for many long days. Why do you still hold love for a man so wicked and corrupt? Your children no longer use his name of old, but call him 'Asotos, the Wastepipe'. But you refuse, still holding him dear to your heart. Why?"

Mihai half expected Ma-we to chastise her for asking such an inappropriate and private question. She was much surprised.

Ma-we rubbed her chin in thought, pondering the moment. She finally eyed Mihai, smiling. "Wisdom there is beyond your years, my darling. Why, even the oldest of my offspring have failed to probe me with such a request. And I see it is not at all foolish at this time. Indeed, you have listened to the music within, which music leads a person to greater wisdom than may be. You have chosen well, I will tell you that."

"My dear child of my dreams, I love your brother because I cannot help it."

To say Mihai was shocked would be an understatement. She could only stare at her mother, mouth agape.

Ma-we took Mihai's hands, squeezing them. "You must understand and believe, for what I say can mean life or death to any man. I still love Chrusion because my heart has not *stopped* loving him. I have no control over what my heart feels, nor do you over what your heart feels."

"I believe that, one day, your brother will do something so vile that my heart will become repulsed to the point of falling completely out of love with him. I have faith in it happening, so I have hope of a release from this constant ache I have. Why do you think I have permitted his wicked world such long life? Until he does such a thing, my heart will continue to yearn for his soul. I must wait for him to ruin that love… completely. May it come soon..."

Her voice became ominous and chilling. "Learn from what I have revealed, for there are some things a heart can never heal from or forget, and will carry in it until the world's ending. Unless love of and need for a certain thing is completely driven from it by some evil deed, the heart will continue to pine over the dream unfulfilled until all sanity it will force from your mind so as to forget the anguish living within it."

"Can you promise to forever lock your heart in a prison, suppressing its desires for all eternity? If not, then do not attempt such folly, for, in the end, it will not only destroy you, but all life that is dear to you as well."

Ma-we said no more of it, and allowed no more questions. She looked into the sky. "It is time!" She took Mihai's hand and departed the balcony.

ဆ   ဆ   ဆ

The inner chambers were unnaturally dim. Or was it only the contrast between that and the bright daylight on the balcony? Mihai thought not. For sure, the worlds of Lowenah's house had grown in darkness. Was it then an omen of sorts, or a warning? Possibly… Mother was known to do such things. As Mihai walked further on, she searched for revealing clues.

It was not long before the woman stopped up short. The place where she and Ma-we earlier lunched was hidden in golden silk curtains. Strangely opaque, they allowed no light either in or, more importantly, out. Ma-we halted behind her daughter, saying not a word. She waited for her child to decide what move to make. Destiny rested with her this day.

Drawing the curtains aside, Mihai entered what was now a tiny chamber nearly filled by the table and divan where she earlier dined. Following closely behind, Ma-we entered, letting the curtain fall closed behind her. Darkness quickly wrapped its arms around them.

Mihai began to sniff the air, as if someone or something was hiding itself within. There was an energy secreted away here, different than any she had ever felt before. Her senses warned her of a power the likes of which was unknown among her people lurking here. For good or ill, it anxiously waited its discovery, calling out a haunting refrain to Mihai's ears, beseeching the girl to reveal it.

A glint of light caught Mihai's eye, soon growing into a glow that cast its golden radiance over the table and the objects on it. As the woman watched, the hypnotizing light slowly descended, gradually surrendering its glory over to what rested upon the table.

Mihai gasped in awe and wonder. "It is so magnificent and beautiful! Mother! What glory you have kept in shadows until this day..." The girl in Mihai could not resist the urge to make a close examination of the prizes in front of her. She walked forward, reaching out to the treasures, picking each up, one after the other, studying them carefully.

The first to draw her attention was a golden scepter about two long cubits in length, tapering in width from Mihai's two fingers in breadth to slightly less than that of one-and-a-half. Made of black organin mountain teak inlaid with acacia wood, ivoriun tusk ivory, carved crimson stature mollusk shell, rainbow jade and countless jewels, the scepter shone bright with majesty and dignity.

As her hands caressed the finely engraved staff, Mihai's fingers slipped around and over its bulbous orb of gold, chrysolite and gemstones, sending a sensual wave of excitement through her body. Like a lover's touch, it aroused her. "Oh! Oh, my! It sings songs of love to me." She then puzzled. "It feels like the music of my sisters' fingers playing upon my flesh."

Suddenly the seven gemstones on the orb's fillet ignited into flaming hues, each one a different color, sending a tingling sensation through Mihai. "My body fills with passion desired..." She frowned, bewildered. "But it is to satisfy my heart with my sisters' love that it sings out to me."

Ma-we stood back, in the shadows, watching Mihai marveling at the gemstones as they began to pulse randomly, one at a time.

Drawing the scepter close to her face, Mihai began to distinguish written script above each of the seven glowing gemstones. She began to read aloud the words, slowly rotating the orb from left to right, reading the inscriptions in order.

"The flaming pink one reads, '*Varda, the flowers in my garden welcome the king.*'"

"The gem that glows copper reads, '*Uma, I shall make the king into mighty nations.*'"

"This one that shines golden, '*Nesya the gift from God I am, to satisfy my king's every delight.*'"

"Here is one whose light is brilliant, glittering onyx black, '*Adaya, I shall haunt my king's dreams with night's love calls.*'"

"The one glowing scarlet reads, '*Sirion, I burn passion-red for my king.*'"

"And look! The one emerald blue reads '*Tzila, come to my shadows, my king, and refresh your spirit with my love.*'"

"Oh! This hurts my eyes for its brilliance of burning, forest green! It reads, '*Sharon, let my breasts excite you, oh my king, and find refreshment in their milk.*'"

Mihai swooned after naming the gemstones, feeling a sensuous passion slowly overwhelming her soul. She quickly put the scepter down, asking,

"What do they mean, Ma-we? What do all the names and words really mean?"

Ma-we quietly answered, "Little I will tell you but this: the names are of ones and also many. The words are but one song, sung by my daughters all. I will say no more."

After thanking her mother for the explanation, Mihai picked up the second object, a golden circlet crown with a raised, pointed, frontal crest embellished with an ivory-white sapphire resting over a green, glittering emerald. Twenty-four smaller points of chrysolite-gold circled the crown, each with a sapphire of different hue.

Light as a feather it was, cool to the touch, but it made Mihai's heart warm with desire for close companions. She became suspicious. "Mother, oh, Mother! My desire grows ever stronger to hold my sister in the fashion a man does. Is the beauty I see in this coronet attempting my seduction? Does its fiery glow seek to entrap my heart with manly passion?"

Ma-we mildly replied, "What you hold was not made anew. It was crafted by mystic hands in secret places long ago, during the carefree days, to be given to the one person who would stand above all others. It knows not your touch or who you are, but only sings the songs given it so many lifetimes of men ago."

Curious, Mihai searched the crown for other clues. Suddenly the green emerald began to glow bright, its flame revealing hidden words. The woman mouthed them aloud. "Ĕlah · Hod · Zakar-Geber · Nasab." (*The words, when translated into the common tongue of your day, are pronounced 'Yehowah-boam', 'the man who stands in the place of God'*).

Mihai puzzled but a moment before her face paled. She read the words again, rereading over and over 'Zakar-Geber, Zakar-Geber'. All too clearly did the woman understand the meaning of the two words, each representing the same identity and being placed together adding double emphasis. The words' translation tumbled from her quivering lips. "The *man*…the *man*..."

With shaking hands, Mihai returned the crown to the table, almost dropping it as she did. Turning toward her mother, her eyes burned with trepidation and fear, shouting out the pain tearing at Mihai's heart.

Ma-we slowly shook her head, speaking in little more than a hush. "My lovely one, first of your kind, bringer of joy to my birthing pains, you have not been unknowing of this day. It was told to you millennia ago by your own sister, Gabrielle, as she spoke to the one who came to be your mother in the Realms Below. Time you have had to contemplate this moment, to consider its worth to you and the others among you."

"Sweet One of my heart, nursemaid to heroes and lords, the time has come to set things in place. My children cry out for a king. A king! For a king can govern in times of peace as well as times of war. The children tire for lack of knowledge. 'Tell us please, oh Mighty One, who shall become our leader to bring us to the end of this wicked time?!' What shall I say to them, to myself?"

Mihai's knees shook and her legs wobbled. She barely managed to find the divan before collapsing to the floor. Her head spun with dread. 'The *man*! The *man*!' The king must be a *male*, child of manliness, 'masculine divine'.

Spasms racked her body as she thought of the change she must have made to herself should the crown become hers. Holding her head in her hands, with mournful cries she pleaded, "What shall I do?! Oh! My belly burns with damnable fire and my breasts ache as if torn away!" She began to weep.

Ma-we settled down next to her daughter, but did not touch her, waiting until Mihai's tears and outcries subsided before speaking. "My dearest daughter, one lovely like the gazelle and comely as the hind with its child, you know my law, and that it cannot be broken by my own hand, for treacherous I would be to do so. You are the one who has gained legal right to my throne. I must offer it to you."

She became silent, waiting for Mihai to consider her words. Although her daughter's outward emotions calmed, Ma-we could still see how distraught the woman was.

Reaching out, she stroked the child's long hair. "Oh, my golden sunshine of lilting song, no more charming voice does the katchberry robin have when she sings to her lover. You must choose for yourself which road to take. Does my daughter accept this crown of glory or not?"

Leaning her head back against the divan, Mihai cried out in angry bewilderment, "Mother! Is it with *evil* that you keep calling out to me, '*oh, my daughter*'?!"

Ma-we said not a word. She kept still and waited.

As Mihai sat, eyes closed, she searched events of her earlier life, cursing her past love and loyalty. Never had she ached so! Even her torture at Asotos' hands appeared distant and less tormenting. She had passed all the legal requirements for the crown - that is, except one - the one Ma-we had not yet spoken of. But there was no need for her to.

Long had Mihai, indeed, had all the children known. The king sitting on Yehowah's throne must be a man. *A man!* How those words burned into Mihai's soul. So much she wanted to give to Ma-we what she wanted, and she knew that, as a man, her mother would still love her... maybe even more than as she was now - a chatty, impetuous, nuisance. Another wave of hopeless anguish swept over her, and she began to weep anew.

Through her tears, the woman attempted to reason her situation. 'Was it really so bad, to become a man?' Why, for several decades she had walked the Lower Realms in the flesh of a man. To this day she remembered the male strength and will, the feeling of might and leadership as a man felt it. 'It was not so bad, was it?' Mihai suddenly doubled up in pain as her stomach churned in tumult.

After the nauseous storm subsided, Mihai sat back, forcing her mind to think past a pulsing headache steadily gaining in strength. What was really so disturbing about her becoming a man? After all, as king, she would have greater power than all others, mortal or immortal, other than Ma-we. Such immortal power should be more than great enough to suppress *any* feelings secreted in a *fickle* heart. But what if she did lose control? Not to worry, there would be many other immortals to hold any foolish actions in check.

Again the girl wretched in agony, but only a little bile reached her mouth. Something was wrong…so wrong. Mihai's heart was in full rebellion, seeking vengeance upon a confused mind. Each time the woman considered accepting the crown, her heart would throw her body into a near seizure, turning her stomach over and over while twisting her innards up in knots.

Leaning back, Mihai rolled her head from side to side in desperation, moaning in agony, "Mother of all living things, Witch of the dawning, why do you persecute me with your offers? Shall a mouse call out to the lion with bold enough words to chase it away? My soul dies from its own distress. Save me the pain of this moment! Allow your child to pass away into nothingness!"

Ma-we did not move or speak.

As her headache reached blinding proportions, Mihai cried out, "What of the prophecy?! What of it?! Shall life go on if the mouse does not become the lion?! Do I doom the universe with wicked reasonings?!" Her mind reeled with a vision of seeing the worlds of all flesh dissolving into dust because the throne sat empty of its king. But she was rightful heir to the crown. What would happen if she declined it? Would all be lost?

'There is nothing else for it! It must be done!' Mihai opened her mouth to take up the scepter and submit to the changes she would be required to make in accepting it. As she did, her heart forced one more convulsion, filling the woman's mouth with vomit, gagging her into silence.

After a bout of coughing and hacking to keep from suffocating, an exhausted and distraught Mihai fell back on the divan, sweating profusely as she mumbled through the spittle, "Ma-we... Ma-we..."

What was it the heart was recalling that Mihai could not remember? Was there something of greater consequence from her younger life that held precendence over this moment in time in value and importance? Mihai thought about it. Only a vow or oath given by the Maker of Worlds could possibly be of greater worth…not to be negated by any later vow.

Struggling to recall times past for some memory of a promise given, Mihai repeatedly cried out as if in labor pains, but no answer came. Desperately she searched, clutching her head and straining to see the ages of her life when the world was innocent and free. Still nothing…

'Remember AsreHalom, my child.' What?! Why could remembering such an evil man at this moment assist Mihai in her hour of need? 'Remember AsreHalom…' Mother's earlier words refused to abandon Mihai's heart. 'Remember AsreHalom, the sorcerer.'

Mihai's eyes popped open. AsreHalom was a sorcerer of wonder, able to induce his own mystic dreams by inner chants and incantations. His visions were profound and insightful, as if he had tapped into a secret world of magic. Mihai remembered him doing it once. How she marveled at the wise knowledge he later revealed.

But, how?! AsreHalom was an ancient of Ancients, his power nearly that of Chrusion. She had to try, though! What else was she to do?! After all, the woman did have the ring of the Firstborn. Maybe it would give her the added power to reach beyond her consciousness and into forgotten places and days. 'Focus on the ring! Focus on the ring and all that it has seen and heard since its making so very long ago!'

Lifting the ring before her eyes, Mihai began a quiet chant of the only words that formed in her mind. 'Strange…' she thought and began singing,

"Ma-we… Ma-we…
oh, my Mother, dear.
Ma-we… Ma-we…
your heart's beat is all your daughter hears.
Ma-we… Ma-w…"

Mihai's head slowly fell back as her hand dropped into her lap. While her lips continued to move, they produced no sound.

Down, down, down the girl was swept, falling back through time and space, to an earlier age, a dark vortex enveloping Mihai's body with freezing chills, followed by almost unbearable heat. The wars of this age quickly whisked into the blurring future, rapidly followed by other personal events experienced through the woman's eyes.

On and on she plummeted, twirling and twisting, every second revealing hundreds of millennia, so many forgotten memories re-burned into Mihai's mind. JabethHull and Nhoset suddenly flashed before her eyes and were as quickly gone, but it felt to the woman as if she had relived every moment with them again.

Instantly, she experienced her first night of loving when she came of age, then that day's celebrating. She was just turned twelve. And then…and then Mihai heard a screeching in her ears just before being slammed into something rock-solid hard as all went dark and silent.

Gradually the world around Mihai regained its focus, as she stared into an afternoon sky, its blue, shimmering brilliance almost blinding. With effort, she sat and looked around, uncertain of what she would see. The woman was disappointed.

Standing, Mihai sputtered, "Must have walked in my vision. Ma-we?! Mother? Are you there? I'm out here on the balcony." No reply came. "Whatever…" Mihai mumbled, disgusted that her vision had fizzled into little more than a mindless ambling, ending in a painful fall. She rubbed her hip, slowly stumbling back inside.

"Ma-w…?" Mihai stopped, gawking at the room.

Where were the curtain, the crown, the scepter? Where was Mother? The table and divan were empty, void of any treasures… and Ma-we? Where had she wandered off to? "Anybody!?" Mihai started for the portico, feeling her mother may have had unexpected business in the reception hall.

Laughter followed by a child singing brought Mihai to an instant stop, "What the…?!" staring off toward a distant doorway, waiting and wondering at what she was hearing. She was not kept waiting long.

A little blond girl danced into the room. Mihai blurted out, "Who are you?!" The child ignored her, pretending she was not even there. Mihai raised her voice. "Little girl! Who *are* you and where is Mother?" Paying no heed to the woman, the child continued on, prancing into the room, singing a silly song, bouncing a ball to the rhythm.

Growing frustrated, Mihai was about to shout at the child when the silly tune caught her attention, it being strangely familiar to her ears. She paused to listen.

The child's eyes twinkled with delight as she began anew the merry refrain.

> *"Mother said we could go today,*
> *Mother said we could do today,*
> *Mother said we could see today,*
> *Mother said we could have today.*
>
> *Mother said we could have today,*
> *Mother said we could get today,*
> *Mother said we would be today,*
> *Mother said we could play today."*

Twice more the child sang these verses, changing them ever so slightly.

> *"Mother said we could have,*
> *Mother said we would be,*
> *Mother said we would have,*
> *Mother said we could be.*

> *Mother said we should have,*
> *Mother said we could have,*
> *Mother said we will have,*
> *Mother said we must have."*

Again the girl repeated the stanzas twice more, shortening them, speeding up the tune, increasing the speed of the bouncing ball.

> *"Mother said we should,*
> *Mother said we could,*
> *Mother said we must,*
> *Mother said we will."*

She repeated the tune the same as the other times, but now, when she picked up the following verse, it became a chant of sorts.

> *"Mother said we,*
> *Mother said we,*
> *Mother said we,*
> *Mother said we."*

The girl's voice grew in excitement until the chant became a cry, like some beast calling out its coming feast.

> *"Mother we,*
> *Mother we,*
> *Mother we,*
> *Mother we."*

Over and over she shouted the refrain, growing in intensity until Mihai thought the child would burst a vocal cord. About the time the words became little more than garbled sounds, the child stopped, clutching the ball. Then, with deliberate slowness in drawing out her words, the girl started a new verse, chanting it only once.

> *"Ma... we,*
> *Ma... we,*
> *Ma... we,*
> *Ma... we."*

All fell suddenly silent. The little girl stared down at the floor, a huge smile beaming on her face. At length, she looked up and over at Mihai. With the tone of voice of a little girl filled with the smug joy of impossible wishes assured, the child announced, "She promised us today! Didn't she?! Didn't she?! She said we would have one, today. Didn't she?! Didn't she?!"

Mihai slapped her head in astonishment as she cried, "This cannot be! You are me, or who I was so long ago!"

The little girl giggled, "I am not who you think I am. I live in a world of promises come true. I do not hope, for I do know it is so. Mother promised. *My Ma-we promised.* She said that when *he* becomes a god, I would be given my wish."

The child bent forward, laughing, "I have never changed, but still live in mystic worlds where no pain can touch me. *Ma-we promised…* Yes! Yes! She did!"

Mihai shook her head. "You're not real! This is a vision gone wrong…a vision gone *terribly* wrong! Mother?!"

The child pouted, chiding Mihai, "You refuse to admit me alive. But I live! Always will! You cannot kill a dream! Never will I depart your soul, for I am who you still are! *You!* You are returning to me, not I to you!"

Mihai's anger erupted. *"You're a dream, a silly, foolish, dream of a vision! You do not exist in my world anymore! Anymore!"*

Now the child's anger was roused and she threatened, *"You will never be rid of me! I will haunt your waking dreams if you betray the promise Ma-we has given me. I will never let you rest! Never!"* She then screamed, "Mother promised*!*"

It was as if the girl's last heated breath ignited a tempest. Mihai was swept from her feet and flung into the air as her world plunged into darkness in the raging storm. Soon all conscious thought faded away into nothingness.

Gradually Mihai's senses returned. Through a pounding headache, her eyes eventually came into focus in the curtained room from where her adventure had begun. All was as it had been, Ma-we quietly sitting beside her on the divan, the table illuminated by the scepter and crown. The woman placed her hand to her forehead and moaned. Ma-we said not a word, her breathing quiet and controlled.

The vision still burned brightly inside the woman, spinning round and round. Pushing it back in her mind, she again bent her attention to the issue at hand. Returning to the table, Mihai began reexamining the crown, studying the inscription once more.

'Elah · Hod · Zakar-Geber · Nasab'… Something was strange about the word placement. Mihai puzzled. The proper wordage layout in the language of her people was out of order. Why would Mother have mixed them around? It wouldn't have been an accident, not from Ma-we. And the first letter of each word was capitalized. How unusual…

'A riddle? Or possibly a hidden message…' That was Ma-we, always playing games with her children, secrets hidden within secrets, the obvious hidden in the mist. Mihai concentrated on the inscription.

Suddenly her eyes opened in surprise. She read aloud the first letter of each word. "E – H – Z – G – N." Putting them together, the woman spelled them out, "EHZGN".

With a jolt, Mihai jumped back, gasping, "It's a word!" In the language of Mihai's people, as with some other languages, usually only the consonants of given words were written, the vowels understood. Mihai's quivering lips reluctantly spoke, "Ehazgeone…"

'Ehazgeone' was a word used when sealing a most solemn oath or promise. In all of Mihai's life, the woman had only heard it used a few times, and most of those were by her mother. In fact, it was Ma-we's use of the word in a confrontation with Asotos that she acquired the name 'Yehowah', the children giving their mother the name in reference to that promise. Now she saw it on the crown. 'Shall worlds pass away before My promise fails.'

Mihai puzzled again. She squinted, seeing another riddle in the letters, 'EHZGN'. Recalling her studies of ancient runes found in Palace City, Memphis, and other scattered parts of the realm, she deduced that those letters were phonetic pronunciations given to certain rune words. These letters were to be found at the base of the throne in the Great Hall.

Thinking aloud, Mihai attempted to remember the literal translation of those letters, pondering, toying with the ring on her finger, giving no consideration to what she was doing. Suddenly its meaning became clear. 'This Man is man as shall is he be'.

There was another place Mihai remembered the word. It was in a little *silly* ditty, part of a very old tune the Ancients often sang to the younger children in her beginning days, before the old songs were forgotten.

"EHZGN

Man by nature,
Man by flesh.
Alive forever,
With manly breath."

Ma-we had said that the crown and scepter were made during the carefree days. That being the case, Mihai reasoned, the crown and scepter were not designed to represent someone's ruling authority, it never being an issue until after the Rebellion. So what was the original purpose of the kingly position Mother had created?

The woman stood, curiosity overcoming any trepidation of the moment. She reached for the scepter, closely examining it for other clues. 'Mother said this was but one song… every woman's song.' Studying each verse,

Mihai came to realize that they were not in proper order, at least if considered by the custom of ancient day. This was not a maiden's tale of love for her sweetheart. No… Two statements caught her eye that had no application to a maiden's love.

First, only the adult women in her realm ever produced breast milk, it being many years after their coming of age and it usually began after being offered the opportunity to nurse one of Ma-we's infants. Second, this song spoke not just of loving, but the making of nations… children… so many children that the women would make nations of them for the king. None of the women in her world had ever birthed even one child.

Curiosity growing, Mihai studied the gems. They did not pulse randomly but in a sequential order. Where to start then? Mihai decided that Nesya, the most prominent of the names, having the most profound meaning, was the most provable starting point. From there, she read the names in their pulsing sequence.

"Nesya…
'The gift from God I am, to satisfy my king's every delight.'

Adaya…
'I shall haunt my king's dreams with night's love calls.'

Sirion…
'I burn passion-red for my king.'

Tzila…
'Come to my shadows my king and refresh your spirit with my love.'

Sharon…
'Let my breasts excite you, oh my king, and find refreshment in their milk.'

Varda…
'The flowers in my garden welcome the king.'

Uma…
'I shall make the king into mighty nations.'"

As astonishing as these revelations were to her, it was the following understanding soon to be revealed that most affected Mihai. She began to reason, 'If the letters on the crown are in fact hiding meanings in the runes of old, then is it possible the scepter does the same?'

Hoping that she had arranged the verses in order, Mihai read aloud the first letter of each word, 'N – A – S – T – S – V – U'. Using the rule for the common tongue first, the woman deduced that the letters consisted of three words, the vowels indicating a word ending, but with only the use of the consonant before it. Doing this, made it easy to see the three words, 'Na – Setousee – Vu', translated into today's common tongue, 'The seed of life shall this man give'.

A chill ran down Mihai's back. She wanted to *receive* the seed of life, not *give* it!

Calming herself, the woman searched now for the possible rune connection. "NASTSVU... NASTSVU?" Where had she seen the letters? Where?! As she strained in thought, Mihai felt her ring tingle. She surrendered to its haunting call and closed her eyes to its music. In the distance, Gradian's Clock chimed the half hour.

That was it! Gradian's Clock! Inscribed upon each planet was its name in the runes of the Ones Who Came Before. NASTSVU was the rune name for EdenEsonbar, the home planet, commonly called the 'King's Planet.'

Beads of sweat formed on Mihai's forehead, beginning to drip down her face. She worked to concentrate on the music the ring was quietly playing in her head. Soon words were coming into focus before her eyes, revealing the meaning of the runes. '*I shall embrace the women forever*'.

A rush of excitement washed over Mihai as the real and original meaning of the kingship unveiled itself before her. It had never been about power or rulership. Ever since Ma-we's birthing her first child, she had been hoping and planning to one day give the power of life to her own offspring. Finally, near the end of the Second Age, she was successful, choosing to first deliver that gift on her new creation in the Second Realm.

For all the ages of time before, from the conception of her first son, she had prepared for the day when her children would be parents, making her Firstborn the giver of that seed to her daughters, making him the father of all the first-born children in the universe. He would continue to be the man from whom all the daughters born of womankind would receive the seed of life, thus making him father of many nations.

There were also other things the ring helped Mihai see regarding Ma-we's future hopes. Now she understood so much the more, the reasons for the festivals and why they were opened and closed with Chrusion and his royal consort, who stood as liege for Lowenah. For all those ages, Ma-we was continually keeping before her children's eyes the promise she tirelessly worked at to fulfill. The crown was to become Chrusion's as soon as he had proved himself a man worthy of his sisters' love. But he had failed...

Mihai slowly placed the scepter down. She understood all too well what she must do if she accepted it and the crown. But she did not want to hold her sisters in the way men did. Not only that, she wanted to be *held* by men, not forever be parted from such manly love. She wondered if she could she survive an eternity. Even if her flesh and mind relinquished the feminine, could she hold in check her heart's desires forever?

The war within was raging ever stronger, but Mihai could already see its final outcome. Should worlds fall because of her decision made this day, it would have to be. Long ago her mother had given an oath to a little child who, as a child yet without breasts or sexual passion, had requested the privilege to produce offspring from her own flesh. A will that strong could never be held in check. It would, one day, either see its desires satisfied or go mad, bringing itself and all with it to destruction.

Mihai stood upright, her muscles stiffening with resolve. She forced down the fear of possible future repercussions from her rejection of the crown. Her mother's heart might break from the loss of having the legal heir refuse the throne. Could Ma-we find a way to sit another? It was too late for the woman-child living in Mihai's heart to contemplate the matter. What she was to do must be done.

But it was still no easy thing to do, to tell Mother of her decision. Grappling with an ever-growing despair over her decision, she turned to face Ma-we, who still sat motionless on the divan, patiently awaiting her daughter's reply.

The look on her mother's face was too much for Mihai's heart. Her legs surrendered to her body's pressing weight, forcing the woman to fall forward onto her knees, supporting herself by resting shaking hands on Ma-we's lap.

"Mother! Oh, Mother!" She wailed. "Should all the worlds fail because of me, remember please that your daughter has loved no one more than she does you! I am come to my end and there is no other hope for me but to do this wretched thing. Please forgive a child so crass and foolish so that she listens not to the wisdom of song, but to the beating of a stupid and selfish heart!"

With pleading eyes, Mihai searched Ma-we's for some kind of reassurance or disapproval, but Mother's emerald green oceans secreted all feelings.

"Mother! Ever have I longed to see this day arrive, a day when all my sisters could sing with the joy of receiving power of life..." she lowered her head in dismay. "But I cannot be the one to give that wonderful gift to them..."

A shudder wracked Mihai's frame as she groaned, "*Please!* Do not hate this request from a wicked and traitorous child, but if there is any love remaining for your daughter, please set aside this offer and grant, *please,* an earlier promise made by your lips, if such a thing is any longer possible."

"Mother, from my young womanhood, I watched you in your birthing pangs as you delivered life to this world, both sons and daughters. Then, one day, you allowed me to hold to my breasts a child of yours to nurse from me. Did my face not beam with unspeakable joy at just her touch upon my heart and did I not ache with happiness at feeling it suckle life from my soul?"

"Oh, my Love! My Cherished Delight! The burning within me has not subsided from the earliest days of my childhood, when I still remained in my virginity. Indeed! It has only become greater, a raging inferno consuming my entire being. Should all things come to pass for me, to go away into nothingness, I would be satisfied if I had borne but one son to feed at my breasts."

Ma-we said not a word, staying silent, hiding any emotion. 'It is not the hour to speak, for I shall not swage my daughter in choices made.'

Mihai pleaded, "If by your hand, the flesh of one kind can be made in to that of another, so that a child of my flesh can become that of my brothers, is it such an impossible thing for you to change your daughter…daughters a little, so that they might become like you and know what it means to be filled with child?!"

"And what of your promise? Is it really such a great thing I have done, so that I, alone, should be given chance to sit a throne and that a man of valor should not?"

Mihai shook her head. *"No! Your child will not surrender what is hers from birth! A woman I came from your belly and a woman I shall remain until the world's ending! It cannot be changed!"* She looked again into Ma-we's eyes, searching for redemption. She found none.

With wails of remorse, Mihai fell upon Ma-we, burying her face in her mother's lap. "Oh, forgive an errant child! *Please*! Let her be damned now, rather than suffer the shame of hurting you!"

At that, Mihai's waking world began to spin into darkness, her flesh unable to carry the weight of the moment any longer, soon to be followed by a deep, painless sleep.

Her mother's tears of joy she did not see, nor hear the gentle words that passed Ma-we's lips. "You have not disappointed the Maker of Worlds, for your wisdom has saved us all this day. Rest for now, my Cherished One. Tomorrow shall come, and with it new joys…" She frowned. "…but also despair."

ಬಿ   ಬಿ   ಬಿ

Mihai awoke to the sound of a twittering bird on her windowsill, as a gentle breeze parted the flaxen shades, allowing late-day light to cascade into the tiny apartment. Gaining her senses, the woman wondered aloud where she was and how she got there. Sitting up, she groaned, "Was this but a foolish dream and am I delinquent in making my appointment?"

A voice from the shadows answered, giving Mihai an unsettling surprise. "Foolish? Maybe, but the hour is young and our appointed destiny still some hours away."

"*Who*?!" Mihai bent forward, peering into a dark corner to find the face behind the voice.

The person, whoever she might be - for Mihai was sure it was a woman's voice - was sitting in a chair propped against the wall, supported on its back legs, two hands clasping a knee that was pressed against the person's chest, her foot resting on the seat bottom. At once, Mihai recognized by the style of boots and cut of the trousers, the person was an officer, but she could see little else.

The woman let the chair fall forward, onto its front legs, revealing her face. It was Darla, all done up in her most handsome of uniforms. "Did we enjoy our sleep, my Lady?"

Mihai grumbled words better left in the shadows as she slowly pushed her legs over the side of the bed while attempting to drive sleep from tired eyes. Little joy remained in the woman's heart, remembering the previous hours and the dread of the decision she had made. It did not put her in a good mood.

Resting her hands on the bed as her feet touched the floor, Mihai grumped, "My darling of sour refrain, how long have you been here?"

Darla casually reached to turn on a wall light, spreading a mild, yellow glow across the small apartment, then lifted her foot, placing it back on the edge of the chair seat, wrapping hers arms around her leg as she leaned forward, resting her chin on her knee. Waiting until Mihai was about to utter some more colorful words before replying, smiling, Darla answered, "Oh, more than two hours ago." Again she waited, flustering Mihai anew. Then, at just the right moment, "Lowenah had Zadar…you do remember our little brother, Zadar don't you?"

Mihai sputtered, "Get on with it, you! Or I'll… I'll… put you on report for withholding pertinent information!"

Laughing, Darla replied, "Since you put it that way, Lowenah had Zadar and me bring you over here. Sure would like some of the stuff you were drinking. You were out cold, but had the biggest smile on your face. Why, I think we could have dragged you over here by the hair on your head and you'd have never known, that is 'til you woke up later."

Mihai shook her head to clear the last of sleep's cobwebs from her brain. "So what a' you still doin' here? Got no place to wander off to, or other people to pester?"

Darla put up a good-natured fuss, declaring her innocence, answering as if offended. "*I* was *asked* to remain here, watching my *ward* until she awoke. Had I known the rude reception awaiting one of such genteel persuasion,

I'd have departed as quickly as Zadar did! He said it was your snoring, but I wonder."

Looking down at the floor, Mihai disagreed. "He must 'a figured the bed was too small for the both of us. That's the only reason he'd leave."

They both laughed, Darla adding, "No, I believe it different. The boy's nose is upon a new scent, I think."

Mihai sighed wistfully, "He does have a way about him," She looked into Darla's emerald green eyes, "…doesn't he?"

Darla giggled, "He can make one wish the night would never end, or is it that day would never come?" She giggled again, her face blushing red as her eyes looked toward the ceiling.

Changing the subject, Mihai noted Darla's stylish uniform. Darla stood, and with arms gracefully spread wide, slowly circled once around.

In the days before the King's War, there was little regulation regarding military apparel, especially formal attire. Darla was no exception in taking advantage of this freedom. Other than its light blue color, there was little else to distinguish it as a Navy uniform. It was natty to a fault, revealing the woman's feminine curves while hiding her sensuality, elegant while not being garish, formal but still fully functional.

"It was just delivered today, just in time for tonight." Darla turned a circle once more.

Mihai asked, half joking, "Haven't you about enough of new uniforms? Only four months ago you were sporting one made, you bragged, by ContorieDamalis, herself, the finest linen maker in the Empire. What happened to make your taste in garments change so fast?"

A black cloud passed across Darla's eyes, Mihai catching only a glimpse of it. Without missing a step, the girl continued her turn, chatting most cheerily, "That thing? I tore it on our last patrol in the Trizentine. Didn't want to bother with a fix, too much work and all."

Changing the subject quickly, Darla laughed and, stopping to face Mihai, grinned with delight. "You know what?! Mother told me to expect a surprise at the council tonight. In fact, she said I would have more than one." She clasped her hands in joy. "Mother's surprises are always so much fun. What do you think it might be?"

Mihai frowned, thinking of her resignation from being field marshal and then her dismal rejection of Lowenah's wonderful gift. Maybe that was the reason Mother had Zadar and Darla deliver her here, to her apartment. Maybe Mihai wasn't wanted at tonight's council anymore.

Shaking her head, Mihai added, "I don't know what it could possibly be, but I'm sure it will be worth your trouble to be there to find out." Then she changed the subject, asking, "Did I really snore?"

Darla laughed, bending forward as she continued to chuckle. "Sister, if you had snored any louder, we'd had to replace the broken plaster in this room!"

A quiet knock directed the women's attention toward the door. Darla jumped up to open it. With a *swoosh*, cool evening air rushed into the room, bathing Mihai in its chill, sending goose bumps across her bare skin. Shivering, Mihai stared into the shadows to see who the visitor was.

"Hello!" Ma-we's cheery voice could be heard among the rustle of wrapped bundles filling her arms. "Well, girl…" speaking to Darla, "are you just going to stand there?"

Darla yipped with joy, "Mother!" jumping like a puppy long waiting for its master.

An instant later, Ma-we found herself being dragged through the door. Almost tripping on the threshold, she cried, "Hey, child! Gravity still works here! Do be careful!"

To say Darla was oblivious to Ma-we's predicament would be to say water flows downhill. She hugged her mother, bundles and all, twirling her round and round, until Ma-we cried out, stubbing her toe, "Please! Little one! Please!" with a painful grimace on her face, "Do be a good girl and put me down!"

Mihai, who had turned rather glum at seeing her mother, could not help but laugh at the antics of her little sister. Forgetting her sullen mood, she sang out part of a little child's tune.

> *"Should the merry pig*
> *dance with the goat,*
> *Shall the swill stay in the trough?*
> *Or will the corn fall off the cob,*
> *To be scattered in the mud?"*

'*Plop!*' A small bundle fell from Ma-we's arms to the floor.

"Little Darling! That is quite enough!" Ma-we sputtered. "Now put me down!"

Darla laughed, spun around one more time, to Mother's fussing, then gently returned Ma-we's feet to her.

What a sight for Mihai! Darla was a big girl, taller than average and muscular. Ma-we, on the other hand, was most demure and only three finger-breadths over three long cubits tall and, also weighing in at only seven stone or so, she was of a stature smaller than most of her daughters. "It makes me more lovable…" She would often say, when asked why she had chosen to be thus among her children.

And Darla? This was a side of her that few people ever saw. In groups she was often shy, as an officer, strictly business, and in combat, ruthless. Today she was with Mother, 'the most wonderful person in the universe'. When with her, Darla could release all her pent-up emotions. She could become the little child again, safe and innocent, free from all the dark memories that haunted the woman day and night.

Darla released Ma-we, only to start rummaging through the securely wrapped bundles. "What did you bring us?!" She excitedly asked, pawing at another package. "What treats are here for your darlings this day?!"

Clutching the bundles tight, Ma-we pulled herself away and turned toward the bed, scolding, "*My little mouse, my little mouse, thou who seeks another's cheese. Run along, run along, for these sweet treats belong not to thee.*"

Dropping the packages on the bed, she turned and, after giving Darla a kiss, poked her with a finger. "*Today belongs to gifts untold, but for you, not here will you behold. To your sister, sweet and dear, these things belong, I fear, I fear.*"

Darla pouted, making a sour retort, "*When birds of spring sing out love's songs, the crow shouts out, 'Be gone…! Be gone!' And off will the tender-hearted songbird fly, crying out, 'Oh, how sad. Oh why? Oh why?'*"

"It's the *raven*, Dear." Ma-we replied, "The *raven*." then slapped Darla on the behind. "And that's what *little songbirds* who don't listen deserve!"

Jumping back, aghast, Darla began rubbing her eyes to cover pretend tears and started another refrain of a child's poem about a little girl rejected by some dancing frogs, then attempted to reach past Ma-we to get at the bundles anew.

Mihai burst into uncontrolled laughter, watching the two struggling in mock combat over who was to get the bundles. Through tears, she shouted to Ma-we, "That's what you get when you spoil the child! Remember, '*The mule will wander far and wide, should a weak-willed master attempt it to ride*'."

Holding Darla at hand's reach, Ma-we, breathless, replied, "I have spoilt all my children… *YOU…especially, you included!*"

Mihai laughed, but a cloud swept her thoughts.

Darla and Zadar were the two youngest children in all the realm. Darla was not three at the time of the Rebellion, with Zadar being born some months after it began. But it was Darla who spent her growing-up-years living in the Palace's shadows, reaching out to few and being avoided by most. Euroaquilo, who frequented the palace during her early years, took a shine to the girl. He was the only man willing to draw close to her.

Darla's affliction was too difficult for Ma-we's other children to handle… and her eyes, those eyes. Few looked into them more than once out of an uneasy feeling of being watched by something unnatural. So it was, when the children visited Mother, Zadar was made their center of attention, while

Darla was politely ignored. Even the woman's coming of age celebration was postponed until she was well into her thirties, Ma-we having found no man willing to trust his dream-share to her.

As she watched, Mihai shook her head in puzzled wonder. Funny, regardless of, or possibly in spite of the way Darla was viewed, she never displayed any outward resentment for the way she was often treated. Her devotion to the cause and her siblings was unquestioned. Throughout the long wars, she had not faltered, even placing her life on the line many times to rescue others from death. It was this selfless devotion to her siblings that won over the hearts of her fellow comrades, especially her sisters.

And then there was Zadar. He had been totally spoiled by the others while little Darla silently watched from a distance. Yet she never harbored any resentment toward him. Truth be said, the two were very close, oft times inseparable. When he grew into manhood, he forced his siblings to accept Darla into their company, even using intimidation or shame.

Mihai was drawn back to the moment when she noticed how quiet the room had become. Darla was resting her hands on Ma-we's shoulders, while Mother gently stroked her daughter's face. Some kind of guttural purr came from Darla's throat, indicating her pleasure with the moment, an ability that was uniquely hers.

Standing on her toes, Ma-we kissed her daughter, asking, "Sweet love of mine, would you surrender the moment to us for just a little while? I do need some time alone with your sister."

Darla stared into her mother's eyes, searching for something secret only to the two of them. Satisfied, she bent forward and kissed Lowenah, and started for the door. While opening it, she looked back over her shoulder at Mihai. "You are to dine with me this eve. I shall wait for you at the tram. If he has not wandered too far away, Zadar will join us at the Kataklino Cafe at eight." She popped through the door into the evening shadows.

Ma-we's eyes followed the sound of Darla's fading footsteps until the evening swallowed them up. With a sigh and slow shake of her head, she turned her attention to Mihai. "My child, your sister loves you too much, loves me too much. She does not test it out, the love, I mean. She hasn't truly searched to see how honest mine is for her, but only bathes in the warmth it produces." She sighed again. "The hour draws closer when her trust will be tested to the full, my child, to the full."

Ma-we said no more of the matter, changing the subject before Mihai could ask any questions. "My Dear!" She grinned. "How wonderful to see you this hour, this very, *very* special hour!"

Plopping in the nearby chair, she wiped a hand across her forehead. "What a workout it's been, didn't realize just how much until I sat."

Mihai was in no mood to fraternize, staring at the floor, still seated on the edge of the bed. What was the use? At a most critical moment, she had failed - failed because her heart refused to listen to the logic of her mind! Now what hope remained for her people, her sisters?

As if understanding Mihai's accusative remorse, Ma-we waxed apologetic. "My tender child, daughter of the New Age and mother to the old, I am very sorry my reply to you this day fell upon sleeping ears. I have caused you much grief, for I, too, became slow of tongue because of the things I heard coming from your mouth."

Mother's sweet tone was too much for Mihai and she scowled. "What are you about?! I…"

"You did the right thing!" Ma-we leaned forward, staring at a very surprised Mihai. "That's right! Somehow…don't ask me how…" she winked. "But for a *selfish, uncaring*…well, you know the kind of person you accuse yourself of being. Somehow you managed to listen to your heart this time instead of your head, which listening to your head is often very wise, but not this time, at least."

She slapped her legs, still grinning. "Michael, *you made the right choice!*"

Mihai was stunned, speechless. She had made the right choice? How?!

Ma-we jumped up from the chair, filled with excitement, and was quickly seated beside her daughter, grasping her hands. "We have drawn closer to winning this day! The danger to my worlds has diminished. Hope grows in my heart that I have made fate wise and it shall do my bidding."

Her head spinning from revelations unmasked, Mihai asked, "What of the prophecies, all the prophecies that must not be dismissed or every good thing shall pass away?!"

Ma-we's reply was merrily scolding, like a child taunting her playmates for not finding her hiding place. "What have you to do with prophecies?" She laughed. "You don't yet understand! *I am the Maker of prophecy.* I invented the game long before your kind walked free upon this soil." She broke into rhyme.

> *"Words there are, many and bold.*
> *Some are new and others old.*
> *And others you'll find twisted and bent,*
> *To fit my mood, I have them sent.*
>
> *Your kind you think are truly smart,*
> *When riddles you discover in the dark.*
> *But for the answer, your braggarts sway,*
> *While the real meaning I whisk away.*

I rarely speak without one of these,
A riddle, a riddle, as I please.
The wise I make to look like fools,
For truth stays hidden in my riddling tools."

Ma-we chuckled. "Prophecies or riddles? Please! They are both one and the same to me. In the days long before your kind, I and others beside me would spend countless hours making riddles of prophecy. Why, there are some riddles we made up that could take months of your time to merely express, not to mention the countless years of your time to figure out."

She squeezed Mihai's arm, grinning with pleasure. "Some riddles that I have been told, so many countless eons of your time ago, I am still puzzling over. That's right! Even *I* am not privy to all the secrets of the universe."

Sitting back, supported by outstretched arms, the Maker of Worlds mused, "Never have I uttered a prophecy that hasn't been twisted up in one or more riddles. Never!" She nodded. "That's right! Even my own children - even you have never been given a clear and simple explanation of what the future may hold. And I have my reasons for doing so."

"First, in the beginning, I could not tell for sure what free will would eventually do to the hearts of my children. Until you came along, I had never felt love in the way you gave it. So love took on new meaning for my children. If I had not known what form it would take, how could I have prophesied it, other than to put it in a riddling prophesy which could have many different outcomes? But my self-said prophecy gave me hope... faith, you might say... that someday I would find the love I was seeking."

"Let me ask you a question." Lowenah's eyes twinkled. "Am I the only source of life in the universe?"

Mihai was surprised by the question and answered abruptly, "Why, yes! By your own words you have said you are the Bringer of all life."

Leaning forward, Ma-we lifted a hand, shaking a finger. "My words you have quoted correctly, but are they not riddling words, themselves?"

Mihai puzzled.

Mother explained, "My fingers have not yet reached beyond forever. I still search for the end of all matters, will for as long as it takes. I live eternal because I have no reference by which to gauge my life. Still, I did have an awakening of sorts, a time when I came to realize I was me. And I do not know all things... yet." She poked Mihai. *"And I hope not to!"*

Ma-we shook her head. "Know-it-alls are so very boring. They never have anything new to speak about. Have you noticed how they act?" She puffed out her chest. 'Oh, now that I have stopped telling you about all the wonderful things I've done, allow me to talk about how wonderful I am'." She laughed. "Boring! Oh, so boring!"

Lowenah quieted. "Allow me, please, one more question. Will life always spring eternal?"

This time, Mihai, uncertain, asked, "Won't it?"

Ma-we glanced away, studying the dials on a corner clock. "Only to the limit of my abilities and life, which, since I did not create me, but have always been there, and because eternity is beyond my vision, how can life eternal be an absolute?"

She looked back into Mihai's astonished face. "That is why you must never take life for granted! It is a gift, filled with riddles of uncertainty and chance. What may befall us tomorrow we cannot know for sure today. Riddles give us flexibility to adjust to whatever may come. Riddles may help keep us living with hope when all becomes hopeless around us."

Mihai was still confused, and somewhat flustered at the thought of 'eternity questioned'.

Glancing again at the clock, Ma-we warned of the lack of time, concluding her dissertation on riddles.

"My riddling prophecies you do not yet understand. Let me say this: what you saw today in the scepter and crown are but an infant's understanding of the riddles and meanings. And it is a very important matter for it to be that way. Without riddles, I would have little means to see into the hearts of my creation."

"So many times I gave gifts to the people in the Realms Below – you saw it for yourself. What happened? The very men rewarded with a tiny bit of *divine* information puffed themselves up with pride, declaring their knowledge of me was divinely great!"

"See! And look at the mess there today. Around the time of the Great War, I handed over to you a man and then a group of men to declare a time of hope. And what did they do with the message given them? They took control, deciding for themselves good and bad, beating any who disagreed with their prattle. Even now, at this very moment, they foment trouble, secretly seeking new power and glory, thinking themselves as the *princes* of a new world yet to come. I shall say no more of them."

"As you can see, riddling prophecy acts like a two-edged sword. It gives hope to the humble who have honest faith in me that I shall carry out my purpose. But, for the proud, it opens up their hearts so they reveal what they really are – revelers without real love, lusting for power and glory, openly displaying a wanton desire to dominate over others of their own kind."

She patted Mihai's hand. "I think we have beaten that horse way far enough. Now on to more personal matters…"

"At the end of the Great War, a new star in your league of followers had risen to prominence. Unlike the former, who had attempted, through honest and humble means, to declare my message of hope to the inhabitants of the

Second Realm, this new saint became an unbendable master, relegating my style of love to protocol and rhetoric, while bullying his masses into line, to do his personal bidding."

"This man, although personally loyal to you and me, reflected the passion of your brother – being proud, boisterous, and arrogant. I did not bring him and the organization he had twisted and bent to his will to nothing because there was too little time for me to start anew. Even though it was now polluted and corrupt with insolence and pride, it could still serve my purpose, to bring forth my Shiloh of prophecy."

"Although still yet to be conceived in the womb, the hour of the child's arrival was clear to me. I could not afford to bring forth another organization in order to bring my prophecy to fulfillment. I decided then to continue to guide this group until my purpose was fully accomplished."

Ma-we sighed, shaking her head. "Although your followers still shout your name and mine, their hour of abandonment is close. I can see that they will not accept my Shiloh when I deliver him, but will stone him and cast him away as an evil and wicked prophet of the Devil."

She shrugged. "But that is the way of men. Good men do wicked things and all must suffer the price for such foolishness."

Snapping her fingers, a fire blazing in her eyes, Ma-we declared, "Well, *my Shiloh does live*, even as I speak! He is still but a child, yet I see him as a powerful lord and king. My faith in his loyalty is strong. My millennia of genetic endeavor have not been fruitless. And *you*" she poked Mihai again, "have opened the way for him to take the throne appointed for him from the world's foundation!"

Mihai jumped back, startled. "What are you about?! My head you filled with words uncertain, dreams of shifting glory, and troubles of fate denied. How am I to understand my trials faced this day? Did the ominous clouds of destruction really hang over the universe should I have chosen the wrong road, or were you only gaming with a weak-minded, foolish child?"

Ma-we laughed. "Riddles, riddles… Fooled you, too!"

Before Mihai could reply, shock growing on her face, Ma-we added, "A game? Yes! A foolish child? No!"

Lowenah stood and began to pace. "When you were young, I watched you play games, some full of pleasure and others full of peril. You were most careless when playing Khoor-ruuk, risking yourself and others, competing in the glider races. More than once you injured yourself, even to the point of breaking your bones and cracking ribs, something that was very rare among your siblings."

She stopped, looking in Mihai's face. "Those skills you acquired then were taken with you into the cockpits of the flaming chariots you flew after the Rebel Wars began. What you played at then often proved fatal to others, even bringing you close to death on occasion. But was it still not a game of sorts that you were playing, a very deadly game, but a game none the less?"

Clasping her hands behind her, Ma-we resumed pacing. "A game need not be pleasant or peaceful to be called a game. It is the pitting of one's mind against another's that makes something a real game. For these many long years, I have gamed against your brother. Is it dangerous? Yes! But there's nothing else for it. If the game is lost, then all is lost."

"My child, dearest in love and caring, I did not mislead you with my riddles, for I asked you not to believe them without question, or to take any action regarding them. When I made request of you to do something for me, I was clear and concise, revealing to you all that you needed to know. But you fell prey to the most tricksy of moves a game-master can make. You *assumed* to understand what I was doing."

She came over and sat beside a troubled Mihai, gently patting her leg. "Child, there was nothing I could do but watch as you and your siblings gathered false reasonings into your bosoms. Misunderstanding a riddle is not damning for an honest, humble heart. Any pain or loss experienced will eventually be compensated for…eventually. In the meantime, I was able to keep your brother in the dark concerning my real purposes and clandestine activities. Your brother assumed, too, but he has acted to his own ruination by thinking he's outsmarted me."

"For these six-thousand years, I have outsmarted him, he thinking you were to stand the throne in his stead. You have taken his blows and must continue to for a little while longer. By my allowing your suffering, I have succeeded in gathering my new creation, my children from the Realms Below, altered and refined through generations of genetic selection. They stand ready, soon to lead this world of yours to victory against all wicked men."

Mihai excitedly asked, "The Swords…? Shiloh…?"

"Yes! Yes, my Dear." Ma-we smiled, sadness in her eyes. "The monster I have created to bring a ruin to all living things, it has been done. What was shall not be. And what is to come shall be the thing unwished for. The storm, even now, is rising in the North. Tonight you shall see the coming breeze, and its cold breath shall chill your heart. Please, my Dear One, do not allow it to destroy your heart."

"What?!" Mihai asked surprised. "Why should I fear the very creatures you have promised me? Do I not love the children you have made for me?"

Ma-we frowned. "Daughter of darkness and death, do not attempt to fool your mother. I see jealousy hiding at your door. Have not your own words this day betrayed your displeasure at the usurper appointed to command your brothers and sisters? Do be careful! Disaster waits for you on the trail. If you do not listen to humble wisdom, a humiliation awaits your fate. Naked you shall be made to look if you do not get hold of your heart, for I see that Time will take a man's hand, and he will reveal all that is secret concerning you and your rule."

"My rule? I chose not the crown today. I have no rule, not even that of army commander." Mihai's heart had focused upon words it chose to hear, pushing Mother's warning of her daughter's jealousy over her own kind into the clouds of willing forgetfulness - a most dangerous thing to do, one that would eventually prove itself fatal.

Ma-we eyed her daughter, but decided that added discussion of the matter would be fruitless. 'Little can the watchman do should the one hearing his warning stuff up his ears to the danger heralded.' She squeezed Mihai's hand. "My daughter, you must learn to learn, for life will teach you many unwanted lessons."

Stroking her daughter's hand, Ma-we confessed, "I have never seen you do one thing out of wanton selfishness, but do be careful. Love, if not checked by wisdom, may well cause a person to make damning decisions. Love without caution, even if it is for me or your siblings, can be as dangerous as pride. I fear your love will act blindly." She slowly shook her head. "But it is not my call to make."

Sitting back, Ma-we smiled. "And now to answer your question concerning rulership..." She snapped her fingers. "But first I recommend a quick bath or a good steaming shower."

"What?!" Mihai was confused over Ma-we's change of subject.

Glancing again at the clock, Ma-we hurried Mihai along. "Time runs ever faster the sooner one needs to complete an errand. I'll explain things to you as soon as may be, but not sooner. If you don't hurry, it will have to be later than may be... much later."

Not asking further questions, a very curious Mihai did as Mother requested. She made quick work of matters, choosing to shower, it being much faster. In only minutes ,the woman was toweling herself dry.

Ma-we met her at the door. Without saying a word, she lifted a hand and *'whoosh!'* a puff of warm air instantly dried Mihai's hair. She grinned. "No good, no good at all. It's much better now."

Squeezing Mihai's arms, Ma-we excitedly asked, "Do you recall the words you spoke so long ago about the master leaving in order to receive a kingship and throne?"

"Why...why yes, I do." Mihai answered, surprised. "But that kingship is gone, or should I say passed along."

"Gone?" Ma-we quizzed, looking up at the ceiling in thought. "Gone? No. It never went anywhere." She looked into Mihai's face. "It's still where it's always been." Saying no more, she hurried Mihai into the bedroom, toward the bed.

"Mother? What?" Mihai was caught up speechless at what she saw.

Some of the bundles had been opened, their secrets displayed on the bed. A beautiful bejeweled, floor-length silk gown was spread out beside an equally long, flowing, purple satin cape, a pair of matching, high-laced sandals and some golden jewelry completing the ensemble.

Ma-we asked Mihai to dress, assisting her as she did. After slipping the shimmering purple cape over her shoulders, Ma-we inserted the gold chained, green emerald earrings through her daughter's ears. With a *'snap!'* Mother locked them in place. "There!" She smiled. "Make sure you release the clasp before attempting their removal."

Turning her daughter around to face the mirror, Ma-we breathed a satisfied sigh. "Perfect, just perfect..." Then looking into Mihai's eyes through the mirror, she commented, "How long I have waited for this day to see my child of fruitful birth stand up as a woman among her kind. To-*night!* It is a good night to be here, when the world is born anew."

Bewilderment grew on Mihai's face. "You confuse me so. Earlier this day, I stood before you, denying crown and throne in order to remain a woman and, hopefully, one day bring forth life from my inward parts. Then you riddle me with words concerning another rulership which is a mystery to me. And then you speak of a new day when you see a favorite child stand up in some kind of glory. Mother, your riddles are too much for me."

Ma-we was busy with Mihai's gown, adjusting a shoulder strap while humming a little tune. She gave a gentle tug and then turned her attention to the cape, fitting it snug around Mihai's shoulders so that it hid much of the dress. As she worked, she stared into her daughter's ocean-blue eyes and began to coo.

> *"A merry sprite went off to walk,*
> *Through a field of crimson wheat.*
> *By chance she met an ogre foul,*
> *Who asked to take her to the ball.*
>
> *In disgust and fright, she ran away,*
> *Hiding low in the crimson hay.*
> *And all the while the ogre cried,*
> *'Please, oh please, be at my side.'*
>
> *As darkness fell, the field she fled,*
> *But the ogre caught her, and to her said,*
> *'Tonight, with me, you'll dine and feast,*
> *For you cannot escape fate with this beast.'*

He took her to the fairy dance,
And into the firelight they came by chance.
And behold, the girl came to see
The ogre was really a prince to be."

Ma-we grinned. "Riddles within riddles within riddles... A riddling book is what I wrote, but truth and honor it is filled with. Did you not believe your sister when, in front of your very ears, before you descended to the world of men, she promised that *you* were to have a kingdom? Think, child! How could I have promised such if I had already promised *my darling* something so different? *You know* that I would not do a thing like that."

"What you believed to be so foul was not...*was not* what you thought at all. I have many kingships to offer. The crown prince over all my universe is but one. *Your* kingdom still awaits you. Tonight I shall have it declared to all the world." She put a finger to her lips. "But they will not be informed as to which kingship it is...not yet."

Staring up and into Mihai's eyes, the Maker of Worlds asked, "Now, if I will give to my daughter - child of my own flesh - all the promises I did promise her when she was but a babe, but has held so dear in her heart all these many days... if I will promise to give her, one day, a son... No! No... many sons and daughters, without number and also to all her sisters besides, will my darling child accept this one other burden and all the woes that are delivered along with it?"

What could Mihai do, other than accept whatever Mother was offering? *Why, for the gift of offspring, she would face, alone, Asotos and all his bands of henchmen. She would accept a thousand years of torture at his hands if she could produce but one soul through which her blood coursed.* "Yes!" She blurted unhesitatingly, *"Whatever your servant girl must do will be done!"*

"Good! Good! My child has promised. *Now it's too late.*" Ma-we scurried to the bed, picking up the remaining bundle. *"What will come to be must be her fate."*

Hurrying back, she handed it to Mihai. "Open it! Open it, my darling little child." She giggled.

"A gift for you
A prize for me
A shock on your brother's face
We'll see."

Mihai shook her head as she opened the bundle. It was good to see Mother so pleased with the moment, especially considering the events of the day. When Lowenah acted so childlike, her daughter knew that all was well with her. Ma-we's quiet moods, something she had been most affected with, as of late, were distressing to Mihai. For as merry as Ma-we was this eve, it must have been a *very good day* for her.

Struggling with the last knot – the bow having slipped when Darla and Ma-we had jousted over it – Mihai placed the package on a small dressing table. Ever so slowly, she worked the string loose, the secrets hidden within the silky wrapping being postponed to near frustration. Eventually the ribbon surrendered, Mihai pulling the wrapping away, gasping.

Ma-we grinned, elated. "Well, what do you think? What do you think? Come… pick it up. Pick it up! What is my darling waiting for?"

Mihai, hesitant, reached out and slowly lifted up a golden crown, cool and hard to the touch, but as light as a goose-down feather. Little more than a band in the back, it widened like two growing waves, joining together in a peaked crest at the front. Aligned along each wave were six gemstones, each of different beauty and power. The two top stones - one to the right and left of the crest – were Cortessoian, a jewel made by combining green emerald and ruby-red sapphire. Beneath the crest there was an engraved roaring lion, under which were words in an ancient tongue, meaning, 'A thousand years may eternal be'.

Ma-we was all so anxious. "Well?! Are we putting it on?! Or must I take it from you and do it myself?!" Not waiting for a reply, she pulled the crown from Mihai's hands and set it on her daughter's head.

*"See! Both your heart and mine are gifted this day.
A riddle answered in a most wonderful way."*

Mihai's head began to spin wildly. Clutching it, she pitched forward, falling into a black void that hurtled her down ever faster into a growing vortex of nothingness. No sight, sound or feeling reached the woman's senses other than that of falling, ever falling. Yet that was only an illusion, vertigo of the imagination, a universe of descending emptiness. Concluding this journey to be a vision, Mihai reached out with her mind to find its hidden treasures.

She soon detected tiny sparkles of color tumbling through the dark nothingness, eventually filling the void with blinding oceans of rainbow hues. "Mesmerizing!" she would later describe this world of living delights. Yes, "Alive!" she said, because of the pulsing messages they imparted to her, even answering questions asked of them with her mind. But this world, too, soon passed from sight.

This kaleidoscopic universe eventually parted, leaving Mihai as she was drawn into an emerald green sea. "Mother's eyes!" Were her eyes not the same in color and warm delight? A sound like the roaring of giant waves on an endless beach filled the girl's mind as she was swept along. Then, down she tumbled again, the roar becoming a deafening tumult. '*Plop!*' Mihai crashed into something, stopping her fall, being knocked senseless.

Was it a fleeting moment or an eternity before Mihai awoke? With a vision, one never knows. In fact, it is a good question not to ponder. She found herself lying upon a sandy shore, pounding surf in the distance. Sitting, she became aware of childrens' laughter coming from down the beach. Getting to her feet, she started off in the laughter's direction.

Struggling up a dune, her feet slipping backward in the loose, dry sand, Mihai eventually made the rise, the beach at low tide stretching out before her. There was a warning cry from someone near the dune, sending dozens of naked little bodies scurrying away, disappearing beyond other dunes. Only one child, a small boy of light complexion and auburn hair, remained.

Slowly and cautiously, Mihai worked her way down the dune, ever fearful the boy would also run away, but he did not. He quietly stood there awaiting her, a living conch in his hands, its shell glistening with colors of the woman's earlier vision. Studying the boy, Mihai could see no fear in his eyes. Indeed, he appeared to be expecting her. Oh how easy it is to forget it is a vision when Mother's fingers play at the game!

Stopping two paces away, Mihai stared, examining the boy in an attempt to understand his part in this vision. He spoke up as if reading her mind. "You wonder who I am, for you see me not in past or present."

Pondering aloud, Mihai asked, "Who are you, then? An apparition from future days? A symbol of things to come?"

The boy shook his head. "I am neither apparition nor symbol. I am a reality though not yet beheld, a promise though not yet fulfilled, a coming dream, a breath of refreshing spring. As you live, so do I, for I am a holy being, born of kings sired by the Cherubs, themselves. I am born from mortal flesh which covers an immortal spirit. My fate is your fate, for you choose my existence."

Mihai asked, very curious now, "Who *are* you?"

The boy frowned. "You still refuse to understand. Oh trouble… Oh trouble… Look at me and see. Are not your eyes and mine the same? Do we not share a common mind and soul? Look, I am the son you wish to have, child of kings, a promise granted."

Crying with joy, Mihai reached out to hold the boy. He jumped back, scolding, "Do not touch what is not yet yours!"

"What?!" Mihai cried.

The boy silenced her. "I am come to give you hope and assurance, because what you see is what you will have, but in latter days, when all that is now is no more. You, my Mother, must hurry to an end this wicked hour if you wish to see your son again. I will mark an end of an age and the beginning of another, a sign that peace has come to all living things."

He handed a surprised Mihai the conch. "But first you must dry up the River Styx and bring the Boatman to his end. He will not halt his ever-quest to bring all souls into his breast until *you* have brought him to a finish. To you has been this burden given, for today the crown of life you took upon yourself."

Mihai protested. The boy hushed her, waving his hand as he slowly faded from sight. "Drink it up and bring it to a finish, for in your hands now rests the destiny of lovers and friends. Bring to an end what your brother created so long ago. Part the waters so there will be a returning for all who have passed beyond."

Alone, Mihai stood on the beach, the tide ever rising, tumultuous waves splashing further up the sand. Or was something else happening? Everywhere she looked, the sea increased in agitation, as if it was being called away from its bed. Looking down at the conch, she saw the shell pulsing its radiating colors in rhythm with the waves. Or were the waves dancing in rhythm with the pulsing shell?

A burning sensation filled Mihai's hands. She let out a cry and dropped the conch, it crashing into the sand, gray, dull and lifeless. Looking at her hands, the woman observed as the pulsing rainbow hues raced up her arms, flooding her body with their radiating energy. Soon Mihai was aglow with power, a living beacon calling to the advancing sea.

Mihai lifted her arms, fingers extended. She stood high on her toes and called out words strange to her ears but understood in her mind, their translation being, 'A ruin! A ruin! A ruin! I shall make it! No more shall your shadow descend upon my people. I shall cut down your living boughs and give what was yours to another. Your heart is for me a sported treasure in which I will exult!'

The raging waters rose high above the woman's head. Just before they enveloped her, she shouted, *"Down with all that is yours!"*

To Mihai's surprise, the tormented sea did not wash her away, drowning her in its wrath. Instead, she discovered, it drew in to her, being torn from the ocean floor. Inward the water rushed, all the oceans and seas, rivers and lakes, until the flood departed, leaving a barren landscape scattered with the wreckage of many broken and twisted ships. For but a moment, the woman stared at the ruined land. She was then lifted up and swept far away, into a silent world filled with glowing spheres of radiant light.

Drifting through this strangest of universes, Mihai felt she was not alone. Gradually she came to realize that life pulsed strong within each sphere. 'Strange,' she thought. Reaching out and touching one as she floated past, a voice called out to her, drowsily speaking her name. Shocked, she jerked her hand away, putting the woman into an uncontrolled spin.

Helplessly tumbling end-over-end, Mihai managed to gently bounce and bump into one sphere after another. Each time she touched a glowing ball, a sleepy voice, as if waking from some deep, forgotten dream, would call out to her, often by name.

"The Web of the Minds!" Mihai shouted, although no sound came from her lips. "Mother shows her child the world hidden from mortal vision!" She marveled in wonder, recognizing many of the voices. Lost acquaintances and lovers sang out to her, and her heart would sing back. Oh, how delightful to be near the ones she had so longed to see again! Yet here they were, still very much alive, waiting once more to be clothed in mortal flesh, so that they, again, could sense the world around them.

"Oh, Mother…!" Mihai cried, only to see the spheres fade into darkness.

Ma-we caught the child up in her arms. Mihai moaned, "What…? Where…?" She had been gone for but a twinkling of an eye from this world, but countless ages and lives had passed before her eyes during that time.

Helping Mihai to stay on her feet, Ma-we steadied her daughter. "There, there, we will soon be fine." She giggled. "Travel sickness, you know. Catches up to the novices quite quickly…"

Rubbing her eyes, Mihai asked, "It was a vision, wasn't it? A wonderful, beautiful vision?"

Ma-we hesitated, grinning. "A vision? Er… well… you might want to call it that… for now, anyway." She took Mihai's hands. "The day may well come when you will understand that visions and reality are often one and the same. You do not always discern matters the same as Immortals…yet."

Blinking in an attempt to regain her focus, Mihai asked, "I'm… I'm really back… here, I mean, or is this another part of my vision?"

Still smiling, Ma-we asked. "Did you like the trip?"

"So I'm back here, in reality, I mean?" Mihai asked again.

"You're *back here*, if that's what you mean." Ma-we answered slyly, nodding. "And I guess you'll be stuck here for some time, so you might as well accept it as *reality*."

Mihai asked no more concerning the matter, concluding the part of her adventure she called a 'vision' was finished. Mother had different ways of looking at things, and when she was in a good mood, it was impossible to get a straight answer from her. Mihai sighed with satisfaction. At least Mother was in a good mood.

Finally addressing Ma-we's question, Mihai answered, "Yes, yes I did enjoy the trip." She reached up to adjust her crown and cried out with surprise when finding it gone. "My crown! Where?"

"It's here!" Ma-we interrupted, touching a finger to the side of Mihai's head. "You possess it within your mind. It is a gift that is only yours. No one can take it from you, nor can you lose it. If you desire it to be seen by others, you only need to think kingly thoughts and it will appear. It would be most appropriate for you to act kingly tonight." She turned away, watching the time. "Once you have wished the crown upon you, it will not fade until you will it away. Oh, yes! It is very real when you wear it... hard to the touch, you might say."

Ma-we turned back toward her daughter. Her jovial demeanor changed. "The position of king is not just an entitlement to the throne over my people. You now have a kingdom that is its own - an everlasting kingdom – but you also act as steward to the throne of the king yet to come. Your obligation is to protect and secure that kingdom until the one entitled arrives to lay claim to it. It is a most serious responsibility."

Ma-we warned, "The hour approaches when you must take the lead over my children. Already I see a great fire in the East that blots out the sun with its smoke. It will silence my lips for but a day, yet in that day all good things may perish. You must stand as a sentinel over my kingdom until that day has passed and protect it until its fate has been determined."

She stepped up to Mihai and began to stroke her satin cape. "You, my child, are but a king...not a dictator. Into another's hand you have surrendered the army. Tonight you will honor that person in front of all onlookers, declaring TrishaQa·Shaib·Jal the new lord over all the armies of the Empire." Lowenah took Mihai's arm. "Child, remember this well: Trisha's loyalty is to *me* and after this night will be also to you. But...but! She is a god over your people at war, not accountable to you regarding military decisions."

Looking into her daughter's concerned eyes, Ma-we explained, "You are the bonding agent that unifies the Empire. Trisha, though, has now become one of the Angels of Death that will bring all things to ruin. Yes, I have chosen others as well. You have the power to hold back the winds of destruction, but once released, it will be your duty to strengthen your people for the storm that will rage upon them. Let the warrior do the slaughtering. *You* do the healing."

She patted Mihai's arms reassuringly. "Today I have bestowed knowledge beyond excellence upon you. You will need it to rule. But I cannot give to your heart the wisdom it will need to survive this coming contest – game, if you will. Thus, the knowledge you have acquired is only useful if you force your heart to become wise with it. A king must think and reason first! Feelings are a pleasant distraction used sparingly and only on the coldest of nights."

Taking hold of Mihai's hands and giving them a squeeze, Ma-we concluded, "Please remember this: A field marshal may lose an army, but a king an entire universe."

The two chatted for a while about some of the things Mihai had experienced, Ma-we nodding and replying when appropriate. Observing her daughter closely, Ma-we troubled inside. 'I must stay the course even though she does not yet understand. Much must be lost before this age ends, much more than I wished might be. But there's nothing for it. Destiny rides the skies unbridled. It belongs to my children to rein it in and force it to do their bidding. There's nothing else for it.'

Seeing the hour was late, Ma-we took her daughter's hand and, to conclude matters on a lighter note, changed subjects. "My Darling so dear, I must be on my way. You should hurry along for dinner. We've kept your little sister waiting far too long. What mischief she attains to at this moment is for the imagination to conjure. Remember times in the past?"

Mihai nodded, recalling that Darla had been known to 'get into a mix' from time to time, especially with some of the more prominent children of the councils.

Touching her head, Ma-we suggested, "Hide your crown for now, until arrival at the council, but wear it when you enter, if you would, please."

Mihai promised.

Smiling, Ma-we kissed her daughter. "I'll see you in a bit…have some little business to attend to before tonight." She kissed Mihai again and darted out the door.

Turning away, Mihai walked over to the mirror. She watched as her crown slowly faded from sight. 'Sorta' like things on Mother's table.' The woman thought, placing a hand where the crown had been.

For a few moments the grown-up girl stared into the mirror, reflecting more on what she had become than as to how she appeared. A new sobriety filled Mihai's heart. The days of her coming of age lay in the long-forgotten past. A new age of violence had long ago swept away any innocence of earlier times. It was now her duty to see to the end of this wicked age and make way for the new – an age of healing.

Glancing around the tiny apartment, Mihai was filled with a romantic melancholy regarding this place. She could remember how it had so long been a hiding place for her soul, a sanctum of security in troubling times. But now there was something different about it. It took her a moment to realize just what.

Now she knew. The woman could remember, just like a person can remember the security of a certain toy, but she was unable to feel that security. It was gone - gone with her innocence that she had refused to admit to until tonight. There was to be no going back now. The world was changed. Mother had made sure of it, and this evening would seal it forever. Whatever was to come on the 'morrow, this tiny dwelling was not to be part of it.

Tomorrow Mihai would remove what few keepsakes she desired from here, delivering them to the Palace. The upper chambers of the Firstborn she would procure, holding them in trust until the man-king promised them arrived. In the back of her mind, the woman understood that this room was but a symbol for all the children of the Empire. Forever was darkness falling on the past. Although the sun was to arrive again, and shine its light on a new and cleansed universe, it would be a different one than the one left behind. Forever gone would be the childlike innocence of the eternal past.

Mihai walked to the opened door, casting one last, longing glance back into the room. She sighed, knowing there was no returning to this comfy nest. Waving her hand, the room fell dark. For the last time, the *child* passed the threshold, quietly closing the door behind her.

ॐ   ॐ   ॐ

Section Two

Of Councils Great and Small

Piercing eyes studied the solitary figure sitting quietly in a distant corner of a great chamber called the 'Hall of Assembly', political strategy room since the beginning of the Rebellion. Those eyes squinted in wondering question, 'So, this is the *wisest of councilors*, personal advisor to the Maker of Worlds? Doddered, unkempt, nervous... Who really is this man, ArdonAzubahKenath? He looks more the part of an Eastern slave merchant awaiting his next client, and he has just recently returned from one of his mysterious deep space sojourns. This person deserves closer scrutiny.'

'Ardon', as he was more often called, had been sitting in the Hall of Assembly for nearly an hour, it being his custom to arrive early so as to observe others entering, and to not be observed, himself. This afforded him the luxury of a silent inquisition of the gathering crowd and time to ponder possible unfolding of the night's events. He had learned long ago to watch warily for clues that revealed motives and intentions. More than once he had managed a coup on some spy or enemy agent sequestered among the loyal children of the Empire. Tonight was special, at least according to Mother, and from the looks of all the military brass and high-ranking officials, Mother hadn't been exaggerating. These people needed his scrutiny.

He frowned in surprise and disapproval watching a lowly naval officer shyly enter, his eyes opened wide in awe at the gathered company of royal officials and leading military officers. For some moments the man stood there, arms hanging limply, with folded hands. The nervous fellow looked more like a trapped animal seeking escape than a captain in the Empire's navy.

Ardon stirred, leaning forward, concerned. 'Now why does Mother trouble our presence with a washed-out captain, unfit to hold the bridge of a cattle barge, or that scrap heap of a ship, the...' It took a moment for him to recall. 'Oh yes, that derelict hulk, Shikkeron? Should have scrapped it out before the Great War... What's Bedan doing at such an important counc...' Ardon snapped his fingers. 'Oh, yes... the Zephath... Sirion... The Shikkeron was a first responder to its distress signals.' He slowly shook his head. 'Why does Mother need Bedan's counsel here? The official report contains everything he could provide.'

Ardon's apparent arrogance was not as it appeared. True, he believed his position on the Head Council was well deserved, and he also believed it would be through the roles of the various councils that permanent peace was to be obtained, the military actions only a necessary stopgap to provide time for diplomacy to win out. Bedan, a captain of peacetime necessity, and one of the countless younger children, made the man's deficiencies loom greater in Ardon's mind. The fellow was just another of the dullards and misfits this war had gathered to itself. The great leaders of the ancient times were the heroes who must bring matters to a finish. And wasn't that what this evening's gathering was all about?

It troubled Ardon to think that Mother - Ma-we - did not bother to inform him or seek his advice concerning Bedan and the Shikkeron. It was not her silence about the matter when they visited in private conference earlier, but her obvious secretiveness that was most disturbing. True, she informed him in somewhat lengthy detail about Mihai's reaction to being offered the king's crown, and she being given another kingship later in the day.

He was also made privy to Trisha's promotion to field marshal, something that also perturbed him as it had Mihai, but for additional reasons. It was Mother's incessant riddling and evasiveness that had been most bothersome. 'I think the girl has the right stuff.' Ma-we had said so offhandedly about Trisha, before adding, 'And she's so pretty, too. Don't you think so?'

Ardon had sputtered about the woman's youth and inexperience, presenting numerous reasons why she shouldn't be given such a high military post. Though not mentioning it, he secretly believed the position should go to a member of the Council, possibly Lord PalaHar, a highly respected military officer and a member of the Council of Twenty-four as was he, who understood the value of diplomacy in conflict. Plus, Trisha being an Off-worlder and so new to this realm led him to suspect the children of this world might resent having to bend a knee to such a person. The shadow of such a feeling already was being manifested by a few in the way they saw Ma-we dote over some of them.

Ma-we had brushed off Ardon's arguments, saying, 'It would be good for some to learn a little humility.' she eyeing him carefully as it was spoken, then, bouncing from her chair, her golden tresses drifting high into the afternoon breeze, politely dismissing him, replying as she turned, 'The hour is upon us when humility may not only save the soul, but may well preserve the heart. It's time some of my children learned that, ArdonZoiathenBethy, *man who sees little use for the titmouse.*'

Ardon scratched his chin over Mother's final words, the name she called him. For hundreds of millennia he had been called ArdonAzubahKenath, 'man of stones'. At least it was the name's original meaning. Ardon ignored the less noble 'the man who abandons the festival of the winds and hides himself in the misty caves' that many of his younger sisters came to attach to it. And that was another thing. His mind wandered... For all his age and wisdom, he being one of the most ancient of the children, he never was able to understand women at all - that was, except for Tashi.

Craning his neck, he scanned the room. Tashi, governor of the Trizentine colonies, was supposed to be here this evening. He searched carefully to see if she had made her arrival yet and been missed. Satisfied it was not the case, the man settled back in his chair, watching the door, but his mind became distracted in seeking the reason for Mother's name-calling.

"Hello there, sweet one!" Startled, Ardon looked up just in time to have two soft hands cradle his face and two full, moist lips smack his. Eyes opened wide in surprise, Ardon stared dumbly into Tashi's face.

Leaning back, Tashi studied the perplexed fellow who was still trying to get his bearings. She frowned, shaking her head. "I've come all the way from the Trizentine, holding my passions in check in anticipation of this coming night to be spent with my lover and you have nothing to say to me? Tsk, tsk. Maybe I should have accepted that captain's request to wile away some quiet hours with him." She pulled Ardon's face close as she bent forward again, planting another kiss on him.

While sheepishly stuttering his hellos, Ardon glanced around the room, concerned that others might have seen or heard Tashi's amorous advances. Satisfied none had, he relaxed and, taking her hands in his, smiled, replying quietly, "It is good to see you, too, Governor…"

Tashi shot him a scolding stare.

"Er, well… of course, of course, I'm overjoyed to see you and… and…"

Though teasing, Tashi's voice was serious to the point of threatening. "I have not contained my feelings these many days to be put off by a stuffed shirt, Lord Ardon. As you have promised… and I will collect on that promise… this visit belongs to me and I shall have my way concerning it. Tonight, and tomorrow, and the next, and the next if I wish… and I do wish… and for all the days I am here on this sojourn of mine, you will lavish you time and energies upon me. *Our* bed I shall warm with you for my entire stay."

She stood upright, shoulders back, eyebrows furrowed, hands still holding fast to Ardon's. "And if you think your phony piety will allow you to show aloofness toward me this eve, I will shout out to the entire crowd your passionate love songs showered upon me in your hidden chambers, songs that others so openly confess to all the world, but you, you stodgy old hermit, hide in secret vaults, fearing your dignity might be questioned should others hear that you also desire the flesh of women with manly abandon."

Ardon's face flushed red with embarrassment and concern. He squeezed Tashi's hands, pleading quietly, "Oh no! No, my… my sweet one! I do want to be in your company. I have been waiting long to see you. It's just that, well, you know this council is so important, and…"

"And?!" Pulling a hand away, Tashi shook a finger at him. "And if you don't behave, I will take my leave with that officer over there…" pointing at Bedan in a distant corner, "and I will deliver my pent-up desires upon him!"

Almost jumping from his chair, Ardon quietly cried, "No! No! I mean… I mean, I do want your company… really. I am sorry that…"

Tashi grinned. "That's better. No more *granny grunt* stuff." She kissed him and turned to leave. "I have other business to attend to, but I will not be far away. Do not leave me alone after this night's council. I will be waiting." She hurried off to see some others.

Ardon slowly settled back into his chair, his eyes ever watching Tashi's sensuous movements as she glided across the room. Not even a muscle twitch gave away his pounding heart, his sweaty palms the only evidence of passions the man was fighting to keep under control. "Oh my! Oh my!" He mumbled under his breath. "How does she manage to do that to me?" He hated and loved that woman, hated her because she could strip him, the *great* councilor to Lowenah, of all his emotional control, loved her because she chose him to be the one she so tortured. How? Strumming his fingers on the chair's arm, Ardon pondered the possible reasons.

The woman's given name was 'TaanathShiloh', meaning 'my peaceful ebony child', but was later changed to 'PurooQanaTashi', having the dual meanings 'mistress of the passionate wildfires'or 'the child who possesses the wildfires'. And the woman, Tashi, certainly lived up to her name. Ma-we had struggled to keep the girl's passions in check until her coming of age celebration. After her release of service from her virgin year, the child had gone wild so to speak, and did chase down her dreams of passion like a consuming wildfire.

Ardon had come upon the woman during one of his many sojourns into the uncharted abyss of the Nebulan Cloud Bank. His need for supplies had delivered him to Exothepobole, a then tiny mining colony on Sustrepho far out in the Trizentine. Tashi was already the elected leader of the mining council - no small achievement considering she was one of the younger children during that time, being only a few thousand years of age.

Sustrepho was a dark, cold planet, being a great distance from its nearest star, where metavideoxide was found. Conditions were harsh and unforgiving. Not only was metavideoxide known to be a dangerous, unstable mineral, mining for it was equally unpredictable. Some of the early veins went two miles deep under the mountains west of the outpost. It was Tashi's job to secure the safety of the miners and make sure they had adequate supplies, responsibilities she executed flawlessly. In fact, Tashi was responsible for turning Exothepobole from a tiny mining camp into a thriving city, provincial capital, and mercantile exchange for the entire Trizentine star systems.

Ardon's arrival at Exothepobole caused quite a stir, few of its inhabitants having met the acquaintance of one so ancient, they being considered almost mythical creatures among the children of the latter part of the First Age. Tashi, being head of the mining council, took it upon herself to make Ardon's visit somewhat of a celebration, seducing him with wine and song, bedding the fellow that night using her sensual wiles and cunning personality, entrapping him into surrendering to her his heart…the only woman ever succeeding in such a feat.

Looking across the room at the woman now, her glistening, black, ebony skin and knee-length, obsidian-midnight, dark, curly hair, Ardon slowly shook his head, his ardor for Tashi growing by the second. How did she do it? It wasn't fair! *He* was in control. How did that woman pierce his defenses? Still, this coming night of passion was looming before him with increasing anticipation. For but a moment, the fellow wished she had clothed herself this eve in more than just her silk lace shawl…for only a moment.

Squeezing his eyes shut in an attempt to regain his composure, Ardon considered why Tashi, the governor of the Trizentine, was here at this council. The reason troubled him. 'The Stasis, those mischievous Stasis!' If the threat of Asotos reneging on the armistice pact wasn't bad enough - an armistice pact that Ardon was most proud of, he being the chief negotiator for the Children's side – the growing boldness of the Stasis Pirates was even more disquieting.

"My Lord Ardon…" a nervous, hesitant voice broke upon Ardon's ears. "Excuse me, my Lord…"

Ardon's eyes popped open, dumbly staring into Bedan's face, the man's hand outstretched in salutation.

Bedan smiled shyly. "It is such a great pleasure to greet you again. I've…"

Ardon blurted out, "Again?"

"Y… ye… yes, my Lord." Bedan swallowed hard. "On Pilneser, after the Great War, I was a courier sent to deliver to you a letter of congratulations from the Council, for your heroic efforts at successfully sealing an armistice pact with our enemy. Of course, you would not remember, my Lord, but it was such a great reward for me to be…"

Ardon politely took Bedan's hand. "Of course, I remember." Really, he was not sure, but it was his diplomatic style. Smiling, he asked, "You're captain of that old, I mean that boat. Let's see, now… oh yes, the Shikkeron, isn't it?"

Bedan nodded, afraid to explain that the Shikkeron was a *ship*, not a *boat*.

Releasing Bedan's grip, Ardon nodded, "Yes, yes, some kind of a brigantine, isn't it? I recall it was in service during the Three Hundred Years' War, resurrected out of the scrap yard for use in the Great War. So it still flies? Interesting… interesting."

Nodding, Bedan added, "Was refitted some dozen years ago, into an imperial brigantine, a much heavier *ship*, Lord Ardon, almost up to frigate class now."

"Good. Good." Ardon replied. Having no desire to hear further about the matter, he changed the subject. "So, er… Captain… er, Bedan, what brings you so far from your duties? Who's tending your boat now?"

Bedan smiled, standing straight. "She's here, at the spaceport, I mean. Orders… came down from the top."

Ardon leaned forward, looking up at Bedan, squinting. "Really? And you? What are *you* doing here?"

Nervousness returned to Bedan's voice. "From Mother, directly from her, she summoned me not six weeks ago. Just got here today, running full out, making smoke all the way just to get here on time."

Ardon frowned, asking, "Why? What's so spec…" He caught himself, asking more politely, "What does Mother want from *you* that requires your presence here?"

Bedan shook his head. "I don't know, my Lord. Mother didn't say. I thought you might know, you being so important on her council and all."

Feeling flustered to think that Ma-we was keeping secrets from him but unwilling to reveal those facts to someone like Bedan, Ardon swept his hand in a motion that signified unimportance, replying, "The world is troubled over so many trivial matters, there is not time to discuss this at the moment. I'm sure Mother had good reason." He looked up to see Admiral NikaoEimi enter the chambers. Wishing to dismiss Bedan without being rude, he pointed, "There's the commander of the Second Fleet… navy, you know. Maybe he can tell you." Then attempting to show interest, he added, "If you find out something important, please let me know."

Bedan bowed low, thanking Ardon for his time, and hurried over to speak with the admiral.

Heaving a sigh of relief, Ardon settled back in his chair, glad to see the admiral was now being troubled with that nuisance officer.

"Lord Ardon…"

Surprised, Ardon looked up to see Symeon's smiling face as he approached, hand outstretched. Ardon stood, grinning. "You snuck in on me, my friend. SymeonKephim! So good to see you!"

Now here was a man in whose company Ardon felt quite comfortable. Delivered here from the Second Realm, Symeon and his fellow brethren from that wild place were quite acceptable companions and conversationalists. True, they usually and willingly spent much of their time in his presence, listening – something Ardon relished. They did, though, have interesting anecdotal opinions that were worth considering. And Symeon? He so much reminded Ardon of Mihai in her younger days, so filled with excitement and that impetuous spirit, always in a hurry, so full of life.

After a warm greeting, Ardon patted Symeon's shoulder, asking, "Has our councilor to the Lady been kept busy this day? You know, with all kinds of court business and important governmental matters?"

Symeon shook his head. "No, my Lord Ardon, Mihai has secluded herself away all day, even choosing to spend some quiet hours with a few close acquaintances for sup. My Lady informed us - Paul, Jonathan, and me - of very little, other than we should expect the unexpected this eve, something I find so curious. She's usually so open and direct with us."

So, Mother was keeping many secrets this day. Ardon nodded approvingly, being informed concerning Mihai's new kingship and Trisha's promotion to field marshal. It made him feel good to think he was so highly trusted that Mother should reveal secrets to him, yet hid them from others. Still, he did not know everything.

"Tell me, please, Symeon, my friend." Ardon asked, probing for added information. "Did our Lady say with whom she was to sup?"

"No." Symeon lowered his eyes in thought, shaking his head. "When she called me earlier this eve, her voice was filled with subdued excitement. She asked me if I would be sure to arrive early at the council because she has a surprise. Then she apologized about missing her late luncheon and that plans were now made to dine with special friends. So, I'm here early, but I don't see her or her surprise as of yet."

Patting Symeon's shoulder again, Ardon grinned, nodding, "Oh, I think you will like the surprise." He winked. "It is a good one, you know, a good one."

At that moment, Zadar entered the council chambers and, eyeing Ardon and Symeon, hurried over. Clutching Ardon in a bear hug, Zadar joyously cried, "Papa! It so good to see you after these many months!" He stood back, his hands gripping Ardon's shoulders. "I have heard of your adventures on Stargaton. Tell me, did the Seimieah Straits deliver up to you the hidden jewels of NiShanderiah, seeing you had deciphered her riddles when last we spoke?"

Ardon took Zadar by the upper arms, shaking his head. "No, no, my little son. NiShanderiah was a witch extraordinaire. I fear I must wait until her return during the after days before I will succeed in having her secrets revealed." He stopped, staring into Zadar's face, pride growing on his. He then complimented the boy on how well he looked in his new army uniform, which led him into a timely lecture concerning what must be done to bring the Rebellion to a finish. Zadar listened intently.

It was only a few weeks after Asotos' attempt at murdering Mihai when Ardon had returned from a deep-space sojourn to Palace City. There he remained with Lowenah after she discovered she was with child and long into the days after Zadar's birth, the first and only child born after the Rebellion began, and one with a most profound and troubling secret shared by his mother only with Ardon. Ardon took to raising the boy up as if his own, even allowing him to journey into some of his secret lands. With Ardon's fatherly mentoring, Zadar became filled with the desire for exploration and adventure. The two became inseparable until he – Zadar - was handed over to Gabrielle, to be brought to manhood by her loving care.

Zadar never forgot Ardon's kindness, his devotion never diminishing for his adoptive father. Now, after all these years of war, and Ardon's outspoken opinions that downplayed the value of the military while encouraging more diplomacy to bring the Rebellion to a finish, Zadar - a man who had devoted his entire life to the military, believing it to be the only solution – always patiently listened to his mentor while he explained the importance of using the carrot over the stick. As he had done before, this night Ardon did not miss the opportunity to lecture his young protege on the subject.

"Now you will see…" Ardon firmly clasped Zadar's hands while he spoke. "What you do is all fine and good, but it is such a waste, such a waste. You are so smart, savvy, I mean. You would do so well as a member of Mother's council. I have clout, you know. Mother would listen to me, you know. Of course, you will have to start out as my loyal apprentice… for a little while, of course, until you get the hang of things. But for you, it wouldn't take long before your voice would be heard in the assembly. And… and, with your military experience, you have a lot to bring to the table."

Zadar, a diplomat in his own right, thanked Ardon, nodding, "Your wisdom I shall seriously consider, Papa. The hour is coming, soon, when your ways will be put to the test. I hope to be there to see their outcome. Mother has hinted to me that such a thing might take place."

Grinning, Ardon tenderly kissed Zadar on the cheek. "You make me proud, son, very proud."

"Watch out for him, boy! He'll make a wuss out of you, and then some!"

Ardon and Zadar turned to see a giant of a man, dressed up in an admiral's uniform, gingerly approaching.

The man smiled, adding, "Make wusses of us all, right, Ardon, old fellow?"

Frowning, Ardon sputtered, "Admiral Euroaquilo, I do not appreciate such…"

Ignoring Ardon, Euroaquilo clasped Zadar's hand, grinning, "Good to see you, my boy! Good to see you!" He stared at his uniform, commenting, "Well, well, so that's the snazzy style of dress for the new army? You look good in it. Not as good as your navy pilot's duds, but still mighty fine."

Caught by surprise, and somewhat embarrassed – a rare moment for the fellow – Zadar stuttered, "It… it… it's…was… is a gift from Mother." Regaining his composure, he added, "This was delivered to me upon my arrival, my being told to wear it at this evening's council. I was told that I was to take leave of the Fourth Fleet and join with the new army commander, but wasn't told who. Asked Mihai about it tonight at supper, but she spoke not a word concerning it."

Ardon, put off by Euroaquilo, knowing it was done on purpose to irk the fellow, interrupted, asking, "You had dinner with Mihai?"

Euroaquilo ignored Ardon, bullying his way in with another question of his own. "So where is that *sister* of yours? Heard you kept some pretty close company since the two of you arrived." He stole a glance at Ardon, whose face was filled with surprise and trepidation.

Still stealing glances at Ardon, he asked Zadar, "So, have you seen our girl, Darla, lately? I was hoping to catch up with her sometime while I was visiting."

Before Zadar could reply, Ardon interrupted, clutching Euroaquilo's arm, "Now see here, Admiral, there are many other, more important matters to discuss this evening than *that* child. There is great need of clear minds at this council. We have many other, more important matters to discuss than *her*!"

Euroaquilo smiled and shrugged. "Have it your way, Lord Councilor. I just wondered where I could find her."

"*Well*!" Ardon harrumphed. "I suggest you search for her after this night's events. I'm sure you will find her slinking around one of the darkened taverns at that late hour!"

Euroaquilo stared down at Ardon, slowly shaking his head. "My, my, you are an old fuss tonight, aren't you?" Although put off a little by Ardon's brashness, he continued on with some lighthearted conversation, catching up on the local gossip and chatting about some of the others at the council.

The Admiral, EuroaquiloIllyricum, was commander of the Navy's Third Fleet, stationed to the east of EdenEsonbar. His name's meaning was, 'the great stormwind' acquired because of his booming voice that matched his size. Six feet plus one-half tall and weighing sixteen stone, he made an impressive appearance wherever he went. Even Ardon, who felt little real respect for the military, was somewhat awed by this man.

And why not? Many were the stories repeated of Euroaquilo's valor in combat. Mihai, a close companion and ally of his, had told Ardon many tales concerning his bravery. "He tore off the castle gate, pitching it at my captor, crushing his skull and providing me with escape." she had confessed to Ardon one day at a council meeting, then demanded he, Ardon, bestow upon Euroaquilo the Golden Medallion of Bravery – Ardon being the purveyor of such awards – a medal the man cherished, and was found wearing this evening.

As he thought about it, Ardon puzzled aloud, "So they still call you 'the twin'?" referring to Mihai's and his close relationship and how inseparable they once were.

Euroaquilo placed a giant hand on Ardon's shoulder, shaking it, grinning. "My dear Lord Ardon, my sister is the sweetest, most wonderful person in the world." He frowned. "There was never found, for me, a more passionate, caring, lover in this world until... until *he* ruined her with his twisted tortures and evil deceit. I have shared the battle against the demons in her mind since that day. Others fear her company, but I... I know who she really is. She and I are still one mind and heart. We are still twins by that very nature."

Looking into Ardon's eyes, he slowly shook his head, softly sighing, "At least she got to see the morning sunrise."

Zadar was about to ask what Euroaquilo's words meant when laughter echoed from the entrance, across the chambers. The three looked over in time to see General PalaHar squeeze through the doorway, TereoAprupneo and PlanetesAntistrate each hugging an arm. The laughter stemmed from PalaHar's dilemma, that of being pursued by two lovely women.

Planetes, better know as 'Planetee', finally leaned forward, looking past PalaHar and into Tereo's face, her eyes twinkling. "You may have managed a coup with your pillow-talk earlier, but an afternoon's delight is more than sufficient for you two. I have forced a promise from this fellow and the after-hours belong to me."

Tereo – 'Terey' – offered up another wicked laugh. "I surrender him up, but shall remain the victor. My sweet scent shall linger in his thoughts and dreams for many long hours. You shall have to force the gate just to be remembered this eve."

The two continued their friendly sparring after passing through the door, PalaHar politely remaining silent. Finally Euroaquilo, grinning with his own brand of mischief, called to Zadar for them to be off to mix it up even more. Zadar, always a willing accomplice to a good game, nodded, and off they went, leaving Ardon alone with his thoughts.

Ardon watched while a battle of wit and winsome words filled the room, it gaining in strength as more of the crowd gathered in, choosing sides and entering the contest. He liked to see such jousting, but could never understand it, especially on such serious occasions as this, but still... let them have their fun. He settled back into his chair, snuggling into its soft leather cushions.

He was no more than settled when another, greater commotion arose among the crowd near the door. All attention was taken off PalaHar and his companions, being given to others who still remained hidden from Ardon's view. 'Who could it be?' That was everyone's question as a flood of the curious descended the bleacher-like seating area to see who was causing the stir, filling the floor with a sea of bobbing heads facing the door.

Standing did little good, Ardon being no man of great stature. As the excitement of the others grew, so did his curiosity. He pushed ahead until he was standing at the back of the growing crowd. This was still no good. When his polite requests for passage were ignored, he finally decided to forge ahead, slowly pushing his way into the mass of spectators in an attempt to see what was happening.

As he advanced, people nearest the doorway began to retreat, allowing whoever was approaching entrance into the council chambers. Ardon managed a peek at the doorway just as Mihai passed through into the room. He stood dumbstruck at what he saw. A collective gasp arose from the gathered company – the effect Ma-we had intended it to have. Even Ardon, although knowing about Mihai's acceptance of a new kingship, was caught up in the moment, being mesmerized by the woman's stunning appearance.

Mihai blushed as she sheepishly bowed, the woman never learning how to take such adoration easily. Her gold and chrysolite crown glittered with flashes of blinding diamond white, sapphire blue, ruby red, and jade green, radiating the woman's face so that it appeared to emit its own divine glow. And the iridescence of the woman's silken satin gown, with its woven, purple lace and kingly, royal-purple flowing cape gave the impression that one the Cherubs had arrived from the outer-worlds to gather with them.

For the longest time, the crowd, including Ardon, stood transfixed, their breathing of silent excitement being the only sound filling the chambers. Eventually, with a great deal of effort, they began to queue up to offer welcome to the new king. As with the others, Ardon found himself shuffling along in the crowd to get in the receiving line so that he, too, could offer up his salutations, a decision he was quickly going to regret.

How he managed to do it, Ardon never could quite figure out, but Zadar had wiggled his way past everyone and was the first to gather Mihai's attention. He, unlike his more reserved brethren, swooped down into a graceful bow while grasping the woman's hand up in his. Still bowing, he looked up and into Mihai's eyes, uttered sweet salutations, and then kissed her hand. Mihai blushed again, thanking Zadar for his tender kindnesses. Zadar then stood up, advancing his attention upon Mihai's escort, demonstrating an equal affection for her, setting the precedent for all the others to follow.

It was when Zadar turned his attention away from Mihai that Ardon noticed the woman's escort. His face paled as he groaned silently within. 'That *woman*! Why her? Why tonight? What deviltry has delivered her to this doorstep this eve? And why was she placed as the King's escort on this important night?' And worse, he wondered why the Fates had delivered him to such a dangerous place at this moment. There was no escape, not so close to the front of the receiving line. He must suffer and endure whatever indignities were to be heaped upon him, hoping only for indignities.

One after another, Mihai passed along the line, the men courteously following along in Zadar's stead, the women bending in a curtsy and then tenderly kissing Mihai on the lips. This was followed by offering the same salutation to Mihai's escort, one RachelOchranNohah, an acquired name, RachelOchlah, meaning 'little charming ewe', that being her birth name. She preferred to be called 'DarlaUmehahAstrni' or 'Darla', she never offering a reason why. Few outside the military ranks knew this woman, and the few who did cared little to be in her close company. For many of them, it was disconcerting to see her here…and with Mihai. So this formal recognition of Darla was often little more than protocol. Still, there were some in the crowd whose love and care for this girl was real and genuine.

After PalaHar's greeting, Mihai reached out, hugging the man. Before standing back, she kissed him tenderly on the lips, saying, "My Lord PalaHar, it is so good to see you." She lowered her voice. "The world grows dark, my Lord, and I see little light to guide my path. It is such a pleasure to know that Mother's torch-bearer is with us tonight."

After some small chitchat, PalaHar turned his attention to Darla. Following his formal welcoming, he leaned forward, kissing her in the way Mihai had done with him. He then drew Darla close in a hug, whispering quietly in her ear as he did, "Child, your journey has yet to begin. The night will become black with evil madness before the sun shall shine upon us again. You… you, my dear little one, must become the star that leads us through that wicked hour. Your valor shall prove to become our rallying cry, our deliverance."

To say that Darla was confused would be a great understatement. She stood back, searching PalaHar's eyes for answers. There were none found. Hesitantly, she thanked him for his kindness, wishing him success in his many endeavors. Then, releasing his hand, she took Mihai's, leading her to the next anxious greeter standing in line.

Ardon waited uneasily, nervous anticipation growing with each of Mihai's advancing steps. Darla, being busy in her attempt to act appropriately as Mihai's appointed escort, paid little attention to those in line, she being so focused on the moment, and did not even notice Ardon until she turned to introduce the new king. Her smile melted away when her eyes finally took recognition of him, quickly replaced by an angry frown and piercing stare filled with malice and hatred. The room went dead silent.

Ardon froze, not daring to move or speak, watching Darla's fingers involuntarily constricting into tortured fists, only to open and then close again. Hair suddenly went up on the back of his neck, his ears picking up a growing insect-like staccato rising up from deep within the woman's throat - the last sound heard by so many of her adversaries.

Mihai, fearing the worst should time delay the coming moment, awkwardly stepped forward and in front of Darla, posturing, "My dear Lord Ardon!" She faked an innocent smile, the scent of a growing tempest flaring her nostrils. "My dear Lord Ardon, how is my lord doing tonight? It is such a pleasure to be graced by your company, your wise insight at this eve's council being deeply appreciated."

"My Lady, I...I am doing splendidly." Ardon stammered, nervously glancing toward Darla, sighing in relief at seeing her forced composure. "And you... you do look so beautiful this night. May I offer to you whatever services I have available to me?"

Mihai thanked him, pressing his hands with hers while placing a gentle kiss on his lips, adding, "The day may well come when I call out to you for them."

Mihai's interruption had gathered its magic to the moment and saved Ardon from a dangerous, possibly life-threatening encounter. Darla had fought down her madness, regaining quiet control.

Just how Mihai and certain others tolerated this *creature* was beyond him. This was not the first time he had witnessed it nor, he feared, would it be the last. As Mihai continued on with her pleasantries, his mind flashed back to the time when he had foiled Asotos' second attempted attack on Mihai, occurring some years after Asotos' first.

There he was, consoling Mother, he leaning over her, they hugging each other, lost in cries and wails of lament, when little eight-year-old Darla entered the room. In a vicious, blind rage, the girl screeched and lunged forward, tearing and biting at the monster attacking her mother. It took weeks for his wounds to heal and many more for the scars to go away. It pained him, even now, just recalling that attack. Although the event was almost six millennia ago, it appeared to Ardon that Darla never forgot, her hatred for him only growing until, again, after the Great War he had been confronted by her, only to be saved that time by Euroaquilo. No! *The girl was a menace and a danger*! Why Mother put up with her was beyond his understanding, and why she had been invited here, on this night, was even a greater mystery.

Mihai backed away, making room for Darla to step forward and receive her official salutations from Ardon. She, though, did not move, her icy stare boring into the man.

For his part, Ardon politely bowed, acknowledging Mihai's escort. "My Lady, may all be well with you."

Darla remained motionless, glaring at Ardon. Mihai finally gave Darla a nudge with her arm, whispering, "Mother will be most displeased to see her favorite daughter acting so rudely. Do your part. Or is it shame you also want to deliver upon me?"

Moved by Mihai's scolding, Darla stepped forward, arms stiff at her sides. She bowed ever so slightly and in a most formal way replied, "Your

Counsel…good evening." She turned away, not even looking Ardon in the face, stepped behind and around Mihai and tugged on her elbow to go.

Mihai looked apologetically at Ardon, addressing him as 'Lord' and wishing him well. She then excused herself, following Darla's direction, and advanced on to the next person. Soon the room was again filled with the quiet chatter of private conversations while Mihai and her escort continued to receive the long line of wellwishers.

As soon as they had distanced themselves from him, Ardon slipped from the crowd and retraced his steps to the quiet, safe world of his perch. From there he pondered the life and history of this *madwoman* who was so bent on his destruction. Ma-we had shared it with him, oft repeating it through the years, but still he was more troubled by the way she fussed over the girl than for the reasons why.

He had heard it all, and not just from Mother. Unlike the other children, Darla had no pleasant memories to cling to. Her world was torn apart while she was but a babe, when Ma-we permitted the child to nurse at Mihai's breasts while she convalesced after Asotos' attack. Mother found it so therapeutic for her daughter that later, after Zadar was born, she offered the job of wet-nursing him to Mihai also. Until the age of eight, Mihai acted as mother and nursemaid to little Darla. All the while, the child's increasing nightmares and panic-filled fainting spells were largely ignored, Ma-we believing the girl had suffered a great emotional shock because she had been nursing Darla when Asotos attacked Mihai, she falling to the floor, Darla crashing headlong into it after being dropped by her. Ma-we had repaired the physical damage and believed the child would eventually outgrow the emotional trauma.

Indeed, it may well have been Ardon's entry onto the scene that saved Darla from going hopelessly insane. Much to Ma-we's dismay, when she discovered the demons growing in the girl's mind, it was too late to cure her. But at least they could be suppressed –for a while, anyway – until a cure might be found. Yes, Darla had been thrown onto the altar of fire and blood from the dawn of her memories. Violence and terror were her earliest companions. Only long after her gaining adulthood had others come to truly fathom the evil buried within her mind…fathom, but not understand.

So why did Mother allow her most dangerous child the freedom she did? Ardon puzzled. True, the child needed love and attention, something Ma-we and Mihai always showered on her. She drew so close to Mihai that the girl refused to leave her bed until the growing sensual emotions that were waking within her forced Mother to make other arrangements. It was understandable that she acted in such a way. She had no companions who willingly shared their lives with her.

Ardon remembered well, he living at the Palace for many years after his return. Oh yes, there were still the parties and gatherings, fewer and less attended, but visitors there were aplenty. Zadar was always the center of attention while Darla would often stand silently in the corner or slink off into the shadows to seek solace with imaginary friends. Euroaquilo's willingness to take Darla under his wing and provide loving companionship not only eased the girl's heart, but also introduced her to the realities of war. Here, Ardon believed, was where Darla's madness worked to her advantage, and he wished she would remain there until her cure was accomplished.

Ardon did not hate Darla. He was ridden with a deep inner sadness concerning her. Still, one was to consider the welfare of the people over one person no matter the cost to that being. At least that was how Ardon viewed matters.

And then there was Zadar, the youngest of all the children. Darla loved him from the start, acting as much his protector as she did for Ma-we. And Zadar? As he grew in stature and manhood, his devotion deepened for his sister to the point of what some came to view as worship of her. To this day, it was wisdom to not criticize her while in Zadar's presence.

And the things Mother allowed Darla and her other children to get away with bothered Ardon so. The last time he was almost attacked by Darla, the last time she had spoken to him, some forty years before, the woman had been in a drunken stupor. At least tonight he had smelled none of the strong drink on her like he had Planetee.

Why Mother put so much trust in Planetee he did not know. True, she was an Ancient, but there were limits and responsibilities. More than once he had witnessed that woman crawling up the Palace steps, reeking with the stink of strong wine and vomit. Never once had Mother turned her away, much to Ardon's disgust. Planetee was one of Mihai's closest councilors and confederates in war. He feared so often for Mihai's well-being because of her. Still, Planetee was a force to be reckoned with, and he felt he was not up to that task. He turned his attention back to Darla.

It was true that Darla lived in a world of satanic madness and pain that was not of her making. And it was true that Ardon's unkempt appearance and long, disheveled hair caused some of Darla's actions. Still, the woman should be watched more closely, especially in a gathering like this. Who knew if the serious matters discussed this night might not bring out the monster in her anew? He must remain alert to the possibility. *He* must act as the peoples' protector if no one else would.

At that moment, a fellow councilor called to him. He stood, smiling, and extending a hand, sauntered over to the man.

଼ଠ ଼ଠ ଼ଠ

"So! This is the world of angels and fools, the blowhards of government and policy making!" The eyes hidden in the shadowy confines of secreted corners of the council chambers studied the many faces in the gathering crowd. Scorn filled the whispering lips of the person behind those eyes, disdain for people of pompous society and highbrow pedigree evident in the creature's bitter frown. Visions of days long ago flooded this person's mind, filling it with the sights of torn and bloodied bodies of the dead and dying, all the while hearing grandiose chatter of an amused audience concerning itself with the glory of the kill or bravery of the defeated.

Turning its attention back to matters at hand, the creature muttered under its breath, "And who, this good eve, is the next to find my blade? And yet, it is not for the cheering crowd I deal death out by choice, but for the voices within that still cry out for the sport. 'A clean kill tonight! Show your skill and cunning, and allow it no second breath! Cleave it to the kidneys, yet let it live long enough to smell your sweet joy in its capture unto death'."

Shaking off the intoxicating vision, the creature sputtered, "It is for the safety of the king and its council. Indeed! The *world* I shall save tonight. Is the death of one not a fair price to save so many?"

And there was another hiding behind secret doors, waiting for someone's message or directions. But the spy was not secret to all, nor would it survive long enough to receive a 'well done' from its awaiting master. Now to wait… to wait and see who shall deliver the treasonous note to the contemptible thief.

Sucking in a breath as though sniffing the breeze, wary eyes examined the crowd as nostrils flared in disquiet. "Too many are the foul odors of mischief and evil in this room tonight! Have all the worlds' vultures gathered here to me, or does the wind itself offer up its putrid scent to offend my thoughts? And yet another I smell whose presence I do not yet discern, but like the Kriggerman on the prowl, it comes ever closer. Its very breath hastens the death of us all."

Quietly, the creature slunk further back into the shadows like a panther waiting its prey.

ଘ ଘ ଘ

"Come with me." Mihai was emotionally exhausted as she tugged on Darla's sleeve, pulling her toward stairs that led high into the upper bleachers. "I need a rest from these well-wishers." She turned her head to look down at the gathering crowd as the two ascended the steps. "We'll take a little breather up here."

"Whew!" Mihai sighed relief, nudging Darla, pointing down toward the main floor. "There, right there, you see where PalaHar and Terey are standing? A trap door in the floor under them allows a person to be lowered out of sight. Well, not just people, but stage props and things like that."

Darla sat up, asking, "Like what? Why would a council chamber have a trap door for props?"

"Oh…" Mihai smiled. "This wasn't always a council chamber. Really, it has been that for less than your lifetime. This was the Palace Grand, Mother's private theater, before the Rebellion, that is. The entire floor was…is the stage, the far wall the backdrop for the plays' settings. Two and three dimensional holographic scenes would accent the storyline and acting, creating an illusion for the audience, making everything so real."

She softly stroked Darla's knee. "There are a vast number of storage rooms and passageways under these bleachers and the many landings scattered about within the seating area. Then there's the wide upper landing above and behind us that circles around in a horseshoe formation nearly to the far wall. All of those things were originally constructed for the actors' use, to bring the plays more to life. Oftentimes the people in the audience would become part of the play itself. Oh, it was so much fun." Then pointing down at the spot earlier mentioned, she added, "I came up through that trap door. I was a flower, blossoming in spring, and I sang a little song after the hidden elevator had lifted up to the stage."

Mihai nodded dreamily. "I was only eight years old and, as I remember, the center of attention, receiving accolades for such a splendid performance." Her face clouded. "That was so long ago now, back in the days of endless peace."

Just then, Governess Anna entered the main doorway, accompanied by two other court officials. Mihai pointed. "See that door? Only the actors came in the way that overlooks the Winter Gardens. The audience always entered from up there, behind us." She waved her hand in the direction of the upper deck and beyond where a set of double entrance doors were now sealed closed. "We would come down these steps. They were lighted, of course, because the chamber was usually hidden in blackness, awaiting the play. Then we would shuffle our way along the different rows of seating. When the lights came up, oh, what a thrill! You would never know what sights awaited anxious eyes."

Darla studied the surroundings, fitting Mihai's tales into what she was seeing. "A person must have been pretty special to get an invite here. There's only seating for about three hundred or so. *You* must have been pretty special to come here so often. I've only been here once before, and that only on business, like tonight."

Mihai squeezed Darla's arm. "No one ever comes here anymore unless it is on business. And yes, I was special, just like every other young child of Mother's. This is where she showed them off to their older siblings. She made them feel *special*. I'm sorry that those days were gone before you had your hour of magic here. I…"

Darla sourly interrupted. "I'm made to feel *special* all right. Every chance they get, someone makes me feel *special*!"

Mihai took Darla's hand and looked into her face, her voice gentle but chastising. "There is reason why you have been gifted with the name 'RachelOchranNohah', 'the ewe that makes trouble her resting place'."

Darla stiffened, peering into Mihai's eyes. At length, after seeing no malice, she answered, "*Old fools* sit on *old councils* dreaming *old dreams!* They care not for understanding or insight. They pine wistfully for the past and torture any who do not understand such useless dreams. I have been gifted that name by the very *fools* who do not wish to forget the past, nor remember the deeds of today's heroes."

Mihai nodded. "Be that as it may, your actions here this eve were out of line, supporting the argument that you have been gifted the name you rightfully deserve."

"What'd I do?!" Darla exclaimed.

Scolding, Mihai answered, "You know full well what you did. This night you were my consort, a lady of this court. It was…is your responsibility to act the part, even if you don't want to. What you did was rude and uncalled for. Ardon is a great councilor in Mother's court. He is well-respected and deserves to be treated that way."

Darla sputtered a nasty retort. "Big bag a' *shit*…!" She chanced to see a scowl cross Mihai's face. "Wind…I mean *wind*… Big words with little meanings that drizzle in a piss pot they are. Chief of the War Honors Council? He wouldn't know a hero if it *bit him on the ass!* I didn't want to waste pleasantries on a fool who would have no real appreciation for them."

She looked down, folding her hands in her lap. "His kind are what ruined this… your world, too blind and unbending, unwilling to see the demons in the hearts of men. And after they were seen, too stupid to act effectively and bring matters to a rapid finish. His kind waited until my kind took to the field and watched as my kindred were slaughtered while protecting those sorry fools. Then, when the body count was delivered up to them, his kind cried, 'What?! You ask that we should also honor your dead for deeds well done? There is no honor in dying. It is the living, the judicious, the wise, who deserve the honor, for they protect the people through councils great and small'."

Mihai's retort was sharp but tempered. "Rachel! You call down evil on our Mother by those words for she, too, fell into such treacherous reasonings. Are you also bitter of soul with her? How could that be? I know of your unquestioned love for her."

Darla stared into her lap, saying not a word.

Mihai thought a moment, asking, "What did Ardon ever do to you?"

Darla shot a glance at Mihai, hatred burning in her eyes. "*Old fool*!" then again stared back down into her lap.

Taken aback, Mihai pondered the reason for Darla's outburst. After thoughtfully considering the matter, she leaned over and wrapped her arm around her little sister's shoulder, drawing her close and speaking softly in the girl's ear. "Today my demons tried to invade my waking hours. They are strong and growing in power by the hour. Do you not also feel their anger, their rage because of being trapped in a mind so filled with love for Mother?"

Darla did not look up or move. No word came from her mouth.

Mihai quietly pleaded, "At least admit to their presence. Admit that you, too, are infected with the Devil's spawn, as I am. Do not deny that they also live in you. At least admit it to yourself."

A thunderous voice shattered the moment as Mihai and Darla looked up to see Euroaquilo stepping over the row of seats directly behind them. "How are my precious children tonight, especially my one and my own?" Before either could move, he had swooped down and gathered them both up in a giant, loving, bear hug.

Like the sun breaking out from behind a thundercloud, Darla's face lit up radiantly. She squealed with delight, stood, flung her arms around Euroaquilo and cried, "I have yearned so for the hour to wrap myself up in your love. My coverlets I have already pulled from the bed in anticipation of your visit. Hurry, my heart is passionate for your manliness. Let's leave these important fellows to their important business and be off to make some important business of our own."

The shock of the moment quickly disappeared from Euroaquilo's face. He grinned, leaning down and kissing Darla on the forehead, exclaiming, "My little roe has missed me so? Am I the only stag in the wood?" He shook his head. "I cannot believe you have hidden yourself away waiting only for me, though it does impress me to think I am so highly sought after..."

Darla nuzzled her head in his chest. "There is no other like you. My dreams are your playrooms. You make my heart sing with passion and delight."

Mihai took Euroaquilo's hand, her eyes searching his, telling him tales of her concerns and the relief of having him there. A sad smile grew on her face. "Lord Euroaquilo…"

Euroaquilo tipped his head down and kissed Darla on her upraised lips. "Dear little one, I am your willing servant, but business first. You know my motto, 'the prison of dreary work only heightens the heart's passion for release.' So let us off with dreary work so we can ride the wind of heart's passion with abandon." Allowing no time for reply, he asked so politely, "May I make company with my two beautiful sisters tonight?"

A giggle rolled from Darla's lips. She leaned up and kissed Euroaquilo again before dragging him down beside her. In seconds, both she and Mihai were snuggled up close to their companion, Darla on his right and Mihai on his left, the man's arms around them both.

Darla buried her face in Euroaquilo's chest, rolling her head back and forth like some puppy nuzzling its master. After a moment she stopped, looked up at his face, a mischievous satisfaction beaming on hers. For several seconds she searched his eyes, her own deep contentment at this moment reflected in hers. Then, with a sigh, the woman became a child again, resting her head on his chest, closing her eyes while listening to the rhythmic '*thump, thump, thump*' of the man's beating heart.

In a hushed tone of mock pity, Mihai lamented to Euroaquilo, "I feel you will not be freed from her from company now. No… No… The Fates have surrendered you up to the child. It's now inevitable. She will not release you until the morning sun burns brightly over the eastern hills, if then."

Euroaquilo rubbed his cheek on Darla's head, stroking her hair with a giant, calloused, hand. "Tsk. Tsk. Oh! A fate worse than death! What is a poor fellow like me supposed to do?"

Darla peered up and into Euroaquilo's face, mumbling something about some earlier romantic interlude or other and just how tortured he had acted. She snuggled closer, wrapping an arm around his middle, and quietly dozed off.

With gentle strokes, Euroaquilo tickled Darla's back, listening for the slow, rhythmic breathing that told him his charge was resting peacefully. He had always been amazed at Darla's ability to sleep almost anywhere at any time, and yet her senses always remained alert. He had watched her as a fighter pilot during one of the earlier wars, how as she waited for her ship to be refueled and rearmed, she would crumple up in a corner of the hangar deck, falling soundly asleep, only to jump back to her feet the second her ears heard the click of the fuel hoses being disconnected. He slowly shook his head in marvel.

Watching the attendants far below, preparing the evening's events, the early arriving councilors seeking out favorite places at ornately carved mahogany tables, they sitting back in the highly decorated wood and leather chairs, Euroaquilo could not stop thinking about who this woman he held really was and just how savagely the Fates had abused her, asking himself if he were any better.

His mind wandered back to the days following Asotos' open rebellion, and his many regular visits he attended upon Mihai during her convalescing years. Darla had taken a fancy to him, and he to her. Few men dared to stand the child's attention for long, her queer gaze being most disturbing to them. It was like something or someone stared out from behind Darla's opaque, pixie-like orbs, always studying them, searching, ever searching. And the child was strange in other ways, too, quirky and elusive, always abstract in speech that was filled with troubling and dark riddles. For some unknown reason, Euroaquilo found himself drawn to the child, but it was more, possibly, out of curiosity than care or concern for her welfare.

Euroaquilo guessed it was for that reason he ignored or rather showed little consideration for the girl's desires or needs. When her coming of age came and went, Euroaquilo gave it little thought, paying no heed to the many flirtatious advances Darla made upon him. Unlike the custom bestowed upon every other daughter of Lowenah's, the girl found no man to take her to celebrate her virgin year, which traditionally began in the girl's twelfth year and lasted into her twentieth. No, Darla languished in silent lament until her late thirties before Mother, through shaming persuasion, convinced him to take the girl for his own - a truth he had ever held secret from the girl, fearing his later affectionate, real love would be thrown in doubt should she discover the truth.

Yes, in time Euroaquilo did fall deeply in love with Darla, and she with him. Eventually he managed to wean the girl away from Mother and the Palace, she being her mother's most fearsome defender. That obsessive protectiveness for her mother carried over into her relationship with him and, later, her fellow comrades at arms. He well remembered how fearsome she was in battle in those early years, a wild rage beyond all reason consuming her, especially if she was defending a fellow comrade.

And then there were the rumors of her escape from the Stasis Pirates. She and a few others managed to free themselves from their captors. Making their way along a stony gulch, they came upon a Stasis encampment, a rendezvous for several Stasis chieftains who were preparing for winter raids upon the local colonies. It was told that Darla went mad, a staccato insect noise growing in her voice that turned into a screeching howl after she crushed a sentinel's skull.

Instead of cowering in fright or seeking escape, Darla and a few fellow former prisoners stormed the crowded encampment, the Stasis scattering like leaves in a gale. Charging with the sentinel's pike, she rushed the camp and, in the gathering darkness, contributed to the slaughter of over eighty of her former captors, the remainder fleeing into the hills or escaping in their ships. Along with those survivors went the name of a new god that haunted the dark passages of their worlds. The 'Therioskotia', the immortal god of war, had become part of the lore that even affected some of Asotos' own army, its reputation flooding the hearts and minds of many a weary enemy soldier on a dark, moonless battlefield.

Euroaquilo's mind drifted on to more pleasant memories, his hand stroking Darla's hair as he reminisced over their few carefree moments the two had shared during the girl's lifetime. Soon the droning chatter from the crowd below and the heated air in the upper bleachers made his eyelids grow heavy. His head slowly dropped as he started to doze.

"My Aquilo..." Mihai whispered as she nudged Euroaquilo in the side.

Euroaquilo's eyes popped open with surprise. Turning his head, his look of surprise turned to concern at seeing the troubling disquiet on Mihai's face. "What is it, sister of my youth? Why does your face carry such a sad shadow on this most joyous of evenings?"

Mihai attempted a weak smile. "Oh, sweet brother of mine, to have your merry heart I would surrender all that is, was and will belong to me, but alas, fate does not bargain for baubles of hope. Listen, please. I have heard reports that do not portend well for us, rumors filled with dark foreboding. I see that you have been summoned away from your fleet at a critical hour, along with other officers of high rank who should be standing their post instead of bantering with old comrades in formal attire. And look, the council chambers are filled with our wisest of councilors, some who have traveled for weeks to attend this meeting."

She shook her head. "No! There is more than meets the eye about this gathering, more than just the formalities concerning another prisoner exchange. The Children of the Darkness are being raised to glory and even now stand ready to bring to a finish what our kind have but dreamed of doing, and in a way that chills my heart. And look..." She pointed below. "Mother hides somewhere in the shadows. Have you ever seen her do such a thing before? Is not her face the first one to greet you at the door?"

Resting a trembling hand on Euroaquilo's knee, she asked pleadingly, "Tell me, oh, brother of mine, do I hide from shadows of fantasy like a child who runs in terror from a sleeping adder, or does evil exist beyond my sight? Please, if you have knowledge, does our world have reason to fear? Can you explain it to me?"

Euroaquilo did not know about the new military arrangements and had scant understanding concerning Mihai's newly acquired kingship, but he was very wise and insightful regarding current and past events when it came to military matters. He stared into Mihai's face, surprised at her question. Seeing how troubled she looked, he ventured a reply.

Answering in little more than a whisper, he began, "All things hang by a thread. This you should already know even better than me...you being field marshal, god over the armies of this Empire."

Mihai lowered her eyes, hiding secrets and her own nagging doubts about coming revelations.

Euroaquilo gave Mihai a reassuring squeeze. "My MihaiAstron, Dawn of the Morning, the Morning Star, did I not bestow that title upon your name those many years ago when you and I stood over the plains of Megiddo, bloodied, but victorious? Did I not hold you, telling you that hope always comes upon a morning light and that you were the morning light for all the universe? You believed me that day. Do you still believe me now when I tell you the same thing?"

Mihai did not lift her eyes to look into his, but she did nod in agreement.

"Good!" Euroaquilo smiled. "Then, as I give my insight, filled with gloom and despair, remember I do not speak without assured hope. Little sister, our kind have lived through endless ages of peace. Our hearts do not - can not - adjust to this new age of endless violence. We continue to seek what is no longer ours, an elusive dream that is never ours to regain. There is our weakness and yet our strength. For, unlike those who surrendered to the new ways of evil violence, who gave their hearts and minds up to the *black vengeance* by abandoning the heart of our mother, our kind hold true to a hope that returns life to this world. But it is not the life that you and I once enjoyed."

Darla stirred, sighing ever so quietly. Euroaquilo knew that the child was awake and listening, but chose not to exclude her from this conversation. Mihai had asked her question in the woman's presence and thus must accept his answer would also fall upon her ears. He held Darla closer, a chill sweeping across his shoulders. "As the hearts of our enemy continue to degenerate, their hatred for all that is good ever grows. At first we did not notice, feeling that for most it was only a great misunderstanding and that they would soon return to their senses. Do I any longer believe this to be really so? For some… maybe. I do ever wish it to be so, but I do not believe it is true for the many."

He looked down at Darla, who was now resting her head in his lap, her breathing betraying the truth, telling him that she was hanging upon his every word. 'Very well...' He went on. "My darling here – Rachel - or as I have called her now these many years, 'Darla', is a product of this new and terrible age. Her mind has been twisted and tormented nearly to the breaking point but, unlike our adversaries, her soul has not fallen into the abyss of evil nothingness. Her spirit remains alive within her. The reason, I believe, is the depth of real love the child has for us… our mother and us… *all of us*. And that includes Ardon."

Euroaquilo could feel Darla's muscles tense up, but she refused to make a reply, pretending to remain asleep, wishing to hear more of what he had to say. He smiled again. "Have you watched our child in battle? She is not like us - you and me. There exists no more fear-inspiring creature upon the field than this woman! She fights with abandon, a madness more like the demon enemy than anyone sane. Her ruthlessness is tempered with kindness in the sense that she chooses only death and not torture for her enemy. She, herself, becomes a demon - a white demon - while on the horrid field. Have you ever wondered why?"

Answering without waiting for a reply, Euroaquilo explained, "My child is consumed with a burning hatred that is so intense, she can feel no other thing when that fever is upon her. That voice, the one from deep in her throat? It is the waking demon seeking release to wreak vengeance upon those it believes has hurt the people Darla loves. It is a madness that consumes this child, a madness controlled by sheer willpower, but unleashed upon the field of honor. I shall speak no more of that monster this hour. It is a story for another day. I remind you of it for reason of explanation."

Mihai shuddered with disquieting thoughts, but remained silent, wanting to hear more.

"Our enemies - those who were once our brothers - are consumed by a similar madness, a hatred for all things good. They, though, have no kindness within themselves; they have no hearts or souls. Their anger is based upon selfish desires and thoughts. Their own degeneration is charged against Mother and those who protect her name. They maim and torture for pleasure and revenge, feeling that it is little repayment for the evil acts done to them."

Euroaquilo shook his head sadly. "We...we, the *enlightened and proud* - proud because we believe in a higher order of rule and honor - we do not seek to understand what our enemy has become. We continue to trust in this...this council and others like it, believing we can negotiate with a rabid dog. Our enemy believes in such councils, too, because it buys him time to gain our destruction. Yes, our destruction! Not our surrender..."

"My Dear One, the Great War was an outstanding victory for us, but it was this greatest of victories that dooms us to failure, has doomed us. Everything our people have sacrificed for, to bring an end to the evil wickedness and cleanse our world of Asotos and his servants, has been brought to naught because of what that war did to us."

Mihai tried to argue that Euroaquilo was mistaken. He shook his head. "No, I am *not* mistaken! We won that war by armistice, a negotiated victory with both sides choosing how to divide the spoils. Why, we even allowed Legion to remain in Memphis, allowed him to keep the remains of our fallen comrades who perished in front of the walls of the city. *Who were the fools that sold the produce to keep an empty storehouse?* For that was all that Asotos permitted us to keep - an empty territory gutted of soul and spirit called the 'Children's Empire'. He walked away with all the gold and the real victory."

Mihai was stung, she having been on the council that decided the fate of that war. She refuted Euroaquilo's statement. "We did what was best for our people. They needed rest. That war had been too costly and our people were worn out and... and... the final hour had not yet come. We needed our energy saved for that day."

Euroaquilo countered Mihai's excuses. "By the very Book of Books, the one held sacred by all living souls, it was our hour to drive Asotos and his horde from this realm. You were at our head, our god of war, the warrior king of prophecy. You need have only driven the fool one more time! He was near the breaking point. Your commanders informed you of that, but you chose to listen to the wisdom of the councilors, the ones who had not lifted up a blade in combat or suffered the blows of battle."

"My sister, you know how deeply I love you. I am your obedient servant. Even now I will follow you to death and beyond if you should only ask me. I hold no grievance against you, or any other man or woman, but I speak the truth as I see it. You asked that of me."

Mihai nodded, eyes closed. "Yes, I did. But must you make it so painful? I did my best. We did our best. I saw no other way through it. My people needed a break from the slaughter, death, dying, the pain - the terrible, ugly agony of it all."

"Your people? *Your* people?!" Euroaquilo sadly shook his head. "We are not *your people*. Never have been and never will be. We are a *free* people. *My kind will live free or die free.* We follow you because we love you, you and our mother, who has sacrificed everything for us, her children. Yet, remember this: should you choose to abandon the field, we - *my people* - will find another leader who will either finish for us what has been started or shall perish in destruction attempting to bring this Rebellion to a finish."

"My fleet stood ready that day, that day you ordered us to stand down. Our tears were many for, in that very hour, we could smell sweet victory. One more blow, one more punch, and we would have forced his hand. His power was gone, sacrificed on the fields of Memphis. The flower of his army lay slain, their blood mixing with that of our defeated brothers who had really won the contest. The universe was ours for the taking. The Great Satan was within our grasp and he knew it."

Mihai's tears began to fall. "I am sorry. I did the best I could. I am no warrior."

Euroaquilo lifted his arm from Darla and with his fingers, wiped away her tears and spoke consolingly. "It is your greatest strength that is also your most vicious enemy. Love, my dear sister, love is a two-edged sword. One must come to understand it or it will devour the things one craves to save. For me, I would rather die forever because your love has caused my demise than to live eternally without it."

He sighed. "Be that as it may, we must now face the present and future, the past being only an object lesson to gain added insight from."

"Our enemy suffered no such trauma as you believe our people have or, if they did, Asotos gave them no time for rest to consider it. All these years since the armistice have been busy ones for the League of Brothers. Their forge hammers have not slowed. Day and night, the people ever slave at rebuilding their world. War machines great and small they produce without number. New and powerful are the ships they are gathering to extinguish our Empire. Every able-bodied man and woman stands in the ranks, waiting upon Asotos' orders, conscripted by him to bring us our own day of infamy. The army is beyond the size of any yet seen in the realms above or those beneath. And when the moment is right, it will strike."

Euroaquilo closed his eyes, seeing in vision that impending future. "And *we* are not ready for it...."

Confused and frightened, Mihai shook her head in reply. "*This cannot be*! Mother has not spoken of this. Her faith is still strong in her children. My people are willing to suffer and die for this cause! They must be ready!"

"You misunderstand, my lovely one." Euroaquilo explained. "Our brothers are willing to die for this cause, but too many are not willing to live for it, do whatever it takes – costs - to see it through. Deep inside they desire the impossible to take place, to see the Rebellion end with everyone going back to the old ways, the return of old lovers, for everyone to kiss and make up. They know it cannot be that way, but they dream it. And that, my dear sister, makes them weak."

He looked toward the ceiling. "Our dreams must die and, when they do, we will lose them forever. Yet, there is no alternative other..." He paused, not wishing to finish.

"Speak, brother of mine." Mihai egged him on. "Speak and keep no secrets. Other than what?"

"Other we suffer the destruction of all living things." He looked into Mihai's face. "Mother knows this is so, oh, so true. You are not the only one she reveals secrets to."

He looked down upon the increasing crowd, lamenting, "The day will soon be upon us when meetings like this one shall be something of the past. Councils waste time, and that is the one thing we are running out of... have run out of." He rested a hand on Darla's shoulder. "To survive the coming hour, we must all become like this child of the New Age. We must all become *mad...mad* for war, for violence, for destruction...*mad* for the sake of being *madmen*."

"We have failed to become mad. Mother has called this council. My belief is she intends to do something to correct that." Euroaquilo closed his eyes again and spoke troubled secrets. "Look, I have seen in my dreaming hours a beast, hideous and powerful, tearing and destroying all things in its path. It cries out to the night in a strange tongue, the tongue of earthling men from forgotten ages past. It calls out for war, the kind of which we, our kind, have never seen. Yet it stands upon the shores of righteousness, bringing life to the dying and hope to those in despair. The flame of God is in its sword and the beacon of future hope shines forth from its shield."

Mihai rested her head on Euroaquilo's shoulder. She wanted to scream out to the sky for it to fall down upon her and consume her in its pity for the fool. Her brother's words were true, more so than he knew. This night would prove them to be so. She shuddered. The age of innocence was past, never to return. It sickened her to think about what it really meant, yet had she not caused it, wished it to be? The monster lived. It would bring to a finish what she could not. It would make Ma-we's children into what she refused to: *monsters, murderers* of all the old ways.

She closed her eyes. In her mind, the world burned. All of their works, their culture, their dreams, their hopes, burned to ashes. Mihai began to feel the pity of a mother watching her children suffer torment and pain. She then looked to Darla, the child of the new and dark age. What had the girl thought concerning Euroaquilo's tirade?

Opening her eyes and turning to ask the woman, Mihai was caught up in surprise. There Darla, laying on Euroaquilo's lap, a smile on her face, was fast asleep.

Mihai rested her head on Euroaquilo for some time, watching the people and pondering what future fates awaited them. A large crowd was now gathered - dignitaries, councilors and officers of high rank, most of the great leaders of the Empire. She was beginning to comprehend just how important this meeting was when a stir arose among some of those standing by the door. Mihai craned her neck to see what the commotion was about.

The crowd suddenly stepped back, parting as if an invisible hand had gently pushed them aside. A restless sea of hushed whispers followed as the curious pushed forward to see what was causing the excitement. Then came a sudden, collective gasp of surprise follow by deathly silence. All eyes were fixed on the doorway. Ma-we peered out from a shadowy corner, smiling. 'My darlings will not doze off this night. Too many questions...' She laughed. 'Too many questions...'

The object of everyone's excitement quietly stepped into the room, a woman, ordinary in stature, beautiful in appearance, other save her officer's uniform and, of itself, it was quite ordinary, too, in most ways. Her fully buttoned, doubled-breasted jacket was light gray with modest amounts of gold braid on the sleeves and lapels, the collar of a red silk blouse just visible about her neck. Natty trousers with a gold stripe along each leg covered high-top, black officer's boots. A gray kepi with a large black bill, pulled low over the woman's forehead, finished her attire.

Oh, how plainly this stranger was dressed, not at all in the fashion of the women of this realm. No jewelry, makeup, or painted lips, something most unexpected for such a royal occasion. And other than the light scent of lilac, a reminder of a recent bath, she wore no perfume. Even her long, curly, brunette tresses were hurriedly gathered together and hung loosely down her back. Indeed, the woman appeared uncomfortable and ill at ease with all the attention being directed toward her.

And why all the attention? The emblems emblazoned on her uniform. A small patch of royal blue encircled with gold thread could be seen on the gore of the kepi, and on the left sleeve and front left breast of the jacket. In the middle of the circle, gold and chrysolite embroidered pomegranates with two ancient runes were woven in mendilevean silver and trimmed in chrysolite-gold…legends in their own right.

The runes were revealed to the people after Asotos' defeat in the First Megiddo War, emblazoned on the ensign of the army's commander, Pontifex Maximus Gabrielle. None of the children knew the meaning of the rune words, for they were from an old and strange tongue known to few but some of the oldest of the Ancients. Gabrielle it was who translated them into the common tongue, 'Jachin', and the second, 'Boaz', telling the meaning to be, 'Yehowah has firmly established in strength'. And it was she who placed the names upon the pillars standing each side of Heaven's Gate at the great temple door in the City of David. And it was she who later cast the pillars down in disgust, handing over the names and their titles to the new field marshal and leader of the armies, Mihai, after the burning and plundering of that same temple in the last age of free men, abandoning mankind to themselves and their own fate.

It had only been their field marshal, Mihai, who had ever possessed the power of those names, some believing it made her invincible in combat. Needless to say, to see the power of the Cherubs decorating the uniform of another - a stranger, no less - did not bode well in the minds of those seeing such a thing. An unsettled murmuring arose among the gathered crowd.

Trisha smiled nervously, politely bowing her head and lifting her kepi in salutation. She stared into a chorus of questioning and hostile eyes. Lowenah had told her to expect the unexpected, but nothing could have prepared her for this icy welcome. Could these creatures really be the angels of story and legend that she had so longed to gaze upon in reverent admiration for all their wondrous deeds of bravery and loyal service? "Oh, for the lot of Steven… Should I be as blessed…" she muttered under her breath as she watched faces growing in disdain and anger.

Mihai was caught totally by surprise, never expecting to see her own kindred acting so rudely. As she stood to go to Trisha's assistance, Euroaquilo took her by the arm, shaking his head. "Give it a moment, Love. There comes rescue on golden wings."

At that instant, a handsome dark-haired man wearing a wide, toothy grin, burst through the crowd, his arms outstretched in welcome, rushing up to Trisha, sweeping her hands up in his. "My Lady! My Lady! You look splendidly beautiful tonight!" Zadar cried just before bending down and kissing the woman's hands.

Turning to the shocked and surprised gathering, Zadar saluted his people. "The hour of the night is begun! Our dreams are awaking to promises fulfilled. Tonight our journey is started. Fate is no longer our master. Let us rejoice with our sister in the new world that stands just outside our door. *'And down the great dragon was hurled!'"*

Bewildered, the people dumbly stared at Zadar who remained there, holding one of Trisha's hands and grinning with delight.

Darla was now sitting up. She leaned in close to Euroaquilo, squeezing his hand. "I knew he was on a new scent. He can smell a fresh roe a hundred leagues away..."

At that moment, Mihai managed to work her way through the confused throng of onlookers. Trisha released Zadar's hand, grasping Mihai's as she drew near. Bowing at the knees, she bent low, kissing Mihai's hand. "My Lord..." Trisha called out in salutation. "Is my Lord well and in good spirits on this festive occasion?"

With all the charm of royalty, Mihai gracefully pulled Trisha to stand. Leaning forward, she gave her a tender kiss on her lips. In a voice just above a whisper but clear as an evening bell, she offered her salutations and congratulations to this evening's stranger. "Let me be the first of my kind to welcome you to this honorable house and to the glory awaiting you here. Our Great Lord has set before us a creation to lead us into our future glory. Praise be to our Great Lord for bringing you to us in our darkest hour."

Trisha winced as if in pain. Looking into Mihai's eyes, she made a quiet reply only for her ears. "My Lord, I am a slave girl, born of the dirt of common stock, a tender of flocks and nursemaid to the snow lilies and brambles. I do what is requested of me to the best of my ability, but shall it be good enough? I do not know. I do not think myself well-suited for this job."

Mihai smiled, kissing Trisha again and then softly replied, "A true soldier rarely does."

Trisha smiled sadly, leaning close. "But will your lips still find mine so pleasant after this eve?"

Puzzled, Mihai stood back, her hands tenderly holding Trisha's upper arms as she forced a smile. "Why… why ask such a silly question?" She then turned to the anxious crowd, raising an arm with outstretched fingers, calling out, "To those of you who have not had the pleasure of meeting her, allow me to introduce to you TrishaQa·Shaib·Jal, a child of secret worlds and hidden lands, raised *god of thunder and smoke*. She brings the morning light, a new day's dawning. Her sword writes red the sky in tumult and power. The hour of our glory draws near!"

She stared into eyes troubled and dumbfounded. Frowning, she cried out, *"Give honor to our Great Lord, our Mother and Creator of all living things! This child she has made in her own image!"*

Mihai's outburst shook the crowd into action. Collectively they bowed on bended knee, answering with the respectful words, "My Lord."

Satisfied, Mihai now commanded, "Now, please, honor me with giving our guest the same salutation you provided me." Motioning Zadar to act as liege, she politely bowed toward Trisha and stepped aside to allow another to come forward.

No one refused to introduce himself or herself to the new field marshal, especially since Mihai had commanded it and, by the time the formalities were finished, the room was again filled with the chorus of carefree chatter, Trisha only a curious memory from an awkward moment. This was when Ma-we chose to make her entrance into the theater of secrets, gathering everyone's attention to her... that is all, save one.

Trisha made her way into the dimly lit recesses of the bleachers, she wanting a quiet respite from her nervous encounters and formal introductions. It was not to be.

"Why, Hello dear! I wanted so much to meet your acquaintance." Anna stepped out from the shadows, giving Trisha a loving hug. "I'm sorry I missed you at the greeting, but I was very busy running some errands for our new king, Mihai. It's so exciting, isn't it? I mean to have a new king and a new field marshal here at one time, in one night! So exciting! So exciting!"

Anna bantered on about all the new things going on, the many dignitaries and military leaders present. "Why, I think I've not seen such a glorious crowd of important people since the end of the Great War. Have you ever?"

Trisha dumbly agreed, not admitting that she knew nothing of the Great War except from books and visual records. Anna lowered her head, half closing an eye while studying her with the other. At length she smiled, changing the subject. After some lighter chatting she excused herself, returning to those who had flocked around Ma-we. When the coast was clear, Trisha made her way to a door hidden far under the bleachers, slipping unnoticed through it, or so she thought.

"Oh!" A woman bolted up from a desk where she had been writing some notes.

"I...I'm sorry. Didn't mean to intrude." Trisha's face reddened in embarrassment as she backed against the closed door. "I didn't know the room was occupied. Just trying to get a breath of air from the crowd."

"No! No! It's all right. I was... was just leaving on an errand... an errand, you know." The woman fumbled for the papers on the desk. "It's so busy around here, you know... you know. Last minute work... last minute." She hurriedly turned to go and then thought better of it.

Turning back around, she approached Trisha. "I'm sorry to be so rude. Got so busy with my work... you know, all the things going on this night... so busy. I'm Eliseah, adjunct to the council. And you must be our new... er... field marshal... er..."

"TrishaQa·Shaib·Jal. Yes, I guess I'm the new field marshal." Trisha extended her hand, opening the door with her other.

Eliseah took Trisha's hand with hers and stepped in, wrapping her other hand around Trisha's back. She swiftly moved close, sensuously kissing a much surprised field marshal on the lips.

Feeling Trisha's troubled reaction to her advances, Eliseah opened her eyes, curious, asking, "Does my Lord not find her servant girl's lips acceptable? Is the fragrance of her breath not sweet enough? I am sorry if I have offended my master."

Trisha had tried so hard to accept the ways of these people. Many times she had watched the way the women made love to each other but, still, it troubled her heart. Even the kissing of her sisters on the lips was only recently an acceptable thing for her to practice. She so much wanted to fit in and not be offensive. It was so difficult at times. She shook her head. "No. No, your lips are soft like petals of rose and your breath is refreshing like a summer shower. It… it is just the night, I believe. So much is on the mind of one newly troubled with heavy responsibilities. It fogs things up."

Eliseah offered an elusive smile, revealing more than what she replied, but Trisha could not figure out its meaning. "Oh, my Lord, many are the secrets hidden in this world of men. A kiss tells us many things, more than one might imagine."

Squeezing her hand, Eliseah offered an alibi for her sudden departure and then hurried through a rear door that led down a long, dark corridor to more chambers, which eventually led to an exit onto the concourse near the Winter Gardens. From there she hurried to a tramwaiter that was to take her out past Palace City, eastward toward the Huushan Rail Stage Terminal. An hour further east and she would depart at the Waldreain Hill Terminal, making her exit from EdenEsonbar. At least that was her intention.

Watching from the shadows, angry eyes observed Eliseah's sensual embrace. A voice cursed under its breath, "The night turns red, but which one will it be?" After seeing the woman's rapid exit, the person behind the voice abandoned the council chambers in hot pursuit, mumbling about Trisha, who remained standing at the door. "It fools them, but it doesn't me. Its blood I shall pour out on the ground. It hasn't a fortnight…."

ೞ   ೞ   ೞ

(*Author's note: The day of the councils was new. It had only existed formally about four millennia, having started after the Great Division. During the Age of Peace, the First Age, people gathered together for festivals and celebrations. Ma-we's Firstborn had held oversight of most of these festivals, with his councilors' primary jobs being the coordination and overseeing of events. Ma-we presided over the bigger, periodic festivals. Everyone was invited to attend and participate. But any one of the children* could choose to have a celebration and for any reason. Its size was only limited by the desires and abilities of the person initiating it. The Rebellion had ended the festivals, and it took time for the councils to evolve into these present official conferences. That evolution came from the secondary aspect of the original councils.

In the First Age, the structure of life was informal. Because of Ma-we's passion for freedom of heart and mind, few laws existed for people to obey. Each person chose his or her own way of doing things. Large disputes were unheard of. If a small one arose that could not be settled easily, it would be handed over to older ones not directly involved. Many of these older children also served on one or more of the councils that existed, starting from the community level on up. Over several millennia, these councils grew to become highly respected for the governmental direction they provided. When a disputed matter was set before a council, its final decision, although not binding, was usually accepted.

After the Rebellion started, it was only natural for the councils to be looked to. At first there was a great deal of confusion. Often the council houses were filled with debate over who should be followed. Ma-we had always deferred governmental responsibility to her Firstborn, having him be the official public mouthpiece for rulership. She would never openly speak contrary to any words her son had uttered. What was discussed privately between them was not revealed. Because of all the false stories generated after Ma-we expelled her Firstborn from the palace, the loyalty of the people was tested. As time progressed, differences of opinion intensified to the point that many communities found themselves with two different councils trying to give direction. Each separate council tried to promote what it believed the truth of the matter really was.

Ma-we claimed to be the Creator, thus being the true God. Her son claimed that he was a co-creator and that Ma-we's power came from the secrets hidden in the Upper Palace. Ma-we claimed that anyone acting independently of the harmonics holding the universe together would eventually die. Her rebel son charged that her statements were a fallacious attempt to maintain control over her people. The people of the Second Realm later came to call the energy force produced by the harmonics 'holy spirit'. Many eventually deified it and made it into another god, or part of a god. It was not until aging and death started occurring among the people of the Second Realm that Ma-we was proved correct. But, by that time, her son had gained a large following, and they did not desire to return to Ma-we.

As with people of the Second Realm, when Ma-we's own children fully abandoned her, they had also cut themselves off from the energy force binding the universe. When proof of her son's lies became evident, they turned on Ma-we, accusing her of evil in the way she made them. They charged she used the power existing in the Upper Palace to change the fabric of the universe, thus robbing them of eternal life. The black vengeance that had already taken root in their hearts prevented them from seeing anything other than their own selfish longing. The desire was already growing strong to find a way to destroy Ma-we and all who still followed her. It was to the Second Realm that Ma-we's rebel son directed his followers, to find a way to bring their desire to fruition.

One of the outstanding differences between the children of the First and Second Realms was the ability to produce offspring. All of the children of the First Realm were the direct progeny of Ma-we, each being born from her. The children of the Second Realm were made with the ability to procreate offspring through reproduction. So even though the people grew old and died, there was an increasing of the population in that realm. The rebel sons started genetic experimentation to make a super race of men who would rule the Second Realm. Their further hope was to eventually make a race of warriors able to invade the First Realm. At that point in time, life was still contained on one planet in the Second Realm. Ma-we was moved to action before this could change. She destroyed the hybrid race along with most of the life on that planet, preserving only a handful of persons and animals alive.

When people started increasing in number again, Ma-we's rebel son attempted another takeover of the Second Realm. Before he could accomplish his plans this time, Ma-we sent a plague into the lands that altered the speech patterns of the people. This was done because she did not have the heart to destroy her creations again, and knew if her son were not stopped, history would repeat itself. Confusion and mistrust destroyed the unity among the inhabitants in the Second Realm, dividing them into nations and races. Ma-we's rebel son found it nearly impossible to unite those people under his yoke again.

Accusations flew back and forth. Ma-we's son claimed that Ma-we was not allowing him opportunity to prove his superior ruling abilities. She accused him of meddling with unreasonable force to coerce people into following him. Ma-we had power far greater than her rebel son, so he attacked her authority, claiming that if things were equal, he would be better able to show himself the more capable sovereign. An agreement was settled upon, stating that Ma-we would no longer use her power to openly assist her children, and her son would not directly interfere with the people of the Second Realm. This forced Ma-we to also withdraw her protective power from her children in the First Realm. Without her power protecting them, the need arose for her children to protect themselves. A form of secondary government became necessary to do this. They turned to the already existing councils to provide the needed governing.

At first, Ma-we maintained command of the central government that came into existence. After repeated accusations and wrangling concerning the contrived offences brought up by her son, she set up a steward who took overall charge. This steward became the head of the council and remained such until Mihai was made field marshal. When this occurred, Mihai removed herself from the council and took her place as its head. For a while, Ma-we continued to conduct many of the important council meetings, but she deferred to the persons in charge for the final decision. After the start of the Great War, Mihai had become the chief over the central council with Ma-we usually introducing the meetings and then handing over control to Mihai.

Everyone invited to a meeting was part of the given council. The entire number of people gathered was called the 'general council'. If anyone had information or an opinion, they were allowed to give voice to it. The decision-making body of the council was made up of twenty-four members. Six were personal councilors of Ma-we. Six were personal councilors of the steward, or the one in command. The remaining twelve were made up of leaders involved in, or knowledgeable of current topics of discussion. For an issue to be resolved, eighteen of the twenty-four needed to approve it, with at least half from each of the three individual groups being in agreement. Ma-we and the steward did not have an official say in the final decision unless it directly involved them. In that case, they had the option to refuse to execute the will of the council. If that happened, the council could choose to reconsider matters until its decision became agreeable to Ma-we or the steward.)

ॐ   ॐ   ॐ

The night's council was already foreboding winds of change. Ma-we had always represented the ruling power of the Council, she standing as King over her children. It had been comprised of twelve members, four standing: Gabrielle, PalaHar, Tizrela, and Ardon, the remaining eight being selected for each given council gathering. In time, after Legion had captured Memphis, a twelve-member Regent Commission or Council was added to the King's Council with Gabrielle acting as head – she being given title of Pontifex Maximus, chief bridge-builder. At that time, Mihai was granted standing membership on Ma-we's council. Later, near the beginning of the Third Age of Men, around the time when PaulNomikos revealed new secrets regarding the Athenians' unknown god to Dionysius at the Areopagus, Mihai was lifted up to replace Gabrielle as head of the Regent Council, she being given the title of field marshal. Tonight that was all changing.

Tonight Mihai stood as king - or a king. Few believed she represented the King, Lowenah/Yehowah, Ma-we to Mihai. Lowenah was present as she had always been except…except this night she wore only her golden ankle-length tresses as her royal garb, something very different from past councils. And she created a forced absence while the children gathered, something so uncustomary for her. She had also maintained a low profile, allowing court officers to stand in for her and make arrangements with the appointed councilors.

Then there was the new field marshal, a stranger to most, not from this realm, and not of their kind. This was most disconcerting to many, angering to a few. And knowing her escort tonight was even more troubling for them, seeing that the one chosen to be escort at an official gathering usually reflected the escorted person's opinions. It was bad enough to have that *troubling child* prance Mihai around the room, surely some of Mother's mischief. But to have her, Mihai, the king apparent, request Zadar escort the new field marshal? Oh, that did not bode well at all...not at all.

There was something queer about that young fellow, Zadar, a most likable fellow for sure, and quite a romanticist with the women, but he had a dark side about him, stories whispered concerning his conduct on the battlefields much like his sister, they had been told. He and that sister of his... he was far too close to her... she having too much of a hold over his mind, some said. It was told once that that girl, Darla, was overheard telling the boy, 'It's better negotiating with a corpse, easier to come to an agreement it is.' And he just stood there, laughing. And that kind of an opinion did not set well with the majority of the Council and their supporters.

So here they were this eve, hundreds of the Empire's wisest and most ardent overseers gathered for a very important, official meeting. The question now was, 'Who would sit the Council?' At least Mother had taken her station at the head table, and it appeared that Mihai was making her way to the head of the Regent Council, and that *girl* still remained sitting high up in the bleachers, bringing a sigh of relief to a few. The court officers were hurriedly seeking out the members who were to sit the councils this night. All waited with bated breath, knowing well that the composition of the clouds often foretells the future weather.

Mihai created no surprises by her choices at first. True, SymeonKephim and PaulNomikos were outsiders, men from the Realms Below, but they had taken well to their new home, likable and respectable fellows, knowing their place in the social order of things, not making a fuss. They had both worked diligently to adapt to the ways of these people, accepting the long-established customs found here.

Then there were the councilors of renown, long-standing members of Mihai's council who were: AnamParedreuo, at times addressed as 'Governess Anna', but better known just as 'Anna' or 'Lady Anna'; Euro-aquiloIllyricum, the 'StormWind', warrior and protector of Mihai in deeds and wisdom, who sat down beside Paul; PlanetesAntistrate, commonly called 'Planetee', a fearsome warrior, drunk or sober; and TereoAprupneo, referred to as 'Terey', best fighter pilot in the Empire, second to none in the TKR – 17, better known as the 'flying corkscrew', but whose exploits had cost the woman her health long ago, forcing her at times to a sickbed with unstoppable nose bleeds and chronic bowel disorders.

Also seated at Mihai's table were some of her long-time councilors well known to children of the Empire: OfhieSanternano - chief construction officer for all civil engineering jobs on EdenEsonbar; CrilenianTorpedee – diplomat and Keeper of the Scrolls of Peace; KyseninaGerzion – Watcher Over the House and secretary for Mihai's council; DarlaRosa – an Ancient whose prescience of insight and foreknowledge offered the council visions into hidden secrets of cosmic wisdom; and DornanceZaboren, troubadour and herald of kingly matters, Maiden to the Crystal Gems and Maker of the Singing Stones.

The one person who troubled many in the crowd was the last seated at Mihai's table - TolmetesRhedEpi – 'the Mad Charioteer of the Sudan'. At least that was the reputation this Off-worlder had brought with her upon arrival into this realm. Tolmetes was battle-hardened by continuous frontier guerilla wars in this realm, in which she had enlisted for over twenty years. The woman's glistening brown skin rippled with muscular firmness while her coal-black eyes burned with wild excitement for adventure. It was said that her mother was an Ethiopian princess and her father descended from the kings of the Heruls.

Tolmetes had already lived up to her name for being mad and wild, at least in a fight. Flying an old T-4 fighter-bomber she, in lone combat, had destroyed four Stasis Pirate fighters over Exothepobole in a skirmish a little over a year before. It had been rumored that the woman had told acquaintances that 'war was a gift from God and not to be wasted with good deeds and diplomacy'. For Mihai to place this person at her council table on such an important evening did not bode well for those who hoped for peaceful outcomes to future events.

Ma-we's - Lowenah's - choices for her council troubled many as well, even some of her older council members. The first four, though, did not threaten the old ways. As expected, Mother had Lord PalaHar and Lady Tizrela seated to her right and left. From days of long ago those two had been called the Cherub Stones (lit: 'music of the gods'). Next to be seated were Lord Ardon and Lady Tashi, also expected to be on the council. These four were advocates for more peaceful solutions to the Rebellion, all being involved in procuring the armistice that ended the Great War. They hoped that, if given enough rope and time, Asotos' League of Brothers would disintegrate under the weight of its own internal strife, leaving the Children's Empire to merely go in and clean up the twisted remains.

But then, to the chagrin of many, the people watched Zadar hurry forward, pulling on the hand of an embarrassed field marshal, Trisha, as she nearly stumbled her way to Ma-we's council table, being seated along side Tizrela who turned and smiled warmly at the woman. Trisha was unknown to most, but not all. A select few were privy to the woman's arrival some years before and her education in the arts of combat. She had taken quite quickly to guerilla wars being fought on the frontiers of the Empire, making somewhat of a name for herself, and advancing quickly up the ranks. Some called her cruel, others ruthless when it came to the fight. If she ever had remorse, it was never revealed, her eyes hiding any and all secrets of emotion.

NoazOhfehr, BruunTaciak, and DinChizki were veterans of the long wars of the Rebellion, heroes of the Great War and advocates for total war. DinChizki was credited with saving the army at Memphis by ordering a daring, suicidal counterattack against Legion's shock troopers in the Battle of the Tower Gate, thus opening a way of escape for thousands of trapped soldiers through the breech of the North Passage Wall. These men were not diplomats, but soldiers, viewed as mercenaries of violence and destruction. Many faces frowned in displeasure at seeing them take positions at Ma-we's table.

Richard Finhardt and Tabitha Copeland were two strangers from the Lower Realms and unknown to all but a few. What was known of Finhardt was that he had been raised in a military society and nurtured in the ways of war. From infancy, his father had trained him to be a soldier. By seventeen he had received the status of fighter pilot, flying wood and canvas warships of his day, and by eighteen he had acquired the title of 'ace', sending seventeen enemy 'flying coffins' to the depths below by war's end. He cast another eight from the skies several years later during another civil war.

Tabitha Copeland was a surprise, well-liked but not trusted by the diplomats in the council. The woman's green eyes cast rays of merriment and mirth when she entertained her new friends and acquaintances. She listened intently to the tales as Ancients told of the world of yesterday, often writing down her conversations at evening's end. An historian, anthropologist, mathematician, and librarian, a 'bookworm' – as she called herself – and... and a brilliant tactician and strategist, it was said of her that she had once calculated the mass of the Orginian Nebula by triangulating different locations from telescopic references on EdenEsonbar and superimposing the factors of the speed of light over time against the gravity effect, doing the math in her head. But why Copeland at this council? Her presence made no sense to them.

And then there was HoiOnarasis, 'Mountain Wolf of the Jahouk', a name given him by his soldiers after the First Battle of Memphis, a well-deserved one. Sweeping south, out of the Pass of Korteniaz, his two brigades slammed into the northern flank of one of Legion's chief officers, General StokJakke's First Corps, breaking up its advance against Mihai's ravaged Seventh and Twelfth Corps, sending it into a rout which was not halted until it reached Memphis far to the south. Light cavalry commander, fighter and heavy bomber pilot, tank commander, tug, tender, and frigate captain, army, marines, navy command - what was there in his long military history that HoiO hadn't been or done? He was a most qualified and able soldier, but he was no statesman. His statesmanship came at the point of a sword.

But most troubling of all was a hooded, blonde fellow who made his own way to the council table. Mother grinned, motioning him a place beside Ardon who politely bowed his head in salutation, he showing no expression to give away his feelings about the man. The mysterious Mr. Garlock, or 'Jebbson' to his friends - of whom there were few - sat, pulling back his cloak to reveal a handsome, bearded man with long hair that fell to his shoulders. What powers or wisdom did this Garlock possess that proffered his presence at the King's table and one so close to the head as to be seated next to a chief councilor? An Off-worlder for sure and said to be curt, blunt, bold, and aloof as to the Empire's strategies at making war – and a close friend of Tolmetes and Darla - *too* close, some complained.

Garlock lived, squirreled away in a laboratory at Oros, coming to Palace City on occasion, and then only to disrupt meetings at the War Department with some brainy new invention or idea he had come up with, or so it was told. And he managed to get Mihai's and Mother's ear way too often. Some complained of him as being uncouth in using his boyish charms to seduce the women of the land into doing his bidding. Others believed the gaze from his piercing blue eyes sufficiently powerful enough to mesmerize the innocent of heart, giving him passage into the victim's soul in order to bend her reasoning to his will. The women close to him would only smile at such accusations while their eyes drifted dreamily upward.

Yes, the night did not bode well for those hoping for peaceful solutions to troubling problems. Still, there was Ardon, chief councilor and close confidant of Lowenah. If anyone could pull a peaceful solution out of the fire, it would be him. He was unflinching in respecting the value of diplomacy, believing it had saved the Empire down to this day and would eventually lead to the end of the Rebellion and a return to a peaceful universe. Yes, Ardon was the key. He must succeed. The future of the Empire rested on his shoulders. Diplomacy was the answer to real peace and a returning to the way it used to be. Oh, for the way it was then! Ardon could make that happen…

೮೮   ೮೮   ೮೮

When the council was seated, the attendants gathered those providing testimony concerning the evening's topics to special seating down on the main floor. Among them was Bedan, uncomfortable at finding himself in such a limelight. Around this time, an attendant had worked her way through the crowded bleachers to reach Darla. In little above a whisper, she asked her to remain for the entire meeting, for Mother had some business she wished to discuss with her. Curious, Darla nodded she would remain.

A hush fell across the room as lights dimmed, the stage illuminating the collected council members. All eyes focused on Ma-we, waiting on her to open the meeting, which was her custom. But she remained quietly seated, her eyes fixed on Mihai who alone stood, casting a gaze upon her mother, both staring deeply into each other's soul. The hour was set. *Time* ruled this eve. It was lord and god over all the people gathered. Mother was waiting upon Time, for it to reveal itself in all its power. When the moment was right, she smiled, nodding ever so slightly.

The theater stage gradually fell dim while lights secreted high in the ceiling cast their white, circular glow upon part of the stage floor, the silence deafening. At that instant, Mihai stepped into the radiant light, motioning with her hand toward the shadows. Slowly, the illuminated part of the floor began to rise. This was nothing new, it being a common practice for such events. What was unexpected was that Mihai stood upon the throne, Mother having always carried the moment at all past moots of her calling.

Mihai looked stunningly beautiful in her royal gown, flowing, bejeweled, silken train, and golden, kingly crown. She slowly turned in place, peering into the shadows, smiling as one does when looking into the eyes of a person she loves. When she again faced the council, she stopped, waiting for the lights of the room to reveal to her the faces of those gathered. The new king then searched the eyes of the crowd, followed by those seated at the council tables, finishing with her mother's.

Ma-we smiled, remaining silent. This was her daughter's night, a sign for future days. Mihai must deliver words to move her brothers and sisters to action. She must ignite a fire in their breasts. It was in preparation for this very night that Ma-we had so anxiously labored. Now destiny lay in the hands of her chosen one, her daughter of the darkness and the light.

Like the peal of a watchman's bell crashing upon quiet waters, Mihai began, her voice never faltering. "We have dreamed of the old world for too long. We, the children of the gods, have folded our hands in rest, sleeping on the soft pillows of self-denial while our enemy has worked laboriously to bring our destruction. The wine of our intoxicating drink has kept us drowsy and complacent. *Wake up!* The universe sits on the very edge of destruction! Each passing day draws us ever closer to extinction. It rests in our hands to save our world... all worlds... from the coming day of fire and fury!"

She lifted a hand, extending it toward Ma-we. "Our Mother, Lowenah – the Maker of men, Yehowah – the Fulfiller of promises, the One who shall become whatever is needed to become – has clearly informed us that she is forced by law - a law twisted by the deceit and treachery of our wicked brother - that she can not, will not directly intervene in the events of this coming hour to correct matters. Our world must wake to it… or… or our kind will die in our drunken slumber. If we do not effect the success of the coming hour, ourselves, all will be lost." She bowed her head in remorse. "But that hour has already passed. Our glory is diminished because of the treachery of our own hearts."

Without pause, she lifted her eyes to the crowd and cried out, "Tonight we must call out a curse upon our own hearts! The discord of evil that is tearing apart the fabric of the universe will soon destroy all living things!"

She lifted a fist high, shouting, "We must act now to stop it! *And damned be the present, past and future of our own selfish dreams!*"

A groaning sigh rippled across the auditorium, the people like a weathered, ancient tree, sagging under the weight of a tempestuous storm. There was no denying the need to prepare for the wrath of the coming fury, and none entertained the idea of shirking his or her personal responsibility. It was a question of strength. Did this people retain the energy to pick up the banner of war and dive, again, into Hell's fires?

Even Tizrela lowered her head, closing her eyes and seeing the grief anew in her weary mind. Well she remembered the hour and the day when she, leading a brigade of DinChizki's cavalry against the advancing enemy at Memphis, was pitched from her mount, her body shattered by a missile blast, how Din, himself, had ridden through the raging horde to provide rescue of her torn body, fearing her already dead. And so many others were never rescued, but lay scattered and broken across the tortured plain, their bones still littering the fields in front of Memphis to this day.

Yes, the aching and weariness from the last war, the Great War, still rested deep within the souls of Lowenah's loyal children. Just containing the enemy for those many years since the war ended had sapped what little energy remained in them. The thought of resurgence of hostilities, and even on a much grander scale, was more than many hearts felt able to bear. It was true, and no one doubted it, the fate of the universe rested on a fickle knife's edge, and they, the children of the gods, must bend that fate to do their will. A collective chill ran through the crowd at understanding what they must do to accomplish that deed, a somber awareness that suddenly made the room feel less cheerful, the shadows cold and dark.

All eyes fastened upon their new king. She, alone, could give them the power and strength to press on, to bring matters to a finish. This was one of Mihai's finest hours, always was when her fire was up. She made mistakes, wasn't the wisest of their leaders, took too many chances, risked everything on a whim. She was impetuous. Yet there was no one greater than Mihai when little hope could be found. She inspired her brothers and sisters to acts of courageous valor by her own outrageous valor.

In raging battles, when all was lost, with no hope remaining, the woman would stand up, raising her colors high, daring any to follow, leading the charge with the fury of an enraged lioness. Just seeing Mihai's ship or banner join the fight could change the outcome of a battle. She was the 'jewel of life, 'goddess divine'. She gave them life when there was no life remaining. She was the 'fire of the heavens' that burned away all doubt and fear. The woman could make her people crave the field of slaughter as one does a lost lover. On her rested all hope. She would lead the way tonight. She would show them how to survive the coming tempest. She would show them how to win this greatest of all battles. This was her coming war. This was going to be the King's War.

The room had become as still as the tombs of yesterday's heroes. All waited upon the moment. Mihai lowered her head, her eyes studying her hands as if the secrets of the future were hidden in them. In time, she looked up into the faces of those sitting in the bleachers, the sadness of the hour carving deep furrows in her forehead, making the new king appear aged like the mountains.

She now began to pace the raised circle, stopping at times to address parts of the audience. From deep within a heart that burned with eagerness of the moment and lamentations of the ages, a majestic power arose in Mihai's voice that signaled the crowd to pay heed to what their ruling prophet was about to reveal. Cold and clear her words rang out. "Prophecy speaks of a great warrior who will crush our enemy to nothing!"

Mihai studied the people's reaction, then shook her head. "*I* am not that warrior." She paused again. "He will come from a realm beyond ours, a realm ever filled with violence, war, and hatred. In his land, love is little more than a word used to speak of the romantic devotion shared between a man and woman. It is a wretched land, having never known peace, plagued with disease and death, the very gifts this warrior will deliver to us. He will ride with a host more fearsome than the enemies we face… have ever faced… and who care nothing for the past we have loved so much. This host will deride the fearful and they will sneer at the cowards and dreamers. Yes, they will look with disdain upon our weaknesses, for our failure to bring to ruin what most certainly should have been brought to ruin. Maidens and old men he will trample as though mere blades of grass."

Mihai lowered her head as if in shame, slowing shaking it. "…Something that we could have done, but our hearts refused to permit us to do."

Lifting her head up to reveal a fire burning in her eyes, Mihai raised her hand high, crying, "The prophets of his world call him 'Apollyon the Destroyer', but our Ancients address him as 'Shiloh'!"

Mihai cast her eyes toward the floor and began to pace anew. "Who this man is, this person, we do not know. Our Mother has chosen it to be so. But I tell you, this man lives even now, as I speak. He is the *Finished Mystery*, the *Sacred Secret*. He will take up the commander's staff and sit down on the very seat of the Firstborn."

She looked into the faces of the surprised council, resting her gaze upon her mother's. "I have neither the strength nor desire to stand such a post anymore."

Turning again to the stunned, silent crowd, Mihai declared, "Today I have accepted the lordship promised to me long ago. This frees up law so that our mother may move ahead with her purposes so that she can, once and for all, bring down the one that tries to destroy us."

Mihai slammed a fist into her opened hand, shouting, "It belongs to *us*, the *children of the gods*, to defend these realms against our brother's evil until Shiloh arrives!"

Much to Mihai's surprise, the room erupted in ecstatic applause, many standing and shouting their approval. Some hugged each other while some cried with joy or shook their fists in defiance. So, the tired and weary were being filled with renewed energy. Mihai had feared the worst, believing her speech would have a detrimental effect on the people. It proved to be just the opposite, for the people were rejoicing in open celebration.

The celebrants fully understood the meaning of Mihai's warning words. They also knew the blow would be crushing for Lowenah's children. What they did not yet realize was that the hammer would strike hardest upon the very ones gathered here this night. Few would survive to see Shiloh arrive, their torn and ruined bodies scattered across dozens of star systems, surrendered to a cause to hold at bay the four winds of destruction until Shiloh's day. Had they known, it would have mattered little on this eve, for the children could see the future promised day as if it had already come and… and their new king would be leading them toward it.

Mihai waited for the energy of the moment to subside, seeking the exact instant to begin again. At length, it arrived. "Faith is not a possession of all. Many of our kind have surrendered to the Fates and whims of doubt, believing it is futile to continue a fight that will only end in failure. But you… you have not listened to the foolish prattle of the Wicked Snake… have not allowed him to corrupt your hearts with hopelessness. You, my brothers, have acted through this desperate age on the faith that all the promises our mother has promised will eventually be realized."

"Tonight… *tonight*…" Mihai's voice was choked off by a nervous constriction in her throat. Her mouth refused to permit the coming words. A heart begging for reprieve from the wanton slaughter and violence screamed out to the mind, telling it to be silent about the matter and to give the people what they wanted to hear…that peace would come some other way, a more kindly and gentler way. Suddenly, two separate visions flashed into Mihai's eyes, each playing its fated outcome simultaneously. Two roads loomed before the woman, one the way of the heart, the other of the mind.

Mihai watched in awe seeing the two unfold before her. First there was the one she and her kind so badly wanted. Easy it was to travel as it swept her along its green and flowered pathway. 'Peace! Peace!' was the cry upon the breeze, promising all a return to the old ways before their universe was torn asunder, with all souls, all lovers, all lives, returned to a glorious, forgetful past. But, as she sped along, an ominous, dark, foreboding, swirling gloom loomed ahead, sending the woman into a stifling, black nothingness from which there was no returning.

Oh, but how much worse the second road was… maddening and destructive! It tore at Mihai's senses, her very sanity. Ghastly scenes of horror and devastation flashed up at her. From every direction, fire and storm enveloped her. The cries of the dying filled her ears while unspeakable sights pummeled her soul. Disembodied voices called out accusingly, 'It is you! You have brought this torment upon us!' At length, a calm settled in, revealing that the road traveled on into gloomy uncertainty, but not total hopelessness.

Mihai opened her eyes to see Ma-we staring at her from a distance. She knew that the visions were no random events of a confused brain trying to grasp reality by sorting out possibilities of future decisions. Ma-we had given her child the visions just now, to show her daughter that there was no guarantee for a happy ending of coming events, but that hope existed by taking only one road, the one most feared and loathed. She nodded at her mother, a resolve growing in her breast to make the right decision, the only decision.

"Tonight…" She began again, her voice sounding with that resolve, "Tonight I present evidence to you that your faith has not been in vain. Even now, the very army of which I have spoken is being gathered for the tempest. Even now, they stand amongst us, waiting to take their places as our leaders, our new mentors." Mihai then shouted, *They will teach us how to gather to ourselves the anger and the rage of God the Almighty!*"

Again, much to Mihai's surprise, the room filled with the wild roar of approval. When all was quiet, she continued. "Long ago, before there was a world of men, the Ancients told of a prophecy that, should the universe fall into darkness, there would be fulfilled upon those who survived to this current day the glory of the ending hour. It has been no secret, but few have remembered it other than in a child's nursery rhyme. A phrase, as you may recall speaks thusly…

'And when the sun is blotted out,
The three moons of Sharon shall give us light.
And by their blades of burnished hue,
They shall lead forth in glory's fight.'

"As you well know, Sharon means, literally, 'Mother of low stones', or 'Maker of lowly light'. It is said by some of the Ancients that there once existed a star system which was ruled over by a kingly race of seers and wizards. Chief among the planets of this mythical universe was one called 'Lagandow', the capital of this race's empire. Hanging high above the sky of this long-forgotten world was a moon surrounded by three radiant rings, brilliant in reflective hues of red, green and yellow, which they cast down upon the fields and hills of Lagandow."

"In the fables told to us when we were children, it was said that the moon's name, when translated into our common tongue was called 'Sharon' and the rings, or children, were named for the color each emitted: 'Ruby', 'Jade' and 'Gold'. Collectively, they were heralded as the 'Blades of Light'. When the moon shown its brightest, the three children would almost disappear from sight. But when dark shadows enveloped their mother, the children would shout out their glory like blazing fires, lighting the night's sky. At least that is as I remember the tale being told." She glanced at PalaHar, who smiled and gave a nod.

"My Brethren, those of you who have supported me upon the field of slaughter, and those of you who I have sat in council with, and all here who have held true to our cause over these countless centuries, the world in which we live has been cast into darkness and foreboding. No longer does our light shine forth, cutting through the gloom of evil that surrounds us. The hour has come. The hour when our *children* must become the beacons of light, guiding our universe toward its final destiny."

"It was also said of the three flaming blades that, should the universe become darkened, should the glory of the sun fade, the fires of the blades would continue to shine upon the ruins of Lagandow as a sign that not all was forsaken, but that hope remained as long as love moved the hearts of Lowenah's children. My brothers…" Mihai raised her voice. "*Our love for our mother has not wavered! Our hope is sure!*"

Again the uproar of approval and applause from the crowd forced Mihai to pause until it subsided.

"There are…" Mihai caught her breath to ease a growing excitement in her heart. "There are three Swords to be taken from the world beyond, the underworld of this universe, which, like Sharon, is a reflection of our own world… our own souls. They have been fashioned into the form of all mankind, but have been tempered in the forges of Hell by the very tortures from our brother's sick mind. To them there is a giving of power and strength beyond that of mortals, beyond our own power and strength. Like their lord, Shiloh, they laugh at danger and distress, for their souls have become like the wizards of Lagandow, their fathers. They do not fear death, for death is become their slave. They are become the wielders of death, the destroyers of souls!"

The room cried out its deafening silence. No one spoke. No one dared. This news was queer and unnerving. Oh yes, the tales of Lagandow were well known and the rings of Sharon were symbols of hope, but other than metaphor? And the wizards of Lagandow, spoken of as being real? True, some related them to the Cherubs, machines of Lowenah's, living machines, maybe, but machines to do her bidding…at least that was the belief of many of Lowenah's children. They, the children, were the *first* real offspring of Mother, the *first* to have a heart and soul. At least that was what many assumed.

Some in the room did not wear an expression of shock, but remained silent, caring not to reveal their personal feelings. Mihai again looked at PalaHar, sitting silently, leaned back in his chair, hands folded in his lap. It was he who long ago told an inquisitive child the tales of Lagandow and of the strange fellows who ruled the worlds from before time. He painted such vivid pictures, the girl even now could see the cities and wonders of that world in her mind.

And there were others: Gabrielle, Terey, Tizrela, and those like them, quirky and different in comparison to the other children, especially the younger ones. They were always aloof, speaking little of the First Age, of when they were children, that is, except for PalaHar. He made story and rhyme of those days. Indeed, as Mihai thought about it, it was from books written by him that what little knowledge of the First Age was revealed to the younger children was mostly through song and riddle.

Mihai had believed those stories until… until the ages of bliss and adventure clouded them from her mind. Only in the occasional dream-share with PalaHar were they revived, but then for only a moment. When cresting the tidal surge during the ecstasy of their lovemaking, how easy it was to believe in strange and wondrous things when only a child. No. Wait! Somehow she felt there was truth hidden in those riddling rhymes, and that was why her heart was forced to speak of them this eve. Was there really a power or force that drove the ships of destiny, and all the children needed do was remain aboard at their stations, staying whatever course those powers chose to take?

And Lagandow was *real*, at least according to the history books. The burning of Lagandow marked the official end of the First Age and the beginning of the Second. All the calendars began with that date, when the fires of the supernova reached the eyes of those living on EdenEsonbar. That was the zero date for all timetables. Even Gradian's Clock was reset to measure from that day forward. There was no official history predating that event, only the fables and tales told by the Ancients living back then. Mihai's heart told her that PalaHar spoke truth concerning the past, truth hidden in mirth and prose. She believed her heart was telling those truths, too, this eve - truths designed to bring hope to tired souls.

Awaking from her inner thoughts with a jolt, Mihai looked up to see hundreds of anxious faces anticipating coming revelations. She did not keep the people waiting. "Of those blades, those Swords, one walks among you even now, hiding in the shadows of your thoughts, observing all ways and searching out our secrets. Her blade strikes like a rapier, plunging deep into the hearts of those who hate us. Already her sword has been baptized in the blood of our enemy, its insatiable thirst only awakening. The manliness of Godenn will be consumed in her wrath, their slaughter extending along the broadways of the stars. She, this Sword, will open the path for the Queen of Darkness who will bring that evil man to nothing during his greatest hour of glory."

A quiet moan of lament rose from the voices of the women in the crowd and a cry of anger arose from the men. Godenn was a notorious, sadistic murderer of Lowenah's loyal children - any child, for that matter, if it suited his fancy. He often skinned his captives alive, torturing them for days before releasing their bodies to death. But he reserved his cruelest practices for the women in the land, he having abandoned their flesh long ago, blaming them for his ulcers and inflammations.

He would cut off the breasts of his sisters, while still alive, cooking them for his lieutenants to feast upon. Often, at these same celebrations, he would deliver the female captives up for sport, heaping upon them every sort of humiliation and violence the mind could conjure, even to the point of forcing them to eat the female parts torn from their fellow sisters. Godenn was the commanding field officer at Memphis when Mihai's army suffered defeat and rout at its gates. He openly meted out to the wounded on the field his most vile forms of torture, forcing Mihai's soldiers to watch, helpless to prevent them.

But who was the Queen of Darkness? Mihai did not say, nor did she know. In fact, when later asked concerning it, she did not recall speaking about such a person.

Hurrying on, Mihai spoke of another Sword, a second. "It is yet to come, but lives as I speak. Her power is in her anger that is yet to be realized. A female cub born, a female cub she is, but to be like a grieving she-bear, crushing and smashing in her madness, she will become. In her fiery fury, cities will melt and lands will become desolate. Woman and old man will quail as she rages forth from her den to bring to nothing all living things. She will devour the flower of Memphis, burning its ramparts and shattering its fortress towers. Only in that hour, when she carries the head of Legion in her own hands, will the she-bear finally find rest, making that city her own."

The crowd sat stunned, many with mouth agape. The ruthlessness of Legion against Ma-we's loyal children was well known. His glory was nearly that of Asotos, but for cruelty, none could compare. Second in command over the League of Brothers, and chief among the wizards and warlocks, few rivaled his secret knowledge of the universe and his uncanny powers at controlling that knowledge. No one dared face him in mortal combat, the man's abilities being extraordinary. Even Gabrielle and Mihai, in their many wars against him, had failed to defeat the man or retake the stolen city of Memphis.

Through deceit, murder and treachery, Legion secured his power within the League of Brothers, finally taking Memphis by force of arms to make that holy city his capital, taking the title 'Sagamore De Warlock' – *the greatest magician* – by doing so, forever corrupting the titles of the Ancients who taught the science of EbenCeruboam. With his proximity to Eden's Gate, greatest of all the portals, Legion immersed himself in toying with the children of the Lower Realms, something he reveled in until the Children's Empire wrested the portal away from him during the Three Hundred Year's War.

Legion was sly and cruel, playing victims like a cat does a mouse. No greater was this displayed than the way he practiced this on the hapless men and women of the Second Realm. For sport, he would use his learned powers to take control of unsuspecting minds and force them to practice upon themselves and others every sort of abominable perversion. He instigated the building of massive arenas used for the sport of slaughter, then offered, for a price, to his rebel brothers the opportunity to feel the thrill of the people's suffering. It was in one of these slaughter pens that the creature destined to bring Legion's eventual demise was brought to birth by the fiery forge hammers of Legion's own hand.

Mihai moved on quickly, allowing little time for the people to contemplate the meaning of her prophecy concerning the second Sword. She lifted her arm, waving her hand to draw the people's attention away from their own inner ponderings and back to her. "I have taken up a scepter of authority given me by the One and Only *true* Authority of this world… of all worlds. Reluctantly it was, with much trepidation, my hand reached out for the power of this kingly duty, knowing how frail a child resides within this mortal body. I ask you, will you honor our mother by also acknowledging the kingship she has given me?"

Euroaquilo stood, shouting, "To the ends of the universe and beyond! See, our king and our god!"

Applause and shouting mingled in a confusing chorus of jumbled approval coming from the crowd. Smiles and tears, nodding heads...not one person disapproved. All here had waited for this day to come. Knowing now what it meant for this universe, all accepted the future it would deliver upon them.

Mihai's face flushed red. She quietly nodded then, turning to her mother, bowed, lowering her crown in symbol of showing who the true King and God of this universe was. Ma-we smiled, holding back tears. This was her chosen daughter, most loved, most cherished. This was to be the second time she would allow her to face the Dragon unto death, if not in the flesh, at least in the spirit. Oh, how her heart ached with pride!

Mihai replaced the crown and stared up at the people. Not hesitating, she cried, "My acceptance of this kingly crown frees up law! Our Eternal King can now hand over to me... to us... Shiloh's Sword, to wield as befits the Children's Empire until that man shall arrive and take up his rightful station on his throne. That Sword will not fail us! Born in the depths of Hell and raised to the heavens, 'Ruby' is the name of this blade, the ring that swaddles her mother in a protective glow. Red is the blood of the enemy it slays as it goes forth in a rage to bring ruin upon those who have ruined this world."

Excitement grew in Mihai's voice. "She will teach us how to hate! She will teach us how to repay vengeance! *She...she will teach us all the ways of the North!*" Calling out with a beseeching command, Mihai asked, "Will you permit me the right to give glory to that Sword so that it might live in power? Will you follow her leadership, unquestioningly, no matter where she may lead you?"

The noise from the crowd rose to a deafening tumult, overwhelmingly approving Mihai's request. The world was now forever changed. The end... the end, the final fury was begun. True, it might take years to bring it to a finish, but this time, this war...this was not a war to merely hold the enemy at bay. The death knell for Asotos was sounded. When the smoke cleared, before they could count their dead, the League of Brothers would be driven from this universe. It was now only a matter of time.

Above the din, Mihai shouted, waving her hand, "*See! See, the Sword in my hand! The 'Smashing Hammer'!*"

A hush filled the room as anxious eyes scanned for this Sword of promise. No one moved. Was the person really here, or was Mihai speaking only in symbols? Time seemed to stand still, even breathing became labored. Yet no one stirred. The look on Mihai's face did not change. No, the king's Sword was real. It must be! But was it? Mihai's arm had not moved. All eyes followed the direction it was pointing, right toward Ma-we's council table.

Finally, after Tizrela nudged someone beside her, a demure woman, small in stature and delicate in appearance slowly stood. Wide-eyed, the shocked crowd stared, the insignia of field marshal emblazoned upon the woman's sleeve, shouting its presence while challenging all power and authority in the room. Some gasped, others moaned within themselves, but most were too overwhelmed with wonder to do more than stare.

This was the moment Ma-we had been waiting for. Before they could gather their senses, she cast a most powerful spell over the room. A vision extraordinary flashed from Trisha's eyes, blazing its radiant storm into the furthest corners of the theater. Like a hurricane, its passionate fury ripped at the very fiber of the people's being, tearing into and through them, sweeping everyone along in its tempest. Out beyond the walls of this chamber, past the city, far into space, until the galaxy itself was only a tiny dot lost in a very large universe, the vision took them, Trisha's fiery eyes glowing blinding crimson red, ever heating the raging maelstrom surrounding them.

A voice, low in tone but powerful in intensity, filled their ears with a disquieting moan, 'You have come to this. There is no turning back!'

Moments became centuries, centuries turned into millenniums and millenniums heaped upon millenniums until time was lost beyond time. The voice chanted out in forgotten song:

"And Sharon weeps because of her daughter, for she has become strong and ruthless.
Shall Lagandow not rise again and bring an ending to all matters?
And look! The bow of the Watchers is broken so that its arrows have failed.
Who will bring a healing into death now so that my children shall stand on high again?

Oh Watcher, oh Watcher, see the Sword that delivers death and brings renewed life.
Your blood shall it seek to bring your salvation, and by your death shall all things live again.
My daughter burns bright with the blood of all men, for she does bring ruin to all flesh.
Give glory to her, for she alone shall rescue me in this hour of darkness.
And Ruby is death, and Ruby is dawn, and Ruby is blood in death and in life."

As soon as the chant ended, another began, this time from beneath Trisha's fiery, burning orbs.

"Shall the moth call out to the eagle and yet live?

I say I am the moth, come to devour the eagle, its young, and even
its prey!
Who shall stand against the crimson tide, or speak against the fires
of a tormented earth?
Who shall defy the gods and yet live, or touch the sun and not
become burned?
Look!'
'I', says the moth, 'shall do all these things and will yet do more!
I shall drink down the tide and pour it out upon my enemy.
I shall catch up the molten fires of the earth and pitch them into the
sea to bring all flesh to nothing.
I shall spit into faces of those calling themselves 'gods' and eat up
their fleshy parts.
And look and become afraid, for I shall quench the fires of the sun
and make the world of men dark and foreboding.
Look and become afraid,
For I am the moth that has become the mountain wall of Yehowah!
In my rage, I will bring all matters to a finish.
Come! See my anger!"

Instantly, before the people's eyes, the universe began to spin crazily, showing them in a moment of time all the days of the First Age, they hearing the warnings of the glowing spirits of God. Along they were taken until the carefree hours of the Second Age had fallen into the turbulent despair of the Third, and on they were swept. With the screeching of a banshee-wind, they were hurried forward, past the final battle at Memphis, the ending of the last war, this very evening, and far through the blackness of unborn time until… until they stood upon the precipice of some future day, to the End of Days.

Spellbound, all eyes peered out into the boiling clouds of sulfur and smoke and down onto the limitless plain below. To their terror and amazement, the people watched the valley plain erupt in fire and ruin as the surging mountain upon which they rode rampaged across the land. Screeching wind covered up the cries of the slain as armies and cities disappeared into the tumultuous storm the mountain chased, only to be vomited out from that very storm as overflowing rivers of blood.

"Deliver their souls to Hades' gates!" a disembodied voice shouted.

At that, the mountain tore loose from itself giant boulders, flinging them down upon fleeing hordes seeking escape, torn asunder or burned to ash when the boulders erupted in explosive flames. Those who escaped the rage of the mountain and the burning missiles were consumed in the mountain's anger as it released upon the entire plain scorpions and creeping things borne from the very mountain but hungry for the flesh of all living creatures.

And behold! Look! To everyone's amazement, leading the battle charge, riding amidst the creatures of the abyss was a helmed, female warrior, mounted on a fiery red warhorse, brandishing a long, blood-drenched sword. Darkened red with the blood of the slain, the woman's hair trailed in the wind, striking the enemy as with the sting of a scorpion's tail, her eyes casting a burning light upon the enemy, dissolving all flesh from off their bones.

Raising the sword high, the warrior urged her army onward, shouting, *"Forward on to death! Faster! Faster! To the end! Fear not their steel nor their blade! Damn them! Send them all to Gehenna's Gate!"*

Despite the maddening speed of the creeping hordes boiling up from the mountain's fiery belly, it kept pace, crushing friend and foe, any who fell behind, caring not for man or woman, wild or domestic beast, the weak or the strong. A voice coming out from the midst of the scorpions and creeping things, following up closely behind the helmed rider cried out, *'Fear not the beasts or those who rule their kingdom! Fear the makers of hosts, the kings of darkness who shed light upon those they choose and bring gloom upon the faint of heart, for we are the kings over your minds! Your nightmares are our playgrounds. Fear us, for ours is the night and the day. Good we can gift or bad. It is our choice!'*

The vision sped along, leaving those witnessing it standing alone upon a torn and tortured plain. As thunderous convulsions of the angry mountain echoed into the distance, a calm and peaceful quiet grew around them, easing the pain and dread that had enveloped their hearts. Dark clouds of a foreboding night gradually faded into a shadowy morning filled with promise.

Suddenly, without warning, a blazing sun burst above the horizon, bathing the world in its comforting glow, to their amazement and joy, the heavens a radiant blue, cloudless, and the air humming with songs of countless birds. At that very moment, a great trembling could be felt as the land literally erupted with life for as far as the eye could see. A jungle filled this musical universe until the land overflowed with every form of growing thing. Never had the eyes of these children seen such variety and color that only a vision of the gods could make. Never could their hearts forget this moment so overpowering in majesty.

While the people gazed upon the surrounding beauty, they began to recognize that a whispering tune wafted upon the gentle breeze, a long-forgotten lullaby sung to them by their mother when they were small, too small to understand all the big things in the world around them. It went something like this:

'Why, my dear one, do you cry,
at the things you cannot see or touch?
I swaddle you in my loving arms,
so no harm can you betide.

Do not dread what you do not know,
or hide from the darkened night.
I ever so much will care for you,
in my worlds of rich delights.

Listen, my child, to my heartbeat,
to the rhythm of love it shares with you.
Nuzzle close to my breasts with milk so sweet,
and hear my heart's love for you.'

The sweet refrains of the melodious tune, dancing upon the fields of honeysuckle, clover and daisies, calmed the children's hearts concerning the previous visions. Soon they were little more than distant memories, like troubling childhood dreams. Working like some powerful drug on a tired mind, the musical words played on each person's soul, each one drifting into his or her private trance or dream. This was the state the people found themselves in, as if waking from a deep, restful sleep, when the vision returned them through time and space back to the Hall of Assembly and the moment.

Trisha had not moved, but was standing quietly beside her chair just as she had been before igniting the firestorm in the hearts of Ma-we's children. Her eyes carried no expression of what the people had experienced, but her face revealed knowledge of the event. Was this woman, small of stature, quiet by nature, and with beauty of face that rivaled the gods, truly as dangerous as the vision depicted? The children stared at their mother, sitting motionless, a twinkle in her eyes the only clue that she was responsible for the previous adventure. Then, what of the field marshal? Who was she, really, and what kind of a person was she?

Before the others could collect their thoughts, a booming voice filled the room, calling out, *"Behold 'The Mountain Wall of Yehowah!' See, the king's Sword, Foe Hammer, does live and stand among us! Kiss the Lady who has given us hope and bow low to her mistress who will deliver it!"* At that, Euroaquilo stood and bowed low at the waist, first toward Ma-we and then toward Trisha.

Other voices broke the silence, shouting, "Give her glory! Yes! Give glory to the One who has promised to become whatever she must to bring all things to a finish. *Give Yehowah glory!*"

Soon the entire throng had broken into laughter and song. The Maker of dreams had given them visions of the future. They would win! The universe would not end nor would their labors have been in vain. The room erupted in celebration unseen since the armistice ending the Great War. Mihai watched with pleasure the joyous tumult. In the end there was little to do other than formally accept Trisha as the new field marshal and pledge all fealty to her, as Mihai had requested. This was concluded by having Trisha take her position on the raised platform before Mihai, she handing authority as Field Marshal and Dictator En Force over to her. When finished, Mihai bowed low and returned to the council table.

There were many matters yet to be discussed and Trisha wasted little time getting down to them. In short order, the minor agenda items were concluded, appointments of deputies and magistrates being little more than formalities. Other items were as quickly dispatched. Trisha's knowledge of the children's customs and protocols was shown in the way she carried out business. Other than the unusual speed at which things were covered, she had done acceptably well, leaving most with the feeling that this outsider understood her place among the wisest of Ma-we's children. Now, though, for the real test… Trisha must prove her leadership abilities in dealing with the upcoming business of the Prisoner Exchange.

Asotos had initiated the idea of a prisoner exchange and even its location, the lonely desert planet, EremiaPikros, that sat on the interstellar border between his nation called the 'League of Brothers' and Ma-we's - now Mihai's - called 'The Children's Empire'… a no-man's land of sorts, uninhabited except for the occasional short-lived ore colony or fur trader searching out the giant phimoosmurna desert rat, trapped for its tough, leathery hide and musk glands located behind its jowls, used in making In-tarajarta myrrh.

Asotos had not attempted a prisoner exchange since the end of the Great War. Oh yes, his treachery in dealing with the children loyal to the Empire was notorious, but always clandestine. Abductions and murder were still favorite tools he employed when the mood struck him, but he always managed to keep his hands clean, feigning innocence in any conflict with or intrusion into the Children's Empire. This time it was different.

Five months before, the howker, PuszzZet, and gun-buses, Gihon and SarahMay, later joined by the cutter, Midnight, out of Exothepobole, engaged the barquentine, Righteous Knight, as it tried escaping back across the Frontier after pirating several merchant ships in the Outer Corridor, southeast of the Trizentine. A heated contest ensued, with the Righteous Knight eventually striking its colors after its engine and boiler rooms were disabled and life support systems failed. The capture of the Righteous Knight and its seventeen surviving crew provided clear evidence that Asotos was clandestinely violating the terms of the Armistice ending the Great War.

Asotos, of course, denied any act of aggression on his part and charged that the captain of the Righteous Knight was acting against orders, an easy accusation to make seeing that the man was killed in recent combat. This would have been the end of matters, the loss of an old barquentine and its few surviving crewmembers, except Legion, Asotos' top lieutenant, was livid, having some very close confidants aboard, including Salak Taqadam, a leading statesman and immediate lieutenant to Godenn, Legion's second in command. He demanded that Asotos return his people to him, no matter the cost, thus forcing Asotos to: one, admit there might have been some misunderstanding on the captain's part as to what his orders really were; and two, find a way to even the odds to make a prisoner exchange sway in his favor.

In the meantime, Mihai had ordered the carrier, DorshanBerry, and its task force to steam hard for the Trizentine in case hostilities should erupt in the region. Instead, Asotos averted a direct conflict by 'picking the plum', instigating the capture of the Zephath's crew by an armed contingency of Stasis Pirates who, for a sufficient price, handed over their prisoners to Asotos' people. By luck, Sirion, a most loved companion of Mihai, was included among the prizes he obtained. It was after this discovery that Asotos began to hatch his big plan, using a prisoner exchange to accomplish it.

The new field marshal was little interested in the details concerning the Prisoner Exchange, she already having formulated a strategy. There was mischief afoot and the woman knew it. For forty years she had studied Asotos' intrigues, concluding that his primary method of operation was intimidation, consolation and finally, if all else failed, play the part of the victim. Few of Ma-we's children were able to one-up his wily ways, but Trisha had a plan, one she had no intention of sharing, especially tonight. Ma-we knew, realizing just how foolhardy, reckless and possibly damning it might be.

No matter what Trisha thought, she was no match for Asotos, her powers still underdeveloped and weak. But would Asotos know that, having never been so boldly confronted other than by Gabrielle, one who nearly equaled him in glory and power? If the new field marshal truly realized what danger she might be in, would the woman be able to pull off such a dangerous coup? Ma-we smiled. Trisha was oblivious to the depth of Asotos' magic, thus ignorant of the danger. She might just succeed.

Trisha scanned the crowd, studying faces, most showing more the curiosity of children watching some strange creature under a looking glass than their new leader. Few reflected the respect or caring that had been given to Mihai when she controlled the stage. Others hid contempt behind placid eyes, wishing for this *bug* to fly away and bother them no more. Most, though, just sat quietly, politely, waiting and contemplating what this human specimen from the forgotten Realms Below had to offer when she stood the platform alone, when Mother did not hold sway with her magic.

Trisha knew, as did all present, that Mother's witchery was finished. Now the truth would be revealed. For thousands of years, prophecy concerning a coming ruler and his three Swords of justice that preceded him had been whispered among the people. For the many, their hope that had been in what was called Mother's 'new creation' raised to life, as was told in the ancient myths and stories, to see the armies beyond the heavens swoop in to save the universe lost. Never was it assumed that children of dust, born in contempt and raised up in sickness and death should be the holy knights brought to rid their world of evil. Now Trisha must wake them to this fact. She and her kind held the fate of all creation, living and dead, in their hands. It had been left up to this woman to prove it, starting tonight.

All these things Trisha could see... feel, you might say. For forty years she had felt it, the sudden quiet of a wardroom when she entered unannounced, the polite dismissal of her opinions during council, even the coolness often felt when at general mess. She had done nothing to deserve such treatment. She should not be the cause of the children's resentment. They had failed to bring evil to its end and their mother, her God, decided to use other forces to accomplish that. Trisha never asked to be brought here. She did not deserve such treatment.

Her eyes narrowed in thought. Weren't these the 'guardians of the universe', the very faces of God that faithful, honest men like John had once bowed to in honor? Who were *they* to look down on her and the others of her kind gathered into their world? Well, tonight they would not dare to look down on her again! The universe was now changed. Trisha's hands closed into tense fists.

Tears welled up in Trisha's eyes. *'Harlot!' 'Whore! 'Adulteress!'* She had long ago paid for that one night of love, one night of bliss out of a lifetime of toil, pain and grief. For that one night, she suffered the stares of the village people, the whispers as she passed, the quiet rooms she entered. For one night - one night when she was held by a man who really loved her, for one night that her heart smiled - she had paid, been forced to pay the bigots and belligerent people who considered themselves so superior to this... this... creature, this *polluter* of their perfect world. Tonight she again felt the stares of those believing themselves superior to her.

Fighting back tears, Trisha forced a smile of defiance. Tonight... tonight was to be different! Tonight the universe would be waked by a force greater than any experienced by these people! When finished this eve, *things would be different!* The people of this world might not love her or respect her, but they would certainly fear her... her and all her kind settled into this universe!

Ma-we frowned in sadness, remembering a conversation spoken in the solitude of a darkened room on a breathless night. 'You have delivered the storm to this world. Did you not know that your children would bleed, theirs souls scattered across the star systems by this righteous evil from the depths below?' And then the final whispers in her ear. 'A ruin, a ruin, a ruin I shall make it. Are they not your very prophecies made upon your own children? Let matters run their course. Allow the girl to grow into a woman. She will one day come to love your children, but the blood must first flow. Death precedes life. Remember? The seed must die to be born again in fruit. Let her winnow the field with an iron rod so that your children shall remember this day and never permit wickedness to rise again.'

Ma-we bowed her head, sighing to herself, "It's time. Lift the sword and unleash the midnight..." Unlike their earlier visions, the people were now to see the *real Sword, Ruby,* unsheathed, its true shimmering metal revealed in all its naked glory.

Clasping her hands behind her back, Trisha began to slowly pace the circular platform, the hard heels of her boots singing out sharply as they hit the polished marble floor. '*Click! Click! Click! Click!*' Round and round the woman walked, creating a harmonic chant that her steps painfully hammered into hundreds of distraught ears. As rushing of blood roaring through a restless mind on a silent night, the piercing tempest grew maddening on the weary souls gathered in the chamber.

At the very moment a body felt it would implode into insanity, Trisha stopped, silent. Then, slowly turning away from the crowd, looking at the closed doorway as though expecting someone to enter, she began, cold and expressionless as a frost-laden morning. The latent power of immeasurable strength hiding within her breasts lay just beneath the surface, each word, each phrase hinting at its explosive anger. They were deceptively innocent to the ears, but they burned with a warning of the power of the beast within that panted to be unleashed.

"As you know, the Zephath fell victim to the vicious attacks of a Stasis Pirate fleet, the crew scuttling it before their capture." She spun around, facing the surprised crowd. "What *fool* believes that!? No pirate fleet in this universe has the power to take on a ship the size of the Zephath! The Stasis are cowards! *Cowards!* If confronted by such a war-craft, they'd *piss* in their boots!"

The people gasped at Trisha's crude way with words at such a formal event. She paid no attention to them.

The new field marshal went on to disclose the extent of information the investigation uncovered, from distress signals to finding the ship's log, Mihai's adventures as she followed the enemy's trail. When the woman had finished providing an overview of the capture of the crew and Asotos' contacting the Children's Empire seeking a parley, she addressed the council as to their responsibilities.

The new commander of Mihai's armies turned toward the wise and the aged, a tone of motherly disappointment dancing on her tongue. "It is not the responsibility of this council to conclude what happened, something, I suppose, that could consume many evenings and mornings of social posturing and debate. You must decide this very eve, and not tomorrow, on what shall be done and how, and who shall confront the Dragon."

Some faces reddened in anger, others clouded with discontent. Mihai frowned, staring down at her clasped hands resting on the table. Ma-we smiled to herself. 'About time someone stirred the fire of self-content...'

Trisha began pointing and waving her hands with appropriate gestures. "The Dragon plays with your minds while he hides his true machinations in the shadows and uses your innocence and naivete to mislead you. He is too evil to lie with boldness, but twists your minds and hearts with truth hidden in riddles and deceit. By leaving you clues that he believes only a fool would overlook, he justifies his treachery and cruelty toward all of you."

The new field marshal was not winning any friends. A cold disquiet was growing in the room, and it would only become more intense. Staring directly into Mihai's eyes, Trisha accused, "Even the greatest of your warriors has walked, do walk blindly into harm's way because they fail - or are unwilling - to understand their brother's tricks."

Mihai looked away, shamed by Trisha's blatant truthfulness.

Trisha paid no visible heed as she spoke to the entire body of councilors, staring first one and then another in the eyes. "You see the signs, but do not understand them. You allow your brother to play the puppet-master over your minds by doing his bidding. Some of you fall to his evil and do not get back up. Some of you have fallen, but still cry loyalty to your cause."

She stared at Euroaquilo. "Others have fallen, do fall, but take the blow and learn, and survive to fight another time." Turning and looking up at the crowd, she cried, *"Any who forget why they are fighting and the evil their enemy possesses will fall!"*

Silence! The beast had stopped disgorging its fire for the moment. Trisha began to slowly and deliberately pace anew. Head down, with hands clasped behind her back, the woman retraced her steps around the outer ring of the raised circular platform. Again, the harmonic rhythm of the *'click'* of her boots played out to the audience, but quieter and more subdued this time. When she stopped, it was to face and again address the seated council.

Trisha's piercing gaze searched the councilors, they reacting as if a personal message was being delivered upon each one of them. Some turned to glance away, others glared defiance and disapproval while still others slowly closed their eyes as if surrendering to acknowledging a secret failure. And a few smiled, nodding approval.

Finally, Trisha's eyes fell upon Mihai. A chill flooded Mihai's mind, like a cold winter wind preceding a tempest. Out of the wind, a voice called, "He is waiting for you… Do you not see the adder at your heel? He has done all these things because of you. Beware the morning of your new life and fear the last hours of your childhood. Accept your death into a new life and be aware of the hour of ascent, the hour of despair."

Mihai tried turning away from Trisha's daunting stare, but could not -

not until Trisha permitted it. The haunting voice pummeled her more. "This time you must face the *beast*... and he will strike you a mortal blow. Take the blow and keep on living. Do not strike back! Do not strike back! Take the blow in death and all will live. Be warned! If you listen to your heart, all will be lost. Be silent and your sister may live."

All eyes looked to Mihai as she let out a cry, lifting a hand to her head. Her hands began to shake as sweat collected on her face, running in tiny rivulets from her chin. The people's eyes slowly shifted away from their beloved king to the ominous figure standing before them. Who was this creature from forgotten lands? How could a woman so unimpressive in stature and, though beautiful, but not outstandingly so - how could she command such power? There was something more about her, something so base and vile, carrying with her the smell of death like the unforgiven souls of the damned, the Stasis and lost, the demons haunting their world.

Trisha cried out to those gathered, "*Stand down and do not listen to your hearts!*"

Was there a tone of love and compassion in this creature's voice? Many wished it would be so, the witch standing before them charging them with the error of ages, condemning their kind for being poor stewards. A shudder ran through the crowd, - a mind, twisted, they could feel. It was as if the madness of the Dragon, himself, was breathing upon their flesh, burning away all hope. But there was more about this woman that seared their bellies and tore at their hearts. Her very words carried the smell of bloodlust upon them, a craving for war, death and destruction. This woman was yearning for war, for slaughter, for the death of things precious to the children of this universe.

Trisha admonished, "You must listen carefully to me and gain discernment so as to find clues hidden in the words you hear. Not everything is as it sounds, and not every soul is true to life and cause. Good air may well smell foul and poisoned air may revive the spirit into death. To choose the right course, one must find the right path. To preserve alive the souls of many, you must be willing to allow them death." She raised her hand, extending a finger. "A *crow* is not a *raven!*"

Murmuring arose among the people. Who was this forgotten creature of so few days to play at their game of riddles? How foolish she was, so immature. Did this little child not understand the depth of knowledge and wisdom carried in the collective minds of the wise and ancient ones gathered before her? Was Mother only toying with them? Some glanced toward her.

Trisha saw their folly. She cried out, "You think me a fool?! Look and see! The *death angel* resides among you!" She pointed toward someone hidden in the crowd. "Until she who carries the Devil's spawn gives birth to a new creation, will your world stand upon the edge of midnight. The Sisters of the Blood*Wind* must pass away into nothing before the great and fear-inspiring day of my God. But, in their rebirth shall all men quail, because they are the trinity of good, bad, and evil. And when the spear of jade pierces the heart of the Queen of Darkness shall all the world know that by evil shall evil be brought to nothing!"

Shocking prophecy! All eyes turned from Trisha to Ma-we, seeking explanation for this outburst. No book of wisdom ever contained such future statements! What was Mother up to? They found no answer, only consternation. Ma-we was leaned forward from her chair, eyes wide open, she herself seeking answers to her field marshal's troubling riddle. She was finding none.

What was it, then? Had this woman dared to tell of future events by using the wisdom of her own reckoning? The children searched Ma-we's eyes. No, her eyes were not accusative. Indeed, what they saw was even more troubling. A cloud of dark recognition passed across Ma-we's face, she hiding it in shadow by lowering her head while sliding back in her chair and staring toward her lap. Something was up with Mother, something so disturbing to her that she found no place to expunge it from her mind. The children could tell she was dealing with some unexpected event that was most disconcerting.

Wasn't Mother the Maker of prophecy? If so, then why was she so disturbed? If the new field marshal had invented it, surely Mother would have revealed it to be so, but she said nothing. Were there other forces at work, forces that acted independently of the Maker of Worlds? How was that possible? But, if there was? If there was, might those forces be using this strange creature for purposes of their own design? As if this collective thought swept the crowd at the same moment, the room quieted to a hush and all eyes turned again to the woman on the raised platform.

Trisha spoke again, and although as sharp and accusative as her words were, no one dared rise in ire against them. A power strange and terrible had filled their hearts and all with wisdom bent an ear to listen to what that power was revealing. Trisha's voice calmed and, along with the passing of any contemptuous tone, she continued.

"You think me a fool? I tell you this, and I tell you this for your own good: you swim so deep you do not see the surface of a tricksy sea. The rocks on the bottom you take while the silent ships of honest fate sail out of your grasp. I sound like a child to you because I speak to you in the simple tongue of a camel maiden, not some great orator. But I can read your minds, lands lost in simple thoughts."

She frowned. "The future promised smells foul to you, the old wine being so sweet in your thoughts. It poisons your minds, making you dream longingly for the past. Oh, you try to do the right thing, but you soon tire because your labors are without objective, your hearts seeking only the warm hearth and numbing wine."

Slamming her fist into an opened palm, Trisha raised her voice in warning. "If you truly desire to see the healing of the universe, *you must put those feelings behind you!* Let the *dead* rest in forgetful bliss. In doing so, you will give them a home to return to."

Trisha again took to pacing, her hands once more clasped behind her back. "To the common eye, two ravens may well look the same, yet both may be so different. One is smart and full of tricks. The other filled with an insatiable desire to fill its own belly. One may destroy your field for reasons untold. The other may seek only to destroy you. By the raven, men have lived and men have died. A raven has delivered meat to feed the flesh and another has devoured the flesh to satisfy itself." She raised a hand in gesture. "To identify what kind of bird searches you out is only half the victory. To identify its motive is the other half."

Lowering her eyes toward the floor, Trisha went on. "There are two ravens among you, but many crows. The crows are ever present, and not are they just in your enemy's camp. Crows seek only their own selfish longing, and are easily led into evil deeds by a crafty raven. Your brother is the raven of which I speak. You must learn how he tricks and riddles with you... and you must learn to see how his crows circle above, waiting upon your mistakes."

"Your Mother is also a raven, and though she may well bring gloom and despair upon her wings, along with those things she carries life through her tricks and riddles."

"Both ravens will use tricks and riddles. Both will deliver you to ill or good. Both will cause you to fall and not get up again. But only one will return life to your flesh."

She stopped, waving her hands. "You must learn how to understand them...*both* of them."

There was a growing turmoil in the room, a restlessness of spirit and heart. How the people viewed this woman was of little concern to her at this moment. Now was the time for action. After all, should this life be any different than her last? Where was this *promised new world,* filled with peace and delights? Had she not seen only violence and war from the very day of her entering this *paradise*? No, better is it to leave people hate you and to deliver their souls than to love them with the gift of eternal damnation.

Trisha did not let up. She continued on with her chastisement of this people. For over an hour she lectured, condemned and chided them for their failures. From the time of the First Megiddo War up through the Great War and down until this evening, she stripped away their clothing of self worth and sacrifice, revealing the naked skeleton of the 'straw man dancing merrily in the light of a blazing inferno'. The people were reeling from the blows of Foe Hammer. It was beating them down, exhausting their resistance, mocking their very existence. One person - one small, demure creature - stood upon the bulwark of destiny, crushing their longed-for visions, pulverizing those visions and casting their dust into a raging sea.

Trisha suddenly stopped her tirade, the silence nearly as damning as her speech. Was she finished? No! The full fury of the tempest was not over. She must yet conclude.

Staring into the faces in the crowd, she declared, "I came to this evil place through no will of my own, I being drawn back from death to suffer this life. My people and their cities… everything concerning them is gone, lost beneath the restless sands. My own sons lie forgotten, buried in the unmarked graves where no tomb recalls their deeds or names. There is no one here to share my past or my memories with, I being of so little value that none of your kind wasted their time to know me then. Still, I ask none of you for consolation for my loss."

"Though unworthy of your thoughts in ages past, *I* will haunt your dreams throughout future days, you wishing I was become a miscarriage in birth. Look! *I* am come from the other side of your nightmares and have gathered them up before me! *I* am everything you hate and everything you fear, a soul twisted and deformed! *I* am your looking glass! See*! I am the Lord of Darkness and I glory in destruction!"*

She turned toward Mihai and spat, shaking an accusing finger at her, "I will not fight to save the past, but I will consume all that is good to deliver the future. You have unleashed the *midnight*, and you can't stop it!" Then pounding her chest, she cried in rebuke, "*I rule this world now, and you will not contend against me! You know what I do must be done, and damn all who resist my will!"*

Trisha stood back, addressing the stunned crowd. "You promised your allegiance to me without question and I shall exact that loyalty with your blood. The fear of me is the beginning of wisdom, because I am only a shadow the one coming after me. *You prayed for this day and I will make you regret it has been delivered upon you…"*

She rested closed fists upon her hips, shaking her head. "And yet this day is not as foreboding as the one Shiloh will collect on to you. Rachel will weep over her own children on the day of his arrival and he will not listen to her plaintive cries for succor."

Trisha's fire was up, she unleashing it upon those present. "I do not ask for your love, nor do I seek your honor or respect, but I demand your souls to do with as I see fit! We…*we* no longer fight for our past, our future or even ourselves, for you live and can remember the past and yearn for the future. We fight only for those who cannot decide the battle, and we will sacrifice our blood to restore them to life! Their destiny rests in our hands! Their future depends on our actions. *If you are not with me, you are my enemy and an enemy to all who have gone before us!"*

She shouted, "Brothers! If we fail, their souls are lost forever! If we do not win this coming conflagration, Elijah will not come, and we shall all pass on to the fate of those who have gone before us!"

Smashing her fist into an opened hand, she proclaimed, "*WE... WILL... NOT... FAIL!*"

Silence like that of an empty tomb filled the room. At that instant, a door opened high in the back of the old theater. Eyes glared down at the troublesome creature below. The thick passage walls may have muffled her words, but her mocking tone and demeaning nature sounded through clearly. "Its *evil* smells putrid to my nostrils. *Foul… foul…* It clouds my vision so bad, it reeks with serpent stink." Shaking its head while hiding in deep shadows, the observer asked itself, "Why do these fools not sense the monster below? Why do they accept such malcontent?"

Just then, the giant wall clock struck eleven bells. Looking up at it, the voice muttered in disgust, "One still warm in its blood I must remove to a secret place. This confederate I shall have to deal with at another time. Another time I shall exact punishment for all the wickedness it does this eve. I will find the hour and place. I will wait, and then… and then..." The passage door quietly closed and silent footsteps wafted away in the darkness.

Silence pressed in on the people with suffocating harshness. What had this woman done? A few were beginning to recognize it. A few…

Knowledge comes at a price. Often little notice is given it because such wisdom comes subtly, like a child maturing into adulthood. Other times it rushes in like a raging storm upon a quiet sea. Those who survive wish for the tempest to have never happened, yet they would not trade lessons learned to make it so. And so it was this night. A great and terrible storm had raged against the collective souls of those gathered here, tearing away flesh and spirit, destroying dreams and hopes.

Still, one day the children of this Dark Age would wear with pride the scars and stripes of the master's rod, pointing to them as proof that he or she had faced the Dragon's wrath and proved their mettle. But that was for the future. They must first survive this night's storm. Was there anyone among them with the strength to save them? Was there anyone who would speak out in their defense?

Finally a person rose, slowly, but like a great giant among men he arose, standing tall as he faced their accuser. Euroaquilo stared into Trisha's eyes, his eyes piercingly sharp with emotion. His furrowed brow and set jaw gave pause to those observing him. All waited for him to release the tempest upon this creature from the depths below. Who could stand against the wisdom and wrath of the mighty StormWind? *He* would speak in his brothers' defense. *He* would put this rabble in its place!

Euroaquilo quickly turned toward Ma-we, thanking her for the many good things she had provided her children over these many lifetimes of men.

Bowing low at the waist, he remained still for several moments, showing her the honor deserved. When finished, he again faced the new field marshal. Now was the moment. Euroaquilo would restore the children's honor, true, but in a most unexpected way.

He bowed low again, much to the surprise of many. When he stood back up, the light sparkled off a tear on his cheek. With his booming voice, the man called out, "My Lord, my Lady, do please forgive this people for our indiscretions we have heaped upon you. Our souls have seen only the pain of a world turned upside down, we losing our ability to see the picture you have painted for us this night. Thank you for your honesty to the point of dealing us a blow that might well save us from ourselves."

Euroaquilo extended his arms, spreading his hands wide as he did so. "I am your humble servant and I hope to speak for all. Our Fates are but one, your breath one with ours. Shall you be cut, we will bleed; shall you cry, we will pine in sorrow. My Lord, you have taught us powerful lessons this night. Teach us, please, how to learn from them." He bowed again, and upon standing, added, "My sister, my blood, in death and in life!"

A shout from above, "Amen! And Amen! Our sister, our blood!" Darla stood, all eyes transfixed upon this *crazy* child. She began to applaud.

Another voice called out, "Our sister! Our blood! Stand and give our sister the glory deserved!"

No one moved.

Frowning, Zadar shouted, "Stand and give our sister her deserved glory or forever be shamed!"

PalaHar, followed by Tizrela and other members of the council stood, repeating Euroaquilo's words. Soon the entire room was standing in applause, expressing their approval of their new sister. Trisha's speech was beginning to take on meaning and understanding. Asotos' spell over the children was cracking. Euroaquilo had broken open the floodgates to this new understanding, but it was the energy and power of the new field marshal that brought the flood. Scales were beginning to fall from the children's eyes. Though not yet realizing it themselves, Trisha had captured their hearts. Their minds and souls were soon to follow.

Trisha did not move, nor did her expression change. What she felt inside remained secret to all. Finally, when the room had settled down, she turned toward Ardon and, in a tone veiling any emotion, she asked, "Lord Ardon, please stand in…"

Without waiting for his response, or looking to the crowd for their reaction, Trisha turned away, stepped from the platform and quietly hurried from the chamber, closing the door behind her. The silent, stunned crowd stared dumbly at the door, expecting it to fly open momentarily, their new leader rushing in to resume her fiery oratories.

৪১   ৪১   ৪১

Zadar was hopeful that the new field marshal was still in the palace, possibly squirreled away in some hidden enclave of this lower section. He had slipped through a side door to find Trisha soon after she left the chamber. Checking with the door wardens, they all told him the same thing - that no woman fitting her description passed their way. Other than the tramwaiters there was no other common exit, and he doubted the woman was familiar enough with this place to know of the more secreted exits.

The Upper Palace complexes had been quiet and subdued, the evening being late and the Council meeting still lasting well into the night. Even down here, along the Grand Concourse, few were the visitors at this hour. Most of the shops and eateries were closed and the few remaining open were nearly empty. As Zadar poked his head in one after another of the taverns and dining establishments, he remained confident that his search would end successfully.

Trisha was little more than a stranger to Zadar, they having met just this afternoon at a late luncheon, and that so casually. Though cordial, the woman had been distant, even cool toward his pleasantries. Yet something happened during that momentary encounter that troubled Zadar very much. And his troubled spirit only intensified as he escorted her around the council chambers earlier that eve. The man's ardor was easily roused, but it was not for that reason he was determined to find this strange creature. If it was for romance or a release of his passions, why put forth such effort? Many were the women available and willing to dance the romantic with this most charming of fellows. No, something burned in Zadar's heart. It called to him with urgency. What it was he did not know, but it grew in power as the empty moments passed.

He was well beyond the Winter Gardens, on the North Concourse, when Zadar felt it wise to pay a visit upon the South Palace Apartments, a complex set aside for visiting guests. Returning along the concourse, he again pondered the reason for his urgency. Could it be he needed to make Trisha understand that his people were not as foolish and selfish as she accused, that she must give them time to learn? True as it may well have been, other forces were busy that night as well. Zadar's relentless search frustrated at least one other soul. Angry eyes soon departed searching for their elusive victim, this fellow being an intrusive nuisance, thus saving the Empire from possible catastrophe.

Retracing his steps, Zadar hurried by the Winter Gardens on his way to the Southern Concourse tramwaiter. The cool, moist air of the gardens bid him to suck in a deep breath as he passed the golden fountains at the apex of the garden's fingers trailing out along each of the four main thoroughfares where the concourses intersected. Zadar could not help but to take in another intoxicating breath of delightful fragrances, sweet and pungent, the gardens ablaze with all varieties of flowers.

He suddenly froze, stopped dead in his tracks. That was odd. Not all the smells floating upon the breeze belonged to the flowers of the Winter Gardens. Jasmine spice mixed with the scent of orange and apple blossoms titillated Zadar's nostrils. The concoction was made by a wizard's hands long ago and given by that wizard, PalaHar, to Mihai as a gift of his appreciation and love. And Mihai was wearing that enchanting fragrance this very eve when she had come to the council. Then how was it that scent drifted upon the breeze in this location, for Mihai was still at the council meeting, it not being finished yet?

Snapping his fingers, Zadar smiled, answering his own question in whispered breath. "My Lady gave the woman a hug this night. That magic of Lord PalaHar's is powerful, clinging to all it touches." He lifted his arm, noting the intoxicating fragrance on his own sleeve. Without hesitation, the man vanished into the garden's thick jungle of exotic greenery.

Melodious splashing of the water fountain was all Zadar could hear in this upper part of the Winter Gardens, making it impossible for him to listen for clues that might reveal where his *prize* was hiding. Oh, she was here. He could smell it and feel it as well. Her spirit haunted him, the woman's energy being strong with emotion, but where she was continued to mystify him.

Not that the gardens were an easy place to find someone even if they were not secluded in a private place. First, it was quite large, being over an acre in size, with a labyrinth of narrow walkways and tiny nooks and crannies where romantic couples could secret themselves away for some special, private time – indeed the very reason for such design. The splashing water fountains, rock formations, trails and terraces had been built so as to create the illusion of solitude in the middle of the crowded world of men. Zadar had to depend on his sight and smell if he were to be successful here.

For over twenty minutes, Zadar searched and, as always, the hunt returned him to this one spot, the restless waterfalls at the northern end of the garden. "Twenty times I've been here!" He huffed. Still, he could find no clue to where this mysterious woman had gone. "She is not some flitting spirit without flesh and body. She must be near, for my nose tells me it is so."

Bending low to study the edge of the flagstone path, Zadar noticed a depression in the soil. Sure enough, a shoe with a hardened sole made it. And there! There was another depression after that, and that one was newly made, for the disturbed earth was still moist and packed by the weight pressing down upon it. Zadar hurried forward, seeking further evidence of the trail's direction. It ran toward the waterfall and then down beside the rushing stream the tempestuous falls created until it narrowed into a little torrent hemmed in by a steep, narrow, hewn granite canyon. From there Zadar worked his way down the stream along a narrow ledge used by maintenance workers to clean debris from the water.

The splashing waters made his going slippery, Zadar almost tumbling into the ever-growing tumult on more than one occasion. From the look of things, it appeared that he was not the only person finding the journey awkward. There were several places where growing lichens were raggedly torn by some misstep or other. Ahead, the man could see a sharp turn in the narrow canyon, this also being the place where several more streams collected, turning the watercourse into a rumbling torrent.

Zadar knew - for he had searched this watercourse many times in his younger days - that the noisy tempest would soon widen, slowing the stream, shortly thereafter plummeting down a giant, carved sluice, taking it far below into an immense cistern, only to be gathered up by huge pumps and returned to the Winter Garden's many water fountains and bubbling pools.

Gingerly working his way around a bend and through some limbs fallen from the dense tree canopy above, Zadar finally managed to find his way around that bend and peer down the stream to where it passed under a foot-bridge before disappearing into the darkness below, that graceful footbridge arched high above, it crossing a ravine at the terrace level of the Gardens. The abutment of the soaring structure, hewn from obsidian basalt, its base jutting out like a bench where the waters were gathered together, again caused the stream to pick up its pace before plunging into the noisy abyss.

Zadar grinned, breathing a sigh of relief that his search was finished. There, hidden in the shadows of the bridge's superstructure was the object of his intense pursuit. Trisha sat quietly, hunched forward with elbows resting on her knees, head down, staring into the chattering stream. Her finely embroidered military jacket and ornate kepi lay jumbled on the ledge beside her feet, and ringlets of the woman's silky brunette hair fell carelessly about her face.

His grin quickly faded. From this distance he could see that the woman appeared to be quietly weeping, or had been. A sudden wave of remorse swept across the man's heart. He had intruded into a very private world, one better left to the grieving soul. Yes, that was it. Trisha's appearance was that of a person in grief. Here was Foe Hammer in tears! This person, this savage and heartless monster of the Children's Empire, a person willing to sink all souls into the depths of Hell for a holy cause, this person was weeping. Zadar could only see a child, a very fragile child trying to save a rebellious, arrogant people whom she loved - or wanted so much to love - and she willing to surrender her heart and soul to repurchase theirs. Zadar became overwhelmed with the urge to cry over this woman's agony. Never before had his heart ached so over another's loss.

Choosing to leave the night to itself, Zadar started to retrace his steps only to be halted by Trisha's bitter rebuff. "I thought if anyone would search me out, it'd be you."

Jolted by her words, Zadar slipped, almost falling into the chilly waters. Trisha did not move or even look up.

Regaining his balance, he blurted out, "I... I was concerned and came looking for..."

Trisha glared, interrupting caustically. "...a *quick* one? A new *rose* to *pluck* for your *amusement*? You wasted no time with that leftenant this afternoon. Had her nearly naked before you were to the tramwaiter..."

Zadar recoiled at Trisha's stinging rebuke, attempting a reply, but could find no words to do so.

Patting the stone ledge as she turned to watch the stream, Trisha sighed in surrender. "Come here and sit down. You have found me..."

Zadar cautiously made his way into the cool shadows, stopping to study this strangest of all creatures before sitting. After doing so, he said, "You've been crying..."

Trisha snapped, "That's none of your business! Now speak of other matters."

Nodding obediently, Zadar asked, "Why did you expect *me*?"

Trisha tossed a short stick lying close by into the water, watching until the stream carried it from sight. "I didn't expect *you*... or *anyone*, for that matter." She turned and stared into Zadar's face. "I believed if *anyone* came, it would be you."

"Why me?!" Zadar quizzed, surprised, "Lord PalaHar, Admiral Euroaquilo, why, even our new king, Mihai, any one of them was as likely a candidate."

Trisha frowned, replying sourly, "You're quite the lady's man, aren't you? Catch a scent and off you go in a rut. You're like a bull in a herd... *sniff her, poke her, pull it out and sniff another*...work your way through the herd until a new heifer arrives, and then it's all attention on her 'til she gets a poke, too."

Trisha's comments hit Zadar like a hard slap in the face. Finally, a little put off, himself, he answered, "It is true that I delight in the field of lilies, my sisters making my love nests many, and me revisiting them often. But *never* have I forced my attention upon a lovely one of Lowenah's, nor have I acted like a buck in rut with my lovemaking. And... and that is not the reason I searched you out this night."

"Oh, *really?!*" Trisha's accusation was nearing the abusive. "I watched you glance at my form, your eyes studying my breasts as we wandered the council chambers. I've seen you stare at them here, while we talk." She eyed him. "Tell me the truth. Should I offer myself to you at this moment, would you be man enough to leave me my dignity?"

Zadar's face flushed red with anger, biting his lip to constrain the retort his heart wanted to offer. 'Better take the blow and look weak and foolish…' Euroaquilo once warned him, 'than to offer battle and prove it'. At length, Zadar replied, "I am sorry that you believe my motives so prurient. Whether I am a man of honor or not cannot be debated between two opponents. The light of sun reveals all secrets. I shall wait upon its light to prove to you the man I am."

Trisha was studying him while he pondered and replied. She felt guilt of heart for accusing the fellow of such beastly qualities, but she could not offer apology - not now, or she might lose all control and fall into a wailing lament. The night was already tearing away at her heart - a woman and mother forced to watch a child die in her arms, to listen to her sons rebuke her, casting lots against her so that the men of the village piously castigated her for one act of adultery against a drunkard and bully.

She turned her head away to hide a tear. In a troubled voice, she commented, "I come from a world where even good men would force them-selves upon a woman, passionately releasing their ardor upon her, forcing her into a servitude of silent torment until she was old and worn out, then casting her aside like some worthless baggage."

A resigned bitterness was carried on her voice. "And then, should we fall during a moment of wishful escape, even the very men who led us in our worship would publicly humiliate us before the gathering, saying that what was done to us by our village elders was but small retribution for such an evil act. And then, those same men who publicly shamed us for our sins would secretly desire our flesh for themselves, repeatedly asking us in detail about our adventurous fornications while, with long faces, shaking their heads in disapproval."

Trisha hung her head in sadness. "I was an old woman when I died in that forgotten land so long ago…well, at least I was considered old by the standards of the day. My friends, few friends, were all gone by then. My husband having taken a younger woman for himself and my sons having abandoned me, I was left to fend on my own, hunched over from rheumatism and unable to work the fields, and no longer good-looking."

She pulled on her jowls. "My wrinkles were many, my skin hanging loose around my chin. My large firm breasts that, as a flirtatious maiden, I would flaunt by the way I tied my robes, were flat and empty of youth, and my belly sagged from the many children I bore. I was a *useless, ugly old woman*. At best, the men ignored me. Others would call me names, 'old hag', 'dung bag', or even worse. I did not regret my passing from that world. I remember smiling when I felt that last breath."

Trisha reached over and took Zadar's hand, looking into his eyes. "When I entered your world, I'd been asleep for over two thousand years. My joy at arriving here was overwhelming. Your mother, my God, and my Lord, Mihai, worked so hard to make me feel welcomed. I truly appreciate the things they did for me, but alas, my past has followed me here, at least in spirit. I have resided here many years but feel much like the worthless old hag I became before my death. Your people have not cared to find out who I am. Their empty and sometimes hostile stares are often my reward for entry here."

"Zadar, do you know what it is like to lose everything that is yours and have no one even remember your name? The desert wind ever blows over the ruins of my village. It was not large or important, but it was my home and life, good or bad, it was what and who I was. No one cared to know me then. Even Mihai did not remember me. Oh yes, your mother knows me and loves me very much. Yet it is her witchery that has delivered me to this tormented land, a place giving me very little refreshment."

She looked around, speaking wistfully. "This place reminds me of home." She took Zadar's hand, squeezing it, peering again into his eyes. "Near my village there was a drainage ditch with a small overhang near the rock wall where the water entered a tiny pool. It didn't always smell nice, especially when the herders brought their animals to town, but it was secluded and out of the way of prying eyes."

She paused to search for the right words. "When I was a little girl, my father… who was really a very good man… would take to beating us when the wine took hold of him. We children would all attempt to find places to hide from his wrath, hoping he would not come searching. I found a haven in that drainage ditch, disappearing under the overhang until it was safe to return home. There I played at whatever I wished to be, creating pretend playmates and going on wonderful adventures. Zadar, it was the one and only place in my life where I always felt secure and free to be who I really was."

Moments slowly passed. Zadar reflected on Trisha's tales of her life, re-living the emotion of her childhood years long ago. Trisha finally broke the silence. "This place makes me feel secure."

She glanced into Zadar's face, exclaiming, "You shed a tear! In my world, a man would be shamed if he cried in front of a woman." Like a caring mother, she reached up, brushing it away.

Smiling sadly, Zadar replied, "The men of this world find no shame in tears or weeping. Our manliness is not based on some emotional premise that women, alone, may exercise freedom of feelings."

Trisha nodded. "That's one example of just how different our worlds are… or were… at least as I recall the world of my day."

Zadar responded, "It's changed little, I assure you."

Gazing into the bubbling water, Trisha wistfully recalled distant times.

"Mihai has told me that I, alone, was selected from all the people of my kind to be gathered here, and for a special purpose. Oh yes, she promised me that after the Ending Days, many of my people would return to the lands of the living, but… but, for the moment, I stand the bulwark of Time alone, a stranger in a strange land. Only one other person do I know from my old days. When I was young and full of zeal for my new religion, I happened upon Paul in my travels to a distant city. He says that he does not recollect me, though I did have a word with him at that time."

She slowly shook her head. "I was a *nobody* in the eyes of my village people and those I worshiped with, a silly chatterer, always thinking sideways of the others. My only true companion, my mother, died before my twelfth birthday, leaving me to the mercies of a father not able to feed all the children he had. I was shuttled around my family until, finally, the old miller took me for a wife and he paid little more attention to me than to satisfy his passions. I doubt anyone noted my passing until the room I died in was consumed with stink… and I imagine they only cursed me for such rudeness."

Sadness grew on Trisha's breath. "I asked Lowenah once why she brought me here, something far beyond my understanding. She just laughed and, with a twinkle in her eye, answered, 'I may have mistaken you for another, oh, someone so much more important, you know. Oops! How careless of me… Well, when I discovered the mistake, what was there to do but let you stay?' That's Lowenah…she always tries so hard to lift your spirits."

Zadar laughed aloud, grinning. "At least you were given a reason. Most who ask find themselves staring into a troubled face looking puzzled. Finally Mother will reply that she really doesn't quite know and, for the life of her, she can't figure out what to do with them now that they're here." His eyes twinkled as a smile grew on his face. "When I was a little one, I asked Mother why I was born. She became serious and, leaning close, saying her words only for my ears, she answered, 'I was so wanting some dumplings for my stewpot. Well, you know, I thought about it with such intent that, oops! Out popped you, my *little dumpling*.' She gleefully rubbed her hands together and then she became oh so sad, lamenting, 'When I went to find the stewpot, I discovered it was missing. When I find it, we'll make the stew then.'"

Zadar laughed. "I tell you, for the longest time, when someone requested stew for supper, you could count on little Zadar taking flight, hiding in some secluded corner of the palace until he thought it safe to come out again."

Trisha smiled, thinking of a little Zadar, much like her own sons, hiding in a secret corner or hiding under the palace furniture, fearing he was being hunted down to be thrown into the cooking pot. She looked into Zadar's eyes, a fading sadness escaping hers. "Thank you. Your tale not only rekindles pleasant memories, but it increases my understanding concerning the ways and thinking of your people."

Zadar asked how that was so. He received no reply. Trisha looked away, returning her stare to the cold waters hurrying toward their eventual fate. At length, she asked, "Zadar, are you good at keeping secrets, I mean secrets that a troubled heart even refuses to acknowledge?"

Puzzled, Zadar pondered in thought. His people played at riddles and guessing games, sometimes in most serious ways, but secrets? Secrets were few, he experiencing them as the tools of war when openness could be fatal. He knew that Trisha was not speaking of a military secret, yet to her, what she wanted to reveal must be as important. He finally nodded. "One secret should be easy enough for me to keep. All right, I promise."

Trisha stared into Zadar's eyes for the longest time, a sadness escaping hers. At length, she looked away and sighed, "I have watched how your men look at me, at least until they discover who I am. They undress me in their mind, seeking to find the flesh hidden under my flowing capes."

Turning her gaze back to Zadar, Trisha bemoaned, "Oh, I know the beauty I possess now. I see it in the mirrors. But… but I feel *old - old and ugly inside, like the hag I had become in my old age*. And… and I have come to despise the looks of honest men, feeling them to be little more than ravenous stares of beasts seeking to use my flesh as a tool to release their passion. I feel like my body is craved for, to become little more than a replacement for a tired hand, working an excited organ of pleasure."

Lowering her head and speaking in just above a forlorn whisper, the woman from lost years lamented, "I wish so badly to feel young again, to trust…to trust like a maiden trusts when a suitor lavishes his attention on her. I want to enjoy what my God made me to enjoy…the love of an honest man…for me to crave his passion and feel his release as a gift given in love and not see my womanly parts as just some repository of wanton lust."

Zadar could not hold back his feelings, groaning in dismay, agonizing over seeing a troubled heart searching release from its own demons. Without thinking, he reached his arm across Trisha's shoulders, pulling her close to him. The woman did not resist, continuing to stare at the water. In time, she put her head back on his shoulder, closing her eyes while releasing a contented sigh. The little stream ever hurried on, its sweet, tumultuous music playing ever on the woman's ears, 'all is well, rest for the world has changed, rest and see your dreams fulfilled, rest for now, Daughter of the Wind. Breathe the universe anew, with life and satisfaction'.

Far away, with the sounds of disenchantment and troubled voices in her ears, another woman smiled with satisfaction. Her son would deliver the medicine. That she knew. Zadar had never failed her before, his spirit being irresistible to her daughters, and this creature from below? Ma-we smiled to herself. A cure…a cure was already in the making.

ಸಿ   ಸಿ   ಸಿ

The tumbling of the musical stream continued, singing relaxing refrains that tugged upon cords binding a troubled heart. It felt so good to have her head on this stranger's shoulder. She closed her eyes, wishing the moment to linger on, but, alas, the woman's mind refused to give her pause. At last, in a quiet, reserved voice she asked, "Zadar, is there time to take council?"

Zadar smiled, his reply courteous and reassuring. "Certainly, what does our captain wish to discuss?"

Lingering in her comfortable nest a moment longer, Trisha answered, "I do know why I have been delivered here and it causes me strife and concern." She sat, pulling away and turning, looked into Zadar's face. "My friend, if I may even call you that…"

Zadar nodded approvingly.

"Well, I am the precursor of the one who will gather himself to your people. I fear that hour, for I have seen it in visions and dreams. That is why I come now, to show your kind the way, to prepare you for the darkness that must arrive on all living things. I must prepare yours hearts for the Lord of Destruction."

Trisha's words puzzled Zadar, for she had uttered similar words earlier that night, their meaning still unclear. He chose, though, not to speak, encouraging Trisha to continue by remaining silent.

"Very well…" Trisha sighed, "Your people dream of a man who will take up the crown of this kingdom and return the world of peace to this land." She shook her head. "I have come to teach your kind many truths - one, that by evil must evil be destroyed. Zadar, through visions I have see the Ending Days of rebellion. Your kind cannot comprehend the great and terrible things your coming king will deliver upon this world and the rabble host. Zadar, this man brings the *midnight*, and he will use all his evil knowledge to bring to a finish what I must start!"

She lowered her head in sadness. "Before the darkness passes, your people will curse the day of their birth, wishing instead for the Silent Tombs of their brothers."

Trisha looked directly at Zadar, pointing at herself, "Zadar, I am a *new creation*, different from all other living beings that have come before, or should arrive after…at least that is how I understand it. There is a hidden power dwelling within my soul that, should I summon it, it would give me the strength of ten men, yet I do not summon it… cannot. My friend, I could tear you asunder this very moment if the mood should strike, but there is a greater power warring within my breast that holds it in check."

"And yet…" Trisha sighed again. "the power of my mind, to take control of your people and lead them, push them beyond all sanity, that power I do have, and it is not restrained by any hidden force."

She squeezed Zadar's hand, exerting enough pressure to make the man wince in pain. Apologizing for having provided him a necessary lesson, Trisha added, "I also feel a strange and disquieting might and glory hidden behind these orbs. Should I wish, I could blind you with my gaze, burning away, forever, your two oceans of wondrous, intriguing beauty."

Trisha blushed, that last statement slipping out of rebellious lips. She turned away, staring at the flowing stream. "I didn't mean to hurt you... really, I do mean it. I only wanted you to see and understand me." Again, a heart betrayed more than the woman wanted Zadar to witness of her soul.

Zadar smiled, rubbing his hand as he watched the red marks begin to fade. "You certainly do have a way of impressing lessons upon your captive students..." He reached out, taking Trisha by the chin and slowly turned her face toward his. Then, frowning so seriously, he queried, "So, if I should stare into your eyes with *want* and *prurient* desire, shall my fate be to behold a most beautiful creature as my final vision before having my eyes burned to vapor? Then it should not be such a bad thing..."

Trisha noted a whisper of tease in Zadar's voice, along with other subtle innuendos. She attempted a teasing return of her own. "*Prurient*? Well, such an insolent act done with selfish intent might raise my ire and bring forth my anger. But...but if it were an honest act of a man speaking only what a *wanton* heart betrays... well... well..." She reached up, gently stroking Zadar's soft beard. "I would so much hate to damage two beautiful spheres expressing so much curiosity and wonder." She winked. "...that is, just yet..."

As quickly as the magic of Zadar's flirting had lightened Trisha's heart, a dark, foreboding, cloud swept over the woman's soul, her eyes losing their flirtatious glow. She turned away, becoming sullen and quiet. Zadar said nothing.

At length, Trisha spoke, her voice subdued and reserved. "There is so little time to learn and prepare, the Dragon already being at your very door. Your brother will soon attack, in ways that your kind are not prepared for, and I speak not just of his wiles at the coming Prisoner Exchange. Satan's army is greater than most imagine, consuming all the lost souls who follow him. He has become great and terrible. There stands but one Fate that checks his hand, and that is Time. He must wait for the right moment in order to bring the entire universe to nothing."

Shaking her head, Trisha hinted at her hidden remorse. "I am come to force his hand. At whatever cost to your kind, it must be done. I must hurry him on so that his attack comes prematurely, so that his strike will only maim and not kill."

Surprised, Zadar countered, "Surely we have the time... must have the time to set matters right... to bring down the beast!" Looking into troubled eyes, his countenance faltered as he asked haltingly, "Don't we...?"

Trisha sadly disagreed. "The hour has already passed, this your mother has informed me. From her I have learned, as she told me through her own tears, that many of her children will needlessly come to naught because of their failure to heed her warning. Even your new king has hidden herself away in denial, wishing for Shiloh to deliver the cure. I am sorry, but it must be by the blood of all living things - your brothers and sisters - that the cure will be made manifest. Zadar, the rivers of blood your people witnessed tonight through vision were not your enemy's alone, but need I say more?"

She squeezed Zadar's hand. "You... your kind must learn how to *hate* the wicked."

"But why?" Zadar asked, his voice filling with uncertainty.

Trisha sat back, surprised. "Zadar! Of all people, I believed you would understand. Is your sister, Darla, the only one with any sense about her? Please... please listen and learn. You and I are not strangers to war. When you and I watch our enemy die, we think not of them as more than a cancer removed from a diseased body. *Good riddance!*" She waved her finger at him. "I know it's so with you. I watched it in your eyes this very eve at the Council."

Zadar nodded it was so.

Trisha placed an opened hand on her breast. "I... we... feel no remorse at such death. Indeed, we rejoice for, like a surgeon removing a cancerous tumor, we see a cleansing taking place. In fact, we *hate* them... *hate* them because we know what they have done to this world, our kindred, our God! It is what *drives* us through the blood, gore, the stink of battle. It keeps us ever willing to fight again, to go on fighting... the hatred, I mean. It keeps us going on to the finish." She looked into Zadar's eyes, asking, "Is that not what I've seen in you? Am I not right?"

Zadar replied, "I see my mother sitting on the stairs leading to the palace courtyard, weeping over the murder of two of her daughters near the Pishon River, not far from Eden. I was little more than a teen at the time, but the river of tears Mother shed at the report of their rape and torture turned all that was inside me into a boiling inferno of jealous rage...an anger that has little subsided down to this day. When it wakes within my soul, the world around me becomes red and my heart seeks the blood of those who hurt her."

Trisha grinned. "You see! We fight for the same reasons! We *hate*! *Hate* the evil that lives and breathes in this land!" She frowned. "Few of your brothers fight for the same reason. Even your Euroaquilo, who is among the bravest of your kind, seeks reasonable solutions in his heart, secretly hoping that peace will be found through wordy councils."

"Well! Tonight I tried to shake the scales from their eyes, tried to help them see the need to put down the gall-tainted wine and sober up, wake up to the reality and dangers surrounding them. I think they did wake." Trisha lowered her head, speaking remorsefully. "Now I must find a way to keep them awake, whatever the cost to them... or me."

Trisha again took Zadar's hand, gently caressing it. "If your people refuse to learn to *hate* the wicked - really *hate* them and all they stand for - their hearts will not be able to endure Shiloh's onslaught. What he will demand from them... for he will cry out in all that is good and evil to bring down the Serpent's house... he will demand that the blood kin become the avengers of blood in the ruining of that house." She nodded sadly. "So, you see, they must learn to hate as you and I have, or their hearts will not survive the ordeal."

As tears welled up in her eyes, Trisha pleaded, "Zadar, I am but a little shadow of the things to come, a rustling breeze preceding the great storm. I know. I have seen it in my waking visions. Zadar, Shiloh *is* the storm! Yes, the very savior that your brothers have yearned so long for is the very nightmare that your brothers have so greatly feared. He will fulfill all the words of all the prophets. He will laugh at war, deride the timid, and despise the weak." She squeezed Zadar's hand. "My friend, Zadar, *Shiloh is the Destroyer!*"

Zadar rubbed his bearded chin, pondering what Trisha's revelations portended for his people. Suddenly his face lit up in questioning wonder as he asked, "Is Shiloh already come?! Does he live here or in the worlds below?"

Trisha closed her eyes, hiding growing tears.

Excited, Zadar pressed her for information. "Do you know who he is?!"

Giving a nod, Trisha hung her head as if in remorse, becoming glum and silent. Zadar said nothing, waiting upon the right moment when the woman's heart would force words to come from her mouth.

Finally, but oh so sadly, Trisha answered, "He is still a child whose opinion is driven by the foolish winds surrounding him. His heart is held captive by a religion led by obstinate men filled with self-glory who seek not the truth, but mindless followers taught to do their personal bidding, binding the peoples' souls by feeding them drops of truth concerning my God, while heaping buckets of drivel upon their starving hearts."

"My heart... I say by witchery, but your mother says by my own desires... my heart is bound up with him, my head already in a tizzy over who this child will become. No other man has, of yet, moved my passions as this one has... and that only in my night visions of our loving togetherness... making me feel all the more lonely and empty of soul and heart."

She looked into Zadar's eyes, pleading, "Please tell no one about what I have spoken. Please!"

Zadar puzzled, asking, "Why all the secrecy? Falling in love is a common thing, especially with your kind."

Trisha glared, eyes squinting, "I speak not of my feelings, though it might embarrass me should my personal feelings be bantered about in public. You should know better than that."

Apologizing, Zadar confessed, "I am sorry, but it was your feelings I was considering. What other reason for secrecy?"

It was Trisha's turn to apologize. Gripping Zadar's wrist, Trisha explained, "It is Shiloh of whom I speak in secrecy. Now, you must promise me with an oath, even of life and death, to even that of ever telling Mihai your king, or anyone who-so-ever, upon your own soul you must confess to never speak of this again until the day of revealing, or I shall take my leave and talk of this no more."

Zadar was taken aback, having never been asked such a thing before. Oaths his people did not take, at least this kind of oath, fealty and honesty being expected by just a word. Still, Trisha was not from this world, her former one being filled with deceit and lies. Was it such a big thing to assuage this woman's fears? Besides, Zadar was filled to exploding with curiosity, needing to know more. He offered his oath in the way Trisha requested.

Satisfied, she breathing a sigh of relief at not having to leave Zadar because of her threat, Trisha revealed her secret. "Upon my arrival to this place, I was whisked away to the outer reaches of this Empire, a certain BruunTaciak being my mentor and companion." She segued, as if thinking aloud. "More a mentor, I guess, I being cold and distant to men... still am, I guess. Bruun was a good fellow and let me have my way, giving me security without romance."

Apologizing for wandering, Trisha returned to the subject. "I was not in this realm yet six months when - I believe I was on post at CharlaBaal, a small military compound south of the Trizentine - when my night visions began carrying me away to the strange worlds below to visit myself upon a young child, oh, such a foolish little boy. Night after night the visions would return, but not the same visions. It was as if I were watching a daily event, each a progressive day, one after the next."

"In time, I mentioned my visions to Bruun. He, being a very patient and discerning man, told me to cherish them in my heart while waiting upon a visit from Lowenah, and that was but a very short wait. Three days hence she arrived at my lodging acting oh, so casual and chatting on about such unimportant matters. Finally I blurted out my constant night visions, asking her what they might be about."

"Lowenah puzzled at first, the twinkle in her eyes telling me so much more. Finally she replied that watching young ones in the Lower Realms was good training for new arrivals to this place, helped to keep an overeager mind occupied and well behaved. At first I accepted her answer, me being too naive to understand your mother's sense of humor and riddling. But as time went on, I became suspicious about this child, he being peculiar in so many ways."

Trisha's eyes searched the little stream as she went on. "It was queer for me to watch him, spooky, some might say. The little fellow was different in how he acted, I mean, in small and little noticed ways. The boy didn't really fit in, always out of place, like a shadow on a cloudy day. He was different, on the inside, I mean." Trisha pointed at her heart. "In here, right here."

She slowly shook her head. "Strange fellow, indeed…! He's grown up in a religion preaching peace and love, that is, until *God* strikes the world with plague and vengeance, but that is to be done at *God's* hand. All those *chosen*, you know, all the good, *saved*, souls are not to get their hands dirty…sort a' like having the reward without getting messy…they'll just swoop in and take over the planet after all the *bad people* are killed off."

"Well, this boy preached all this with his mouth when talking to others about what he believed, but he was one hellacious warmonger when left by himself. That's all he ever was about, warring at this, fighting at that. He made little flags for himself and led imaginary armies on to great victories. Most of his toys became war machines, clay became soldiers and sticks became weapons. Yes sir, he talked *peace* and studied *war*… all the time he did, reading and watching about it… all the time."

Trisha lifted her hand while extending a finger to make an added point. "I studied him in my dreams and came to believe it was not by chance the boy acted so odd in the way he did things, thought things. Lowenah, I came to feel, had been dabbling with this boy, weaving his chemistry while in his mother's belly. Over time I found that others were paying more than the usual attention to this child. Your Gabrielle has spent more than her share of time investigating him."

Zadar nodded with understanding, rubbing his beard in thought, finally commenting, "Gabrielle has long been absorbed in the lives of your kind. She is not one to idly wile away the hours on trivial matters. Her attention given to the boy betrays his importance to us… at least in some way."

Trisha agreed, "I came to feel so out of place, my seeing the boy and all of these important people in my visions, and my visions being so real. Eventually Lowenah told me that my visions were real, that my mind was being transported to my old world and what I saw happening, even playing a part in, was really happening as I saw it."

"These visions have carried on down to this day. I have spent many years watching him. Not more than a week ago, I visited the boy. Oh, he's like most boys his age, and at times quite ill-behaved… sneaky, if you know what I mean. But something in him, I think a love for Lowenah, a kind that's rare among his people, I think even among your own… I believe that's what draws me to him."

Trisha cast her eyes away, embarrassed. "I took to dreaming about him, as a man, I mean, seeing him and me together, loving each other. It became so bad that I found myself waking in heated sweats, my heart pounding for his touch, his embrace. He was so gentle, always so gentle, in my dreams, I mean." She looked back at Zadar. "Whether it was real or not, I found myself falling in love with the man I hoped he'd become, have fallen in love. When I confessed this all to Lowenah, she smiled and went to chatting about other very unimportant matters."

She looked up and into Zadar's face, her eyes welling with tears. "It was only this morning that your mother, my Lord and God, revealed her secrets to me concerning this boy."

Zadar could not contain himself, blurting out, "What did she tell you?!" He quickly apologized for his intrusive brashness.

Smiling, Trisha answered, "I intended to tell you the rest, and shall. You are so strange in many ways, so ancient and so youthful, old and young, man and child. Do you understand what I mean?"

He replied he believed so.

"Well…" Trisha began. "allow me, please, to first digress. I must take us back to the days when your sister, Mihai, visited my world as a man, grown in power, glory, and wisdom, being the greatest of all Yehowah's prophets to men. Well, the world that Mihai was born into was ruled over by kings whose bloodlines were considered of greater worth for rulership than other abilities. For that matter, the man who dictated law over her mother's nation was an illegitimate king, having no right to rule a *toadstool* let alone a divine nation."

"Mihai's birth mother and adoptive father were both in the bloodlines of those having the rightful rule of your mother's earthly nation. Thus, through the trickery of your mother, Mihai, being born a male, and being the firstborn of that bloodline, possessed the right to be king over that people, and any future people of that nation."

Zadar acknowledged, already being fully aware of those events, but what Trisha said next was surprising and chilling.

"There was trickery afoot long before that day, trickery that Asotos believed remained hidden from the eyes of Lowenah - but that was not really so. Long ago there was a woman, a Moabitess, already a Hormaxian full-blood child, her mother being a child of rape by that cult and then she - Ruth's mother - herself, having produced Ruth by similar means. This woman, Ruth, the very person who became ancestress to Mary, Mihai's birth mother, was, herself, impregnated by a man filled with Hormaxian blood."

"For it was not Boaz who made Ruth pregnant with child but *so-and-so* who, through trickery, seducing Ruth into believing he had taken her as wife, took her and had relations with her and then, the following day, rejected her publicly in the city gate, when he realized that he was to produce a seed - a child through brother-in-law marriage for another man - and that he would not receive the landed inheritance he had expected."

"Boaz, later learning of the matter, chose to remain silent and took Ruth's child for his own, telling no one the reality. And so your mother, my God, she keeping the truth even from the prophets of that people, allowed Asotos to believe he had contaminated the bloodline of the promised seed that was to bring to ruin his rebellious world."

Trisha slowly shook her head. "It was on a pretense that Asotos led the Babylonian wise men to king Herod, he wanting Lowenah to believe he truly desired to kill Mary's son, thus hiding the fact that he was preparing the child to become his own agent to do his eventual bidding. It wasn't until Asotos fully realized that Mary's firstborn was not a child of the earth, but born from the heavens and was Mihai, herself, in a man's form, that Asotos, in his anger, brought the child up to death before Pilate, he having no idea that his scheming ways were never secret to your mother, she using his treachery to her own advantage."

"When Mihai, as a man, was murdered by Asotos' agents, because she died having produced no heir, the right of kingly rulership passed on to Mary's next oldest son, James. Thus, by law, Mihai lost the right of being king over the Second Realm."

"What?!" Zadar's excited voice carried a tone of confusion. "That's not so! For all of Mihai's brothers and sisters have been in wait of her kingly power, which she presented to us this eve, to remove forever wickedness and establish an everlasting kingdom."

Trisha smiled to herself. So, the information she was privy to was secret to Lowenah's children. She savored the moment, basking in the thought of being so favored by the Maker of all things. "My friend, it is true what I have said, but you must hear me out and listen to all of your mother's riddling before you will understand the great deception she has heaped upon the Wicked One's head. Now please pay attention."

She patted Zadar's hand, breaking into a toothy smile. "Tonight, Mihai received a legal kingship over a tribe, not over a nation. In doing this, your mother has given Mihai power and glory over her brothers and sisters, but she has not received the majesty of Firstborn, could not unless she changed the very nature of her being and returned to the likeness of her former flesh when in the Lower Realms. And even then she would have no right to claim an ancestral connection to Shiloh and his kingdom either, except... except for..." Trisha's voice trailed away, she being reluctant to reveal further secrets.

Zadar refused to be put off... not now, not after all his tingling ears had so far discovered. "Sister! Now is not the time to play games with me. It is not fair on your part to string this fellow along to only leave him hanging high in the breeze. Be a good soldier and tell your brother the rest of you tale."

Trisha replied, shocked, "You called me sister!" She thought about it for a moment, finally smiling. "Thank you. What I have to speak about is secret to all but your mother and… and a woman from my world who resides even now in the shadows of this one, for she is hidden from all but Lowenah and now me. Yes, from her very mouth has the truth about your sister, Mihai, and her adventures in my world been fully revealed. Even Gabrielle has no knowledge of this, Lowenah blinding the eyes of her children until the coming hour."

"Please… er… my brother." Trisha grinned, it feeling good to call someone by such a family name. "Mihai, born of flesh as a man, perfect in the flesh as a human man, born from the genetic makeup of her mother, allowed her, as a man, to legally repurchase the sons of Adam for the wickedness of that man, the first man. Still, it did not give her the right of kingly power over Abraham's children or any other men. That must come through the bloodline of the seed, as promised by Gabrielle in the Garden so many ages ago."

"James, Mihai's younger brother in the flesh…you know James. He walks with us in these realms. Well, James received legal right to carry the line of kingship through his children and did so, his family's bloodline mixing with that of mankind. Your mother… er, my mother…" Trisha grinned again. "Mother? …mother, whisking her seed away from Asotos so that he could never threaten it again. So, from James, will… has come Shiloh, the promised king. Well, almost…"

Zadar squirmed with impatience, Trisha laughing, delighted at seeing his childish antics. When he had settled down, she continued. "Mother was not satisfied with this. She wanted Mihai to have legal right to the throne of her brother, that is, if she really wanted it. To do that, Shiloh must also be of her legal descent, her human bloodline. Now here is where wisdom extraordinaire comes in, for nothing is impossible with Yehowah. Isn't that the very reason for her children to gift that name upon her?"

Zadar nodded.

"Yes." Trisha went on. "As I said, Shiloh must have Mihai's blood, but how? Here is the truth, a secret told to me by the one who was carried along by spirit to become the very Sacred Secret of my God. You see, as I recall it being written by our friend, Paul, who spoke of Mihai in the flesh, saying that she… he… after he had been made perfect, became responsible for everlasting salvation. He, Mihai in her human, male flesh first needed to become like Adam, fully perfect."

Now Mihai, in the flesh of a man, but with the knowledge of her heavenly flesh, took, by the command of our mother, a woman of clay and celebrated with her the rite - just as Adam did with Eve in the Garden on the day the woman was brought to him - thus making Mihai complete... perfect... in the sense that she now fully understood the makeup and emotions of a man, thus making her a priest to all mankind. Here is where the promise given to Rahab in a dream became fulfilled. 'The harlot will give a blessing to all mankind'."

"So it was, the following day, when Mary, the sister of Lazarus, oiled the head of her Messiah, she, for her part, was celebrating the marriage of flesh between her and the man she anointed. This one final act, the manly act of taking a woman and sharing in her love is what made Mihai perfect in all ways, her womanly and manly qualities fulfilled to the full measure. But it did more, and that is what is the *greatest of all secrets...*"

"Shortly after the death of Mihai in the flesh of man, her younger brother, led by spirit, took Mary for a wife, he never knowing the reality of the matters. In due course, she bore him a daughter, she naming her 'Shi-loShani', meaning *'bloodline to peace'*. But truly, the daughter – as Mother will attest to – was not Jude's but Mihai's from her manly flesh, something she does not yet know down to this day. Mother was responsible for this, using the girl's bloodline to mix with James' in order to give Mihai the legal right to being Firstborn."

Zadar was completely taken aback, his head swirling with confusion and insight. He exclaimed, "Do you say that one of us, my kind, have children of flesh?!"

Trisha looked surprised, she never contemplating that only her kind made children and... and that Lowenah's children had any real desires to produce their own. "Why... why yes, several are Mihai's descendants, mostly women, because only from Mihai's birthing mother did Lowenah take the genetics to make Mihai in the flesh. But what is most important is that Mother could now physically mix the blood of her most loved child with that of Shiloh's ancestors, giving her an eternal gift and legal authority to take up the crown of the Firstborn."

"And..." Trisha poked Zadar's arm with her finger. "And this very day Mihai declined the crown, so this evening she legally became king not as Firstborn, but king over a new and different people, another tribe, so to speak. That tribe is of my kind." She pointed toward herself. "There are many thousands like me, destined for immortality and incorruptibility. Some, like me, are already here, living in this world, some still reside in the worlds below, and others yet rest in the Field of the Minds. One day we shall all be gathered together in the last hour to unleash our vengeance upon the wicked Snake and bring to a finish all evil in a great final war."

"By Mother handing over to Mihai the king's Sword, she has given her daughter authority to rule over everything that will become Shiloh's, at least as a great steward for him. Yet the common understanding is that Mihai is king over all things, Gabrielle, a most loved and trusted confederate, being the only one of Lowenah's children knowing differently."

Pausing, Trisha took a breath, sighing with satisfaction at having shared such a powerful secret, she hoping that Mother would understand. "You see, it is the coming great warrior, Shiloh, one yet to arrive here, who is the very person intended for the crown of Firstborn. Now that Mihai has rejected it, he stands next in line to possess it. He is the one who will sit Mother's throne, 'Yehowahboam' – 'the man who sits in the seat of God'. This is he, the very heir to that throne, this Shiloh, whom I have been watching these many years."

A puzzled look crossed Zadar's face, he blurting out, "Wait a minute! You were at the palace this morning, you told me so yourself, and Mihai… this I know… was at the palace later in the day…Darla and I returning her to her apartment later. So how is it that you know what she did regarding the crown?"

Trisha frowned, taking her fist and lightly tapping Zadar's head with her knuckles. "Block of wood! Are all your kind this dense or are you, alone, made of marble-teak? I arrived only minutes after you left the palace, I being summoned back there. That's the reason your pursuit of the new game hen was futile, at least until the late day luncheon when you attempted to impress me with your manly… *boyish charms*. You are *quite a charmer* when you're on the hunt."

Puffing his chest out and huffing in his manly pride, Zadar responded, "Well! At least your day didn't turn out a complete waste, then."

Fire erupted in Trisha's eyes, they boring into Zadar's as she leaned away. Zadar could not tell his fate, watching her double up a fist while preparing to strike him a blow. With a soft punch to his midriff, Trisha let out a laugh, a real, deep laugh, an act that was as surprising to her as it was to Zadar. In the freedom of the moment, she leaned close and kissed Zadar on the cheek, hugging his arm.

Nose to nose, Trisha looked up and into Zadar's twinkling eyes. Laughter melted from her face followed by embarrassing shades of red that crept up to her ears. Releasing Zadar's arm, she sat back while sliding away to a more respectable distance from the man, but her eyes continued to betray the woman's inner feelings, she repeatedly glancing over at Zadar to see what his reaction was. It felt good to do something spontaneous and fun, especially with someone who allowed her those feelings. She sat silent for a long time, savoring those moments.

Finally, in the most authoritative voice she could muster, Trisha admonished, "Zadar please, no more clowning. The hour is late and I have more to tell."

Zadar could feel Trisha's body language and her continual glances belied her tenor. She was having a good time, relaxing in the company of a man, enjoying his presence, something, he believed, the woman had not done in many long years. It made him feel good to think he could do that, but at the same moment he puzzled about himself. Something stirred within him that he was not at all familiar with. So odd... Later! There were currently more important matters to discuss. Smiling, Zadar promised he would behave.

"Thank you." Trisha returned his smile and then went on. "That right to kingship over a people and, in reality, the right of Firstborn, has passed on from father to son, along with a little mixing of Mihai's blood from the daughters' side, down to this very day, for two thousand years. And it was accomplished right under Asotos' nose, why even with his help, and he never caught on."

Zadar wrinkled up his face, wondering aloud, "How?"

"Easy!" Trisha exclaimed. "Like you and the others, your brother was searching a race of people to deliver the seed, the same race your kind paid way too much attention to even after your...our mother warned you, through Paul, that the seed was being delivered into the nations. But unlike you, Asotos continued to purge that race, which were even my distant kindred, bringing one pogrom after another in hopes of slaughtering them off. Down to this day he has sought their murder, hoping to thwart Mother's ambition for a coming seed."

Zadar began to ask another question. Trisha hushed him. "Please! Allow me a breath without you butting in. The children of Mihai's half-brothers, James and Jude, all married outside their race, seeking gentiles of common mind and belief. From those of Roman stock to that of the Gauls, Franks, Celts and... and all the other wild and unfettered lovers of freedom and war that my world could conjure up. Even some from the Isle of Meric were chosen by Mother to add their gene stock to James' lineage."

"All the while, your brother is off butchering a people too foolish to realize that they no longer even have a kingly line to look to salvation for. Their own arrogance in thinking that their savior is yet to come has led to so much untimely destruction, Asotos believing them to still be chosen in some way." Trisha laughed bitterly. "And he need look no farther than the end of his nose to find the real heir, the future king who will take his crown, glory and title. Not only is the heir under his nose, but the child is being guarded and protected by his very might and strength."

Zadar exclaimed in question, "Why would Asotos want to protect Mother's seed, especially when that seed will bring all that is his to a finish?! This I don't understand at all!"

"Oh, that's easy to explain." Trisha grinned. "The fool is so full of himself he refuses to believe the obvious. Stick an onion under his nose and he will declare its sweet fragrance. Place a rose before him and he will cry out, because of the thorns, that he has been made a victim of an evil and wicked plot to destroy his house….that is, if the mood is upon him to do so. He thinks so much of his own wisdom he forgets that of others, just like your kind who search so deep so as to be blinded by the obvious."

"Your wicked brother has tried to discover Mother's secrets, especially concerning her kingdom and its day and hour. But Mother is not unaware of Asotos' intentions, and his blind pride. She set up a people not so long ago… About the time of your own Great War, as you know, there was one raging in the Realms Below, too, whose leader of these people declared a period when this war was supposed to begin, and Mother helped that come about, doing so to trick your brother."

"As time went on, Asotos began to believe that Mother was moving these people along by her spirit whereas, in reality, they were just bumbling their way along in their arrogant pride. But the ruse worked, to the point of Asotos delivering his own seed into those people's company, eventually taking over the leadership of that brotherhood with his own chosen Hormaxian followers. After years of searching in the most intimate corners of that order, he could discover no specific person or group that appeared to be chosen or set aside for a special purpose."

"To top it all off, after the Great War ended, those same leaders got so full of themselves that they screwed up every prophecy they interpreted, they aggrandizing their ignorance to the point of deifying their personal opinions while persecuting anyone with a different view. This was too much for Asotos, he not being able to understand how a chosen people could act so… so… stupid unless Mother wasn't really helping them. Disgusted at feeling tricked, he abandoned his search there and returned to the original promised seed, reserving that order to serve him in other devious ways, one of which was to bring his *own* seed to full maturity."

Zadar could not suppress asking, "But the seed still remains within that order, one abandoned by Mother? How can that be so?"

Trisha countered, "I did not say the order was abandoned. Even though many among its leaders have fallen into darkness long ago - their *gentle, loving* words and actions only covers for evil and wicked deeds - the common folk, those who give heart and soul to what they have been taught about our mother and her promises, they are good stock, worth our mother's time and consideration. It is the common folk who influence the boy the most, persons of little wealth but having big hearts and a love for truth, which, sad to say, they get little enough of."

"Anyway, despite the order's leadership, Mother keeps sprinkling little truths into the garble distributed among the common folk, giving them more to digest than most of the poor souls in that retched realm. This also keeps them different from the other orders, odd you can say, what with all their proselytizing and refusing to celebrate and participate with other orders and groups in what most consider appropriate behavior. All this helps keep the boy in a constant state of confusion, his mind desiring one thing and his heart tearing at his soul to act differently. An odd duck is an easy thing to hide in plain sight."

Zadar was truly intrigued, but he wondered, "Why the odd duck, now I mean? Why all the secrecy concerning the boy? The time must be close for his revealing, at least I'd think. And…and wouldn't it be good for us to know so we could aid in his protection and guidance?"

Trisha shook her head. "Honest, caring people may make mistakes. The wrong word might prove disastrous. Also, any undue attention might make Asotos curious about the boy. That's why I and the others have only visited him through the visions in our minds, so our presence wouldn't be felt. But…but there's even more important reasons to keep the child hidden."

At that, Trisha stood, stretching her arms high as she tensed her body to squeeze out the tired blood from her muscles, making room for new, oxygen-rich blood to replace it.

Zadar studied the woman with rapt attention. Her sheer blouse did little other than shade Trisha's olive-brown skin, so distinctive a color for people of her race, and the woman's shapely form burst through her raiment like the sun on a cloudy morning. The man feasted on the moment with a growing passion and desire, dogged by a strange and disconcerting fear, one he had never before experienced, a fear that should he speak the wrong word or make a misguided gesture, the moment would be lost forever, his aching heart filled with lonely bitterness. What was wrong with his head?

Trisha turned and stepped in front of Zadar. She bent forward, resting her hands on his knees, her face only inches from his. "Well?" She asked. "What do you think?"

"Think?! About what?!" Zadar's body erupted with emotion of a magnitude he had long forgotten existed. Even Gabrielle, on their first nights of loving, had not moved the man's explosive ardor to greater heights than he was experiencing at this moment. He struggled with every fiber of his strength to keep his arms in check, they seeking to tear themselves from their shoulder sockets so that wanting hands could explore and fondle the boundless beauty presented to them. Beads of sweat formed on Zadar's forehead as he fought with all his might to keep his eyes on hers and not stare at the two swaying spheres of sensual intoxication singing their hypnotic, impassioned lullaby.

Zadar forced his attention upon Trisha's face, searching the woman's eyes. Was she teasing him, flirting with his senses? No, the woman's eyes betrayed the innocence of a little maiden. She did not see herself as beautiful, so how was it possible others did? Her question had been honest and not related to her appearance or romantic charms. There was more. He could see a sadness buried deep within those eyes, a loneliness sown by years of toil and grief, those scars still open and raw.

All these things Zadar found hiding behind Trisha's obsidian orbs made his heart ache in a terrible and wonderful way, both beautiful and terrifying feelings tearing through him at the same moment. Trisha was special, precious - a rare treasure to be won or lost upon a breath, a word, or the tiniest misstep. Hard as granite mountains but fragile as the finest porcelain, that was this woman. The man shuddered with concern realizing how perilous the moment was. One false step and Trisha would turn away and walk out of his life, and that thought set a fire in Zadar's heart so intense he nearly cried aloud.

Though his eyes continued to peer into Trisha's, Zadar's mind drifted into other worlds of thought. He wished he could make time stand still, the two of them frozen forever as they were, becoming statues eternally placed here for the whole world to see, to admire. Happy would he be to leave for the Forgotten Lands having shared but this one moment with this woman. A sigh of contentment secreted his mouth as he pondered what had become of his heart and why it so troubled him.

"Well?" Zadar was jolted back to reality by Trisha's question. It took a moment to sink in. Shaking his head to clear the fog, he apologized, feigning some lame excuse for his actions. After mildly chiding him, Trisha asked, "I know the night has been long, and we could conclude matters another day, that is, if you wish, or…"

Zadar bolted upright, taking hold of Trisha's arms as he did. "Oh! No! No! Please go on. Your were discussing… reasons… reasons for…"

"Reasons *why* the boy must remain hidden, at least for the moment, the most important of reasons…" Trisha looked into Zadar's face, seeing his fleeting confusion slowly retreating. "Do you want me to tell you?"

"Please!" Zadar nearly shouted, catching himself before he did.

Trisha smiled, her own heart stirring with long-forgotten feelings. "Zadar, this war is a *blood feud*, a *brother war*. Feelings get all mixed up, are all mixed up, and few are the numbers of your kind who have been fully tested out to loyalty and trust for this cause. Indeed, Mother warned me to keep a wary eye out for possible traitors among us."

Disbelief filled Zadar's face, he blurting out, "Impossible! *Impossible! It can't be!* Not now. Not since the Great War that…"

"That did nothing except get millions of your kind killed. Nothing…" Trisha shook her head. "The Great War was a travesty, solving nothing and accomplishing little other than giving your people a stay before the next and greater war - one that must now be fought as certainly as the Second Great

War that was recently waged in the Realms Below. And, oh yes, treason did play a major role in your Great War. From the Day of Tears to the slaughter at Memphis, treasonous voices brought about ruin and devastation."

Trisha stood, glancing at the bubbling waters, "Not all who allied themselves with your wicked brother have fallen into eternal darkness, not yet. This, our Mother did tell me. She said that a wicked act might not betray a wicked heart, for it is not the heart that tears life from the soul, but spirit that is born of the mind. A heart might well seduce the soul into wicked acts, but the mind must surrender fully to the machinations of the heart before the spirit will consume all hope and goodness, casting the soul into eternal darkness."

She frowned. "Do I not repeat what you have long come to already know?"

Zadar agreed, adding, "True, but you have woven your words with an understanding found only among our most wise and exalted Ancients. Their clarity is beyond the peal of a bell on a crystal night." He wrinkled up his face in question. "Why, then, do you trust me with such secrets…me, a stranger so newly introduced to you?"

Trisha thought a moment before answering. "There are many reasons, few tangible, most emotional. First and foremost, I have listened to your mother's heart when she speaks about you. Oh yes, many have been the times when your name has drifted into our conversations, your mother being extremely fond of her youngest child. I feel her trust in you. I trust her feelings. And then there's the sweet music, harmonics, I feel when I'm near you, the same as I felt when Darla stood close to me. Strange how such melodious refrains can come from hearts so torn and twisted by bloodshed and violence."

"And… and I feel no discord when I'm around you. Oh yes, my friend, you have not hidden well your passion for my flesh. I can *smell* your desire for it."

Zadar started to apologize. Trisha placed a finger on his lips, hushing him. "I did not speak of it in disdain, only in passing. Little do I yet know if and when I could accept such overt suggestions, but I believe them to be honest and filled with restraint, your heart seeking my good and not your own. I guess that's also part of the reason I trust you. Few men from my world, even good and honest men, would have been able to control their manly passions had those passions been hurled upon them as yours were upon you. I am sorry. My actions were innocent, but still I should have been more careful, me knowing full well that you are not a god but only a man."

Trisha stepped away, facing the little stream. "It is quite difficult for innocent persons to discern wicked discord in its early stages." She faced Zadar. "My friend, neither you nor I are any longer innocent."

"How so?" Zadar asked, he being more absorbed with her earlier statement.

Noticing, Trisha admonished him to pay closer attention to the moment. "You and I are so different than most I have met in this world. We become suspicious and wary when confronted with new situations. We question things when others see no reason to. My heart has been twisted by the old evil that still lives in my former world, and I believe you also have a heart twisted to those same harmonics. Though not evil ourselves, we feel evil in all its convoluted ways. I cannot hide those evil harmonics, it being one reason, I fear, for having acquired so few friends in this place."

"You project the same harmonics, but the people like you, trust you, so they disregard the evil they feel, eventually forgetting it is there. And that's the danger. Others carry similar evil vibrations within their own hearts, I think for more dubious reasons, but the people ignore them also, thus allowing the traitor easy access to the secrets hidden in their minds and hearts. I know this as fact, for I felt it tonight at the Council. Evil resides among us, the room echoing its warning, but none, not even Mihai will listen to their own hearts and accept its presence…that is, except for your poor sister, Darla."

"What do you imply?" Zadar asked, confused.

"This…" Trisha waved her hand as she spoke. "Your harmonic finger-print rang clear for me because of your close proximity to me and length of time I was given to study your scent so to speak. I felt the scent of others but could not trace them, they being smothered out by Darla's, which is almost overpowering. Whatever evil resides within her is so grave and venomous, even a dullard can sense it, making many people think the woman is cracked, if you know what I mean."

Zadar nodded.

Trisha sadly shook her head. "I don't believe that to be the case. Darla is badly damaged, partly from the evil - I have heard some say demons - but also from the way she has been made to feel the outcast. The woman lives, I believe, a waking nightmare, constantly battling something within her mind that seeks her enslavement or destruction. Still, I feel a sweet music flowing through her, from her, and I see that those who also feel it, as you do, draw ever closer to her in strange and lasting bonds."

She looked Zadar in the eyes. "I have been told that there exists a love-bond between her comrades at arms and herself, a bond of blood and loyalty. It is the leadership, the wise and Ancients among your kind who resist the woman's advances for companionship. They treat her with polite disdain, grudgingly indulging her company – at Mother's request, of course – while carefully avoiding the creature's *contaminating* touch. Like a leper from my old world who is loved and hated she is, loved for pity's sake, her siblings wishing to see no one suffer as she, and hated out of fear of contamination, that somehow they will catch their sister's disease."

Shaking her head in wonder, Trisha confessed, "I don't understand your kind, so confusing they are to me. How can they consign a child to such emotional tribulation and still be the very sons who men like John and Abraham held in such esteem? Darla is a sweet, caring woman, she being willing to sacrifice her own life for anyone in that room tonight, even Ardon. I know her spirit that well, can feel it. I trust her with all my heart, the same as I find myself trusting you."

Reaching out and taking Zadar's hand, Trisha added, concerned, "There were other evils there this night, evils of malice and deceit, evils unrestrained by loving and caring hearts. Such malcontents can cloak their evil behind benevolent faces and kindly posturing while lying in wait to strike, like an adder on a shaded path. That, my friend, is why the secrets I have told you this eve must remain that… secrets. Should word of this boy leak out before the coming hour, all that Mother has worked for may be in jeopardy. It must remain our secret."

Zadar was still full of questions. He was about to ask another when he saw Trisha yawn drowsily. She raised her hand. "Please, my friend, I feel the sands of sleep descending upon me. This has been a long and draining day for me on both my mind and heart. We will pick up our discussion at another hour."

No sooner had her words been spoken than a sudden wave of exhaustion swept over her. Sitting to avoid stumbling and possibly falling into the chill waters, Trisha let out a sigh, closing her eyes. "Dear one…" she offered groggily, "give me a moment and then we shall return to the Council."

Drifting off to sleep, Trisha leaned into Zadar's shoulder, snuggling her face against his chest. As the rhythm of the woman's breathing turned into the melody of a sleeping song, Zadar wrapped his arm around her shoulders, pulling her tight.

He smiled, pleased with the moment, no desire to return to the others, no desire to ever leave this place, never, not as long as this woman remained here. Never before in his long life did he the man feel as content and satisfied as he did now, and he wanted to savor this time for as long as possible.

The little stream bubbled and blurped along its merry way, its crystal clear waters eventually cascading into the blackness far below. Tirelessly, continuously, the tiny tempest sang its sweet, merry song to the tired sojourners sleeping upon the stone bench hiding in the shadows of the narrow draw.

'*Sleep on. Sleep on.*
Tomorrow is soon enough to wake.
Sleep on. Sleep on.
Find peace in a troubled world.'

ဆ   ဆ   ဆ

The Council's business lasted well into the early morning hours. First, details of Asotos' offer were disclosed, requiring much open discussion, at times appearing to be little more than the desire of certain Ancients to extol their assumed wisdom regarding the subject. At length, attention was turned to the series of events that occurred up to and the taking of the Zephath's crew. Of course, each individual account needed to be scrutinized for fear some *important* detail might be overlooked. Even Ma-we eventually tired of such games but, out of polite etiquette, remained silent.

Captain BedanSheba of the Shikkeron was grilled to distraction. He patiently attempted to describe the Shikkeron's part played in this adventure, but was constantly interrupted by questions, more often caused by ignorance of navy procedure than actual relation to events. The man was never in good humor, hadn't been since first being snubbed for promotion many long wars ago, something that had repeated itself throughout his less than glorious career. When Ardon questioned Bedan again about some trivial matter, Bedan's temper almost got the best of him. Embarrassed and tired, he finally was dismissed, skulking away into the shadows.

Tashi, governor over the Trizentine, was well received. Being an Ancient, few dared question her account of matters. Her testimony went quickly, accounting the seemingly random Stasis attacks against the settlements in the colonies on Sustrepho, the most distant, inhabited planet in the Trizentine star systems. Her description of kidnap and torture of innocent settlers stirred many a heart to righteous indignation.

Mihai also took the stage, even sheepishly describing her encounter with the droid, including her rescue by a mysterious ally. Then there were other eyewitness accounts from transports picking up strange communications and peculiar sightings of ships being where ships shouldn't be.

It was Euroaquilo who stole the show. He could not speak unless his entire body was consumed in it. His booming voice, wild exuberance, flair for theatrics and love for the poetic made him a favorite at the Council, and he was at his best this eve. When finished, he had touched every level of the audience's emotions, from heights of laughter to the depths of despair, drawn the people into his account, tugging at their heartstrings with his vivid renderings of the pirate scourge until no dry eye could be found in the house.

Of course, Ardon needed to have his say, he being more knowledgeable than many about this most inhospitable place in space. He was long-winded, self-aggrandizing to the point of braggadocio, consuming time with seemingly endless, minute, unimportant, detailed accounts liberally peppered with anecdotal illustrations rarely related to the night's subject. Still, there was great value in the things the man said. As Ma-we was often heard to say of his counsel, 'If you dig deep enough, you will find water, but dig quickly or you will certainly die of thirst!'

When Ardon finally paused to sip some water, Mihai politely interrupted, requesting she be allowed the privilege of summing matters up, it really being the fear that soon the audience's snoring would overwhelm the speakers. At length, the matter was taken to the table, meaning it was time for open debate and, hopefully, final consensus.

It was during this debate agreement was reached that, first, the capture of the Zephath's crew was not a random act and, even though carried out by Stasis Pirates, it was an act perpetrated by Asotos; second, that Mihai must accept Asotos' request to moot with him on the chosen planet, EremiaPikros, she accepting; and, third, that a peaceful solution was better for the welfare of the prisoners than warlike threatening. Ma-we accepted this in principle, but strongly suggested Mihai retain a small contingent of soldiers to accompany the entourage, a fatefully wise decision.

Ma-we had also chosen to go, she telling that her presence had also been requested. PalaHar and Tizrela were to be her color guard, with Tashi and Ardon among the chief councilors to follow in her train. She also requested Zadar be allowed to go along, she not providing reason other than he needed the training.

And then, to everyone's surprise, Ma-we requested that Darla come along as well. The room erupted in angry debate with a few staunchly defending the girl, but most condemning it as recipe for disaster. For twenty minutes, the arguing persisted, almost to the point of riot. Finally, Ma-we stood, her own anger silencing the people. There was no place for debate, she declared. The choice was final. With or without the will of the Council, Darla was to accompany her, being her personal horsemaiden. Ardon still attempted a coup, he ranting on for five minutes before Ma-we silenced him. It was settled. No more debate.

What of Darla? She had weathered the storm in silent, stoic fashion, the same as she had done so many times before. At length, when everything quieted down, she slipped out a side door, disappearing into the night. Few noticed; fewer cared. After all, it was well known the girl did not have feelings, at least feelings like the rest of them. She never cried or laughed when in their company…no emotions, no emotions at all, 'poor thing, poor sick, cracked, little creature.'

The Council continued its business of preparing for the Prisoner Exchange. There were to be numerous ships - one battle cruiser, two frigates, four barqs and a few smaller transports. For some unknown reason, Ma-we requested the Shikkeron be included, she wanting it for herself and her party. Then she requested a dozen fighters be assigned to the taskforce. Some grumbled, but Ma-we won out, citing the enemy's need to be shown force while extending an opened hand.

When complaint arose another time concerning the growing army being taken to the Prisoner Exchange, Ma-we's temper flared. "I will not lift up a hand in defense of my children… cannot! If your brother has set a trap for you, who will escape if all you have are threatening words to exchange for missiles and swords? *Don't be complete fools!* Even an *ass* knows when danger lurks down the road!"

Finally, plans were set, the date of departure decided upon, the exchange goods and enemy prisoners used for trading. The biggest hurdle was the need to surrender AsreHalom, now better known as 'Salak', back to Asotos. There was little choice. The murderer of multitudes was to be returned to Asotos or there would be no exchange and, worse yet, Asotos threatened to give his hostages back to the Stasis Pirates if Salak was not given to him. With settling of this final issue, the council meeting was concluded.

Being such a late hour, few lingered in the council chambers after being dismissed. Some had unfinished business, others desired to capture a fleeting moment with a dear companion not seen for a while. Mihai? She remained seated, elbows resting on the table, hands holding an aching head. Her experience with Trisha was troubling enough, the pain from being pummeled by the woman's telepathic attack still hammering the back of her head. And then the fiasco over Darla had delivered a migraine that made Mihai's forehead pound with a nauseous headache.

Ardon smiled to himself as the raised platform descended into the floor. In a few moments, he and Tashi would be exiting into the night in search of spending a few carefree days at the mountain hot springs on Diamond Ridge. It was not to be…

"Lord Ardon!" Surprised, Ardon turned to see Ma-we approaching, her face stern and filled with displeasure. "Lord Ardon, a word." At that, Ma-we's hand went up, signaling Bedan to come over.

This was not good. Ardon attempted to excuse himself, claiming some important errand. Ma-we dismissed it. *"Listen, you old snipe, I want a word with you!"* She walked up close, looking into his face. "Your actions were uncalled for tonight! My girl has done nothing to you, other than display greater dignity when humiliated by you and the other silly fools here!"

Surprised at Ma-we's curt remarks, Ardon defended his actions. Placing an opened hand over his heart, he pleaded, "I only spoke up about a matter the others here held in their hearts. I…"

Ma-we brushed him off. "Horse*shit!*" She glanced over at Bedan, who was nearing. Lowering her voice, she warned, "You pull a stunt like that again and I'll make sure you regret it!"

"You wanted to see me, Mother?" Bedan offered salutation as he approached.

Ma-we shot another warning glance at Ardon before turning toward

Bedan and taking his hand as she smiled, answering, "Yes, dear, I did. Just a moment, please."

Hiding her frown, Ma-we politely addressed Ardon, asking, "My son, would you be so willing as to do your mother a tiny favor?"

Having already forgotten Ma-we's recent threat, Ardon graciously bowed, answering with a grin while glancing out of the corner of his eye to make sure his audience - Bedan - was paying attention. After all, it was only proper for the fellow to see just how important a councilor Ardon was in Mother's eyes. "It would be my greatest pleasure, my Lord and Lady. Whatever you wish..."

Ma-we curtly snapped back, she not even pretending a smile. "*I wish a lot!* But I will keep my task for you simple, *something* at your *level* of manageability. Wisdom is as wisdom does..." She cast a quick eye toward Bedan whose shocked expression was telling of her success at insult.

Ma-we's affront to Ardon had been worse than a stinging slap to the face, wincing as if receiving such a blow. There was no wish on his part to see Bedan's reaction - the greatest part of Mother's insult - to have a common officer witness such a rebuff. Gathering his wits about him, he stuttered a polite response.

Ma-we's tone changed little, her displeasure at Ardon's earlier actions still troubling her. "Lord Ardon, you are to go as soon as may be to Chrusion and obtain for me some of the chrysolite stones from the Black Mountains. They must be from the Black Mountains."

Ardon's jaw dropped in shock and surprise, quickly making a flustered reply. "My Lady! My Lady! It's yeoman's duty you are requesting of me! Certainly you must be mistaken. I have many important matters to conclude before leaving for the Prisoner Exchange. It will be nine days' hard running just to reach the planet and return. We leave on the tenth day. That gives us less than one day to accomplish our mission. I will have no time to prepare for..."

Ma-we cut him off in a curt retort. "All I need is a breathing lump of flesh to stand beside me at the Prisoner Exchange, someone to look *official*. I expect nothing more than that from you. It will take no time to pack your things for the trip, seeing that you've already done it, *haven't you?*" She lowered an eyebrow, staring accusatively into Ardon's face.

Turning to Bedan, Ma-we's sweet smile returned. "Son, I want you to deliver this...this sneak... to Chrusion and make sure he does what he's been told."

Bedan frowned, still stinging from Ardon's uncalled for grilling earlier that night. "Mother, I have been stationed on patrol for eighteen months. I was hoping to take a day or so and visit friends in Oros. Plus, I have the Shikkeron to ready for the trip, it in need of extensive maintenance."

"You've plenty of time to meet with old comrades when we finish at the Prisoner Exchange." Ma-we patted Bedan's shoulder. "Hopefully, this trip will keep you both out of mischief."

Bedan said nothing, his eyes telling Mother of his disgust at taxiing the *great Ardon* across star systems. Ma-we stretched, giving the man a soft kiss on his cheek and began to play with a button on his uniform. "Son, I know the Shikkeron is in need of repair and I have already taken counsel with Euroaquilo to have that assignment given to a qualified officer. The Starlight has just been refitted with a whole bunch of new toys and its crew has not yet been assigned their commander. You take the little cutter and run it through its paces, shoot a target or two to test out its arsenal."

She looked up and into his eyes. "Remember, as captain, *you* are in charge of this mission. *All those aboard* must do the bidding of the *captain*." She stared at Ardon. "That includes *everyone!*"

Looking back at Bedan and gently stroking his upper arm, Ma-we flirtingly cooed, "Now be a good son and deliver back to me the baubles I have requested. If Lord Ardon should dally, you have my permission to leave him there." She laughed.

Ma-we then addressed a very disgruntled Ardon. "Thank you, sir, for volunteering for this very dangerous mission, though I believe it safer there than here for the moment. Leftenant Darla shall be charged with the repairs and equipping of the Shikkeron for the trip. I believe that will keep my child busy enough to prevent her hunting you down in the depths of space."

She warned Bedan, "Do be careful and keep a good eye out for possible attack. But let me warn you, Darla is an excellent fighter pilot! It would be better to surrender up the councilor here than risk a confrontation. No one would slight you for trying to protect the rest of the crew, given the circumstance."

Ardon was thoroughly miffed. He detested the dressing down, especially in front one of the *lesser children* like Bedan. And to have *him* placed in charge?! That was almost too much! But it was Darla who was most troubling. Why all the fuss? Still... Mother was in a mood. Better leave things go...

Ma-we's eyes filled with sadness as she turned her attention back to Ardon. How could he not understand the importance she placed on having Darla's presence at the Prisoner Exchange? True, she had confided in no one the reasons, but Ardon was not dense - that dense - to see that it was not on some emotional whim that the girl had been selected to make the trip.

'Pity...what a pity, he cannot see the forest.' Ma-we attempted a smile and, in a gentle voice, suggested, "I know you planned to share some quiet hours with Tashi. Why not take her along with you?" She glanced up to see the woman loitering near the door. "She's been too long in the outer reaches of the universe. The lady needs a little special attention. I know you can deliver that. She will love the trip and cherish the company."

Ardon's gloominess dissolved in an instant. He hugged Ma-we and, after giving her a gentle kiss, hurried over to Tashi. Arm in arm, the two disappeared through the door leading to the outer balcony and into the darkness.

ଡ଼   ଡ଼   ଡ଼

Darla's embarrassment had quickly turned to anger nearing that of rage, but she was a good girl, never allowing her inner feelings to betray her to others. She quietly slipped from the auditorium into the night shadows. Euroaquilo had not at first noticed her leaving, but there was little he could have done at that moment anyway. Finally, after finishing business with Ma-we, he bid his adieus and hurried away to search for his girl.

There was a place where Darla would sometimes go when the dark mood took her. It was quiet and out of the way, a place where the world did not intrude, where she could be alone with her feelings. Euroaquilo was taken there once when Darla was still a maiden, she showing him her secret garden, her private place. He believed she might well be sequestered there at this moment, an ancient garden about two furlongs northwest of the old palace…at least that was what it was at the time. Mulberry trees, holly, mistletoe and thorny rose vines dominated the ruins of what the Ancients called a 'Cherub's Chatue' or 'Gate', its blue-green, iridescent stones charred and burnt as if by some molten blast, along with the remains of a northern wall, now overgrown with black lichens and hoary ivy. Upon its inner face were the rune letters that, when translated in the ancient tongue, read, 'Druid Zodiak Doract Tosommia' meaning 'So shall come to all sorcerers who apostatize'.

It was a gloomy place, said to have fallen to ruin during the day of quaking, the night the burning of the Great Star, Lagandow, first appeared in the evening sky above Palace City. Few children visited the garden, it being so foreboding and ominous. PalaHar once wrote of it, 'It reminds one of living death. Even animals avoid the place. Never does the sun reach through the gloom of the upper foliage. And when you stand in the desolate center circle, there comes upon your heart a feeling of unwelcome. Few can tolerate more than fleeting moments in that dismal garden.'

Struggling his way through the thicket of thorns and twisted vines, Euroaquilo finally reached the edge of the inner circle of this most dismal of places. Darkness was pushed aside here by an eerie glow that radiated out from the charred ruins and up through the lifeless soil. Searching the green gloom, his eyes focused on a lone figure, slowly pacing back and forth, wrapped in its own arms, mumbling curses and oaths.

Darla was in an abnormally foul mood, so deep in vindictive thought she had not noticed Euroaquilo's arrival. The man slowly backed away from the clearing, shaking his head sadly. This was no time to intrude upon the woman, not this way. He quietly made his way from the garden and sat at the curb of the lonely, narrow street that wound its way past, pondering what to do next. He decided to give the girl some time. A few minutes, a half hour maybe, and she just might be willing to accept a little company. Maybe...

Ardon's actions were totally inappropriate this last eve, but so was that of the entire Council. And what of him? Had he not done more than stand once in the girl's defense? Had he bellowed out in his commander's voice her innocence, might things have ended differently? All were guilty of inaction. Only Terey and Planetee and that fellow from the Second Realm... yes, that Jebbson Garlock fellow...they, alone, other than Mother, had stood the storm of protest with vigor and determination, defending Darla to the end.

Still, Euroaquilo was not head of the Council, only an invited member. There had been protocol to follow. Ardon was placed in charge after the new field marshal departed. He clenched his fists in frustration, angrily shaking his head. Protocol would never buy his silence again!

When he hoped sufficient time had passed, Euroaquilo made his way into the thicket, stomping and crashing his way while calling out Darla's name. As he burst out of the twisted, jungle-like tangle of foliage, he looked up to see the girl frozen in place, angry eyes staring in his direction. The woman did not run. It was not her nature. Had the person arriving been unwanted company, even Ardon, she would have quietly dismissed herself and slid away into the darkness. That was Darla's style.

But this was *Euroaquilo*. Even if she had wanted to flee, it would have been impossible. Euroaquilo was her mentor, her god, the man who gave her life and breath. He was her reason for living when others around her were surrendering to the evil of the moment. Through glazed eyes, she stared at the man she so loved, pressure of hidden tears pushing at her eyes until it felt as though they would explode. She refused to cry. No...nor run to the arms she so wanted to encircle her. The pain was too great for that now. Not now... The furnace of wrath building in her chest was still heating up, waiting to be unleashed in all its fury.

Euroaquilo smiled innocently. "Oh, there you are! I have been searching everywhere. Now that business is finished, I'd hoped we could enjoy some private time...you know, go do something together, just the two of us."

Cross-armed, Darla stood erect with both feet planted like pillars rooted in granite. Other than a quiver in her upper lip and puffy, red, tormented eyes, the woman refused to surrender up the roiling emotion torturing her. *She* was lord of her destiny! No power in this or the Realms Below could force the woman to act against her iron will. She, the child of a hundred wars, standing countless battle lines when others around her fled…she, the maiden of secret terrors, refused to give up this moment, this victory over mindless fools, to her own lack of control.

Sadness swept over Euroaquilo, watching Darla struggle for mastery of her inner self. What strength and majesty and power of will! Who among all of Lowenah's children was of greater constitution than this woman, who more perfect in discipline and might? This was no unstable, unpredictable woman of fragile spirit who would put the success of the coming Prisoner Exchange at risk. Now, more than ever, Euroaquilo wished he had spoken with greater boldness in Darla's defense at the Council meeting.

The woman was dangerous to herself, though. Euroaquilo knew this child well, but what of the depth of her inner strength? There were limits to one's ability to subdue emotional stress. He had seen it all too often on the field of battle. A person's sword might well succeed in bringing to ruin its enemy, only for their mind to shatter when the moment of rest arrived. To this day, he paid visits upon close companions who had not yet regained control of their minds, they residing in the shadow-worlds of random dreams and frightening visions.

Darla was truly stressed to the limit, more so than he had seen in recent memory, the Council's uncalled for verbal abuses having been severely cruel to her. Euroaquilo must play this carefully or his girl might just snap. Few any longer held her trust. Did he? The man frowned, sighing, deciding to face the *beast* head on. After all, that was his nature. Isn't that how he acquired his name in the first place?

He extended his hands, softly speaking so apologetically, "My DusmeAstron, my heart yearns for your approval. Have I caused you harm this night? Have my actions damaged your tender heart?"

Darla cast her gaze toward the ground, two giant teardrops falling into the shadows. 'DusmeAstron', Euroaquilo's name given to her the day he took the child for his own…'Western Star', 'Sunset Star', he had said it was so fitting that she carry the name of the last daughter of the night, the brightest star after the setting of the sun, it bringing hope of a night filled with light and promise.

"Please, my Lord, do not kill your servant girl with fair speech."

Euroaquilo began again. "My DusmeAstron…"

Darla spun around, hiding her face as a sob escaped her. "Please, my Lord, do not kill your daughter with your words!"

"Should I die instead of you!" Euroaquilo blurted out, his voice strained to cracking. He stepped forward, arms outstretched, pleading, "You and I are children of but one blood. We are one, you and I. Will not my heart bleed if yours is wounded? If you are sad, will I not cry? My heart weeps over the widowhood of my beloved sister. Please! Please! Allow your own flesh to weep in anguish over your loss."

Darla slumped as quiet sobs increased, having surrendered for the moment any control over them. "My Lord... please... My Lord... please don't..."

In a heartbeat, Euroaquilo was standing behind Darla, his arms wrapped around her shoulders. He could feel convulsive energy coursing through the woman's body, the wound upon her heart intense as he heralded his regrets in her ear. "My darling, had I known the agony this passing eve was to heap upon you, I would have stood the line to the death in your defense!"

Pulling away and spinning around, Darla stared at Euroaquilo, her teary eyes glaring their anger. No longer could the woman contain her fiery rebukes, unleashing them with full fury. "*Damn* their worthless skins! *All of them*! *Ardon...! Damn* his no good hide! *Old bag of shit*! Windy shit, *useless dung heap!*"

She nearly choked, taking a breath. "I have drenched my sword in the blood of all living souls to preserve their *asses* while they romance diplomatic behind the safety of distant walls! I have stood the line while the *bravest and noblest* of my kindred fled, pissing in *fright* from nearing death, my own flesh standing as a shield of safety for them!"

Shaking a fist in anger, she cried, "*Four times* I have lain in my own blood while my spirit sought escape! I have crawled miles in the filth with ruined legs, dragging my sister's corpse so the enemy could not desecrate her temple! Through the ravages of famine, fire, fear and fury, I have carried out my sacred duties in order to bring this *goddamned Rebellion* to a finish, a rebellion I share no responsibility for starting! What *goddamned right* do all those miserable ingrates have in declaring *who* is sane and fit?!"

Euroaquilo sadly nodded his head.

Darla was not finished. In anguish, she cried, "My sword has consigned hundreds of souls to the fires of Hell! Do they think my heart doesn't weep over such murder?!"

Turning away, she put her hands to her face and sobbed, "*Never* have I requested *one thing* for myself from any of those *bastards,* not even a straw pillow for my head! Their council I do not seek; my opinions I keep to myself. Did I intrude tonight, placing my name high up above the others? My soul sought escape from this night. But no! The Lord of Lords commanded my appearance there, and then it was by request of the new king that I acted the part of consort, escaping to the shadows when possible."

She shook her head. "Many are those who, not by design but by fate or circumstance, have received greater glory and rank. Never once did I complain unless it was one of my brothers who deserved the recognition... and rarely was that even delivered. At Avery, my troop of less than thirty held a force of four hundred at bay for six hours, preventing our flank from being overrun. All but six I left behind on the frozen sands, digging their shallow graves myself with bare, bloody fingers. Who of those so wise and noble reflected upon the sacrifices made to stay the line that day? Not even a *note* placed in the official records for such gallant valor could I get them to write!"

Turning to look in Euroaquilo's face, Darla lamented, "What of me? 'Oh my! We must be so careful, mustn't we? She's *cracked*, you know, unstable, unpredictable. She may say something wrong and offend the Great Serpent…' *Wicked WastePipe! Lord of the dung heap and the flies!* 'Oh! We must be so careful to not upset him! Ardon must stay close to the brattling for fear she will put others at risk!' That… *that*, my Lord, is *my* reward for countless years of sacrifice and bravery!"

Darla rested weary hands on Euroaquilo's upper arms. She was exhausted, but the fires of distress were not yet extinguished. There was another storm building, hopefully the last, but he could not tell. "My dear Dusme…"

Darla stepped back, livid with rage. "Where were those *great leaders* when we lay in the ruins of Mordem, huddling in desperation to warm the dying as the winter winds screamed and bombs burst all around?!"

Tears finally gushed forth. Like a mother filled with grief, she wailed, "I should have perished on our day of lost valor at Memphis! As least I would have fallen with those who were real heroes. Jared died, pierced through by a lance, pulling my broken body from the charging, horned beasts. Tifara, my dearest companion, was torn asunder as she shielded me from a rogue missile, my leg being nearly severed at the knee when it exploded. Our reward for holding that gap on that day of infamy was seventy slaughtered companions and an ever-aching injury that hasn't healed completely down to this day. And not one *goddamned 'thank you'* for all our suffering…!"

The color had drained from Darla's face, her energy quickly waning. She stared up and into Euroaquilo's eyes, searching…searching. Falling onto his chest, fingers clutching at his shirt, distraught, she cried, "What good is my life?! If I should die tomorrow, will I be remembered only as the woman whose mind is demon-bent?!" She buried her face on his shoulder and wept.

Euroaquilo embraced his child in burly arms. He could hear her labored breathing as tears sapped what little strength remained. A moan came from the woman's lips, indicating a powerful headache was brewing. Soon Darla's knees began to buckle, no longer having the ability to sustain their load.

Mustering the last of her energy, Darla looked into Euroaquilo's face, whimpering, "I have tried to be a good child… so hard I've tried. You do believe me… don't you? Don't…"

Darla collapsed, fainted maybe, Euroaquilo catching her up in his arms before she fell. Carrying her to a grassy corner of the garden under a mulberry tree before laying the girl down and sitting beside her, he looked around at the things the eerie light revealed to his eyes, finally studying the runes in the broken wall. Funny, he had avoided this place like all the other children did, but now he wondered why. There was a quiet comfort hidden here. It wasn't foreboding…it felt secure. That was it, restful and secure, like none of the evil in the universe could penetrate the opaque jungle surrounding this private world. It was a safe place.

At least that was how it seemed to be for Darla. Already she was fast asleep, her breathing deep and peaceful. There appeared to be a force of some kind watching over the girl. Euroaquilo could feel it, too. She would rest comfortably tonight, nestled in this thorny fortress. No bad dreams would invade her mind. The mysterious forces of this place would see to that.

Euroaquilo began a little song, attempting to force his rather loud, bass voice to sing in a hush. At length, the merry tune - one he had so often sung to his lady when she was still a maiden in the palace - came to a finish. He looked up to see a glow in the eastern sky, knowing a new day was quickly approaching. Well, what the hurry? No one would think to search here for him and… and his duties could wait a little while.

He lay down beside Darla, whispering in her ear:

> *"May the Star of the West sail on to worlds trouble-free.*
> *There is not another like you,*
> *nor will there ever be.*
>
> *You have taught us how to live in the shadows of death,*
> *and to die while finding treasures of life.*
>
> *Teach us,*
> *No…teach me your ways so that I, too,*
> *may become wise like you.*
>
> *Be patient, be patient with us and allow us,*
> *please, to also grow up.*
>
> *You are not forgotten and unloved,*
> *never will be,*
> *never will…"*

A mist arose from the fading light, smothering Euroaquilo in a drowsy embrace. His head fell, resting against Darla's shoulder. There they remained, long into the following evening, the ever-shade of this protective jungle hiding them from all the sights and sounds of the busy world of Palace City.

ಜಿ   ಜಿ   ಜಿ

The evening had not been kind to Mihai. Her earlier speech was now all but forgotten due to later events. And her kingship? Only a few visited their congratulations upon her after the council meeting was finished. Few remembered, she supposed. A confusing kaleidoscope of visions and words spun around in her head. Trisha's warnings still painfully echoed in her thoughts, acting to jumble the tortured recollections of earlier proceedings.

What was clear, though, was the fact that the world was about to change, was changing…had changed. The new field marshal had seen to that. Tomorrow, war would arise, and this time it would not attempt to contain the enemy by treaty or armistice. No! This woman spoke of *total* war, a battle to the finish either by annihilation or expulsion of Asotos and his people from this realm. One or the other, or by their own extinction through the same combat, there was no other option offered this time - *total* war, leading to *total* victory - or *total* extermination. Oh well, she was to sit this one out, only having to decide when the slaughter was to begin. 'Not tonight! Ponder it another time.' Mihai forced her mind on to other matters.

What of Darla? Mihai shook her head, thinking about the humiliation heaped upon the girl this eve. The councilors were blind to the reality of this person, Darla being outstanding in loyalty and resolve. She was loved and trusted by those who stood the course of battle beside her, but the Council? There were few upon it, truly, few at the meeting tonight who understood war let along actually having shared in making it. Valiant mighty ones like Terey, Planetee, Euroaquilo, and PalaHar were rare among the councilors.

And of Tizrela? Mihai didn't know. From the battle of Melas, the Black Pit, during the Third Megiddo War until Memphis, she had been one of the outstanding proponents for total war. But something had changed the day they carried her shattered body away from the blistered plain in front of that city. Maybe it was the destruction of her regiment in Din's counterattack – so many of her closest companions slaughtered - or the severe injuries that took years to heal. Or was it the cumulative effect of seeing so much death and destruction from the endless wars? Whatever it was, the woman seemed to have lost her edge, her subdued support of the new field marshal or of Darla a reflection of it. Did she still have the mettle it took to lead armies? Mihai wondered.

What of herself? Darla received little support from her, the person who should have been the girl's most loyal confederate. Why, even that Garlock fellow, a man never sharing the blade with the woman, stood defiantly in Darla's defense, describing her as the 'most ardent supporter of the innocent soul of all of Yehowah's children', a statement that rankled more than one at the Council. Mihai? Well, she acted *kingly*, staying aloof and not openly choosing sides. Mihai hung her head in shame. But that was no excuse! Even her throbbing head gave leave to absolution. She just had not thought it that important, that is, until she watched the devastation grow on her sister's face. By then it was too late.

A smile of shame grew on her lips. At least Euroaquilo stood up for the girl. And Terey and Planetee, why, they were ferocious in their defense of Darla! Had more, just a few, possibly just she, herself, raised a fist in support, the crowd might well have been swayed to see it Mother's way without her being forced to cast humiliation upon her daughter.

Ma-we had done the best she could, seeing her new king did nothing. Not wanting to usurp the throne, she worked out a compromise that still permitted Darla's presence at the Prisoner Exchange while salving the concerns of the child's opponents. Ardon would stand in as guardian, being near just in case his *protective services* were needed. But protecting whom? *The 'WastePipe'?!* Mihai rested her head in her hand, slowly shaking it in sadness.

What of Darla? The woman proved she was tough as nails. Mihai had looked into her eyes when the pronouncement was passed by Council vote that she must submit to Ardon's oversight. She had been pummeled for over twenty minutes, one councilor after another publicly extolling the child's *unstable sickness*, which statement was always followed apologetically by 'through no fault of her own'. Then to be crushed by Mother's request she promise to respect and obey the Council's decision? How devastating and humiliating!

What made Mihai feel the worst was the fact that Darla stood alone through all those insults, only slipping away after the Council was finished with her and had moved on to other subjects. And Mihai? The new, *great and wonderful* king? She had not even noticed the girl leaving.

A gentle hand touched Mihai's shoulder, stirring her from those thoughts. She looked up into Terey's face, forcing a smile. How old Terey looked - that is, if the people of this world ever looked old. No, it was more like worn and tired, like a weathered tree that has seen too many winters. She sighed, "Well, my Dear, we have survived another one."

Terey smiled oh so lonely, and took to gently massaging one of Mihai's shoulders. At length, she asked, "The Chisamore pulls out tomorrow. I will be leaving by shuttle from the Palace City Spaceport in the morning. Will you come to see me off?"

Mihai stared at her, a questioning gaze growing on her face.

Terey answered without being asked. "They are short experienced pilots, so I volunteered to help them out for awhile. After all, I wasn't needed at the Prisoner Exchange, me only being here tonight to offer support to you and that new field marshal of yours. The Chisamore is an old tub more ready for the bone-yard than a front line carrier, but it's the best we've got, seeing production's behind schedule on its replacement. It's been refitted as best as could be. I don't think its engines will blow."

'How tired she appears, almost pallid.' Mihai thought as she looked into Terey's troubled face. Terey needed some rest, a break, but could she survive one? Maybe the woman's body needed rest, but could her mind take it? No, Mihai doubted it. 'Better to keep busy than have idle time to think.' The mind might take a person to places it rather not be. Still…

Mihai was concerned for Terey's safety. The Chisamore was a relic by any stretch of the imagination, better suited for a museum than for fighting. Originally built as a capital ship, it served valiantly for several decades until being torpedoed with the loss of half its crew during the GrayStone Debacle. It was salvaged from deep space and refitted and then rebuilt into an attack carrier, it remaining on front line service for over the next three hundred years, until the end of the King's War. Its list of honors included every major engagement of the Fourth Fleet during that time.

'Wheel within a wheel…' Mihai grimaced at the thought, last of the Korvikion class carrack, designed for ramming but upgraded to dreadnaught. Four times it had been decommissioned and once written off for scrap. But the endless need for ships to patrol their vast empire necessitated the need to revive it. She believed it should have been long gone to the scrap yard, but when Admiral Sujin was Commissioner of Salvage over the navy yards, all that was brought to a halt. Every ship thereafter that came off line, no matter its condition, was either placed in mothballs, parted out, or refitted and sent back to work in some other capacity.

Mihai questioned Terey's decision to go on station with the Chisamore. "Why that boat? Even with a refit, it's still a flying deathtrap…was when it was new, more so now. Why, a modern frigate can outgun it, could turn it into a Roman candle before it could bring its own guns to bear. There are several other carriers in desperate need of qualified pilots. Why the Chisamore?"

Terey frowned. "Dear…my dear, you know full well the sacrifice each of us must make to keep this kingdom safe. Is my soul better or more important than the other hundreds who are also sailing on her? They needed a good fighter pilot. My 17 was sitting idle, so I offered to fill in. For life or death, is the way I see it."

Mihai turned to stare at the table, she feeling selfish for wanting to keep Terey safe for herself, to satisfy her heart's needs. Terey and Mihai went way back, the woman having been Mihai's personal flight instructor in the days of the glider races so many eons ago. The two were wing mates since the Second Megiddo War, flying in the same squadrons, sharing the same bunks, rations, facing the same dangers. Mihai did not want to lose her dear companion to an accident caused by a piece of flying junk.

At long last and in subdued voice, she asked Terey, "Where are you headed?" looking back into Terey's eyes.

Terey stopped massaging Mihai's shoulder, stepped back and sighed. With effort she answered, "Eden's Gate…"

Mihai looked at the pain that crossed Terey's face. Bitter were the memories from that place. Hundreds or possibly thousands of good, brave, fighter pilots had come to their end protecting that portal. 'Portal to the Universe' it was called in days of peace. 'Passage from Hell' was the name often heralded by sailors now, it being constantly in need of protection from an enemy who wanted it desperately and was willing to expend their own thousands to get it. If the children lost Eden's Gate, they might well lose the Empire. The issue had long been settled by high command. 'Hold Eden's Gate at all cost.'

"We… we are to rendezvous with the Fourth Fleet at some undisclosed location." Terey frowned again. "You know Admiral Sujin. He's the one who renamed the Chisamore after her last resurrection from the abyss… was the old Argototh, named after the Battle of Argototh Heights on Stargaton…" She shook her head. "I'm sorry. Why am I telling you? You were there. Well, anyway, Sujin is all about giving *need to know* commands. He's a queer duck, always wary, never trusting anyone. The old 'what the enemy doesn't know' thing… Guess I shouldn't complain, but ever since he was appointed to the Chiefs of Staff, he's pushed for all this secrecy. Makes old guard people like me feel shoved out, if you know what I mean."

Mihai nodded. She knew, yet she had given her final approval to the admiral's appointment. Gabrielle was adamant about the whole thing, having been Sujin's mentor and companion for many long years and believing he was the right man for the job. In some way, considering how fussy he was concerning doing things just so, Mihai felt a little more secure about Terey's safety while aboard the Chisamore.

Terey sighed again. "Once on station, we will relieve the Merimna, transferring some of its fighters to the Chisamore. From there, we will patrol parts of the Southern Ring, including Eden's Gate."

Mihai stood. She began to gently fuss over Terey's silky blouse, carefully working the wrinkles out of it. Looking down at her shirt, she quietly crooned so resigned and motherly, "You and PalaHar shouldn't romance in something like this. It gives you away you know." Then staring into her eyes, she asked, "How long will you be gone?"

Terey closed her eyes. Watching the loneliness on Mihai's face was too troubling. She opened them to see Mihai's fathomless blue eyes still fixed on hers. A feeling of guilt swept through her heart as she answered. "Three months… maybe a year." Then shrugged, "You know, it depends on how soon the new carrier is finished."

The selfish child in Mihai could no longer contain itself, its frustration carried on accusing questions. "Why? Why are you going now?"

Catching the child up, Mihai suppressed her selfish wants, waxing selfless. "You returned from your last patrol only two weeks ago. You need more rest, more time away." She fussed again, the little girl escaping once more, "I only returned this very day and… and… we've been apart eight months now. We've…"

Terey put her hand up to silence Mihai, the stress of the moment reflected in her curt reply. "You know full well, dear one. Our people are tiring out. They're losing their will to fight. Every day dozens of our best flight crews retire from active duty, or request extended leave. And that doesn't include our rapidly dwindling army. For the grunts it's even worse, all the privations forced upon them for lack of supplies and the growing indifference of their officers."

She stepped back, shaking a finger in gesture. "If that lady, Trisha, didn't cast a powerful enough spell over the people tonight, there will soon be no army left to protect this city, let alone this Empire!"

Mihai tried to object.

Terey stopped her. "Don't misunderstand me, dear. I have not surrendered to the darkness yet. Mother will succeed. I have full faith in that fact. But you know her ways allow us to create our own destiny. She will permit us to fail, maybe already has, will provide rescue some other way… maybe already has… to our eternal shame."

Terey shook her head, echoing remorsefully, "The prophets called us the 'sons of light', that we could never fail. They wrote of our presence with hope, writing of us as the 'warrior guardians of the universe'. What would they think of us now?"

Angry, she smashed a fist into an opened hand. "Mihai! We were the rulers of these worlds! Just one of us could strike fear into the hearts of thousands! Look at us now! We need a woman born in the realms of backward ignorance to wipe our noses and dry our eyes! I fear our brother was right when he accused us of being too weak of mind to see things through. Look at us! What have we become?"

Mihai stood, dejected. She knew that Terey was not accusing her for the many failed attempts of her people to bring this rebellion to a finish. Still, wasn't she the warden of war, for two thousand years deciding how the game was to be played, and always falling to the wiles of her adversary? As Euroaquilo had earlier stated, even in defeat, Asotos managed to come out winner.

Returning to the moment, Mihai forced a smile as she caressed Terey's arm. "I will be there to see you off on the morrow. I promise."

"Well, hello!"

Mihai and Terey turned to see Paul and Symeon ambling up, offering cheerful and congenial greetings. The two had been patiently waiting and had become tired of pretending to be studying some maps and drawings scattered upon the council tables. At length, at Symeon's prodding, they made their polite intrusions. Seeing the men's attention was focused on Mihai, Terey quickly excused herself, feigning her need to finish preparing for her early departure, kissing first Mihai ever so sweetly and then doing so with Paul and Symeon, but much more formally.

Mihai was tired, moreso weary, the night having taken a toll on her constitution. Pushing that aside, she entertained some time with the men, they being eager to discuss earlier events and, of course as always, having many questions. Besides that, she was beginning to feel a lonely melancholy enveloping her spirit. The thought of Terey's leaving hurt more than expected. Smiling, Mihai tenderly kissed her two closest of companions. "Please, I'm sure this night has provided you with many more questions than answers."

Paul and Symeon waited for no additional invitation to begin. They rifled one question after another at Mihai, Symeon taking the lead. This was the first time either man had witnessed Lowenah's Grand Council and both were excited over it. What was surprising was not the men's excitement, but what they were excited about.

For the children of these realms, Trisha's visions and rousing speech were troubling, offensive, and/or profound. To Paul and Symeon, it was little more than expected, the children from the Realms Below long anticipating those very prophecies fulfilled. Mihai was pummeled with questions concerning the leading members of the Council, who they were and some of their history. They wanted to know more about the Prisoner Exchange, what was to be expected of them, how they were to act, what the enemy might do.

Mihai was forced to repeatedly slow them down, attempting to answer all their questions, one at a time. What else could she do? These were not foolish chatterers. The men had legitimate questions that needed answering. Mihai began to ponder if waiting so long to deliver her two close friends to these realms had been such a good idea. Ma-we waited until only four seasons ago to deliver Paul here, Symeon a year later, she saying they would serve her purpose to keep them bright-eyed and bushy-tailed for coming events. Well… maybe they were a little too bright-eyed for the coming Prisoner Exchange.

In time, after answering a couple of questions twice and having some others asked that made little sense, Mihai began to conclude there were other subjects these men wanted to broach, but feared doing so. Although tired, Mihai patiently waited upon the moment. When they were ready, it was Symeon who betrayed himself first. His fidgeting only increased to the point of nuisance. Finally, stopping Mihai in mid-sentence, he stammered, "You know… well… ah… you know… well, in all these years… you know, I've never seen him."

Confused, Mihai asked, "Who?"

Sheepishly, Symeon began, hesitated, embarrassed and began again. "Ah, well…" Then rubbing his hands in self-consciousness… "The 'Snake'… You know, the 'Serpent'. You know, Satan, your brother."

This was the one question Mihai should have expected, but she was the least prepared for. Swallowing down bile and attempting to ignore a sudden nauseous feeling growing in the pit of her stomach, she stepped back, resting a hand on a chair.

Symeon and Paul both apologized for their rudeness. Mihai motioned them innocent, indicating they wait until she caught her breath. After all, it was not their fault. Long ago she had been warned that as mentor she would be called upon to reveal all the secrets of this universe to her former companions from the Lower Realms. She owed it to them. Besides, if these newcomers were expected to stand the line facing such an insidious foe at the Prisoner Exchange, they needed to be prepared for it. Now was as good a time as any to introduce the matter.

Taking another breath eased her stressful stomach. At length, she began. "There are things… things… you want to learn if you are to be success-ful in the coming days. We do not often use titles like 'Snake', 'Serpent', 'Devil', 'Satan', and so forth to describe the Wicked One. They are only words that partially describe him anyway. In our language, for that matter in any language, there are no terms that can accurately portray the evil man he is. In fact, there are those among us who curse with an oath when his name is mentioned. The injuries he has delivered upon his brothers and sisters, especially Mother, are so deep and the pain so great… Well, I hope you can understand."

"I will tell you the truth, but you must remember not to speak aloud to others what I say now, other than this: The name for this man is no longer spoken by my people and, since the Rebellion he has come to have an open disdain for it. Around Mother, we use the term 'brother' when forced to mention him. It helps to soften the blow to her heart." She admitted. "Mother speaks not of it, but her heart still aches over the loss."

This was truly noteworthy information, making Paul and Symeon's ears tingle. Mihai reminded them of their promise to remain silent and then continued. "The name you will hear his fellow conspirators address him with is 'Theshileo', or 'Alithea', their root meaning coming from your common tongue 'AletheuoPhileO' – 'The tender Father who is faithful and true'. We will not honor him in any such way, using only 'Adelphos' – brother – when we do have to address him. It eases Mother's heart to have it so, and it is a truthful title, he having once been our brother… and in the flesh still is."

She wagged a finger in warning. "The rest of what I am to reveal you must not speak aloud in the company of any, other than, save your closest and most trusted companions. Should your tongue slip at the Prisoner Exchange, not only will you trouble Mother's heart, but you may well bring the wrath of the Evil One down upon us, thus threatening the very souls we seek to rescue."

"You have heard some of the children use the name 'Asotos' when referring to the man. It is the name given to him by Mother's faithful house, meaning 'the one who lays waste by riotous living', from the root words 'waste pipe' or 'sewer pipe'. He is well aware of its use, hates it so much that it is unlawful for his people to speak the word 'waste' aloud upon pain of death. It will be wise to remember my warnings should you have need to address him at the exchange, though I doubt the arrogant fool will trouble you with his attention."

Symeon asked. "So should he trouble us, how do we address him?"

"As I have said..." Mihai pointed a finger at Symeon. " 'Adelphos'! Nothing more! Nothing less! He is our brother by blood. Show honor for that blood, for it is our Mother's blood that flows in him. Show honor to her."

Pondering Mihai's answer, Symeon rubbed his bearded chin. "I can only see ugly evil, a deformed twisted monster." He looked at Mihai, asking, "How does your kind manage... I mean, how do you manage to speak in such affectionate terms?"

That question troubled Mihai. She wanted to scream out her deep revulsion for the man, the woman having more hatred for Asotos than most. With considerable effort, she forced those feelings aside, hiding from Paul and Symeon her emotional struggle. Looking into their faces, she realized they needed to be given understanding into how this world thought and reasoned.

"Please..." Mihai began. "Be patient with me and I will give you under-standing and wisdom. You have not yet the age of the rings of a very small tree, but you make judgments as with tongues of men borne along by the ages. Let me remind you of the facts."

She spread her fingers, touching her heart. "In this world, I am con-sidered little more than a child, there still being those sitting the Council wondering why such a new birthling be given such undue power and glory. Yet I - I walked the haunted worlds of distant star systems long before your home of old was little more than a burning mass of boiling fire. In my own time, I have seen the mountains rise to new heights between Palace City and Oros to the east."

"Lord Ardon, I must tell you...Lord Ardon remembers when there existed no mountains there at all, but a huge fresh water sea that lapped at shores no more than a day's walk from the city's eastern wall. He has also told me of the time in his youth when a jungle filled all the area of the inner wall, with only this Palace butte existing within the ocean of green."

Mihai frowned, resting her tired weight upon the table. "Asotos… Adelphos… remembers far more. Through our dream-shares, I have seen the massive translucent dome that once covered this castle enclosure. Indeed, I have see all seven of the Crystal Cities that once covered this plain, each with an equally impressive wall system, each designed for reasons of life experiments, bringing new life into existence on this planet, all of it built by the hands of the Ones Who Came Before. All that - the domes and scientific activity - were gone by the time of other Ancients, the mysterious Tolohe remembering but little of the previous days of glory."

Symeon blurted out. "But you say you *saw* those things!"

Mihai nodded. "I said I saw them through my dream shares with Asotos."

The consternation showing on Paul and Symeon's faces forced Mihai to explain. "Yes… and you must remember the ways of my people… I have also shared Asotos' bed. For many years I did, as have all my sisters, other than Darla. He was our lord, our mentor, the giver of the Dream of Dreams. That is how he could take control of our souls…that is until the darkness took him. Burned to ash are his powers of lovemaking, though a few refuse to believe it down to this day. It is through what you call 'intercourse' that the dream-share is fulfilled, as you have already come to witness."

Symeon blushed. Paul said nothing, staring down at the floor.

Mihai fussed. "Grow up, you two! I have shared the bed with the both of you and given many pleasant dreams to you. Did I not promise such a thing long ago when I spoke of drinking the wine anew in this very realm? Well, Asotos' powers were far, far greater than mine. He could transport a woman as though in body to any place in the universe his mind might conjure. And, as a child, his ward, he showed his glory to me, I seeing through his eyes the world as it was in his youth."

She swept her arm in gesture. "From wall to wall, the Great Dome of radiant hues shielded this place from the surrounding world. Asotos remembered the giant man-things heaving on cables and cranking huge wheels, delivering the sea monster up to its watery home. Yes, the very seas once lapped upon this mountain butte. Here was the home of many living creatures, Asotos having been witness to much of it. How long he has lived is secret to all, other than himself and Mother, and neither has ever revealed that secret."

"Asotos – Adelphos - was, still is the greatest and most knowledgeable of all our wizards or scientists. He assisted in the creation of life on your old planet, directed most of it. The major varieties of life existing in your world of old came from his fertile mind. He was given a free hand with few restrictions regarding how things were to be, carbon-based life being one of those things. Mother had her reasons at the time. He even had limited access to the Web of the Minds." She pointed at her head. "…the reason for Darla's and my sickness. It is a power he has long lost."

"It was told me that he personally designed the body and soul of your first ancestor, the man called 'Adam', making him in his own likeness and personality. It was said that he even wove his own DNA…" Seeing the confusion on the men's faces, Mihai added, "Blood, it's like blood, in the blood. He created a man-son in his own image, an exact likeness of himself in Adam. That is why no hope exists for that man, for his heart rebelled in like nature to that of Asotos, forever cutting himself off from the power of the Web of the Minds."

Both Paul and Symeon responded together in nearly shouting. "That's impossible!"

Mihai's bitter laugh was chiding. "You are *fools* to not believe me! Yes, that's right. You, yourselves, are sons of the Devil. The blood of the Great Satan flows in your veins. And if it wasn't for the wisdom of Mother, there would be no hope for all your kind, because the nature of his wickedness in an imperfect body would lead any man to damnation. So many of the things you call impossible are so commonplace for my kind. Your obstinate refusal to accept that all things are possible with God, and nearly so with our kind, has led your kind down the path of manipulated calamity several times."

Paul attempted to argue. Mihai cut him short. "My friend, I love you… loved you so much that I risked losing you when I revealed my true nature to you on that desert road many years ago. You believed in me, but never once wrote or spoke of the matter to anyone - even Symeon here - or your close friend, John. Why? I will tell you why: you were afraid…afraid of being totally discredited among your peers, possibly being stoned by the very ones you had shared in converting to believing in me. If I sent you in fire and glory this very day to my people on your home planet to declare to them the truth about me, who would listen and not ridicule you, or even accuse you of blasphemy and say you were sent from Beelzebub?"

"Now let me tell you this, so that you both will have a little understanding and appreciation for my mother, your God. Mother did not allow Asotos permission to design your ancestress, the woman Mother named 'MihaiAstron', after me - a name I acquired long ago in the days of peace. JabethHull bestowed that name upon me in one of his rare, affectionate moments. It is a name I have cherished down to this day. In my exact likeness, using my own blood, you might say, Mother created that woman, using only a small portion of Asotos' nature in the woman's making, taking the rib from his invention to build only the woman's physical structure. That is why there still rests hope for her future days, my blood being so strong within her."

Mihai wagged her finger again. "And that is why there exists any hope at all for your kind. My blood flows in all the bodies of all men, some to a greater or lesser extent than others. It is by the blood of the Wicked One that all men are condemned and by the blood of your sister, here…" She pointed at herself, "that all mankind is saved. Now you see the need for me to have made a personal appearance upon your planet so long ago. I needed to lay legal claim to that right to activate my blood's saving power. Had Asotos had his way, only his blood would have been found in both your father and mother, thus, through its corruptive energy, all mankind would have dissolved into the same hopeless evil manifest by that snake."

Mihai returned to the moment. "I have wandered from the path. Listen, please, and learn. Do not underestimate the power of this fallen hero. His special might is still greater moreso than most, possibly all. I do not know. His mind is dangerously powerful, enough so that what appear to be minor, winsome comments can get inside your head, taking control and manipulating your thoughts. And he has other powers of mind and spirit control that are still beyond any of his siblings. Mother made the man very strong in mind and soul."

She reached out, taking hold of Symeon's arm, warning, "Do not! I repeat, do not attempt a coup on this man! Few have survived unscathed while doing so."

The visible pain that raced across Mihai's face gave pause to both men. Paul especially felt guilty for bringing up the subject in the first place, he telling Mihai so. She waved him off. "This you needed to know. It would have been such a disservice on my part to not have warned you. You did nothing wrong. Tomorrow, when I am rested, will be sufficient to discuss further with you these important matters."

"Well, well, how are my little darlings this morning? It is morning, you know, bedtime for my babies." Ma-we's voice startled Mihai and the others, she having silently approached while the three were in deep conversation.

"May I join this pleasant company?" Without asking, she crowded in, wrapping her hands around Mihai's arm. Looking into her daughter's weary face, she cooed, "My dear, I do feel you need some good company this evening. I suggest you not forget to take my boy, Paul, with you when taking this morning's leave. It is so good for the soul, you know."

Mihai smiled weakly but, before she could reply, Paul spoke up. "Mihai has been pummeled with our questions concerning the Prisoner Exchange and… and other related subjects important for us to know. I believe we have worn out our welcome. She may well not abide any more company." Symeon nodded in agreement.

"Nonsense!" Ma-we then addressed Mihai, telling the others not to leave. "I have some important business to attend to in other parts of my kingdom and shall be on my leave for several days. Tell no one of my absence. I will certainly be returned before our departure for EremiaPikros. Now, I want you to care for things while I'm away, seeing that you have taken over the chambers of the Firstborn… or so I've been informed."

Mihai said that it was so.

Squeezing her daughter's arm, Ma-we smiled. "All the necessary locks have been reset to accommodate your entrance… and this fellow's here." She pointed toward Paul. "I have left the place a mess." Her eyes twinkled mischievously. "Been so busy, I have. It's in need of a good cleaning, has been for some time. It would be nice if you two would tidy it up a bit." She grinned. "Who knows what treasures one might find lost in such a mess."

She turned to Paul, warning, her eyes still a' twinkle. "This little lady should not be expected to do all the work herself. After all, if you expect her pleasure in the bed, she should expect your elbow grease in the kitchen."

Paul's face flushed red. Symeon laughed.

Ma-we went on, putting on an oh so serious face. "Be a good dear, please. I so much need to hear a good report about this when I return."

At first, Paul was taken aback, until he observed the twinkle in Ma-we's eyes. He smiled, offering a slight bow of his head. "I shall do all you wish, my Lord, and more should this beautiful lady only ask me." Then he waxed poetic. "Shall she seek a star from the heavens, or a jewel from the oceans deep, it would be as asking for but a drink of water for my soul to seek it for her."

Ma-we laughed, pointing at him. "Be careful, for what you offer may well be taken up by her on a whim. She does have a selfish streak in her, you know."

Mihai fussed at her mother's comments.

Ma-we laughed again. "Please help my girl with her move into the Palace. Do take the time to run some errands for her. It will help you learn the city better. And…" She glanced back at Mihai, "help her with her bath, please. The girl has such a hard time getting all those spots that need scrubbing. We want our child all bubbly clean now, don't we?"

Embarrassed, Paul promised he would, Symeon grinning from ear to ear.

Ma-we turned her attention to Symeon. "You… I want a word with you…in private!"

Symeon was shocked and concerned. Ma-we's countenance was grave, her voice so serious.

As she took Symeon's arm, Ma-we ordered Mihai and Paul, "You two stay here. I may need you soon. I'm sure you can find some meaningful conversation to occupy your time."

It was so difficult for either Mihai or Paul to concentrate, what with Ma-we and Symeon only a few paces away, and Ma-we acting so serious. It was easy to see the expressions on Symeon's face - first those of serious concern, then curiosity, then deep sadness, when suddenly it exploded in an astonished grin. Symeon whooped with glee, doing a little dance of excitement. He hurriedly started for them, but Ma-we's strong arm stopped him, she whispering something in his ear.

Then, slowly and deliberately, the two returned to the curious couple ridden with need to hear the latest gossip. Symeon was beside himself with anxious desire to reveal all he knew, but Ma-we would have none of that. She was a master at suspense and savored the excitement of the secret as much as the revealing.

Eventually, holding Symeon's hand as if in comfort, she explained, "I'm sorry my dears, but your friend will not be journeying with us to the Prisoner Exchange. I have great need of his services elsewhere. This will certainly be a loss to all of us, but there was nothing else for it. And… and, I'm sure it will be a disappointment for Symeon as well." She reached out and took Mihai's hand, speaking so consolingly. "You will just have to find a way to do without him."

That was it. Symeon could contain himself no longer. He blurted out. "I can't go… because… because…" He let out a joyful cry, "because she's *coming*! My little girl, my daughter child is *coming, coming back to us, here! Soon! Here!*"

Symeon began to laugh and sob at the same time. He bent his head as his hands came up to meet his face, crying tears of joy. Ma-we hugged him around his waist, nodding while wearing her motherly smile. "I think my boy has had a full night. He needs some well-deserved rest. I'll see him home."

As they were leaving, Ma-we turned back to Mihai and Paul. "Life should never be taken for granted. Even forever is never long enough to do everything one wishes. Don't waste your life chasing impossible dreams. Take what is yours for the moment and drink it to the full." With that, she led Symeon to the door, exiting the chambers.

"What did Lowenah mean by her words?" Paul asked, while taking Mihai's arm.

Mihai sighed with tired satisfaction, smiling. "Sometimes even we children forget the value of gifts we possess while we search the shadows for others that are uncertain. Life is not to be measured by what we might accomplish tomorrow, for tomorrow is not guaranteed, but full of uncertainties. No, joy comes to those who understand the treasure that exists within our grasp while life still courses through our souls, while it remains ours to possess."

She looked into Paul's eyes. "My Lord, master of my dreams, will you please take your servant girl home?"

Paul nodded, smiling. With that, the two journeyed up the stairs to the upper deck and through the doors leading to the outer balcony. Stepping into the cool freshness of early morning, Mihai watched the gray of that early morning battling with the blackness of night. For some time the two stood there, silently watching the distant warring.

At length, Mihai asked, "Has my Lord ever seen the sun rise from the battlements of the eastern tower on the outer wall?"

Paul looked into Mihai's face, saying not a word, his eyes seeking her lead. The two stood motionless for some time, appearing as silhouettes painted upon a darkened screen. Finally, still gripping his hand, Mihai motioned their leave, whispering, "The cooing of the morning dove is so sweet from those towers, Love, its scent like that of lotus blossoms."

They walked down the stairs into the darkness of the night, disappearing into the courtyards far below.

ℬ   ℬ   ℬ

(**Author's Note:** *I have gleaned these notes from the thesis,* <u>The Glitter of Gold</u>, *written by Queen Adaya near the beginning of the Fourth Age of this universe. It reveals some little known facts about one of Lowenah's chief councilors:*

Ardon was one of the oldest of the children, growing up at the time when the Upper Palace was the only structure in the universe. When he was a child, he would busy himself playing in and exploring the thick jungle growth surrounding the palace. He had also journeyed deep into the tunnels under the butte, sometimes being gone for days at a time. It was from those explorations in the tunnels that he had developed an insatiable desire to explore rock formations, especially crystalline and mineral. When the knowledge of space travel had been sufficiently developed, he was one of the first children to abandon his home planet and reach out to find secrets in the stars. He would disappear for centuries at times, squirreling himself away in some mountainous planet, deep underground, studying its different rock formations. In fact, when the Rebellion started, he had been busy examining strange crystals found in the depths of an obscure planet in the outer reaches of the Trizentine. When news reached him, he had rushed home.

The details of events leading up to the Rebellion had devastated him. He discovered few of the oldest children had remained loyal to Ma-we. As time passed, the number of those abandoning her increased. Ardon had immediately joined himself to Ma-we, offering to provide whatever support he could to her. He became the only former councilor to his older brother who had not joined in the Rebellion. Ardon's laboratory had never been revisited and, to the best of his knowledge, it lay quietly undisturbed, awaiting his return.

Ma-we eventually made Ardon one of her personal councilors. She took advantage of his slow, deliberate ponderings when complex and difficult situations arose. He was meticulous in thought, always trying to examine every minute detail. It was the way he reasoned that caused him to dislike riddles. He found himself constantly over-thinking their context, something that made him the brunt of more than one joke. Someone would ask a trick question and Ardon's response was often some wildly long dissertation totally unrelated to the answer. They would allow him to go on and on with his reply. All the while, smiles of fellow conspirators were growing bigger and bigger. Only when he had finished was he made privy to the way he had been set up, much to the humor of the others. Never the less, it was difficult for Ardon to see humor in things he spoke about, he always being so serious concerning such things.

Ardon's slow and deliberate thinking often caused him to miss the point when a quick decision was needed. Once Ma-we had jokingly said to him, after he had laboriously plodded his way through one of his obvious solutions that, now having received his input, she at least knew the direction not to proceed in. This wasn't always true. For example, the recommendation he once offered, to confuse the counsel given to a certain king of the Second Realm in order to bring him to defeat, had been accepted and had proved quite successful. Having managed such a success once, though, did not diminish his oft-deserved reputation.

He also hated riddles because his mind did not grasp the mathematics of how they worked. To him, riddles were like long detours on the journey to finding the correct answer. When his mind was focused on a subject, it consumed his thoughts. Anything that obstructed his desired goal was, at best, a nuisance, something to be labored through in order to achieve his goal. On the other hand, Ma-we and most of her children enjoyed riddling. They were happy to spend many hours idling away the time, playing riddling games. This was so deeply ingrained in their minds that most of them thought in riddles all the time. Because Ardon did not think this way, Ma-we found his views and observations strikingly different from many of the others, offering glimpses into things from excitingly new perspectives.

Ardon did have some outstandingly useful qualities, too. His natural ability to observe and scrutinize the slightest details was not focused only on his study of rocks. When he applied his skills to people, he could often discover what was hidden deep in a person's mind and heart. His eyes and ears were always alert to many subtle changes of voice inflection and body language of people being observed. From their posture, eye movement, speech patterns and the way they breathed, Ardon recorded each detail in his mind. He would later review information to develop a profile of the inner person of the one being observed. Such insightfulness often helped him draw correct conclusions of someone's future actions.

The way he revealed his insight was also one of his assets. Ardon had no way of expressing himself other than to be open, up front and honest. His candor frequently bordered on being blunt, finesse being one of his unlearned arts. He was also willing to offer his observations publicly, without being requested. Although this did cause some disquiet, Ma-we found it extremely useful. It gave her a colorful insight into people in ways that even she sometimes overlooked.

These qualities, along with an inexhaustible desire to gather details, coupled with unlimited patience needed to accomplish his task, made Ardon the person of choice when complex issues arose. He was willing to spend the necessary time and effort to gather all the required information that would provide him with a correct answer. Then, with precise words and well-defined and logical reasoning, he would explain his findings to interested parties. It was only on rare occasion that Ardon would find himself at a loss to understand an issue when he had made it a subject of investigation. This was also true of the people he chose to study. Few could remain a mystery to him, and it deeply disturbed the man when that did happen.

         

SirionSandevar's <u>Letters in Defense of Love,</u> written not long into the King's War, discloses the earlier history of Terey and her role played in the making of an empire:

During the First Age, the Age of Peace, Terey had busied herself in the study of language. Although only one language was spoken among all the children, the original vocabulary was basic and limited. As need arose, people would coin words to describe new things. This method worked fine while all the children lived in reasonable proximity to each other. When exploration into the stars became common and colonies grew in number at distant locations, people could be isolated from their mother planet for hundreds or even thousands of years. Over time, each colony might develop a myriad of different words for their local vocabulary. Not only this, but words tend to acquire altered meanings. Although two people from separate locations would speak the same language, the meanings of the words might be totally different. Terey took it upon herself to deal with the problem.

For thousands of years, Terey traveled to all the major colonies and many smaller ones. Over the course of time, she recorded a massive encyclopedic dictionary of words and their meanings as understood in various parts of the galaxy. Through exhaustive effort, she developed what came to be known as the 'universal tongue'. She defined word segments and root word concepts, explaining their meanings and uses in all aspects of written and spoken language.

Terey redefined the common theory of speech, placing more importance on using a series of root segments to invent a new word than creating a new word by itself. She undertook the task of designing a simple alphabet, so that a few letters could replace the many hundreds of characters used in standard writing. This contributed to the mass printing of literature, thus creating quick and easy access to all varieties of written material, including Terey's. Her printed volumes on language became the foundation for all official and scientific writing.

After the attack on Mihai, Terey went into a serious depression. Her nervous disorder made her physically sick, something at that time unheard of. Eventually the depression ended, but her physical sickness continued to dog her. She remained sensitive to many foods and her hands would often tremble. Persons thinking this weakened her ability to fight often paid a high price for such foolishness. She was a cunning strategist.

Terey also had a constitution of iron and her sickness did not slow her down. In fact, she was one of the best fighter pilots in the entire navy. During the Great War, she had flown as Mihai's wing pilot on several occasions. Only outstanding pilots were able fly with Mihai's squadron because they flew a TKR-17, commonly called by other pilots the 'dancing corkscrew'. An upgraded design of the TKR-14, it was a difficult craft to fly and inexperienced pilots were afraid of it. But, in the hands of a highly skilled person, it was one of the most deadly ships ever built.

ॐ ॐ ॐ

This explanation of the fighters used during the King's war was taken from Copeland and Garlock's, The King's War: A History:

"When exercising routine fighting maneuvers, the TKR-14, the standard attack fighter needed to be manually operated, thus requiring the pilot's complete concentration to manipulate the craft. The pilot's hands rested on right and left spherical control pads. Each pad contained identical command inputs, except being mirror image in design, thus the same fingers on the different hands executed identical functions. The hands did not have to move, because the impulse of the neurological charges racing from the brain initiated the response of the plane. The pilot needed to remain focused on handling the ship to avoid sending mixed signals to the controls. For this reason, a safety feature had been included in the 14. If a pilot did lose control when in manual mode and flying became erratic, the quickest way to stabilize the ship was to lift his or her hands off the pads. This done, the plane would automatically correct itself. In doing so, it would slow down until the pilot again assumed command of the helm. In a dogfight, though, when the enemy was constantly seeking to get a lock on their opponent, such a maneuver could get a person killed.

The TKR-17 was designed directly off the TKR-14. The two planes looked similar, starting with a long, sleek, pointed nose, tapering back into a rakish, cigar-shaped body, with small tail side-fins and one vertical stabilizer. Below the bubbled pilot's cockpit, midway down the ship's sides, were two small, lateral wings. The wings enabled the craft to utilize the atmosphere of a planet when flying in sub-space. They also served as cooling radiators for the engines which were located in the lower midsection of the fuselage. The primary thrust of the rockets was rearward, but the fighter could move in every other possible direction, even backwards. That is where similarities of the 14 and 17 ended.

Fighter craft evolved slowly. The first true fighters were seen about thirty-five centuries earlier. By current standards, they were slow and awkward. It had been difficult to convince the pilots who flew them to upgrade to better equipment. Most people do not like change, and the fighter pilots were no exception. Many of them had flown the earliest of the ships and had been reluctant to modify what they were used to. The TKR series had been first designed well over a millennia ago, and the model 14A was already a little over a century old when the Great War started. Yet it was still the primary attack weapon of the navy.

When Mihai started setting up combat commands prior to the Great War, she felt the need to have a better plane than the 14. Changing the physical structure of the current fighter would be expensive and time-consuming, because most of the navy's carriers were designed for optimum space, using the TKR-14 as their primary attack support machine. Time was something Mihai did not have.

The prerequisite physical shape of the new plane was already set. Mihai and her design team, which Terey was part of, chose to confine the changes within the framework of the 14. Two prototypes followed that were eventually produced, but were only special adaptations of the 14 called the 'TKR-15' and '16', and only a few were built. After a disappointing start, the team chose to scrap everything about the 14 except the exterior structure, which was outstandingly well designed. The control system, armaments, engines, computer system, even the cockpit were brand-new in concept.

Two of the most noticeable changes were visible. The pilot's cabin was moved three feet forward, primarily to make room for the additional size of the engines, but also for better visuals. Second, to meet the desired acceleration increase, the twin engines had been made proportionately larger than the 14's. To properly install them, the belly of the new plane was expanded, creating two slightly bulbous extrusions on the lower right and left sides. The remainder of the changes were unseen, yet were the most evident in combat.

The TKR-17 not only mounted laser cannons and energy burst rapid-fire guns, along with racks for exterior ordnance, it also had two solid projectile, forward-fixed cannons. High-speed attack ships rarely mounted solid pro-jectile guns, for it was all too easy for the pilot to fly into his or her own fire. Mihai's team accepted that risk because of the armor-busting effect solid projectiles had over energy blasts. There was another reason the solid pro-jectiles were desirable. Counter energy beams and fields had been developed that could often neutralize laser and other energy weapons. This was one reason the sword was still a standard weapon of the infantry; energy side arms might be disabled. Solid projectile guns still used mechanical mech-anisms for operation, and dry chemical reactions to create the energy to propel the bullets, all of which were unaffected by the counter-energy fields.

The other outstanding feature of the 17 was the way it was flown. Hand controls were of similar design to the 14, but had a more sensitive reaction to the neurological impulses contacting them. Located in the pilot's helmet were probes connected directly to the main computer. These probes would do continual brain scans of the pilot, and then it would respond to the scanned signals. The artificial intelligence level of the computer was almost equal to the pilot's intelligence in certain respects. It would even react to the different emotional signals the brain would transmit. An almost symbiotic relation-ship often developed between a pilot and plane, causing the ship to take on the personality characteristics of the pilot. This was one of the reasons that, during the Great War, the enemy knew when Mihai had joined the fight. For those able to master the needed thought processes to properly operate the 17, the plane became a beautiful and deadly tool. But for those unable to do so, it could become their coffin.

Land based fighter units were later provided with a modified version of the 17, but with similar controls of the 14. These ships were designat-ed 'TKR-14G'. The greater weight and increased fuel needs limited their use with the navy. Later, more compact engines were designed with similar power and acceleration of the 17. These and other improvements were in-corporated into the 14, the new model being designated ' TKR-14H'. By the time of the latest council, it had become the standard navy fighter.

∽ ∽ ∽

This material, taken from the periodical, <u>Ottawa,</u> reveals some inter-esting details about Terey during the time of events being discussed by the author of this book, it being written shortly after these events occurred. Excerpts are herein quoted.

- "Terey's skills and courage had been demonstrated on many occasions. During the Great War, she was engaged in every major battle involving the main fleet, often returning to the war while still nursing injuries received in

previous encounters. Two of her planes were shot out of the skies, and many times she had brought others home, crippled. If a person flew in Mihai's squadron, they expected such danger. Captains like Terey fought with the same desperation as their commander in trying to beat the enemy down and drive it out of the Empire. There had been no other squadron that was more often engaged in battle or suffered heavier losses than Mihai's. Yet it was that determined desperation displayed by so many that finally forced the enemy out and won the war.

The skills of a statesman and councilor were not lost on Terey. She manifested outstanding insight in political, social and military matters. In the early days of the Rebellion, her insight was sought from governors and princes. Her voice helped to persuade many who were indecisive to remain loyal to Ma-we. Eventually she became a permanent member of Ma-we's council. Officially, Terey was still a member of that council, but upon Mihai's request for assistance, Terey had joined her council and had remained there since."

- "She sat there, silently contemplating the outcome of changing events. Showing no outward emotion, her smoky, blue-grey eyes revealed a fiery concern burning deeply within her. In Terey's mind, the events of the past and present were one and the same, a continuum of only one much larger event conceived thousands of years before, whose labor pains were not yet completed. She saw a universe soaked in blood, rivers overflowing and seas flooding from it, with no end in sight. A new round of slaughter was about to begin. The crown Mihai was wearing had sealed their fate. Asotos' jealous outrage would explode against all living things when he found out, and Terey knew it.

Two thousand years had passed now, but the memory was still crystal clear. When her rebel brother learned that Mihai received power over the peoples as a chief steward, he reached out to destroy those of the Second Realm who followed her. Failing that, he influenced those same people to deify and worship her, hoping Mihai would destroy them, herself. Again failing, he raised up another group of worshipers who reveled in holy war. For nearly a thousand years, the Second Realm ran red with the blood of destruction. But he had failed to understand the spirit of these creatures possessing the realm below. Even a polluted worship of the real God made them stronger than people who worshipped a make-believe one. Eventually, in the name of their deified messiah, they crushed his grand army of followers, forcing them to flee into the cracks and crevices of the planet to hide, awaiting the day when he would awaken them to again unleash a reign of terror upon the planet.

The victors of these wars lifted high the cross of battle and proceeded to plunder the planet in the name of their God. They eventually returned the breath of life to an ancient beast by returning its heart to it. The last ruler over that beast had seen its demise coming, and he had created a great religion to preserve its heart alive. While others concluded that it had died, the men in the sacred cathedrals knew better. They were only waiting for the right leader, to give it to a man who would continue to recognize their power and greatness. Eventually one came. They made him king and declared a kingdom of a thousand years had started. But their revelry did not last.

In their newfound power and glory, these people finally crushed the infidels. Shortly thereafter, their grand kingdom fell apart. The Great Rebel tried to destroy them from within by raising up differing sects inside the kingdom. Again, the world ran red with the blood of innocent people. After generations of murder, one kingdom succeeded in wresting the heart of the old beast away from the others. It used that heart to gain control and expand its influence across the planet. When one of its former estates rebelled against it, war erupted between them. When that war ended, there were now two powers sharing the same heart. Down to the day of this council, it had remained the same."

- "And what about her own part during all this time? Terey thought about the many battles and skirmishes she had survived. Wreckage from countless engagements lay scattered across the galaxy. Many lovers and companions were gone now. People she had shared lifetimes with had become crumbling piles of bones moldering on some desert planet, or had been blasted to dust in cosmic conflagrations.

Most of these battles were defensive actions, done to prevent the Rebellion from progressing too fast, too soon. They fought the enemy for the sake of a timetable, to prevent things from happening too quickly. It wasn't until the Great War that they had gone on the offensive, and more had perished in that war than all the others combined. It, too, had only been one more step in the grand picture. The period of time between then and now was only for rest, a breather until the next storm; but they had rested too long. She could now see the storm brewing. Ma-we had waited for her children as long as possible, could wait no longer, and was preparing to hold up the bait to draw Terey's rebel brother out. He would react quickly to crush it with all his military strength. Terey could see that her people were not prepared for the fight to come. She now also realized that her brother was going to strike first..."

৪৩   ৪৩   ৪৩

Section Three

Legend's Heroes

happy, crackling fire spewed forth a shower of golden sparks as a hickory log erupted in a blaze of light. Shadows danced to and fro across rough-hewn timber walls, leaving much of the room hidden in darkness. The fire was warm and the building sound, creating a comfortable, cozy feeling that all was well even though the winter winds should blow. And blow they did.

Driving snow pelted the tiny windows as howling winds battered the door in its angry fury. Yet, for the lone figure slowly rocking back and forth before the glowing hearth, all was at peace, the snapping and popping of a roaring fire and the 'creak-*creak*' of the old wicker chair the only melody falling on the person's ears.

Hidden within the shadows, two emerald-green eyes peered deeply into the burning light, a sweet, gentle tune being hummed by half-closed lips…

"No hurry… No hurry…
Let the night winds cry.
No hurry… No hurry…
For tonight brings on a happy sigh."

Hands relaxed on the chair's gnarly arms, fingers curled over and around its knobby ends. Naked feet resting on the hard, oaken floor would slowly push down, sending the person in the chair back into the shadows until, tired of the struggle, they would surrender to the moment, sending chair and rider up into the firelight. Back and forth, back and forth, the musical creaking of the chair blended in melodious harmony with the little humming tune.

"No hurry… No hurry…
The night is young.
No hurry…"

The mellow light of the musical fire revealed a tiny brown furry creature scurrying across the floor in search of fallen crumbs, also being rewarded with small pieces of cheese scattered among the morsels. Eyes closed as a contented smile grew across the face of the 'oh, so untidy person' listening in the shadows. Moments of peace such as this had been all too rare over many centuries. It felt good to have the antics of this little mouse be the biggest intrusion into their cozy dream-world.

In the middle of a bite, the mouse froze. Then, still holding tight its treasure of well-aged cheese, it sniffed the air as if searching for an answer to a disturbance in the cabin's restful ambiance. For a heartbeat, the creaking of the chair ceased, the person also hearing the harmonic shift in the winter stormwinds. All so soon the chair began its music again, the shadowed figure displaying no concern. But the furry little creature hurried away, holding fast its trophy of the night. Something approached, its power great, and the little fellow wished not to be found in such an open, conspicuous place no matter how inviting the banquet.

Above the unyielding pitch of the blizzard, distinct sounds of hard-soled boots on tired wooden stair treads echoed across the room. The one seated in the rocker appeared to pay no notice, and continued rocking to the little tune being hummed.

"No hurry... No worry now...
The night is young...
The night is very young..."

The heavy iron door handle began its mournful cry as rusty tumblers resisted being awakened by a determined hand seeking the latch's surrender, allowing the hidden power escape from the fury of the storm. 'Sha...*clack!*' The ancient bolt broke free of its rusty prison, surrendering up the door to the whims of the night. With glee, the winter winds pummeled the door, seeking to breech the walls of the one unconquered fortress in this vast, desolate world.

Exerting great effort, a hand held fast the tempest, engaging in a contest for the gate. A struggle ensued, the winds beating relentlessly against flesh and wood, seeking to best the lone sentinel refusing it entry. At length, the battle ended, the warrior taking control of the pass, entering the warm solitude of the comfy cabin, but not before the storm's flanking guard managed a coup by slipping between the legs of its protagonist, sending a chilling blast into the room.

The fire roared to life, sending a swirl of sparks upward through the hewn stone chimney, flames soaring high in defense of the warmth it had birthed, driving down the bitter winds to defeat, consuming any of the chilling breeze that stood defiantly before it. '*Slam!*' went the door, quickly followed by the crack of the bolt being driven home, securing the latch. At that, the winter tempest began a howling of angry frustration that lasted several minutes, but to no avail. The battle was lost.

Nervously peering out from behind an old musty trunk, the mouse, still holding close in tiny paws its cheesy delight, watched closely, eyeing with trepidation the giant standing in the shadows at the edge of the fire's light. Nary did this giant move, not until tiny rivers of water and chunks of melting snow falling from cleated boots puddled the floor upon which it stood. Still, the person rocking said nothing, watching intently with sea-green eyes the crimson blaze beyond the hearth. At long last, the tiny furry creature tired the wait and turned its attention to the cheese, keeping a wary eye on possible danger while savoring the feast secured in its grasp.

At length, still tingling from the cold, the newly arrived visitor strode toward the fire, extending chilled hands while stamping frozen boots to free them of any remaining ice. As the person stood there, rubbing life into numb fingers, a voice quietly asked, "Did you slip away unnoticed?"

There was no immediate reply, just the sound of hands being vigorously rubbed together. In time, the person at the fire stood erect, pulling back a fur-lined hood with slender fingers now returned to life and feeling. With one graceful movement, the cape, with hood attached, swept from handsome shoulders, revealing the comely form of a woman goddess. Tall, muscular, sensual, the fire could not disguise this woman's beauty. As young in appearance as a sprite, but with a haunting face and furrowed brow as ancient as the mountains, this woman was no child, but an ancient of Ancients, a witch from before the dawns of time.

Firelight flickered across ghost-grey eyes, revealing a latent power held in check by an iron will whose struggles had weathered such a handsome face into stone-like beauty. But the eyes burned bright, full of spirit, even as the body gradually withered from a cancer slowly consuming its might.

There was no smile in the woman's reply, no emotion or energy, it having been consumed by the winter storm. "I took the lone night patrol along the Nebulan Cloud Bank. It interrupts our inter-ship communication as well as our scanners. No one is expecting to hear from me for many hours."

Looking around the room, the woman shook her head, recalling innocent days of long ago. "I have not visited this place since the constellations of the AntonSodoney rose in celebration over the southern hills of EdenEsonbar and Gradian's Clock chimed the coming hour of rebirth. That is nearly twenty-six thousand years past. Was I the last of my kind to seek the solace of this haven, for I sensed my spirit still lingering upon the handle of the door?"

Green eyes twinkled, recalling fond memories, while a head nodded dreamily. "Yes. Yes, it is so. Do you not yet know that you, alone, have been my only love to have discovered this place? I built it for you, my dear one, long ago, when the universe beyond EdenEsonbar still belonged to the Ones Who Came Before. It is full of mystery and secrets that only you hold the key to. I had envisioned it as a gift to you when the secret of life was revealed to my children." The person saddened, shaking her head. "Alas, it shall never see such innocent mirth as I purposed. This place will, instead, become your sanctuary in future days when the worlds are again at peace. I am but the caretaker of it until that hour arrives."

The woman nodded but made no reply. She looked around and, spying a stool half hidden in the shadows, pulled it near the hearth, sat down and quietly removed her pilot's boots. With a grunt, followed by a relaxing sigh, the last boot was pulled from her foot. She then busied herself in gently massaging life back into cramped toes.

As practiced hands soothed the flesh, a tired voice went on to speak of other matters. "The storm is most intense. Had I not felt your presence, I doubt it would have been possible for me to find this place tonight. As it was, I made my way through a mile of frozen drifts, having to abandon my ship in a distant field, I fearing the danger of a collision should I pursue further travel with that machine."

A smile crept across the face of the person in the rocking chair. "Few there are who could have mastered the elements this eve. Do you think it by chance the weather is so outrageous? My dear one, there are many evil forces who have great power. Spies abound in your world. Only a fool would have dared follow you into this maelstrom… save only one…and he is far from this place at the moment. I can feel it to be so. It was important for my heart to seek you out in secret tonight. I desired no one, not even an innocent, to interrupt our meeting."

There was a long silence in the room. The woman sitting on the stool hung her head as if in tired disappointment, her long, flowing, silver hair falling almost to the floor. Staring at the worn planking, she finally replied, "I am your servant. Please, my Meter, what is it your heart wishes to speak about?"

The person in the chair turned her head, smiling. "Long have your lips been silent with that name, my Tolohe." She returned her gaze to the fire. "Tolohe? Tolohe… 'Pillar of the Sun', 'StuloHelios', Tolohe. You do recall it is a name given you by the gods of ages past, when you still suckled at my breasts. Few speak of you by that name anymore. Why do you hate it so?"

Tolohe raised her eyes toward the flames, searching for a reply. "When the world was young, it was so beautiful. There were but the two of you, my Meter and Chrusion, my lover and mentor. Oh yes, I do recall the strange beings that flitted in and out of our lives, sometimes so handsome as to outshine Chrusion, and yet at other times taking on wild shapes that could be laughable or frightening."

"I knew you only by the name I gave you, 'Meter'… 'Mother', until I was well in my teens, when those same gods spoke in secret to me their own fond words for you, and how deeply they cared for the one giving them life so long ago. It was long ago, beyond the ages of time, and yet I feel that I, too, have lived beyond the ages of time. So long my heart has ached over lost love, long before this Rebellion. I have hidden my heart in a shadow-world until it stands alone in a desolate land. Few are my lovers. They fear my sickness lest they may fall prey to a diseased mind. My beauty faded long ago until it is little more than a ghostly ruin of its former self. Chrusion broke my heart before the First Age was passed. When it died, along with it went the beauty of the wondrous name given me in that forgotten time."

Tolohe looked into her mother's face. "And should I complain? Has not your heart been ripped from your own bosom, being crushed by the man we both loved for so long? Does not the very name given you by my young siblings testify to the changed world that exists around us? *Yehowah!* God of the new age, King of the Throne of Salvation, Bringer of Rage and Storm! I stood beside you the day you declared to the man who was once our lover, '*I shall become whatever I need to become in order to crush you... you belly-walking worm!*' From that day forward, my sweet, innocent Meter has carried the name of war and death, 'Yehowah' ...a name so unfit for the person I love so dear."

Again there was a long silence. "Meter... it is a name that is so comforting to my soul." Meter – 'Ma-we' - looked into Tolohe's eyes. "My dear, I am no ruler, never have been. The Ones Who Came Before did not see me as a ruler or a god. I was but one with them, they having come from my very essence. I do not like to rule, and that is one secret you know better than all the others except... except... we shall not speak anymore of him."

She reached out, touching Tolohe's knee with playing fingers. "Tonight, for a few fleeting hours, Tolohe needs to again become the Pillar of the Sun, the pillar for Meter to rest her weary head upon."

Tolohe gripped Ma-we's hand, tears filling her eyes. "I am your servant, your lover, your companion. Whatever your slightest wish, I shall move the heavens to bring to you. You ask so little and deserve so much more than your child can possibly give."

Ma-we leaned her head back, resting it against the chair. She closed her eyes in silent ponderings, the crackling fire the only sound coming from within the tiny cabin. Peeking out from its hiding place, the skittish mouse, overcome by hungry desire for more crumbles of cheese, chanced the moment, hurrying forth to abscond with another of the morsels scattered upon the floor. If anyone heard, no one paid heed. Cheeks full of rich reward, the little fellow happily scampered away to its hiding place.

At long last Ma-we took up the conversation. "I have brought you here tonight for many reasons. Some, as you know, are fraught with personal and selfish desires. Still, had it not been for other more necessary ones, I would not have troubled a soul weighed down with the needs of the universe. The future of all living things hinges upon decisions soon to be made. I fear you, alone, will have the power to force those decisions onto the correct path."

She sat forward, turning her chair so as to face Tolohe. "I'm sorry. Such a rude host, you know. My mind's been off in a fog. Please, can I offer you something to warm your tired soul and feed a hungry belly?"

Tolohe smiled, nodding. Soon there were hot cakes and jam, along with steaming jasmine sweet tea to tempt the palate. As the newly appeared dishes magically filled with sumptuous delights, the woman wryly commented, "My powers are greatly diminished through this sickness of mine. No longer can I conjure such a repast without the aid of machines made by ageless hands. Little more than that cup could I produce for this meal. The witchery of my mind, though, is still sharp and I can see deep into the heart of space and time."

Ma-we grinned reassuringly. "My daughter shall be made new again, that I know. For now, let us pretend... pretend that things are so different. Now then, tell me of my concoction. Does it titillate the senses as it once did?"

Tolohe took the cup of hot brew, inhaling its delightful fragrance, a smile growing on her face, and then sipped. "*Ahhhh*...you have outdone even yourself. None better have I ever tasted in all my days. You are the greatest witch of all, making the simplest things treasures to behold." She looked deeply into Ma-we's eyes. "You, Mother, make the best tea. I do so miss it when I am away."

Ma-we grinned again, lifting up her own cup. "Then we shall drink it to the day when there will be no need for us to part!"

For a while the two became lost in innocent chatter, each one outdoing the other with rhyme and song, stories from happy days long forgotten. The little mouse danced with glee at seeing the countless crumbs falling to the floor, a feast in the making.

At length, the hour had come, the food consumed. Ma-we's face sobered, her dark thoughts harkening other speech. "My dear child, there are many dangerous roads we must travel before innocence will again rule the worlds." She looked toward the fire, a newly placed log having freshly ignited the sparking flames. "The Prisoner Exchange is but a few days future. I do so wish your company at that time, but I know it is not possible."

Tolohe nodded, asking for another cup of tea, stalling for time. As she stirred the fresh, hot brew, she asked, "So, do you intend to continue with your plan, even after the last council?"

Ma-we nodded. "I can wait no longer. I have seen into the demon's mind and watched him stew in his anger. I must force his hand now." She looked into Tolohe's face, the age of troubled times reflecting on her own. "It is no longer an issue of 'are we ready?' It matters not the cost to us, for it shall be high. Chrusion must be made to move, show his hand in power. He must be goaded into action before he is fully prepared."

Tolohe studied her tea as if stirring it was most important. After sniffing in the satisfying aroma, she quietly recommended, "May I suggest you take Tizrela and PalaHar with you as standard bearers? Neither fears the Worm, each having contested against him on the field of honor. They also understand the hour and the day, counting no guilt toward you, but hold themselves accountable for the evil that lives among us."

She set the spoon down, staring again into Ma-we's green eyes. "It is true, we have become weak and, as at other times in the past, not heeded your council or listened to your wisdom, but trust me, there is still a fiery strength hidden within your loyal children. We *will* weather the coming storm."

Ma-we slowly shook her head. "Strength like an aged, weathered tree… Your kind will, as you so often have before, take the blow, but that age is passed into meaninglessness. Your kind must become the aggressor, the monster that tears up its prey. I doubt such a feat still exists with them."

After taking a sip and giving time for her palate to luxuriate in its robust delights, Tolohe replied, "I trust you have a remedy to deliver a cure, for never have I heard you pose such a dilemma without having searched out a solution."

Nodding, Ma-we answered. "Oh, yes! But a bitter one it is! A long night is coming, and I fear that the Field of the Minds shall fill to overflowing before the daylight again arrives. My children…" She was so remorseful. "…my *children*…so many will sleep the long sleep before the evil hour's hunger is fully satisfied."

Looking down at her hands, she lamented, "I have the power to bring this madness to a finish, but I cannot, for then I, myself, should become the greatest of evil serpents! The blood of freedom of all my children, of all I stand for, cries out from beyond the abyss, condemning me for even thinking such selfish thoughts. No! The victory must come at the hands of my children even to the destruction of them all." She began to quietly weep.

Placing the cup down and taking her mother's hand, Tolohe promised, "My dearest one, my love, please do not torment your tender heart. Such calamity will not happen. I will not allow it. Dear one, your children will not fail."

Ma-we's pleading eyes looked out from a tear-stained face. "How can you promise such folly when I have seen your very demise in fire and smoke? How can you know with such confidence that my children will succeed?"

Shocked at first by Ma-we's revelation, Tolohe quickly recovered, answering, "The blood of our mother flows in each of my siblings. She is not weak from fear and neither are they. Foolish? Yes! And also dull of senses, drugged by the happy days of ancient bliss."

She squeezed her mother's hand, leaning close with a pleading answer. "We love you with such intensity that each one of us would eagerly sacrifice all things, forever, rather than see our dear one hurt. We lack wisdom, must learn how to pull victory from longing hearts, but it can…will be accomplished. There is too much love within us to fail. Show us how to love and we shall conquer all that is evil, bringing it down to Gehenna for all time!"

The flow of tears eased and soon stopped, Ma-we watching the fire surge in intensity as the winter winds cried out in empty frustration. The heat of the blaze, along with the sweet smell of flaming apple-wood newly placed on the hearth, refreshed her spirit. A sudden '*pop!*' sent an army of tiny sparks up the chimney. Ma-we watched until the last one disappeared from sight. "You know… I believe I lit a fire under my children at the last council meeting."

Tolohe silently nodded, not wanting to intrude where uninvited. Mother was oftentimes a secret person, the reason for riddles. So much she kept to herself, always had, feeling she did not have the words to convey the real meaning hiding in her heart.

Tonight was different. Ma-we wanted her daughter to see, to understand all that lay beneath the surface of her outer soul. "I have revealed to my children the third of my three Swords, TrishaQaShaibjal. I am sorry to have not sought your council in this matter, but… but, still, what do you think of my choice?"

Tolohe rubbed her chin in thought while staring into the half-empty cup of tea. "Well, I detect that not everyone was pleased, including my sister, Mihai. Meter, I trust to your wisdom. As for the woman? I do not know her well. She served under my command for a time, but only as a common officer. When observing her, I find few secrets. She hides herself so well in shadows of mystery, something that I believe has been the doing of your hands."

She frowned. "There exists a power within the woman that troubles my spirit. It is dangerous, barely contained, and smells of evil. Had it not been at your very hand she was delivered here, I would say a demon raised from Hell the woman to be. Yet I know her not to be such, for you have sealed her heart in lasting life. I trust you."

Ma-we smiled, nodding, "Others of your kind have not been so generous with my choice. They see her as a bastard child of these realms, an unfit usurper of privileged powers."

Tolohe picked up her cup of tea, drinking the remainder down, offering, "You have purposes secreted from the wisest of your children. PalaHar has spoken of this to me. He is both troubled and amused. He and I trust fully in your actions and accept this child of the earth into our inner circle. My hope…no, I am certain that my brothers and sisters will come around and not only embrace her as our new leader, but become willing to learn at her feet the ways of the North."

Thanking Tolohe, Ma-we added, "You speak with discernment. The child's heart is twisted by the very forges of Hell that have engulfed her old world in violence down to this day. But it is by such a twisted heart that salvation shall come to your people in later days and… and at the Prisoner Exchange."

Tolohe wondered, "PalaHar says the woman has no feelings, but stands as emotionless as a mountain wall. How will my people trust her if they can see no love or compassion flowing from her?"

Ma-we grinned. "Oh, she has love and passion. And I have already begun the process to reawaken it from within. My little boy is busy at work on her heart. I sent him away on a scent that he will be unable to shake from his nostrils. Soon Trisha's ardor will grow beyond control for…well, you know how Zadar is."

Tolohe laughed. "You need not given him the witch's potion to boot. He has the power to make a woman surrender to his wiles even should she be upon the field of battle. Once the dam has burst, will Trisha have the fortitude remaining to lead your children to war?"

Answering, Ma-we shook her head. "It will take a great deal of witchery to deliver that child to Zadar's bed. She is a tough case. In the years since her arrival, she has refused every offer of romance, be it dream-share or otherwise, she feeling repulsed by even the thought of her sister's touch. No, it will be no easy matter for my son to carry the gate to take her heart, but I trust he will… and at the right time, too."

"Are you sure *you* sent him?" Tolohe asked, chuckling. "She is quite comely, more so than most, and those stodgy clothes can hide only so much. Zadar would have sought to uncover the woman's secrets soon enough if left on his own."

Ma-we laughed. "True! True! Still, this child is so different, badly damaged, I feel…so much so I fear that Zadar would tire the chase if left to his own powers. Oh, he will struggle with her, with his personal feelings… already is. Who knows, he may well fall in love."

"Zadar fall in love?!" Tolohe laughed. "The world is not prepared to deal with that man captured up in love."

Ma-we also began to laugh with Tolohe. It felt good to laugh, and if someone could bring on her light spirit it was Tolohe. When the joyous tumult eased, she became serious, resting a hand on Tolohe's knee. "He loves you. Always has. Why do you dismiss his advances? You know how sweet his kisses are and how they revive your soul."

Tolohe frowned then smiled. "You're right. I have been derelict in my duties. I will not refuse the boy his advances the next time he offers. He has a way that can make my heart sing on the dreariest of nights."

"Good! Good! Please do so, for my sake." Ma-we went on to other business. "Mihai also revealed the secret of the other Swords, pointing out that the first was already walking among them, hiding in the shadows."

A chill swept across Tolohe's heart. "Meter, this one is very dangerous. Only by your reassurance have I come to trust her. Even I have trouble remembering when she passes. More like the mist is she - an angry mist filled with vengeance. There is good reason she is called the 'Death Angel', the 'Gravemaker'. Hairs rise on the back of my neck when she comes into my presence. Like living death she feels to me. She is there and then gone without a trace. I cannot find a soul within her. Is she truly real, a child from forgotten lands, or is it a machination of your witchery sent to test us out?"

Shaking her head, Ma-we answered, "She is very real, very damaged... far beyond Zadar's repair. Her owner will one day rescue her heart. A danger? Not to you or your kind, but to those who rebelled she is most deadly. A heart more corrupted than the Stasis is hers, but still filled with a sweet love for all that is good. A formidable force is she to your wicked brother. Even now she haunts his worlds, walking unseen in his holy places. There is an hour coming when a crack will rupture in the wall surrounding her heart...a sad hour, but one that will begin the healing."

Tolohe was curious. "So you created this being when making her new in these realms or how?"

"No." Ma-we again shook her head. "Chrusion has created a demented world filled with pain and sorrow. It bends and twists the hearts of many so that even my powers cannot mend the damage. I must trust to Time for the cure. Until that hour, I can use the destructive forces instilled into the Worm's victims to wreak vengeance upon his world - just reward for what he has committed against these innocents."

"With such a foul-smelling heart, my child can enter in right among those evil miscreants, they sensing no abnormality in their harmonics. For the moment, my Sword's heart releases a harmonic song that cannot be detected even by Chrusion's powers. She has even put pig piss in his omen cup!" Ma-we laughed derisively. "She is become a shadow-dancer. The rebels believe a traitor walks in their midst and they know not what to do about it. She is a very trustworthy spy."

Leaning forward, Tolohe asked, "So she keeps close in touch?"

"Oh, yes!" Ma-we answered. "Your brother's war councils do not remain secret to my ears. I have learned much about the coming Prisoner Exchange from my attentive daughter."

"Meter," Tolohe asked, "why put her at such risk? She is still mortal and inexperienced. Have you no better way to gather needed information?"

Ma-we pondered aloud. "Risk? Mortal? Inexperienced? Well yes, you might be correct, at least about the *mortal* part. Inexperienced and at risk? That I must argue. First, I do not put her in danger. She is a creature of free will and chooses to do as she wants, merely delivering to me information pleasing to her. And" She squinted, searching Tolohe's eyes, "the only *danger* is to *Chrusion and his people*. The child has powers greater than yours - many latent, for sure - but still sufficient to deal with the likes of those rabble. Indeed, there has never been a child with greater glory than her and those others I have delivered to these worlds. But for now the glory remains to be found in my Swords, new creations of untold strength and might."

Leaning back in the chair, Ma-we sighed. "Even as a mortal, there is no force to be found among the enemy that can stop my child. Why, she could create heaps upon heaps of bodies should Chrusion's elite guard attempt her capture. That woman could walk through a company of his best like a whirlwind through a wheat field. Only could Chrusion check her hand."

Ma-we offered more tea. When the cups were full, she continued. "As for the spying, I refuse to steal freedom even from the wicked. I will not stoop to such loathsome antics as searching hidden rooms with my mind, nor steal another's thoughts for my purposes, even if they are well intended. The ends do not justify the means. A game is a game and a riddle is a riddle. No matter the cost, rules must be followed. It is the root-law of freedom."

Tolohe agreed.

Taking first a sip, Ma-we added, "It is by this *fly on the wall* I have come to know many secrets, and, by law, I can use this information against him. You will see him fail. This Prisoner Exchange will not be to his liking. What he learns there will set matters in motion that will force him to act prematurely, leading to his final defeat."

The two lost themselves in discussion concerning the Prisoner Exchange, the latest council, the attitude of the children regarding the newcomers from the Lower Realms, and any pertinent gossip relating to current events. Tolohe was not satisfied with the state of preparedness of the military, making recommendations while listening to several suggestions from her mother. She was most attentive to Ma-we's detailed account of Ardon's actions regarding Darla, saying nothing for fear of stirring a troubled pot.

Finally, Ma-we revealed the real reasons for requesting Darla's presence at the Prisoner Exchange, asking, "Was I remiss in pushing so? Did I do the right thing?"

Tolohe defended her youngest sister. "Darla will cause you no injury, but beware, she may well destroy herself should truth be twisted beyond reason." She frowned. "The child is a misfit, a queer thing, spooky, but she is not dangerous other than to herself. I believe you have chosen wisely. What this world needs are more like her. Had she been a million, this war would never have begun."

"At Memphis she saved more on that day than perished in fire and torture. She held the gap – how, I do not know. Against odds of a hundred-to-one, her band stole the enemy's glory, surrendering up to him a hollow victory filled with his own countless dead." She clasped her hands, remembering, "Twice I have carried her shattered body from the field, thinking the child no more. At Fortress Mordem, we found her nearly frozen, she refusing to abandon Depais' body to the wolves and vultures. We were forced to promise to gather the dead before she would abandon the field."

Shaking her clasped hands while nodding, she added, "Darla is an outstanding leader. A shame she has never been recognized as such. She is the bravest soldier I know, and smart. Godenn underestimated her once and nearly lost his head for it. If she survives this coming fury, may she be honored with the glory she deserves."

Ma-we eyed Tolohe. "She will survive! Must!" Then turning away toward the fire, added, "As for the older councilors, Darla is not refined or smooth, with diplomatic speech. She speaks her mind when offered the moment. Few of the oldest on the council have seen, first hand, the horrors of war, or have they smelled the distress of battle. If they could witness her heroism, they might well feel differently about her."

Tolohe asked, curious, "So you have chosen to keep the child alive so that she cannot die?"

"Not I!" Ma-we waved a hand. "There are forces at work in this universe that even you have not come to fully understand. You, the child of the Cherubs, should realize that I do not enforce law as some king or dictator would. There are those whose council *I* even pay close heed to."

"No, I fear not the loss of Darla's body, but that of her mind. The demon grows in might by the day, consuming more of the child's mind into its own. Already it has done lasting damage. How much, I cannot tell. When rid of that monster, she will be forever changed. How much is for the future to tell. At this time, I must set wheels in motion that will bring to a finish what grows within."

Concerned, Tolohe asked, "Is there no cure other than a sojourn into damnation?"

"There has ever been only one other, and none of my daughters will release their control over that destiny long enough for me to bring it." Ma-we sadly shrugged. "So it must be a journey into damnation to receive the cure. But my child does not go alone. Her friendly host is most caring. Never has she been abandoned to the darkness, never will she. Trust me, though heaven and earth should pass away, my girl's rescue will arrive in time."

Ma-we continued, dismayed. "When the evil of Chrusion's corrupt mind entered the world, I could well see it in Michael's mind, but I became so preoccupied with her that I abandoned my responsibilities with Darla, *my dearest Rachel*. When I discovered the demon growing within her, it was far too late to make a cure. I soothed her as best I could, but had to allow the monster its day. And because of it my child has suffered in so many ways." She sighed. "Her suckling did save Michael's mind, though, it slowing the demon's growth."

"Meter! Is there nothing we can do? What of the powers beyond this universe?"

"No!" Ma-we bemoaned. "Only by some great orgasmic reaction exploding from within her own soul will such a deed be accomplished. It must be so great as to threaten her very existence. It must happen soon or we will lose her anyway, and then I don't know… I don't know."

Tolohe nodded, understanding all too well. If Ma-we failed to deliver the cure, and her child fell into damnation, she would see herself as a mother unfit to even live. Could she contain those feelings for eternity? She was immortal, having life within her personal being. Death could not come to her, but… but, she feared, would her heart sink to such levels so as to destroy her mind, bringing on an eternal forgetfulness and a ruination to all living things? Long had the possibility troubled her. Only Tolohe understood its depth.

Staring at the floor, Tolohe answered reassuringly, "You will succeed." Looking up and into Ma-we's eyes, hers reflecting that same sadness, she promised, "We will succeed. The blood that my brothers and sisters have shed will not be wasted upon some empty victory! We will do whatever is necessary to carry the future to success. You will not falter, cannot. My little sister will win her contest. Mihai will learn wisdom. Meter, there is much more to you than you wish to see. You say you do not want to be ruler. I say there is none better to rule than you. Your strength of will is far greater than even your heart. You can hold all the fires of torment in your bosom for all the ages and never waver in your purposes. There is nothing that is impossible for you. Nothing! When you feel at your weakest, your strength is only then made evident. I have seen it. It burns in your children, in the gods beyond this world, and in you… the Maker of our souls. Meter…my Love of loves…*you will succeed!*"

Ma-we's fingers gripped the arms of her chair. Little could she hide from this intuitive creature, her troubled heart exposed by distressed words. "Thank you for such kindness, but you know I have failed my children… still do. But you…your leadership is unmatched by anyone living or dead. I wish you to have been my firstborn. You can calm a troubled soul… have. You bring me real refreshment." She looked sadly into Tolohe's eyes, confessing, "I have used you up, depended too much on your might, to the point I have kil't your soul by my many demands."

Tolohe shook her head in denial, but said nothing. The cancer was hers to carry, the stress of the ages having destroyed her immune system. The woman would not charge against another the burden she had chosen to carry so long ago. Still, Tolohe hoped a cure. There was another who might save her, but that request must come at the proper time, for he saw not the ways of mortals and understood little the panderings of a selfish heart.

Silence filled the room, the fire not quite as comforting as before. Ma-we wished to change the mood and bring back the warmth. She spoke of other matters. "Michael Morning Star has rejected the crown."

Tolohe perked up, smiling. "It's good! Did you succeed with your other offer?"

Ma-we nodded. "The child is now king over a tormented land that she, alone, can secure and return to brightness. I have set in motion the tools necessary for her to accomplish the task."

Looking into Tolohe's eyes, she asked, "Now that it has come to pass, will you not accept what is - what should have always been yours? You are the second in line to the Firstborn and have proved yourself fit and worthy. Will you take the crown offered Michael and deliver the blessing up to my daughters?"

Laughing, Tolohe answered, "A woman born was I and a woman I shall remain until the breath passes from my lips. This you've long known. Besides, you've already chosen the King of kings in your heart, did long ago. It should go to the one woven by your magic. He is the one deserving the crown, being so much like you."

Surprised, Ma-we raised an eyebrow, squinting the other eye, asking, "Why do you speak in such riddles?"

Tolohe cautioned, "Don't play innocent with me! I know your heart nearly as well as you do. Need I tell you the tale of the world beyond? I will anyway."

"At one time, in the Realms Below, you wanted a nation to be built, made to show the rest of mankind how generous and loving a person you really were. Alas, you put your daughter here to the task, resulting in what I believe to have been disappointment. From the days of Abram down to glory's hour, I led them and directed them. What happened? The world of men came to think of you as a cruel, demanding and aggressive God, one to be worshipped out of fear. To this day, they call down evil on you for the acts of war I delivered upon wicked men."

She shook her head. "I am a warrior, will die with my hand on the sword before any sickness will take me. Valiant and harsh are my ways. You call me 'Pillar of the Sun'. Your own children have named me '*HierosEchidnaMnema*', '*The Holy Serpent that brings down to nothing*'. No! My ways are harsh, almost evil. You are too pure for me to represent your spirit. I have grossly misrepresented you."

Looking into the blaze, she continued. "Later you delivered Mihai upon the scene. Through her love, she has changed the world of men, but not their understanding of you. For many, Mihai's God is weak, unable to do anything but love, unwilling to bring justice. May I add there is some just reason for them to think so. When the hour chosen was delayed - as it has been now for so many centuries - the men of that world tired out, feeling your promise only a metaphor, the hope only remaining at some other place after death. For this and other reasons, I do not feel Mihai a truly suitable person to represent you."

Ma-we disagreed. "It was not the fault of my daughter that the hour of salvation was delayed. I could not risk her demon's glory over her, and your brother's treachery with tricksy words fooled even the hearts of many of my loyal children, and… and there were so many other reasons I allowed the universe to wait upon a moment. I still wait… still wait."

Tolohe leaned forward, resting a hand on Ma-we's forearm. Her reply was filled with love, but it could not hide bitter disappointment. "My Meter, no matter the reason, the delay has been most costly. For three times we drove the evil of Hormax and his confederates down, bringing devastation upon the lands of Mizraim, Magog, and Javan, desolating those worlds of men. And only then, in the end, as the blood of Haudenosaunez's kindred and your own loyal children made holy the field of slaughter – our dead counted by the thousands of thousands - he and I, side by side, felled the last of the Anakim at Camorra Heights, bringing the first breath of freedom since the days of Japheth to those tortured lands of demon possession. My Love, your children cannot survive another delay. I cannot survive another delay. My hour is close, for I have seen its wretched end should time fail me."

Tolohe sat back, ashamed of her rueful accusations. How well she knew the sacrifices her mother had made, but only here, in this one place, in the company of this one person, could the great Pillar of the Sun become the tired, lonely, disheartened child. For this reason Ma-we remained silent, allowing her daughter time to grieve over the loss of her own virginity - innocence.

Shaking her head to clear troubling memories, Tolohe returned to the subject, a stoic appearance of weathered granite clouding her face. "Neither Mihai nor I are qualified to carry the Horn of Rachel before the universe of men. We are the extremes of your personality. No…no, the king who sits your throne must be just like you. Your blood must flow through his veins."

Ma-we leaned back, replying in thoughtful consideration. "So, you've put me in a pickle. Who is there remaining, fit and qualified to take up the scepter and return to my daughters their youth and dignity?"

Tolohe chided, "Don't play the part of an innocent waif. You may well have tricked with the foolish, dumb and blind, but your riddles have been secreted by me from this world's founding, for well I am aware of the unholy union and its offspring. And long have I known that you wove your own blood into the belly of the woman who bore the Son of Salvation, and I do see that that blood still flows rich in the veins of a man born from darkness and light. You have not hidden well your intentions in our dream-shares together."

Cocking her head to the side while shaking a finger, Tolohe postured, "I harbor no ill will concerning these matters. You are the Maker of all things. You are Law. Whatever is your slightest desire is my most impassioned want. So then, I recommend what will satisfy most your heart, a man-child who shares your soul, heart, and yes, even your blood. For the right man, you have held in abeyance the four winds down to this day and he, I believe, you have now discovered. '*Yehowahboam*'… 'The Man Who Stands In the Place of God'…Shiloh…'Sword-King Over Heaven and Hell'." Tolohe's eyes wandered as she described the man, her face blushing rose while two lips struggled to hold back a girlish smile.

Patting Tolohe's leg, Ma-we stared into her eyes, squinting. "The scent of a storm's coming ever heralds upon the approaching breeze and a maiden swoons at the thoughts of her hero's embrace. Has my daughter been smitten by the breeze that tells of a coming man who is but still a child? Does her heart yearn for love from a hero yet to prove himself? I detect feelings of love hidden in the music of your words. Love… such a dangerous possession for the heart to contain while the stallion is yet running the plain, unbridled."

Tipping her head back, Tolohe closed her eyes, sighing sadly, "Oh, but this stallion has the heart of both its mother and father, fire and ice, power and tenderness, rage and compassion, tumult and peace. Hidden in the self-doubt of a frightened sheep there dwells a demon-monster waiting to rise, it awaiting the day its power is unchained. Dangerous he is, King of the Dragons! Lord of the gods or slave of the Serpent, himself… We must wait to see. Still, his scent excites me in ways long forgotten. My heart is bound with his to our glory or our ruin." She leaned forward, clutching Ma-we's arm, pleading, "The boy must not fail! For shall that happen, then I wish no longer for life itself."

Ma-we caressed her child's hand. "Death? Death is not yours to choose, for your fathers have purchased your soul and will do with it as *they* choose. But this I do know: I, too, trust in his success, but I have seen that in his glory will come your destruction. In his hour of test, in his greatest victory, he will call out to a woman who will not heed your council, but will attempt a coup upon her brother. A trap! A trap, I say, has already been laid at his door. Death to her is its intent. You will not let that happen for my sake and the blow will fall upon you."

Ma-we slowly shook her head, tears falling. "To save my Michael, you must die."

Tolohe bowed her head in silence. At long last, she whispered, "He will succeed. There is nothing else for it, or all heaven and earth shall pass away."

Ma-we smiled, wiping away tears from her eyes. She finally asked as though speaking to herself, "So, has it come to this? The future existence of all my worlds depends upon the loyal love of a child not yet grown from his teens? We risk everything on the merits of a good heart borne along by a free will of a wild stallion let loose upon the torrid field, trusting that he will act in wisdom when his hour of darkness falls instantly upon him?"

Turning to stare into the crackling blaze, Ma-we pondered the coming hour when all of her works hung upon such an uncertain thread. It was all or nothing…always had been…but never violently exposed and violated to be spoken of with such openness. Still, it was the truth, the only way to bring absolution to the argument that she – Ma-we – was not wicked in the way she had made her children. Freedom must win! And she must prove that her way was the solution to bring real freedom. Looking back into Tolohe's passionate eyes, Ma-we softly pronounced her willingness to stay the course at all cost. "*Then so be it!*"

Ma-we quickly changed the subject. "As I have said, Michael has accepted the kingship and will wield the King's swords until he arrives. Because of this, I find myself in a most peculiar position in which there is need of your assistance. I have a serious request." Tolohe bowed low, looking up and into her mother's eyes. "Why do you need to make request? To my dying breath, all that I have is yours for the taking."

After showing her gratitude with a kiss, Ma-we asked, "Please sit up and become my steward. The hour of the prophets draws ever closer and battle, this time, shall ruin all my wonderful works. Indeed! My womb shall cry out for its children who lay slain like fallen chaff upon an overripe field of grain. My grand ballrooms will become a lurking place of the dust mite. The spider will weave its tapestry across the doorposts of many great palaces that will echo only the sound of the fruit bat as it seeks refuge from the sun. It is a bitter hour. Who will survive?"

"In the middle of this maelstrom I have set my child, Michael. She will gather the storm and set the forest ablaze. Her hand will decide the time that this world shall die. But I have set up a protection for this child, should she listen to its wise council…which I doubt. The girl is reckless, unpredictable - a quality I will soon be using to my advantage – she will little tolerate the back seat when the cry for blood rents the air."

"The crown and kingdom I have saddled her with will force my child to stand the throne while the world goes mad around her. But she is feisty and, if pushed, will enter the battle of warcraft. This is something that must not be allowed, at all costs. I cannot afford her capture and enslavement."

Tolohe stopped her mother, asking, surprised, "I know you choose your words carefully. Why do you speak of her capture and not her death as being the worst of calamities?"

Ma-we glanced toward the door as though fearing the wind might carry away secrets to listening ears as she softly answered, "She cannot die..."

Aghast, Tolohe asked, "She has not yet passed into the worlds of the immortals, has she?! It is still for a future day, is it not?!"

Tolohe's excitement set the mood. Ma-we relaxed. "No. No, she is not yet immortal, but she has been changed as have a few of the others. You see, her spirit cannot escape the girl's flesh. When Michael first returned from the Realms Below, I created a new body of flesh for her. When she accepted her rightful place in my kingdom by taking the crown, I set it aflame, waking its power. So, until the day she is gifted with immortality and is given authority over the spirit of the flesh, she is locked for good or ill in the body she now possesses. And that body cannot be fully destroyed. Thus is finally fulfilled the words of my prophets, 'Death, where is your glory, for you have been made subject even to me.'"

"So here is the dilemma: should Michael be captured, or should her body be found as though dead upon the field, your brother will demand it be sent to him, there to be desecrated in horrible ways. Once it is discovered she possesses an indestructible mind and heart, when it is seen that by the very hidden energy of the universe the woman's body would regenerate back to health, think of the tortures he will heap upon her until her rescue was secured. Then think, also, of the countless number of my children who will perish in fire and destruction attempting that rescue."

A visible shudder ran down Tolohe's back. "What, then, is my part in securing freedom from such a fate for this child?"

Ma-we's answer was quick and sharp. "You must stop her from such folly! Whatever the cost, keep her safe!"

Tolohe shrugged in wonder, her arms outstretched with question. "How?! To her has all authority been given. She rules as king, lord, master over all living things. Yes, I am older than she, and my witching powers are far, far, greater, but what authority do I possess that will make her subject to me?"

Ma-we, too, shrugged but all so casually. "Then I will have to gift you with *greater authority...*" A blinding light flashed across the room. Tolohe cried out in surprise and pain as a fire-like ache exploded in her right hand, racing up her arm. When her eyes could again focus, why there, shining every color of the gemstone world, rested a signet ring that, when the runes were translated read, 'Yehowahboam'. Tolohe was stunned, speechless. She struggled for words while fighting back welling emotions growing in her breast.

Ma-we broke the silence, pointing. "That, my Dear, should satisfy your needs. Being the King's signet ring, no one will question the steward wielding its power. And power it does have, enough to rule successfully over this universe… all universes." Cupping Tolohe's shaking hand in hers, Ma-we grinned. "It is yours to use as may be, but also a gift that you will bestow upon your King on the Day of Celebration."

Tolohe burst into tears, sobbing uncontrollably as she hid her face in her hands. Ma-we gently squeezed and then rubbed her child's knee, understanding all so well the emotion of the moment. It was not the power or the authority the ring carried that so moved the woman. Indeed, it was not really the ring, but what her mother had said regarding it. "… bestow it upon your King on the Day of Celebration." Oh, to come of age again! To become a maiden in the arms of a man who would never shun her love, a man so much like her mentor from the Elder Days but always faithful and true to the end of time! Yes, there was to be a rebirth even for her…

When Tolohe had finally composed herself, Ma-we smiled, cautioning, "Keep it hidden well. You do know how to hide it, safe in your mind. Please, for the moment, keep it secret. Use it only when all other hope is lost, when winsome words have fully waked the demon's pride in my child, not before. This ring is very dangerous, made for an immortal's hand to wield its power, and you, my Dear One, are not yet immortal."

Nodding as final tears fell from her eyes, Tolohe promised to be oh, so careful with such a precious treasure. She leaned close and kissed her mother on the cheek. "I love you too much, my Meter, too much for my heart to bear. Should I fail you, how could I survive another day?"

Ma-we grinned, getting up to stretch as she did. "You? Fail me?! Child, more like your father are you than you do know. I should have delivered you up to immortality long ago, but…well, you know what I mean."

Yawning loud, Ma-we lifted her arms toward the ceiling while standing high on tippy-toe. She was tired, and the ebbing flames reflected her mood. Walking across the room to the window beside the door, she stared into the wild and confused storm outside. "You know, it still looks mighty angry out there, an unpleasant night to forge through frozen drifts to find a half-buried ship." She tapped the windowsill. "Now, if I were one to forecast the weather, I'd say that the morning will bring a break to this madness, but the clouds should still cover us with enough gloom to get you away unseen." She began to hum a pleasant little tune.

Tolohe looked up to see not her mother but a tiny sprite of a woman-child, someone little more than in her teens. How beautiful this woman was when the weight of the universe lifted itself from her shoulders! Tonight was such a night. For a few fleeting hours, the troubles of the ages might be forgotten. Tonight… tonight sweet memories of forgotten days, when the world was filled with innocence and wonder, might fill this cabin with the music long unsung in Lowenah's heart. Here stood the Maker of Worlds so longing to be a flirting maiden in a land of bliss.

Ma-we turned to Tolohe, firelight dancing off enchanting eyes. "Must you brave the cold outside so soon and leave go the warmth of this humble abode? Can you wait upon the day and hold close these fleeting hours in the quiet of this room?"

Tolohe laughed. "Did you really believe I journeyed these many miles only to fend my way off into this storm after such short council, one storm, I may add, that appears to be assisted by tampering hands? No. I could not depart at this hour should the Lords of Lagandow call out my name. Tonight is our night, yours and mine. We shall share it as we once did in days long ago when, as a much younger and innocent woman-child, I first unlatched that very door."

Two lips touched, two souls embraced, the fire peacefully fell to slumbering. In but a short while the tiny cabin was filled with the sweet music of hearts reunited. To lands long abandoned but not forgotten journeyed the souls of time fulfilled. For the hour, for the moment, Time was but the boatman ferrying lovers upon an endless river to which the further shore could not be seen.

Soon all fell into silence, other, say, than the sounds of gentle breathing while stormwinds tired of their fury and… and a little mouse sat back on its haunches, happily munching on the feast of crumbs and cheese that had been so carelessly scattered upon the floor.

ဢ ဢ ဢ

An ear-splitting scream tore into Paul's quiet dreams like a savage beast ripping at his soul. In a panic, he leaped to his feet, eyes bulging with terror of the unknown, wondering what had ever perpetrated such a heart-stopping sound. Instantly there crashed upon his ears another even more diabolical screech of terror, this one coming from the bed where he had been sleeping.

Spinning around, hands raised in preparation to battle with some monstrous evil, Paul stared in shock to see Mihai thrashing about, crying out in agony, all the while tearing at her face and hair. "Mihai! Mihai!" He shouted, plunging toward her in an attempt to prevent her added injury.

It was he who suffered the wounds, as Mihai slashed out at him with long fingernails, cleaving crimson trails of destruction as they cut across his chest. The moonlight betrayed a story of anguish being fought out within the woman's mind. To her, all things this night were evil and if she were to survive, she must fight with all her strength.

"Mihai! Mihai! Wake up!" Paul's tearful pleadings went unheeded.

Into a void of long-forgotten nightmares Mihai fell…fell until she crashed into the one time and space the woman wished most to forget, yet journeyed there often when the moon was full and the night refreshingly sweet. And this night? It was the worst night of the year… the worst so far. For it was a reminder night, a precursor of the moment yet to arrive, a troubadour heralding her new birth to come… *her birth into Hell*.

Deep into the vortex of sordid memories of long years gone Mihai tumbled, crashing through one horrid nightmare after another, her demon struggling to remove all remaining sanity from her mind. Smashing hard upon her shoulders in a thorny brier patch, the woman found herself at a long ago time and place, the putrid smell of death filling her nostrils to a nauseating extreme.

Wild laughter and foul curses erupted in her ears as violent hands tore at her flesh. All the while beasts violated the woman's body in most obscene ways as her lover… yes, lovers… tormented her with the every kind of debased and lurid act. Then, if these attacks were not enough, there comes to her the one man - her mentor and god - the man who made her into a woman. He seeks not only to release his unholy passion upon an innocent heart, but with it deliver a horde of unspeakable demons to rule over her withering soul.

And then the monsters within! With the unleashing of his power, Mihai's mind reels as an army of unspeakable filthy things crawl into her secret worlds to forever seek control of the girl's inner peace, to eventually possess even her waking thoughts until she becomes little more than the walking dead, knowing, but unable to prevent any act committed by her debased body of flesh.

Another scream shatters the night as Mihai refuses to go quietly into tormenting depths. With all her strength she fights back as the fire-blackened monsters bore into brain and muscle, their fangs and claws shredding breast and bone. She watches, helpless, as two thumbs bore deep into eye sockets, crushing sight from her world, hears the curses regarding the child's birth, the chants singing the uselessness of her life. Finally, as the last of her power wanes, the woman cries out, begging, "Oh, let me die! Oh, my God, please let me die!"

But the child's heart refuses to surrender. It screams out, *"Damn you! Damn you all to Hell! I shall take the river and bring all the world to ruin! I shall bring you down! I shall bring you all down to nothing!"*

As she continues to struggle against the monster within, there comes the cry of reinforcements upon the quiet breeze, a voice calling out her name, seeking her return from the worlds of the damned, "Mihai! Mihai, my love! Wake up! Come back to me. Come back to me." Though it sounded so distant to Mihai, Paul was in reality screaming in her ear, "Mihai! Mihai! Wake up! Wake up! It's a dream! It's a dream!" He began to violently shake her as he continued to call out her name.

Gradually, as if rising from beyond the Silent Tombs, Mihai nodded the dream away, hearing more clearly her lover's words. She took up the battle cry and stood fast her ground upon the sordid field. Eventually the demon hordes were pushed back into the darkness as she gained control over her mind. As the moon's glory waned, giving it up to the power of coming morning light, Mihai came to sense the growing day, a harbinger of hope and life. With one final cry of defiance, Mihai collapsed into a deep, deathlike, sleep.

ῴ   ῴ   ῴ

Mihai opened her eyes as the first rays of morning sunlight filtered through the curtains and across the bed. Paul was gently rocking her, giving her tired body the occasional shake. Still groggy, she beseeched him through tired lips, "Oh please, Love! It's quite enough. You're shaking me to jelly. I'll live! I promise… promise… I'll live another day."

Worry lines cut deep into Paul's face, his frustration at the night showing in troubled eyes. His concerned smile and shaking hands puzzled Mihai, commenting at what the fuss was all about. Paul said nothing, soaking in Mihai's complaints as if life-giving air to starving lungs. Finally, with tears in his eyes, he cried, "Oh, my Love! My dear sweet Mihai returned from the dead! My Love…!"

"Oh, what's the fuss?!" Mihai sputtered as she struggled to sit. "A bad dream is all it was. One little…" She gasped aloud looking at the surrounding destruction.

The bed was red from her bloody sweat. Littered about, like chaff in a field after a storm, countless golden strands of her hair clung to the wet sheets. "Up! Help me up ple…" Mihai let out another gasp as her eyes focused upon Paul.

It was now her turn to carry a worried question. "What beast has haunted these rooms this night?! You look no better for wear than I feel. Tell me, please, what has come of us?"

Paul shook his head, somewhat relieved at hearing the *old* Mihai speaking. "It was the demon of love, my dear, the monster who strikes out blindly when all hope is lost. But you have returned to me! I remember no struggle, only hope restored to my heart."

Paul had been a good boy like Ma-we had requested, and stayed with Mihai throughout her ordeal, Ma-we having told him that his presence, alone, should such an event occur, would do wonders at warding off the demon attacks. 'The time is close for the haunting hour when darkness shall rule for but a moment. It is your duty not to leave my child's side until that time has passed into nothingness. Do not leave the girl's side until the witching hour is gone."

"Help me up, please." Mihai again asked, almost pleading.

With Paul's assistance, she managed her way from the bed to the mirror at the far end of the room. Mihai leaned close and, peering out through bloodshot eyes, studied the tortured creature staring back at her. She groaned with disquiet. Standing there was the most pitiable of living things, a face scratched and puffy gray from the bruising struggle, a head of hair disheveled and torn, bald spots where clumps of golden tresses had been violently yanked from their nests. Mihai looked a mess. To top this off was a bleeding wound that oozed crimson from the corner of a blackened, swollen lip.

She turned around and, catching Paul's worried gaze, sputtered, *"I look like shit! Draw me, please, a bath... and fill it, please, with those mineral spirits I keep in the cupboard."* Turning back to the mirror while touching a finger to her lip, she fussed, *"This is great! Just great! We leave today and I look like the losing hen in a fight over an old cock rooster! Shit!"*

Paul stood back, aghast. "Here I thought you were about to die! In fact, I thought you already so! And all you're worried about is how comely your appearance?! What is it with your kind anyway? Is the whole world crazy?"

Mihai continued to study her wounds in the mirror, saying nothing. At length she turned, replying through a painful smile. "It's about time you noticed one of my better qualities. Yes, we are all quite mad here. How else do you think we could tolerate your kind at all? Always so quick to jump into the pot your kind, not testing the waters first and, speaking of water, will you be kind enough to fix me that bath?"

Reaching up to examine Paul's injuries, Mihai put on a pout, cooing her remorse that her gallant hero had suffered so this last night. Tilting her head so flirtingly to the side she kissed him, whispering, "Come, my warrior saint, and assist me with my bath. You, too, should be refreshed in the healing waters of the sacred springs of Diamond Ridge. There's plenty of room in the golden tub for us both. Come, my dear, I shall heal your soul while you also do mine."

Throwing his hands up in confusion, Paul exclaimed, "I don't understand! After all this you seek love's cure? What...?"

Mihai silenced him, taking his hand. "How little one understands. Come refresh your soul and spirit. A hot bath of mineral delights helps to heal the flesh. A potion of male delights helps to heal my spirit. Come and I shall seek ways to heal your flesh and spirit as well. We both need a bath."

ဢ   ဢ   ဢ

Oh, a soak in the tub, what a cure for sore muscles and tired flesh! And the songs of love, what a cure for weary hearts that needed reassurance and healing as well. Closing her eyes after passion's glory had swept away the night's troubling dreams, Mihai drifted into a swaddling sleep. Once she glanced a look into Paul's concerned face. She squeezed his hand, offering a sleepy, toothy grin. "Give me a moment, Love. I rest in a world of lilacs and apple blossoms and wish not to be waked until the morning high."

Mihai closed her eyes again, falling into an enchanted sleep. All the while Paul stood guard, holding her hand and softly singing little ditties of love in her ears.

ಶಿ   ಶಿ   ಶಿ

With a *snap* and a *whir*, the two ornately engraved doors of the tramwaiter opened onto a courtyard filled with the early morning noise of a hurried spring day. The sun had recently peeked its head over the eastern garden wall, waking insects, they busily singing happy tunes to the golden rays of light. Bees of every kind made musical love to the colorful spring flowers decorating the deep, rich, jungle-like greenery in this secluded enclave of beauty.

Out from the tramwaiter and into this joyous symphony of sensual delights jumped a handsome man seeking the company of a most elusive lady friend. His feet merrily tapping a happy beat upon the cobblestone path, Zadar hurried his step toward a humble door still hidden in morning shadows. Unable to hold his excitement in check as he neared, Zadar broke into a little song while his feet skipped along keeping up the beat. Oh, how the world had changed in the past few days, he filled with emotions never before experienced.

Stepping up to the door, the young fellow patted his new smoky-gray blouse and trousers, and then tilted his officer's kepi – its waxed bill and wide black band glistening bright, even in the shadows – until it was just right. Clearing his throat, he leaned forward and gave an ever so soft rap on the door.

(*Author's note: Trisha liked the new dress colors for the army uniforms. Hers was similar to Zadar's except it was less ornate and she did not tuck the pants into her boots. Also, her blouse was more formfitting, thus accenting her delightful figure. At the moment, Trisha was not wearing a sash or jacket, but the blouse did have the emblem of her rank sewn on the left sleeve and front left breast.*

The design of the emblem was the same as the one Trisha wore at the Council meeting, but the coloring was different. At the meeting, she had one that was blue with gold embroidery. The new one was the same color green as Zadar's shell jacket and instead of the rune representing 'Boaz' being embroidered in gold, it was done in a shimmering, burning copper-green.

The rune for 'Jachin' was done in a metallic, sky-blue thread. The green 'Boaz' stood for the Army, the blue, 'Jachin', for the Navy. The division had come about when Mihai resigned as field marshal, which was a command over all military forces. The separation of Army and Navy command created two supreme commanders: field marshal and admiral. This was part of the new military that was emerging in the First Realm.) Excerpted from Tabitha Copeland's work, Dogs of War.

"*Who is it*?!" A sharp, almost annoyed voice on the other side of that door asked.

Surprised but alert, Zadar made a quick reply. "It's Leften... er... Lieutenant Zadar, reporting as requested!" He reached for the door handle.

The same curt voice shouted through the door, "*You wait there!* I'll be out in a minute."

Scratching his head while screwing his face up in questioning wonder, Zadar pondered the moment. He did not understand this Trisha creature at all. For nine carefree days they had wandered the wilderness of Diamond, carrying only the packs on their backs. Trisha was more like a child on holiday than a new commanding officer in charge of the Empire's army. She and Zadar spent endless hours splashing in the mineral pools, spelunking in hidden caves, and just frolicking in the high desert thickets and canyons.

He smiled to think of the time that Trisha, refusing to listen to his mentoring ways, attempted the crossing of a theoxified streambed - *a mineral brook formed deep underground when its waters pass through a substance the children called 'theoxian', which, when diluted with water, lowers the temperature of the resulting liquid far below freezing, it taking several hours to detoxify after exiting the depths below.* The woman had fallen into the chill waters, she being swept along by the torrent until becoming totally soaked. A warm fire, comfy wool blankets, and a few loving hugs – to chase away the cold, of course - and Trisha was fully recovered and ready to take on other adventures.

Like two children on a quest, two peas in a pod, that was how Zadar felt about his relationship with Trisha. Anytime there was a break in the schedule of meetings and official procedures, she and Zadar were off on a run to explore this exciting new land. Trisha was more childlike than even she could remember. Life was fresh and fun, a joy it was to be alive. For Zadar this was a most intriguing time, filled with new and unexplained emotions.

He smiled to himself. So, this was Heaven, or what it was meant to be? If so, might it never end...

Then there was the journey to Pyre Mountain. Time afforded the duo opportunity to pay a visit upon one of the Diamond's most outstanding residents, Pyre Mountain, an ever-erupting volcano far to the north of the wilderness' bubbling springs, nearly a day's journey by pack animals, but well worth the effort. Beneath the glowing summit, Sulfur Lake lay nestled between two high bluffs, its many boiling springs and excitable geysers creating a wonderland of delights. It was a matter of folklore that one who spent a night resting upon the lake's misty shores or swam in its deep iridescent pools was forever changed. Zadar contended the folktales to be more truth than fiction.

It was a long, tiring day making their way to the lake and, after setting up camp for the night, the couple did little other than stroll the shore searching the many steaming pools for sand nuggets, tiny crustaceans said to thrive in the lake's tepid estuaries. Not only were their shells of beautiful hues, but also it was rumored they were to be savored for their excellent flavor when steamed. Having eventually returned to camp with rich rewards for diligent effort, Zadar had cooked up a feast. They ate until bursting to satisfaction and then reclined in the warm sands near the southern end of the lake.

Long after the sun set and the golden mist was gathering to shroud the shore in its foggy embraces, the two sat, staring at the glowing reflection of Pyre Mountain in the shimmering stillness of Sulfur Lake. Finally, Zadar broke the silence. "I puzzle at my feelings. It is said that this place forever changes people, and the feelings I am now experiencing are definitely strange to me, but I don't believe them caused by my presence here."

Trisha leaned close until her shoulder touched his. She asked him to explain.

"Well, I feel strange, like part of me is missing, yet when you're near me the feeling subsides. My heart hurts, too. Never have I felt it so. Do you know what might be?"

Trisha only smiled, offering no hint for a solution.

The following evening, when the sun escaped behind the cliffs, Zadar and Trisha took a long, swimming soak in the frothy waters near a hot spring. Trisha dared the darkness to be seen as she truly was made, enjoying the bubbly foam in the way Lowenah intended for her children. The night was warm, the air sharp and sweet. Saying not a word, she took Zadar's hand and then tenderly kissed him on the lips. That night they shared their first romance on a moss-laden beach, resting in each other's arms well into the night. Then, just as silently, Trisha rose, bathed in the nearby cove and, alone, returned to camp.

The following morning Zadar found Trisha to be distant almost to the point of being rude. She spoke few words and then only of business yet to be finished and the anticipated journey back. After their return, Trisha was off on official matters, ignoring Zadar until later in the evening, even then, at dinner, speaking to him only in formal conversation. When the meal was finished and the other officers and guests were retiring for the night, a very nervous Trisha asked Zadar for council. They strolled along a grassy path that led down past a peach grove and far from the lights of the lodge.

At length they came to a parting in the path, an obelisk long fallen at the center of the fork. Taking Zadar's hand, Trisha asked him to sit. She searched her thoughts for just the right words. "Zadar, this is such a strange world for me, for should we have loved in my old world like we did just yes-ter-eve, my people would have condemned me a harlot. It is so troubling for my heart to relearn that what is really such a beautiful thing between a man and woman is treated with such disgust in my world of old."

She began to nervously rub her knees. "I love and fear your world…love it for it allows me breath and freedom…freedom to think without guilt. I fear because I am confused…confused into believing that I live but a dream and shall awake to the accusations of angry men, cursing me for enjoying life. Is this life real, or will I awake only to find I, too, dreamed here only to have any honest hope for love dashed and ever destroyed?"

"Zadar, I have watched the pleasure your people find being lost in acts of love that would be considered lurid and obscene by my people of old, even of those in these current days. And yet your kind practice for others to see the very acts my kind hide in the darkness, behind curtains thick. And to speak of such sensual acts aloud? Why a woman could get her tongue removed for merely whispering such things in secret. And yet here I sit, I, too, at a cross-roads, deciding my future fate."

She took Zadar's hand, wrapping it up in hers. "I am very fond of you. I dare not say it any other way for now. My eyes have watched. I've studied your love-making with the ladies, and many there are. They stand in line as if waiting turn, caring not whose bed you have recently departed, desirous only to be next in sharing your love. Your passion is unbridled with them, yet you were so gentle with me. In my old world, few men cared for my pleasure, even the best being demanding and harsh. To them, a woman's body was little more than a warm piece of meat to be skewered upon their manliness."

"Still, old feelings die hard. The thought of one man and woman among my kind was absolute, at least only one man for a woman, she being his property. It is such a strange feeling to overcome, to see and feel love that is based upon what is found in the heart and not in an act of intercourse. So strange to have many lovers, but to be in love with but one, or hold just one so close while sharing the bed with many. It hurts my mind."

Zadar nodded his understanding. "I was born into a world forlorn and dismayed. The carefree days of romantic bliss were long trampled in the sands of lies and betrayal. For me, my coming of age days were filled with explosive sensual desire for the satisfaction of my flesh, I learning not to love a woman as she needed until long into my adulthood. But the women of my early days were patient with me, pandering to my *prurient* desires until my flesh became filled to satisfaction. Then I began to learn how to love, sensing what my lover wanted without speaking a word to me."

"As I grew, I learned reasons for the laws Mother made to protect your kind in the worlds below. Little more than slaves your kind became, and so badly treated, may I add. If it had not been for such taboos, what would have been the fate of womankind? Slave pens and brothels, at best, would have been your fate. Anyway, I do see what needs you have and I so much wish to make you happy. I will try to adjust to your feelings, just as my sisters did to mine. I…"

"No! No!" Trisha shook her head. "That is *not* what I want from you! You must understand that it is me who must rethink my life and this new and strange world that I now live in. Someday I may have many lovers, though the thought of it troubles my heart for the moment. But I *do* want you to care for your sisters. I see the way they look at you. I would be worse than a thief should I steal you away from them. No, better is a sip of brandy than an empty cask full of dreams. You create much joy in the hearts of many. Desert your sisters and I will be shamed into deserting you."

Trisha spoke not another word. She took Zadar's hand, they slowly journeying back to the lodge, saying their good nights outside her stateroom door. At parting, she kissed her young fellow on the lips, thanking him for a wonderful few days, and then quickly slipped through the door into the darkness within.

Zadar stood stunned, the ever-growing ache only increasing in strength. He departed in a tizzy, his heart floundering between explosive happiness and burning sadness. For these several days hence he had found no room for passion with his sisters, feeling the witch's touch had already condemned him to both their loss and the loss of this new, strange creature his soul found so entrancing. What spell had this woman placed over him and, and why did Mother take so long to give a woman such wonderful powers? May he die happy if he never awoke from such dreamy thoughts…

It was in this trance-like state that Trisha found her new lieutenant before her door. "Well! Who are *you*?!" She scolded, he not having noticed the door opening.

Zadar jumped to attention, almost hitting Trisha in doing his salute.

Trisha dodged a flying hand, laughing a reply. "I think you'll do!" Putting hands on hips, she scrutinized her new officer. Zadar's uniform of smoky gray was most becoming, and the long-sleeved, double-breasted blouse and green shell jacket helped him cut quite the picture. Topped off with knee-high riding boots into which his pants were neatly tucked, an ornate kepi, neatly trimmed beard and insignia of adjutant lieutenant, Trisha felt he made quite a good-looking officer.

Zadar's uniform was new standard issue for the field marshal's staff and other non-field officers. After some refitting done to Trisha's uniform at Mihai's request - Trisha said 'orders' - the field marshal's comely appearance was much more evident, something that met Zadar's full approval. In fact, he was about to comment on its sensual comeliness when Trisha caught him up short.

"*Lieutenant!*" Trisha's voice fell stern on Zadar's ears, her eyes having turned cold, her face sober. "I want you to understand me clearly. It was not by my request that you were chosen to be one of my staff officers. Of course, I accepted the recommendation, the ones making such reassuring me of your fitness as to loyalty and duty. Let me set this straight, there are no favorites in my command. I'll place you before the skewer as soon as may be if it is your turn to die. As a junior officer on my staff, I expect you to play the part of one."

"You, I have been told, have built up quite a record for military prowess and heroism. I tell you, that is behind you for the moment. A 'go-fer' you are, 'little errand boy', 'do this, get me that, another cup of tea, please', and you will smartly reply, saluting, 'Yes, General', 'Right away, Captain', 'Whatever you wish, my Lord' and so forth. I will show no favoritism to anyone, especially you. I expect you to act in accordance with all the rules of protocol your position calls for, setting an example for all the other junior officers."

She looked down, rubbing her chin as though in thought. "Of course, a good staff officer…" She stared Zadar in the face, hers betraying a new softness. "a good staff officer should feel free to offer opinion – at the proper time, of course – but still, if that officer were discerning as to when and how it were expressed, that officer would be quite valuable." She smiled and then quickly frowned.

Quite flippantly, Trisha flatly stated, she waving her hand as though the outcome of her comment was of little concern, "You are a volunteer, as are all officers. As such, you may choose to resign your commission under my command at any time, and may do so now if you wish. Until such time, I am your supreme commander. You are to obey my orders, whatever they may be! Does this junior officer understand clearly?"

Zadar had remained motionless, unable to gather what this woman was all about. He stared down into stern eyes watching his for any visible betrayal of the man's inner emotions. The fellow was very much upside-down in his feelings. Studying Trisha's face revealed nothing other than sheer determination to contest anyone who questioned her authority. What was she about? This was truly a strange and dangerous creation, a woman Zadar could neither read nor understand. Not since his younger years had he experienced such opaque emotional feedback from his feminine companions. What was really going on in this person's mind at the moment?

Zadar thought he was prepared to face whatever his new friend might deliver, despite Mother's warning. 'Son, you may one day well regret the assignment I've offered you. Trust me, it will make you grow, if you survive the ordeal.' She had laughed and then became serious. 'There are black secrets that you do not know. Even you will be tested to the limit, for the Age of Darkness is much closer to you than you possibly may realize. Truth revealed - and it all will be - may well destroy a soul, untaught and un-pummeled in every emotional way. This woman may well save your mind and soul when that evil seeks even your heart.'

He swallowed hard. Well, if he were to be pummeled, at least it would be by the one he had come to be so fond of. A lash on the back by a person so cared for was better than a glass of wine given by one hating you. And he knew that Trisha did not hate him. He suddenly came to the realization that this woman was not ordinary for her gender. She had come into this world changed, made into a great weapon, forged while she slept those many years in the Field of the Minds. Her heart was still that of a tender maiden, but her mind? It was hardened into that of a destroyer with a purpose: to bring to nothing all that was become evil in this world at whatever cost to friend or foe alike.

Trisha's eyes bored into Zadar's as he contemplated all these things. Finally, after fully accepting the consequences, he smartly saluted, replying, "Lieutenant ZadarFahyVel reporting for duty! Your dutiful servant!"

"Good!" Trisha snapped as she frowned again, attempting to hide a smile creeping from the corner of her mouth.

Staring into Zadar's eyes, Trisha's face took on a reddened hue and she turned to look away, commenting, "Of course, I do not require my officers to be so in their off-duty hours. You, like the others, have freedom to choose how to occupy your time in whatever idle pursuits your heart desires when not on call."

Suddenly, taking hold of Zadar's arms, Trisha whirled him around, pushing him against the apartment wall. Pressing her body against his, she snuggled her head on his chest. At length, she looked up and into Zadar's eyes, her own twinkling while half pleading, "I do so hope you will take notice of me in your spare hours. I do need to be loved and want your soul to refresh mine. I have an ache within me that you have ignited and I hope that you will satisfy it until the fire dies."

Her face flushing red, having not believed the secrets her heart betrayed to this... this man who was still such a stranger to her, Trisha pushed herself away, patting his uniform smooth. Embarrassed, she stared at her feet. "We are expected at breakfast momentarily. Will you honor me with your company?"

Zadar nodded, smiling, "My Lady, I will honor you in whatever way you desire."

Placing her hands on his shoulders and pulling herself up on her toes, Trisha gave Zadar an impassioned kiss, she not caring if anyone saw. No one did. Standing down, she took his hands. "We must take our leave, though I wish it not be so. Tonight I ask your company so that we may discuss what you should do in you off hours." She winked, and sought out another flirting kiss. Finally, after lingering in each other's arms, hand in hand, the two departed for the tramwaiter, seeking out the company of friends and officers who were patiently waiting them.

ઉ૭   ઉ૭   ઉ૭

Mihai, too, had lingered with her bath, soaking long in the healing waters filled with minerals from the Diamond. Then, applying more Diamond Cream to her cuts and bruises, she began to dress. When finished, she washed away the cream and examined her face in the mirror. Although the swelling was greatly diminished and her scratches less pronounced, the woman still fussed about her appearance and her need to look proper for the day.

Paul puzzled aloud about her dream, asking for explanation. Mihai politely refused, saying the constraints of time could not do the conversation justice. Paul could tell that she harbored no intention of discussing it, now or later. He finally surrendered to the notion that Mihai was still in a sour mood and, should he pursue the issue further, might well receive more than a gentle rebuff concerning it. Nodding, he commented that it was time to leave anyway.

As they prepared to go, Paul asked Mihai the reason for such tantalizing garments, a reasonable question for a man from the Realms Below. Mihai's royal finery was deceptively sensual, at least for Paul - red silken pantaloons held up by a wide black leather belt, laced, heeled sandals, giving Mihai an arch to her back that accented her voluptuousness, a long-sleeved, billowy blouse of sheer spider silk and a half-sleeve jacket fitted to clasp tight at the waist while opening at mid-waist height, fully exposing the wonders of Mihai's delightful form. Although common dress for these people at special events, Paul could not help but asked why so fancy and ornate in the morning, and for a breakfast appointment.

Mihai harrumphed, opening the door to leave, "Mother expressly asked me to *womanize* myself for the journey this day, and there isn't time for my return here after breakfasting with the others. So I have chosen to look *womanly* from the start, though I feel more *beastly* at the moment." Then touching her side, added, "She had also just delivered this jacket to me but yesterday and begged me to fashion it for her. I'm killing two birds with one stone. Now let's go!"

Paul followed quickly though his desire was to help Mihai off with that finery and linger a while longer in the seclusion of the bedroom. But it was a wonderful jacket, he forcing his eyes away from other, more sensual delights, a rich royal purple covered with all sorts of gemstones and diamonds. Laced with gold and chrysolite were numerous runes, some understandable, while others were from a time even the Ancients understood little about. It was something the likes of which only the Maker of all living things could have designed, and it was truly kingly.

The labyrinth of rooms and corridors that comprised the living quarters of the Firstborn were many and complex, Paul having little time to explore there much, but the path Mihai was taking to arrive at the Royal Chambers was a mystery to him, roundabout, Mihai seeking time to put on a better mood before seeing the others. Eventually, after many detours, hallways, banquet rooms, gardens, and whatever other out of the way passageway Mihai could conjure up to travel, the two arrived at a narrow set of doors leading into the center palace.

By this time, Mihai had managed to compose herself and improve her disposition, even chitchatting with Paul about her childhood when these worlds were her private wonderland where she ruled as princess. In short order the two stood in the portico facing the grand balcony that overlooked the inner gardens, she saying that one last look into the plush greenery works wonders for her soul.

Pushing aside the silky curtains, Mihai walked onto the balcony over to the marble balustrade, its polished surface demanding to be stroked. She looked out and down upon the Wonder of Wonders, the most unique and delightful of botanical nurseries in the universe. This was the world of but one mind, the Garden of Feelings, a place where, as Ma-we once stated, 'the thoughts and dreams from my heart become reality'.

Inhaling the sweet, healing scents wafting up from countless varieties of colorful blossoms and pungent greenery forced any foul mood Mihai harbored into swift retreat. A second breath and the woman was becoming intoxicatingly lost in the musical smells and sights, forgetting the reason for her visit. Paul wandered close, she taking his hand and delivering a gentle kiss on his cheek. Oh, the delight of this paradise! If only the two could stay secreted away in this place until time came to a finish! She tipped her head back, luxuriating in this hypnotic world of symphonic emotions.

A welcoming voice from the shadows below startled Mihai. "Hello up there. I thought you'd waste the whole day in dreamy lullaby. You know, Paul – hello, Dear – will still be around tomorrow and…and he will only get better with time."

Mihai stared down to see Ma-we, who had returned to rummaging some thick undergrowth, fussing, "I did see a new one here, just so cute, so cute. Musn't get distracted next time."

"*Mother!* What are you doing? And..." Mihai frowned, surprised, looking down at Ma-we, now on all fours, pawing the rich mossy ground. "And what are you doing here? When did you return? I didn't expect you 'til later."

Not stopping, Ma-we called back, "It's a bug of some kind, a new one I think - cute little fellow, bright yellow with green stripes, lost sight of it when I heard you stomp'n about. And, of course, you didn't know I was here, or else you'd not been so bold to be a snoopin' around here."

"*I've not been snooping around here!*" Mihai retorted, smiling at the sparring going on. "You told me to watch the place whilst you were gone. That's what I've done, though I doubt I'll receive any gratitude for it..."

Ma-we stood, her face, knees and hands smudged with dirt. Grinning, she held up the tiny prize. "I'll put it away safe..."

After tucking the bug in a little cage, she stepped into a fountain, washing away the grime. As the water splashed upon naked flesh, she replied to Mihai's defensive report, "What you say may all be well and good, but I have found broken ferns and crushed grasses that speak of more than just watchin'. And I also smell the scent of romance, not that you'd know anything of that, would you? Should I ask your gentleman friend there about the matter?"

Paul's face flushed red, but before he or Mihai could answer, Ma-we called up, "No time to argue... Bring that fellow conspirator of yours along and hurry down here. I've business and can't waste another moment on the likes of you."

Mihai squeezed Paul's hand, cautioning, "Careful, she's up to something. I can smell it. Keep your smarts about you."

For the children from the Realms Below, Ma-we was a very tough person to figure out. A 'quirky personality' was a common description given her, for those countless riddling stories, outrageous humor, and the way she thought sideways - at least in the eyes of those *normal* people from the Lower Realms. Paul smiled. And when she and Mihai conspired together, woe to any hapless victim caught in their sights! Shaking his head as he followed along, Paul knew it was his day to be targeted.

Both Mihai and Paul were impressed with Ma-we's surprise. It was most pleasant. There was no one better at conjuring up magical meals than the Maker of tasty delights, herself...this morning a breakfast of sweetmeats, cheeses, fruits, nuts and roasted grains, served with goblets of fresh juices or spicy hot drinks. The three feasted until bellies were full and appetites satisfied.

As they laughed and chatted on, Paul looked around to marvel at the beauties of this mythical place. The laws of the universe were even servants to these wondrous gardens, so filled with unimaginable living things. As he mused over the endless variety of plants and creatures, he looked over at Mihai to make comment, his mouth dropping open in surprise at what he saw. The ravages from Mihai's preceding nightmares were totally gone! Even the worry lines from the woman's constant stressing over the coming Prisoner Exchange had disappeared, replaced by a radiant glow like that of a maiden awakening into womanhood. Paul's mind was nearly overwhelmed by the mystery of this place, he pondering, 'It's magic! It must be the magic from this place!' While contemplating the moment, he was rudely shaken by a spoken reply.

"No, Dear, it is not the *magic* of this place." Ma-we smiled. "I do have powers, too, and use them when the hour calls out need for them. I cannot allow my child to arrive in public so broken in appearance, not this day. I fixed her up just like I did you."

Paul was aghast! "How? What?"

Ma-we took up a tiny crumb of sweet cake from her plate, popping it in her mouth, answering, "You have many things to learn yet, like keeping your emotions hidden behind your lawyer face." She grinned. "You also need to gain mastery over your mind, else it will be the ruin of us all, you shouting thoughts so painfully loud."

Paul attempted a response with further questions.

Ma-we stopped him. "My son, you must learn to walk before you can run. Have you not become studied in the many ways I and my children communicate with each other, sometimes over great distances? Have you not studied the physics of what your kind call the 'avenue of prayer'?" She shook her head, feigning sadness, "My boy has so much to learn..."

She began to explain, gesturing with hands and fingers. "As you know, Dear, we... even you... speak also with our minds. You know this. You should also recall that there are specific places in the brain that transmit these thoughts just as someone uses the mouth to transmit thoughts vocally. Now, Dear, you must remember to strengthen those parts of the brain - practice, practice, practice - so that you do not shout out to all what you wish be left secret. I do not pry into the private world of your inner mind, but when you publicly declare inner feelings, well... I have the right to respond. And this morning you have been quite vocal, even hurting Mihai's head."

Mihai took a sip of her fruit wine. Setting down the glass, she looked at her mother, replying so casually, "He's been pestering me all morning, giving my mind no time to rest. 'Tell me your dream!' 'What happened?' and on and on." She looked Paul in the eyes. "He believes me to be in a sour mood, afraid to ask me outright."

The perplexed expression on Paul's face revealed the man's confusion. He had spent too little time pondering the wonders of telepathy in this realm, and that he sat in the presence, at this very moment, of the person to whom he and his fellows in the Lower Realms had silently cried out to so many times in fervent supplication. Although being learned in the ways of mental communication, the fellow all too often still relied on his mouth to relay information, forgetting what parts of his thoughts were being exposed to others.

Ma-we smiled so impishly, she hearing in her mind all these things. "My lovely one, oh, dear Paul, you must take the time to learn how to speak so that your mental words flow as eloquently as your tongue's" She laughed. "...though I feel we will miss the grand entertainment provided by you when that hour does arrive."

"No!" Paul cried, his voice nearing that of squealing like an animal caught in a trap. "Not I! How have...? In what way?"

"Well, you did ask me." Ma-we grinned. "So I shall tell you just one thing I have heard from you."

"I took on a body that is strikingly handsome, more so than my daughters. Oh, the physical beauty of it is common for the women of this world, but I placed an aura – scent - about it that is so bewitching. I made myself allur-ingly seductive so that my children would never tire of my company." She frowned, but said nothing.

Smiling again, Ma-we added, "I truly enjoy my children's stares and the endearing affection received. That is why I created the festivals, to con-stantly remind my children of the value I place on romancing the sensual, both the heart and flesh. Oh, but you do speak with such boldness as to make my ears turn red from your boyish candidness. 'She has such beautiful tits! Should death await their touch, oh well, such a little price...'"

In a panic, Paul cried out, "Please! Please forgive the rantings of a fool! I..."

Staring into an anxious, distraught face, Ma-we grinned. *"You are no fool!* I am charmed, I assure you. And I do hope for the hour, when time permits us such interlude...and much, much, more. In that day you will come to understand what *Heaven* truly is."

Paul began another round of apologies. Mihai reached out a hand, quieting him, nodding to her mother while speaking to Paul. "Dear, this is not what it's about."

Ma-we agreed. "Yes. Yes. I am so pleased with you finding me so sensually attractive, truly charmed. Yes, and the day will come when I expect us to share in the bed of romance. But that day is yet future, for prophecy must first be fulfilled. Please, though, do not cloud the issue at hand, that being your mind has been opened to work in the way of the children living in this world. If you do not gain control over it, then disaster may well be lurking at your door."

Paul was crestfallen, recalling the many prurient thoughts that had flooded his mind since first observing the naked delights of this universe. Could he ever face the crowd again and not feel the fool?

Sensing his dread, Ma-we comforted Paul. "Only very recently have I heightened your telepathic abilities. Rest assured, you have not *yet* become the court jester. Still, I believe that my little demonstration this morning has awakened your awareness to the dangers awaiting an unlearnt mind. And, I'm sure that with a person like yourself, such a lesson will not go unheeded."

Mihai squeezed Paul's hand. "After the council meeting, Mother discussed with me the need for you to enhance your mental abilities, it being the feeling that such powers might help at the Prisoner Exchange. You will find, if you haven't noticed already, that the world around you may appear a bit sharper – more focused. You're more sensitive to the happenings going on around you - something that will serve you well when mastered."

"That's right, Dear." Ma-we smiled, her eyes serious. "The hour is rapidly approaching when all the children I have gathered from the worlds below must stand up and bring to a finish all that is and all that will be, you not being the least of the ones to do so. Mihai needs time to teach you how to collect the spirit of the mind to yourself, she being able to begin that training on the way to the Prisoner Exchange. I feel the experience you gain there will be a good dress rehearsal for future days."

She leaned forward, touching Paul's hand. "I did not wish for hurt feelings, but... you're a big boy and well... I guess that I wanted you to know how fond I am of you, too. And, I believe this lesson learned will be remembered much longer than if you were forced to suffer a lecture from Ardon."

Everyone laughed.

Mihai lifted Paul's hand, clasping it with both of hers. She became serious. "Love, I will teach you well. I will escort you into the land of the mind by way of our coming dream-shares. You'll be ready for the Serpent by the time we arrive." Flirtingly, she added. "I don't recall you finding our dream-shares being arduous on mind and soul."

Paul blushed, he still not comfortable with such sensual openness displayed by Lowenah's children. Mihai and Ma-we did not carry on as though anything out of the ordinary had been said. After sheepishly thanking them for their consideration and concern, he chided Mihai, "You told me she was up to something! *I didn't think you, too, carried a skewer for my roasting…*"

Mihai laughed. "Only a fool or one ignorant comes without an appetite to a roast! I am neither. I didn't even know Mother was here, do you recall? But when she invited us for breakfast, I knew there would be the bill to pay. I just didn't know who would pay it. When I saw the way things were going,

I went along. Better you than me when it comes to the skewer, and trust me, many are the times Mother has roasted me, and not often in such private settings."

Ma-we stood, spinning around so sensually while the breeze caught her hair up to reveal all her enchanting beauty. Paul and Mihai could not help but be mesmerized at her stunning appearance.

As she slowly twirled in silent dance, she flirtingly crooned:

"I have given to man a visible sign, that proves to all his arousal for me.
My hair is my clothing, enough to be had, and my daughters are true shadows of me.

When to me a fellow is rude and uncouth, I shadow that beauty from him.
But when wistful fondness my heart does awake, then all my secrets I'll offer to him.

Oh, Paul, my dear Paul, what you say about me, is so cute in a passionate way.
It tells me you have the heart of a man that even Ardon's company can't steal away."

Mihai burst into laughter. Ma-we stopped, grinning at Paul. Paul stared, amused but wondering, "Why is poor Ardon often found in your comments when you speak of men? I mean…"

Mihai took up as teacher. "My dear Paul, Ardon has the reputation for becoming so consumed at the game of spelunking deep within the souls of the planets, he finds no time to do the same for his sisters, which is most troubling now that so many of our brothers abandon us to follow Asotos into the wilderness of rebellion. We have been left empty, starving to be filled to the limit with the love from the few men who remain among us. Ardon still doesn't get it. Other than Tashi, who can raise the ardor of a stone, the man thinks nothing of abandoning his sisters to the wiles of other adventures."

Ma-we added, "The fellow's been known to squirrel himself away in some wilderness for years, seeking no companionship at all. Tashi brings out his fire, but she, too, would starve if the girl solely depended on him for satisfaction."

Gradian's Clock chimed the hour.

Ma-we glanced up, sighing, "We have frittered away the morning. I must prepare for the coming journey, seeing I must travel as a mortal on this occasion. And you two must play catch up, for the others are still waiting for you. Don't mention this meeting or our discussion. Play your *lovebird* thing with them. They'll believe it." She winked and then pointed toward her head. "And that mind stuff, speak not of it to anyone…our little secret."

After giving each a giant hug and smacking kiss, Ma-we waved the two off. "I'll be along shortly. My council and I are shipping aboard the Shikkeron." She winked. "Second class helps to keep Ardon humble." She laughed.

Waving goodbye, Mihai and Paul exited the garden and hurried away. Hitching a ride at the nearest tramwaiter station, they were soon off in search of impatient companions.

ಬ   ಬ   ಬ

The earlier jovial clamor was greatly quieted now that most of the breakfast party had departed the eatery to attend to other duties. Some had lingered, awaiting Paul and Mihai's arrival only to surrender the hour up to unfinished work, often making good-natured comments as to Mihai's increased tardiness since she had taken a shine to that 'Paul fellow'. The number remaining was but five until Trisha and Zadar arrived fashionably late, surprising some and raising the eyebrows of others. They had tucked themselves away in the corner of a tabled booth, soon to be joined by the few who still waited upon their wayward friends.

Symeon had arrived to see the others off, but his mind was so troubled with coming events as to be of little company to anyone. Having moved to the booth at Eutychus' request to join him, he now fidgeted with some tiny trinket picked up from the table. "His mind's been in another place ever since learning of his girl. Isn't good for anything…" Eutychus whispered, leaning in close to Trisha so Symeon wouldn't hear him.

Trisha nodded, glancing down in surprise to see she was holding tight to Zadar's hand. She chose not to let go. Then, looking around the table, she began to muse over the people seated in her company.

Well, there was Eutychus. Everybody knew the story of the sleepyhead boy who fell to his death from a window only to be returned to life by Paul – a tale many were eager to recount when in the man's company. But a boy he no longer was. Eutychus was a giant, even dwarfing Euroaquilo, but ever so shy was he, as well as mild-tempered and soft-spoken. She once heard Paul speak of him as the man who would apologize for you hitting him. Still she felt there was something about the fellow that needed more attention. It might do well for her to get to know him better.

Jonathan sat next to Zadar in quiet conversation. A reclusive man, naturally so, he just did not reveal his inner self. Trisha knew little about him outside his earlier writings except that he and Anna were attached at the hip so to speak, they having journeyed throughout the Northern Rim colonies for parts of several years on diplomatic missions. Upon his arrival in these realms, Anna had taken such a liking to him she nearly begged Lowenah to be his mentor. After receiving approval, the two became inseparable, Jonathan also becoming very fond of her.

"I refused to give him quarter! And, on my next turnabout, drove the bastard from the sky!" Planetee hit her fist on the table at the last exclamation, having finished telling a very distracted Symeon about one of her recent military escapades.

Trisha nodded. Planetee was a warrior of pure blood, but what was the price for her loyalty? She was bone and spirit with Mihai. As if one breath were the two. Should something occur at the Prisoner Exchange, on which side would she stand? Close Trisha and Planetee were not, she having soundly dressed Trisha down in public over some misunderstood comment long ago. Neither was ever more than cordial toward the other since that time.

'Drinks too much. I smell it on her now.' Trisha thought. Still, the reports of her stalwart defense of Darla in front of the Council and the woman's unbridled bravery, coupled with her tactical mind, also Lowenah's private considerations, this Planetee could be very useful, if she survives the Prisoner Exchange.

"Now be a good fellow and let me have a look-see." Anna nudged ever closer to Jonathan, he just having been given some little bauble by Zadar.

Trisha frowned. Anna was most charming a companion... when the mood took her. She was well respected by all the children and deeply loved by Mihai. Trisha was uncomfortable around her, especially when alone in her company. Anna always seemed too attentive, seeking more than casual intercourse with Trisha. A shudder ran down the woman's back - a mixed feeling of disgust and arousal. Anna had cornered her once and delivered such a passionate kiss on her lips as to make the woman swoon. Had it not been for her old taboos, Trisha was sure she would have made her way to Anna's bed that very hour.

It was the sensual power Anna had over others and how she used it that troubled Trisha. She was only beginning to understand the mind share. Anna was a witch extraordinaire at using it. Oh well, the children of this world and their ways. Anna had always been stellar with her and helpful when Trisha needed her assistance in kingly matters. Trisha shrugged, 'I must learn their ways and accept their customs, for I am stuck here.'

A man broke away from some officers and their small talk, making straight for Trisha's booth. Planetee recognized him immediately, calling out his name as he approached. "Well, Major Garlock – it's still major, isn't it – haven't been demoted since our last meeting, have you? It's good to see you!"

Jebbson laughed, taking up Planetee's hand as he gracefully bowed. "Only in my self-esteem, my dear General, only in my self-esteem, that is since you have never entertained my proposal for dinner and song at one of our fine eateries in Oros." He kissed her hand, offering sweet disappointments. "The sun is so beautiful as it breaks upon Oros' high peaks. You should stand there with me at morning break to gather in its many splendors."

Planetee grinned, offering gentle rebuff. "As legend has it, I would have to pick a number and wait many long mornings to have my turn to view it with you. Besides, I have been to Oros when it was a lush garden city, the Iris Sea spreading to its very gates. Countless were the times my lovers and I viewed those high peaks, long before the morning chill swept…"

The smiled vanished from Planetee's face, she hesitating for but a moment. Shaking Jebbson's hand, she thanked him for his generous offer. "You stir up many memories with your pleasantries, Major. Oros, oh Oros, if not for your harlotry with war there should be little more than decaying ruins of you now. In many ways you have become much like many of us, empty shells of glory past, hiding the decay within." She shook his hand again, bidding her goodbyes.

Jebbson bowed so politely, understanding far more than his words implied. "My Lady, the invitation still stands, and no number for *you*." He offered his adieus to the others and hurried after two other officers departing the diner.

Trisha quietly mused. Now *there* was a man after her own heart! She had need of his abilities and must seek him out right away. He might prove very useful at the Prisoner Exchange.

Idle chitchat soon turned to the topic of the hour, the coming Prisoner Exchange. Anna managed to pester or cajole the others into explaining their roles in coming events, Anna beginning, smiling proud. "As you may know, Michael personally asked for my company, she depending so much on my counsel. With such an air of uncertainty as exists at the moment, she felt it especially important for me to be at her side. We took council together for the preparation of this trip, wanting nothing to interfere with its success. Isn't that correct, General Planetee?"

Anna's charming smile and cheerful speech did little to hide the gloating tone in her voice. Planetee had long since tired of the silly game Anna played, needing to remind everyone how important and valuable she is. True, Anna stayed loyal to Mother after the Rebellion began, even as her glory of former days faded into the shadows when the festivals ceased, lavishing her attention now upon Mihai during the woman's long convalescing. And she had treated Darla with a great deal of kindness, much more than most of the others did. Also, her loyalty to her brothers and sisters had cost her months of torture and rape at the hands of enemy captors during the Gihon War. Still, couldn't she leave it go, just this *once*?!

Planetee and Terey were the engineers behind the strategic plan for the children's part at the Prisoner Exchange. They had gathered the intelligence, collected the ships, crews and materials, supplies, barter goods, and everything else needed. Yet Mihai had chosen not to use either one of them in an official capacity during proceedings at the exchange, asking them instead to act as little more than body guards for her – the real reason Terey chose to book aboard the Chisamore, resentful for being pushed aside after all the work she had done for coming events.

As Planetee pondered her reply to Anna's question, an anxious foreboding began to fill her heart and a shadow was cast over her mind. It was as if she could see the prophecy of future days arising from the ashes of the coming storm, ignited by nearing events. Something was telling her that this Prisoner Exchange was to be no ordinary one, and the future Armageddon of her world would be triggered by it.

In an instant of time she saw a woman-child with serpentine eyes and fanged teeth crying out to the heavens in anguish, seeking revenge and death at the same moment. Planetee watched also to see that this woman stood at the fork of two different roads, one leading into uncertainty and the other into nothingness. Suddenly, a smoldering spirit appeared between Planetee and the woman. It called out to Planetee in words unuttered, 'Will you, too, deliver your soul up to the Queen of Darkness?' At that, the spirit lifted a sword and drove it into Planetee's heart.

Planetee jumped, the vision vanishing before her eyes. She looked around to see everyone staring, waiting for her to answer Anna's question. Gathering her wits, she quickly replied, "I have a contingent of fighters that will be in my charge. Protection of the fleet and all, you know." She turned away, a feeling of gloom growing ever stronger in her heart.

"And you, dear Eutychus, what is your part in this adventure?" Anna cooed affectionately.

Eutychus blushed, shaking his head. "I guess I'm just along for the ride."

Anna kindly chided him. "No need for such modesty, Dear. You must realize just how important a *valet* is to this council. Your services are most appreciated. Why, I have been told that Mihai personally requested your assistance."

Eutychus sheepishly nodded, grinning at the attention such an important person as Anna was giving him.

Jonathan explained he was replacing Symeon for reasons that were still somewhat unclear and that little was expected of him other than putting in a formal appearance. Everyone already knew what responsibilities Zadar had, they being loudly broadcast to everyone soon after his arrival at the dining hall.

"And of you, Dear, our new field marshal…" Anna smiled so politely. "What will *your* duties be?"

'*Snoop!*' Trisha thought, smiling so sweetly in return. Was Anna prying for information, or needling her because Mihai had left Trisha out of most of the preparations? Anna could get jealous at times. Maybe she was taking out on Trisha her displeasure over Paul's intrusion into Mihai's life. Or possibly Anna was 'just being Anna', if there ever was a 'just being Anna'.

Trisha's smile grew into a grin. "My duties are to do whatever it takes to return our people back to us safe and sound, by whatever means necessary."

The tone in Trisha's voice abruptly ended the conversation, Anna not attempting any more questions. Quickly changing the subject, Anna went on about a few unimportant matters relating to the day's events, some of the others chiming in with little tidbits of news to share.

Planetee's gloominess was growing upon her to the point of distraction, the vision only the more troubling for it. Eutychus, having observed the woman's sudden sullenness, asked if something was amiss. The woman smiled sadly but, before she could reply, a joyous shout came from a man entering the door. "Hey there, General! I've a parchment for you. Smells pretty. Some blonde-haired fellow handed it to me, asking I give it to you."

Planetee turned, smiling, calling back her hellos, that smile fleeing from her face when a woman accompanying the man stepped out from behind him to offer her salutations. Then she, too, when realizing who sat at the table, became somberly quiet.

Planetee's mind raced to past events. '*Bauglow...* Has she ever forgiven me? Why, when I ruined her in body and mind?'

The woman, too, thought of that long ago event when all Hell opened upon her regiment, delivering slaughter upon eighty percent of those under her command in what came to be called the 'Battle of Bauglow'. 'How can she ever forgive me for the waste of souls I allowed that day?'

The man saw none of that, and when the woman feigned her need to deliver the packages she carried to the culinary workers, he waved her over. "An attendant can wait upon that for you. We've only fleeting moments before work separates us. Now come here and be a good fellow. Long has it been since I've companied with some of these folks."

Reluctantly, the woman surrendered her packages up to a nearby counter and, forcing a smile, followed the man over to Trisha's table. Wishing her best upon the new arrivals, a very distraught Planetee begged her leave, giving up her place at the cozy booth, saying there were many duties for her to finish before ending of the morning watch. Concerned over Planetee's welfare, Eutychus offered her his company. She gratefully accepted. Tucking the parchment into her blouse, Planetee tipped her head, saying her pleasantries, and departed with Eutychus.

As they waited for a passing motor coach to hitch a ride out to the fleet, some three miles' distance, Eutychus attempted some small talk. It was futile, considering Planetee's frame of mind. Although it was a pleasant, sunny day, Planetee stood shivering, rubbing her hands up and down her arms for warmth.

"Here! Take my coat." Eutychus quickly removed his uniform jacket and draped it over Planetee's shoulders. Smiling her thanks, she pulled it tight, wrapping up in it as though it were a giant cocoon.

The mood was quiet for some time. Finally, Planetee broke the silence. "I'm trying to stay off the stuff, you know, at least for the Prisoner Exchange." She looked into Eutychus' face. "Don't tell anyone. Promise?"

Eutychus nodded.

Planetee cast her eyes toward the ground. "My friend, I'm sick, I mean really sick… inside. Something's wrong, a cancer or something, maybe worse. I hurt all the time. That's why I take to the drink. I coughed up a lot of blood last night."

She looked into Eutychus' eyes. "The healing machines help some, but I never have enough time to make a cure, if that's possible. My friend, tell no one please. And my head is all screwed up with frightening dreams and wild visions. Sometimes I can't tell what's real. Oh, I don't mean reality, like us being here right now. I mean what's made up in my head, like a dream or something, and what may be coming from someplace else, like a vision or something. Had one just a little bit ago in the eatery. I still feel a burning in my heart from it."

Reaching out a hand, Planetee grasped Eutychus' upper arm. "I may be sick, but I am a *witch* and still have my powers of wit with me. I fear… I fear there is a great evil lurking among us. I felt it this morning when I went into this place." She pointed back toward the diner. "Something tried to cloud my mind, succeeded in some way, that is until we came outside. Now I fear for the journey. If not for Mother's company, I'd say we were sailing off into damnation!"

She looked up, not noticing the fluffy white clouds of a summer morning hurrying away toward the east. "My friend, there is a storm brewing as I speak. Ferocious and vicious it will be. I feel it… inside…" She put her hand to her heart. "I will not survive this one… see this coming conflagration on to its end. This war will be my last, for good or ill."

As her eyes filled with tears, Planetee turned toward Eutychus, pleading, "If your kind do not succeed, no one will survive what's coming. We, the children of this universe, have no power left within us. We're burned out, burned up. There has been too much death, murder and treachery forced upon us. Your kind have been blessed with such short lifetimes, for your tribulations quickly pass. Ours never end. Please! Eutychus, promise me you will not fail me… me and my people!"

Eutychus stared back, wanting to ease Planetee's concerns. Before he could reply, an open motor coach loaded with exuberant sailors turned the corner. Seeing the two people standing at the curb, the driver quickly veered toward them, noisily stopping right beside. Crying out cheerily, the driver asked, "Looking for a ride? Heading out to Staging Area Two, if that's where you're going, or can take you on to Staging Area One, whichever. Got room for two more."

Planetee nodded, smiling. "Two is fine."

As the driver opened the door of the motor coach, Planetee turned to Eutychus, gripping his hand while softly beseeching, "You will stay with me today, at least for a while?"

Eutychus grinned, "My duties are finished until everyone's boarded. I'll stay as long as you like."

The two climbed on, squeezing into the crowded machine. The driver called out a warning and throttled back into the street, hurrying for the far end of the spaceport.

ᗿ　ᗿ　ᗿ

Trisha had been patiently listening to the animated conversation at the table. She discovered that the woman was a delivery person for the postal, responsible for packages and boxes. The man was an engineer of some kind, highly regarded. He struck up a conversation with Symeon about some kind of a project the fellow might be interested in seeing. No one bothered to introduce the new arrivals, so the best that Trisha got from the conversation was the name 'Chess' for the woman – a nickname no doubt, and 'Sweetheart', 'Love', 'Dear', and other such terms of endearment for the man, mostly from Anna. Zadar used the name 'Chess', and only in passing. The woman added very little to the conversation. The man merrily returned Anna's flirting comments with suggestive remarks, indicating the two had a long relationship.

Looking at her timepiece, Trisha decided not to wait longer for Mihai and Paul. 'Screw her all day, if he had the chance…' She was about to ask their leave - quite a chore considering the number crowded into a booth designed for four and she and Zadar were tucked in the far corner - when Euroaquilo suddenly burst through the door, heading directly for the kitchen.

In a moment, he returned with a bagged meal. "Hello!" He called out to the party in the booth, stopping to offer some quick salutations.

"Hey, you!" Zadar complained. "You just left here, having stuffed yourself. What ya' doin' with more? Afraid there won't be anything to eat on the trip?"

Grinning, Euroaquilo ignored the comment and, staring at Trisha, warned, "I'd be careful the company I kept, my Lady. Some'd say you're risking a sordid reputation, socializing with some certain fellows. Won't say any names, though he's pretty close. Hard to wash his reputation off once it gets around you're with him."

There were a few chuckles.

Zadar struggled to stand, spouting threats. "It's a good thing the table's between us or I'd give you such a thrashing as you'd not forget for a fortnight! For the sake of this lady, I must restore my honor. This means war!"

Euroaquilo stepped back, raising his hands as he quailed. "Oh, please forgive me. Oh no! Not that! Don't hurt me! It's the sun that's been on me. I'll be good! I promise!"

The following antics of the two men put everyone in stitches. A boisterous Zadar made phony attempts to escape his corner prison, swearing oaths of vengeance for such disrespect, and Euroaquilo for his show of cowardice, he crouching with his hands covering his face, crying for mercy, promising not to act so foolishly again.

When the laughter died down, Euroaquilo leaned on the table, explaining, "My little girl has been working day and night to get the Shikkeron ready for departure. She refused to join me for breakfast, saying 'a good captain remains aboard until relieved of duty'. Bedan's not arrived yet. I promised her some of the chef's delights, she being fond of his cooking. Then I went off in a rush, forgetting them. Can't face the girl's wrath without them, so…"

He sighed. "I've not seen a ship's crew work this hard in years, 'six-to-six, spit, polish and paint. Clean the boilers, check the generators, double-check the gages, mixers, exhaust systems… and when you're done let's have at it again'. I tell you, the Shikkeron's the best-prepared ship in the fleet. Mother sure picked a good one for this trip."

Anna grinned. "It's a good thing that Mother put Darla in charge of readying the Shikkeron for the journey, else Ardon might have seen misfortune come visiting."

Euroaquilo leaned past Chess, addressing Anna, the humor escaping his face. "My Dear, don't underestimate our little girl. She is far stronger than most can imagine. There's something about her that makes me wonder… Well, anyway, I feel there are days coming when we might all wish to be made of her mettle. If Ardon comes to any misfortune, it will not be at her hand. She would choose death before hurting the least of Mother's loyal children. She's a real gem."

Anna sadly agreed. "You know my love for the child. It hurts me to think what she has never experienced and the demon that resides in her. Well, a cure may soon come. We can only hope."

Taking each other's hand, the two became silent, sharing some private thoughts. After a few fleeting moments, Euroaquilo stood back, smiling as he looked toward the door. "I must be off. Time waits for no one." Holding up his meal-bag, he confessed, "First I must deliver this and then there's an entire fleet I have to check out before our departure."

Hearing the sound of a nearing motor transport, he hurried away, shouting for the driver to wait up. "Good bye, all. See you later." He waved before passing through the door.

Jonathan looked at Anna. "I guess I must be going, too. The hour is late, and there are still a few things need tending."

Anna offered to leave with him, seeing they were to board the same ship.

Grunting as he stood, Jonathan asked wistfully, "I wonder what my berth is like?" Passing the woman who was now standing, he offered his pleasantries, shaking her hand. "It was a pleasure… er… Chess… to have met you. I look forward to our meeting again."

Chess smiled. "In our world, we give a kiss goodbye." She gave him a little peck on the cheek.

The remainder of the group followed Jonathan and Anna through the door and into the bright morning sun. Chess waved the others goodbye as she pulled away from the curb. Jonathan and Anna hurried along, hailing down a small motor-cab. The others stepped to the edge of the street to await another coach. Trisha looked down, surprised, and then smiled. Zadar and she were still holding hands.

ℂ ℂ ℂ

The open motor carriage quietly cruised down the thoroughfare, its stratified-thermo engine producing little more than a slight hum, while passengers chatted on about many unimportant matters, the pleasant weather, delightful breakfast at one of Palace City's finer restaurants, and just about anything else in general. After all, soon they would be departing for the Prisoner Exchange and, after a few formalities, would be returning with their newly released companions to a richly deserved hero's welcome. Was this not the way it had played out so many times before? Diplomacy worked so well…

Ardon leaned back in his seat after conversing with OfhieSanternano and CrilenianTorpedee concerning the time-space vortex vs. quantum particle logic theories – concepts in the study of EbenCeruboam. He laughed, looking out at the fruit trees lining the roadway. "Have it your way, Crilenian, but I will sorely miss you after you have released those subatomic particles into the theoxen-chlorine chamber. If you're wrong, you'll be little more than space dust."

Crilenian vehemently protested, defending his idea, finishing by smugly stating, "You just wait, Lord Ardon! When I can find someone to build my propulsion system, I'll prove to everyone the validity of my concept." Then shaking his finger toward him, he added, "You are a great wizard in the council. None can question that. But you do seem to come up short when dealing with *real* science. Someday all the great starships will be powered by the Crilenian Positronder."

Ardon only smiled, sucking in the aromatic fragrance from the surrounding trees and flowers. Oh, the joy of just being alive! What a wonderful day! He sucked in another invigorating breath while pulling Tashi close and squeezing her in a one-armed embrace.

DarlaRosa raised an eyebrow, asking, "Too much of the wine so early this morning, Lord Ardon, or does the fragrance of the roe smell like that of gemstones and success in the chase? You know, 'the lord conquereth all and rides to make it complete…'?"

Ardon pretended no offense, but he did lighten his hold on Tashi as he answered rather smugly, "I do not prefer to *ride* anyone. It is a far too aggressive way to pretend a conquest. Indeed! I wish for no *conquest* at all. Love and the intimacy of romance must remain *refined* and *dignified*. It is not a subject for *common* discussion, like one might discuss some *sport* or *game*. I do not share such privacy with others, as I have never shared our secluded moments with any of my other lovers."

DarlaRosa sat back in the carriage, laughing. "How could you? As I recall our last *secluded moments* together, I spent the night seducing you with flirtation and wine only to feel your manly power within me for but scant moments before you exhausted yourself and then collapsed upon me in a snoring stupor. Oh, yes! *That was some real, refined lovemaking you did then.*"

Tashi giggled while the others smiled or laughed, some offering an additional comment or two.

Ardon harrumphed. "Now do you wonder why so few men share your bed, and why you must drug them up before they are willing to make passage into your dreams? But I would be remiss to continue on with such uncouth folly. Let me tell you this: yes I did conquer, but in a way that most of you would find little delight in. I found some of the purest chrysolite ever discovered in a natural state. Those crystals were so harmonically perfect, I was forced to pack them in vacuum chambers so as to not have them interfere with the ship's navigation system. Mother was especially pleased."

Tashi sat forward, the wonder of her experience showing on her face. "What we saw in those caves was breathtaking! Our lights reflected off some of the most beautiful formations of stones, gems, and crystals in every shape and color as to dazzle the eyes. And then the tales told me by Ardon of hidden planets and rivers twisting throughout the universe, and… and so much more. Our journey flashed by as if mere moments. Darla, truthfully, you must make a journey with this fellow someday. He will show you a side of himself few have seen."

Darla was polite enough to Tashi, she being considered one of the great governesses of the Empire, but she could not help making reference again to Ardon. "What you say, Dear, about the universe and caves may all be well and true, but it was not Ardon's *side* I was interested in - I or my sisters. There are few enough men in this world to go around, and for one of those few to be as lame as an old duck can be frustrating, to say the least."

Ardon was about to make retort, but Tashi stopped him, she putting her hand on his knee and sweetly replying to Darla, "Oh, my fellow here has a powerful ardor for the women. He must be teased in the right way to make that nature within him manifest. Besides, Dear, I have heard that you are not in short supply of comforters. Why, it is said that the men find you so mesmerizingly attractive as to pine away, awaiting but a moment of your company. You are so beautiful, you know."

DarlaRosa was taken aback by the flattery. Had it come from anyone else, she might have become offended, but Tashi was such an honest woman, and her tone so sincere. Snuggling back into the seat, Darla soon began a discussion with Crilenian, who sat directly on her left. KyseninaGerzion, who sat facing her, soon joined in, taking up the subject. Ofhie leaned back and decided to nap, leaving Ardon and Tashi very much alone with each other's company.

It took a little coaching for Tashi to turn the conversation back to yester-morn's return trip from Chrusion when Ardon filled her head with tales of hidden planets and galactic adventure. He had relished telling her of his exploits in those wee hours when the wine was still on him and he had tired of romance. But since that time he was quiet as a mouse concerning them. She had asked once, when they were dressing for breakfast this day, but the man had instantly changed the subject.

Tashi was determined, her curiosity being earlier piqued. She gently massaged Ardon's hand, flirtingly pleading, "Please, Dear..." She spoke barely above a whisper. "You have teased me these many days to the point of distraction. Why are you so secretive about some nameless rocks floating off in space somewhere? You have put my head in a spin concerning the wonderful, but leave my heart feeling empty for want to know more."

Ardon eyed the others. Seeing no one paying attention to them, he quietly answered, "The universe is a strange and wonderful place. Truth be said, I have tried to share my adventures with others. Yes, it was long in the past, but I still remember well. You know, there are times when romance takes on a different level of lovemaking than what is base and sensual. There are higher levels, intellectual heights where the thrill of the physical is overshadowed by the philosophical and theoretical. Gabrielle and I once went there, once, a long, long time ago, but most women companions have detested the mathematics, instead longing for the sensual."

He looked Tashi in the face. "Women just don't get it. The mathematics, I mean. My mind lives there all the time. And all the men want to do is romance the women. You get them away from a female for a week or two and they start a lathering up for a good rut. Then it's off they go to chase down some doe in heat, following the scent half way across the universe to find her. You are the only lady I've found who cares at least something about the world of measured learnings, but I fear I might burn you out if I talk too much of my adventures."

Tashi squeezed Ardon's hand, smiling. "Dear, I love where you take me in our dream-shares, and I so much desire to have you carry me away in them more often. Whether it is the philosophy of physics or absolutes, I do truly enjoy the way you play with them when we are together. And I would listen to you expound the marvels of this and any other universe, and happily travel to your mysterious worlds even if you sought not to have a single dream-share with me. I do so love the way your mind works."

It always seemed that Tashi knew just the right words to say when she was probing for information, though with Ardon she was being sincere, at least in heart. Her reputation with men left her former confession of celibate loyalty somewhat in doubt. It mattered little to Ardon. Tashi loved him for who he was and not for someone she wished he would be… something he believed most of the other women desired.

He smiled, squeezing Tashi's hand. "All right, I'll tell you a little, but not too much to fog the brain."

Ardon spoke quietly, though sometimes with exuberance, all the while making small gestures with his right hand. "You see, space is not empty, but filled with anomalies and cloud masses that disguise or hide planets, sometimes entire solar systems. One must understand the mathematics of space and time to find what is hidden away from the senses of the flesh. A person must enter the world of thought, leaving behind what is considered to be common sense, and journey into the abstract and illogical."

"Most people would say - if they watched how I came upon my discoveries - that it was accomplished through pure accident. I know…" He tapped the side of his head. "Though having never witnessed the world of the Immortals, like Tolohe and some of the other Ancients, I know those worlds exist. And I believe that my mind works similarly to that of Mother's. Then, if that is the case, I must think beyond the mortal and into the worlds of the Immortals to find what is secret to my physical flesh. I believe the mind is capable of functioning upon the immortal plane, even if it must function in a metaphysical one. At this level, you gain a seventh or possibly it's an eighth sense. And that's how I have made these strange discoveries."

At this point, Ardon went on about the way the universe bent in and around itself, thus the reasons for the jump portals. "You see, a distant star may appear to be afar off, if one studies the light patterns in the sky. Should another less reasonable or even illogical set of calculations be applied, it might well be discovered that star system is very much closer than it physically appears. The dynamic construction of the universe, I believe, is the greater fractal of our brain's design, like wide flat sheets all wrinkled up to fit in a tiny space."

He grinned, lifting a finger. "Now, how did I come to that conclusion?" He looked into Tashi's eyes, but did not wait for an answer. "And I know for a fact that is how the universe is constructed." He frowned apologetic. "I really did try to share my discoveries, at least long, long ago, back when the world was innocent and sparse."

Ardon shook his head, forlorn. "It wasn't part of EbenCeruboam theorem. The wise of that age had better things to do than listen to a dreamer. So how did I come to that conclusion? I used logic to discover the most illogical of universal secrets. I studied Mother's ways, watched her real close, her every move, how she did things, even the most trivial of matters I studied closely. I figured if everything was invented by Mother, then even the Immortals, the Ones Who Came Before, would have thought the same as she."

Leaning back and placing his arm around Tashi's shoulder, Ardon spoke quietly into Tashi's ear. "What I discovered was this: Mother has a very interesting personality. Patient as a stone she is when the mood is upon her. She will sit and watch a rock erode into sand one speck at a time, and never once show a need to hurry. And that is what everyone sees her to be, stone-slow patient. Many feel she has only hurried up at this final hour because time forces her to do so... and that might be. But Mother is only slow when she *wants* to be. When she doesn't want to be, watch out! She will hurry along in a blur. I tell you a fact: Mother has no patience when the mood hits her."

Tashi whispered, she copying Ardon though she did not understand his reason for being so quiet. "This is not uncommon knowledge, Love, at least for us older children. Mother has driven us all to the point of distraction with her antics... hurry here and then do nothing, or go a playing while there's needed work to be done."

Ardon cautioned, "Now listen and learn if secrets will become yours. It is not how *we* view Mother that is of value. It is how *she views herself* that reveals the hidden nature of all things. Mother keeps many secrets, but the person of her heart she wears upon her sleeve. Her nature is who she is. Now, please, follow my logic."

"When the mood is upon her, Mother will remain upon the path to reach her destination, but when her disposition for the path changes, she will skip away and take a short cut. With everything she does this, everything. So then, I thought to myself: she lives in our world because the mood is upon her, but when the mood changes will take the shortcut. I then watched to learn the properties of her short cuts, am still studying them carefully, but what I have learned has led me to the making of many of my discoveries."

From this point on, Ardon escaped into his private worlds of adventure, carrying Tashi along with whispers of the mysterious. There was no other way for Tashi to go, Ardon's explanations sprinkled with so much of his own mathematics and strange words of his own invention. The woman did try so hard to pay attention, her senses wandering to the different sights and smells wafting upon the breeze as the coach passed tiny shops and city orchards on its way to the spaceport. But Tashi's ears did not fall completely deaf to Ardon's loquaciousness.

"…and the strangest of all the proxmoaidian planets is not far from here at all. I discovered it quite by accident, I did. See, I was searching for a nuroain-cluster… a series of gaseous ice nebulae orbiting super-dense dark matter… when the largest of the proxmoaids I've seen set off my ship's collision warning systems. Slammed on full reverse thrusters to keep from smashing right into it. It lies out there, right under our noses and I'm the only one who knows of it."

Tashi's ear went a'tingle as Ardon went on about his planet. "You first see a yellowish glow like that of a distant lantern on a foggy night. Drawing closer, say two or three hundred leagues, you begin to notice individual shining pools of light radiating from the shadowy surface. When you are within fifty league's distance, the shapes become distinct. From this altitude you can clearly see that the planet emits colors of every hue from the spectrum of jade greens to sapphire reds to onyx blues and, oh yes, the golden yellows that are most intense."

Raising his hand and pointing upward in exclamation, Ardon revealed what to Tashi was so intriguing. "Ah, but that isn't the best part. Like the vast majority of proxmoaidian planets, there is no apparent life on its surface, the atmosphere being too harsh for anything other than possibly some very small microorganisms or bacteria. On the inside, though, it is honeycombed with caverns, caves, water-filled tunnels, some stretching and twisting for thousands of miles, plunging hundreds of leagues toward its center. One such labyrinth system I have discovered has a chamber over ten leagues wide and is nearly one hundred eighty leagues long."

"Yes, and the colored crystals…they are woven throughout the planet like a rainbow spool of yarn, looking as though the molten core angrily threw them off in a giant convulsive fit, they bending and twisting into brilliant, lighted tubes that later reflected the energy boiling within that very core. The exposed crystal tubes not only produce kaleidoscopic hues of daylight dreaminess in those giant underground caverns, they draw up enough heat from within to create a mild greenhouse temperature. Added to this, the continual release of gases that produce an acceptable atmosphere, you have all the needed elements for life as we know it on EdenEsonbar."

Clasping her hands together, squealing with delight, Tashi exclaimed, "Oh, so wonderful! It sounds so wonderful!"

The others in the coach started, staring at Tashi. She apologized, claiming as excuse her exuberant joy over some pipe music being played in a gazebo they had just passed. She then looked down, embarrassed, staring at the floor.

After the others had reoccupied themselves with previous activities, Tashi turned to Ardon, again taking his hand, and whispered, "Tell me, please, where is this wonderful place?"

Ardon looked Tashi in the eyes, his furrowed brow speaking more than his words as he whispered back, "That is *my little secret!* A secret is only such for as long as it is kept so. And I intend to keep it so for the moment." He squeezed her hand, looking toward the sky. "I promise, when I'm ready, when the right moment arrives, I shall gather you up there. Then you will truly attest as witness that all I have spoken to you about this place is so, that I have not exaggerated one little bit." He lifted his hand, bringing his thumb and pointer finger close. "Not one little bit."

Then, with the excitement of a little boy growing on his face, Ardon quietly explained, "The reason it is secret is that I'm not finished with my playing there. You see…" He grinned so impishly. "I have made this planet my Eden." He nodded. "Yes, from this planet, EdenEsonbar, I have gathered all manner of life forms and delivered them to the caves and hidden seas of that planet. This I have done over three thousand millennia of time."

Speaking like a proud father, he went on about his wonderful works. "Oh yes, my world flourishes with grasses, grains, trees of every kind, and insects, creeping and crawling, winged and web-making. All abound in the many varied worlds secreted under the surface of 'KruptoGinomai', my name for it. Anyway, there are also fishes, tadpoles, lizards and salamanders in my rivers, streams, and lakes. Also the sky, as is what you can call 'sky', is filled with every winged beast that may be. Oh yes, the rodents, squirrels, conies, and every other kind of furry animal plays upon the fields of flowers and clover."

Lifting a hand in gesture, he added, "Just before the Rebellion, I delivered upon the land the deer and mountain goat, along with the wolf and bear to keep them in check. I have not returned back since then to see what has become of that match up, but shall do so as soon at these times permit."

Tashi squeezed Ardon's hand, shaking it ever so gently, her eyes radiating childlike glee. "You have promised to take me! Do you still mean it? Will you take me to your wonderland?"

Ardon laughed ever so quietly. "Yes, yes, I promise, with all my heart. No matter what may come, I will take you to my wonderland of delights."

Tashi giggled ever so childlike, squeezing Ardon's hand tight while pressing close and delivering a tender kiss upon his cheek.

His heart jumping with delight, Ardon tipped his head back, releasing a sigh of satisfaction and sucking in the fragrant breath of early summer in Palace City. Closing his eyes to the visions of yester-hour, the realities of events from but days ago flooded the man's mind - he and Tashi exploring the hidden caverns of the Black Mountains in search of the perfect chrysolite, Tashi's sensual teasings and constant inquisitive questions, and her abandoned willingness to hang on to every word when he extolled his knowledge of the world around them.

Ardon sighed again, smiling. Tashi's company when exploring the mountains was deeply satisfying. No! More! It had been fulfilling, making him feel complete in some way. When the time came to depart, a sadness assailed his heart, one the likes of which he could not recall, he at first concluding it being little more than the normal emotional reaction to the end of such an exciting time. Now, though, Ardon thought it to be his desire not to leave Chrusion, but remain behind with Tashi, lingering in the misty mountains, questing for further adventures.

It would have been fun. At least Ardon's heart told him so. For the first time in the man's long life, the desire to linger with a woman, the two alone, abandoning themselves to the universe, appealed to him. A shadow swept across his heart when the thought of Tashi's returning to Exothepobole, the capital of Sustrepho in the Trizentine, crossed his mind. He did not want her to go, as she would have to after their return from the Prisoner Exchange. A desire was growing in his soul to keep her with him, at least to linger without leave until his soul could understand its new feelings.

The sudden roar of hurried turbines jolted Ardon from his wistful dreaminess. A giant tractor pulling several heavily limbered freight barges wheeled around and past the rather tiny coach as it leisurely made its way toward the main terminal of the spaceport. All eyes searched far to the south for the fleet that was to take this great council to the exchange.

At last, after passing through one final gated checkpoint, the grand armada for this momentous event spread itself out before them. Ardon harrumphed quietly, he having expected a more impressive display of power and dignity. Looking over this *dismal* collection of *museum pieces,* he puzzled quietly, "Couldn't Mother at least have given us one fine ship like the Sophia to deliver the dignitaries of the Children's Empire to that forsaken land? Cattle barges and flea traps, the lot of them. Embarrassing it is. It really is…"

Well, yes, there were several barges there, transports called 'bilanders', bulbous ungainly-looking ships used to transport animals - this time horses, as close to horses as may be. These were military mounts, super hybrid, genetically re-engineered creatures. Unlike its common stock cousin, the

KreissonKtenos, meaning 'better beast', were specifically designed for war. Its digestive system permitted it to utilize food better. A handful of concentrated pellets could keep it healthy for days. It needed less water, could also eat hay and roughage, was impervious to pain, difficult to frighten, bonded well with its master and, as one veteran once stated, 'is still quite tasty in a pinch'. On long sojourns like this one, the KreissonKtenos was a precious asset seeing that all food and most water must be transported to EremiaPikros, a desolate desert planet.

Ardon watched, musing. In the mix were also some camels and pack mules. He shook his head wondering 'why all the silly fuss with animals?' Every mechanical invention known to the Children's Empire lay at their fingertips. Oh yes, the occasional ride through a wooded glade or trotting romp along a sandy shore even appealed to him, but to depend on beasts for war when smarter, more powerful, comfortable machines existed in number was beyond his understanding. The motor coach and rail-stage were more to his liking.

Passing the second bilander, EnGlorious, Ardon spied other animals that gave him a start. Twenty of the renowned KaminosKtisis were being queued up to board. Literally meaning, 'Furnace Creation (*Ordnance*)', they were the most fearsome and powerful hybrid horses in the universe. Mother's personal creation, bred and raised on one of her mysterious planets and ferried here by one of her 'trade ships', as she called them, these beasts were most to be prized. A single animal had been known to serve as a ransom for an entire city of men and women.

Ardon had heard rumors telling that Mother was delivering some of these animals up for possible exchange, but to have twenty? Who among the prisoners held in Asotos' camp was of such value to Mother? Certainly not Sirion! And the trade ships? Again, the tale of seeing such a ship - if not ships - had fallen upon Ardon's ears just the other night. Long had it been since reports were made of seeing Lowenah's mystery machines near Palace City… not since the Great War, and those accounts were unverifiable.

His mind drifting in whimsical longing, Ardon recalled the one occasion many eons ago when he personally stood close to one of those ships. He was returning with NhosetHebel from a frolicsome adventure in the EthoHule Jungles, having just forded the MouesCennie River, when a beautiful silver ship silently drifted into sight. In moments, this shimmering machine was settled down some twenty paces away, a door opening in its side and a ladder descending. Momentarily, JabethHull bounded down the ladder, sweeping up a very pleased and excited Nhoset in his arms.

Ardon closed his eyes to remember, his heart jumping as he saw the long ago event in his mind. Nhoset was his first real love, or at least a love like what he felt for Tashi. She was already ages old by the time of his birthing, but she never treated him that way. 'Ah, those wonderful carefree days in that wonderful ti…' He frowned, his daydream broken by the memory of her fiery death soon after the Rebel Wars began. Collateral damage, the fickle winds of war? Murder…at least as far as he was concerned.

He pushed that aside, seeking his earlier vision. Oh yes, the trade ship… JabethHull revealed little, but did explain how Mother permitted a select few of her children passage into some of her secret worlds, to assist her with certain projects. That was where he and Nhoset were now off to. He also mentioned there were others with them, but was unwilling to reveal who or what was aboard. The two climbed the ladder, sealed the door and the ship lifted off, silently rising and then, just as silently, zooming out of sight in an instant.

DarlaRosa suddenly sat forward, arms waving as she shouted to some officers huddled together in conversation on the tarmac. Behind them were parked two barquentines, commonly called 'barqs'. Ardon was about to ask Darla which of the officers, or how many of them, were included in the latest of her amorous intrigues, he thinking better of it while his eyes studied the barqs. He had been forced to tarry aboard one once, on some diplomatic journey. It was, to say the least, an uncomfortable and cramped imprisonment.

Barquentines were nothing new to the Children's Empire, the term itself only denoting the volume - carrying capacity - of the ship. When the wars began, and needed vessels for fighting came off the 'ways' - another carryover term from water-borne sailing days - the old words used to qualify cargo ships carried over into the navy.

ဆ ဆ ဆ

(*Author's Note: This author uses colorful terminology found in the classical writings that are cherished down to this day. Credit for the inclusion of ancient nautical words of the Lower Realms to describe the sky ships from the Rebel Wars can be attributed chiefly to a woman from that world, Tabitha Copeland. After the wars had long ended and well into the beginning of the Fourth Age, when children of the innocent years were becoming numerous, Tabitha took it upon herself to become a poet extraordinaire for the children of that time.*

Along with the many historical works, i.e. Copeland and Garlock's, The King's War – A History, to name just one, Copeland put her pen to songs, ballads, and – as she is best known for – a series of adventure novels accounting the tale of a fictional character by the name of MarySanne, her great-grandmother's given name. Generations of children grew up on those stories, the collection today called The Tabitha Letters, this old, romantic ter-

minology being liberally dispersed throughout her novels. To the non-technical reader, these descriptive words and phrases conjure up vivid pictures of those wild and dangerous days when the life and death of a universe hung upon a thread and hope was often little more than a dream.

I have chosen to follow along in the style of this famous author, writing my historical narrative with a flavor for the youthful adventurer. Although my accounts are historically accurate, the colorful oratory of a troubadour is used to paint an emotion and understanding that history, coldly written, sadly fails to deliver.)

ജ ജ ജ

What Ardon knew was that the class of ship denotes its interior space, thus a cutter of around 500 tonnes was much less comfortable than a capital ship or carrier of from 40,000 to 100,000 tonnes. A barquentine of some 4,000 tonnes was a huge ship while parked in a spaceport, but was cramped and *very* uncomfortable in space, what with its crew of sailors and marines, the extra stowage of supplies, and all those ugly weapons. He was so glad Mother had not chosen one of *those things* for her delegation to travel on.

Thinking of what Mother chose did sour Ardon though - the *antiquated Shikkeron with that washed up Captain Bedan.* It was a brigantine class warship more fit for the scrap yard. And it was not much better than those barqs…an 8,000 tonne antique. Oh yes, it was refitted to the class of imperial brigantine, meaning that more comfort space had been stolen for battle armor – needing larger, more powerful energy machines - and weapons.

"Why couldn't she have picked one of those?" Ardon grumped under his breath as the imperial cruiser, Flagellum, came into view. He was told it was a 20,000 tonne warship, the largest class ship able to fly atmospheric and use planetary spaceports. It had comfortable staterooms and private officers' cabins. 'She could have at least given us a frigate.' He fussed to himself, thinking of the one they passed when first entering the spaceport. Displacing 12,000 tonnes, it was able to carry *some* creature comforts. 'Won't even be able to breathe in that rust bucket we're taking!' He sadly shook his head. 'And to have to share the shower and head with the common sailor on such an important mission?! I just don't know what's got into Mother.'

Looking longingly at the cruiser, Flagellum, Ardon sat upright, surprised. The ship's name was now changed just since he had departed for Chrusion less than two weeks ago. "*DusmeAstron*?!" He blurted aloud. "Why did they do that? Evening Star? What could be the reason for that?"

OfhieSanternano barely opened an eye, answering offhandedly, "Oh, that Euroaquilo fellow must be up to some trick or other. He's supposed to be admiraling this venture. Never can leave well enough alone, always changing things. They say that he commanded it long ago, his first ship, and that was its name back then. Confusing gentleman to say the least, always living in the past, but the Navy likes him. In charge of the Third Fleet, you know." He returned to his napping.

Ofhie's answer did not satisfy Ardon's question. The Navy didn't just go around changing it ships' names without reason, nor foregoing proper channels. Even if the Flagellum once was the DusmeAstron, one did not go changing names back for no good reason, and this trip was not a good enough reason. That much Ardon knew. Still…it was not long before the DusmeAstron was forgotten, someone calling out they were soon coming upon the Shikkeron.

What Ardon did fail to recall was one reason for such an unimpressive fleet taking them to such an important event. The Great War had been very costly, not only in loss of life, but in machines and ships as well. The last great naval engagement of that war was a running battle lasting eight days and costing the lives of millions and ruining both navies, something the leaders of the Children's Empire had not bothered to correct during the following peacetime. To that day, the littered debris fields from the Day of Tears remained choked with untold destruction.

Lowenah chose not to deplete what little navy still existed, allowing it to carrying out its primary responsibility, that of protecting the territories and colonies of the Empire. She used what was available and expendable at the time, part of her nature. So, this greatest of delegations was to ride to valor upon the backs of broken and discarded machines not needed elsewhere for the moment, a fate that would immortalize their names into legend along with the heroes of flesh that manned their decks.

ಶಿ ಶಿ ಶಿ

(*Author's note: During the Great War, the cruiser, DusmeAstron, was refitted after major battle damage, being reclassified a heavy frigate and renamed 'Flagellum', the ship displacing only 17,000 tonnes after the refit. When Admiral Sujin was Commissioner of Salvage, he ordered the Flagellum be refitted again, returning the original width and girth to its superstructure and increasing the ship's overall length by eighteen feet, bringing it back up to its initial displacement of over 20,000 tonnes. The ship was then reclassified a light cruiser.*

Under its new name, the DusmeAstron served with valor throughout the King's War, and assisted in the final assault on Memphis, some years after the King's War ended, it being Commander SarahCnidus' flagship during that campaign. Decommissioned from active service shortly thereafter, the DusmeAstron was renamed 'ReaDameia' and became a deep space *freighter. Garlock's ballad, <u>Never Shall They Forget</u>, ignited a fire in the children of those veterans of the Rebel Wars to create memorials honoring the sacrifice and valor of the ones who toiled to bring the Rebellion to an end. The old cruiser, DusmeAstron, was once again returned to its former glory and delivered to the Memphis War Museum where it sits to this day, a salient monument to the heroes of those turbulent times.)*

₧   ₧   ₧

"There! There it is!" Crilenian shouted, stretching his arm, pointing as he did.

DarlaRosa and KyseninaGerzion looked up and moaned. Curious, Ardon chanced a glance over his shoulder, groaning. Ofhie, who didn't even bother to open his eyes, just muttered, "It's been on deep space patrol for over eighteen months, had no servicing for that long or longer. Heard a lot of work's been done to the inside. *Still looks like a dung heap, though...*"

Ardon's heart sank. *What a dump!* He imagined if it appeared so ratty on the outside, what must it be like within? It was true, the Shikkeron did look a sight. The ravages of deep space patrol were hard on any ship, but the demands placed upon the Shikkeron over the last year and a half had really taken their toll. Hasty repairs were all afforded it during those months and, other than the ten-day makeover recently given it, little else was done with her. The ship looked tired, old, and defeated. It certainly was not a ship to host such an important delegation as was Lowenah's council!

"Curious..." Ardon spoke aloud, observing the nearing brigantine. Unlike the hustle and bustle he saw around the other ships they passed, the Shikkeron was strangely quiet. There was a small cargo tractor waiting behind an unloading lorry, a water tanker charging the ship with its cargo, and a small gun-buss with its crew of three at watchful ease - oh, and several nattily dressed sailors standing about the different open entryways. Other than a brightly colored tent some twenty paces from the main loading ramp with a few people lounging in its shade, there was little activity to observe.

The coach pulled up close to two tiny, motorized flat trucks, their baggage handlers snapping to attention, hurriedly attending to their duties as soon as the driver came to a stop. Ardon jumped down quickly, smiling to the attendants who politely bowed his arrival. Turning, he offered his hand, assisting first Tashi and then the other women out of the coach.

In less than a minute, the luggage was loaded on the flat trucks and whisked away, the motor coach quickly following, off on some other de-termined errand. The small party stood, silently viewing their surround-ings, tumblers of iced, cold ale presented them by one of the ship's officers. The sun shone brightly in a cloudless, deep blue sky while an occasional chickadee darted in and out of view. Other than the muted noise of some exhaust fans and the distant hiss of an engine room steam vent, all was quiet except for the sound of the morning's gentle, warm breeze.

The officer was called away by someone under the tent, she suggesting new arrivals follow her. Instead, Ardon, having now taken on the role of guardian, directed the group toward the boarding ladder at the Shikkeron's bow, seeing the main belly ramp was still closed. Ardon waved his pleasantries to the junior officer there who smiled and bowed his salutation.

Extending his hand in greeting, Ardon offered a cordial hello, he knowing the officer from his recent journey aboard the Starlight. "Why, Crilen, what a surprise! I'd not expected to find such a fine steward as you booking passage on *this* barge. Or did Mother press you into service for our journey?"

Crilen grinned, shaking his head and pointing to the braided ribbon on his sleeve. "No, my Lord Ardon, neither. Captain Bedan offered me a post as midshipman if I should join his crew. Mind you, serving as a steward aboard that fine schooner was delightful, but rather dull. I wanted some adventure and, feeling the Prisoner Exchange with its deep space travels to EremiaPikros – I've never been there – might satisfy the desire, I took up the good captain's offer and shipped aboard."

Ardon laughed. "Well, if its adventure you want, then may it be so. But I doubt you will find it on this tour of duty. EremiaPikros is little more than a hot, sandy planet filled with nothing other than nasty creatures that bite, sting, or just irritate the senses. As for the Prisoner Exchange, I expect little difference from past escapades. We'll go and haggle ransoms and who's to blame and for what. Then we'll trade whatever for whomever and return home with our freed brethren. Nope, I think you may be disappointed with this trip if it's adventure you seek."

"True that may be, my Lord." Crilen smiled good-naturedly. "But I've already made my mark and signed on for this tour of duty. I'll have to wait until our return to decide my future fate, though I think I'll have a grand time anyway, seeing all the important dignitaries taking passage with us."

Patting Crilen's arm, Ardon looked over his shoulder, asking, "Why is the ramp up? Doesn't the *good captain* know his guests have arrived? We'd like to board and freshen up a bit."

Crilen apologized. "Captain Bedan is yet to arrive, my Lord. The ship's officer in charge has decided to wait his arrival before boarding passengers. We have set up a spacious pavilion for your waiting comfort, filled with sweet dainties and refreshing drinks. Two of the Shikkeron's musicians are there, at the ready to titillate your ears."

Frowning, Ardon stepped toward the ladder. "No…my party and I need some *private* refreshment time. If the ramp is closed, then we shall enter by this means."

Crilen did not move, he standing between Ardon and the ladder. "I'm sorry, my Lord. Please, take some refreshment at the tent. The captain will be along soon."

Taken aback and embarrassed, Ardon's face clouded, his voice betraying inner feelings, blurting out, "Crilen! You know who I am! Who we all are! Now let us pass so we may settle aboard!"

"I'm sorry, my Lord," Crilen was shaken, but stood his ground. "but I have my orders."

Anger clearly sounded in Ardon's voice. "*Forget* those stupid orders! Look! *I* take responsibility for your actions. Step aside and let this party pass!"

Shocked at Ardon's outburst and, though quite intimidated, Crilen still refused to allow Ardon to pass. "I am truly sorry, my Lord, but you do not have the authority to negate the orders of the ship's officer in charge."

Furious, Ardon waved his arms, rendering insults and threats to the officer, Crilen, and the Navy for permitting such fools to be placed in charge. His ranting drew the attention of everyone within earshot. Even the baggage handlers stopped to watch the goings on. Tashi stepped back, embarrassed and surprised at her companion's actions. The others remained as they stood, some nodding approval while others said not a word.

Someone hidden in the darkness of the Shikkeron shouted down, "Midshipman Crilen! Give me your report! What's going on down there?"

Crilen did not look up. Standing stalwart against the rising tide of intimidation, he calmly answered, "There are those here who wish to board, Captain."

"*Captain?!*" Ardon shouted angrily. "*That's not the voice of Bedan. Who are you?! Show yourself this instant!*"

No sooner had he finished speaking than a black, polished boot appeared on the highest rung of the ladder, followed on the next rung by another. Then, in rapid succession, those boots flew down the rungs, their owner with her back turned as she descended. Instantly Ardon recognized the uniform. His heart sank. It could only be that misfit, *Darla*. Why, oh why her? Anyone, but that creature… And she was a fright to see, being all dressed up for war, carrying a long dagger strapped to her right thigh and a holstered lanner fastened by a wide black belt high to the left on her waist, set up for right-hand cross-draw.

His face growing red, fear of possible humiliation, embarrassment, and increasing anger at not being shown the proper respect for their - his - lordly station, Ardon decided that *this creature* was going to rue the day she crossed the line of propriety. This would not become another travesty such as occurred at the last council meeting! He would not be on the receiving end this time!

Darla's feet were just touched the pavement, she beginning her turn to face toward the people there, when Ardon attacked. Stepping forward to within inches of the woman, as her eyes met his, he unleashed a venomous string of scathing rebukes. "Enough of your silly games! Has the titmouse forgotten its place behind the hearth and decided to rule at the table?! This is the *King's council* and we have *more important matters* to attend to than to *wait upon the panderings of a shrew rat!* Now let us pass and stop acting akin to the Lord of lords!"

Taken aback by the mind-numbing assault for but a moment, Darla stared dumbly into Ardon's angry face. Gradually, as the reality of the moment began to sink in, she came to her senses. Devastating as it was, she refused to allow it to affect her actions. After all, Darla was a first-rate officer. Duty came above feeling, and duty at this time was to display the qualities of a first-rate officer.

Pushing hurt and rage aside, except for the furious blazing in her eyes, Darla calmly replied to Ardon, "My Lord, I am but the steward of this ship until its captain arrives. He shall choose who will board and when, it being a courtesy granted seeing he is responsible for the fate of those in his charge. My orders were to remain the Shikkeron secure until the captain arrives. Midshipman Crilen was only obeying my direct orders."

"*Stupid orders!*" Ardon screamed, veins bulging in his neck. "*And what did you make up such stupid orders for anyway?!*" He waited for no reply. "*No! No! You're playing captain, lord and god!*"

His face mocking, Ardon swept his hand wide, asking haughtily, "What is this to you? Are these people your *little toy soldiers* in your *own little kingdom of power?* They stand so pretty in their neat little uniforms. And we? Are we *your peasant crowd,* expected to bow to your command so as to get the crumbs of a blessing from your table of boastful delights? Has the sun got to you so early in the day, or does the fragrance of the fermented grape still linger heavy on your lips?"

Ardon threw his hands up to his mouth, leaning back as though afraid. "Ho! Maybe we're at risk for our lives! *One of us may be an evil saboteur seeking this ship's destruction…* if there's anything left of it to destroy. Look! We've important business to finish, and we don't have time to waste on the childish antics of a half-crazed drunkard…"

Darla remained the good soldier, though how is uncertain. Standing as if a line in battle, she steeled herself and quietly answered, "The officer in charge does not drink while on duty. I am not drunk. As for the danger, Lord Ardon, of all people I would believe your knowledge the greatest for why we need to be wary. Even now, assassins linger in our crowd, a murdered courtier discovered not three leagues from here only eight days ago. It is necessary to be prepared for every danger…"

Directing the party's attention toward the tent by extending a hand in invitation, Darla forced a smile. "There are prepared drinks and treats from our excellent galley cook, music for your listening pleasure and, should you desire, there are some chilling fans to keep you cool. My attendant here will assist you with your every need."

Tashi, who was dumbstruck and thoroughly embarrassed, began to follow the attendant, soon to be followed by DarlaRosa and Kysenina. Ardon shouted for them to stop and turned, enraged, back to Darla, shaking in anger. "The only danger here is *you! You* and that *sick head* of yours! Now get out of my way, *misfit!* Let us board!"

Before Ardon could blink, he found himself looking down the barrel of a drawn lanner, Darla's finger squeezing back on the trigger. "Lord Ardon, may I suggest you reconsider?" Although her voice was calm, at the moment Darla could only see red, Ardon being little more than a shadow painted on a crimson landscape. And then she felt it, the waking monster within.

Fearing the worst should matters escalate, Darla pleaded with Ardon, she feeling another being reaching out to take control of her soul, the monster of the battlefield. It had many times been her savior, but today? Today it might well spell her ruin. Then from deep down in the woman's throat there arose an insect staccato noise. Darla was on the verge of panic.

"*Please! Lord Ardon!*" Darla cried in an unrecognizable, deep guttural voice, "*Please,* obey my request!"

Ardon chanced a glance into Darla's eyes, gasped and fell back in terror. Orbs of smoldering red fire burned into his mind the most unholy of sights the man had ever witnessed. Was this creature even one of Mother's children, or an abomination from the dark abyss of Asotos' twisted mind…or worse? Was the demon of her nightmares finally consuming the soul of this woman and only her flesh survived to house the beast?

The others stared dumbly in stunned silence, Crilen standing aghast, eyes bulging with fright and uncertainty. As Darla composed herself, the monster slowly retreated, returning mastery of the moment back to its rightful owner. At length, she found her voice and, forcing a returned calm to her speech, reconfirmed her authority. "The Shikkeron is currently under my captaining. No one boards without my permission. Should it be attempted, I will put that person down by whatever means practicable."

Ardon was retreated some distance by now, cowering behind a very distraught Crilenian who was unable to avoid his predicament. From the safety of his reluctant fortress, he opened anew his verbal assault against his protagonist. "*You're crazy!!! Flippin' crazy! Fallen from your tree, you have! The demon's taken you for sure! You'll kill us all!!!! Kill us all!*"

The sound of an approaching motorcoach did little to assuage Ardon's vicious attack. It was not until Euroaquilo shouted out his booming hello that the man quieted. Upon seeing the admiral, he hurried over to greet him, beginning anew his rant regarding his attempted murder at the hands of that 'crazy woman'.

Euroaquilo patiently listened, finally asking as he scanned the crowd, "Which one is the *crazy* woman?"

Ardon's temper flared again, he poking Euroaquilo in the chest and then pointing. "Don't play that game with me! You know who I am, and you certainly know who that *crazy* is. But, for your benefit, in case your senses have left you, too, it's the one holding that terrible gun over there."

Following the direction in which Ardon pointed, Euroaquilo saw Darla and very quietly replied, "Oh..."

"Don't just '*Oh...* '!" Ardon shouted. "Do something! Now!"

Euroaquilo nodded and then slowly walked over to Darla, who was still holding the lanner high and in the direction where Ardon had first accosted her. He stopped up close. Darla did not speak or move, she fighting to keep her wits about her. Lifting the bagged food, he quietly commented, "Hello... Sorry I'm late. Here's the breakfast I promised to get you."

Darla lowered the lanner, but her eyes never left Ardon. Her reply was polite but sour. "I'm not hungry, thank you."

Ardon jumped forward, now using Euroaquilo as his new shield wall. "Dismiss her now! I order it! That *creature* is a threat to us all... and to our mission! *Dismiss her!*"

Lowering the bag of food, Euroaquilo innocently asked, "What'd she do?"

Ardon was incensed. "Not you, too! She... she... that *creature* tried to kill me! She stuck that ugly thing right in my face! If I'd not jumped back, she'd 'ave killed m..."

Euroaquilo turned and smiled so seriously. "My Lord Ardon, this woman needs never try. Had she decided you dead, then I would be asking the others what happened here. You are indeed most fortunate. Never have I seen this woman ask to parley when she has decided to kill someone."

Ardon became sarcastic. Euroaquilo ignored him, pressing Darla for an answer. "Leftenant, what happened here?"

The woman sighed in an attempt to finally compose herself, closing her eyes as she did. When they opened, she replied, "I had ordered that no one was to board the Shikkeron until its captain chose to do so. Lord Ardon apparently misunderstood those orders. I was presently assisting him with their clarification."

Ardon broke in, shouting and gesturing wildly. "*Lies! Lies! She tried to kill us! Kill us all!* All we wanted was to board this boat and refresh ourselves!" He then grabbed hold of Euroaquilo's shirt, tugging on him, demanding, "*Order it to let us board! Then dismiss her... or shoot her! Just get rid of her!*"

An eyebrow went up and then another. Euroaquilo gently removed Ardon's hands and, pretending to fuss with the councilor's clothes, answered, "According to the rules of engagement, this officer stands this ship until its chief officer or the person placing her in command relieves her of duty. I do not have such authority and am, in this case, outranked here."

Looking around at the others and then staring Ardon in the face, he loudly added, "The good leftenant here has the right to keep anyone she chooses off this ship, including me. She also has the right to use whatever force she chooses to prevent someone from boarding. My friend, that *creature* was within her legal rights to put you down, to kill you when you attempted a coup on this ship. We are in the Navy here, on this tarmac, not the council chambers. We play by different rules than you do there. For the time being, Leftenant Darla is commander of this ship, and *you* are whatever she chooses you to be."

"My fellow…" Euroaquilo pointed toward the Shikkeron. "*that* is the good leftenant's ship!"

Ardon was dumbstruck. He was furious, to be certain. What was wrong here? Was Admiral Euroaquilo so taken by this… this urchin that he, too, had become demented? Was Darla's demon so great so that it also gained control of the girl's lover? Dangerous it must be, but Ardon was not a complete fool. He would be silent for now. Mother was soon to arrive. He would find an audience with her and expose this folly and get the matter corrected. And then they would learn respect for a councilor of Lowenah.

"Come, now!" Euroaquilo waved his hand high while putting an arm around Ardon's shoulder. "There looks to be dainties aplenty for us all and… and, why there are some fine musicians to play us a ditty or two." With that, he ushered the party toward the tent.

Darla, her anger beginning to bubble up from within, finally threw an insult in Ardon's direction, speaking loudly while handing Crilen the lanner, ordering him, "If that peasant should decide to board without Captain Bedan's permission, shoot him!"

Ardon hurried his step, fearing to look back. Better to stay his distance than to have the demon revealed at his expense. He would wait his time to be exonerated. It would come soon…

ಬ   ಬ   ಬ

Mihai and Paul gingerly stepped down from the carriage and hurried toward the dining hall door in hopes of finding the members of their breakfast party. They were stopped up short by two others. Richard Finhardt and Tabitha Copeland, blocking the eatery door, were deeply absorbed in a lively discussion concerning a Lower Realm war from the past.

Tabitha poked a finger at Richard. "You can't tell me differently. I've read enough about it. That Bismarck of yours was full to blame for it all, he and his dreadful need for power and glory."

Richard raised his hand, pointing for emphasis. He was interrupted by Paul's calling out, "Enough! Enough!" Waving a smiling salutation, he asked if any of the others were still inside.

Although surprised to see the late arrivals, Tabitha was quick with the wit, she being quite good at such things. "You've got forever, Paul. We've got a powerful day ahead of us and you've been dallying in the parlor. Can you keep it in your pants long enough to give our lady a breath so as to make her passage on time?"

Paul was caught off guard. Embarrassed and speechless, he stopped, staring dumbly into Tabitha's laughing eyes. Mihai wrapped her arms around one of Paul's and offered a flowery retort to Tabitha. "It is not the buck who chases this doe, my Dear, but the doe who eagerly pants her lover onward. I am just such a lucky woman to find a fellow with an ardor strong enough to satisfy my desire."

Tabitha tipped her head back, laughing out loud. "I shouldn't know, my Lady, seeing you have kept the man sole prisoner for yourself. Still, one day I may take my right to see if what you say is truly so. Until then, well, I'll just have to make due." She leaned forward and kissed Richard on the cheek. "Just have to make due..."

Richard blushed, stepping back, shaking his head. "Whoa there..."

"What is it with you men, anyway?" Tabitha harrumphed. "You think of little else other than romancing a woman into the bed. Then, when you finally succeed, you have to show off your manhood in hopes she will act impressed. Your size, prowess, and stamina are all put on display in some way to seek her approval, for her to exclaim that you're the best, have the biggest, and can last the longest..."

She wagged a finger first at Richard and then at Paul. "And then, when you get out of the bed, you become embarrassed should sexuality even be mentioned in mixed company. Tell me, what's your problem?"

Mihai stepped up to Tabitha, taking her hands in hers. "The ardor of a man from your world is strong and can be so exciting, but he has so much yet to learn about the music of sweet lovemaking. I believe it is that lack of maturity in that art, such as my kind have practiced from the days before the lives of your kind... that lack that drives them to ever seek approval from the ones they wish to impress so much."

Giving Tabitha a gentle kiss on the lips, she crooned, "Someday they may learn how a soft and gentle touch at the right time and place can excite the heart as much as their manly ardor." She reached up, stroking Tabitha's upper arm. "My sisters are not ashamed of their desires. They openly confess them for all the world to see."

It was Tabitha's turn to blush, Mihai's openness being a little more than she was used to. Still, the woman was not embarrassed by what was spoken. Tabitha was no stranger to Mihai's loving arms, they sharing intimate moments on more than one occasion. But it had been a while, Paul consuming most of the new king's time over the past several months.

Quickly regaining her composure, Tabitha smiled and, while taking a finger and softly stroking Mihai's cheek, whispered her reply, "My King, should the hour have been less cruel, I should have sought an audience with you to discuss this matter further. The tongue, I have learned, is an instrument for much more than speech, and softness may at times defeat the ardor of any hero."

Mihai sighed from the touch, but her mind betrayed her feelings, raising the image of another lover into her visions. She frowned, forcing her thoughts back to the person standing before her. After all, had she not been the one to introduce the tease this day? It would be so improper to offer the intoxicating wine and then only deliver its fragrance because a yearning heart craved another's touch.

Cupping her hand over Tabitha's and staring into her dancing green eyes, Mihai purred, "It is several day's journey in the cold depths of space to reach our destiny. Should it be so, then we do ride the same comet together in its flight. Come hither and warm this roe's heart, keeping it safe this night from that frigid expanse. Let us draw close to see into each other's dreams and passion away the lonely hours between wake and sleep."

Tabitha blushed again, nodding.

Before she could speak, Richard piped in. "Well, if we don't hurry, you can be doing all that stuff on the curb here! Taxi's waiting and we're the last to board. Come on with it. Let's go before we're left behind."

Waving him off, Tabitha chirped, "Oh bother! We've lots of time. Lowenah's not even made an appearance yet, or so I've 'eard. Now be a good sport and leave us two a moment, and then we'll be right along."

Richard motioned to Paul and the two headed for the open-air taxi. Tabitha and Mihai kissed ever so softly and spoke a few private words to each other. In short order, they, too, joined the troupe waiting in the motorcar.

ಲಿ   ಲಿ   ಲಿ

The little taxi scooted past offices, barracks and storage buildings, and finally the giant hangars that bordered the spaceport proper. By the time it reached the final checkpoint, the heat of the afternoon was upon them, the breeze no longer filled with the fresh cool breath of morning. There was still a lot of activity, mostly that of work trucks, lorries, fuel tankers, and a few motor-coaches making their return trips from the harbored ships scattered about. The driver zipped in and out of the traffic, hurrying along and taking shortcuts whenever possible.

Some two miles away, the imperial frigate, DishonPele, the 'wonderful antelope', awaited its nearing entourage, Mihai having requested the ship because it had two relatively large wardrooms for conducting meetings, something she felt need for during this coming journey. It was one of the newer vessels in the fleet, receiving a complete rebuild less than thirty years before, but it was already tired from constant use and lack of needed refitting.

The driver hurried along as best she could in the growing traffic. Mihai sat back in her seat, eyes closed, just soaking in the day while the wind lifted her golden locks, sending them a-twirl, she paying no heed to the possible growing tangle of knots the tempest was creating. The woman smiled with satisfaction. Hopefully there would be little to do in the remaining hours before the tiny armada departed and she could catch a catnap before dinner.

The driver suddenly swerved to miss a passing tanker truck, it sounding its trumpeting warning just as she did. Mihai chanced a glance to see all the fuss. Turning her head to watch the truck, she spied a distant figure walking across the tarmac. Something felt amiss. Looking closer, she saw it was Darla. 'Strange. The girl doesn't take to strolling when on duty. Out here, she's always on duty.' Getting the driver's attention, the taxi turned hurried off in Darla's direction. As it neared, Mihai called out, waving.

Darla looked up, surprised. She had not noticed the motorcar until Mihai shouted. This was the *last* person she wanted to see right now. In fact, she wanted to see no one. "*Just leave me be!*" She sputtered under her breath, disgusted. "Oh, Death, come take me so I need not suffer more torment..." Motioning the taxi away, she turned and started heading in another direction.

Mihai frowned, but was undeterred. That child was not going to put her off! It was time to show some *kingly* authority. Asking the driver to stop a distance away, she climbed out of the auto, telling the others to travel on, she catching up with them later. As the machine sped away, the woman took to matters at hand.

"Leftenant!" Mihai called out in her commander's voice. "Halt and be addressed!"

Darla clenched her teeth, more out of dismay and frustration than anger. She stopped up short, but refused to turn about. Casting her eyes skyward, she quietly waited the approaching intruder.

Mihai hurried forward, coming to within a few paces before stopping. When Darla continued to ignore her presence, she entreated the girl, "My lovely Rachel, why do you find me abhorrent? It's your sister, Michael, the one who loves you so. How is it that you do not know your loving companion?"

Following a flock of birds in the distant sky, Darla finally offered reply, commenting ever so casually, "It is such a beautiful day to start our journey, isn't it? The sky is so blue this time of year, and the smells..."

"Darla, look at me!" Mihai stiffened her stance, hands on hips. "That's an order!"

Ever so slowly, Darla obeyed.

Mihai sighed in dismay. It was all she could do to not reach out and hug her little sister. Darla looked a fright – swollen, reddened eyes, distraught countenance, a tear-stained face, revealing the appearance more that of battle fatigue. The girl had been crying, so much as to have stained the blouse of her dress uniform.

"Oh, my child!" Mihai exclaimed in sorrow, the words involuntarily escaping her lips.

For two long hours after Ardon's vicious attacks, Darla had managed to contain her feelings, she concentrating fiercely on ship's duties until Bedan finally arrived. When relieved of command, she had quickly departed, barely making it out of earshot when the torrent of tears and quiet wails erupted. Darla tried to smile, but just looking at Mihai brought a returning flood of tears. Stoop-shouldered, she stood there sobbing, no longer able to fight back her inner emotional warring.

Mihai, herself, tearing up, stepped forward, arms outstretched to embrace her little sister. She was abruptly motioned away, Darla crying out her warning. "Leave the dead bury themselves, lo you may well become consumed with their madness! I seek only the solace of the Silent Tombs. Leave me be to such glory. I feel even a dog deserves that kindness..."

Surprised, Mihai quipped, "Darla! Don't think that way! I..."

Her fists clenched, Darla leaned forward, crying, her face defiant. "*Is death such a bad thing to wish for?! So many of my companions have I already buried, there are none left to do so for me. I wish only for their glory. At least they stand as honored by those in this contemptible house.*"

An angry fire flashed in Mihai's eyes and she snapped back, "There is no glory in a death wish! Only cowards and those with no souls seek its release."

Wailing, Darla shook her fist. "*I am no coward!*" She shouted in anger, lowering her head in grief. "I have no strength left to live. Go away and let me die! Leave me be. Cracked and broken was the child made, and even more so has the brattling become. Now leave me go... please..."

Mihai would have none of that. She plunged forward, wrapping Darla in a bear hug of an embrace. There she remained all the while the child wept, holding her close, singing gentle, soothing melodies in her ear. To Mihai, it seemed as if the world had stopped, paying its silent respect by restraining an intrusion upon them. For Darla, she remembered little other than the total despair in her heart.

After long moments had passed, Darla stood back, patting her uniform. She looked down at her soiled blouse and, with a sad half-smile, asked, "Do you really know why I wore this fancy uniform today?" Mihai replied she did not know.

"My Lord, you should understand." Darla looked into Mihai's eyes. "I was charged with commanding the Shikkeron until Captain Bedan returned. You know that it is only proper to prepare for the ship's crew to show respect by officially honoring that officer on his arrival. It was my duty to honor Bedan in that manner."

Mihai agreed. "Any good officer would…"

Darla looked away, interrupting, her face grave. "I had nothing else to gift him with that had not been soaked in the blood of the ones I love. The uniform Contorie made for me lies buried in the fields of Hailar, wrapping my loving sister, SaleenHavson, she having died in my arms in that barren wilderness shortly after we were attacked by Stasis. Indeed, I have no other garments of quality other than this," She pulled on her blouse, "that has not been soaked with the blood of the ones I've loved."

Looking back into Mihai's eyes with her own pleading orbs, Darla mused with wistful sadness, "I had so much wished to journey this day for once feeling clean, washed, innocent."

Then fear began to grow on her face, a dark cloud nearing panic. "But now it has found me! It has waked to take power over my mind. Even now it is clawing at my sanity. It laughs at me in derision, sarcastically accusing me of being the fool for allowing Ardon to live. It nearly took control of the monster within today, making me go blind with rage, its ugly laughter and my hatred for it all that kept my sanity."

Mihai now felt her own panic rising. She clutched Darla by the shoulders, asking in desperation, "How long have you been resisting the demon's advances? How long has it sought you out in your waking dreams?"

Shocked, Darla dumbly stared into Mihai's eyes. How did Mihai know about her waking dreams? She had told no one, even keeping them hidden from Euroaquilo in their dream-shares. Finally, casting her gaze down and away from her sister's searching eyes, Darla answered reflectively, "Off and on for many years, they becoming strong during the Great War, then retreating into hidden recesses for a while. But now they grow again, the demon being insidious and bold."

An involuntary shudder ran down Darla's back. "These last three nights have been most cruel on my constitution, the demon giving me no rest at all. Its very breath I feel upon me even now. I cannot escape it."

As Darla's own words began to sink in, a new fear grew in the girl's heart, one she could not contain. Tears of terror brimmed in her eyes as she desperately pleaded, "It's the blackness, isn't it - the blackness that consumes all the damned, eventually driving them mad like the Stasis!"

She shook her head, whimpering like a little child. "I failed, haven't I? Failed to love enough and care enough, to hate my own wickedness, my own evil. I tried to be good, but this last hour's convulsions of wrath have driven me over the edge. It has come for me, hasn't it? And I can't stop it this time, for I have damned myself to it." She bowed her head and began crying anew.

"No! No! No! That is not true at all!" Mihai shook Darla, her needing to deny her sister's wicked evil as much for her own sake as Darla's. "It is not what you think! Cannot be! Cannot be! It is another evil warring inside you. You're a good child... good child. Mother loves you more than most! I know! I know, for she told me so, herself."

Darla mourned, resigned, having heard nothing of what Mihai said. "It calls to me, seeking my love. It yearns for my attention, gifting me with dreams of dismay, telling me it offers me only what I deserve. I am damned, and there is nothing for it. I should end it now before I bring the ones I love down to the pit, for that is what the demon seeks, yearns for me to desire."

Mihai was beginning to panic. She saw not Darla, but herself slowly sinking into the abyss of damnation with every word the girl spoke. Inside her own head, she could hear sniggers and quiet laughter and, further away, from somewhere near, she heard the mournful cries of another beast calling out to hers, seeking solace from it. Darla's demon was trying to contact hers! Mihai almost cried aloud, terror growing in her heart at that revelation.

Was she, too, going insane? Was it too late for Darla... for her? "No! No! No!" She shouted in desperation. *"It cannot be! I will not allow it! Damn all the world! I will not allow it!"* Squeezing Darla's arms to the point of pain, Mihai demanded, *"Tell me! Tell me, now! What about your dreams?! Tell me about your dreams!"*

Through the fog of her own inner terrors, Darla heard little. Was she lost to the souls of the damned? The thought was so disturbing as to make beads of bloody sweat form on her forehead. She mumbled something incoherent.

Mihai's heart was racing. She had to know. For her own sanity, she had to know. Violently shaking her sister, she screamed, *"Tell me about your dreams! Fear me, for my wrath is worse than the fires of the abyss! Tell me of your dreams! Look at me! Look at me now and tell me about those god-damned dreams!"*

As a caged animal fears the fires of its tormentor, Darla cowered in fright, she having shrunk up to a mere shadow of her stately stature. Those emerald green eyes so often filled with mirth staring wildly into a world of darkness and horrors. Hideous sights filled her head as the demon within sought control of her senses. But Darla was a strong child and she would not go quietly. Struggling to regain power over her mind and soul, she swore vile oaths and rebukes to all the worlds of the living and the dead. Slowly, through curses and beseeching pleadings, she regained possession of her senses.

Finally, she felt the shaking, Mihai's shouting. Now she heard the questions Mihai was asking. Dreamily, she answered, "My lovers, all my lovers, are crying out to me, accusing me for all the death and tribulation heaped upon them. I see a river of blood as it reaches out for me…my lovers, all dead, rotting corpses with taunting voices, seeking my destruction, to drown me in that river of blood."

"*What else?! Tell me, what else did you dream*?" Mihai shook Darla again. "*Tell me!*"

Darla nodded, she still being lost in a mind-numbing fog. "I feel the loathsome maggots feasting on my flesh and the scarabs chewing on my brain. They ever eat me up, constantly chewing, ever eating. And my… my insides are spilt out upon the ground where the dogs are consuming them. Oh! And my head…my head is being split apart by some power from the inside. Yes! By unspeakable visions! Oh, my head… My eyes have been crushed and my nose torn away. My very womanly parts have been ripped from my body. Oh, the agony!"

Wrapping her arms around her sister, Mihai cried out in remorse, "Oh, my dear little one, I am so sorry for the tribulation I have cast down upon you. You, the most innocent of children! It is I who belong with the damned for, if not for me, you would not have suffered these terrible things."

Staring into Mihai's eyes, Darla asked, confused, "What are you about? Has the universe all gone to rubbish? Are we all dead and not know it yet?"

Mihai smiled, holding her iron embrace on Darla. "It's all right. The demon has not taken over your mind, nor have you slipped into the worlds of darkness and damnation."

Darla did hear what her sister said this time. As if coming out of a stupor, she gently pulled away from Mihai's embrace and stepped back, asking, "How are you so sure that it will be *all right*?"

Darla was listening, waiting. Mihai relaxed a little. "The blackness has not taken you or me… *nor will it*. Mother loves us and would never let those with the powers over the abyss harm us. That I know. And I also believe I can help you understand your torrid dreams, or at least the concept of them."

Pulling her sister close again and speaking in little more than a haunted whisper, Mihai confessed, "You have seen my terror, what was done to me in that evil hour long ago. How, I do not know, other than the creature our brother planted within me is highly intelligent and able to reproduce itself, or at least once was able to do so… or, maybe, there was more than one planted within me – I'll tell you why I think that is possible – and one has entered into you by traveling upon a strand of my DNA that you drank as I suckled you."

Mihai frowned. "A terrible evil has enveloped you, one that I believe may be far worse than mine. You know of my demon and I know of yours, or at least that you have one. Now I'm beginning to understand something far more sinister. I can feel their camaraderie and ability to communicate to a degree through the mind. I also believed that he gave to me those demons on the day of his attack, but now I think I may have received them over time, he practicing his subversion during his many dream-shares he showered on me in the weeks before that damnable day."

A chill ran up Mihai's spine. She thought of the possibility of others being gifted with such evil during that same time period. But few were visitors then, he being so busy planning, only... there was another, and... No! Mihai could not bear to think it possible.

She forced that nightmare from her thoughts and continued. "I fear that I have added to the madness hiding inside you. Through our many dreams shared, while we opened ours minds up to each other, the demons may well have had the ability to do the same, taking advantage of our openness to communicate freely."

"You see, my Lovely One, Mother gave to our brother power extraordinaire, and she shared many of her sacred secrets with him, she being so blindly in love with the man. I do not blame Mother, but allow me to continue. Our brother was given the ability to mix his genetics with that of his lovers, or at least his women lovers. Why he turned to hating his sisters so badly and giving his passion to his brothers is a question I have pondered many times. Anyway, Asotos could give the gift of himself to any woman he shared his love with, bonding her to him in a special way. Some women, like Anna, grew to loving him with a drunken craving. Whether it was him or the woman who cast or allowed to be cast such a spell, it was real, very real."

Darla asked, curious, "So it was through the act of intercourse that Asotos contaminated the mind of his sister, or could do so?"

"Well..." Mihai thought about it. "I feel it might have been that way, possibly, but he could have accomplished such a feat through any physical exchange of genetics, even through someone's food, I believe. It is, or was, the spiritual aspect of matters, though, that set the stage for seeing his *gift* come to fruition. He had to get into your head. That is what your older sisters have called the 'dream of dreams'. The man could get right inside you, become part of you, and then he could play upon your soul the sweetest, most exciting music a woman had ever experienced."

She shook her head. "That power died when Mother took it away from him shortly after my assault, thus depriving him of additional victims."

Inquisitive, Darla asked, "So who can offer up the dream of dreams today? Who has the power? PalaHar maybe?"

Mihai denied it to be so, answering, "The power is not with us at this time. It has been promised to us by Mother that she shall resurrect it at a future day. For now we must wait, or pine, as some have the habit of doing."

Releasing Darla and stepping back, Mihai confessed, "All that is in the past now. The blissful life we once believed could never end, the countless dream-shares, even the tiny garden that so many of us came into womanhood in is gone, covered by the thorns of Time. But I digress."

Reaching out and brushing a strand of Darla's wavy black hair from her face, Mihai smiled reassuringly. "There are ways to rid ourselves of demon terrors, or at least ease them. And needs be it shall become for you to have such a cure. You see, it is nearing the anniversary of my attack, the hour of my coming of age, the moment when my heart and mind were forever torn asunder. I believe this prisoner exchange has been set to that date so that our brother can offer up some of his special deviltry that he's so good at doing."

"My dear child," Mihai took Darla's hands in hers. "as the hours progress, the demon will increase in strength and viciousness. This happens to me every year about this time, but this anniversary, I fear, will be worse. Maybe I'm just tired. I have been busy, you know."

Darla shivered with growing trepidation. "So will it consume me... us, or is there something we can do to hold it in check?"

Mihai said there was. "Yes, yes there are positive things we can do, and not so difficult to manage, either. Seek out the attention of Euroaquilo. Make him keep you at his side for these remaining days before the prisoner exchange. Tell him your need for protection from your dreams, from your demon. Many are the nights he has already acted gallantly in your behalf, even in mine. Go to him. Mother has given him the power to protect you."

"What of you, my Lord? Who will protect you until then?" Darla asked, more concerned for Mihai's fate than her own.

Mihai fussed, "You worry about *you*. Your demon has been acting a bit unruly this day. Have Euroaquilo put it in its place. Besides, Mother has given me a fellow who's pretty good at holding back the goblin. He may not have learned how to be the best lover... yet... but he knows how to take on a fight with that demon and best it! Like *that!*" She snapped her fingers. "Like *that!*" Secretly she wished to herself to have Euroaquilo by her side, but it could not be.

Seeing and understanding, Darla insisted that Mihai be with Euroaquilo. Mihai resisted fervently. "No! That must not be. If the demon gains success, it may never be rid from you, and that may well bring you to the damnation your most fear...a living Hell for a long as breath exists within you."

As her own words sank in, Mihai's countenance failed her. She lowered her head, tears falling. "I am so sorry. Except for my selfish desires, my dearest little sister would not face these dragons. Her fate rests in my hands, and those hands have brought her to the edge of destruction..."

"Sister..." Darla tugged at Mihai's jacket. "Sister..."

Mihai looked up to see a serene, smiling face and sparkling eyes staring into hers. "Does the doctor never need a cure? Is it not true that the most fearsome of wild beasts will one day spread a grand feast for the lowliest of creatures? My sister, one day we will feast upon the evil creations of our brother, and he will shudder because we will then rule the worlds of men and gods."

It was Darla's mouth that formed the words, but Ma-we's voice that Mihai heard when her sister spoke again so reassuringly. "The most terrible of trials may one day become the greatest of gifts. Those who pass through those unspeakable fires forever are bonded together as but one person. Mihai, you and I have shared the blood grape, we have loved in its passion. We are one, you and I, never to be torn asunder."

"We, you and me, are also bound together by a living evil, married to a fiend that seeks our destruction. Yet it is we who feed upon its malice to accomplish our own desire for vengeance. We crave our demons as much as they crave us, for the power beyond what is normal for us from them we attain. Their blood sustains us when all others' powers fail. Their spirit drives us onward when the bravest in our midst quail in fright. No, they are the host upon which we feed to our own glory. Our demons cannot win for they are abominations of a corrupted mind. We, my sister, cannot fail, for we are the progeny of an immortal spirit."

Darla gave Mihai a tender kiss. "We have but one soul, mind, and heart. We are the Daughters of Darkness, borne to rid the universe of all that is evil. By evil shall evil be brought to nothing. My Love, we are the Queens of Darkness, the gorgons who ride Shiloh's flank in the coming War of Wars. The price? We fear not the price for this success, for we know the future treasure is of far greater value than our frail bodies."

"Should I die tomorrow, I will feel no regret, for you, my sword and shield, have comforted me during all this time. You have given me life and breath. Your milk has given me life and power, for with the power of Asotos' demon, I shall bring his house down to nothing!"

Kissing Mihai again, Darla crooned, "Oh, my sister, my flesh and my blood, I do love you so much."

Their embrace was unhurried and soothing both to soul and heart. When the two women finally released their loving hold, the weather was changing. Billowy clouds were filling the sky, being driven along by an agitated breeze. It was mid-afternoon and the time, like the clouds, was racing along toward a determined destiny. Still, time must wait for Mihai. She had some unanswered questions that troubled her.

As Mihai wiped Darla's face with a clean, white kerchief, she puzzled over the girl's earlier comment concerning Ardon and wondered aloud about her soiled blouse. She had been so absorbed earlier so as to forget the reason for her sister's dismay, but now she wondered the why-for of it.

Darla was a good trooper, brushing it all off as nothing, a mere misunderstanding.

Mihai would have none of that, she pressing her little sister until, bit by tiny bit, she squeezed the account from her. As details grew, her countenance became greatly agitated to the point of seething, but she dare not reveal it to Darla. At length, she asked for a close look-see at the blouse.

If Darla had a fault, it was her desire for quality and her meticulous passion for detail. This shirt had been hand-woven of a blend of the finest silks and jewelion threads. It was the value of at least a month's leftenant's wages, possibly more - not counting the golden and chrysolite weave in the embroidery and tassels. It was now ruined, Darla's tears staining the dye of the fabric. Mihai doubted it could be repaired, even with another month's officer's wages.

"Give me your blouse, please." Mihai ordered, her tone reflecting her mood.

Shocked, Darla asked why.

Mihai reached out a hand and demanded it, telling of her need to make a closer examination of it. "Now be a good servant and do what your king requests." She would not accept 'no' for an answer.

Reluctantly, Darla pulled off the shirt and dutifully handed it to her *king*.

Thanking her, Mihai studied the blouse. Sure as she had suspected, it was of the finest quality, and made by expert hands. Looking up to comment, she could not help to study the beauty of her sister as well. Few men dared Darla's company, they usually feigning some great need or other to be about important business, but at what a loss! Darla was a natural athlete and well-practiced in all the martial arts of the day. Her rippling muscles, proud stature, voluptuous curves and deeply tanned, olive-colored, golden skin made her something to behold and desire.

Mihai smiled, waxing sadly, "What a shame to cover such stunning magnificence with these rags of stodginess called 'clothing'!"

Darla shivered, not from the cold, but from her nakedness. "My Lord…" she said, nervous, glancing around, "I'm on duty. You know the rules. 'Officers must deport themselves as such at all times while on duty'."

"*Oh, poop! Piss on those orders!*" Mihai laughed. "I'm king and I can make or discard any orders I wish! Besides, if you recall, *I* was the one who made up those orders not that many years ago, when I was field marshal." She grinned. "Maybe I'll order that all officers should prance around naked while on duty. You know, I'll have them tattoo their ranks on their butts…"

Both women laughed. It felt good to laugh. Then Mihai took off her kingly jacket made for her by Ma-we. Handing it to Darla, she ordered, "Here! Musn't break some silly rules now, must we? I've a fine blouse to conduct my business in and have no need of this at the moment. You wear it like a good officer."

Darla fussed, but finally relented. Mihai helped her sister. It fit a little snug, the revealing cut of the jacket acting like a lifting bodice, hiding none of the woman's round, full bosom. Tightening the laces across Darla's belly, Mihai grinned. "This'll squeeze you in and push you up. Dear, you'll be a sight to behold."

When finished, Mihai stepped back for a better look. She good-naturedly fussed, "You make me jealous, my Love. You are rounder, fuller and bigger than the owner of that jacket. You are *gorgeous*… just *gorgeous!* It is said by the poets, 'more perfect than perfect are the breasts of the one born last, and far sweeter are they from the maiden having not yet given suck.'"

Darla blushed, "You say that only to ease my spirit. I am a handmaid, not a maiden. Your golden locks and bouncing breasts stir passion's desire in the hearts of all. And your pink delights that deliver the creamy elixir of life to the tongue are far more refreshing to the spirit than the finest of Medeba's wines. I am but a tempting vessel offering up empty promises. You can satisfy both heart and palate."

Mihai laughed. "You tease my heart, too, but tonight is not the night for satisfying our flirtings. Now hurry along and find your man and tell him all that I have commanded you to tell him." She patted her on the behind. "Be off! And do not allow any cad to lure you away from your destiny. Many will take notice of you this day, and few will forget the sight, a kingly waif in kingly garb speaking with kingly authority. No! No one will forget my darling this day." A mischievous smile danced across her face as she pondered people's reactions.

Darla nodded, curtsied, and then kissed her sister so tenderly. "Thank you. Thank you for loving me." Off she went to find her manly hero, Euro-aquilo.

"And now for some other unfinished business..." Mihai fumed under her breath. Clutching the ruined blouse, she hurried toward the distant Shikkeron.

஀   ஀   ஀

"Ahhh…" Ardon sighed in tired relief. He was finally packed away, his *teensy* room stuffed with the treasures he had brought along to make this journey more bearable. The cabin, designed for four or more midshipmen, was filled to overflowing with his and Tashi's baggage until he had managed to harangue Captain Bedan into removing the mattress from the hinged upper bunk. Stuffing the space behind the now closed panel with clothing and other whatnots tidied up the place, making it more livable.

The room was very small, only seven by seven feet. The two bunks, each being less than three feet wide, were usually shared by two officers, rotating in shifts. This was often increased to three during wartime when extra personnel were aboard. But, for Ardon, this was way too small a place for him, alone. And what of Tashi? Certainly she would find such cramped accommodations *deplorable*. Oh yes, she had been a good girl, saying nothing when being delivered here. In fact, she was being strangely quiet since lunch, just dropping her things and leaving, saying she needed to discuss some important issues with some fellow councilors.

Looking around, Ardon fussed, "Can see why she didn't want to stay. Miserable little hole in the wall! Could have given us the first mate's room… It's a little bigger and further away from the engine room. At least it would have been showing a little more respect."

Ardon looked around, unhappy. "Oh, bother!" And then smiled, spying the mug of hot brew recently delivered. He stepped over to the tiny foldout desk/table, easing himself into a small wooden chair across from the opened doorway. Grinning, he picked up the mug. "A just reward for a job well done…"

His musings were interrupted by a hammering echo of hurried footsteps on the metal deck plates in the hallway. He turned to see Mihai stopped on the threshold. Smiling, he was preparing to offer a salutation when his world suddenly exploded around him.

"*Bastard!*" Mihai cried.

Ardon's chair spun around, smashing into the cot before it folded up and crashed to the floor, his mug twirling from his fingers, flinging its liquid contents everywhere, loudly shattering on the paneled floor. The scattering of papers and books the man did not notice, having the breath knocked from him when the *monster* in the doorway lunged in and crushed him against a wall locker.

And monster it was… When the blinding pain eased from hitting his head at being slammed against the cabin wall, Ardon saw only a seething, red-faced beast staring at him, its chest heaving with an angry passion. The malice growing in the monster's eyes was too overwhelming! He panicked, seeking escape, his feet slipping in his struggle to get away. At last, he whimpered to be let go.

Enraged, Mihai drove her weight into Ardon, her arm pressed across his throat. She screamed in his face, "*Shut up, you fool, or I'll kill you now! You worthless shit-weed!*"

Ardon could not shut up, nor could he desist in his struggles, the man being too terrified to even think of anything other than a looming death if he did not get away. Mihai's insults slowly subsided with her energy, she finally realizing that Ardon might really be dying.

By now Ardon stood limp, Mihai pressing him against the wall, keeping his feet under him. His face had turned purple and his eyes were glazing over as they blankly stared up toward the ceiling. Calming somewhat, she realized what was happening and, it not having been her intention to hurt

Ardon in the first place, Mihai eased off on her grip to give the man a chance to breathe.

It took several moments for Ardon to regain his senses. His breath remained raspy, but his face was recovering its color. The man was still in too great a state of shock to speak a word. During this time, a crowd had gathered at the doorway, they having come running when the sounds of a struggle were heard echoing down the corridors. At seeing Mihai, none dared to enter or even speak. Some slunk away while others stood bewildered, watching events unfold.

Mihai angrily spat, *"Only godless demons publicly rape a woman!* Do you seek also my sister's murder?! What kind of a creature are you?!"

Ardon was dumbfounded. He shook his head in confusion, totally befuddled over what Mihai was talking about.

Shaking in frustrated rage, Mihai shouted contemptuously, *"You ignorant... worthless...bastard!* Do you think *my little sister,* Darla, has no soul?! That she is some heartless wild dog, to be beaten and driven away?!"

Pushing herself back, Mihai turned and stepped toward the doorway. Ardon slowly slid down the wall 'til he sat on his haunches, clutching his throat and blinking away a growing headache.

As she reached the doorway, Mihai spun around again, her eyes a blazing inferno. Her hands shaking in contempt, she leaned forward, pointing a finger at him.

Ardon cowered, squirming. Throwing his hands up, his face a fright, he begged, "Please! Please! My Lord! Don't…"

Mihai was furious. "Don't 'my Lord' me! You're not one of mine! The dung heap with you! If you were not one of Mother's favorites, I'd not let you live this long!" She made a fist, shaking it. "Ardon, *nothing man,* I swear, as I live, *if you ever mistreat my sister again, I'll rip you open from gizzard to gonad and scatter your guts across a field! I swear it, Ardon! As I live, I swear it!"*

Spying Darla's blouse lying on the floor, Mihai picked it up and flung it into Ardon's face. "You get my girl a new one, or repair this like new! Don't even think of seeing my face until you've made it proper. You get it done right and bring it back to me!"

She stormed out, the gathered crowd scattering like leaves before a tempest. In all the confusion, Mihai nearly bowled over Captain Bedan, who was just arriving after being informed of trouble aboard the Shikkeron. Jumping back in surprise, a dumbfounded Bedan stared speechless at the advancing woman.

Mihai made no attempt to slow down. As she brushed past him, she fumed polite, "Permission to board!" a courtesy she had failed to offer earlier.

Still hurling curses under her breath, thinking of additional denunciations she wished to have cast, Mihai hurried down the Shikkeron's belly ramp, her hands still clenched in angry fists. She glanced up to the sound of someone quietly singing a merry little tune. Ma-we was fiddling with one of the wheels on her personal carriage.

Looking at Mihai as though surprised and then at the darkening sky, she chimed cheerily, "Looks like a storm's approaching. Well, I guess I arrived here just in time."

Eyeing her mother, Mihai sourly replied, frowning, "I'd say you waited for the storm to end. Let me make a fool of myself first, and then you arrive so innocently."

Ma-we grinned the culprit. "Mother gets so busy sometimes, she just forgets the hour. I did intend not to be late, you know. And I think I wasn't, either. Now, tell your dear mother what you're all about. What storm?"

Mihai saw right through Ma-we's sweet innocence. She began to laugh. "All right! Have it your way." The sound of distant thunder rumbled across the spaceport. Looking into the sky, Mihai asked, "Will you take me to my ship, or at least allow me use of your carriage?"

Being so polite, Ma-we graciously offered her child the use of the machine. As Mihai started away, she called out to her, "Send it back, Darling, as soon as you're done. My luggage is still in it."

Mihai waved, shouting back she would. Ma-we turned toward the Shikkeron and made for the ramp. "And now for my other darlings..." She slowly shook her head, smiling, "Tsk, tsk... So much to do... So much to do..."

ῴ   ῴ   ῴ

Darla dutifully obeyed her big sister's command, but finding Euroaquilo was no easy task. She played a game of chase 'n tag for the better parts of an hour. Hitching a ride on a motor coach with a very willing driver, she searched several ships, each attending officer saying that the admiral had just left and was off to 'such and such a ship'. True to Mihai's words, Darla's outfit caused quite a fuss. Mihai's kingship had been quietly broadcast through the gossip channels, nothing official having been declared.

When Darla arrived with the king's jacket – a garment that could not be mistaken for less – it caused a real stir. Curious eyes peeked out from behind loading trucks and darkened doorways. Hundreds of people took to seeing what the rumor mill was spewing out. What caught them so by surprise was the stunning beauty of this woman. Many were the ones among the military who personally knew of Darla, respecting her heroic bravery, even if others knew nothing of her at all. But, oh, how handsome she was! That was another story.

Then, when tales of Mihai's visit to Ardon made its rounds through the rumor mill… well, Darla was becoming quite the celebrity. By the time she reached the EnGlorious, news of her escapades were well circulated. The ship's crew and several service personnel did not even bother to pretend their attention upon her visit. And when the captain had sent her off toward another transport, all eyes followed her departure.

This, by the way, was all great fun for Ma-we. It fit in to her plans so well. 'Just wait, my darlings, when you see what I have done with your little sister by the time we arrive at EremiaPikros. The sight you'll see then!'

What of Euroaquilo in all this chase 'n tag? He truly had been busy making his rounds of the fleet before it departed. Still, he could not help but feel fingers playing behind the scene. Long after the news had reached his ears about Darla's searching for him, circumstances continued to prohibit them from making contact. Twice he determined to wait for her, having told others of his whereabouts, only to be called away at the last minute. So, eventually surrendering to the moment, the good admiral returned to the DusmeAstron, his flagship for this journey, and waited for Darla's arrival.

There were other reasons Euroaquilo wished to be with Darla. Throughout the day there was a growing disquiet in the man's heart, an anxious tightness similar to when a person feels danger surrounding them. And then there were the haunting voices whispering, apprehensive, in the back of his mind all afternoon. No…he concluded there were forces beyond his wisdom fating the coming encounter. Good or bad, this *evening child* was to play a part in the destiny of the Empire. The future of all living things might well hinge on coming events. He could just feel it.

Euroaquilo purposely arranged for his meeting with Darla to occur on the now empty captain's bridge. It was located on the upper most level - deck five - and far forward. Having ordered all other ways closed off, there was only one entrance available for his girl to take. That was from far abaft ship. He leaned against the elevator rail, waiting and listening for her arrival.

(*Author's note: The battle bridge and captain's bridge were located on the upper levels of the DusmeAstron, it being the custom of ships built in the era of that ship to have the battle bridge in open view, below and directly in front the captain's bridge. From the captain's bridge, all ship's activities could be monitored and commands could be given. The Shikkeron was designed similarly, it being of that vintage.*

There were four ways to gain access to the bridge - from a single door abaft the bridge, two small hatchways that opened through the floor, and an elevator that ran from the loading ramp, near the hold, to the bridge. It ran up and down on four large tubes, one located at each of its corners. There was no shaft, just openings through each floor, thus requiring a removable safety rail be placed around the opening on each deck. This design allowed the elevator to second as a heavy freight mover.

Under the passenger compartment there was an open platform. When the compartment was on one deck level, the platform was on the next deck immediately below. This required a hole be placed through the inner hull above the bridge, to accommodate space for the freight platform to reach the bridge. When battle conditions existed, the elevator was raised to the bridge, plugging tight the opening in the inner hull, the bridge and the deck below it. The other decks had semicircular plates mounted to the elevator shafts. These would be rotated into place at such times, closing tight the lower decks. These older style battle wagons had been built with large windows, permitting observers to see outside without the need of screens and monitors. Ref: Fires in the Sky, SirionSandavar, pp. 294-7)

There was a stirring at the distant end of the long hallway that extended the spine of the ship, and then a muffled clunk of an iron hatch being carefully closed. Leaning forward with the anticipation of seeing Darla soon appear out of the shadows, Euroaquilo was shocked by the bewildering sights that flooded his eyes. "How strange..." he said aloud, rubbing his eyes and looking again. "How *strange...*"

Emerging from the darkened bowels of this metallic denizen of destruction there approached an apparition of such hypnotic splendor that it took Euroaquilo's breath away, he gasping at the sight. Clutching his heart as it began to pain in wild palpitation, the man's mind raced with long-forgotten memories of passionate moments in a far away time and place - haunting dreams of summery nights under a mystical planet's hallowed moon, Sharon, wrapped in the loving arms of a bewitching enchantress singing intoxicating melodies in words foreign to his ears while enraptured by the dizzying, drunken spell created by finely fermented blood-grapes.

Tolohe! Could it be? No, though once she had shared such witchery with him, when he was little more than a lad. But not now, not Tolohe... Her powers of magic and the song were long withered away, these wars having destroyed that magical energy. Then who or what was entering this world of flesh, for its radiant glory transcended that of flesh or spirit, at least on any level Euroaquilo ever witnessed.

The excited passion of the moment pressed forward until it stood but a hand's breadth away. Then a voice called out to him from the blinding luminescence, a voice like that of a thousand doves taking to flight, countless waterfalls cascading from unreachable mountaintops. "My Euroaquilo..."

At that instant, Euroaquilo was swept along by a vision profound. Gone was the captain's bridge, the ship, the spaceport, even Palace City. He found himself in a grassy field filled with brightly colored wildflowers, the sun still in the high noon sky, no breeze, no breath, no singing birds or buzzing insects. All was as if the man stood upon a world frozen in time.

'Strange...! So *strange...!*' The man exclaimed, but no sound came from his lips. Then he began to remember.

Poof! With that first recall of his youth, this silent world around him sprang to life. A breeze tingled his skin, birds flew overhead and bees merrily buzzed among the swaying flowers. Sucking in the invigorating air brought a surge of childlike excitement to Euroaquilo's heart. There he was upon the crest of a low mountain so long forgotten, but well remembered. He turned. Surely, Tolohe must be near, for this was the land to which she delivered him in his youth, during the years she mentored him after his coming of age, a secret land known only to her.

No. No. Wait... Yes, this place looked and felt the same, but it was different. There would be no Tolohe, not today, nor maybe ever again. Things had changed, the world had changed, and now he faced a future uncertain.

Now Euroaquilo recognized where he stood. It was the realm belonging to Time, a realm hidden deep within the mind, for only in the mind can there be a past, present and future. Time, in reality, is only moving forward, yet people are always living in the past, because they are only reacting to what has already happened. True, people may dream of the future, plan for the future, even attempt what the future may bring. Yet all that is based on past experience or happenings. But here, in the Realm of Time, Euroaquilo could become the master of past and future, king of his own destiny.

The world around the man rapidly began to change. Clouds came rushing in from the western sky while the sun raced forward to greet them. Moments later, the winds of Time hit upon Euroaquilo's ears with a deafening roar as the sun plunged beneath the distant horizon only to rise above the eastern plain a heartbeat later.

Faster and faster, day melted into day, until the world was ablaze in a streak of white fire. Winter came and went, then came and went again and again, until the seasons fused together as though but one moment in time. Mountains sank and oceans flooded above their peaks, only for the mountains made anew to arise from the depths of the seas to begin again the process of growing old. And old they did become, over and over. Deserts became jungles, jungles became swamps, swamps became oceans, repeating this cycle until Euroaquilo lost track of time and space. All the while, he and his little knoll upon which he stood altered nary at all. The flowers, birds and bugs all happily continued on as though nothing was amiss.

As quickly as it had begun, it came to an end. The sun slowed until it lingered, high in a clear blue summer sky, and fields of green spread down the mountain into a rising mist far below.

"My Euroaquilo..." The mystical voice called out once more.

Turning, Euroaquilo cast his eyes upon a shadowy form, so entrancing, it features hidden by a radiating light following up close behind. Suddenly, at only a handbreadth away, this glorious light entered the form, it bursting into a brilliant flame of dazzling beauty, taking on the appearance of a woman hauntingly familiar, yet so peculiarly strange.

Euroaquilo stared into a face placid and sublime, at peace. Golden hair danced upon a silent breeze, its afterglow as if taken from the burning sun itself. And the woman's eyes were radiant, glowing, emerald-green furnaces of fire and ice filled with a passion for life. As he stood, transfixed by this wondrous flame of beauty, he began to see a sight both troubling and enchanting to behold. The face was that of the one he called 'DusmeAstron', but it was crowned in hair of splendid gold and had the eyes of a serpent and fangs of a beast.

Surprised, Euroaquilo found his heart filling with passionate desire for this creature. Losing control, he reached out to take hold of the woman, but instead, his hands passed through the ghostly form, he falling ever forward into a blinding abyss. And on he fell - for a moment or an eternity, he could not tell - for he was falling through the realm belonging to Time.

As the wind rushed past, he came to realize that he was not falling, but rather flying through endless space upon the wings of Time. His emotions exploded, having reached their limit in his frail body, flooding over into the expanse around him, creating a melodious crescendo of feelings. Laughing and crying, singing and talking, the man spread his arms and sailed upon the blue nothing faster and faster until he, too, had departed his frail body of flesh and was now one with the universe around him. He was becoming all things - the wind, the moon, sun, the sky, and even the stars. He was part of this universe as much as the universe was part of him.

Ever onward toward Time's destiny Euroaquilo flew, his passion for life growing stronger with each beat of his heart. Soon he saw a distant horizon looming in the mist. Was this his destination, the reason for his journey in this magical vision? He reached out to hurry his journey onward. As he did, gentle words fell again upon his ears.

"My Euroaquilo…."

With a *poof!* the vision ended, but as the last fleeting glimpse passed out of sight, another voice echoed in his ears. 'It all rests in your hands…'

"My Euroaquilo..."

Blinking to chase the last of the fleeting vision from his eyes, Euroaquilo stared into the face of a very troubled Darla. He smiled, his face filled with loving concern. 'She is so beautiful. So much her appearance is that of an innocent babe. How do I save her, and from what? How is my wisdom so great that it should be able to preserve a soul from destruction when Mother's wisdom can find no way to bring it?'

His heart suddenly took a shocking jolt. In that instant, Euroaquilo understood that he must find the answer himself and, if he would listen to his heart, he could find it. At that he smiled, answering, "My DusmeAstron, you have come."

Darla had taken a half step back and, as her radiant emerald-green eyes stared into his gentle hazel orbs, she reached out taking the man's hands in hers. Those same dazzling eyes begged him as her lips pleaded, "My Euroaquilo, only you can save me from this demon within. Help me, please, before all sanity retreats from my soul and my spirit shrivels into the netherworld of nothingness."

Euroaquilo stared at Darla, studying the woman-child as though for the first time. This creature was truly the most beautiful *madwoman* he had ever known. Indeed, as he pondered that beauty, he concluded there to be none ever more charming in appearance other save Tolohe or possibly Mihai. No, Darla was truly of greater beauty than either. How strange he had never noticed it before. The man looked closer.

Darla's face was strong and sharp-featured, yet soft and gentle, with full rich eyebrows, her hair thick and luxuriant. But that was the woman he had always known. Maybe it was the deep, bronzed tan, she being naturally a flawless ivory-white. Or was it the stunning king's jacket, made by Mother's own hands? Such a garment could have magical powers sewn into it. It truly was magnificent, from its thousands of tiny gemstones to the luminescent fabric and mystic runes. Possibly it was the way Darla filled out the jacket. Euroaquilo felt his heart begin to race with a desire that was not appropriate for this moment.

Darla started to speak again. Euroaquilo pulled his hand from hers and placed a finger over her lips. "One moment, please, child. I need a moment."

For the first time in their long relationship, Euroaquilo felt the uncertainty of the moment or their future. The woman was falling into shadow before his very eyes. It was as if he could see an impassable chasm widening between them. As his heart grew fonder of her by the second, she drifted further into distant nothingness. Oh, how he had always taken their relationship for granted! From the day of her coming of age celebration until now she had always been there for him, and he for her.

Now something stood between them. *Time!* It was now the Master over their destiny. It pointed a cruel finger at him, declaring the man delinquent in and negligent of his duties concerning this woman's heart. How much remaining of their hours was Time willing to give, and at what price? Was there already a blade or arrow waiting to remove the two from each other? Destiny…how tricksy it was. It allowed one to choose their own road, but had fated that choice to satisfy its own means.

Like a flash of lightning across an angry sky, Euroaquilo understood the true destiny awaiting them at the Prisoner Exchange. Fate was to decide the hour, but the deed was as good as done. Darkness and uncertainty awaited this woman, for good or evil. Fate cared not, for it was delivering two roads upon the universe, and Darla was the person who would choose which one was to be taken. He also understood that both roads were damning and both dangerous. Both also led off into a dark abyss. Yet the one road held out a glimmer of hope, for it, too, branched off onto other roads, and others beyond that.

And then he saw it, the juncture. Should Darla choose the road of hope, then he must set its course at some uncertain future date. A fiery holocaust loomed up in his mind, along with the realization that her life rested in his destruction. And then the mental intrusion faded away, leaving him alone with his disturbing interludes. Fate was sure tricksy, for it hurried on, keeping further secrets to itself. As it passed, it softly called back to him, 'It rests with you...'

Euroaquilo released Darla's hand, and sweeping his arms around her, drew the woman-child close in a gentle bear hug. He had nearly forgotten how much he loved this person, what with all his responsibilities and concerns regarding navy duties. Oh yes, they had romantic interludes recently, before she reported for duty aboard the Shikkeron. But he had also been with others in the meantime, giving Darla little thought while in their arms.

Now Euroaquilo stood there, holding a most treasured gift, realizing that soon a great chasm was to come between them. How little time remained? An aching pain rose in the man's heart. He looked into Darla's eyes. Already he missed her...her touch, her warmth and her love. Then it struck him, something Mother told him long ago. 'One day, my Darling, that child will get under your skin, and then you will not be able to rid yourself of her. Son, my Rachel, in her own way, has greater love than any of your other siblings. She is closer to my own image than even Mihai.'

So, this was Mother's secret kept from all her children. Mihai's love was but the 'shadow of things to come'. Darla was the treasure that all living things were to seek out to become like the Maker of Worlds. This Euroaquilo now realized in his heart, though no words could he conjure in his mind to truly grasp it. What he did comprehend was that this greatest of all treasures was not assured. All could be lost, first, at the Prisoner Exchange and, if the woman survived that ordeal, then later, but when? Fate refused to disclose that truth. Euroaquilo must wait.

Releasing his grip, Euroaquilo took hold of Darla's upper arms and stepping back, studied her closely. He could see in her eyes the love and trust she placed in him. And, for the first time, he felt that same emotion. Now he was beginning to understand the depth of love he had for her.

After an awkward silence, one which Darla waited ever so patiently upon, Euroaquilo asked, "What must I do to save you from such a terrible demise?"

A tear rolled down Darla's cheek. She was not used to asking for help, and this request the girl saw as begging, an admission of failure. The woman's pride was strong. It had brought her severe tribulation many times and close to death on more than one occasion. Indeed, had Mihai not ordered it, Darla would not have searched out Euroaquilo, but would have sought out some other way to best the demon by herself, no matter the cost. Pride, angry pride, was not finished with this woman yet. For now, it surrendered to the moment, but continued lurking in the shadows for another opportunity to take mastery over her soul.

"My dreams..." Darla so much wanted to run away. Why did she have to ask this man? Had he not fought with her in the land of the Abyss many times? Had they not bested the beast-men who resided in that damnable world, fighting side by side in glorious combat? Why did she have to beg when he should know her needs, offering to take up the battle with her? Her heart pained as feelings of self-pity grew. No! Something had changed in those desolate lands that the woman no longer had the power to control. Looking up into Euroaquilo's eyes, Darla's heart jumped with an aching need for this man. She loved him, wanted him, his touch, his affection. But why did she have to beg?

If the king's command did not burn in her mind, Darla would have darted from the ship, but she was a good girl. "Mihai said you could save me from the evil growing in my dreams."

Smiling, Euroaquilo took hold of Darla's hands. "You honor me with such a request, but I find I have been remiss, for I find that you are saving me from my own guilty dreams."

Confused, Darla asked, "What do you mean, I...?"

Euroaquilo interrupted. "For many days I have known of this coming hour, and I was going to speak of it to you this very morning, but was distracted and forgot. And then I became so occupied with my duties that I lost track of the time. I do beg your forgiveness for my failure to warn my sweet darling. We are nearing the evil hour of Wickedness' birth, and this being the beginning of the Harmonic Years, your demons will only gain in power. My love, few are the living beings, if there are any, who will be able to enter into those dismal lands alone and survive the evil lurking there."

He kissed Darla on the forehead. "You honor me with the request of joining you in the coming battles. Only the bravest and foolhardy will best what is hiding within. Thank you for your great trust you have placed in me. My dear..." He laughed as if in victory. "I will battle beside you and we shall tear down the Devil's house!"

Darla smiled, Euroaquilo having salved her feelings again. He was so good at doing that, but she puzzled, "You speak in riddles. Is the ending hour arrived so that prophecies have come to their full, and what are the Harmonic Years you speak of?"

Euroaquilo's face clouded and his voice became grave. "No, my child, I do not speak of an ending, but a beginning. You see, fourteen days from this very hour will begin the anniversary of the first great act of defiance and the beginning of the Third Age, the Age of Rebellion...the day of our sister's attempted murder and when the world, as we know it, came to an end."

"That's the day and hour of the Prisoner Exchange!" Darla looked away in thought, finally looking back into Euroaquilo's eyes. "How does such a fate bring us to that time?"

Euroaquilo sputtered bitter. "It's not fate! It's Asotos. He doesn't just *happen* anything! No, Dear. Every detail of this little adventure has been carefully orchestrated. By now, I suppose, he knows our plans, too, who will be there and how many." He shook his head in dismay. "He has spies every-where. It has become difficult to trust anyone anymore."

Taking Darla by the upper arms, he warned her, "My Dusme, the evil living within the heart of this man is far beyond your ability to comprehend. The things you have been told or witnessed are nothing compared to what Asotos is willing to do. If he could, he would take all those whom he hates and surrender them to a living Hell for all eternity, paying the occasional visit upon them to make sure they were suffering appropriately. This is what he has already attempted with Mihai, and you suffer the effects. Dear, he wants Mihai... and you... to go mad forever, and will stop at nothing to accomplish that."

Darla put on a bold face of defiance. "I have raised the sword against many wicked men. I have found little to fear other than from the steel in their hands. This *Asotos* is little different."

Euroaquilo frowned, "Do be careful! This man is not like you or me. It is said the power of the Cherubs resides within him, given as a gift to him by Mother, herself. He still retains much of that power. Why, with his mind, alone, he could disarm you and rip the flesh from your bones. He can control the weather, my Dear. It is even said that he knows the secrets of life itself. That's how he made the demons in your head."

Darla sputtered. "He's a man... a fool of a man! He is not immortal. I have witnessed the coward on the field of battle, how he hides behind the others, using them as his shield-wall while hiding in caves. Powerful? Yes, I suppose, but like the mythical Cherubs to whom all creation owes its existence?" Darla laughed. "They are no more real than angels of Mareemah...tales for little children they are." She laughed again.

Cautioning her, Euroaquilo wagged a finger, "Do be careful! The Ancients did not tell us those stories merely to entertain little children. There is often truth hidden in tales…tales, may I add, that were oft told us for a purpose. Indeed! Had we children truly listened to those *fables,* the evil may never been borne upon us."

"All right… All right…." Darla raised her hand, waving off the matter.

"No! Don't think yourself so wise!" Euroaquilo scolded. "Asotos can get in a person's mind with his warped and twisted reasonings. When you were but a foolish babe, I watched so many of our wisest leaders fall into darkness following his winsome words. Some of my closest companions and lovers surrendered up all reasoning, believing the twisted lies of that murderer. Oh yes, I say *murderer!* True, Mihai did not die, at least in body, but she was devastated in mind and spirit, and has only been a shadow of the woman she used to be ever since. But also, within days of that torture, Asotos did murder several of my sisters in his rage and anger."

He wagged his finger again. "Do be afraid should you need to face this man at the Prisoner Exchange, and well may that be the case. Mother does not deliver you up to this event for your entertainment! Darkness looms ahead for anyone confronting this man, and that includes you if it has been chosen to have you delivered up to him. Life and death will both walk the edge of a very sharp blade that day. If one falls, then there will be no hope for them. I must warn you, for I have witnessed it. There are those with greater faith in Mother than you who have fallen to him."

Taking hold of Darla's hand, he explained, "Our new field marshal spoke of two ravens among us. She warned us of just how tricksy they are. You know of Mother's riddling, tricksy ways. Do you believe that the one made in her image and receiving so many of her sacred secrets does not possess many of those same tricksy powers? No, Dear One, Mother comes with us into this storm because she sees the danger within. Pray that she will act the raven to the limit, or total disaster awaits us there."

Euroaquilo kissed Darla on the forehead again. He leaned back, so concerned. "I fear your loss at this exchange, for I feel you have been set up to answer to Fate's desires. I have heard accounts today concerning you, and now I see that you wear the coat of the king, made by the gods them-selves, the very ones you deny. All afternoon I have been troubled in spirit concerning you. My head has been filled by waking visions with confound-ing meanings. My Dusme, you are a star-child, fated to a road that leads to life or damnation, not just for you, but also for all living flesh. The journey you have has already been decided by Fate, but the road remains of your choosing."

Darla countered. "I am a woman with free will! *I* choose my fate. It does not serve as lord over me!"

Euroaquilo offered a quick retort. "You are a fool if you think fingers do not dabble in your life! You chose to do what you did? *Really?* You are as predictable as the sunrise to those who know you well, and Mother knows you better than anyone else."

Darla did not argue, but had no desire to discuss the matter further, so changed the subject by asking, "Please tell me, if all this is so important to know, what are the Harmonic Years?"

Resting his hands on Darla's shoulders, Euroaquilo shook his head. "*Strong-headed woman!* I will not be dissuaded from this discourse, but will return to it. I will only tell you this concerning the Harmonic Years, seeing you have not learned your history lessons well. There will soon come upon this universe - on all known universes - the Great Juncture, a time when all things are made new or are renewed. That, even a wayward student of history should know about. The Harmonic Years precede that time. It is a period of great unrest and change. It's as though the universe is preparing for coming events. During the Second Age, it was a time of great celebration because our spiritual insight became heightened, our visions sharper, our self-awareness keener."

Euroaquilo frowned. "But when the darkness came into our world, a fear fell upon the children, they realizing that another Great Juncture must come before the evil would be brought to a finish. It is believed that evil will be heightened during the Harmonic Years, growing in power until it threatens to consume all good found in the universe. The evidence of that reality can already be seen with you and Mihai. Those demons you have are growing stronger with each passing day."

"Now!" Euroaquilo put on his mentor face. "I will conclude the previous matter..."

Darla harrumphed. "I was *not* destined to come here! I had free will to choose the course I took! Since it was a reasonable one, I decided to come even though it was not made easy by you."

Closing his eyes in growing frustration, Euroaquilo replied, "Dusme, do you really think the events of this day have only come about by *blind chance*? Why, the gossip among the entire company is about you - this morning, and the king's jacket that you're wearing, and about this most beautiful of women seen flitting from ship to ship. And your comely appearance? The men have been able to speak of nothing else since your visits upon them. Even I, your long-time lover, find an aching burning within my soul to be consumed by your love. To not take you at this very moment is taxing my constitution to the limit."

"Then *take* me!" Darla peered into Euroaquilo's eyes, teasingly. "Pick the flowers of my love. Leave off this *horrid* conversation for the bed of delights and passion."

Euroaquilo looked longingly at Darla, sliding a hand off her shoulder and across her breast, caressing it with a gentle squeeze. He looked back into Darla's eyes with desire, but his face clouded over. Disgusted, he spun around and walked some distance away before turning back.

An angry edge remained in his voice as he shot back a rebuke. "*Fool!* The women in Asotos' camp sell their charms to remain alive, but you *whore* yourself to only put an end to a conversation. Whether it is for money, survival, or meaningless gain - even if it is with your lover - it is upon the altar of the prostitute that you place your vile offering! You sell yourself so cheaply… for but a word!"

Euroaquilo fumed, raising a hand in gesture. "Do you think my words to be little more than verbal flatulence?! That I speak like the dimwitted chatterers, only to listen for the echo of my own utterances? You believe you think for yourself? *You are little more than a puppet dancing to the tune of others.*" He thumped his chest. "I fated you here, to this very spot! Yes, even I, a simple man, manipulated you into doing his will. You are *so easily manipulated...*"

Stunned by Euroaquilo's rebuke, but unwilling to surrender the moment, Darla retorted, defending her actions, "I *was not* destined to come here! I had *free will* to choose… *to do as I please!*"

Euroaquilo dropped his hand in frustration. Looking toward the floor, he sadly shook his head. "Pride comes before a fall, and fall you will unless you learn wisdom. Do you think for one minute that Mother is unable to know your very thoughts, how you will act, whom you will listen to and obey? You *did not* come here of your own free will. It was as if hooks had been set in your nose and you were dragged here by force. Never have you disobeyed Mihai. We all know that. When ordered by her to find me, you would have moved heaven and earth to carry out the command."

Darla lowered her head and tears fell. She was shamed by Euroaquilo's accusations. It hurt so to be called such an abhorrent thing, but it hurt almost as much to be told that she didn't have control of her life. She survived by that belief, to think that she controlled something - her own soul - that she did as she chose.

Euroaquilo returned to Darla, taking her hands ever so gently. "Look, we all are predictable to Mother. I'm not saying that our lives are planned out and our journeys prepared on some mystical chart that satisfies some grand divine purpose, but we are players on a huge game board, allowing ourselves to be moved about as our Master sees fit. And our Master knows us well, better than we, ourselves."

He squeezed her hands. "I fear for you because I know better than you how much a puppet-master Asotos is, too. The man is so clever. He can get inside your head and twist reasoning until the absurd becomes normal, good becomes bad, and right become wrong. I have witnessed it many times, and I even see it in your eyes as I speak. Your demon is a manifestation of its master. It is very intelligent and plays on your desire for love and respect. It will be very strong by the time of the Prisoner Exchange. Its mission is to hand you over to its master."

Darla's tear-filled eyes stared into Euroaquilo's. "But you called *me* a whore, not my demon. Do you know the pain you have inflicted upon me?"

Euroaquilo proffered, waving his hand, "Better is it to tear apart the heart than to see soul, flesh and heart burn forever in the fires of Gehenna. You may hate me on the 'morrow, but if that should be the cost to me to save your soul this day, then it has been worth the price."

Darla buried her head in Euroaquilo's chest. "No… No… I cannot hate you! I love you too much to hate you. My Lord, *you are my life and breath! I will not, cannot live without you!*"

Euroaquilo warned, "That confession may well be used against you in future days. Fate listens at all times. Your love for me is your weakness, which means it is the enemy's strength. Already they know of it. If they choose to destroy you, they already have their weapon. It is now but a choice as to who will use that weapon first, and in what way. Even in this our Fates are sealed."

Darla looked up, eyes pleading for Euroaquilo to deny his last statement. He refused, adding, "There is no planet upon which men have trod that the sun does not come up in the east, for by our very nature the sun must do as we declare it to do. You think yourself wise? I have lived more millennia than you have lived years, and you wish for me to desist in offering my wisdom? I will risk even your hatred, if that's what it takes to save you."

Euroaquilo shook his finger toward her. "Your pride seeks your glory before its time. Great will be the tribulation to one holding, alone, the torch of battle. Listen to my wisdom and learn so that upon wings of Cherubs you will be lifted up to that coming glory."

With that, Euroaquilo began to explain the depth and height of his secret wisdom, at least secret to this child of such *tender years*. Darla's ears tingled, her heart aching from the intrigue. She discovered quickly that her lover was no *simple* man, but a wizard of mind and tongue. Long before the Rebellion, he was recognized as an outstanding leader among his kind, sitting with the Great Lords on Ma-we's council of the Twenty-Four Elders. He was seated to that Council and given powers far beyond normal when he was little older than Darla was now. And she learned it was he who took to the caring of her after the Rebellion began, tending to the girl's injuries and reviving her soul from death while Ma-we rested in a fitful coma after Mihai's brutal attack.

Euroaquilo went on to reveal many unknown secrets concerning Mihai's attack and its aftereffects, the things Asotos did to prepare the woman for that hour, to make her even more vulnerable to his attack. He explained in detail the evidence found that showed how Asotos planned for months, possibly years, to bring Mihai to ruin. He also confided his belief that Mihai's death was never intended, but that something far more sinister was Asotos' purpose.

He concluded, "My sister's soul was destroyed in that hour. Everything in her life, from her twelfth year unto that moment was stolen from her. You see, she loved that beast even more than you love me. Her entire life revolved around pleasing him, something she strived for but never accomplished. She still seeks his approval down to this day, yet does not know it. My Dear, you and Mihai are so close for many other reasons than you know: one is that she was born anew on that wicked day and is but your age in mind and spirit. You understand her in ways that no other person can."

The man smiled. "Our sister speaks secrets to you that she cannot even speak to her own heart. There is hope alive even now, because she trusts you beyond measure. *You* are her hope. That you remain standing gives her faith that she, too, will survive this ordeal."

Darla asked, "Of the Exchange, you say it occurs on the very hour of Mihai's violation and torture? This Mihai must already know, and thus be preparing for. What can the Great Serpent achieve by all his reckoning?"

"The miscreant is full of mischief!" Euroaquilo answered, adding, "His intent, I believe, is to goad Mihai into some kind of foolishness so that he can slaughter the prisoners and as many of Mihai's troops as possible. And he will attempt the capture of Mihai, herself. We believe the attack on the Zephath was not random, but carefully orchestrated to obtain Sirion's capture, or at least that's what was first believed. I think now it was to capture another soul who was much closer to Mother's heart."

"Oh yes, Asotos will use Sirion to get Mihai's dander up, but it will only be a ruse to obtain his true objective… to *destroy Mother's heart.*"

Darla asked, pondering, "You speak with concern for my welfare when all that is told me betrays an assault against our sister and Mother. Where does this pertain to me when I do not even go with Mihai? I stand a horse-maiden for Lowenah in her entourage, not even knowing the reason for my presence."

Rubbing his bearded chin in thought, Euroaquilo answered, "I do not know, but I feel it may deal more with who you are…or aren't. You see, among Mother's daughters, you are the only child to have not shared Asotos' bed. He has not given you his dreams, nor does he have your signature. Every woman he has known he keeps a mental note of, and he does not forget. You will be a puzzle to him, an enigma, a distraction."

"So I'm just a decoy, then?" Darla grumped.

Euroaquilo grinned, shaking his head. "No, I think not. If I am correct - for I know Asotos is a very curious man - when he discovers something is amiss with you, he will pursue an answer. That may well prove to be a pivotal moment at the Prisoner Exchange, but a *very dangerous one* for you. My Darling, all day my spirit has been agitated over you. There is a shroud of impenetrable gloom surrounding you. I feel Fate is allowing you to choose, and the decision you make may well affect far more than the Prisoner Exchange."

Angrily, Darla retorted, her tone bitter, "*My* decision?! With that fool, Ardon, beside me, I will not have a choice of when to relieve nature!"

Euroaquilo shot Darla a warning rebuke. "That's quite enough! It is true that Ardon has many lessons yet to learn. Today's was one he will likely long remember. Do not cast away an ally because he smells bad to your nostrils. One day you may wish to have Ardon's…"

Darla spat, "*I wish that old bag 'a shit dead!* Should have done it when I had the chance…"

"Oh, do you really?" Euroaquilo asked smugly.

Darla squinted, spitting venomously, "*Yes*! I mean it with all my heart…"

Speaking as if a prophet, Euroaquilo raised a hand, shaking his finger in her face, "You betray your feelings. Beware! If you survive the coming tribulation, you may well be thankful you saved his life this day. Possibly, you may well find that it is *he* who will one day save you from the bottomless pit. This I do know and believe…you could not have hurt that man this day anymore than you could have hurt Mihai. Rather would you have stood the blast from your own weapon than to hurt one hair on the head of a person so loved by Mother."

"That is not so!" Darla fussed. "One more step and he would have been a dead man! My monster within was gaining control over my flesh…"

Euroaquilo disagreed. "You did not meet by chance this day. Mother set you up to be there, she arranging for the Shikkeron to be the council's transport. She trusted that you could do him no harm, you knowing full well his loyalty to her in her early days of distress. He defended your sister to the point up to death when Asotos attempted to assail her as she convalesced behind the Palace walls. He even stood vigil over your bed, helping me with his healing songs as you fought back the fires of an infectious fever. He did not violate your sister - that you know - and he did not, with evil intention, violate you today."

Darla's eyes betrayed her hatred for Ardon.

Gripping tight her upper arms, Euroaquilo warned, "*One who hates a child so loved by Lowenah does despise the very soul of the one birthing that child!*"

Darla's eyes flashed fury as she cursed Euroaquilo. "*Never say that to me again! You've no right to interfere, you son of empty words!*"

Euroaquilo moved faster than a heartbeat, clutching Darla tight in his iron grip and slamming her against the elevator rail, setting Darla's head in a spin. He angrily spat, "*I will speak as I damn well please! No urchin of self-pity can stop me! I am the StormWind, and don't give a good god-damned for the soul who forgets that! If you are stupid enough to believe I speak folly, then there is no hope left for you. You will perish within a fortnight, and rightfully all flesh will curse the day of your birth!*"

He began to lift the girl. "Better is it to chance a rebirth with the revived demon than to send you to certain damnation before the Prince of Lies! I shall risk my soul to the eternal abyss and hope a cure will become yours in future days by pitching you to the depths below than to hand you over to such a fate! Your damned self-pity has destroyed your heart! *I will not allow it to destroy your soul…*"

Darla cried out in pain when an upper rail post cracked a rib as Euroaquilo pressed hard upon her. He lessened his iron grip for just a moment, giving time for reflective thought. What good would such an act of chivalry really accomplish? If Darla was already lost from the Field of the Minds, nothing could save her. If she was not? What would her murder really accomplish, her momentary destruction, possibly leading to an abysmal eternity in a living Hell secreted in her mind? And what of him? Would his own destruction prove anyone righteous? Asotos would surely presume himself justified when learning of the dastardly act, declaring Mother unfit to rule.

Darla broke the silence. With tears of pain running down her face, she begged, "My Lord! My Lord! Do not waste your treasures on a *maggot* like me! I am not fit to be counted among the stupid ones. Allow me, please, to bring this all to an end on my own, and save yourself innocent."

In a panic, Euroaquilo yanked Darla into his encircling arms, crushing her to the point where she cried out again in agony. Tears streaming down his face, he pleaded, "Please! Please promise me, first, that you will not do such folly! *Promise me!*"

A faint was growing upon Darla's mind. She little remembered her reply other than to promise, and then asked before being whisked away into the blackness, "Will you help me with my dreams?"

Euroaquilo gently lowered Darla to the floor, sitting and cradling her in his arms. Moments passed quickly and the woman soon recovered from her fainting spell. Resting there, looking up into the face of the man so dear to her heart, Darla whispered, "I love you…"

అ   అ   అ

Mihai's transport frigate, the DishonPele, sat quietly on the tarmac, its crew having finished most of their duties, resting, awaiting orders for departure. Out front, just beyond the ship's nose, a half dozen of the crew were busy taking down the two tents where guests were entertained before boarding, they carefully packing up to stow these materials for future use. Mihai had sent back Ma-we's carriage. Now it was returned, parked near the ship's belly loading ramp to be used to transport the remaining well-wishers saying their goodbyes to companions traveling to the Prisoner Exchange.

Symeon gave Jonathan a giant bear hug. Stepping back, he grabbed him by the shoulders, smiling as tears grew in his eyes. "I really did want to go, you know. We've been through a lot in times past and it felt good to see us take on another adventure again. I'll miss you."

Thunder rumbled across the spaceport, everyone looking heavenward to watch the ominous clouds threatening a downpour. Jonathan looked back at Symeon, smiling, "Come now, not so glum, old fellow. Not everyone gets to have all their wishes given up to them so fast. First, your girl here..." He pointed toward Hanna. "And then the child you love so much? Hey! I think it's a fair trade."

Hanna wrapped her hands around Jonathan's arm and kissed him on his bearded cheek. "I'll miss you, too. Do be careful. I've heard things, and do believe our coming adventure is far less hazardous than yours."

"Have no worry, my dear, sweet lady. Mr. Fuddy-Duddy here will be in my company for this journey." Jebbson Garlock pranced down the loading ramp, releasing Tolmetes' hand. Stepping up behind Jonathan, he slapped him on the shoulder. "The poor fellow will be quite safe from the bogeyman." He squeezed his shoulder. "Won't you, Boy' O?"

Jonathan offered a perturbed reply, looking at Jebbson, frowning. "I am quite able to care for myself, thank you. And should I need assistance, it will not be in your direction I'll be calling. And stop using those big words with little meanings that neither I nor any of the rest of us understands."

"Oh, s'cuse me, Captain, didn't mean to ruffle any feathers." Jebbson winked at Hanna. "Just wanted to make this charming lady here feel reassured that we'd bring this ol' granny grunt back to her, safe and sound."

Jonathan snorted disapprovingly. "Don't call me 'granny grunt'! And if you want anything from *this* lady, it has nothing to do with my welfare... or hers."

"Well!" Jebbson pretended offense. "I should be insulted, and in front of mixed company."

Hanna laughed. "And might it be so if his arrow didn't strike so true." She extended her hand to Jebbson. "I will permit a knightly kiss for your promise to return my gallant squire safely home to me, but a kiss is all that I will surrender up to you. My heart, tonight, belongs to my prince, and all that is mine I freely give to him."

Jebbson glanced at Symeon, who was putting on a blush. He then gave Hanna a tender kiss on her hand, extolling his remorse at having lost the battle to such a worthy foe. He grinned. "My lovely Hanna, you are a charm.

Few are the women from this world, let alone ours, who have ever taken such pains to learn the history and culture of so many people. You honor me with your whimsical poetry."

Before Hanna could reply, Jonathan asked, "By the by, why did you manage your way over here today, and shouldn't you be on your way, seeing we leave shortly?"

Tolmetes stepped up to Jebbson, hugging his arm. "This good fellow came to deliver me to the Shikkeron, not wishing I have to make such a journey all alone. I've pressing business with Tashi that needs immediate attention. Mr. Garlock has been gracious enough to offer me assistance and accommodations for my visit."

Someone commented about the 'frying pan and into the fire'. Everyone laughed. Jebbson grinned, giving Tolmetes an affectionate glance.

"Oh yes!" Jebbson snapped his fingers as if remembering. "I've need of transportation for two. Seeing it is some distance, and it's about to pour, I'd hoped I could call upon your mercies to deliver us to the Shikkeron when you take your leave today."

Hannah hugged Symeon, asking, "Do you think it prudent to allow such a cad take up company with us? You know, Dear, there are *those* among us who might feel our reputations would be sullied by doing such a thing."

Jonathan harrumphed, "Now you two? Have I any allies in this camp of villains?"

Anna had been chatting with some companions when she heard Jonathan's complaints. She called out and came over to him. "I'm still your companion..." She brushed a hand through his thick wavy hair, smiling, "I've business to attend to momentarily, but would so much like your companionship for dinner tonight. Sweetheart, will you be so kind to join with me in the captain's cabin at seven? It's a small group, but it'll be a fun way to begin our journey. Then, at nine there's music in the main galley where there'll be a little dancing. I could use your company."

Jonathan grinned sheepishly, nodding. "It would be a pleasure, my Lady."

Jebbson slapped Jonathan on the back as Anna hurried away. "There, Boy' O, you got at least one close friend. I'd 'av invited you for dinner, myself, but none of that danc'n stuff afterward."

"You're incorrigible!" Jonathan snorted. He turned and looked Jebbson in the face, wearing such a serious frown. "And I dare say you would not do a dress any compliment either!"

Everyone burst out laughing. Jebbson nodded his agreement, but defended his appearance. "My knees are quite handsome in kilts, but that's as close as you'll all see me in a dress, I'd say."

At that moment, Paul stepped into the group, putting his arms around the shoulders of Jonathan and Jebbson. "This is what makes the parting of ways more tolerable. Remember these moments, my friends. The memory of mirth warms many a heart on cold winter nights."

Symeon piped in. "True, true… But a box unwrapped can fill a heart with joyful anticipation. My friends, a salute to the future! This is only the beginning of the Day of Dreams. Who knows what surprises await us on the 'morrow. With companions like you, it will be all the more joyous."

"Yea! Yea!" came a return chorus of approving shouts. Someone produced a flask of rum and passed it around, thus starting a tradition that has lasted down to this day.

᭓   ᭓   ᭓

(*Author's Note:* '*Passing the Circle', or 'Dancing the Circle Rum', as some call it, a hearty farewell celebration practiced when good companions part for distant places, had its humble beginnings on that stormy afternoon so long ago. Some say it was because it was the last happy departing of friends before darkness fell upon the universe. Others just say it was remembered because people like to remember good things. I personally believe it is because there is a child inside all of us that seeks reasons for parties and one for departing companions is as good as any.*)

᭓   ᭓   ᭓

A gust of wind pelted the gathering with a cold blast of swirling rain just as the sky opened up its watery tempest, accompanying the deluge with a cacophony of thunderous crescendos. Many in the crowd scattered, some hurrying up the ramp while Jebbson and Tolmetes headed for the carriage, Jebbson doing his best to protect Tolmetes from the whipping showers. Hanna hugged Symeon as he wrapped his hooded cloak around her. Mihai turned her back, shivering from the chill blow, she wearing no coat or jacket. Paul called out to her, pulling her close. Zadar took hold of Trisha and joined Jonathan, all huddling together to wait out the initial attack of the storm.

Out of the driving rain, a small baggage truck approached, its large round headlights appearing suddenly through the frothing downpour. Stopping up short, just beneath the belly of the ship, the machine's side door opened and two very drenched passengers crawled out. Eutychus turned back to Planetee as she struggled to wrap his soaked coat around herself, he extending a hand to assist her.

Planetee laughed when Eutychus caught her up after she slipped and nearly fell on the wet tarmac. Eutychus beamed, clutching Planetee's arm to prevent her from having another spill. Planetee snuggled up close, allowing the fellow to play the part of her hero. Then, after waving a 'thank you' to the driver, the two hurried over to the others awaiting their arrival.

"Well, it's about time!" Mihai shouted to Planetee. She looked a sight, hunched over, hugging herself, shivering from the wet and cold. But other than being cold, Mihai was in a surprisingly good mood, chiding the two for being late. "I was about to send out a search party, my suspicions growing that my duty officer had run off with our steward."

Tipping her head back, laughing, her dark satin hair glistening from its soaking, still holding tight to Eutychus, Planetee defended their tardiness. "We have not arrived late! It is the *storm* that arrived *early*, catching us in a torrential maelstrom. Had not that wonderful lorry driver been kind enough to deliver us from that tempest, I believe we would have both drowned... nearly did, anyway."

Jebbson pulled aside the curtain window of the carriage and called out his salutations, waving andPlanetee smiled back. Looking around at the others, she jokingly fussed, "Is there no sense among you? Drowned rug rats, that's what the lot of you look like. At least we had an excuse, getting caught out in this storm, doing our duty and all. What a poor and pathetic picture you fellows make..."

Eyeing Planetee, Mihai teased, "Couldn't leave you go alone with our steward, now could we? Especially after hearing that the two of you took off alone this morning, we were about to call the port authorities to have them find you, thinking you might stow away in another ship just so as to have him all to yourself for this trip."

Paul piped up, eyeing Eutychus. "Oh, I wouldn't blame the lady. That Eutychus has a devious way about him, all innocent and bashful on the outside, a real lady's man on the inside. I feared he'd taken off with our councilor here, and whisked her off to some secret lair." Eutychus' face reddened. He had a good time with Planetee that day, but the thought of romance never entered his mind, and to have the subject brought up in such a *provocative* way was really too much. He managed only to stutter his innocence, much to the amusement of the others.

Planetee retorted, "That's enough, right now!" adding smugly, "If you cannot respect my gallant hero, then I shall just have to keep him safe for myself!" Shaking his head, Zadar chimed in, "You only want a personal servant, leaving me to be the lone steward to tend to the needs of the others." Smirking, Planetee replied, "Well, if they haven't the ability to treat good help courteously, then I wonder if they deserve a steward at all. I shall be kind and undemanding."

There were whoops and cries aplenty, some expressing the unfairness of such treachery, others of a more questionable nature. Finally, Planetee declared, she pulling on Eutychus as though being her possession, "This eve, my gallant knight belongs to me. I shall reward him for his valor and treat him with the honor he deserves. On the 'morrow, I will decide if *you* deserve his attention."

More fussing ensued. Mihai, who by this time was thoroughly soaked and chilled, put an end to the friendly jousting. "Enough of such foolishness! I shall not die here debating the duties of our stewards. Come along now!" She pointed at Eutychus while addressing Planetee. "We waited upon you to be able to finish our business. You may choose to keep your *hero* to yourself *after* our business is finished. Bring him along for now and let's get out of this terrible weather." She turned and hurried toward the ship.

Starting up its ramp, Mihai snapped her head around, calling, "Be safe, Symeon… Hanna. I'll see you when we get back." She motioned to Trisha and Planetee and then hustled along, disappearing into the welcomed warmth of the ship.

Paul stepped up and kissed Hanna, warning, "Do be careful, now. I've doubts about the nobility of your companion. He may be kindly and look innocent, but his winsome words can persuade worlds. I fear his concerns for your welfare are not all as chivalrous as he implies." Jonathan adding, "You would have been safer if you had taken up company with that gentlemna in the carriage." He tilted his head in the direction of Ma-we's machine, and then stepped up to kiss Hanna goodbye.

Symeon sputtered, "That's quite enough of both of you. You're hopeless. At least Garlock there lets you know what he's about. Calls you out for who he thinks you are. I'll take his company any day over the likes of troublemakers like you two." Jebbson shouted out to Symeon after hearing what he said. "Spoken like a scholar and a gentleman. Now, come on and let us be gone, before the Shikkeron leaves us so's I'll not be around to protect Jonathan when he needs our help at the Prisoner Exchange." Jonathan pushed his hands away toward Jebbson, telling Symeon and Hanna, "Take him with you and I'll make it worth your while upon my return."

Hanna reached out, taking Jonathan's hand, grinning, "I'm so sorry, but our business will consume all our time. Besides, I feel there may be some truth hidden in Mr. Jebbson's humor. We must be off." She pulled Zadar over and kissed him on the lips. "Be safe, my friend. You make the world a wonderful place. There are so few like you. I love you… love all three of you. Take care of my sister, please. She carries the world on her shoulders. This is not like past prisoner exchanges. This one's different. I feel it in my gut. We, the Children of Darkness, have not arrived in your world to return its former glory. A new day dawns red on the universe."

Zadar smiled sadly. "My Lady, you… your kind has made my world a wonderful place. Too bad it is that your arrival must usher in the darkness that was prophesied to come. We have failed. Your kind must win. I believe your sister is going to put the universe on notice that a new game is going to be played, and this time it goes to the finish. No more armistices. I shall willingly surrender up my life to preserve hers, but I feel it is an unnecessary offer."

Thunder rolled across the spaceport, shaking the ground. Zadar hugged Symeon, wishing him well. With parting pleasantries, he waved Hanna and Symeon off as they hurried toward the carriage. He, Jonathan and Paul silently watched the tiny machine fade into driving rain, its amber taillights winking out their goodbyes.

The three hurried toward the ship. Starting up the ramp, Zadar stopped and turned. "I do not understand your kind at all. Your people are so much younger, like shoots of spring grass, yet your depth of heart and mind defies that age. Here I find a woman of your kind who messes up my head, sets ablaze fires in my heart, and fills me with longing for her company. Never have I felt this way. Has Mother cast a spell over me?"

Paul patted Zadar on the shoulder, laughing. "Bewitching, isn't it? Look, it's cold out here. I think we need to discuss the matter in greater detail over some hot buttered rum."

Jonathan nudged Zadar. "We may be ages younger than you, but we do know that hot food and drink along with good company can make any riddle easier to solve."

Zadar smiled and nodded. Together, the three scampered up the ramp in search of an early meal and hearty drinks, and Zadar getting answers to troubling questions.

జ   జ   జ

Darla and Euroaquilo rested in two of the folding command chairs on the captain's bridge, the surgeon having recently departed after tending Darla's injuries. No one questioned the couple's flimsy excuse of her stumbling against the elevator handrail. Long ago the ship's medical officer learned not to pry into other's business, not when they were soldiers like Darla and Euroaquilo. Besides, it would do no good. They had disclosed what was necessary to make out a report, and that was all there would ever be to it, ever.

With her ribs wrapped and having taken a mild pain killer, Darla relaxed with her steaming beverage, attentively listening, while Euroaquilo filled in details concerning the early days of the Rebellion just after Mihai's being attacked by Asotos. There was a sudden explosion of blinding light that flashed through the portholes and across the bridge, instantly followed by crashing thunder that shook the entire ship, jolting both Euroaquilo and Darla.

When the rumbling subsided, Euroaquilo wryly commented, "These are really quite flimsy machines without their energy shields. In fact, I doubt the best of our dreadnaughts could hold up to the stresses of the jump portals without 'em. When you're all wrapped up in those protective swaddling bands, you forget just how fragile a world we have created should those shields ever fail."

Darla nodded, saying nothing.

Lightning again flashed across the darkened bridge, quickly followed by another rumble of angry thunder. Euroaquilo smiled. "This storm will delay our departure. It gives us a little more time to chat before I have to get the crew up to do their preflight checks. Come on, let me show you something."

Taking Darla's hand, the two walked forward, stopping at a large porthole. Euroaquilo rocked back, supporting his weight on his heels. "The first time I stood here, in this very spot, I saw a tarmac filled with countless warships, hundreds of big cruisers along with thousands of smaller ships. For as far as the eye could see, there were ships preparing for war." He rocked forward. "Yep, right here on this very spot."

Darla slid her arm around Euroaquilo's waist, asking, "So you have been on this ship before? When?"

Smiling, Euroaquilo answered, "This was the first big dreadnaught I captained. I also commanded a half dozen tenders and support ships, something typical back then for a capital ship of this size."

He stared out the window, watching the lightning dance in the ragged sky, but his mind wandered to past events. "I was so nervous, being sure that every captain in the fleet was scrutinizing me, judging me as to fitness for such an important position. I wanted to do everything just right. Well, when I looked out across the gathering armada, I could not believe in anything but a swift victory. Nothing this big had ever been assembled, and it wasn't just here. Why, we were collecting everything we had. At every port in the Empire, warships were assembling."

Looking at Darla, he asked, "Do you recall hearing about Operation Willow? It was a grand operation staged in the latter part of the Great War, leading up to the Day of Tears."

Darla replied, "No, I was serving in a combat platoon stationed at Mordem at that time. I had taken a stint in the army for a change of scenery. What was Operation Willow?"

Euroaquilo explained, "It was command's idea that the war might be decided in naval combat if we could concentrate a large enough flotilla of ships in one general area. By hitting the enemy with overwhelming force we, it was believed, would decimate Asotos' defending fleets with little loss to ours. Then, we would roll up the fence, taking out one after another of his scattered armadas, thus driving him out of our Empire. With the skies cleared of his intrusions, we could bypass his stranded, landed forces and proceed with our own invasion of his territories."

He shook his head sadly. "It might have worked if we hadn't been betrayed by spies. Asotos got wind of it in time to make counter preparations. The day we sallied forth into these skies, singing our victory songs as if the battle was over, the die had already been cast. We were sailing off into the biggest bloodbath in the history of all our wars."

He asked, still looking out the porthole, "Do you know much about the Day of Tears?"

Darla said little. "A little… I was there for some of it." Then, in the same breath, she requested, "Please, tell me about your part in it, you know, things you have never shared with me in your dreams."

Euroaquilo raised an eyebrow, pondering. Darla's interest concerning his part in the Day of Tears debacle was curious, seeing she already knew so much about it through their dream-shares. Still, he would fill in a few details first, and then probe for other answers after.

"As you may already know, our battle group of thirty-some fighting ships, under the command of Admiral Lonche, had been running picket duty to the Q South and West of point during the first three days of the contest. Action was light, mostly skirmishes among our outrider patrols. Well, just after midnight, we received distress calls from Admiral Nachliel-iTzach's Fourteenth Fleet that it was under heavy attack and falling back with mounting losses."

"Fully understanding the need to maintain our fighting line in that sector to prevent the main body from being flanked, Admiral Lonche ordered our battle group to advance to the Fourteenth's aid. My attack group being the furthest south made contact with the enemy first. We joined the contest in support of two damaged carriers that were under heavy attack, flying right into a slaughterhouse. It appeared as if the entire enemy navy was upon us. We mixed it up as best we could but, by the time the remainder of Lonche's battle group arrived, half my fighting ships were destroyed or disabled."

"The DusmeAstron had taken several hits, but was holding strong. Then, about three hours into the fight, a missile tore into our already damaged port engine room, tearing the outer pod to pieces, killing everyone in the engine room and condensing chamber. Our boiler rooms and reactor went offline, leaving us with only our auxiliary backup systems."

"With weakened energy shields, we became more susceptible to enemy missiles. The ship absorbed several smaller strikes, fouling our ventilation systems, damaging the gravity machines and starting fires. Then we took a hit right outside the hull, here, where I'm standing, sending a concussive blast filled with thousands of metal shards across the navigation bridge. Six of the crew were torn asunder from the explosion, several more severely wounded."

"I was standing behind the navigation tower, back there, when the missile hit, saving me from death. Still, my eardrums were ruptured and I was in a daze, having hit my head on the bosun's rail. I staggered to my feet, making my way forward to explore the damage and stopped here to catch my breath, glancing out this porthole as I did. What I saw made my heart sink. There, before me, while fire crews fought to save the ship and medics did the same to save lives, in silence I stared into the face of our coming doom."

"What was it?!" Darla asked, eyes big with wonder. "You've never told me about this."

With furrowed eyebrow, Euroaquilo stared at Darla. "I guess we *all* have our *little private secrets…*" and he returned to his account. "There, I'd say about five miles out, the ancient carrack, Ambrosia, was making steam for the DusmeAstron. That old capital ship was designed for slow speed ramming, and it was bearing down on us at about the speed of a horse's trot. I could count the seconds until impact, seeing in my mind's eye its jagged ram ripping a hole the size of a house through our already weakened hull. Death would be quick. But the living - as I waited for the coming end - was nearly unbearable. I could only stand there, helpless, and watch. No calling 'abandon ship!'… no time… no running or fighting back. Just stand there and wait to die."

Euroaquilo leaned forward, placing his hand on the porthole. His head sank in thought, remembering that day many years ago. Darla believed he again stood his post, seeing his coming doom. Or was it something else, an understanding of future events suddenly becoming clear in the man's mind? Before she could utter her trepidation, Euroaquilo lifted his head and looked into her eyes.

A sad smile crept across his face. "I learned a most important lesson that day, one that I hope to never forget."

Euroaquilo sighed, looking out the window again. "My Dear One, the true heroes drink not from the victory glass, nor do they tell the tales of their adventures. The true heroes lie moldering under the grassy glade or ever drift aimlessly amongst the frozen stars. The true hero, with free will, surrenders up all for souls in his charge, the broken and helpless who have no choice over life or death, but have only hope - a fool's hope - a hope for a hero to come rescue them."

Darla began glancing out the portal as if she, too, might see the giant carrack pressing ever closer. Excited, she asked, "Tell me, please! What hero happened by you that day?"

As misty eyes stared through the portal into distant memories, Euroaquilo answered, "The Ambrosia was maybe a quarter of a mile away and approaching, having maintained its speed. Suddenly, our of the corner of my eye, I caught sight of Admiral Lonche's flagship, the LorrieMay, as it flashed past our hull, back-drafting its engines to overload its reactors as it went over us. An instant later, I was blinded by a horrific firestorm when the LorrieMay tore through the Ambrosia."

He looked over at Darla with tear-filled eyes. *"Admiral Lonche blew that son-of-a-bitch into a million pieces!"*

Taking Darla's hand, Euroaquilo added remorsefully, "We were as good as dead, useless for battle, no one of any importance aboard. There was no reason to save us. The LorrieMay was still in fighting trim, we, just sitting ducks. Admiral Lonche surrendered up everything that day for us, because he could. He gave to us life when we had no life left within ourselves. Now that's a real hero..."

He shook his head, puzzling. "To this day, I ponder his reasons for saving us. He had so much to give, being an Ancient, among the first to sit the Council of Twenty-four, even a healer. Why he wasted it all on us, I don't know. I sometimes wonder if the Empire would be in such a pathetic mess as it is today if we had not lost so many heroes like the good admiral..."

The loss of Admiral Lonche had been a blow to Darla, too, she having served under his command aboard the escort carrier, DamonShoals, during the Persian Insurrection, some fifteen-hundred years before - another major defeat for the Children's Empire which ushered in hundreds of years of darkness for the Second Realm. Little had been chronicled up to this time as regards to the Day of Tears other than the roster of those killed, wounded and missing. So Darla knew only that the admiral and his entire crew were killed during the battle.

⁚   ⁚   ⁚

(***Author's Note:*** *Finhardt, Copeland, and Sandevar's exhaustive work, <u>The Slaughterhouse Chronicles,</u> details the six day battle, events leading up to it, and the aftermath. It is the most comprehensive account to date, the University of Memphis listing it as one of the ten most important histories of the Great War.*)

⁚   ⁚   ⁚

Darla lowered her head, looking at the floor. "I, too, suffered his loss, he being such a great man, gentle and caring." She then stared into Euroaquilo's eyes, questioning, "How, though, can you say his loss and the loss of others like him has placed us in such a precarious situation, other than those who direct us from afar are weak and afraid, wishing always to surrender us up to defeat by *compromise* and *diplomacy?*"

Euroaquilo responded, "You speak wisdom about some of our councilors and political generals, but I think that may soon change. What I talk about is *leadership*. You see, the Great War was terrible, with weapons of mass destruction being implemented to monumental degrees. I believe it was the loss of the old guard that helped that along, also. Many of them were wizards of sorts, having extraordinary powers. They chose the sword and buckler, you know, hand-to-hand combat over mechanized weapons. We entered the Great War following those leaders who were soon swallowed up in death because of the very battle tactics they decided upon."

"One hears whispers that some of the Ancients were not like the other children, like us. Rumors there are that they possessed special powers, connecting them to the secrets of the universe...the reason for their uncanny abilities. Gabrielle still possesses such, like her talent of being able to communicate through the mind, far across the galaxy. But even an uncanny mind is hard-pressed to stop a missile cast from miles away, or halt a bullet once unleashed for the hunt. The enemy changed the battle plan while our leaders resisted with vigor...still do. So, like young shoots in a blistering heat, our old guard, taking the lead at the head of our armies, withered away under the fiery rage of modern war."

Shaking his head, Euroaquilo sighed. "It was a terrible loss. Oh yes, many brave soldiers perished, too, but with our healers, healing machines, and our own rapid self-curing abilities, the vast majority of our people survived the combat. By a disproportionate number, our leaders did not, leaving a void to be filled with less able and inexperienced leaders. They're still brave - some foolishly so - but they have not learnt the lessons from past conflicts. The sword, crossbow, and catapult are subjects, still, of their favorite songs... The glorious cavalry charge is the supreme form of valor to our romantic samurai. And they still have the ears of the Council."

Darla frowned, thinking of the many contests she and her companions had bested in. "It has been my experience that most of our leaders give little more than directions. It is the warrior on the ground or in the fighter's cockpit that extinguishes Asotos' flame. We stand alone upon the sordid field, facing the enemy, our *leader* the raised sword, and our *champion* the smell of our enemy's fear in our flaring nostrils."

Euroaquilo leaned back from the porthole, reaching out and tussling Darla's hair. "My Dear, if our armies had more of your kind, I doubt that Asotos would have an army left to defend his castle, let alone hold his empire together. He would be hiding in the rocks right now, trembling in fright concerning future days."

Euroaquilo then offered that they relax in the bridge chairs. After doing so, he went on to explain, "You have seen or have heard reports of how the people follow Mihai in combat. Why, just her presence can turn the tide of battle. Entire armies hiding behind crumbling breastworks and cowering in defeat will stand defiant when they see her battle flag rise before them. With cries of victory, they will charge into the thickest of fights because she leads them on."

He shook his head, saddened. "Many were the leaders like that when the wars began."

Darla responded, respectfully defiant, her eyes ablaze with passion, "Never have I been gifted to follow such a leader. My kind have not cowered behind anything, waiting to be led! We have taken the battle to our enemy, waiting not upon a master to direct us. We fight for a cause that is greater than any of us. We stand the gore and stink of the field, the dread and destruction of that wasted land for that very cause. My kind need no leaders to follow, only men wise enough to allow us to finish our duties."

Euroaquilo nodded. "What you say has great merit but, sadly, few of our brothers and sisters have such power within themselves. They need someone to give them that power."

Darla disagreed. "I don't understand this at all. From my perspective, what I've seen is that the *leaders* receive accolades for the victory while the ones who have forced the battle lay silently rotting upon the field or convalescing behind curtained walls in a secluded hospital or sanatorium. There are few leaders who would dare stand where I have planted my feet in final contest. Repeatedly, my companions and I have reaped the whirlwind, leaderless, they falling like leaves around me while we stood unmovable at our post. We waited for no one to give us power, but found it within ourselves."

Euroaquilo asked, curious, "Do you view Mihai to be such a leader as you've described?"

Darla was quite adamant that was not the case.

Leaning forward and taking Darla's hands in his, and then resting his hands on her knee, Euroaquilo explained, "Not everyone is like your kind. My child of few mornings, you are a leader, too. Many there are of the leaders not yet recognized, but they are still leaders, none the less."

"My Dear, there are many brave souls who do not know how to lead... even themselves. They need someone to show them valor so that they can understand it. They need to see bravery to find it within themselves. A good leader, by chance or by knowledge, manages to tap into the hearts of those who follow, building up their spirit, for at least the moment, so that they, too, can do heroic things. It is to those leaders that accolades should be given. They have earned it."

Squeezing her hands, Euroaquilo added, "I have watched and observed. By your very nature, you are an outstanding leader. I imagine the reasons for you to be surrounded by so many brave and stalwart companions are that they have fed off an uncanny power you also exude. You are a wonderful example of leadership. I have watched it from afar for many years. And...it was that kind of leadership these many wars have stolen from us, leaving us so deficient of it."

He smiled. "Still, we do have some good leaders among us, and that should bring us hope…Mihai, Gabrielle, Lord PalaHar and Lady Tizrela to mention only a few. And some of those delivered here from the Realms Below, I'm quite impressed with them. Our new field marshal, Trisha, and the others who sat the Council the other night? Quite impressive, indeed… Indeed… They will turn the tide of battle for sure and, I believe, will have an impact on the councils of the future. They will also, like your kind, take the battle to the enemy, giving no quarter, demanding total victory."

Darla sat, reflecting on Euroaquilo's thought-provoking words, wondering why he should call her a leader.

During this silence, Euroaquilo took opportunity to advance a brewing question. "My Dusme, many are the dreams we have shared since the Great War, yet never have I found revealed your adventures of this great and terrible battle. Now you speak to me concerning your experiences regarding the Day or Tears in such an off-handed way so as to dismiss it. Please share with me the moments of your glory during that conflict. Why hide it from me any longer?"

Darla's jaw stiffened and her expression soured. At length, she relented. "To you I will speak of this matter, but you must not tell another soul for its pain is too deep for my ears to hear it repeated. Until the healing day, it must remain secret."

Euroaquilo promised he would keep it so.

Darla slumped as if in remorse, tears welling up in her eyes. Resigned to her fate, she began her account.

"My platoon had been together for just over a year, I being its senior officer. We had already participated in six major engagements up to that time, having lost eighty percent of our original complement and, even with replacements, were currently down to only seventeen troopers reporting for duty. Our acting company commander, First Leftenant Ricteer, had ordered us dug in above Mordem Heights, which we held from spring to mid-summer. The constant soaking rains and lack of sanitary conditions were making us all sick. By early summer we were calling ourselves the 'Mudpuppies' because of how badly we stunk and our deplorable living conditions we called 'home'."

"When High Command asked for volunteers to man transports for a gathering invasion fleet, I offered up the Mudpuppies, seeing we should all die soon if we remained in those filthy trenches much longer. We shipped aboard some wreck of an ore freighter converted into a transport… I don't even recall its name… our job being to support the crew and maintain the safety of the ship. It was little better than what we left behind. Not really.

We had hot food, warm showers, dry bunks to sleep in, our duties weren't overbearing and we had a good ship's captain. In short order, we'd settled into keeping things safe for the six hundred men and women of the Eleventh Infantry Battalion, they suffering far worse from their overcrowded living conditions."

"Twelve days out, we were joined by six other transports and their support ships and were only hours away from Commodore CythereaNo-ah'ha's Third Teleohodos Battle group. The captain had just heaved off the lines from a supply ship and had called down my fire crew when all Hell broke loose. Several squadrons of enemy fighters and heavies slammed into us without warning. We were sitting ducks, eight lightly armed transports, a half dozen merchantmen, and all defended by two cutters, an ancient barq, and a handful of antique fighters, facing over thirty frontline enemy attackers."

"Our fire station was aft the main hold, near the stern. After refusing stays on the refilled canisters of thallium oxysulfide, my crew of nine departed, leaving the remainder of the stowage work for the incoming fire crew. Following the captain's shipboard combat zone protocol, we remained suited up and on internal life support systems until we were safely retired from the fuel storage compartments. It's a good thing we did."

"We had only just entered the second deck safety locker, in process of closing the lower hatch, when exploding torpedoes ignited the thallium oxysulfide, creating a massive firestorm that engulfed the hold, incinerating everyone below and aft of us. The ship's energy systems couldn't take the strain, rupturing our shields and buckling the first deck, which tore everything on that level asunder. Corporal JasmiKusbi and Private SoshieZulita were instantly sucked out through the hatch, while the rest of us were slammed about like rag dolls in a whirlwind until the hatch fully sealed. Had it remained opened one more second, none of us would have survived."

"Things happened so fast. The floor of our locker buckled, twisting its walls up something dreadful, but somehow it held long enough for us to escape through an emergency hatch into the boson's pantry and out through the officers' mess. We were very fortunate because our fire suits were not only self-contained, but made of much tougher material than ordinary suits, being designed for harsh duty. Those suits saved us that day. I later heard that our platoon sergeant, LeviaBritt, was cast to the skies when the ship blew apart, being rescued several hours later by search scullers."

Darla's mind drifted into private thoughts, staring off into space as if reliving some particular moment in her life. When she realized what had happened, she tried to make excuse. Euroaquilo nodded politely, acting as though he had not noticed, commenting about how warm the room was getting while handing her a kerchief to wipe her sweating forehead.

Thanking him, she then went on. "As we stumbled along the debris-filled companionway, searching for a means to reach the upper levels, we heard cries and screams of the trapped, injured and dying, also shouts of others trying to escape or assist those in need. There was nothing we could do to help, what with the numerous fires breaking out, filling the passageway with noxious smoke, along with terrified soldiers packing the narrow walkway. My current duty was to save my fire crew, realizing that the entire second deck could collapse at any moment, sending us all into the bitter cold of deep space."

"With only flashing emergency lights to see by and the deafening bleating of alarms in our ears, we found it very hard to locate our escape from the second deck, which was rapidly tearing apart. We were moving forward along the main passageway, expecting at any moment to be crushed by collapsing bulkheads or swept from the ship through a buckling deck. To our left we could hear a constant tearing and screeching of metal as deck plates and compartments gave way to the ever-hungry vacuum of space."

"At length, we took a narrow passage that went to the right, I recalling it led to an emergency hatch that went to the third deck. Finding and opening the hatch, we assisted two dozen or so who'd followed us up to that third level. Being the last one up, I secured the hatch, fearing we would lose the seals on the second deck at any moment. My heart ached to think of my brothers and sisters trapped below, but could only hope they might find another way of escape."

"Exiting a tiny containment chamber, we found ourselves on the shuttle bridge. Already it was packed with people, nearly impossible to move. Everything was rushed, my mind racing, occupied with responsibilities for my fire crew and the need to locate the others in my platoon, so much so that I ignored the people around me as best I could, only reflecting back on those events in the lonely hours while awaiting my rescue. To this day guilt haunts me, for what I witnessed there makes me feel that much more the miscreant and coward."

Euroaquilo attempted to make excuse for Darla by calling attention to the fickle winds of war. Darla would have none of it. "I watched the real heroes that day…the crew of that tramp freighter fighting so hard to save lives, the duty officers and other marines assisting the injured and confused, calming others in a panic, and… and sacrificing everything so someone else could hope for a chance to live."

"A midshipman feverishly worked to help load one of the shuttles, she clothed only in her officer's kepi. Another sailor surrendered up his oxygen suit to an injured soldier before assisting her into a shuttle. There was no panic, the officers in charge refusing to permit that. No. While I scrambled about to find escape, those brave warriors stood their stations. I doubt few of them survived, and yet how many of my comrades owe their lives to them?"

"Give me a minute, please..." Darla excused herself and walked toward the back of the bridge and past the elevator. Euroaquilo believed he heard quiet sobs, but remained where he sat, waiting upon Darla's privacy. Eventually the woman returned, sitting again, but remained silent for some time. Finally, through reddened eyes, she looked into Euroaquilo's.

"I could not locate any of my other platoon members, so I attempted to get my fire crew queued up to board the shuttles. The lines were very long. It was decided that my 2nd duty officer, Corporal AsteiosAllotrios, and I would go up to the fourth deck to search for our remaining platoon members and, if unsuccessful, make our attempted escape via one of the several tethered craft riding piggyback on the ship's hull."

"With the elevators and all the main portals secured, we made our way aft to where the shuttle bay bulkhead separated the bay from the ready chambers, which were still intact. There we found an escape ladder going up through an emergency hatch that remained operable. We scurried up the ladder as best we could, what with the bulky fire suits and extra life support tanks we were still carrying. Asteios spun the mechanical locking system release, pushed hard open the hatch, struggled to get through the opening, I helping by giving her a gentle shove up."

"Asteios had made it just halfway when another explosion racked the doomed ship. The hatch triggered automatically to close, slamming down a smashing blow on Asteios' back. I heard her scream of agony in my headset before she passed out. Then everything went crazy."

"The shuttle bay was still holding, as well as the chamber above us, but the power died, leaving us in almost total darkness. Then the gravity machines failed, at first intermittently, which was deadly dangerous. I heard the cries of those injured and dying when some crashed back to the floor or were crushed by falling objects. How I remained on the ladder, I cannot recall."

"Finally, the gravity machines failed completely. Fortunately, the red, flashing firelights activated, helping us see a little bit. In that eerie, pulsing world of mayhem, I somehow managed to push open the hatch, freeing my unconscious companion - an easier thing to do without the gravity systems working. My biggest fear during this time was that those machines might start up again, sending me plummeting into the living morass below. It was a struggle, but I managed to seal the hatch while holding firm to Asteios' suit, something that, I believe, saved many lives, seeing what soon happened to that fourth deck compartment."

"The area we entered was called the 'aft ready transfer station', one of the ship's several docking bays with access hatches to tethered shuttles riding piggyback on the transport. It was a ghastly sight to behold. An earlier firestorm had ravaged the place, killing anyone in this area at the time. The only living souls on that deck were recent arrivals like us. Seeing the situation, I decided to attempt our escape by way of one of the tethered crafts, hoping there might still be one able to give us safe passage from the ship's coming doom."

"Searching the destruction, I found most of the exit hatches lighted up red, or flashing red, which indicated empty tethers or ruined shuttles. The ones where I saw no lights at all I never attempted, not knowing what might be there. My heart sank, feeling that we were come to our destruction. Then, just about the time I was beginning to surrender our fate, I spotted a green glint out of the corner of my eye. Holding my duty officer snuggly by her harness, I pushed off for the light, only to come crashing down to the tortured deck some feet away because the gravity machines began working again."

"Having twisted my ankle in that fall made it very difficult for me, but thankfully the gravity machine was not operating at full power. I managed to hobble my way through the tangle and up the twelve-foot climb to that shining green ray of hope above us. After what seemed an eternity, I was up the ladder, with a semiconscious Asteios tied off to my fire line, lying on the deck down below. Hesitantly, I pushed the release button, fearing there was no rescue on the other side of the hatch, only to be sucked into the black cold of empty space."

"But no! There was rescue…what, at the moment, I could not tell. About four feet away was another closed hatch that opened into an escape craft, its safety light, too, still green. Crawling into the connecting tube, I hit the switch and the most pleasant sound of servos met my ears, revealing the cockpit of an old T-4 fighter. It only took a minute or so, but it seemed like hours after I had crawled into the tiny ship and managed to pull Asteios up to safety."

"Asteios' feet had just cleared the hatch when I felt a terrible rumble and heard a roar and then someone crying for help. I looked down the connecting tube in time to see a hand reaching up through roiling smoke. An instant later all was quiet, the entrance hatch having slid shut, its sensors automatically closing us off from the destruction below."

"There was no time to think about the fate of that poor soul who was so close to escape. I frantically worked removing Asteios' life-support tanks and firefighting gear so I could secure her in the fore navigator's seat. I also had to remove my helmet and extra gear because of the tight spaces there. She groaned so in pain as I secured the harness over her shoulders. I knew I was torturing her, but there was nothing else for it."

"I was almost finished, leaning back, when I was startled by a sudden *thud!* On the fighter's canopy, next to my head, I glanced up, almost falling over in shock. For just an instant of time, I stared into frozen eyes that were blankly staring back at me. My mind can still see it as clearly now as I saw it then. The most beautiful of white marble statues looked in serenely upon me, smiling so carefree. It was carved so flawlessly perfect in every detail, the work of a master sculptor. Then it was gone, my mind having not been able to comprehend that it was not a statue but a once living, breathing woman with the same hopes, loves and desires I possessed."

Darla looked into Euroaquilo's eyes. "She must have been already dead when cast into those icy seas, for the death that awaits those thrown into a vacuum alive is often much more gruesome."

Euroaquilo only nodded in agreement.

Darla continued while fidgeting with her fingers. "Though the corpse quickly passed by, it was instantly replaced with the most horrific and macabre of scenes I ever witnessed. Many are the fields of slaughter I have stood upon, but nothing ever to compare to that hour, that place, that horror. My demon cannot conjure up a more horrific nightmare than what appeared before me in that hour."

"Debris of every description continued to erupt from the dying troopship. Fiery smoke filled with litter, machines, flotsam and jetsam, and yes, bodies, dozens upon dozens being thrown from the monster's belly, whole and in pieces. The men and women on that ship were being consumed by the ever hungry emptiness of space. At times I would see people, alive, being flung from some newly erupted hole in the beast, they thrashing about only seconds before silently drifting away, frozen forever in their last gasp for life."

"There were a few shuttles detaching from the ship, getting away safe for the moment. But there were other shuttles, still secured to the hull, or held loosely by some tether lines that never moved, their passengers eternally waiting rescue. One, less than ten yards from my fighter, drifted free of its mooring though it was still attached by guy wires to the hull. It lazily rotated round and round, the gaping holes in its sides revealing the fruitage of the slaughter, dozens of more names to be inscribed in the Silent Tombs. And this nightmarish vision was but one of so many that overwhelmed my senses. As if in very slow motion, I was watching the end of the world… one person at a time."

She hung her head in remorse. "And there was nothing I could but watch it dissolve around me…"

Euroaquilo started to offer some comforting words.

Darla's head snapped up with tear-filled, angry eyes staring into his. "You shall not interrupt me or, for a certainty, I will refuse you this tale! My heart is already overwhelmed to the point of breaking. My words, my way, or the struggle will be too great for me to relive with my speech. Better it is that I should have died that day. Then, for absolution I would not have begged these many years."

Nodding with understanding, Euroaquilo remained silent. He knew Darla was guilty of no sin requiring absolution, but he could well fathom the remorse and guilt that often floods a warrior's heart when the winds of war allow that person life while it rips it away from so many others. Only now did he begin to comprehend why this woman never shared these dreams with him. If only recalling events by speech were ruining her so, how could she have survived the trauma that a dream-share would produce?

The rage over her own guilt did not diminish in her eyes, or the self-loathing in her angry tone, as she went into a rant. "You think me innocent?! Well I *damn well* am *not* innocent! I did nothing! *Nothing!* There I sat, in a most fearsome fighting craft, one like I had flown countless sorties in, and I could not gather my wits to leave off the panic of securing my rescue and escape. Oh, *I* the *coward*, standing the breach with power unimagined, and I could not think to use it for other than a pardon from death. I am so ashamed..."

She broke down crying, releasing pent-up energies that had built up over these many years. Euroaquilo did nothing, keeping his promise, he fully understanding that 'upon every soldier must the night watch fall'. Alone, the picket must stand the post, on to death or the morning light. It is the battle each sentinel must undertake.

Gradually her tears subsided until, after one final whimper, Darla continued, "I tell you, many were the soldiers who kept their wits about them. If it hadn't been for the insane actions of those brave warriors, I doubt anyone would have lived to tell the tale of that day."

"The gun crews on the transport never left their stations to make an escape. As the madness unfolded around me, I saw the fiery spray of red, blue and green tracers lighting up the blackness, those gun turrets ever swinging back and forth to pour iron and death upon the enemy. They stood their posts to the end, dying with their fingers frozen on the triggers."

"And our fighters! Those heroic pilots fought with a madness few have ever witnessed. Many of the scrap heaps they flew were relics when we charged Memphis' gates during the Third Megiddo War, but in the hands of those warriors, they were first-rate killing machines. Why, sometimes one would take on five or six of the enemy's best, breaking up one attack after another."

"A fighter blasted past, guns all ablaze, it just clearing the transport's hull. I watched amazed, seeing the pilot paying no heed to the fire and smoke belching out of the gaping holes in it. Others I saw took on the heavies, hurtling themselves against the overwhelming onslaught with careless abandon. They dove like hornets upon evil intruders, holding back the unleashing of their ordnance until right on top of the enemy. And when their guns went empty, some made their own fighters into missiles of destruction, turning those heavies into caldrons of flaming death."

"The troop ship was lazily spinning larboard, round and round, providing me a panoramic view of this world of chaos. Slowly, like a full moon rising over the hills, I witnessed a sight my eyes could not believe. In the distance, I could see two cutters circling three of the troop transports, their defensive fire keeping many of the attackers at bay. One of them, I believe was named 'Cranberry'. I recall that because it was moored alongside our transport before our departure."

"The cutter was an old squat thing, a converted collier possibly from before the Three Hundred Years' War. Anyway, when it came around and turned hard to starboard, I saw that everything in front of the fore bulkhead was a twisted jumble of wreckage, with similar destruction on the upper decks all the way back past the captain's bridge, the outer hull being completely blown away over the communications and battle bridges."

"The Cranberry was slowly dissolving into nothing, just like our troop ship, but it was still heavy into the fight. Somehow, the remaining crew managed to maneuver that ship, keeping it between the enemy and the transports. All the while, the gun crews heated up the sky with their cannons and torpedoes. I never knew what became of that gallant ship and its brave crew. The annals from the Day of Tears don't even list the Cranberry on its roster nor does it mention this horrific little battle."

Darla's words became sharp and bitter. "I watched a sky full of heroes that day. They fought with abandon, not to save their own asses, but to save the helpless and weak! No *battle flags* waved them forward. No *glorious words* to assuage troubled hearts. *They* were the leaders, the wonderful throng who stood the line without orders, defending this Empire…if it deserves defending. Their names are forgotten, not worthy of the Council's attention, *worthless little people* who did only what they were supposed to do, nothing more, nothing less. Why, isn't that what they signed on to do, anyway?"

ଚ୦   ଚ୦   ଚଓ

(***Author's Note:*** *The Cranberry survived the battle Darla witnessed, but was abandoned because of extensive damage. Of the seventy officers and crew, thirty-two were lost, another twenty-one wounded. Salvage crews eventually took the ship in tow, delivering it to the DowHardy Navy Depot, on Stargaton. There it languished in the salvage yards until broken up for scrap in the days just before the King's War… See* The Slaughterhouse Chronicles*, pp. 892-4, Vol. II.)*

ଚ୦   ଚ୦   ଚଓ

Darla sighed long and sad, becoming quiet and morose to the point that Euroaquilo believed she had finished with her account. She had not.

Looking across the bridge, through the window at the lashing rain, she continued. "I finally came to my wits and released the securing pins locking the fighter to the transport's mooring station. We were just floating free, I about to charge the engines, when two enemy fighters swept over the ship. One opened fire on us, six tiny red tracers blurring across my vision. The fighters blasted past, leaving us and not returning. Whether we were considered a valueless target or they were out of ordnance, I don't know, but the damage done was sufficient to be devastating."

"Computer systems, communications, hydraulics, electrics, the main thrusters, even life support systems were damaged or destroyed. There we were, tethered by a single line, unable to escape certain death should the giant holding us fast decide to shudder in fear or erupt in anger. And then smoke began seeping up from the bomb bay compartment into the cockpit. I needed to do something, and it needed to be done fast."

"I rummaged through my firefighter's gear, finding a Plesso wrench. I took its claw end to rip loose the pilot's power control panel, and then used its side cutters to snip the lead wires going to the computer. After stripping the insulation, I managed to short out the security system, releasing us from the tether line. Then I took to jumping wires to ignite the engines, which didn't happen. When I was about at my wits end, I finally located the main switch wires for the vertical lift retro-rockets."

"Touching those leads together set all four of the rockets ablaze, sending us cart-wheeling away from the troopship. Fortunately, it was away and not toward, because I couldn't shut the rockets down. It took me forever to jimmy the retro-switches before I gained enough control to stabilize the fighter, much of the wiring harness having melted when I touched those leads together, having been forced to bypass the fuses in my hurry. By the time I got the retro-power under control, we were hundreds of miles from the fleet, drifting alone in the stark emptiness."

"While I was still struggling with the controls, about four miles or so from the transport, there was this blinding orange fireball that lit up the cockpit. Looking up, I saw the fore and aft ends of my troop transport tumble off into space, leaving a glowing white cloud of burning debris where the ship had once been. It's funny, as I think about it. I was working so frantically to get that old T-4 under control, I gave that event little notice until now."

"Sometime after the Armistice, I was visited in the convalescent hospital by Corporal SaleenHavson, the platoon's clerk and my bunkmate. The corporal was part of my fire crew, escaping on the last shuttle to make it out before the troopship exploded."

Darla hung her head in remorse, speaking in little more than a whisper. "Saleen was killed by Stasis Pirates less than two months ago."

She then wiped a tear from her eye and cleared her throat. "Anyway, Saleen filled me in on the fate of that ship."

"The gallant crew saved nearly three-fourths of the troops aboard the ship, losing over half of their own doing so. They surrendered up their lives to save over four hundred others. Of my platoon, everyone other than the fire crew did not survive the initial attack, their barracks being one deck above the main boiler which blew up when the fuel storage hold was destroyed. Of my fire crew, only four, including me, survived to tell of that event, Saleen being the only member to survive totally unscathed that day."

"Two of my crew, Privates TeleoZugos and DeuroHorkos gave their fire suits to some injured comrades and remained behind to assist the ship's company. With the death of Saleen, Sergeant LeviaBritt and I are the sole remaining survivors from the Mudpuppy Platoon, and Levia was so badly damaged later at the Battle at Memphis that she cannot recall her own name. I visit her at the High Banks Sanatorium, up north of here, whenever I get the chance. I can tell by the look in her eyes that she recognizes me. I think it lifts her spirits when I come."

Darla groaned as she stood, her legs aching from sitting too long, making her way back to the elevator, leaning over the rail to view the sights below. The DusmeAstron was equipped with multi-leaf safety hatches on each deck so that, spreading out like flower petals, the hatches would close off the elevator opening and seal the separate floors of the ship up tight. When opened, like it was now, the exposed parts of the hatch wings pulsed green with hundreds of tiny lights. When the lights began flashing red, it was a warning to stand clear the elevator shaft.

Euroaquilo watched Darla from his officer's chair. She was always so beautiful in form and comeliness, so concerned about how well kept she appeared. Yet today, the woman looked old, aged like the mountains, haggard. The long wars had not been nice to her, she having fought in nearly all of them. How many of her lovers' and companions' names were written now on the Silent Tombs? He pondered. She had lost so much, given so much, endured so much. Could her frail body continue to weather the persistent storms hurled against her? He shuddered to think of his visions and the coming Prisoner Exchange. Would that day be her Armageddon? Would she survive to tell of its passing?

In time, Darla returned to her chair. Staring out the distant portal, she noticed that although the driving winds were diminished, the rains still ruled the sky. Looking into folded hands, she continued her account.

"By the time I got control of the retrorockets, we were alone in the galaxy. All I knew was that we were somewhere in the Oreion Shelf Region, a most unhealthy place to be. This was still very much enemy-held territory, and was a well-known haunt of the Stasis Pirates. But we did have patrols in the area, and a few military encampments scattered about the star systems. There were also some neutral colonies within range where rescue might be afforded. Still, even that was a reach. I needed to find help soon or there would be no worry about who found us. Asteios and I would only be a couple of frozen castaways drifting through a cosmic wonderland of an eternal evening."

"The smoke and toxic fumes were gathering in force. If it hadn't been for the chemical filter canisters on our fire suits, I doubt we could have survived. I locked Asteios' helmet on, she crying out in pain at my slightest touch. When I explained to her what I was doing, she begged me to let her die. I could not."

"I figured we had ten good hours of clean air from those filters…longer if we conserved our energy. I foolishly attempted to do without my canister, thinking it better to save it for Asteios, if need be. After I puked twice, almost passing out the second time, I had no choice but to use the apparatus. My radio was broken in my helmet, so communication was impossible. I have no idea the suffering Asteios went through. I was heartbroken that I couldn't even speak consolingly to her. At least she was staying alive."

"I am a child of this wicked age and have few of the witching powers of my older siblings. Still, I attempted to focus in on the energy of the universe around me. It was so difficult, what with my growing fatigue and my ever-aching ankle. I drifted in and out of sleep continually. It was during one of my waking times, when I was adjusting the retro-thrust that I realized I wasn't alone in that wilderness."

Darla smiled. "As I slowly manipulated the thrusters, ever so slightly changing our course, I began to notice a quiet tune playing in the back of my head. The more I altered course, the louder the tune played. I discovered that if I stayed on that course, the music would play hauntingly loud and clear, it diminishing when I veered from it. It was the same music that has always been with me, my companion when the world around me is going to Hell, when all hope is lost, when nothing is going right. That little tune will start playing, guiding me down a safe path, if I should make sure to listen to it. I did this day."

"I was so tired… Every bone in my body ached from the stress of the day and my lungs burned from breathing so much poisoned air. I finally fell into a silent stupor, having no idea how long I slept. I awoke to sudden quiet. No music. I began to panic until looking out the canopy. There, much to my surprise and relief, I saw a beautiful blue-green planet."

She looked at Euroaquilo, wondering aloud. "I lost track of time, I know, but after I was rescued they told me the name and location of that star system. There is no way that broken T-4 managed that distance in only ten hours. Even with full thrusters and hard running, it was a good day's journey from where our troopship was attacked."

"Anyway, trusting to the fact that the music had delivered us here, I prepared to attempt a landing on the planet. I worked my way forward to Asteios, opening her helmet long enough to communicate my intentions. She was groggy, offering little more than a nod and a weak smile."

"I had to close her helmet because of the toxic air, but when I strapped her into the seat, oh, the pain she must have endured, me twisting her broken back the way I did. I cried out to Mother, tears streaming down my face to let me, please, take Asteios' pain and carry it for her. I believed Asteios was dying, her injuries more severe than I'd realized. I wanted so badly for my companion to pass away in peace, dreaming of happier times and more pleasant places."

With tormented eyes, Darla lamented, "There are times when I have wished that death take me. This was one of those times. You know, the devil takes his own, but I guess nobody finds me desirable..." She broke into a little rhyme.

"Heaven and Hell both reject this waif.
So she wanders the world on a midnight broom,
Seeking solace with the wolves and snakes.

Ever, ever onward goes the wayward child.
Chasing Death as it flees her wiles.

Oh, my dear love, why do you run from me,
When in your sweet arms is where I should be?

So sings the sailor lost on desperate seas.
With all hope gone but the breath she breathes."

A sad smile crept across her face. "That Jebbson fellow gifted me with that tale. Said he made it up oen night when the schooner he was on was taking water and everyone thought they'd all drown. Jebbson said an old Indian medicine man told him that 'if you seek death, it will flee you'. So he made up that little poem and shouted it out to the storm. Well, he and the ship survived the tempest. After that, he would sing that little ditty when Death walked with him, for he said that Death is like a flirtatious lover who ever seeks to catch but never be caught."

"I changed the words a little, but... well... I don't know why I thought of it just now. That Jebbson is a strange fellow. He can get into your head – deep, I mean - like he knows who you are and what you're about without you ever saying a word to him. I like him a lot."

Euroaquilo agreed. "He's a good man. He's a lot like you. Likes a good fight and wants to see it through to the end. He's a scrapper, can stir the pot with the Council. Doesn't make a lot of friends there, doesn't care to. If I was Death, I'd be afraid of him, too..."

Darla smiled, nodding. She then shook her head as if to clear it of these and other distractions. She planted her hands on her knees, leaning forward a bit. "Let me get on with it."

"As you know, and I learned that day, the T-4 is a stout ship, designed back in the days when the welfare of the pilot was more important than the ship's. Its wings are massive enough to permit a dead stick landing if need be, and for us it was need be. With retrorocket propulsion, we would be able to enter the planet's atmosphere without overheating. Then, with the fighter's generous wingspan, I should have time to search out a reasonable landing place."

"There were many worries that crossed my mind in the fateful moments before making the final maneuvers into descent. I had one shot at this. There could be no turning back, so I wondered: 'Would I find 'friendlies'? Was there truly breathable air down there? Not knowing the damage to the ship, would it hold together after entering the planet's heavy atmosphere?' "

"Some gauges still worked, like altitude and air speed, but few others. I had already chosen the landing location in the northern latitude, but close enough to the equator to offer some seasonal warmth. Visuals looked good, low mountains with broad valleys that, hopefully, offered several safe landing spots. I waited for my descent window and then committed us to whatever the Fates offered us down below."

"The retrorockets held long enough to get us through the most dangerous part of the entry. Much to my joy, the batteries maintained a strong charge all the way down, allowing me reasonable flight control over the air wing. My calculations were quite adequate, bringing us down on deck at a perfect altitude and slow enough descent to study the general terrain. I saw no signs of civilization, no cities, communication towers, power dams, nothing… at least yet..."

"Narrowing my search to just north of a line of rocky outcroppings, I swept down in a wide, arching circle and lined up at what looked to be a broad valley ideal for my purpose. Well, I guess that others also found that valley to be the ideal for similar reasons."

"I'd dropped in real low, hiding myself from possible hostile eyes. But that trick had also blinded me to my landing spot because of several high hills to my immediate north. Passing just south and west of a tall rocky bluff, I lined up on my landing zone, nosed down a little and set up a gliding trajectory for the location I'd decided on to land. About six miles out, I noticed some strange shapes hidden among the scattered giant conifers up ahead. At just over two miles, I recognized those shapes to be camouflaged fighters and buildings. I'd chosen to drop in on an enemy encampment!"

"I know I screamed in panic and frustration. I don't remember it, but I know I did, because I felt my heart rip right out of my chest, I was so terrified. 'Get away! Get away! Get away!' I remember me shouting those words to myself over and over. I almost tore that old joystick right out of its socket to turn away. Yanking the nose up and rolling that T-4 over, I gained enough altitude to clear those same bluffs and make my escape south."

"We had been drifting straight in toward the enemy's camp, apparently on their same flight path. They took no notice until I banked hard and retreated the scene. It would only be a matter of time before they'd scramble their fighters and come after us. Still, I guess they'd believe we were skedaddling, not thinking we were coming in for a crash landing. And we were going to crash, for sure."

"The question was, 'how far could we get away before it happened?' As I hurried south, I hit my retros again, hoping there might be something left in them. There was - about a four second burst, enough to get us another eight or ten miles away. The terrain was also dropping, maybe several hundred feet, but it looked real ugly. We'd tear ourselves apart if some better landing sight didn't appear soon. By now I was flying the valley, hills above us on either side. Seeing nothing but death approaching, I chose to follow a narrow canyon that ran east between two tall buttes, and prepared myself for a hard landing."

"After turning hard to port and descending into the canyon, I noticed that up ahead was a tiny patch of gray and green several hundred feet long filled with pebbles and sticks. I dropped the flaps and lifted the nose to stall out. I don't remember the rest of the ride. I just remember holding back on that stick with all my might, and then everything going black."

"Things got a little fuzzy after that. I woke to the stink of smoke, not much, but a real bad noxious stink. It was then I realized my helmet was missing. How or when it came off, I've no idea. My fear of dying from the poisonous air was quickly assuaged. The cockpit was smashed all to hell, with the canopy twisted beyond recognition, its glass shattered to the winds. There wasn't enough left of that old T-4 to know it had ever been an interstellar fighter."

"The clearing I landed in was really a volcanic wash filled with boulders and broken trees. The ship piled into that field at over a hundred miles an hour, ripping itself to pieces as it skidded through that jumbled mess. Little was left other than the cockpit, upper hull, and part of the tail section. At least the fighter had cut a straight path along the skid way, not flipping, it finally slamming to a stop against some ancient giant tree trunk."

"It was eerily quiet, other than a little hissing of a steam vent and the popping sounds from tiny electrical fires. I figure my fuel dump before we started our descent saved us from a fiery inferno that would have surely enveloped us had the tanks not been emptied. As it was, there was little to burn. The fires died quickly."

Darla blinked several times, shaking her head as her heart returned to those fitful hours. "I was waked by a burning sensation in my leg. Also, the fingers on my left hand were crushed and broken, and blood ran down my face, half blinding me. I was a mess! Blinking away the blood, I saw that Asteios' navigator's seat was torn loose, pinning her between it and the control panel. I bolted forward to help her, instantly falling back in screaming agony."

"When I regained my senses, I checked to see what the matter was with my leg. Shocked I was to find a barb of metal sticking three inches out from where my kneecap should have been. It was then that I realized how close to death I'd come. My pilot's seat was skewed and twisted, but it had held... how I don't know, what with the wreckage piled into it. Our sudden stop into that tree must have broken all kinds of things loose behind me, driving the rear of the ship into the cockpit. One jagged spear-like piece of metal punched its way through the lower panel of my seat and into the back of my leg, ruining my kneecap." Feeling with my hand, for I could not see the damage done to me, I discovered that my leg was skewered, the spike of the shaft sticking some three inches out the front of my knee."

"'Oh, *this* is a sweet one you've done, *fool.*' I said to myself. What was I to do now? My sister was possibly already dead, and I? I was near to being little more than a trophy for the day's hunt, my head the guest of honor at the night's festivities, it garishly staring down from the pike at the end of the feasting table. This was not good. I must do something quickly. I must get away, but how, what with my leg already being skewered upon that spike?"

"As our friend Jebbson has been heard to say, 'desperate times call for desperate measures.' Well, I was desperate. The only way I was going to escape torture and certain death was to get unstuck. The first attempt racked my body with such nauseating pain that I wretched into passing out. When I came to, I was sweating profusely and breathing hard. I began to panic, feeling there was no escape."

"I fought down the panic, reasoning that any pain I might inflict upon myself would be far less than what the enemy would do when they found me. Pain was my friend for the moment. Pain offered me freedom. All I had to do was reach out and embrace it, seek it like one does the arms of a lover. I gripped the front of my seat and, with all my strength, lunged forward."

"Well..." Darla smiled, grimacing with the memory, "It was no lover's embrace." She admitted, "Having my belly ripped open at the Battle of Argototh was nowhere as cripplingly agonizing an experience. Pain was no lover, but it did save me that day, freeing me from a certain, even more painful death."

"While the world spun around me, turning ever gray, I stumbled forward, falling over the wreckage to get to my sister. I'm sure she was already dead, but I refused to accept it. 'I'll get us out!' I screamed. 'Hang on! Hang on! We'll get out of this!' I then began slamming my shoulder into the cockpit side door to smash it open."

"I have no memory of the following moments or hours. When I awoke, I found I was free of the fighter, a pilot's pistol and my life support system beside me. There, only feet away, Asteios lay, looking like she was resting, so peacefully resting."

She shook her head. "How I – we - got out of the fighter and down to the ground, I cannot imagine, and with all the emergency supplies scattered about, too. There was food and water to last for a while, and whatever tools and equipment I might be able to haul away with me... us. Yes, I refused to leave my sister behind to have her temple desecrated by those animals. I cared not the cost to me. It was all or nothing. And *that* was *that*."

"I believed it to be late in the day and possibly the season to be high summer. The air was dry and dirty with dust, enough so that the sun was setting in an orange haze. That explained why we were not yet discovered, and their possible notion that we had not crashed, but hightailed it away. I was sure when they found no trace of our ship on their radar screens they would conclude we were hiding out somewhere, but maybe not so close as we were. Still, it was only going to be a matter of time before search parties would come calling."

"Rummaging through the emergency gear revealed a treasure trove of valuables. The medical kit contained everything from gauze, bandages and painkillers to surgical equipment. I soon discovered that the T-4 was captained by a 'Major somebody or other'... the name I don't recall. It was in transport to Commodore CythereaNoah'ha's flagship, Cyrene, to be delivered to the major."

"I tell you this because of how well stocked I found the fighter to be. The major must have personally stowed those treasures aboard before departing with the fleet. Well, whoever the person was, I'm grateful to 'em. Those supplies saved my life." She paused, quiet in thought.

Euroaquilo patiently waited.

Ω Ω Ω

(*Author's Note: I recently received a letter from NikaoEimi, who served as a liaison officer aboard the Cyrene during the Day of Tears battle. He was pleased to inform me, after reading a transcript of this section of the book, that he believed he was the major mentioned by Darla in her account. I quote a few of his words to me regarding the aforementioned T-4.*

"My fighter I had named 'ChrimsonKnight', was a relic assigned to me during the Three Hundred Years' War, I obtaining it for my personal use after the war ended. For most of the Great War, I served aboard various navy ships as a staff officer, coordinating activities between the sub fleets, Special Forces, and the main carrier fleet. I left the T-4 at my home base on Stargaton, feeling no need for it aboard the new carrier, Cyrene... that is until I was told about Operation Willow. I immediately requested base to have the ChrimsonKnight transported to me as soon as may be. The manifest I received after the demise of the T-4 says that it was being shipped aboard the troop transport, Shallie."

"You may possibly find more information on that ship in the Archives De Loriet, at Tilgath, on Pilneser, the Navy's Archival Museum for the Great War."

"From Adaya's (Darla's) description of events, I believe the Shallie was the troopship she sailed on and the fighter she took rescue in was my old T-4, the ChrimsonKnight. If it is, I am proud to think that my old battle tub helped to rewrite our history by saving such a renowned hero and leader.")

₧ ₧ ₧

Darla sighed, returning to her account. "I hurried as best I could in preparing to get away, not understanding why I'd not heard or seen any search craft. Then there came the sound of the muffled roar of distant wind, along with hot, stifling air and a hazy, dust-filled sky. There was a storm coming... a massive sand storm. Now I grasped why no one was searching for me. It didn't make me feel better. I had to git, which meant braving hurricane force winds, driving sands and suffocating dust. No holing up for me."

"It took me a little while before I was ready to leave. I modified my breathing apparatus to filter the air. My helmet was intact and I borrowed Asteios' left glove, seeing mine was destroyed. She was so kind, offering no complaint. Well, let's see... oh, yes, I took what few supplies I could carry, tethered my sister up to my harness, and began the painful crawl south, down the canyon."

"The storm was the worst I've ever been in. I couldn't see three feet at any time. My directional finder kept me on a southern track, but my biggest fear was to crawl off a cliff into an abyss. That's how bad the storm was."

"By morning of the third day, it was easing enough to prevent my traveling in the daylight. I figured we were about two miles from the crash site. The canyon was now spread out into a rock-strewn valley about a quarter mile wide. There were several overhangs, outcroppings, and a cave or two, making it easy to find some hidden shelter. I holed up in a little tunnel cave made by a pile of jumbled rocks and waited for night to come."

"This was the first real rest I'd had since leaving the wreck. I heated some rations with a chemical heater, and risked the removal of my helmet and breathing the filthy air to enjoy eating, unencumbered, those delicious, cooked morsels. That was probably the longest day of my life, my not having a clue as to where I was or how to contact anyone, wondering where I was trying to escape to, and believing it was all useless, because I was going to die anyway. It was only a matter of time."

"Later in the day, after the heated red glow of a tortured sun made its arrival, I heard sounds of machines coming in our direction. They had discovered the wreck and were out in force, looking for its crew. For the remainder of the day, wheeled and tracked machines roared up and down the valley, and search craft flew overhead. Fortunately for me, they did not realize the extent of my injuries. I'm sure they expanded their range much further a-field, thinking the escapees were making time, hoofing it hard south. Whatever the case, I saw no more search parties after that day."

"Later that night, I pulled out and made my way further down the valley. The hot winds picked up again, making things difficult, but it did cover our tracks from any pursuers. Tracks? I mean snaky, crawling marks. I couldn't walk, but was on my elbows and pushing with one knee, those painkillers numbing me up good."

"I don't know how far I made it that night and remember little of the ordeal. I do recall sheltering in some rocks through most of the next day. By now my water was almost gone. I stopped eating in an attempt to retain as many fluids as possible. Worse, I took the last of the painkillers that morning. By afternoon, I was in such numbing agony that I doubt I cared if I lived or not."

"I took up the escape again that night. By next morning, I'd cast away my helmet, gloves, all my gear, only saving my pilot's pistol to blow my brains out with if I got caught. Of course, I still dragged my companion with me. I refused to leave her behind. Not now, not after all this! We would die together if need be, but I would not leave her behind. That day I didn't even bother to hide. I didn't even care anymore. Why, the pain was so great, I reached more than once for that pistol to end it right there. But for some reason, each time I'd put it away, thinking better of it."

"That's really the last I remember of things other... other than one night. One night, the winds were howling, blowing choking sand in every direction. I was so thirsty, so thirsty. And then I heard it... my tune. It was clear and pleasant, so sweet, beautiful, but it wasn't in my head. Somewhere out in front of me, someone was playing my tune. It sounded like a flute. The hypnotizing spell that it cast over me urged me on, ever on until, suddenly, I found myself splashing in a wonderful pool of clear, cool water."

"I drank and drank until I felt my innards would burst, and then I fell into a deep sleep and dreamed." Darla leaned forward, staring intently into Euroaquilo's eyes. "The most beautiful dream I'd ever dreamed! I remember floating in a silent world of glowing spheres where all my long-lost companions called out to me in loving chorus. Why, even Asteios sang sweet songs to me. I felt hands touch my face, voices telling me how beautiful I was, how much they loved me. My heart ached with the joy of being in this wonderful world. I wanted so much to stay."

"And then I heard the music again, it playing loud and clear, but this time I discovered words in the hypnotic refrains. 'Come now, little one, we must leave. For you, this journey does not end here. No, not for you, not for you.' Then I heard Asteios laughter, such joyful laughter. When it faded away, the music began again, singing, 'For her, child, for her, not you, child, for her.' I recall nothing more until waking to blinding lights boring into my tormented eyes."

"I cried out in panic, fearing the worst. A hand touched my arm and a gentle voice called out my name. Squinting, I saw Zadar standing beside my bed. I do not recall my reaction, but my heart was so relieved to see him. When I calmed enough to listen, Zadar explained that I was aboard a medical packet accompanying a large convoy of troop transports on their return to MueoPoros. When he had received the news that I was the pilot rescued from that planet, he requested permission from his commanding officer, Major Chasileah, to pay a visit upon me."

"Zadar remained by my side for several days, and made continual visits even after we made port at MueoPoros, he finally departing when his regiment was deployed to what's become known as the 'Spider's Lair'. I heard tell later that he was wounded badly during our attack on Memphis, I not receiving the news until several months after the war ended."

"Getting back to my account, during one of his visits, he brought me up to speed with my rescue. I was told that a pilot on a scouting mission got confused when his instruments went berserk and, fearing it was the enemy jamming his navigation systems, dove to ground level to escape it. As he came down on deck, the sunlight reflecting off something below caught his eye. On his return pass, he came in low and slow. It's said that I shook my fist at him, apparently thinking he was the enemy. A little while later, I was aboard a rescue ship being transported toward the medical packet."

Darla laughed. "They said I put up such a fuss when the rescue team tried to leave Asteios behind that they threatened to leave me behind also. Anyway, I persevered." Sighing sadly, she added, "They eventually brought her body back to EdenEsonbar. I visit her grave there from time to time just to renew old memories."

Then slapping her hands on her knees as she tipped her head up, Darla sighed relief for nearing the end of her confession. "The surgeons fixed me up right quick, most of my injuries being minor. My knee was not broken and, with the use of those healing machines, I was up and about in no time. Eventually, I was returned to my old company now stationed near Memphis, pestering the doctors into madness to release me. My captain refused me active duty in the trenches, though, feeling I needed more time to recuperate from my injuries. I did finally manage to get permission to do courier duty for the regiment, along with several other convalescing members of my company."

"It was that tiny group I managed to gather in front of Memphis, along with a small contingent of other brave souls, that held the Gap (*officially called the 'Battle of the Tower Gate'*) until reinforcements arrived. It was in that skirmish that Tifara died, blown to pieces, protecting me from a missile attack. I was broken up real bad that time, spending four months in intensive care, and another year in rehabilitation, long after the Armistice. By the time I recovered sufficiently to address the Department of Records, requesting Citations of Valor for my fallen comrades, I guess everyone was tired of the war and didn't want to think about it anymore."

Darla became silent, staring at her folded hands. At length, quietly standing, she slowly made her way back to the elevator rail. The woman peered down into the abyss of the elevator shaft, again taking on the stature that reminded Euroaquilo of a weathered old tree, tired and defeated.

Eventually Euroaquilo, too, rose from his chair and joined Darla at the rail. He reached out and lovingly took her by the arm, pondering these secrets revealed. Who was this woman, DusmeAstron, child of the evening hour? Many were the tales of great valor that had tingled his ears, but never such as they had now received. These were profound, not only worthy of the Book of Records, but worthy of the Book of Books! Fear-inspiring they were!

Darla turned her head and looked up into Euroaquilo's eyes. She had aged this hour, Euroaquilo being so reminded of Gabrielle. How close was Darla to being consumed by the same crippling cancer that was slowly destroying many of the great warrior witches of this Empire? Or was Darla merely tired, tired of the passing whispers, the pitying nods, the disregard for her valor and battle cunning, the distrust of her mental constitution, her own self doubts as to whether all these things said about her were true?

Euroaquilo smiled. If she was sick, there was little he could do. But if she pined over doubt, well, he had the power to revive her spirit and self worth.

He reached up, lovingly stroking her face. "My child, my dear, wonderful child, if the gods of ancient days do exist, then they most certainly cast their gaze upon you, marveling with awe at this mortal goddess that walks among men. You have not chanced to be alive this day to relate to me your tale. No! For a certainty, I perceive that the powers beyond this universe have preserved you down to this time. How great you must stand in their eyes and our Mother's, for legend speaks to the motives of those gods that they seek always the healing of Mother's heart. You must be very precious in her eyes."

Darla blushed, laughing. "My Love, you make my heart sing. When I'm with you, I feel like a princess divine, like I was meant to be born, not some accident created by a random, passionate moment."

Euroaquilo stepped back stunned, but dared not ask why she thought of herself that way. The dark secret Darla had never revealed to anyone was the angry remarks of an Ancient, who long ago accused her of being such an abomination, unplanned and unwanted, an abortion of flesh that Mother had refused to reject. Darla was but six and two years old, and the Ancient was a standing member of the Council, that is, until he fell into the darkness of Asotos' world. But Darla remembered it well, and wondered still if the old sage's words rang with some truth.

"My darling lovely one!" Euroaquilo took Darla's hands in his. "You are the most wonderful of creations! Few are the women born of my age who have beauty to compare to yours, and that is of the flesh. Your heart? Why, I feel there is none greater than you who has such devotion to our Mother and, yes, to all of her children, too. I know she loves you with such heartfelt passion that she would bring down all the heavens to save but you in her bosom."

Darla just shook her head, blushing all the more. "Please, please, my Lord. This jacket is already too confining. Should you boost my ego any more, my chest will puff out to the point of bursting Mihai's kingly finery."

Euroaquilo gazed down upon her beauty. "And what a pity to have thrust upon me your full naked comeliness should such a terrible catastrophe happen. But I shall do as you request except, except for this one other matter I must address."

Darla puzzled, curious. "Yes?"

"Well, you see..." Euroaquilo stepped back, releasing Darla's hands, and began to quietly pace, his hands clasped behind him. "er...well...just let me come to the point. In my haste to gather the needed machines and materials for this journey, and considering all the important dignitaries traveling along, what with all their special needs and all to consider, well, I failed to assign a bridge officer to assist me and to take over command of the fleet should something untimely befall me."

He stopped and turned, waxing apologetic. "Well, when I got wind of your searching for me, it dawned on me that here was the answer to my dilemma which I had so foolishly placed myself in. Realizing that you are an experienced naval officer of some rank, and highly qualified and schooled in its procedures and protocols, I would like to ask your assistance with getting me out of this little bind I'm in. I'd like you to support me on this expedition as my deck officer, adjunct to the admiral."

"What?!" Darla began to laugh as though Euroaquilo was joking with her. "Listen, I'm a leftenant second class, you know, just *above* latrine duty officer, a *termite* or *wiggle worm* being my superior. Please, Love, give me a break. My heart is not in the mood for such jesting right now, though I appreciate your attempt to lift my spirits."

Euroaquilo did not respond in kind, his face remaining serious and sober. He shook his head. "I am *admiral* of this fleet. I do not take lightly my responsibilities for its crew and passengers' safety! I do not joke about such serious matters. Now, I can order you to take up this post, but I do not usually act as tyrant over those in my charge. I want you to accept out of your own free will. Please?"

Darla's face filled with disbelief and consternation. She leaned forward, hands opened with palms up, gesturing as she answered. "Look at me! Take a good look! *What do you see?* I am no *officer,* fit to command a fleet! Why, I can't even keep my tears from ruining the only uniform I have. I have been delivered here because Mother asked me to be her horse maiden...a *horse maiden!* Even she sees me not as a soldier, but someone only fit to tend a beast."

"My Euroaquilo..." Darla sighed, dismayed. "how could I even think to command a bridge dressed like a Consort Divine and not a soldier? Who will respect my authority when I walk this bridge? What officer will listen to my orders?"

"Hmmm, let's see..." Euroaquilo stepped back further, playing with his beard. "Hmmm...the bottom half of you looks like an officer, - a pretty glitzy one, I admit. Oh yes, and that jacket, I hear, belongs to none other than our new king, Mihai, and I'm told that she personally ordered you to wear it today. I'm also sure that your little discussion with Ardon has made the rounds. You put him in his place right good, or so I understand that's the way the gossip puts it. Made some of our officers pretty happy, hearing he got his comeuppance. I dare say, I believe there will be few officers bold enough to even risk questioning your appointment as my adjunct, let alone refuse to obey your orders."

He winked. "And, I believe there might be quite a few officers like me who'd rather see you out of uniform completely, if you know what I mean."

Darla harrumphed, blushing anew. "You're always like that with me..." She smiled shyly. For some reason she felt shy around this man. "I like you wanting me. It makes me feel special."

"You *are* special!" Euroaquilo nearly shouted those words. "Why do you think I asked you to stand the bridge in my stead? Now, I ask you again, and answer me directly this time. Will you support me in this request or do I have to give you a direct order?"

Darla lowered her head, grinning. She quietly whispered, "Yes…yes, I do."

Beaming, Euroaquilo reached out with his burly arms. "Great!"

Darla squealed in delight, diving forward and circling her arms around him. The two became wrapped in love's embrace, she pillowing her head on his chest, he resting his chin on the top of her head.

ဆ   ဆ   ဆ

The golden glow coming from the opened door of the elevator cast itself upon the two still locked in silent embrace. A tall, slender man quietly exited its doorway, quickly followed by several equally quiet officers and crew. As the others hurried to their different posts, the tall man approached Euroaquilo and Darla. He stopped at a respectable distance and patiently waited to be recognized.

At length the two released each other, Darla giving Euroaquilo a tender kiss on his lips as they parted. Euroaquilo turned to the man, extending his hand. "Captain Asarel, I am grateful for you kindly indulging me on this whim. I am forever in your debt."

Captain Asarel grinned. "No, Sir, the pleasure has been all mine! I should not have intruded upon you two, but I have received communique from Mother suggesting we may want to prepare for departure. It will take a little time to get the boilers up and ready the ship. I waited as long as possible. Sorry I had to interrupt."

"Yet," The Captain raised a hand, shaking a finger high. "I will remember your offer of debt! It is a very important matter to remember favors. Never can tell when an admiral can come in handy."

Euroaquilo burst out laughing, slapping the captain on the shoulder. "You haven't changed since our days together, flying those Coriveon fighters. In fact, if I recall correctly, you may still owe *me* a favor from that time. Remember Leah and all the kissing up to the brass I had to go through to get her as your bunk mate?"

"Well…" Captain Asarel grinned. "then let's call this one even." The two men squeezed hands tight in greeting, giving each other a one-armed hug.

Euroaquilo spoke up. "Captain, I'd like to introduce you to my adjunct, DarlaUmehahAstrni. She will be standing in as bridge officer in my absence."

Captain Asarel clicked his heels together, bowing politely and taking Darla's hand. "It is my pleasure. No, we have not met, but I feel I already know you well. The winds have spoken your name many times this day. Please, Commander, permit me to officially welcome you aboard my humble ship. Treat it as if it is your home while you're aboard. Please, whatever we have here is at your disposal."

Darla was shocked, her jaw dropping in surprise. Commander?! That was a much higher rank than a wiggle worm. This was almost too much for Darla. She fought back tears while replying, "Th...than...thank you, Captain Asarel. Thank you very much." She squeezed his hand, smiling, respectfully bowing in return.

Ignoring Darla's unsettled countenance, Captain Asarel politely bowed again and then, after releasing her hand, turned to Euroaquilo. "One need not do a lot of kissing up aboard this ship to gain favors. May I suggest we put Commander Darla up in the commandant's stateroom, right next to your quarters? We have no marine officers of rank on this journey, so the room is currently empty. It is well furnished and should live up to the needs of your adjunct quite well. Also, I would like to request you both to accompany me in my cabin for dinner this eve."

Euroaquilo chanced a glance at Darla. It was obvious the day had been very stressful on her constitution. He nodded a bow of thanks. "You are most generous in your offer. Moving my officer to her new quarters will be a minor undertaking, and seeing we must also press the time with private consultation, may I suggest such an offer on the 'morrow? I also believe my officer needs nutrition soon, for she 'as not 'et this day and must be famished to fainting. I request your leave, to allow you to man the bridge for departure, while we seek out some refreshment to satisfy a craving stomach."

"As you wish, my Lord." Asarel smiled. "Tomorrow night will be your night." he smiled, looking at Darla. "I will send my cook around with the menu. You choose for the rest of us. Decide for us the mouth-watering delicacies we shall all feast upon."

Darla stuttered her gratitude.

Euroaquilo also thanked the captain, adding, "Please, with your permission, notify us of the hour of departure. I do wish to share the bridge with you as we leave."

Captain Asarel promised. He motioned to those quietly waiting. Soon all was a' bustle with hurried officers and crew. Lights blazed across the darkened bridges while monitor screens flashed to life. Servos hummed and motors whirred. Soon the entire upper deck was awash in activity.

Amid this hubbub, the captain and his guests strolled toward the elevator. Euroaquilo broke the silence, addressing the captain. "Thank you for the permission to return the name of this ship back to when I captained it. It means a lot to me, you know. It was very kind of you."

"No, my dear Admiral. The pleasure is all mine." Asarel grinned. "To have you walk beside me again, like in the old days? No, you honor me to think you still care enough about this old hulk to put you special name back on it."

He looked up, thinking aloud. "DusmeAstron? DusmeAstron? Western

Star? There's a song in that name, mysterious. It's so beautiful, so beautiful. You know, you never did say where you picked that name up from."

Darla stared up into Euroaquilo's face, his arm around her waist, wondering his reply.

Euroaquilo glanced toward Darla and then looked at Asarel, nodding. "I guess I never did say, did I? Yes, I agree. It is a most beautiful name."

Squeezing Darla close, Euroaquilo kissed her on the forehead. The captain smiled, knowing some questions must wait to be answered.

Arriving at the elevator, its golden lights entreating entry, Euroaquilo and Darla obeyed its siren's call and stepped inside. Asarel shook Euroaquilo's hand one last time. "You will be promptly informed of our departure. I am looking forward to our standing the bridge again, together."

Euroaquilo thanked him as the door slowly closed. Servos whirred to life and the elevator began its descent to the lower decks. The captained turned to his crew, watching with satisfaction their smooth efficiency. He smiled again, saying to himself, "A well-oiled machine."

Outside, steady rains washed over the newly painted name of the cruiser, DusmeAstron. It would faithfully deliver it passengers to EremiaPikros, and to a certain person below, who was seeking a pleasant repast, an unexpected destiny. For good or ill, it dared not say.

ೞ   ೞ   ೞ

Section Four

The Forges of Hell

"**C**an a butterfly flapping its wings on one side of a planet eventually lead to a typhoon on the other?" Questions such as these are often thrown out by armchair philosophers when they cannot think of logical responses to reasonable questions. Still, is it not true that very small, miniscule causes often, in time, produce astronomical effects?

No better example of this can be found than the union of two very tiny cells that join to create a new life. From one fertilized egg no bigger than the head of a pin have come all the great orators, poets and leaders known to our universes. In their turn, the worlds of men have been changed for better or worse.

On a warm summer evening, while balmy breezes drifted in from the sea and the gentle glow of a waxing moon filtered down through tamarisk trees, a young maiden offered her love to her strong, handsome beau. Their passionate embrace was not unlike that shared by countless other lovers throughout the lives of men, and with similar outcome.

Above the clouds and beyond the sky, watchful eyes waited to see if their many centuries of effort and labor were soon to be rewarded. For thousands of years they had played in the genome pool of this race to create the perfect warrior priestess, one who would share a throne to rule a universe.

For generations, fingers had busied themselves weaving the web of life in the bellies of countless mothers by gathering the desired threads from countless fathers until satisfied with the finished blend. Faces smiled with pleasure at the results accomplished. But other faces took no delight in the little child.

Given a name belonging to the gods by her father and mentored in the new religion of her uncle, the Forces of Darkness swore revenge for such disrespect. They skulked in the other world, waiting the day when their enemies wearied of protecting the girl. At last, such a time arrived.

I start this account back in that day and hour when, for but a moment, the demon forces thought the battle was theirs. In an age of empires and gods, of gladiators and prophets, the flap of tiny wings against the tempest of madmen began a storm that would one day bring down Satan's entire house, beginning with Legion, his chief lieutenant.

No one person can start a firestorm of the proportions witnessed at the end of the last age. Yet, the collective spirit of persons like this child proved to become an unstoppable force, eventually crushing a superior enemy before he could cover the universe in eternal gloom and destruction. The history of Heaven's War does not, then, belong to one hero. As you will see, *all* who fought in it are heroes.

It was the beating of countless wings, through death and sacrifice, that has delivered us to this Fourth Age, the age of rebirth.

⁞   ⁞   ⁞

"Isn't she a pretty one! I'd like to fancy whoring w'th the likes o' her for a n'ght!"

"You best leave that lovely alone, Perk!" protested the grimy, balding man known as 'Tanner'. He was standing next to Perk, also peering into the cell. "She's saved for the party tomorrow and if you 'ert her, me and you will be dog food 'fore the next nightfall."

Perk glowered at Tanner. "Stop your whining, ya' ol' bastard, or I'l rip yor own guts aut an' feed 'em ta the dogs, meself! No one's goin' ta hurt the pretty, but if opportunity should just happen to come ta 'ave some fun – well… we's just'l 'ave ta watch an' sees – won't we?"

Tanner backed away from Perk and shut his mouth. He had worked with him in the prison for many years and didn't doubt a word said by him. He was afraid of Treston, captain over the governor's personal guard, including the prison, but this man terrified him. Perk was not only a senior prison custodian, he loved his job, taking pleasure in his work and the pain he could inflict on others, calling it his 'bonus pay.' As he eyed the child huddled in the corner of the stinking cell, his nostrils flared as a greasy drool dribbled off his jowls.

Perk reached his arm out and put it around Tanner's shoulder, drawing the older man up close to him so that their noses almost touched. With a semi-toothless grin, he hissed in a hushed whisper, "I don't knows about you, but I ain't never seen nothin' like what's in there in here 'afore. In my whole life's dreams, there hain't niver come to me somthin' as sweet as that thing in there. If Hell come tomorrer for me, it 'uld be worth it. I'm achin' already for it, an' that pretty can make the achin' go away."

Then lowering his voice even more, his eyes glowing with lust, Perk offered, "Now Tanner, my bosom fr'nd, we has worked heres a lon' time. I has always shared with you. I'l save you some. Why I'l even guard the doors while you fun w'th her." He paused in thought, his eyes staring at the ceiling. "I can make it wurth yor while – wurth our while. Now goes about yor w'rk, and keep that flapper a' yors buttoned up."

Tanner's eyes spoke of his fear. Perk knew he would keep quiet. Tanner turned away from Perk and went about feeding the prisoners. Perk opened the cell door and entered. On the floor, a dirty dish sat in maggot-infested filth. He threw down some moldy bread, then, with a cup, reached into a greasy pot, took out some lukewarm slop and poured it into the dish. He cast a leering look at the girl in the corner and broke into a hideous grin, hissing, "Eat up, darlin', best the feast is what yu g't fer yer last sup. An' try ta rest som, fer a l'ng night's comin'."

He turned, exiting the chamber, slamming the door shut. Stopping, Perk swung around, pushing his nearly toothless, grinning face up to the bars, blowing a little kiss, "Sweet dr'ms, pretty..." and then walked away down the hall, his whistling growing fainter until all fell silent.

ঙ঵ ঵঵ ঵঵

Her hands were not shaking as badly now, her breathing more relaxed and less shallow. The girl's prayers had a calming effect. In the least, they took her mind off the burning agony gripping her belly, but tonight they seemed to be soothing to flesh and soul as well. The terror of earlier hours when Perk had returned was decreasing and she was starting to feel the dull pain of repeated beatings. Drying blood mixed with human filth left over from previous inhabitants covered her naked body and caked her hair. The airless chamber had already been chokingly thick with that rank smell, but now the stench of sweat and sexual exhaustion emulsified with the other stink to produce a stomach-wrenching odor. She heaved up more bile, but there was nothing else left.

Perk had waited until Treston had retired for the night. Then he had quietly slipped out the side door of the prison chamber. At Perk's departure, Tanner lit a small lamp and paced back and forth in front of the cell door until he returned. When he came back, four other men accompanied him, all of them filthy and unkempt – men who worked or slaved down in some other part of this *hole* of a prison.

Perk threw open the door of the girl's cell and stepped in, holding the lantern high to look over his prize catch for the night. "My, my, whut a dainty we 'av 'ere. The gods 'av luk'd on us t'nite." He then cooed, "I 'ear yu got a nam, an' quite a fan-see on', too." Turning his head back over his shoulder, he grinned. "*Ish-tar*... can yu baleeve it? We g't us a goddess right 'ere in ar li'le 'ome. Ya ev'r see a *goddess* 'afore?"

As he clumsily reached for her clothes, the child threw up her hands to stop him. Perk lunged forward, driving his fist into the side of her head, sending her spinning into the far wall. Before she could fall, Perk's giant paws were around her throat, squeezing the life out of the girl.

Tanner wailed. "Stop it, Perk, or yu'l get us all kild!"

"Shut your friggin mouth you!" Perk growled.

Tanner's cries did have their effect, though. Perk caught his breath and calmed down. Easing his iron grip, he pulled the girl close, opening his mouth in a sinister grin, cautioning, "Well goddess, yu win fer now. I dn't want ta spoil th' goods. Now be nice, or next time, I'l rip that sluttin' 'ed of yur's right off."

"Let's 'av a see at what a goddess looks like…" Perk reached down and ripped Ishtar's tunic off, the force flinging her across the room. She caught hold of a post in the wall just before falling. Tanner lifted the lamp high to get a better look at the naked girl. A hushed gasp rose in chorus from the men as they watched, staring, transfixed, looking at the most strikingly beautiful form they had ever seen.

Not only did this woman have an astonishingly attractive face, her other features were of equal grandeur. Ishtar's hair was a brilliant orange-red. In the lantern light, it radiated red, then gold, copper, and back to red. Her perfect figure was enhanced by a silky-smooth, light olive-colored skin, while dancing shadows made the girl's generous curves and firm breasts appear as those of a goddess come to earth.

Perk was aghast. "Well I …well ain't that …sooo." He dropped his eyes pondering his good fortune. Drooling like a hungry beast, he grinned. "I bet you ain't never had it 'afore neither, 'av ya?"

Hooting, Perk turned to the others and asked, "What's she worth now, gentermen? Clean as the driv'n snow. What will yu pay to be the first driv'r? A goddess, no less..."

What happened after that was a blur. Aside from the explosive pain rending through her head and the burning agony in her belly, she could remember little detail except for Perk. He was brutal. His animalistic abuse was beyond description. The more she cried out, the more intense the pain he would inflict. When she resisted, he would beat her until she would nearly pass out. After he had finished, she lay on the floor, her eyes rolled back in her battered head, oozing blood from her nose and ears.

Tanner was petrified with fear, believing the child would die from Perk's abuse. Perk shouted for him to shut up and went after the child again.

After thoroughly exhausting himself, he forced Tanner to perform the final insult to her. When he declined, Perk angrily threatened, "You'd better get it up, or I'll cut it off!" Taking Tanner by the shirt, he pulled him into the cell, flinging him at the crumpled body on the floor, mocking him. "You'll kill her! You'll kill her!"

Tanner timidly obeyed, finishing his deed as quickly as possible. The girl quietly moaned but offered no resistance. When finished, he jumped up, and while still fastening his clothes, scurried away.

Laughing, Perk shouted after him, "If the lit'le bitch dies now, you'll 'ang for it, too!"

The other men had long since retreated to their own hiding places. If the girl was going to die, they wanted to be a far way from the scene. They were well aware how much value Treston placed on her appearance in front of the emperor's magistrate the coming day.

Perk lingered a while, staring at the body sprawled in the corner then slowly turned to go, stopping in the door for another look. Ishtar opened her eyes - now filled with malice and rage - only to meet his. He kicked the filth from the floor in her direction, cursing, "And damned be your god, too!" and stormed off down the passageway, taking the lantern with him. Soon a shroud of the darkness enveloped her.

Ishtar struggled to her knees only to be caught in nauseous convulsions. Driven by uncontrolled heaves, hot liquid forced its way up her throat, spewing out her mouth. As the child gasped for air, a shooting pain racked her body, racing up her back, exploding into a million stabbing spears at the base of her skull. In a muffled scream, she pitched forward, falling face down into the filth and dirt.

ဆ   ဆ   ဆ

"There ain't been anyone out here in hours. It's cold and damp, and my feet are tired. What's all this big deal 'bout us bein' here, anyhow?" The guard shivered, rubbing his arms with his hands.

The second guard continued his searching vigil of the deserted street while chastising the first guard. "The cuckoo bird's got in your head! We got some big prize locked up and the sergeant ain't wantin' no problems. If he got loose, all of us would be feedin' lions tomorrow."

The first guard nodded. "I don't doubt what you're sayin', being a big prize and all that, but…" He glanced around to see if others were near, then whispered, "All them followers of his aren't gonna bother here. They'er all them kindly, peaceful people. They don't hurt nobody."

"Watch your mouth!" snapped the second guard, glaring at the first. "Those kinda words could get us both killed! Just shatup and watch for somthin'. That's our job." He returned to scanning the darkness.

The first guard sniffed the air, wrinkling his nose in disgust. "Why in Hell's name don't someone clean that hog pen?!"

The other agreed, staring into the empty animal pens across the street then suddenly jerked his head up and froze. Wide eyed, he excitedly whispered, pointing, "Somethin's mov'n there!"

The second guard reached for his spear, squinting into the blackness. A cackling echoed off the surrounding buildings, shrill and disjointed but somewhat musical then was quickly followed by equally shrill musical words.

"By night it walks to hunger still,
To find sweet meat, its belly fill.
It smells the blood, so warm with heat.
It'll drink it down, and saves the meat!"

A cry rose from the darkness, followed by painful whining. "No! No! I won't hurt them! Agguuh! I won't hurt them! I promise! I promise! I am your child… your little servant child. Please! No more! No more!" It grew quiet for a moment, and then the voice sputtered, "Not hungry! Not hungry now!"

"By the gods!" The first guard wailed, jabbing his spear toward the hog pens.

A black shape slowly emerged out of the darkness as if rising out of the very filth of the ground and wobbled straight for the two guards. Hobbling and weaving from side to side, a hunched-backed, two-legged beast from the underworld made straight for the pen's gate, all the time cackling and cursing its complaints for need of food then declaring it wasn't hungry.

The foul creature was forced to stop at the gate, it being tied shut, letting go vile curses and oaths, damning the worlds of the living and the dead, finally muttering, "Sees if I shares my feasts with them again!" And then it became silent. A hand almost as black as the creature's ragged robe poked out of a fold, reached up and untied the rope. As the gate slowly creaked opened, a mouth hidden by a faceless hood cooed with a hissing cackle, "He said they would be pretty… he did say… he did." The creature laughed. "They are pretty… they are… they are. He said they would be fresh and juicy… he did…"

The creature then fussed in disgust, "But I don't like *fresh!* I *don't like fresh!* I like ripe…sweet…soft and ripe." It made a smacking sound and started toward the two guards.

"Stop there! Stop there!" The guards yelled, shaking so badly they had trouble holding their spears.

The putrid creature hidden in stinking rags halted. Lifting its head as if to examine them, it indignantly threatened, "Master said you would be nice boys… yes… he said it. He said you would be good to me," adding with a bitter hiss, "not like the others. They were bad, bad little boys." The thing cautiously looked around, making sure they were alone. Finally comfortable that 'whatever' wasn't there, it lowered its voice and laughed, "but they was tasty… oft and tasty." More smacking sounds filled the chilly air.

"Get back, you devil! Get back! I'll stick you! I will! I will!" The second guard's spear shook so violently it nearly fell from his hands.

The creature hissed back, "Yes, yes, you know me? That's good! My lord said you would… yes, yes he did." Its voice changed to that of a waffie on the take. "He said you like money. I have money, good money. Not to hurt the pretty boys, he said. I have money."

A dirty, bony hand poked out of a fold in the ragged robes, this time with a little leather pouch. Another hand reached out, its fingers rummaging around inside, eventually pulling out two silver coins glinting in the cold starlight, throwing them on the ground near the guards, who jumped back in fright.

The tiny, dark figure fell silent, patiently waiting for the guards to respond as they cautiously watched this smelly creature, occasionally glancing at the two shiny objects near their feet. "Get a light!" The second guard ordered.

The first guard backed away, opened the prison door and reached in, taking a half-burning torch from the wall. Holding it at arm's length, he looked toward the creature, but could see only shadows under the hood. He then stared at the two stater coins tossed on the muddy bricks - nearly a week's pay for each man.

The creature laughed, slowly rocking from side to side with glee. "My master says there's more, yes more, but I must do master's will first."

Holding his spear high, just in case, the second guard reached down and picked up the coins. After studying them in the torchlight, he exclaimed, "They're real! Look!" He handed one to the other guard.

Hefting the coin and then rubbing it between his finger and thumb, he thought for a minute. Eyeing the creature with caution, the second guard finally asked, "What do you want?"

Shuffling closer, until threatened again, the creature leaned forward and just above a whisper, hissed, "You have a man in there. He makes fun of the gods… he makes fun of master. Master is unhappy. Sends me to talk to foolish man."

"And what is his name?" The second guard asked suspiciously.

The hooded figure laughed. "We call him 'Talker', because he does not know how to shut up. But others call him, sh… sh…" It nervously held its hand up to the faceless opening and, first letting go with more curses and oaths, whispered as if in pain, "Cee...phasss.."

"Who?!" The guards howled, pointing their spears as they did.

The second guard stepped forward, shouting, "Be off with you, you… whatever you are! Take your money and go away!" He threw his coin at the creature.

It howled in anger and turned to leave, and had only taken a step when it cried in pain and fell back, wailing, "No, please, not my fault! Not my fault!"

Ranting on, flailing its arms, it cursed the guards. Suddenly, as if warding off a blow, the putrid thing raised its hands and cried, begging for mercy. "I tried! You said they were nice boys. You said they like money, money!" then angrily howled, "They are not nice little boys, they do not like good money!"

With the same suddenness, the creature quieted and stretched forward. "What? Yes, yes, they would." and giggled as it turned back toward the guards, asking, "But how?" Then it cocked its head as though being whispered a reply. There was a burst of laughter and, "Worms? Yes, yes, worms. It makes them tender, nice and tender."

The guards listened, terror gripping them as the creature argued over what was to be done with the two. There were sounds of laughter, followed by, "Yes, yes, that is good."

With disgust, the creature jumped back and fumed, "No! Don't burn them. It tastes better cold and soft." There was a smacking sound again. "Better for my mouth..."

Terrified, the guards cowered, pressing their bodies against the prison wall.

The creature moaned, bending low, like a dog seeking mercy from its master. It whimpered, "Not good boys. Don't like money. You said they would like money." then perked up and laughed, asking, "Leprosy? Give them leprosy?"

Slowly turning its head toward the guards, it let out a manaical hiss, "Yes, yes, worms, but first leprosy. Bad little boys..." starting to raise its arms and begin some kind of a chant.

An invisible hand reached out and grabbed the creature, snapping its head back and swinging it around. Half-sobbing, it cackled, "You said I could, you did, you did!" then becoming quiet as though listening to someone. The creature started to argue, "What? More money? But they don't like it! What? Gold? Gold money? You will give *bad* boys gold? Let's eat them instead. Eat them!"

Again it whimpered like a whipped dog, but soon quieted. After what seemed ages to the guards, the creature shrugged, "All right." while turning and shuffling in their direction, stopping just outside spear-thrust range. It cackled, "Master will give you gold money, good money...to good little boys." rubbing its hands together, rolling one coin over the other. "Yes he will, he said. He promised."

"How much money?" The second guard asked, barely controlling his panic. "How much money do you give us?!"

The creature laughed as it slowly bobbed up and down and from side to side, turning its head away from the guards. "Good boys, good little boys. You said they would like the pretty money. Yes, yes you did." It looked back and started to shuffle forward.

"Stop there!" Both men yelled, dropping their spear points in front of the opened hood.

The creature halted, whining, "You asked! You asked me! How much money? How much pretty, shiny, money?"

"Tell us! Tell us how much!" The second guard shouted, his voice belying his fear.

Excitement grew in its shrill voice. "I will show you! Good boys. He said you are nice little boys. Not to hurt good little boys. He said to be nice. Master says to be nice to little boys… I will, I will… Please, see my money. Master says see it."

As the creature silently swayed from side to side, the guards could see clouds of steam escape from under the hood. Finally, the second guard told the first to move closer to see the money.

"Why me!?" Cried the first, clutching his spear tighter. "It may attack me!"

The second reassured him, "I'l hold the point of my spear in its face and keep the torch high. If it tries somthin', I'l stick it." Then turning to the creature, he bravely demanded, "No tricks!"

The filthy figure cowered, lifting its arms for protection, the leather pouch swinging from its hand. "Don't hurt me. Master said be good. Little child is being good, very good." It shook its head. "Not hungry now, not now. Promised I would be good, be good."

The first guard hesitantly inched forward, stopping about arm's length from the creature's hood. The stinky thing appeared so small at this distance. How dangerous could it really be? Courage started to build in the guard's heart…

"Put your hand out!" The creature hissed. The guard jumped back, startled, his bravado dying before it could show itself. "The hand, I say! Put out your hand for the money, the pretty money." He wanted to bolt, but the second guard chided him for being a coward. Very slowly, the man extended his hand, palm up, fearing giant fangs might rip it from his arm. The little creature croaked with delight, lifted the bag, and emptied its contents into the guard's opened palm.

He jumped back quickly, staring at the coins in his hand. The creature cackled with laughter. "Good money. Master said it is good money, pretty, shiny money." Wide-eyed, the two guards examined the coins. There were eleven more silver stater coins, making a total of thirteen. A frown grew on the second guard's face. He glowered, shaking his spear at the creature. "Wait here! You said there was gold money. This ain't gold."

"Gold! Yes gold!" The creature chirped, bobbing up and down, "Pretty gold money…later." then lowered its voice to a menacing hiss, "When done with master's will. When done with my job."

"Give it to us now!" The second guard demanded. "Now or we'll stick ya!"

Raising its arms and angrily growling, "I'll give you! I'll give you…" its voice suddenly cut off as the creature pitched back, nearly falling to the pavement.

The guards shrunk back against the wall, throwing their hands up over their faces watching as the creature gaggled and coughed and started to whimper as though being beaten by some invisible hand. Finally, it cried out, "No more! No more! Little child will be good! Good little child! Please! Please!" It fell to the street as though being released. Painfully standing, rubbing its side, the creature faced the guards and whined, "Gold, yes, gold money. Will make you rich." It then threatened, "Master is tired of playing. First must talk to foolish man, must talk!"

The guards argued over what to do, fearful of the demon and its master, but equally fearful of the prison's commandant. Finally, the second said, "You stay here and I'l see the head man." The first started to complain, but was cut off by the sharp retort. "Shat'ap, fool! Yu'l be alright. Just keep your spear pointed at it." Without waiting for a response, the second guard turned and hurried through the prison door.

His returning seemed to take ages. All the while, the little stinky creature continued to slowly rock from side to side, humming some tune just under its breath. The wary guard stared at it and then down at the coins in his hand. As time passed, he looked more at the coins than at the creature, moving his fingers, making the coins slide from one side of his hand to the other, and then back again. What wealth! What wealth - more money than he had seen at one time in his entire life! He began to dream of the good times he could have with such wealth - the women, wine, and power the money could bring. Hurried footsteps jarred him back to reality.

The commandant of the prison burst from the door. "All right, what's the… Whew! What is that god-awful stink?" He looked at the black shape rocking to and fro in the torchlight, and let out his breath. "Have the souls of the slain risen to offend us?!"

Laughing erupted from under the creature's hood. "Yes! In a way, yes." It smacked its lips then grumped, "Not hungry now."

The commandant was taken aback, falling over the second guard, nearly toppling the both of them. Quickly regaining his balance and attempting to do the same with his dignity, he demanded, "What do you want?! Tell me now, or be off!"

The creature raised a bony hand and pointed it directly at the commandant as it hissed contemptuously, "You took my money, you did, you did. Now give up your end to me, to me. Now!" It cackled. "Or be forever cursed!"

The stunned commandant's face reddened in anger. He was about to order his guards to attack this beast when the torchlight flashed off the two coins given him by the second guard. He blankly stared at them. His anger was now turned toward the guards. "How many did it give you?" When no answer came he shouted, "How many?"

The first guard started fidgeting with his fingers, while his face twisted up with consternation. At long last, he stuttered, " 'Leven, yea, 'leven." then pointed toward the commandant's hand, "Plus those two."

"That's thirteen, you stupid fool! Thirteen!" The commandant glared at the creature, "What curse do you bring tonight? Why the devil's wage?"

The creature raised its hands in dispute, shaking its head. "No curse, no curse... Good little boys, pretty little boys. Not hurt pretty boys. Master said to give more money, more money. Will remove the curse..." The creature lowered its voice and shook its finger. "if little boys are good... yes, master will remove it."

"Give me a lamp!" The commandant demanded. "Now! Get it now!"

The second guard hurried through the door, soon to come back with a flaming, oil-wick lamp. Taking it and motioning for the creature to come closer, the commandant bent down, shining the light so he could peer inside the hood. He let out a short gasp, but lingered to have a good look.

Coal-black eyes stared out from a death-white, pockmarked face with caked chunks of mealy skin hanging from it. The creature's mouth was a gaping black hole of a laughing smile, out of which some kind of juice drooled. The commandant could also see strange marks and runes carved in the creature's flesh.

The commandant stood up, waving his hand while making a face. "God, it stinks... like something dead!" He backed away, keeping an eye on the creature which patiently remained there, swaying side to side.

Nearing the guards, he whispered, "It's a witch of the Devil, himself, all right, or worse... maybe a demon." In little above a whisper, he attempted to reassure the others. "If it had wanted to kill us, we'd all be dead by now. I really do believe its business is not with us tonight, else you'd not have received the money."

He asked the creature, "Who are you? What do you want here?"

It hissed in anger at the question. "I have spoken to the little boys.Not nice boys. They were supposed to tell."

The commandant was stern with his reply. "I want you to tell *me!*"

After muttering more curses and fussing that it had already told the others, the creature grudgingly obeyed. "My lord has business with a bad man - his business, not yours." It then softly cooed, "I am his little child. Good child, nice to pretty boys." It extended its hand, slowly pawing the air. There was a sharp cry and the hand vanished under the creature's ragged garment as it unleashed some more curses and then moaned, "Not hungry, not hungry now."

The commandant spoke up bravely, but his voice could not hide his trepidation. "We won't let you hurt Cephas."

The creature jumped, thrashing it arms about. "Don't say its name, its *name!*" crying in pain, *"Call it 'Talker', 'Talker'!"* uttering more oaths and calling out incantations, seeking to ward off some sort of evil because the man's name had been spoken aloud.

It soon calmed, satisfied that any possible danger was now passed and shook its head. "Not hurt bad man. Not hurt him. You can do that, do that tomorrow." It giggled. "Yes, yes, that's for you. Must talk to bad man *tonight*, while he still lives."

The creature again fumed in disgust. "He insults the gods!" then reassured them, "Just talk, yes, talk business, my master's business."

Turning and motioning with its hands, it pleaded, "Be Patient! Patient, I say. Don't hurt them. I promised you wouldn't hurt them." Turning back to the men, it clasped its hands and waited.

Although fearful, the commandant remembered the coins. "The money - what of the money, the *thirteen* coins that brings a curse? And what of the gold you promised?"

Laughter filled the cold night air. "Yes, gold… gold money for the good boys, and more silver." The stinky thing held up its bony fingers. "Three more silver coins… Three! Bring good luck to little boys." Then its voice suddenly became threatening. "But first, business. Must do master's business now! Or master will not be kind to little boys."

The three men huddled in deep discussion over what they should do. If they received no more money, then a curse would surely befall them, but if the prisoner were hurt, the governor would throw them to the lions or even worse. They also reasoned if they didn't allow the creature in, it might put a spell on Cephas, possibly killing him. Then they would be thrown to the lions anyway. After several minutes of arguing, it was concluded they best chance the witch. At least there was a possibility the creature would hold up its end of the bargain.

The commandant finally motioned the creature forward. When it got close, he asked, "You promise no funny stuff, not to hurt him? You promise us more money, too?"

"Yes! Yes!" It sputtered impatiently. "And more money for good little boys, too. But first business! Master's business!"

The commandant gave orders to the first guard. "You stay here and watch." while he told the other to come with him.

The first guard complained about being left alone. The commandant silenced him with a few expletives and threats, after which he ordered, "Now keep a good watch and don't fall asleep!"

ଔ　ଔ　ଔ

'Remember, my Dear, there is a reward beyond this life for those who remain loyal to Yehowah. You must be willing to sacrifice all things for it.'

Ishtar could hear her uncle's words echoing in her head over and over again. Each time they did, her pain would ease, freeing her mind to think.

'Yes, Uncle, I know. But I need no reward. I love my God. I will serve him without reward.' How many times had that statement crossed her lips? Was that really so, or had she only said it to impress others?

There was a sudden rustling near her. Ishtar's eyes popped open in fright. The dim, golden glow from a light filled the cell. Who was there? Was Perk returned to ravish her again? The girl's heart pounded in rising panic. She squeezed her eyes shut, afraid of seeing Perk's garish grin. Nothing…no foul voice or brutish hands mauling her flesh…nothing. All remained silent.

Eventually, the girl's curiosity overcame her fears. She needed to know what was happening. Her heart needed to know what fate was to befall it, should it explode within her chest. Cautiously and ever so slowly, she pushed up and back onto her knees. Still nothing. Gathering up courage, she opened her eyes. Nothing…no shadows or sounds… just a comforting, golden glow filling the room.

Strange, Ishtar could see no lamp or torch. In fact, the light source seemed to be everywhere and nowhere. She rubbed her eyes, thinking herself dreaming. The light remained, still illuminating the room. But where was it coming from? Seeing no sign of its source only made the girl more determined to find what was making the light. Ishtar struggled to stand, moaning as she did.

The golden light shone out from her cell into the darkness of the prison, but from where? Ignoring her pain, the girl began to explore for its source, searching nooks and crannies everywhere in the little cell. She was stooped down in a far corner when sound of a gentle footfall echoed in her ears. Sucking in a breath and crying aloud in fright, Ishtar spun around, terrified of who she might see.

Words cannot describe Ishtar's shock at seeing a young woman appearing no older than her standing just outside the prison cell. A smiling, gentle face crowned with dark hair was pressed to the bars, twinkling, emerald-green eyes of almost hypnotic brilliance peering at her. The light revealed her ivory-colored, silky-smooth skin wrapped in a white satin, sleeveless gown, pinned at the shoulders by two silver brooches.

Ishtar stared in disbelief and surprise. The woman did not move, nor did she speak. Who *was* this person? Was this only a vision or a dream? Was the girl dead and gone to her promised glory? Was this her soul looking back at her as it prepared to leave for other worlds? The girl began to drift toward the haunting enchantress, extending her hand as if it were leading her along.

Slowly she drew near until her face nearly touched the woman's. Ishtar knew not whether it was seconds or an eternity that the two remained there, eye to eye, frozen in time. A spell held the girl in its grip, refusing to give her release. All the while she could feel some kind of energy flowing into her beaten body, soothing her heart and mind.

The woman finally broke the spell. In a musical voice, talking just above a whisper, she spoke to the girl. "Ishtar, I must have a word with you." Startled, Ishtar stepped back. The woman quietly opened the cell door and entered. The girl marveled in awe watching this person. The grace and beauty of the woman was beyond description. The fluidity of her movements could not be described as walking, but more like a drifting swan on a summer breeze. And her beauty was so great, the girl's heart started to burn with such a passion she feared it might burst. She stood transfixed, unable to remove her eyes from this magnificent goddess.

The woman reached out a hand, touching Ishtar's shoulder and, with two fingers, let it drift down to the girl's elbow. A raging fire and a freezing cold raced through Ishtar, starting at her shoulder and spreading like a tidal wave across the girl's flesh. The woman's fingers continued down the girl's arm, stopping at her opened palm. She then reached out with her other hand and cupped the girl's hand between hers.

An ecstasy of emotion erupted in Ishtar's head and her heart filled with joyous sensation the likes of which the girl had never experienced. Was this feeling the same as a woman enraptured in the arms of her lover? It was but a fleeting thought as Ishtar was swept along in this surge of intoxicating joy. The rush of emotion crested with the girl's cry of delight and then slowly ebbed, leaving her feeling satisfied and refreshed.

Gone were the earlier terrors of the night, having drifted away like some nearly forgotten dream. Perk's evil was little more than a memory, horrid and chilling… but still only a memory. She felt clean. 'The peace that excels all thought.' Those were the only words she could think of. 'The peace that excels all thought.' She then glanced down and received another shock. The child was clean, cleaner than if she had bathed.

The woman held up a gown, similar to hers. "Here, my lovely one, take this. Put it on and come with me." With the woman's assistance, Ishtar managed to dress. The gown's fabric was iridescent, shimmering with rich hues of blue, green and gold. It also had two silver brooches that glittered in the golden light. The woman then drew out two golden sandals like her own and slipped them on Ishtar's feet. She grinned, pleased, "There! You're now ready for our stroll." and gently pulled Ishtar from the cell.

As they walked along the passages, Ishtar noticed how quiet it was. Everyone, even the guard, was fast asleep. But what was even more spectacular was that the golden light remained in their company, illuminating the rooms and hallways. No person barred their path. Even the heavy iron door was swung fully open. The two gingerly stepped over one of the sleeping guards as they exited onto the foggy street.

The woman glanced around, lifting her head up as if smelling the breeze. Her voice filled with urgency. "Come, quickly! This fleeting hour will soon pass. Much there is to do and so little time to do it." She pulled Ishtar along, and both disappeared into the dense haze.

The fog was so thick, Ishtar could not tell how far they had traveled, nor did she know how long a time they walked until coming out of it. When it broke, she saw they were standing on a little hill overlooking a broad, moonlit valley filled with the scents of a warm spring evening.

The woman permitted the girl little time to luxuriate in the tapestry of the delights surrounding them, squeezing her hand. "Ishtar, my sweet one, we must talk." The girl was so caught up in the moment, the woman had to repeat herself twice more before getting her attention.

Reluctantly, Ishtar pulled herself away from this enchanting dream world. "I'm sorry, but I have never seen such..." She was stunned into silence. The light that was accompanying them was now emanating from the woman, her skin and clothing radiating with a golden glow, lighting the area around them. "Wha... Wha... Your... Who ar..." Ishtar stared into the woman's emerald-green eyes, reedy pools of green so deep. She felt another universe must be hidden within those eyes.

Ishtar was becoming aware that she was standing in the presence of a creature not of her kind. As the realization filled her mind, she grew fearful for her life. Should this person truly be a messenger of God, how could she survive? The girl fell to her knees, clasping her hands together and raising them high, crying, "My Lord, forgive me for my insolence. Forgive me, please, for looking upon the face of God!"

"Ishtar, stand up." A gentle but firm voice responded. "I am not God, just an ordinary servant of His house. Now, please, my sister, there is much to be done. I have no time for this. Please, stand." She pulled Ishtar up. "Child, I am not from your world, that is true, but I am still your sister. Are we not all children of God?"

Ishtar was nearly beside herself with anxiety. The woman wiped tears from the girl's eyes and held her shaking hands. "My child, blessed you are among women. Had you not been found delightful to God, he would not have bothered with you. You have nothing to fear from me, but there is reason to fear."

That statement caught the girl's attention. The woman smiled. "My child, I have been sent to offer you a choice." She swept her left hand in the direction of the hills. "Look, please, to see your future. There are two roads being offered to you. Each contains a blessing and a price, but one may be greater. You choose." The woman opened her hand, revealing a tooled leather pouch. Ishtar gazed down at its opening. The purse was filled with silver and gold monies, a king's ransom. "Here..." The woman placed the purse in Ishtar's hand. The girl gasped. A person could live a lifetime and never acquire such wealth. "What is this all about?" She asked, not able to take her eyes off the money.

The answer came quickly. "You may take this money and go. Travel north, then east, continuing on until the roaring sea faces you. There you will find peace for the rest of your many days in this realm. A husband of valor and kindness will be waiting for you at the end of your journey. He will fall in love with you and refuse to leave your side. Never will cruelty and suffering befall you again. Your womb will become fat with children and your breasts will swell with the sweet milk of life. No enemy will enter your gate nor will famine or thirst find you. That is the gift of the first road."

A sweet smile crept across the girl's face. She imagined what her life would be like, her husband of valor, the many fat and happy children she would nurse, and then the smiled faded as she considered the cost. As she slowly closed her hand around the money as if fondling a dream, the girl frowned. "What is the price? What is the price of that road? What does it cost me?"

The woman closed her hands around the girl's, hiding the money from view. "For you," She looked away. "being a good wife and mother will not always be easy." Ishtar was not satisfied with the woman's answer. She could see her skirting the question. Once more she asked, "What is the price of that road, and what of the other? You do not tell me yet what the second road is. How shall I choose wisely if you do not tell me?" The woman was surprised. "Is the first road not good enough for you? Why must I tell you of the other? Enjoy your gifts. You have earned them. They are a reward for all your sacrifice."

Ishtar was becoming impatient. "What is the second road from which I may choose, and what is the price demanded for taking it?" Slowly shaking her head, the woman sighed, "So much like your uncle you are. Little knowledge is a dangerous tool." Ishtar pressed her for an answer. The woman surrendered to Ishtar's will. "All right, I will tell you. Your Lord said that some of his servants would speak before kings and governors. They would stand in front of crowds in defense of his God. They would prove his enemy a liar. That is the blessing of your second road."

The woman grasped Ishtar by the arms and stared into her eyes. Great sadness grew on her face and a tear rolled down her cheek. "Take the monies and go. Unsung is the hero who succeeds in secret, but a hero that person is nonetheless. Yet to fail while attempting the sublime will only bring one shame and humiliation. You have run your race to the full. Enjoy your reward."

Ishtar was quick with her reply, and her tongue sharp and scolding. "You offered me two roads. It is my choosing as to which one I take, not yours.

Now, please, it is your turn to confess to me what the fate of the second road is. It is my right to know."

"Yes…yes, I did." The woman softly replied. She could not look the child in the face. "The tiller man is not kind when the tempest descends upon the sea. He exacts a high wage to deliver one to safe harbor. There is no safe harbor to be found on this second path. Only the black abyss of death awaits the sojourner. There is no escape from that destiny." She looked up into the girl's eyes. "So why trouble the spirits with such a fatal choice? Enjoy the blessings already offered you."

Ishtar was not swaged. "I have a right to know! I choose my own fate, not you! You offered me two roads. Must I barter with you… or is mine a *free choice*?" A warning filled with indignation crossed the woman's lips. "Shall a child rebuke its father and not be chastised? Dare you show God's servant such disrespect and not fear retribution?!" The reproof was not wasted on the child. She humbly begged forgiveness, apologizing for her flagrant disrespect. Still, she pressed the issue, pointing out that she had been *offered a choice*.

"Yes, my little one, you have been offered a choice." The woman thought a moment, adding, "It is sometimes better to not know the price until it has to be delivered up. Would you be able to see it through if you did know?" Ishtar was more respectful, but still firm in her resolve. "The tiller man cannot exact a thief's price if his charge knows the journey's route. I will not travel the road blindly when knowledge can light up the dangers I must face."

The woman shrugged, resigning herself to telling Ishtar everything. "All right… The price that is to be paid is not yours alone. It will be demanded from both you and your uncle, and it is high. He will be tested to betray his love for his God, to preserve your life. If he remains loyal, you…" She shook her head. "you will die a most horrible death in the arena, torn apart by beasts. Should he fail in his test, your death by wild beasts will be delayed but for a day so that vile men may have their way with you."

Ishtar groaned in dismay. "So that is my test? The price I must pay to take the second road?"

"No…" the woman answered. "You, for your part, will have no control regarding the outcome in this approaching test. It is your uncle's to decide. Your test will arrive sooner. The finality will be the same, should you fail or succeed, but it will either be death in victory…or defeat."

Ishtar silently pondered the matter then asked, "What of my test, then? If I am to die, do I not deserve to know what it will be?"

"You pose a question I cannot answer." The woman softly replied. "It is great, because your enemy will continue to offer you a way out. If your heart is not complete toward your God, you will not succeed. Easy it is to fool the heart when a door of escape is opened for you. And gentle speech may well hide a deceitful tongue."

She closed Ishtar's fingers around the purse. "Here. Take the money I give and leave. Enjoy your blessing to the full." Ishtar watched the woman turn away and then mutter as if to herself, "This war is not hers to fight. How can you ask this of the child?"

The girl reached into the pouch and played with a few coins. Her mind could not conjure up visions of the treasures this money offered. The coins suddenly felt dirty, unclean. She dropped the money back into the purse. Indeed, everything about the first road felt wrong, like delicious food that turns sour in one's belly.

As Ishtar reasoned over the things she had been told, her mind filled with suspicion. She felt compelled to ask, "You did not come from above the stars to wish a child well and give her a gift of gifts. I do know for a fact that God does not work in such ways. So tell me, please, should I take the monies and depart, upon whose head does the duty fall?"

The woman did not answer. She continued to look toward the east, tears trickling down her face as she pleaded with Ishtar, "Take the monies. We will work things out."

Ishtar grabbed hold of the woman's arm. "I can make no commitment without understanding! Now tell me! *Who* pays the bill for my happiness?" Covering her eyes with her hands, the woman sobbed, "My Lord and my God pay the price, for your uncle is needed elsewhere in this realm. It is not his day to die. If you leave, they will destroy him."

Ishtar lowered her head, thinking aloud. "So, my soul in place of his..."

The woman turned to the girl, distraught. "No one deserves to be asked what has been of you, but there is no other way. My soul instead of yours I would gladly offer, yet it is not to be. Only you have the power to save your uncle on this morrow. He must prove his worth. His destiny demands it of him."

Ishtar released her hold on the woman. "Here, take back your money. How can a man enjoy a warm bed and a full belly when his family starves in the cold? I am *not* that wicked!" She pushed the purse into the woman's hand. "Now return me to the nether world and the demons who await me." A shudder ran through her as a sickness grew in her stomach. "I will wait there for my time to come."

There was no stopping the woman's tears. She kissed the child, promising, "The spirit of my God will stay with you, and I... yes, I swear, as I am alive and do live... I will remain by your side to comfort my cherished sister in her distress." She embraced the girl and gave her another kiss. "Until the day when we will share the wine and the good times..."

The woman began to fade into a rising mist. Ishtar cried, "Who are you?! What is your name?! I need to know! What is it?!" As the woman became little more than a fleeting shadow, she sadly called from the mist, "To many I am only 'the troubling one'. To others I am known as the 'child of pain'."

Fog swept in upon Ishtar. She reached out for the woman, but could not find her. Air swirled around the child like a cyclone, its sound as though thousands of birds taking flight. Up into the whirlwind the girl rose, spinning faster and faster until her head became dizzy and faint. Eventually the windstorm subsided, gently dropping the girl down in a pile of soft straw.

The surrounding sounds and smells told Ishtar that she was again in the prison cell. She began to wonder if she had ever left. Maybe it was but a dream caused by the blows Perk had delivered to her head. Still, it was a beautiful dream. Could it have been a magic dream? A vision? Her uncle had told her of visions. But visions were something special, reserved for men of great renown, not her. The girl shrugged. Not to matter. Whatever it was, she felt refreshed by it.

There was no light for the child to see with, no window to let in the moonlight and no lamps even in the distant rooms to permit any sight. The sound of heavy sleeping was all that disturbed the silence. Even the rats had apparently decided to take a holiday.

Ishtar leaned back on the straw. Strange…it smelled fresh and her pains from the night's beatings were gone. The girl began recalling the details of her wonderful dream, not wanting to forget a thing about it. She pulled her knees up to her chest. Wrapping her arms around them as she did, her heart jumped in excitement. Even in the blackness, she could tell the feel of satin, the smooth, silky satin of her beautiful dream gown.

ಬಿ   ಬಿ   ಬಿ

The dark of WacxGonn trees with their low-hanging evergreen boughs gave Darla little solace. She darted along the path, flitting in and out of their protective shadows. The gown, so effective in dazzling Ishtar, acted like a beacon every time the woman stepped into the moonlit night.

Searching eyes could be anywhere now. There had been no time for Darla to gather her flight suit and weapons. She was sure they, along with all the vision gadgets, were long since discovered. Legion would not be pleased to have someone messing with his 'special toy'. The woman was beginning to regret not waiting for the remainder of the mission team, but what else could she have done? If they had failed to make contact with the child this night, the entire mission would be in jeopardy.

Darla pulled the communicator from a hidden pocket in her dress. A series of tiny blue lights flashed to life in rapid succession only to fade, one after the other. Again they would flash, searching for an incoming signal. Still nothing... 'They should at least be here by now. What's taking them…?'

There was good reason for Darla to worry. This was a strange and curious world she found herself wandering alone in. Long years before, Euroaquilo, her mentor and intimate companion, had journeyed with the woman into this place. His warnings, recalled, did not bring comfort. 'This is a world that defies all known laws. It's quirky, doing as it pleases, and biding no intruder's commands. You would do well not to wander here alone.'

Euroaquilo had informed Darla of some of the known and imagined history of this place, most still a dark mystery to even the oldest and wisest of her kind. It had been said that time and space matter little here. Sojourners navigated it by linking up complex mathematical coordinates with existing star system charts, adding in galactic rotational calculations and then, as Euroaquilo said, 'would mix in a little gut feeling' and there was their destination.

Her successful and timely arrival had been no small miracle. She managed the rendezvous point at Eden's Gate after losing two bandits intent on her interception. After waiting several hours for her contacts, she had ventured through the jump portal, trusting to her own ability in finding the single portal stream out of millions that would deliver her to this one location.

She arrived in time by chance, she thought, to make the two league's distance from the ship to the city and then still have time to change into the gown and set up the vision gadgets. Although never actually leaving this Middle Realm and transferring into the land of humans, often called by her people the 'Second' or 'Lower Realm', by using the vision machines and her very limited mental abilities, the girl successfully completed the mission, maybe not as good as Gabrielle, but *damn good,* anyway!

The crisp snap of a twig alerted Darla to possible danger. She slunk back further away from the trail, under the trees. It could have been one of many things causing that disturbance. Her heart raced with fearful anticipation.

Attempting to calm her jitters, she contemplated the possibilities. After all, there was a menagerie of huge beasts in this land. One might very well be tracking her, more out of curiosity than ill intent. Then there were the 'People of the Mist', one of the names given the mysterious race who existed long before her kind were born.

The accounts of these people were both mythical and intriguing. They were referred to as 'Spirit Walkers', 'Guardians', 'Cherubs', 'Blazing Wings', to name a few. Darla had always liked the term 'HootinSmokers', a name given them by some of the most ancient of her race who claimed to have actually seen them. The wild antics of those storytellers had caused her, as a little girl, to roll in laughter as their tales were acted out.

Legends told that when Darla's kind began growing in number, the People of the Mist withdrew into the hidden lands of this Middle Realm, becoming little more than ghostly shadows on moonlit nights. It was said that they slept in silence until their Master would wake them to glory in the last trumpet call. Well, that was one of the stories she had been told when a little child. The woman hoped the intruder might well be either of these two things.

A shudder ran down her spine, as she thought of Euroaquilo's warning given her so long ago. 'It is also a very dangerous place since the Rebellion. Every debased, vile creature frequents these haunts, making it necessary to never travel here alone.'

After the Rebellion, war had broken out in the Middle Realm. Although its expanse appeared limitless and much of it was still unexplored, key locations had been fought over for many centuries. In fact, this was where the major part of the wars had been fought up to this night. Darla was no stranger to these wars. She was a hardened veteran, having fought in all three Megiddo Wars, the Persian Debacle, the MedoGrecian Crusade and the Maccabean Decade. But she had been one in a crowd of countless thousands then. Tonight she was alone and naked, bereft of weapon or comrade.

Listening to the continuing night noises and detecting no other unusual sounds, Darla decided to chance a run for her ship. Considering the gown to be a hindrance, she kneeled down to unlace her sandals, quietly removing them. With a grunt, she stood and began pulling the dress over her head.

"Got'ya!"

Darla spun around and dropped into a crouch, her arms and head still wrapped up in the gown. She was preparing to be assailed by hands intent on her capture. Legion would be most pleased with such a prize and could be counted on to give a rich reward to the person delivering her.

'Cr-a-ack!' Whoever wielded the club had no intention of taking his trophy alive. The blow caught Darla just below her right eye, lifting her off her feet and sending her sprawling, face down, onto the pathway.

A rough hand yanked Darla over onto her back a she groaned in pain. Another person pulled off the gown and exclaimed, "She ain't dead, Yulackk! You must be losin' your touch." Yulackk bent close to examine the damage his attack had done. Darla's eye was little more than bloody pulp, her upper jaw crushed and her nose split, but she was still very much alive.

He glanced at Darla's upper arm and noticed its awkward angle. "The bitch's arm got in the way. Ain't my fault!" He laughed, "Did a number on it, though..."

The second man stepped closer. "Get outta the way, Yulackk, I want to get a look at who we have."

"She's just a *bitch*, Gihon, some worthless little *nobody*." Yulackk grinned. "I was right when I said we'd get the same for her dead or alive."

"Outta the way, you!" Gihon demanded. "I'll decide if it's a *nobody bitch* or not."

Yulackk grumbled, wanting to finish her off so he could get back to more important matters. Gihon motioned him away, saying to wait. He knelt down on one knee, straddling one of Darla's legs, and leaned in close to her face to get a better look in the dim light.

Giggles and laughter filled the night air. Two women came jogging up the trail. When they got near, one of them called out asking if the men had found the intruder. Gihon ignored the woman's question. He scrutinized Darla's face, but could not identify it with anyone he knew.

Just as he was about to reveal his findings, a hand flew up to his ear. Gihon screamed in pain as Darla dug her nails in and began tearing it off while driving her knee hard into his groin. Yulackk jumped forward shouting, kicking Darla in the side of her head. Knocked senseless by the blow, the woman's body went limp. Gihon rolled on to his side, groaning in pain.

"Has our lord Gihon's *tool* been broken?" One of the women teased. The second woman derogatorily accused, "How does a chieftain in Legion's house explain his being bested by a man without balls?" Both of them erupted in chiding laughter. They went on with their insults until Gihon, still clutching his groin, rolled onto his knees and, swearing and cursing, ordered them to shut up. He finally sat back on his haunches and lifted his kilt, glaring at the women. "You watch and see what my *tool* can do… and wish you hadn't. For when I'm done with *this*," He pointed at Darla. "I'm going to do the same with you two!"

With that, Gihon began to work up his manhood by brutalizing Darla with his hands, after which he started to violently rape her. "How do you like it now, you miserable piece of dog shit?! You could have made it easy on yourself and died quickly, but *no,* you wanted to make me the fool. I'll show you who's the fool! You'll soon wish you were already dead!" He dug his nails into Darla's breasts, angrily tearing at them.

Darla cried out in agony. It only made Gihon more sadistic. He bit and chewed at the woman's face. He tore off her earlobe, chomped it into tiny pieces and spit it into her face. "Pray to Mother, you ugly shit worm. Maybe she'll let you die!"

Darla turned her head to the side and coughed out blood and broken teeth. She could make no reply.

Gihon laughed. "See! The Mother of harlots cares not for her children…" He released his passion in one heaving outburst and then fell on Darla's chest. As he panted, he ridiculed her, snidely whispering in her ear, "Or is it just you…you *worthless dung meat!*"

After catching his breath, Gihon sat back on his knees, viewing with pleasure the results of his labors. He rested his bloodied hands on Darla's legs, nodding his head. "You're a delight to behold, nearly as beautiful as that tramp, Michael, was that day outside the palace. My artwork is nearly complete." With that, he motioned to Yulackk. "Smash in its skull!"

Yulackk grinned. "I won't hav'ta do it twice…" He swung his cudgel high over his head in one graceful move that transferred his body's power into the weapon.

Gihon stared at Darla's broken face, waiting to see Yulackk smash it to nothing. "Do it good, you! I want a big splatter!"

'*Sh...ur...rr flu...unk!*'

Yulackk yipped like a startled dog as the club fell from his hands.

"What the...?!" Gihon looked in time to see Yulackk grab his face and stumble backward, a glistening black jillson bolt sticking from his face just below his nose.

'*Sh...ur...rr flu...unk!*' A second arrow slammed into Yulackk's mouth, punching its way up through his skull and protruding out the back of his head until its waxy tail feathers disappeared into the man's face. Yulackk let out a gasp as he spun around and fell, face down, in the dirt.

"*Beetle dung!*" A woman in a silver-metallic flight suit came running out from the shadow of the trees, drawing forth a long double-edged battle sword as she advanced, its green, ghostly flame identifying it as a fearsome derker blade.

"*Gabrielle!*" Gihon quailed as he threw his hands up over his face.

Gabrielle halted beside Darla's bleeding body. She lifted her sword high, shouting, "*Master's whore-maiden! Be off into damnation!*"

With a grunt, Gabrielle swung the weapon down and across, cleaving Gihon's head and hands from his body. Blood squirted into the air as the lifeless corpse slowly keeled over, falling to the ground.

A woman screeched, "*NasiSair! NasiSair!*" (meaning '*Prince of the Warlocks*'). She and the other woman ran off, screaming, into the night.

The whooshing sound of several more jillson bolts followed them into the darkness, at least one finding its mark. There was a cry followed by a crashing thud of a body hitting the ground. The other woman continued fleeing, all the time sounding the alarm, "*NasiSair! NasiSair!*"

Tossing her sword aside, Gabrielle dropped down next to Darla and began searching for signs of life, gently resting her hand on the woman's chest, relieved to feel a weak heartbeat. The girl still lived, but for how long? Gabrielle tenderly cradled Darla's head in her hands and wept. "Oh, my child, my child... Forgive me! Oh, please, please forgive me!"

Sound of hurrying footsteps echoed in the darkness, the night air soon filled with groans of dismay and lament. Gabrielle was inconsolable. Her tears ran in rivers, mixing with the blood on Darla's face. "I'm sorry, Mother, I'm so, so sorry! My soul instead of hers, I promised you! I promised... promised!" She looked up at the sky and wailed, "I have murdered your little daughter! Forgive me, please, Mother, please!"

Gabrielle paid no heed to the hustle of the others in her troop as they secured the area. One voice sounded above the others, giving orders and directions. "Periste, you and Chisamore stash these bodies. Planetee, take the others and set up a perimeter. Sirion, stay with Gabrielle."

Planetee motioned to the others her orders. In moments they had faded into the darkness. Before doing the same, she asked, "Michael…er'…Mihai, what of the woman? If she's alive, do you want to take her prisoner?"

Mihai shook her head. "We will take no prisoners, understand?"

Planetee acknowledged and departed. Mihai turned her attention to Gabrielle and Darla. Periste and Chisamore were just returning from disposing of Gihon's body, having very unceremoniously tossed his head and hands into a thicket. They then grabbed hold of Yulackk and dragged him into the shadows. Mihai tried to ignore the hacking sounds and curses coming from that direction.

Sirion mentioned it, though. "Periste can be mighty expressive when you get her temper up. They'll have to bag him to bury him after she's done!"

"That's enough, Sirion… please!" Mihai softly scolded. "Help us with Darla and forget the night."

Gabrielle had stopped her open weeping. Through subdued, heaving sobs, she was choking out a healing song. The woman was the oldest of all the daughters in the First Realm. It was said her powers of healing were second to none and that she had been known to restore life to those whose breath had long left them. Tonight this wizard worked her magic in order to prevent Darla's breath from passing away.

Mihai leaned over Gabrielle, gently placing a hand on her shoulder. "Honey, please, our child will live. I promise you. She will be delivered home safely into Mother's arms."

Darla groaned and moved her head. Mihai squeezed Gabrielle's shoulder. "See! Already your cure is having an effect! She will survive, I promise you. With your help, our daughter will pass through this fire."

Gabrielle continued her healing songs, all the while caressing Darla's injuries with her fingers. In time, she and Mihai could see a positive response to what she was doing. Gradually, the girl regained consciousness.

Suddenly a hand shot up and gripped Gabrielle's arm and Darla's undamaged eye opened. She struggled in an attempt to communicate, rolling her head from side to side while pulling on Gabrielle's flight suit. Gabrielle held Darla's head in her hands and softly whispered, "It's alright, my lovely one… it's alright. We'll have you out of here shortly. The fleet's not far away. Don't fret, you'll be fine."

Darla violently shook her head, crying out in pain from doing so. She struggled to speak, but only coughed out blood and more broken teeth. Mihai reached down and touched the girl's shoulder, trying to reassure her. "You're safe, Darling, you're safe. No one's going to hurt you anymore." Mihai's intended encouragement only frustrated the situation. Darla began to thrash about, forcing Gabrielle to restrain her. "This is no good!" Gabrielle moaned. "If this continues, she'll damage herself even more."

"Is there something you have to tell us?" Sirion asked Darla, catching her eye as she did. Darla quieted and painfully nodded her head. After several failed attempts to communicate, the girl's face being so broken she could not move her mouth, she let out a cry and tears started.

Mihai pondered in thought a moment. She finally leaned close and whispered in Gabrielle's ear. "Don't you have the power to share with her in a waking dream?" Gabrielle frowned, whispering back, "I have not attempted such a thing with someone in this condition. Her brain is badly bruised, and she's hemorrhaging. Besides, the waking dream is most often shared between bonded lovers - men and women - if you know what I mean."

Mihai was at a loss for ideas. She felt a waking dream was their only hope. "You must try something! Our girl is nearly beside herself with a desire to speak. I'm afraid she will die from anxiety should we fail her at this moment."

"*Do you understand?!*" Gabrielle asked in fearful concern, still whispering. "A waking dream requires intense concentration on the part of both parties. I'm afraid that it will kill the child for me to do such a thing." Darla squeezed Gabrielle's arm. She had overheard the conversation and was revealing her willingness to take such a risk. Gabrielle argued awhile with Mihai and Sirion, but to no avail. She finally surrendered to their persuasion.

"I'll try not to hurt you, Darling," Gabrielle sadly crooned to Darla, "but it's very dangerous." Darla indicated her willingness. Placing her hands on each side of Darla's head, Gabrielle bent over until her forehead was touching Darla's. She stared into Darla's face and began to hum an enchanting tune. Darla attempted the same. Gradually, the two women sank into a harmonic trance, becoming oblivious to their surroundings.

It was only a matter of seconds, but for Darla and Gabrielle it was an endless encounter. The two drifted in worlds of time and space, sifting through the thoughts and memories of many ages of men. Gabrielle struggled to focus her concentration on the issues of the moment. Darla, on the other hand, drifted in and out of consciousness, flitting from one dimension of thought into another.

With herculean effort, Gabrielle managed to break away. Pushing herself up, she let out a cry. "I have tried! I have tried! I am sick and my world spins with senseless riddles of confusion." She dropped her head from exhaustion. "Give me a moment to sort things out." The sickness rapidly passed and, as Gabrielle caught her breath while mulling over the visions in her head, she explained what happened. "A waking dream is casual, something used by romancing lovers as they flirt from afar. It was designed to transmit emotions and feelings, to increase passion and desire in the lovers' hearts."

A shudder ran down Gabrielle's spine. She shook her head. "I have never searched for other than feelings before. Hard... very hard to find words... and meaning. Give me... some time to think." She leaned forward, resting her weight on her hands, drooping her head.

People came and went in the camp, bringing Mihai information and seeking instructions. Tzidohn and Depais were approaching as Gabrielle revealed what she had learned. She sat on her knees, head up and hands on her legs. "Darla's already made contact with the girl, but she took license with the way the encounter was orchestrated."

Gabrielle's tone sent shivers of foreboding across Mihai's shoulders and down her arms. In a halting voice, she asked, "What did our child do?"

"Darla was to give Ishtar a vision and offer her a way out. Whether she understood the proper use of the machinery, I'm not sure. She transferred material from this realm directly into the Second Realm, something that was only to be done if Ishtar chose to depart the prison."

Mihai asked, "So what..." Gabrielle cut Mihai off.

"She produced a real gown for the girl, and left it remain with her and she filled the prison cell with fresh straw. When the guards discover it in the morning, well, I don't know how it will change matters." Gabrielle raised a hand, shaking a finger. "But that's not the worst! Funneling her own mental powers through the vision machine, Darla cured the girl of the damage delivered her body earlier this night, giving the girl's flesh a glowing vitality uncommon in humans. During this process, Darla linked her mind with Ishtar's and then she promised to be with the girl to assist her this coming day."

Mihai finally asked her question. "So what are we supposed to do now? It sounds to me that Darla's attempt at helping the girl may well add to her woes. The governor is a tyrant, having little respect or concern for anyone other than himself. I had hoped that Ishtar's beaten condition would lead the man to have pity on her. Now he will likely obsess over her beauty, seeking some way to take her for himself." Frowning, Mihai added, "If my worst fears are realized, Ishtar will not survive this test without being linked to one of our minds."

Gabrielle agreed. "And Darla has already made that link. Unless one of us can accomplish the same task, Ishtar will not receive that needed support."

"But the spirit will be there." Sirion answered. "She won't be completely alone."

"True, true..." Mihai replied, agreeing, turning to Gabrielle. "But from what you've learned, we now are dealing with a woman having near perfect beauty. How will the wolves of her world react to such a thing? Indeed! Could a good man keep his honor around her if given control over her soul?"

She looked back at Sirion and moaned. "The girl's test was certainly great to begin with. Now it may well be impossible for her to survive it alone, even with all our spirit. Indeed, I think the only way she will succeed is to do something that will make herself ugly in the eyes of her oppressors."

Mihai gripped Gabrielle's arm and spoke with urgency. "We must make contact with the girl ourselves and link our minds with hers!"

"It's too late now." Tzidohn stepped closer. He pointed into the distance. "The element of surprise is gone. That's what we came to tell you. Gihon and his clowns were not here by accident. They were part of a much bigger hunting party. What our little sister has done did not go unnoticed. Legion has his scouts out searching for the intruder or intruders. The size of the search parties makes me think he feels there are many opponents." He looked over his shoulder. "The door of opportunity is now closed. We would have to fight our way through at least a company of enemy hosts to get to her. There are only ten of us here, besides Darla." He looked at Gabrielle, "Even with your strength, I doubt any of us would survive such a battle."

Gabrielle slowly lowered her head in defeat. "We have lost. There is nothing we can do now." Darla would not be counted out so quickly. She began to thrash, pointing toward her head. Gabrielle was apprehensive, but surrendered to Darla's demands. She again began a waking dream with her. This time it seemed easier and less exhausting, a connection having already been made. Gabrielle soon struggled to sit up.

After a moment's rest, she told the others what Darla requested. "Our child wants us to take her to the hanging cliffs, a promontory some distance from here. She believes with my help she will be able to communicate with Ishtar from there."

"Why there?" Sirion asked. "Why not here? What's the difference?"

Interrupting, Mihai answered, "The promontory has a strong energy field, helpful when using mind communication. Plus, the place is mathematically the nearest location to the prison and governor's palace, making the possibility for a mind link more successful."

"Not only that," Depais added, "they know, or soon will know where we are. We were unsuccessful at stopping that screaming meemie. She's sure to bring Legion down on us. We need to be on the move, and soon!"

Mihai added, "Then we'll have to make haste. Depais, you and Tzidohn help with Darla. I'll..."

Gabrielle cut Mihai off. "I'm not moving this child, 'less it's back to our ship. She's half dead, and I'm not going to risk her life on a fool's hope."

Sirion piped up. "It was a *fool's hope* that sent Darla here alone. We didn't consider any breakdowns on our end, so never gave her directions should we fail to arrive. I believe she wants to finish her assignment, no matter the cost..."

"You tend your duties, little one!" Gabrielle snapped. "I've been given charge of Darla… promised Mother. I will not suffer her loss on a futile whim!"

Sirion countered. "It's Darla's wish. She has the ri…"

"That's enough, now!" Mihai snorted. "This is not the time to…"

"I'm taking her back to the ship! And that's final!" Gabrielle leaned over Darla and began another healing song.

Sirion muttered on about their dilemma and what they should have done. Gabrielle sat up, scowling, anger growing in her voice. "It might have been better if you had stayed behind, little one. I thought you might learn something here, on your first sojourn into this valley of darkness. I regret our breakdown." She moaned aloud, "Why, oh why this day?! Why did our engines have to fail on this most important day?!"

Mihai glared at Sirion, her stare telling the woman to remain silent. She then rested a hand on Gabrielle's shoulder. "Honey, there's no need to make the decision at this moment." She looked up and asked Tzidohn, "How much time do you think we have before Legion arrives?" He raised his head as if smelling the breeze. "Oh, I think we're safe with an hour, maybe a little more."

Depais offered to return to the ship and get some medical supplies. Mihai watched as the woman and Tzidohn disappeared into the night then looked into the sky. "We have two hours or so before daybreak. Sirion, go get Periste then meet me on the trail. We'll scout on ahead to see what's up."

Sirion hurried away and Mihai turned to Gabrielle. "It'll be alright, Honey. Mother wouldn't have approved this mission if she didn't believe in our success. You do your magic for now. We'll see what comes of it."

Gabrielle returned to her healing songs. Mihai met up with Sirion and Periste, and hurried out of the camp. The moon sank behind the hills, filling the surrounding world with blackness. Soon the only sound to be heard was the quiet tune of a healer desperately working her magic.

ℂ ℂ ℂ

Cackles and laughter echoed off the walls and fell on the ears of the prison population, along with occasional smacking sounds, followed by "Not hungry! Not hungry now." This was too much for many of the prisoners. Not only were most very superstitious, they believed the jailer had brought a demon here to play sport with them.

An uproar grew among the inmates. Many began crying out to their gods in fear and invoking them for protection. Some called down evil on the commandant, crying out curses that his soul burn forever in torment for bringing this abomination against them.

In frustration, the commandant shouted to the prisoners to quiet down, telling them there was naught for them to worry about except his wrath. Finally, forgetting his fear, he turned toward the creature and angrily threatened, "Shut up your face! I can't have a riot in here. If you don't quiet down, I'll... I'll..." The commandant began to ponder what might become of him if the creature felt itself in danger.

The creature lowered its voice. "Yeesssss?" It suspiciously asked.

The commandant swallowed. "I'll... I'll say his name."

The stinky little creature froze, put its hand up to the opened hood and cried, "Sh! Sh! Not talk, not talk now. Not loud, must be still." It crouched, putting both its hands up like rodent paws. "Must be like a mouse... er... er... Will be like a little mouse... a quiet little mouse."

Having gained some confidence, the commandant spoke up boldly, wagging his finger. "When we get there, I don't want no loud words, neither. Nobody's to hear what you say. Nobody!"

The little creature could not understand. It asked, troubled, "Nobody?" "Nobody?!"

Somewhat exasperated, the commandant explained. "Only the man you go see. That fool Ce..."

The little creature flung its arms about. "Sh! Sh! Not his name! You promised if little child was good. You promised!"

"All right! All right!" The commandant fumed. "You know what I mean, right?"

The little creature laughed. "Yes! Yes! Only to foolish man..." It threw its hand up in front of its hood. "Sh... Sh... Will be quiet like a mouse... Pretty boys... good... nice boys will not hear little child. Noooo... not hear little child at all."

"Good!" The commandant snorted, and then threatened, "And keep it that way, or the guard will stick you with a spear!"

Both men heard a little hiss escape the hood, followed by, "Like a mouse, a little baby mouse. Good child will be quiet, like a mouse."

On the bottom-most level of the prison, at the end of a musty, putrid smelling passage, the three came to a large iron door. The only light was from the guard's lamp, which appeared to gasp for air enough to remain burning. The commandant took out a large key and slowly turned the rusty lock, its tumblers squealing in contempt at the intruders, finally giving way with a loud *crack!* It took the combined efforts of both the guard and commandant to force the heavy iron door on its hinges.

Finally, with audible grunts from the two men, the door gave way, allowing the guard to enter with his lamp. The light fell upon the single occupant in the room beyond. He sat, motionless, feet firmly secured in massive wooden stocks. The person covered his eyes with a hand, the light momentarily blinding him.

The little creature yipped with delight. "It's him! It's him! Master will be so happy with little child. It's him!"

The commandant scolded, "Quiet now! You promised to be quiet."

The creature's hand popped up in front of its hood, nodding in acknowledgment. "Sh… Sh…"

The commandant leaned forward, into the room, calling out to the man, "Fancy that! You have a visitor, but I don't think you'll be much happy about it."

He motioned for the creature to come forward. "It says its master has some words for you. Do be polite… and no screaming."

Shaking a threatening finger at the creature, the commandant ordered, "Don't hurt him. You promised. Or else…or else I'll say his name!"

An angry hiss escaped from under the creature's hood. It started, as if remembering to be good, then, as it shook its head, promised, "Not hurt him." It extended a bony finger. "For you… for you."

The creature turned away from the commandant and stared through the doorway. It began its happy little bobbing from side to side, humming some little nonsensical tune, followed by, "Like a mouse, a little tiny mouse."

Satisfied, the commandant turned to go, ordering the guard to stand watch at the door. After he departed, the guard cautiously inched his way forward, until he stood just inside the room. Holding his lamp high, he motioned the creature to enter, "I'll be watching!" his hollow words an impotent threat.

As it passed him, the creature snarled, its fingers brushing the man's leg, the guard recoiling in near panic, stopping just short of crying out in fear. The creature swept its hand back in disgust and mumbled something under its breath, then focused its attention on the prisoner, smacking its lips and singing little chants.

Symeon sat on the stony floor, arms behind him, lending support. For six days his feet had been shackled in stocks, his food and drink scanty at best, and his cuts and bruises untended. Still, his sight was clear and his mind sharp. If this was some trick of the governor, he refused to fall for it.

When the noisy little creature was just feet away, he sarcastically asked, making sure the guard would hear, "So, what do you intend to do, eat me?"

The creature put its hand in front of its face, speaking in a hushed voice. "Sh… Sh… Must be quiet like a mouse. *Symeon* must be quiet like mouse."

"What the?!" Symeon cried out.

The guard lifted his lamp and craned his neck. "Hey, there!"

"Sh! Sh!" The creature was urgent. "Must be quiet like mouse, like mouse."

A dim, flickering glow reflected Symeon's curiosity.

The creature stepped in close so that its opened hood was only inches from Symeon's face. "Who do you think would waste their time coming to see the likes of you, especially when you can't even remember to keep your promised appointments!"

Symeon's eyes grew big with surprise as he whispered, "Is that you, Hanna?"

The creature pretended insult. "Who *else* have you stood up? Of course, it's me! What did you think I was, some kind of *demon*?"

Symeon wrinkled up his nose, shaking his head. "You smell like one. Whew! And I thought I stunk."

The man reached up and took Hanna's hand, careful the guard didn't see. Although happy to see his long-time friend, his concern for her welfare was reflected in his voice. "It's too dangerous for you to be here. Why have you taken such a risk?"

"There are many reasons I have come -" Hanna started rummaging under her tattered robe. "to help you, inform you and to *warn* you." She glanced up, catching Symeon's eyes, hoping he didn't see the pity in hers. "The world has changed outside. Clouds of violence against our people are growing everywhere. They seek to destroy our faith by forcing you to recant yours."

With some noticeable effort, Hanna pulled out a leather-like flask from under the robe. "Here, drink this. It's some herb soup." She apologized. "Sorry, it's cold, but it was the best I could do. And I'm sorry I stink so. I couldn't think of any other way to get in to see you."

She looked over her shoulder at the guard, still standing in the door, and growled. The guard quailed, but said nothing. Hanna went back to digging in her robe. "They are afraid of me. They think I'm some kind of witch or demon. It's amazing what a little flour and stink can do."

Symeon shook his head and sighed. "The poor, ignorant fools. I feel sorry for them at times. They're so wrapped up in superstition about the gods, they fear every shadow and every wind." He took another drink from the flask, grinning with satisfaction. "But it does work out in our favor at times. It's so good to see you."

Hanna withdrew some dried figs and pressed fruit. "Here. Don't eat these now. Later...save them for later." She retrieved two small loaves of date bread and gave them to Symeon. "I have little time to tell you many things." Symeon took another drink, thanking Hanna for her many gifts.

The woman gave Symeon a water bottle, telling him to save it also. Taking his hand, she began, "Tomorrow is a big festival day. The emperor's magistrate is visiting. They intend to break you in the arena. Already, soldiers have arrested many of our elders. They plan to have them witness you recanting your faith."

Symeon interrupted. "I trust my God, Hanna. He will provide help to me." His voice was filled with confidence. "I am prepared to die this day."

"It won't be that easy, my friend." Hanna warned. "They don't intend to kill you."

He argued. "Should they choose to torture me to make me confess and recant, I shall not give in. It will be a fool's attempt on their part."

Hanna countered that it was not so. "Now listen. Please! Two days ago, the governor's personal guard came to your sister's house. They took Ishtar away with them. When your sister complained, one of the soldiers cuffed her with the back of his hand, saying to stay put, because they were returning later for her. We believe they will use your niece to get at you."

Symeon clenched Hanna's arm. "They can't be that cruel! Not even those animals can be that cruel!"

"Stop it, Symeon! You know full well the governor's men have no souls. The demons pale in comparison to them." Hanna took the empty flask and put it under her robe. "The guards were overheard talking about Ishtar being given to the dogs if you don't give up your faith. Now do you see why I had to tell you? You cannot stop what will happen. But could you have withstood surprise and shock of seeing the one you call 'daughter' being dragged into the arena? And what would you say when given the choice to save her or keep your faith?"

Symeon bowed his head, tears in his eyes. "No...I don't know...I don't know if I can. She's only a child. She has cared for me when my own sons despise me. I don't know..." He groaned. "Your words cast doubt on my faith."

"You have no choice but to *keep* your faith!" Hanna was adamant. "If you fail, the governor will send a wave of terror onto our people unlike anything we have yet seen. You are a *leader* among us. Paul has been sent to prison and may already be dead. There are few of the old ones left. Every day that passes, you become greater in the eyes of the people. *You cannot fail! You will not fail!*"

Hanna consoled Symeon, wiping away his tears and comforting him with supportive comments. Gradually the rush of emotion passed. Symeon eventually changed the subject. "What of you and your daughters, my dear Hanna? For sure, they will track you down. Can the storm of injustice pass you by? The entire city knows who you are."

"Do not fear." Hanna stroked Symeon's hand. "I have sold our home. After tomorrow, we are leaving Ephesus. I doubt we shall ever return. My late husband's uncle, Gallen, has come down from the North Country. He is with my two youngest daughters outside the city as we speak. My oldest daughter, Leah, and her husband, Midian, departed Capernaum some time ago and arrived during the past week. They helped me get my things together and are going with us. Gallen suggested we travel beyond Bithynia, cross the straits near the Sea of Marmara, and continue on north with him to the frontier."

Symeon felt uneasy about the news. "I have been told many stories of the Barbarians on the frontier. Are you sure it is wise to go that far?"

"Symeon, Gallen's grandfather was one of those Barbarians. My daughters have cousins residing among them." Hanna explained, "Look, the frontier is dangerous to the legions because they are so heartless and cruel. They rape and plunder for fun and profit. Most of the captives brought here as slaves or sold to the arenas are innocents kidnapped from their homes. Many of the atrocities are committed against the peaceful border towns or even within the territory itself. It is little wonder the north people seek revenge when opportunity affords."

She gently squeezed his hand. "As a wedding present, James gave his son some of his own father's carpentry tools. Midian is a skilled carpenter, too, just like his father and grandfather, and the north people will pleasantly accept his craft. Leah is almost three months' pregnant. If we do not leave now, she will not be able to come with us. Gallen has relatives living in Thrace. We will be able to winter there and then move on in the spring."

Thinking of his old friend, Symeon asked, "How is James?"

Hanna lowered her head. "His health is bad, Symeon. Leah wonders if he will survive the winter. The death of his wife and mother in the same year took so much out of him. You remember how he adored them so."

"Yes," Symeon sighed, recalling. "I remember watching him, eyes all aglow, while his mother, Mary, described her early years, how the family had to flee from home, the strange visitors giving them all that money, even Anna's prophecy regarding his oldest brother." He waxed romantic. "And Alba's eyes could hypnotize anyone, and her smile..."

Sadness grew in his voice. "When the fever took her, something inside James... inside all of us... died. He put himself into the work of building up the friends, but his health has continued to decline from that time on. I would so much love to see him once more."

Hanna agreed. "If he had been better, James would have journeyed here with the children." She went on to relate the current conditions of Symeon's hometown. "It's bad in Capernaum, real bad. The Zealots have overrun the countryside, forcing the people to join the resistance or be burned out, sometimes even murdered. I was told that the emperor is raising a large army with a new general to retake the territory. Most of the friends have left or are leaving. Those who have family elsewhere are traveling to join them."

For but a moment, Hanna allowed her personal distress to slip into the conversation. "The world has turned upside down. What the future holds for us is anybody's guess. I hope and pray that things will work out in the end."

"They will, they will." Symeon smiled, attempting to boost Hanna's morale. "Look, this will all be over soon. Then you and I can be reunited. I have so many things to say to you."

Hanna closed her eyes as tears fell. "May it be so. May it be so..."

Symeon squeezed the water bottle and patted Hanna's arm. "What you have done tonight has built me up. With God's help, I will not falter. Please be careful, and may our God protect you through the coming tribulations."

"Hey in there!" The guard's anxiety was growing. He had waited as long as he dared, fearing the demon creature's wrath. But the time was late, and he knew the commandant would be growing impatient. He called out with timid bravado, "Come on, gotta get goin'. Time is up. You gotta leave."

The little creature hissed. "It's not done talking! A curse it is on them! No money for pretty boys if master becomes angry."

The guard's voice quivered in fear as he warned, "One minute, then. That's all you can have."

Symeon cautioned, "You better go. You got in here on your wits, but the door of escape is not yet opened to you. No need creating suspicion." He took her hands in his. "Oh, how I do thank you for being here tonight, and for all the things you have told me!"

"Good bye, my dear friend." Hanna worked to hold back tears. "Someday... I don't know when...but someday we shall be together again. God bless." She slipped her hands from his and slowly turned to leave.

The stinky little creature instantly returned. "Hee, hee. Sh... sh... like a mouse." Then it quietly giggled some more and slowly waddled toward the door.

The guard raised his lamp to see about the prisoner. When the light revealed Symeon to still be alive and apparently well, he let out a sigh. As the creature neared him, it raised its hand to its hood, "Good child! Good child! Not hurt bad man... promised... promised." It looked at the spear and then up at the guard, angrily hissing as it passed.

Closing the door behind him, the guard followed the creature up the stairs and along the many hallways until reaching the commandant's chambers. The commandant turned away from the brazier, his shadow falling across the little creature. He grinned while extending his hand. "We've done our part. Now give us what you've promised. Where is the money?"

The little creature hesitated, glancing around the room. A little hiss escaped from under the hood. "Master said it would cheat the others. He said the man with the bossy mouth would steal all the money for himself." It cocked its head and asked. "Where are all the good boys I promised the money to? I see only one."

The creature, pointing a finger at the commandant, threatened, "Master has the money! Your soul for the dammed if you should try to cheat the good boys. I will give you the money where master can see me give it, outside the gate!"

It then cooed in a nasty hiss. "Or shall you buy the way with your soul?"

The commandant was indignant. He raised his voice, shaking a fist as he declared his innocence. In the middle of his tirade, the creature coughed, spewing some dark liquid onto the floor. The commandant gasped and stepped back. The creature cackled with laughter…

"The blood of jackals at your feet is laid.
In the hand of the helmsman your soul is weighed.
A ransom of gold must now be made.
'Ere the sun does rise, your debt must be paid."

It pawed the air. "Come! Come with me and I shall show you the way to the boatman. He waits for you. Hurry! Hurry! I know him well. He will like you… hee hee… like you."

The commandant put up a brave protest, swearing oaths and making threats, but his voice betrayed a growing fear. Finally the little creature, acting disappointed, shook its head and asked, "Doesn't loud boy want to go with little child? Too bad... Too bad... Then must come and get money… good money."

Without hesitation, the commandant called to the guard as he ushered the creature from the chamber. Up the last set of steps and into the cold of the foggy street, the commandant didn't stop until they were all outside. The guard keeping watch there hurried over to the others. Now, breathing the fresh crisp air, a renewed boldness entered the commandant. He hailed the creature. "There now, we kept our end of the bargain. What of our money?"

"Money? Yes, yes, money." It turned back to the three men and laughed. "Will get money for nice boys, good boys."

"What do you mean *get!?*" The commandant cried, thinking more of the curse the little creature had pronounced on him. *"Where is the money?"*

Defensively, the creature replied, pointing into the darkness, "Over there, over there."

"You're lying!" Shouted the commandant, desperation growing in his voice.

The creature shook its head. "Not lie… no… no… not lie. Little child does not lie." It bobbed up and down. "Master promised. Yes, yes he did."

Looking into suspicious faces, it pleaded, "Come with nice child, good little child. Will get money."

Finally, the commandant, nodding the guards to accompany him, followed the creature as far as the gate. The little creature began humming some strange tune as it passed through the opening in the fence. It turned back and beckoned, "Come, come with good little child, nice boys, good boys." Reaching out for the arm of the first guard, it begged, "Please."

The guard screamed in fright and jumped back. "I'll stick you! I will! I will!"

"Come!" The creature cried. "Come get the money, the pretty money! Master says to give you the pretty money."

The commandant ordered the guards to follow the creature. They refused to move. Every curse word and threat the commandant knew could not force them to budge. Finally, he snarled at the creature, "You get the money and bring it here."

The little creature turned, muttering to itself in disgust. "Go get money… Not come with child for money... Must bring money to silly boys… silly foolish boys." It cackled while smacking its lips, catching itself up short. "Not hungry. Not hungry now."

The creature dissolved into the darkness. The men could hear it talking and complaining about the gold and the bad little boys as it moved toward the far end of the animal pen. A little while later a heated argument ensued, the creature complaining about the bad little boys and how it didn't want to give them the money. Then came a loud smack and all was quiet. Moments later, a small purse was flung past them, hitting the stone pavement with a *'plop!'*

The second guard scooped up the bag, which was promptly confiscated by the commandant. With shaking fingers he opened it, tipping the contents into his hand. Out fell three silver and two gold stater coins - a half-year's wages.

The guards hopped with joy, chattering about their newfound wealth. The commandant gleefully handed a silver coin to each guard and began to pocket the rest, that is, until the one guard reminded him of what the little creature had warned about, sharing and all. A lively argument broke out, lasting until the sun peeked over the eastern hills.

The outcome was uncertain, at least for Hanna, for she had quickly disappeared, parting the scene through a sewer grate on the far side of the pens. By the time the sun arrived, the stinky little creature was little more than a memory, as Hanna was now preparing another charade.

     ഇ   ഇ   ഇ

"Wake up, you old fool! Something's a'foul, and I want to know why!" Treston kicked Tanner's cot, jolting him out of a restless dream.

Tanner's sleepy eyes popped open, filled with surprise. At seeing the anger in his captain's face, he threw his hands up in front of his own. "What? What? My Lord! What's the matter?"

Treston was in no mood to be pleasant. "That girl's the problem, you *ass!* What did you do to her last night?"

"It's not my fault!" Tanner cried, sitting up on the raggedy old cot. He began to fidget nervously. "Perk wanted it done."

"Wanted *what* done!?" Shouted Treston. "*What* did Perk want done?"

Tanner was awake now. Fearing he had said too much already, he fussed and fretted, pretending to be confused over the question. Treston grabbed him by the shirt, pulling him to his feet. "You come with me, shit weed! I want to know the reason for this mess."

Torches set along the passageways were all alight, casting their flickering blazes into corners long hidden. Treston had called out his entire guard, which was presently assembling in the prison, leaving little room to navigate the narrow corridors.

Tanner was already unnerved, being dragged from his sleep and rudely manhandled by Treston, the chief of the guard. Treston was head of the governor's judicial police, over two hundred soldiers. He rarely visited the governor's prison this early in the day, and when he did it was often at a high cost to some unfortunate. Tanner was beginning to fear that he was this day's candidate.

"Sergeant of the guard!" Treston called out.

A grizzled soldier, a flagellum tucked in his belt, hurried toward him. "Yes, my Lord..." He stopped and saluted Treston.

Treston motioned the man into line. "If he doesn't have the right answers, maybe you can help get some."

Tanner cowered as the sergeant sidled up next to him. The man frowned. "Has our little *titmouse* been up to some mischief?"

"No!" Treston shook his head. "I believe our *watchdog* has been *sniffing the bitch* 'stead of guarding the door."

Tanner cried out, "My Lord, I h'aint sniffed nothing! I just done my job is all!" He began to whimper. "All poor Tanner's done's his job. H'aint smelt nothing."

The sergeant poked Tanner in his side. "Shut up, fool! Lord Treston was only makin' a point. You ain't dead...yet..."

Treston stopped outside one of the prison rooms and looked Tanner in the face, politely asking, "Now would you be kind enough to explain to us just what happened here last night?"

Tanner began to shake. He feared Treston's reputation. The man had been known to disembowel a person or gouge out their eyes on a whim. The 'brand of Treston' - a deep scar across one's cheek, with the lower earlobe removed - was an all too common phrase bandied about the governor's house.

But Tanner feared Perk nearly as much, possibly more. Perk always had his way behind these sullied walls. The sergeant left Perk to himself, allowing the man to run the night watch much as he wished. Poisoned food and drink had taken the life of more than one guard who had crossed the man. Perk pretty much remained in the shadows when the sergeant was about. The sergeant preferred it that way.

Tanner shrugged, sweat running down his face, "Tanner doesn't know what my lord wants...doesn't know what to explain."

Treston flew into a rage, screaming out vile curses. He seized Tanner by the neck, dragging him into the room and flinging the man against the bars. "Explain *that* to me, you moronic ass!"

Tanner grasped the bars, pulling himself up as he slowly turned to look into Ishtar's cell. Expecting to see a bloodied corpse on the filthy floor, he was preparing some alibi for his defense. Instead, he gazed upon a beautiful young woman in a silky, satin gown, quietly sitting on a clean pile of straw.

Gasping aloud, Tanner stared in disbelief. His eyes bulged as they filled with terror. "By the gods! By the gods! I didn't know! Please! I didn't know!" He fell to his knees, beseeching the forces of heaven with tears and incoherent babblings.

"Please! Please! Forgive me!" He wailed. "I didn't know. No! No! Please! I didn't know!" He looked up at a very confused Treston, sobbing and weeping, invoking the spirits to forgive him. "I didn't know! I didn't know!"

"What is wrong with you, fool?!" Treston backhanded Tanner across the face. "Tell me! *What is this all about?!*"

Tanner paid no attention to Treston. He continued his laments and woeful outcries. Treston finally had enough. He shouted, "Go bring Perk! I want to him here!"

When the man didn't move, Treston gave him a hard boot to his side, knocking Tanner to the floor. "Now go get me Perk or I'll feed you to the lions right now! Tell him I want answers, or you'll both get it! Go!"

Tanner slowly stood, pulling himself up by the prison bars. He was nearly hysterical, in fear, but not of Treston. Why, his eyes were not even focused on Treston, but on something far more distant. "The gods! The gods!" He cried.

Treston screamed into his face. "*I* am your god! Now go get Perk, you good for nothing ass-wipe, or you'll wish you were dead!"

Tanner started to recognize Treston. His pale lips quivered. "I... I'm already dead." His face, pallid white and distorted with fear, showed his understanding of Treston's command. Quailing, he turned and darted toward the passageway to get Perk. The others could hear his incessant pleas and constant blubbering long after he was gone from sight.

Treston turned to the sergeant. "Follow him. The fool's near cracked."

Perk was sprawled across his cot, snoring loudly, an empty wine skin lying where he dropped it. Tanner burst into the room crying, "We're damned! We're damned! To a Hell of a thousand deaths we're cast!" He fell on his knees next to Perk's cot and clutched hold of his shirt, shaking him.

Perk grunted in anger as his eyes popped open. "What the...what the

Hell!" His eyes began to focus. When he recognized Tanner, he broke into a rage, clutching him by the throat. "You wanna die?! God damned fool! I'll kill you, myself, for botherin' me!" He released Tanner and rolled over.

Tanner lunged forward and violently shook Perk, renewing his cries. "The world of damned! The world of damned! That's 'ar curse! The world of the damned!" He fell forward and began to weep.

Perk angrily pushed Tanner away and sat up. "Fool! Old woman! Waking me that way, I oughta kill ya! What's in yor head? Shut up your hole and tell me!"

Tanner sat up on his knees, clasped his hands together in front of his face, and wailed, "That girl! That little girl... She's...she's a goddess! A goddess, I tell you!" Lifting his head up and extending his arms heavenward, he cried, "Forgive me! Oh you mighty gods! I didn't know the Hesperides was her home!"

Perk was becoming perplexed. "What's this about?! Tell me!"

Lowering his arms, Tanner stared at Perk and exclaimed, "Wer goin' to the Land of the Damned!" He buried his face in his hands and began to weep. "That child is one of the gods! She's sendin' us to the world of the damned!"

Perk's face clouded with fear. "Is she dead?"

Tanner did not reply.

Perk clutched Tanner's shirt, ripping it, screaming in Tanner's face, "Is she dead? Tell me! *Is the little bitch dead?!*"

Tanner let out a howl. "Don't call her that! I tell ya, she's a goddess! A goddamn goddess! And wer' dead men! I tell ya! Dead men!"

Perk backhanded Tanner across his face and then threatened him with his fist. "Is she dead?! Fool! Is she *dead*?"

"No! No!" Tanner shook his head, sobbing. "She's a goddess from the Isles of the Blessed and we're gonna burn in the pits of the damned!"

The sergeant, along with another guard, stepped into the room. "Perk! The old man wants ta see ya... now! He ain't happy!" Pointing at Tanner, he added, "And bring that bag o' shit with ya!"

He and the other guard dragged Perk and Tanner from the room and hurried them back down the passageway.

Treston was pacing the floor, muttering to himself. Tanner was running nuts, out of his mind. The girl in the cell stared at the floor, mute as a stone. And Perk? Maybe Perk would provide him with some information. At the sound of footsteps echoing from the corridor, he smiled and hurried to the doorway.

Confronting Perk, Treston angrily queried, "Is your head also in your ass..." he pointed at Tanner. "like this fool?! Or do you have a mind to tell me what happened here?" He grabbed Perk's ear and yanked him into the chamber.

Perk was taller than Treston, with a thick, muscular body and a flabby gut. It had been this mass that Perk had used to his advantage, to bully others. Treston paid no heed to it and Perk knew it. The big man cowered before the captain of the guard, knowing full well how valueless his life was in Treston's eyes.

Treston shoved Perk up against the prison bars, twisting his face in Ishtar's direction. He gritted his teeth and hissed in Perk's ear, "I don't like secrets and you're hiding one! If you want all your body parts, you'd better start talking!"

Perk stared blankly at Ishtar. She was still alive…and able to sit! What was the problem? Gradually, his senses came to him and he began to take in the surroundings. It was too much for this simple man's mind to comprehend. He was dumbstruck.

Treston exploded, "Enough of this charade! You better give me answers, or I will have someone's skin!" He squeezed Perk's neck, shaking him. "And I mean now!"

Perk became nearly as incoherent as Tanner had been, but not invoking the gods. He blubbered on about how he didn't know anything, that he was sleeping all night, and how good a servant he had been. This did nothing to appease Treston's growing wrath. He cuffed Perk across the face, making the man's mouth bleed. "Look at me, you dumb ass!"

Treston pressed his face against Perk's. His suspicions were growing. "How much did they pay you?"

A stupid look crossed Perk's face. "Who?"

Treston screamed curses and vile oaths filled with threats. He finally calmed a little, shouting, "The people you allowed in here last night to dress the girl up!" He glanced into the cell and back at Perk. "She didn't bring them clothes with her and for certain wasn't hiding that straw in her ass! Now tell me, who paid you to do this?"

"Nothin'! I mean nobody!" Perk was sweating profusely by now, thinking of something to say that would get him off the hook. He stuttered, "Nothin'! I… I mean… er… Nobody! There weren't nobody here! Nobody come in here last night!"

"Well…" Treston reached up and squeezed Perk's face. "Somebody dressed up the little lady. It didn't just happen!" He lowered his voice to just above a whisper and snarled, "If you think you can take a bribe and not share it, you're too stupid to live, at least as a man. I think it wise for you to 'fess up, and quick!"

Perk was beginning to panic. He beseeched Treston, "My Lord, I don't know nothin'! Nothin' at all! F'rgive me, Lord, I don't know nothin'!"

Treston grabbed Perk by the ears, slamming him against the cell bars and screamed, "What did you do, you miserable excuse for life?!"

Perk quailed, but stuck to his tale of ignorance.

Treston turned to the sergeant. "I'll have you feed his guts to my dogs this very hour if he doesn't come up with some answers!"

Perk fell to his knees, raising his hands high, seeking mercy, "I don't know, my Lord! I don't know nothin' at all! I ain't lyin'! Honest, Lord! I ain't lyin' at all!"

Treston gave up. *"Dumb ass!"* He motioned to the guards, and they pulled Perk from the floor. He put his hands on the bars and pressed his face against them. In a soothing, fatherly voice, he asked, "Please child, what happened here? Tell me, please. It will go much better for all of us if you do."

Ishtar sat there, staring at the filthy floor, deliberately ignoring Treston. It enraged him to the point that he started screaming and violently shaking the bars. *"You little piss-wart! Do you know what I can do to you?"*

Ishtar started. She glared at Treston, defiance burning in her angry eyes. Standing up, she stepped closer and contemptuously spat, "What would you do, *take the virgin and hole her?*" She reached down and picked up her old, torn, filthy tunic, smelling of blood and sexual exhaustion, flinging it at him. *"You're too late!"*

Treston reeled like he had been punched and struck dumb. He slowly turned, facing Perk and Tanner, seething with rage. He shook his fist. "Did we have some *fun* last night? We didn't do *nothin'*..."

Taking the sergeant's flagellum, he angrily whipped the two men, shouting vile threats and accusations. Then, shaking the spiked end of the handle at them, asked, "Does someone want to start talking now? *And no lies this time!*"

Tanner started his blubbering, confessing everything, making sure Perk received the blame. "You *shit!*" Perk bellowed, punching Tanner in the nose.

Blood splattered everywhere as Tanner tumbled back, falling to the floor while screaming in agony. The guards quickly subdued Perk.

Treston was beside himself, furious. He clutched Perk's face in his hands, digging in with his nails until the blood flowed freely. *"You slimy bastard! No good son-of-a-bitch! Why'd you have to go and ruin the girl for me?! Do you think I would follow the likes of a shit like you?!"* He cursed and swore until his energy was drained. In disgust, he pushed Perk back and turned away. "I ought to cut your balls off and feed 'em to Tanner!"

Treston ordered the sergeant to take Perk and Tanner away. He called after them, "Make sure they're locked up secure. I'll deal with them later!" He straightened his uniform, examining it to be sure it had no stains or tears, muttering as he did so. "Now to the business at hand..."

Treston turned his attention back to Ishtar. He found it difficult to believe that the things Tanner had spoken were true. If Perk had really attacked the girl, she would be lucky to still live. He looked at the bloodied tunic. Sure enough, it had been a violent night. And then there was the girl's implied accusation of rape.

The thought of Perk having touched the child troubled Treston. From the day of Ishtar's arrest, Treston had dreamed of having her for himself. He came to the prison early this morning on some lame excuse, hoping to secret her away just long enough to take his pleasure with her. Then Perk had to ruin it. But, oh, how good she looked.

"Damn it all!" Treston fumed under his breath. There wasn't any time now. Never would be, if the governor carried out his plans against her.

But what of the clothing and straw? Those questions needed answering, at least enough to satisfy the governor. Treston fought back his growing passion and attempted a charming inquiry, asking, "Please, child, tell me how you got this beautiful gown."

Ishtar looked down at her hands, pretending to take special interest in them, turning them over to see the fronts and then the backs. She appeared to completely ignore the question. But out the corner of her eye she watched, waiting while Treston's impatience grew. Just as he started to rise on his toes and his lips began to quiver, she spoke. In a tone showing casual disregard for Treston, she nonchalantly answered, "An angel gave it to me…"

Treston was taken aback. Uncertainty and fear of unknown things began growing in his heart. Perk was ruthless and cruel, he was deceitful. But he was not stupid, leastwise about Treston. If someone had bribed Perk to get to Ishtar, he would have offered to buy off Treston's anger with some of the reward.

And there was the girl. He knew she had been violently raped. Perk would have done it no other way. Rape was a common thing in these prisons. Few women survived more than a week in them from the brutal treatment meted out, and young boys or effeminate men suffered similarly. That was the reason Treston had threatened such severe punishment to anyone touching Ishtar. He still had half-expected her to be abused.

The blood on the dress must have been Ishtar's, but there was no visible sign of the violence she received, not even a tiny bruise. How had the girl managed such a transformation?

There was one possible answer. The governor or some other power baron had sent people to examine her. Finding her in such straits, and fearing the wrath of the governor, they hurried her away to be made presentable. Perk would not have dared to mention such a thing if he was ordered to remain silent about matters. Even Treston's dire threats wouldn't have pried such information from him.

Treston was troubled. It made no sense to have the governor request such a thing. After all, the man had not even seen the girl yet. Besides, if such a thing were ordered, Treston would have been the one to carry the order out. No. No. It was no one from the governor's house who did this. Then who did?

Treston motioned the guards. One came forward and unlocked the cell door. Treston stepped in, a guard entering behind with a brightly lit lamp. Ishtar did not move. She continued staring down at her hands, half expecting more violence.

Shimmering light cascaded across Ishtar's shoulders, revealing her near perfect figure hidden only by a semi-sheer garment. The woman was flawless in every way, from the curved bridge of her nose to her rounded hips. Why, even the girl's dazzling white teeth were as straight as if chiseled by a master sculptor.

"Who are you?" Treston asked with a faltering voice. "For this is not the child I delivered to this place." His mind began to whirl with stories of gods and goddesses. The haunting tales of his mother flooded the man's mind. With a shaking hand, he reached up to touch the girl, but stopped short, fear gripping him. Treston's heart began to ache, not from passion, at least he thought not. No. It was something new and strange. Here stood a kind of untouchable divine beauty, something unearthly and above him. He was insignificantly small in comparison to it.

Ishtar reached up suddenly and clasped his hand. "You will take me to my fate, for this day the eagle shall fall from the heavens and the sea shall turn to blood. My hour is near and you, Lord Treston, must deliver me to it. You must bring to ruin my flesh in order to deliver your own."

Treston was shaken from his trance. He became gruff and defensive. "I am here to deliver you to the governor, for you to answer certain charges brought against you. Do be good and I will see no more harm comes to you in this place."

Ishtar was curt in rejecting Treston's words. "Your governor has even now judged me. Can you not already hear the dogs howling for my blood?"

She poked Treston with a finger. "In a dream I have seen all things. Your grief is my reward and your savior. Today your soul dies with me, so that tomorrow it will lift me up, for my God has said of you, 'His sword shall become a defense for you, a shield and a fortress, too. Against the one who murders you shall he stand with you in the day of darkness.' "

Treston was shaken, but put on a bold face. "I serve my governor and king! The gods' business belongs to scholars and prophets. Should you live or die today is no concern of mine." He motioned to the guard with the lamp. "We must not keep the governor waiting."

Ishtar stared at Treston. "I shall forget you in the Field of the Minds. It is my reward." She shook her head. "But I shall haunt your waking moments. Never will my spirit depart from you until you know that to the Maker of all things does prophecy belong."

Not wishing further discussion, Treston hustled Ishtar from the cell.

As they hurried along the passageway toward the palace stairs, Ishtar again grabbed Treston's hand. "I shall take hold of a serpent and he will keep me safe!" She stared at him in wonder and puzzlement, adding, "For shall one serpent gulp down the many and thus save all living things." Treston remained silent.

The sounds of their footsteps soon disappeared as they circled the staircase leading from the prison up to the governor's palace.

ভ০ ভ০ ভ০

"Gabrielle… Gabrielle..." Sirion gently shook the woman's shoulder. "It's time."

As if drifting in some drunken stupor, Gabrielle pushed herself up on her arms. Shaking her head, she muttered something incoherent and slumped back over Darla.

Sirion shook the woman's shoulder again, growing anxious. "I'm sorry, but there is no more time. Mihai sent me back to tell you that we must go now or it will be too late. The enemy is on the move!"

Gabrielle struggled to sit, more alert this time, but still determined to keep Darla where she was. "I am not finished! I fear she will die if we move her." She sighed, "I have had too little time to heal the child's massive injuries. A doctor must have time to finish a cure."

Darla stirred, laboring to speak, but Gabrielle hushed her. She bent low, close to the girl's ear and whispered, "Not now, my Dear. Don't try to talk." Raising her head and looking around, Gabrielle asked where Mihai was.

Sirion pointed. "We found a good location. Mihai sent me back to tell you to get ready, said she'd be back momentarily, leaving the others to secure the site."

Gabrielle looked in the direction Sirion indicated and nodded. "Tell me when she's back." She returned to her healing song.

Sirion was frustrated and worried. Mihai had impressed upon her the need to move as soon as possible, but Gabrielle wasn't cooperating. Gabrielle was in command, but Mihai was the newly appointed marshal en force of the army, a position Gabrielle held until recently.

It had been at Mihai's request that Sirion and Darla were included in this dangerous and very important operation. Gabrielle had protested, feeling there should only be highly trained and experienced personnel on the team. She finally surrendered to Mihai's opinion after Anna and others of Mihai's new council assured her of the security measures that had been put in place. She had even accepted responsibility for Darla's and Sirion's safety when Lowenah had questioned the validity of taking them along.

Now, with everything in shambles and Darla at death's door, Sirion did not know who would decide their final destiny. Mihai still leaned heavily on Gabrielle for support and guidance, she being among the oldest of all the children, and Gabrielle was in charge of this mission. On the other hand, Mihai was accountable for the success or failure of said mission, being its chief architect and having personally chosen the team to execute it.

Sirion said nothing more to Gabrielle, fearing a scathing rebuke. She began to nervously pace, all the while fidgeting, afraid of Mihai's response for her failure to obey orders and equally afraid of Gabrielle. The sound of snapping twigs alerted her to Mihai's return, the woman questioning Sirion with a wondering look. Sirion nervously shrugged and pointed, indicating her attempt to persuade Gabrielle of the need for haste. Mihai walked over and rested a hand on Gabrielle's shoulder. "Please, Honey, we have to go."

Gabrielle did not move, mumbling, "I'm not taking her there. She's too hurt."

Mihai's face went ashen. "You must! The enemy may be upon us at any minute. We cannot dally! Darla needs to be taken to Ishtar."

Slowly, Gabrielle sat up, gritting her teeth as she forced strained muscles to obey her will, staring at Mihai, repeating, "The child is too hurt! If we take her, she will die!"

The woman could not believe her ears, sputtering incredulously, "You can't mean that! If we don't take her, she will die anyway! It was her request, and *I* will honor it!"

Laboring to stand, groaning in discomfort while stretching to get the blood flowing again, gripping Mihai's arm and pulling her along like a mother with an unruly child, Gabrielle snarled, "Let's talk!" leading Mihai some distance from the group.

In no mood to play lieutenant to a *bratling* sister so much her junior, she released Mihai, putting her hands on her hips, glaring into the woman's eyes, wasting no time mincing words. "Darla is not in any condition to be moved, let alone be taken an hour's walk and then made to sit for who knows how long. The child has three broken ribs, rupturing her lungs. Darla has a severe brain hemorrhage and two vertebrae in her neck are fractured." She paused for effect before stating her final intentions. "I will not accept responsibility for her death. I am taking her to the ship!"

Mihai was furious. "You have no right to decide her fate! She has made clear her desire. If you prevent her from carrying it out, she will never forgive you, forgive me," she poked Gabrielle in the chest with her finger. "...or forgive herself!" then pressed her face close to Gabrielle's, snorting, "What has been asked of you is not to decide her life or death! You have been requested to channel your power through her to assist Ishtar!"

Gabrielle pushed Mihai away, growling, "This is not a question of feelings! If she dies, we will have accomplished nothing except the loss of a child I could have saved. That will be too much for my conscience to carry!" Turning away, the woman muttered, "She is *my* little sister, too. I promised Mother I would care for her. She would have never allowed the girl on this mission if she had not trusted me with her care."

Spinning around, fists clenched, Gabrielle stood defiant. "I'm taking Darla to the ship!" Mihai spread her feet and, reaching across her waist, grabbed the hilt of her sword. "You will have to go through me to do it! If you choose to abandon this mission, we will accept that! But you *will not* stop us!"

Although shocked and surprised, Gabrielle did not lose her composure and shot back with a fiery retort, "Mihai, do not think yourself my equal! I can cut you down before your sword is drawn! And for what purpose? To feed more blood to this soil? Look! Death is what I am trying to *prevent!*" She began to advance, motioning Mihai away. "Now stand aside!"

Mihai clenched her sword, her left hand taking hold of its scabbard. "I mean it! This is no threat!"

Gabrielle's face clouded with anger as she took a battle stance. "Don't make me…"

Sirion, approached unnoticed. Already the girl's sword was drawn, its radiant green flame dancing along the blade. With tears in her eyes, she cried, "You may kill one of us, but can you best the both of us?!" brandishing her blade, threatening, "Darla has a right to die for the cause *she* chooses! *My* blood shall soak this ground before I will allow *you* to steal that right!" Tears gushed forth as the girl choked out, "You cannot take away her freedom to pacify your soul! Death's reaper comes to us all. *It* chooses who it will take."

Gabrielle stared in disbelief, glancing first at Sirion and then Mihai. "Are you two *insane?!* Look! If Ishtar fails her test because it is too great a thing, it will be overlooked. It's happened before when our mission's failed. She's but a child. Her age will give her pardon."

Sirion and Mihai refused to be swaged. Gabrielle pleaded, clenching her fists in desperation, "It's not worth Darla's death!" as she cast a glance in Darla's direction, groaning in dismay when she saw Tzidohn and Depais busy assisting Darla onto a litter while Chisamore, having heard the commotion, was hurrying over to give Mihai assistance. "Is the whole world against me?!"

A hand still on her sword pommel, Mihai retorted, "It is not an issue of forgiveness! Ishtar was promised she would have help! On my soul, never have I failed to carry out a promise! As God lives, I will do this duty! Should it bring death to us all, it is a small price to pay for our success!"

Gabrielle protested anew. Mihai stopped her, eyes pleading. "Sister! Please listen! I do not believe Darla will survive this ordeal, but I swear, as I live, her blood and mine shall soak this ground together before I allow her to fail! I owe it to her! For God's sake, I owe it to Ishtar! And you do, too!"

Desperate, Gabrielle searched the camp for someone to offer support. Her eyes darted from one face to another. All were as resolute as Mihai and Sirion. She muttered under her breath, "There is no logic to this folly! No one need die!" then cried aloud, "Mother will understand! She will understand! Look! Who's to say that our girl will not prove herself without our help?! Others have many times!"

No one spoke. Mihai, Sirion and now Chisamore, too, stood a wall against Gabrielle's protest as others in the camp busied themselves with Darla or preparing to move out.

"What is *wrong* with you?!" Gabrielle shouted. "This is not an issue of the mind with you! Your hearts tell you tales filled with deceit and trickery! How can you fall prey to such seductive reasonings?! You do not listen with an opened mind! Mihai, do not let your newfound glory go to your head! Think things out!"

Mihai glared, her lips curling in anger. "Should I be a titmouse before an eagle, I would not stand down in this instance! If your heart yearns to regain the glory of marshal en force, it's yours with my blessing, but I shall not stand aside if you were king of the Cherubs!"

Gabrielle was frantic. "A fool falls upon his own sword, or threatens the life of a companion and ally! Can you not see the hopeless folly of your actions?! If we depart now, Darla will survive. If she dies, how will I ever face Mother again?! I promised her the child's safety!"

Rleasing her sword, Mihai pointed an accusative finger. "So, the truth is revealed! It is not your mind that speaks for you, but a heart filled with fear of failure and rejection. Is your resistance really based on *logic* of the mind, or have you filtered it on the dregs of emotional fervor, playing Judah's fiddle to gain food for your heart's belly?! You are more pitiable than I because I am jealous over my sister's feelings while you think only of your own!"

"It is not so! I speak only for the child's…" Gabrielle choked silent as her mind recalled an ancient warning. Her thoughts flashed back to a long-forgotten age, beyond the edge of time, to a mystical planet of fire and ice. With but naked flesh, she stood upon the mountain peak, staring into bottomless canyons filled with raging rivers of boiling sulfur and brimstone.

As she teetered on the brink of doom, searching for a trail down, her companion and mentor warned, "Your heart is the window through which you see and interpret all things. It will show you what you wish to see, making excuse while it induces you to drink the sweet wine that dulls a wary mind. It ever seeks your well being, encouraging you to take the easy path, but for sinister reasons. If you give ear to it when hope wanes, all that is good will be lost and all that is evil shall overcome you. The easy path, my daughter, is rarely the wise path."

Her mentor, a prince from the Beginning Days, added, wagging a finger,

"Do beware of the heart's treachery should the darkness overtake your race and the Incubus rises from the smoldering abyss. It will seek solace from duty, musing that one will succeed avoiding the inevitable, whispering its haunting refrain, 'be good to yourself, for this calamity need not befall you'. The light you must force because the darkness never wearies."

But it was her duty to protect her charge… or was it? Gabrielle knew in her mind that statement to be false. Darla was no babe, innocent and unknowing. Many a battle had the child contested, bloodying and being bloodied. Had Gabrielle been there for her during those moments? No! And had she not volunteered, without Mother's request, to protect the child on this mission? Yes, it was something new for Darla – but not the dangers accompanying it. Then why was she so adamant about her need to protect the child?

Logic! That was it! Logic! But Gabrielle could find none except that crying from her heart. So carefully she had analyzed the moment, believing it wise to abandon the mission to whatever the Fates permitted. Was that logic or… or was it guilt… guilt at having failed Darla for missing the appointed rendezvous? Was she attempting a way to find absolution for her own failure?

Gabrielle's head spun with doubt and confusion. Had only the others chosen Fate's course through the emotions of their hearts, or was her heart also manipulating the moment? That thought alone was tormenting the woman's mind.

"Well?!" Mihai intruded into Gabrielle's pondering. "Do we die as enemies or allies?!"

Gabrielle lowered her head, mourning, "What do I do?! It is better for me to never go home than to return with a dead child who was in my charge! How could I ever face Mother again? Mihai, I have never failed in a promise given to her! It is better you destroy me now than to make me live forever with that torment!"

Mihai's pent-up tears burst forth as she made rebuttal. "Do you think Darla's promise less worthy than yours? You… you have the power to choose your own destiny, but that child does not! Indeed, without your assistance, she has little hope of succeeding, yet she will not die alone. If our Mother's disapproval is all you fear, then go! I command it! Tell her that it was upon my order that you abandoned your charge. You are absolved of all obligation."

Mihai's fiery retort struck like a burning missile. Shocked into seeing her own selfish reasonings, Gabrielle wailed, "Does a dog not return to its master after it is beaten?! My Lord, do not strike your foolish servant again by sending her away! Please! Allow me a chance to prove my worth." She stepped forward, arms beseeching as she pleaded, "If we are to die this day, it will be as one soul not a house divided. My shame is too great for me to carry alone! Allow me, please, to attempt a healing on our sister, so that she may succeed in helping Ishtar. Here I have wasted so much precious time thinking only of myself. Allow me to make amends."

Mihai also stepped forward, arms reaching for Gabrielle. In tears, the two women embraced, wailing and moaning as if reunited from death. At length, Gabrielle pushed herself away, taking hold of Mihai's arms. "Sister, we must go now or be forever late."

The women turned, slowly making their way back to Darla, Sirion and Chisamore following up closely. In a few minutes the litter-bearers were ready, Gabrielle quietly talking to Planetee when Chisamore glanced around and called her name. "Your blade still lies in the dust, my Lord. You might need it if trouble is afoot."

Gabrielle stuttered, "Th… thank you." while staring down at her empty scabbard. 'How brave the wolf when it sees no hunter with the flock'. Retrieving it quickly, she hurried assisting Darla. Taking the girl's hand while gently caressing her forehead, she ordered the litter bearers away. "Be off! Quick now! The Devil is not a patient person."

℠ ℠ ℠

"Your Worship," The governor politely bowed as the emperor's magistrate entered the palace throne room. "I pray your sleep was restful and breakfast satisfactory?"

The magistrate angrily began waving his hands in disgust, his shrill, effeminate voice piercing the morning air. "I thought I was bedded in the *slaves'* quarters, with all those bugs flying around! Then, I was awakened early because of the noise coming from the street! And that god-awful stink that entered through my window last night! I think you should move the fish market. A wise man would."

Ogust, the Great Councilor, cousin to the Divine One, was never satisfied with anything. Rumor held that he was, in truth, the emperor's bastard son, born of a sister barely into her teens. Held ever captive within the palace walls, Ogust grew up tormenting and threatening family and servants with his abuses, both verbal and physical. Finally, in desperation, the emperor assigned the boy – now a young man – to position of magistrate. It was said that Ogust relished his new job, raising his abusive talents to even new levels of wickedness.

Governor Claudesius was about to respond when Ogust started on breakfast. "I do not know how anyone could become fat on the worm dung served as food in this place! If this were my home, the cook would have been taken and roasted on a spit and served for supper. He certainly should taste better than the filth he gave us this morning!"

Claudesius felt need to pacify this moronic maggot quickly, or he might find himself being the main attraction at this evening's celebration. Folding his hands in respect and bowing humbly, he apologized. "I am so very sorry for the *great tribulation* suffered by my lord this last night. I will make sure matters are corrected this very day."

Glancing up, he observed Ogust's sour expression. More must be done. "My Lord, the castle is yours, for your pleasure. Tell me, please, whatever chambers you delight in are available for your choosing. I will give personal attention to them being arranged comfortably for you. And…" he lifted a hand, shaking a finger, "I will close off the streets near the palace."

He turned and stared toward the seaport. "As for the fish market, ah, well, it is located near the harbor. I really think it would do little good to shut it down or move it. I've tried…" he lied. "You see, much of the stink comes from the rotting things in the river itself. I can go to the temple and invoke the gods to change the breeze, but other than that, I am helpless to do a thing."

Ogust still frowned.

"And… and I will deliver several more servants into your hands this night, so that you might have the bugs fanned away."

Rubbing his fat chin with a chubby hand, Ogust mulled over the governor's offers. He soon smiled, making a condescending reply. "Invoking the gods might serve us well. After all, I know there are some things we must leave in their hands. Make sure you see to it." Claudesius nodded, saying he would.

As his eyes flitted about the chamber, thinking of the coming eve, Ogust mused, "I will scour the palace today, in search of better accommodations… possibly yours will do. We will see. We will see." He took a few steps, stopped, twisting his head around until he faced the governor, threatening, "I *do* want those servants! And don't give me any *tit-hangers!*" He curled his lips in disgust. "Boys… healthy, *young* boys. Understand?!"

Claudesius breathed a sigh of relief. "Very good, your Worship. It will be my pleasure." Seeking to secure the magistrate's approval, he returned to the morning's breakfast. "I am so disappointed that your meal was unpalatable. If you choose, I will prepare roasted cook for your evening's enjoyment, but…" He tapped his finger on a nearby table.

"But what?!" Ogust cried, shivering in anticipation. "But what?!" The man's fat face and bulging eyes made Claudesius sick to his stomach. How much more he would enjoy roasting *him* for supper. 'No oven wide enough!' he thought, looking at Ogust's triple chins and bloated belly. Drumming his fingers, Claudesius lingered with his tease until he dare not risk it any longer. Then, drawing his words out, he slowly began to inform Ogust of the evening's festivities.

"Tonight, after the day's circus, Ephesus is to come alight with celebration over the demise of our great protagonists who have insisted on defaming Artemis and our other great gods. Several of these *blasphemers* have been rounded up and are locked securely in our prisons. If you wish, they can be our guests tonight, to help us illuminate our courtyards in glory."

Rocking back and forth on his heels and grinning, Ogust rubbed his hands in delight, asking, "You do have *tit-hangers,* too… *big-titted* tit-hangers? Oh I do so much love to see them burn!"

Trying to cover his shock, Claudesius forced himself to answer nonchalantly, "I am sure there are women among them. As for your *big-titted* ones, I will have to investigate."

Ogust clapped his hands with glee. "They are so beautiful! So beautiful! When their oiled hair shoots up in showers of flame…oh, it is such a beautiful thing!" He drooled spittle, commenting in orgasmic delight, "And their screams… long, chilling screams!" Shaking a finger, he warned, "You must keep the fire clear of their faces… clear, so they can give us a longer show. Mustn't kill them too soon… not too soon."

Ogust began to strut, one hand on his hip while waving the other, describing with relish one of his most choice visions. "I must tell you the truth, a tit-flame is the most beautiful thing a man can witness. Have you ever seen a tit flame?"

Claudesius shook his head.

Surprised, Ogust replied, "Well! I will have to show you one this very night. Do, please, find me a big-titted one… a young big-titted one. First, what you do is cut a long wick from a linen garment, then wind it round and round the titty, tying the end securely around the titty's nipple. Now the fun begins. Take a mixture of hot tar and wax and paint it thick on the titty. Oh, the excitement! Their screams from the blistering burns… so entertaining!"

"But you must remember, tie their hands to an upper post or they will try to scrape the burning tar away or worse, they may become faint and fall down. If they are hanging, you can continue at your pleasure. Do this earlier in the day, say the early evening, before the sun sets behind the hills, then you can have added sport for you and your guests. And they will be delighted, I promise you."

"After the tar-wax is at least finger thick, allow it to cool. Now give your tit-hanger out for sport - dogs or prison slaves will do quite well, quite well. Don't worry. The tar cannot be damaged by their gaming. It won't crack or come loose."

"When finished with your sport, take the tit-hanger, tying its arms to a cross-post. Now pull its hair back, knotting it through a heavy weight. This prevents the tit-hanger from breathing the smoke. We don't want to ruin the show by having it die on us." Ogust clapped his hands. "If you do it right, you can keep the titties aflame throughout the night, the creature sharing in the festivities with its passionate cries."

Claudesius smiled weakly. He thought about his own wife and teenage daughter. Both women were buxom. 'Oh, what fun would Ogust have with them?' Suppressing his disdain, he casually replied, "Yes, yes, your Worship, we will have some women there this eve. I will personally search to find some large-breasted ones for you."

"Wonderful! Wonderful!" Ogust cried in delight, as he squinted, eyeing the governor. "You will also have some little darlings there, too, won't you? Innocent little children are so much fun at a party. They do so make a celebration come to life."

Quietly nodding then quickly changing the subject, Claudesius asked, "Could your humble servant interest my lord in a goblet of excellent wine? It is extra sweet, being slowly boiled many days in huge lead pots."

Ogust blushed at the governor's offer. "You are such a generous man, which surprises me greatly. After all, I see that you appear to be happily married and have adorable boys. Few men having that weakness are as considerate and caring of others as you."

"You are too kind, your Worship." Claudesius smiled, knowing that Ogust dismissed his daughter as nothing more than a tit-hanger. 'Better to leave it there, for her sake.' He ordered a servant to fetch some wine. Offering the magistrate a chair, he also sat, suggesting, "While we wait for the wine, may I inform you about the day's events? There is a young creature you might find interest in and, if she survives the day, you may well delight in practicing your magic on her. I am told she is quite shapely and a virgin, too."

Ogust clapped his hands with glee, rolling his eyes as he lifted his head, envisioning his magic being practiced on such a sweet thing. Finding a stool, he plunked himself down with a tired grunt and then asked excitedly, "What of the circus?! What have you arranged for my pleasure this day?"

Claudesius slowly paced the floor as he detailed the day's activities. While it was true that Ogust gasped, cried, and crooned with joy and excitement over the things he was hearing, making the governor cringe in disgust at times, Claudesius did relish listening to his own echoes of the violence and mayhem offered by the arena. When he arrived at some particularly gruesome part of the story, his arms would flail descriptively while his face beamed with excitement.

Saving the best for last, he finally came to the part Symeon and the girl were to play. At that moment a servant arrived with more wine which Ogust greedily gulped down.

Pausing with his tale, Claudesius kindly cautioned, "My Lord, the day is young and you would not want to miss any of the fun prepared for you, would you?"

Ogust's eyes flashed his contempt as he closed his lips in an angry pout. He studied the governor closely, wine dribbling from the sides of his mouth. Finally, placing the empty goblet in the servant's hand, he coolly replied, "Yes, yes, you're right. There are too many things afoot this day that I wish not to miss. I am sure your concern was only for *my* welfare, governor."

"Your great and lofty Worship…" Claudesius humbly clasped his hands and made a polite bow. "though our years differ widely in age, I perceive your wisdom is of far greater wealth than mine. You see things from on high, while my tongue speaks only in the ways of lowly men."

The governor glanced up at Ogust. The man's eyes were slowly losing their angry edge. 'Good! Good! A little more of this horse dung and the fat ogre should be pacified.'

Opening his arms wide, Claudesius begged the magistrate's pardon, explaining, "A child can see only through the eyes of a child. I, the child, could see only the wonders of the day, and wishing that my most distinguished guest might enjoy it to the full, I, through my childlike eyes, offered advice to you as only a child could. Your insight is far beyond my humble abilities. After all, the blood of the gods flows in your veins."

He reached out with his hand in a gesture of humility, "Please forgive the child who has spoken so brashly." then motioned for the servant to hurry with more wine. "Your Lordship, wine is best if kept on the dregs, and I have obtained some of the finest aged this way from the forbidden northland vineyards. Far beyond our territories was it grown, my Lord. At great risk was it delivered into my hands and… and…"

"Yes?! And…?!" Ogust's eyes were bulging with bated excitement.

"And…" Claudesius pointed a finger into the air, smiling. "and among the treasure there remains a sealed keg, small enough for you to take along with you when your journey begins anew from this place, that is," He quickly added, "if you enjoy it enough to wish to do so. My servant is getting some for you as I speak."

Ogust hooted with delight, happily clapping his hands. "Oh, so wonderful! So wonderful! I know you spoke foolishly because you did not understand. That is so good! So good! It is so important that you are my friend."

Claudesius smiled again and bowed. 'Pigs and swill. Fill their gullet and they'll always grunt with delight.'

Easing down into an engraved, teakwood, high-backed chair, the governor offered to continue his tale of the day's events. "As I have mentioned earlier, there exists a certain Symeon in my custody, who is both an enemy of the state and a rabble rouser. He has filled this city - the entire world - with his blasphemy, saying that our great gods are but contrivances of men. He tells all the people that there is but one true God, the Maker of all things."

Frowning, Claudesius shook his head. "Not only do his followers preach that this *God* must alone be worshipped, they no longer offer up sacrifice to the great Artemis, refusing to pay the temple duty charged upon all the good people of this city." He leaned forward. "My Lord, I have tried, through every kind act possible, to silence these people. They will not and, with Symeon, their leader's arrival, they have become very troublesome."

Ogust leaned forward, squinting, "I have heard of this Symeon. There are others! Paul and a 'John' fellow and a brother, I believe. I've heard my mother speak of him. At least he's not around to bother us – did right by hanging him up. So, tell me, why haven't you hung this Symeon up and gotten rid of him, too?"

Leaning back in his chair, Claudesius began to drum its arm with his fingers. "I have studied this strange sect, my Lord, and have discovered that death and torture does nothing but encourage its followers to become more delinquent in their obedient service to our emperor. If one is executed for his vile conduct, twelve more will stand up to take his place. No. No, my Lord," He pointed at his heart. "we must destroy them here. Then they will lose their will to remain in this crazy religion."

Watching the breeze upon the billowing curtains, he grinned, "Symeon shall be the tool used to accomplish this. Today he will deny his God."

Ogust scoffed. "You have enjoyed too much of your own wine! Symeon is of the old house, one of the twelve. He will not crack. Should he face a thousand spears, he will not surrender his soul to you."

"So right, your Worship, so right." Claudesius grinned again. "But should his heart fall into despair over the loss of the one person he does love? Well, I do have to wonder."

Shaking his head, Ogust argued, "Only the threat to a wife or child could have such power, yet this Symeon is a man alone, often little more than a shadow, flitting about in secret, first here and then there."

Claudesius stood, closely watching Ogust's eyes, waiting for just the right moment to speak. Then, just before the magistrate cried out to know the governor's little secret… "There is one whom Symeon loves more than life itself and the gods have delivered her into our hands. In this very city the child lives. She carries the name of our most precious god and yet dishonors that name by her own mouth."

"Not every worshiper of this strange new sect is as true of heart as you might expect. Some can be bought quite cheaply. Others might take more persuasion, but enough come around. We find out what we need."

"This girl – Ishtar is her name – resides as a guest in my prison. Today she will pay a social visit upon a very surprised Symeon, as he stands to defend his faith before a number of this sect's leaders that we also managed to round up. No man lives who will surrender a virgin child up to the execution dogs of Ephesus… at least no man with a soul…especially if it his own niece, one whom he calls 'daughter'."

"What if he doesn't recant his beliefs and deny his god?" Ogust asked. "Will his cult of followers not be emboldened?"

"I highly doubt the man will surrender his child to the dogs." The governor flicked some lint from his robe. "Even if he does, the death heaped upon the girl will be slow and gruesome enough to dissuade others from joining with them. We will keep their leaders in prison where they will languish in a slow death, Symeon included. With no more direction and with the fear that they, too, may suffer the same demise as the girl should they decide to continue such folly, this *ulcer* of miscreants will soon fade away."

"And if Symeon recants?" Eager anticipation was growing in Ogust's eyes. "And if he recants?"

"Then," Claudesius spoke nonchalantly, "you will have opportunity to listen to the child's sweet songs as she lights the evening's festivities."

An exciting chill raced down the governor's back as he envisioned coming events as he thought of the child being torn apart by dogs or seeing her burning in agony. It was as though a power within was stoking the flames of passion in his heart, crying out for him to carry out its will – he being rewarded with even greater ecstasy of emotion than he could normally achieve watching the circus.

A shrill, effeminate, voice of someone calling out the magistrate's name shattered the governor's sadistic visions. "Ogust…?! Ogust…?!"

Out of the shadows, emerging from the bowels of the palace, a young man strolled, his lacy, silk chiton revealing far more of the person's appearance than Claudesius wished to see. Stopping upon spying Ogust, he called out cheerfully, "Oh, there you are. I had wondered if I'd find you alone or not." He turned a gaze at the governor and then back to Ogust. "I guess you are."

Ogust's face lit up in delight as he jumped from his stool, arms outstretched, and hurriedly waddled forward. "Jusslin! Oh, has my Jusslin slept well!? I wished not to wake my little beauty this morning. You looked so peaceful, so peaceful and pretty."

Jusslin waited impatiently for Ogust, a hand resting on a slowly swaying hip. After an affectionate hug, he began about how disappointing the morning had been. He went on about all the privations suffered since their arrival in the city, occasionally eyeing the governor with an accusative stare. Eventually, Jusslin arrived at what was most annoying.

Lifting a limp hand and pointing, he sputtered, "They fetched *girls* to care for my bath! *Little bitch girls!* Can you imagine that?! Well! I had to make a fuss! The slaves in this household…" he shook his head, "they have much to learn about attentiveness to their duties. Well, they finally brought me two boys to assist me. But, my, oh my, scrawny, sallow, dark-skinned creatures more fit for the stables than a noble's house. What, are there no pale, full-fleshed, blond children to be found here? Anywhere?"

Ogust frowned as he eyed the governor. Not wanting to face another bout with him, Claudesius bowed in apology, a remorseful expression on his face. "My Lords, my heart fills with great sadness regarding the terrible ordeal my ignorance of your needs has heaped upon you. This land is very foreign to your refined culture, it being filled with the refuse of inferior people made our slaves so long ago."

"It has been over twenty years since my eyes have seen Herculaneum, the home of my birth, and many more than that when I walked the stairs leading to the emperor's palace in Rome. Old men tend to forget what the good life is like after being lost so many years in these recesses of iniquity, as this rabble makes this land." He lifted his eyes toward the ceiling. "Ah, but the willing sacrifices one makes to preserve our empire."

Claudesius now addressed Jusslin's complaints. "I assure you, now that I am aware of your needs, I shall personally see to making the remainder of your stay here as pleasant as the gods will allow. It is a dark-skinned race that thrives in this despicable place, but I believe I can find you more desirable servants. I will send out my guard to search for some attractive, full-fleshed, blond boys. They will be arrived here this eve, to serve your wishes as you see fit."

Stroking Jusslin's face like one does a wounded puppy, Ogust softly warned, "I certainly hope our day goes better than the morning." He glanced menacingly at Claudesius and then turned his attentions back to Jusslin. "I have been in such a fair mood today, despite all our misfortune. I don't wish to become troubled in my spirit so that my mood is ruined. You do know what I mean, don't you, my dear Governor?"

Ogust's threatening tone carried chillingly cold on his words, implying that his patience was near an end. Claudesius was beginning to feel his efforts at appeasement would not be successful. Maybe Ogust had been sent to depose him. It was a common practice of the emperor to do such things, especially if he had another person, friend or relative… someone due a favor… who was in need of a political position. If that was the case, there was nothing he could do. An official magistrate of the emperor wielded the same power that the emperor would, should he be present.

Claudesius could be dismissed from his position at the whim of the magistrate, with no provision for appeal. Indeed, an appeal was usually impossible, given that the one deposed was often executed after being accused of some treasonous act. Before a lengthy torture and humiliating death, the offender's family would be subjected to degrading indignities, including rape, torture, brutalization, and other selected forms of punishment, which usually led to the death of the victims. The governor shuddered, thinking of the games Ogust would surely prepare for his family, especially now that he saw how great the man's hatred was for women and his fondness for blond-haired boys.

But! But if this was just Ogust's way of demonstrating his authority? Claudesius offered a polite bow, folding his hands together in respect. "My Lord, sovereign to the emperor, your day will certainly be most joyous. As I have mentioned, there will shortly arrive here the girl I have spoken about, Symeon's niece. If you wish to start your festivities early, I am sure she can make you fine sport. What you desire to do with her… well… that is totally up to you. As I have informed the great magistrate, it is hoped to use her to bring down the evil house, should she still live by your kindness."

Jusslin whined, patting Ogust's hand, "Why must we suffer the bitch-dog at all? I have had my fill of those *creatures* already this day." He stroked Ogust's arm, cooing, "I think her uncle a much more worthy prize, even if he is an old man."

Ogust affectionately squeezed Jusslin's arm. "My Dear One, it is part of the tribulations that we officers of the court must face. At times the law makes demands upon us that are most troublesome. It is at those times that we must rise to the occasion and make the sacrifices needed, for all the good people of the land. Besides, knowing a criminal of the state has been fairly judged before being thrown to the beasts satisfies the soul and conscience that justice has been served."

"Oh, I suppose you're right." groaned Jusslin. "But must we remain here while the governor interrogates the *creature*? Do we really need to see its flesh stripped bare and worked like one does a beast? There are other things I'd rather be doing." He gazed longingly into Ogust's eyes.

Claudesius politely interrupted. "The subject of this coming interrogation is young of years, and inexperienced in the ways of wicked craftiness and shrewdness. Your *outstanding* knowledge and wisdom, though much appreciated in this case being as simple as it should be may not be necessitated. May I suggest that you, my Lord Ogust, and your distinguished statesman, Jusslin, remain here until the girl is delivered to us and then you decide, for yourselves, how we proceed with this case."

After pondering the governor's suggestion in his mind, Ogust smiled. "That will suit us well. We will decide the matter for ourselves. If the case is worthy of our time, then we shall stay. But if it is of little concern, well, we will allow you to decide."

Jusslin was quick to add, "Being a bitch-dog that will stand on trial, I doubt it shall take us many moments to conclude if we should waste our time on such trivia. Your offer to us is a wise one."

The discussion was interrupted when a house guard entered the room, saluting by sweeping his arm across his chest and snapping it back to his side after which he stood silently at attention, waiting to be recognized. Claudesius excused himself and walked over to the guard who quietly spoke in the governor's ear.

After sending the guard away, he returned to the others. "I have a minor issue that needs tending to before our interrogation of this young rabble begins. Permit me, please, a few moments to set those things in order. In the meantime, my servants will entertain you with some delightful music and magic tricks. There are also more fine wines and delicious fruits and cheeses to tease your palates."

After receiving nodded approval to leave, Claudesius quickly departed the governor's chamber and hurried through the palace until reaching its southernmost open portico. Treston met him there, saluting and then bowing in respect.

Claudesius was in no mood for games. He growled, "I'm sitting the Devil's playpen this morning and can't afford to let his children out of my sight. You'd better have good reason to call me away, or I might just offer you up to them for something to play with, to take their minds off me."

"My Lord..." Treston bowed again. He spoke calmly and quietly, but the concern on his face could not be hidden, nor his continual glancing around as if they were being watched. "My Lord, I have a matter of grave concern that I felt you needed to be made aware of before I delivered the girl into your hands."

"You haven't killed her, have you?!" The governor angrily responded. "I need the little tramp alive and walking! If she's dead, I'll dress *you* up like a woman and feed you to the dogs today!"

Treston shook his head, replying in a hushed voice, "No! No, my Lord, the girl is... is... fine, my Lord. It's... it's just that... I believed you would want to know what I discovered when I went to fetch her. There are fingers in the pudding, if you know what I mean, fingers hidden in dark secrets. I felt you needed to be made aware of the matter and not be taken by surprise."

Taking his cue from his lieutenant, Claudesius lowered his voice, demanding. "Tell me, then, what is the story you wish to feed me?"

Treston was a most trusted officer of the governor. He had served as captain over Claudesius' personal bodyguard for over ten years and knew better than to ever lie or twist the truth. More than one servant in the governor's household had discovered the hard way that it was far better to suffer the flagellum's biting talons by truthfully speaking of one's foolishness, than to hide behind lie's curtain only to become the night's entertainment for the governor's lions.

"My Lord, I had many duties that carried me late into the night. So I arrived as early as may be to the prison this morning, to make sure everything was in order so that the girl could be promptly delivered to you, and in respectable condition."

"You wanted to *hole* her, you!" Claudesius ridiculed. "You'd hole a hanging sow, given half a chance. *Don't tell me different!*"

Treston made no attempt at defending himself. Few were the servants and common people in the palace's district who didn't know the man's reputation, nor had experienced or witnessed some form of his licentious activity. Few of the younger slave women had not been bent across the table by him, the common locals having faired little better. There were also times when the wine was upon him and there were no sweet things available, he would turn his attention to some charming young lad.

"My Lord," He softly replied. "even if that had been my intent, I wouldn't have hurt the girl. I know just how important she is to you…to be alive and healthy, I mean."

"Then what are you about?" Claudesius demanded impatiently. "Tell me so I can finish this and be about other business!"

"My Lord…" Treston quickly went on to explain about the surprises he encountered in the prison that morning, emphasizing his diligence in attempting to collect the facts and the uncooperative actions of the prison keepers. "The two night wardens, having been of no help, are locked up awaiting further questioning, but I think they will have little information to offer. One appears to have swallowed too much gall and gone out of his mind. The other?" Treston slowly shook his head. "I doubt he'll give up his secrets to any but the Reaper after crossing over the River. I needed to hurry the girl here for her examination, so had no time to pursue the matter any further."

"You say she's not dead or badly damaged?!" Claudesius' face was grave, thinking of his personal wellbeing. "You know how I placed my trust in your ability to keep her safe."

"Oh no, my Lord!" For the first time the governor saw a glint of fear in Treston's eyes. "The girl is fine, no, more than fine, like lilacs in the full blossom of spring or like…" Treston's voice trailed off in thought.

"Like what?! Like what?!" Claudesius nearly shouted. "Like what?!"

Treston answered just above a whisper. "Like the summer goddess just risen from the jasmine fields of D'arth."

"Has the river fever overtaken you?!" The governor asked, not bothering to keep his voice down.

Treston snapped to. "No, my Lord! It's just that I… well I've never before been unable to explain what happened to someone in my charge. And the gown she wears, my Lord, it's as if someone - or some ones - came into the prison last night and prepared this girl for her meeting with you today. And I know for certain that at least one man was in her cell with her and was violent with her, too. But there isn't a mark or blemish to be seen on her at all."

Troubled and curious, Claudesius asked, "What of the girl? Did you question her?"

"Only with words, my Lord, only with words." A look of fear flashed from his eyes again, and quickly faded. "All she would say was that an angel visited her in the night." Regaining his composure, he added with suspicion, "I feel someone was bribed or threatened to let visitors in, but I can find no proof… yet. That is part of the reason the night guards still live and have not been executed for falling asleep at their posts."

Resting his hand on Treston's shoulder, Claudesius pondered the moment, finally nodding. "You have done well, Captain, once again showing my wisdom in choosing you to be in charge of my house. I, too, may wish to question these men you speak of. But as long as the girl is saved harmless, I think it better to not make a big fuss over this. After all, with patience and long-suffering, your ear may well hear loose lips that will reveal many secrets. Then we will know for sure."

The governor did not mention his own unease. After all, he did have enemies, many of whom would be more than willing to assist him to an early grave. Might this be some plot of an opponent to spoil his great plans of bringing to ruin this new religion? If Ogust watched him fail, after all the brags made this morning, would he and his family survive the night?

Smiling, he quietly asked, "Where is the child of controversy? Take me to her so that I may judge for myself the good and bad of the matter."

"In the shadows of the dungeon gate, my Lord. Follow me." Treston turned, the governor staying close.

As the two men neared the upper entrance of the palace prison, Treston motioned for his soldiers to fetch Ishtar. When they came forward, the bright morning sun revealed the young woman in all her radiance. Treston stopped up short, staring in disbelief at the beauty standing before him, he having only seen her in the light of the torches.

Nearly crashing into Treston, Claudesius huffed with disgust, "Be off with your foolishness!"

Stepping around and forward, the governor found himself face to face with the girl. He cried out with a gasp, clutching his heart as it painfully rent itself within his chest. Like a man caught in a witch's spell, Claudesius froze, unable to move.

⁖   ⁖   ⁖

Sirion had just met back up with the party carrying Darla. Out of breath, she conveyed Mihai's orders to Gabrielle. "It's been recommended we take shelter near that outcropping of rocks, giving us some protection from the countless eyes searching for our whereabouts."

Frowning, Gabrielle disagreed. "That copse of trees in the distance will suit our needs much better. I can sense the energy being stronger there. Darla is very weak. The nearer we draw to a cosmic portal with the Lower Realms, the greater our chances of success. This place is far too far away."

Remaining respectful but determined, Sirion argued against such a move. "The leeches are gathering to the blood-feast! Mihai says she has never seen such a huge crowd of these miscreants collected together other than in war. She feels that Legion, himself, is here. And that means his private army is here, too."

Tzidohn, helping with Darla's litter, agreed. "Yep, I've heard that since the kataschesis-aulos has been improved upon, making it easy to control a human's mind, a vast number of Pseudes have made pilgrimages to the Second Realm to prey upon those innocent and reckless of heart. But if Legion's really there, something else's afoot."

Gabrielle informed them, "The reason for our mission... When it was learned that Legion planned to break Symeon in order to bring down Mihai's house, we immediately took counter measures. Now, well I don't know if we shall attain success."

"We needn't fear, Sister." Depais chimed in. "It's our effort that matters most. Should the universe burn in flames and yet we have held true to all that is good, our mother will have a report to make against Asotos' lies, and the world will again be made right."

Casting a glance toward the outcropping, Gabrielle sighed. "Then let us choose death over there, by those rocks. At least we may affect the moment, and that just might change the course of battle." She lamented, "'It is ever the dream of the sun to chase forever away the shadow, but the shadow will out when the bitter night arrives too soon'. Let us hope the *bitter night* is delayed today."

They struggled over broken ground covered in jagged boulders and twisted thorn-berry shrubs until coming to the low rock face. Telling the party to stop, Gabrielle looked around. "Guess this'll have to do. There's good cover to the west and north, and those trees to the south are thick enough to hide us." She glanced east, staring into the distance, seeing little protection other than the giant rocks strewn across the valley. She pointed. "If trouble arrives, it'll come from there first. We'll need to stay low to keep out of sight."

After placing the litter on the ground, Gabrielle sent Periste to report to Mihai and asked Sirion's assistance with Darla while having the others set up a perimeter around the camp. When finished giving directions, she and Sirion busied themselves with the task at hand. After blankets had been laid on the ground they, along with Tzidohn, succeeded in transferring Darla off the litter and onto the blankets.

Gabrielle smiled down at Darla. "There, my lovely one, you just relax and I'll crawl over top of you, and we can get started."

Darla shook her head, drawing Gabrielle's face close to hers.

Gabrielle frowned. "You're far too weak! We must try it this other way."

Darla persisted with her request. Finally, grudgingly, Gabrielle relented. "All right, but for only as long as I permit it."

Nodding, Darla pulled on Gabrielle, and with Sirion's help sat, bending her knees up while spreading her legs. Gabrielle wiggled down to the ground until sitting, slithered up to Darla, spreading her legs and locking them around and behind the girl's torso. When she had finished, Darla, suffering a great deal of pain in the process, did the same with Gabrielle.

Sirion unzipped Gabrielle's flight suit, pulling it off her shoulders and down to the woman's hips. "There," She smiled. "let me cover you with a blanket so you don't catch a chill."

Gabrielle turned to Sirion, the look in her eyes apologizing for her earlier harshness. Sirion said nothing, unrolled another blanket and gently draped it over Gabrielle's shoulders. When finished, she settled down behind Darla, pressing herself close, so that Darla could rest her back against Sirion.

Darla swooned in pain, adjusting her body to this new, cramped, position. She wiggled her back into Sirion's chest and worked her head until the neck brace fit better. She mumbled her readiness.

"Good!" Gabrielle grinned, her eyes belying a troubled heart. "We shall begin."

Reaching out with naked arms, Darla and Gabrielle locked them together, hands grasping each other's elbows, leaning forward until their faces almost touched. Looking into Darla's eyes, Gabrielle considered the moment. There would be no more conversation until this trial passed. 'If the child dies during it…'

Gabrielle smiled. "You are the bravest woman I have ever known. No matter what this day brings, it will remain one of honor for you and all that you have done. I love you."

Darla smiled back. They closed their eyes, reaching out to the surrounding harmonics, seeking its bonding powers. Gabrielle strained to find Darla's thoughts. Gradually, a fuzzy picture began to grow in her mind. In a few moments she could see a woman's face as it entered into the bright sunlight of morning. At that she started a low guttural tune, pushing the notes up and through her nasal passages. Soon Gabrielle and Darla were mated in a binding trance, lost to the world surrounding them.

৪০ ৪০ ৪০

Mihai was lying on her belly in the ashen dirt, watching from behind a charred tree stump overlooking a volcanic wasteland in the valley below. Long lines of enemy Pseudes were making their way from the landing depots to the cosmic arena, a built up area nearest an opened energy field that permitted them easy access to the gathering crowds in the city below.

Startled, Mihai jumped at the sound of someone approaching. Periste, crawling through the thorny underbrush, let out a muffled cry when she drove her elbow into a woody brier. She looked up to see scowling though much relieved eyes staring at her. Quickly, she slithered up beside Mihai.

Staring down at the moving throng, Periste quietly let out, "Whew! I haven't seen so many Pseudes in this realm since the Greco-Maccabean Wars. Can they just be here for the one reason, to watch Symeon recant his faith?"

(*Author's note: 'Pseudes' was the name given to the followers of Asotos by the loyal children of Lowenah who joined together to form the Children's Empire. The name was derived from Pseudin-Posades, meaning 'false witness' and/or 'liar', and later gained the added meaning, 'to make oneself an apostate through fornication (lusting with falsehood for something to which one has no right)'.*

By Ishtar's day, Asotos' followers had elevated the use of mind control over earthly men to an art. By use of newly refined and contrived machines, the common Pseudes was able to take limited control over the minds of ignorant and/or willing men, thus causing them to act in ways so subhuman and demonic that later historians came to write with disgust concerning that particular generation of men.

The Pseudes also developed machines that could greatly enhance pain and panic in chosen victims. Through implantation, they could feel the emotions and fear racing through these persons as they suffered any torments being heaped upon them. This was the reason they gathered together above the arenas of Greece and Rome, to not only watch the slaughter but to feel the thrill of terror and agony of the people in contest and to revel in the bloodlust of the crowd.

For these truly corrupted servants of Asotos – for not all of his followers sank into this eternal abyss – there were no feelings of love remaining within. All emotion, then, had to derive from sordid means, or there was no emotion at all to be had.

The main reason for Perk's violent rape of Ishtar was to implant thousands of the Pseudes' malicious bugs into the girl. These devices would have heightened Ishtar's personal fear and agony, but also made it possible for anyone tuned in to the harmonic frequency of the bugs to feel, along with her, the child's tribulations. Legion, himself, had perpetrated this deed, part

of his reason for hating Darla so. For, when she purified Ishtar, healing her,
all of Legion's efforts came to naught.)

"Here." Mihai whispered, handing Periste her vision/listening machine.
"See for yourself into the world of *Hell and damnation*."

Placing the headpiece over her temples, Periste worked the tiny lever
on the handheld control, scanning surroundings in Ephesus. Eventually she
found the frequency that allowed her to spy in on Ishtar. At length she pulled
the headset back, whispering concern. "I though Mother's directions were
to only remove Legion's machines from Ishtar, her healing only enough to
prevent death so as to receive pity from her tormentors. Here Darla has made
the child perfect in flesh, almost as much so as we are. Had she made her
a little more so, the girl would have become a weapon of destruction, her
beauty rupturing the very hearts of lowly men."

Mihai nodded.

"And did you see the dress?" Periste put the headset back in place. "She
was not to leave the unearthly garment with the girl. Nowhere in that realm
does such a thing exist. Magic it may well be perceived by those creatures,
possibly lifting the girl up to godship."

Glancing away from the crowds below, Mihai replied, "Don't cast blame
on Darla. This was her first clandestine mission, one in which she was to have
received guidance. We failed in providing promised support, not only endan-
gering the girl's life, but possibly altering the history of men. Whether it was
by mistake or intention, Darla's actions must now be taken into account. We
must work with what we have. It may be the governor will now take pity on
his own heart, seeking some way to preserve such a ravenous beauty from
the jaws of death."

Mihai was offered her headset, she motioning it away. "The power of this
ring allows me limited vision of current goings on. You use it for whatever
needs you may find. I desire to watch the enemy below. Some of Legion's
personal guards have passed this way, maybe in search of us. You, too, keep
a sharp eye out for them."

Periste replaced the headset, adjusting it to fit. She crawled forward
enough to watch the gathering crowds below, then settled down to see other
events. Motionless, she and Mihai watched the world above and beneath.
As the Pseudes continued to collect themselves, the test of Ishtar slowly
unfolded within the palace walls. With bated breath, the women waited to
see what the outcome would be.

ଔ   ଔ   ଔ

The burning ache in Claudesius' chest was diminishing as the group walked along the palace portico, but his recent shortness of breath persisted. The governor never did fully recover from this initial contact with Ishtar. Taken fully by surprise at seeing the girl, and being an older man, his heart was sorely stricken, which led to his eventual death.

Try as hard as he might, he could not stop staring agog at this spell-binding creature. But what disturbed him most was the feeling as if a voice within continually called out for him to tear apart the flesh of this 'putrid thing' and burn it with fire.

Treston maintained a reserved appearance, though his ardor was intense enough so the arteries in his neck bulged. Having survived so long amid political vultures was no accident, but taught behavior. This learned self-control made it easier for the man to restrain his emotions. There were also no quiet voices urging him on to carry out lascivious or violent actions against Ishtar.

Never had Treston been a man having great reverence or fear of the gods. He had not set foot into a temple in years, other than to find certain sensual gratification or at the behest of his superiors. In fact, after the untimely death of his daughter, Treston had silently warred with the gods, condemning them in his heart for their wicked acts.

Once, when the wine loosened his lips, he declared to a companion, "The keepers of Hell shall not my soul peacefully abide, for I will not accept them as a slave does his master! Their prisoner I may well become, but to do their bidding? Never! My voice shall castigate the gods for all eternity!" With such a strong-willed man, Legion's machines had little effect.

Of the guards accompanying them? A motion of Treston and one sharp glance was enough to keep them under control. Better to die from wanton desire than at the hand of a man known to watch prison inquisitions while eating his dinner. Suffer as they may, the guards stood vigil over their own souls and acted as good soldiers should.

Claudesius searched for ways to stall his return to the justice chambers. Not only did he wish to have this child's' attention, but the thought of sharing her with the two ugly stooges, Ogust and Jusslin, was so much more than repulsive. Using the pretense of gaining needed background information to fairly judge the case, Claudesius busied himself in small talk with the girl.

As they strolled along, the governor casually looked toward the porch's ceiling, musing, "Ishtar, um, Ishtar… Now that is such a strange name for a child of the Jews and one who has Cephas for an uncle, don't you think so?"

Although suspicious of Claudesius' motives, Ishtar's innocence could see no treachery in his question. She cautiously answered, "My mother is a Jewess, that is true, sister to Cephas. But my father was from a city in Phrygia, not more than thirty leagues from here. He was a man of honor, serving as a captain in the fabri, the engineers, and second assistant to the praefectus fabrum, none other than Vitruvius III, grandson of Vitruvius I, overseer of the works, personal servant of Caesar Augustus. My father was so favored by Vitruvius that he gained citizenship at his behest."

The governor stopped, staring at Ishtar. "So, you, too, are a Roman?"

Ishtar shook her head. "It was after my birth that the gift was bestowed upon my father, a gift for his valor to duty that led to his fateful accident and crippling."

"Your mother is a *Jew*, but your father a Phrygian." Claudesius quietly drummed his fingers against a supporting column of the porch. "So how did such a *happy* relationship develop, come about, I mean, between your father and mother?"

With indignant undertones, Ishtar answered, "My mother is a *Jewess* and she met my father while he was in the Decapolis, on king's business. He *did not* hold the Jews in disdain as some men do but found them most fascinating. He fell in love with my mother, taking her for a *wife*, not some *plaything!*"

Treston instinctively stepped away, expecting to see the girl backhanded and flung across the marble floor. But, no, much to his surprise, Claudesius brushed off the child's insolence, carrying on as if nothing out of the ordinary had been spoken.

With his hands clasped behind him, the governor politely asked, "So, tell me, daughter of a... a Jewess, how is it you have come to reside among us in this humble city?"

Although her ire was still up, Ishtar replied calmly, "After my father's accident and subsequent retirement from the fabri, we journeyed here where he established himself as a very successful dealer in trade goods, for both the Temple Artemis and foreign merchants. Before the fever took him, my father had secured enough wealth so that his family has not come in need or want."

Nodding, Claudesius smiled, "You have still not explained your name, other than your father was not a Jew and that he dealt in trade goods for the Temple Artemis. Is there more to tell?"

"There is more." Ishtar responded. "My father was a man who feared the gods... that is, all but two. The God of my mother's ancestors he respected, but the god of his mother's endearment he came to love. So he gave to me, his only and most cherished child, the name of his beloved god, by the name with which his mother called out to Artemis, and that was 'Ishtar'."

Staring into the girl's face, and lifting a hand in question, Claudesius asked, "Why does a child who holds to this new and strange religion and, I may add, bears the accusation of blasphemy of the very god for whom you are named... why have you not reverted to your *Hebrew* name, one I am sure your mother has bestowed upon you?"

Ishtar raised an eyebrow at the question. "Many men, worms of the earth…" She chanced a glance at Treston. "have carried honorable names, while there are many good men who have owned names filled with evil and foreboding. For me, the name 'Ishtar' is filled with sweet love and bitter sorrow. My father valued me as if a son in his eyes, and wished I remember it should he pass into the world of darkness. I am proud to carry the name for my father's sake, not for some impotent god of stone and dust."

There was anger in his voice, as Claudesius quickly chastised the girl. "Do not think yourself wise, ridiculing the creators of this world! My powers of discipline will arrive quickly upon the heads of such blasphemers."

Ishtar's retort was swift and stinging. "No man has any power at all unless the Maker of all worlds grants it! You breathe life, as do other men and beasts. Not one hair's breadth can you add to it, other than what *my* God has given you!"

Claudesius' hand was just a blur as it swept the air, smashing across Ishtar's face. "*You insolent shit weed! Whore-maiden of an evil apparition! I control your destiny! Fool! I can make your next breath your last!*"

Though blood gushed from the girl's nose, she took no note, breathing fire and threat. "*Then take it now and I shall wait for you beyond the River for my revenge! I control my own destiny, not a man who quakes in fear at idols of wood and stone!*"

Claudesius was not hearing Ishtar's reply, for he was absorbed with wonder, staring at the girl's gown. As blood dripped from Ishtar's face, it fell in rivulets onto her dress, spattering on the stones at her feet. In disbelief, he watched as each drop of blood rolled off the fabric as if thrown away in disdain, leaving the dress unblemished.

"What the…?!" He reached out to examine the fabric. It was smooth to the touch, the weave something he had never before seen, and it felt warm and cool at the same time. And it was not white, but danced in every color of rainbow hues when the fabric moved.

"Where did you get this?" Ishtar remained mute. Claudesius screamed, "Where did you get this?!! Tell me now!" He raised his hand as though to hit her again.

Fire in Ishtar's eyes burned into the governor's as she leaned forward, nose to nose, seething in angry defiance, whispering her rebuke, "*Strike me again, old man! It takes a strong hand to hide a weak mind. If you had eyes, you would see that your shitty gods have no power, else they needn't rely on the likes of you to protect their worthless names!*" The girl braced herself for the coming blow. Nothing happened.

The governor's hand began to shake. He so much wanted to smash this insolent pest, but he could not. Even through the oozing blood and a growing bruise on the girl's face, Claudesius stared at such beauty never before seen.

He could feel his ardor for the girl growing by the moment. The heat of her breath inflamed his desires. Hate, passion, and fear were a'work all at once in his soul.

At length, Ishtar stepped back, wiping a hand across her bloodied face, spitting crimson saliva onto the stones to clear her mouth. Glancing first at Treston and then back at the governor, she smiled coldly, answering defiantly, "As I have already said to one of your *servants*, an angel gave me this dress."

Claudesius glared at Treston as if to say, 'Why didn't you tell me this?' He then turned his attention back to the girl. She was only a child, eighteen years at best, but her stare was unnerving – as though someone else was looking out from her and peering deep into his soul. Who was this woman? Did the child really have power over the gods? Impossible! Still, the governor chose not to debate the issue further.

"We must hurry!" the governor called out in his most official voice. Motioning Treston to him, he ordered, "Take this… this person and clean her up. When finished, you shall personally see to her deliverance to my chambers. Have one of your men come with me to assist in making things ready."

Treston saluted, bowing his head, "Yes, my Lord. It will be done quickly." his heart pounding with desire as tiny tremors raced across his shoulders and down his arms. Forcing an excruciating ache into submission, he took Ishtar's arm, leading her away.

Claudesius disappeared into the shadows, placing a trembling hand over his palpitating heart.

℠ ℠ ℠

Ogust's head lolled from side to side while Jusslin gently rubbed his shoulders. Opening an eye when hearing Claudesius' return, he noticed the man's reddened face, smirking. "Oh, there you are! I was beginning to think you had fallen into the lions' pit!" Silly laughter followed, Jusslin joining in with some senseless comment. Ogust did so much like to laugh at his own humor.

The governor grinned, sheepishly pretending to appreciate Ogust's comment by joining in the laughter. 'Fat puss-face!' he thought to himself, smiling at Ogust as he crossed the chamber. 'Could feed a hundred lions for a month on that blubber, if it didn't kill 'em first.'

Sitting, Claudesius cast a gaze out the window and across the river, but his eyes saw nary cloud, sky or ship, for the vision of the child, oh, so beautiful, commanded his attention. Passion swept over him, one so great he believed his manhood would rip asunder, and the pain in his lower back grew intense. Only could that girl give him release from this agony. He must find a way to take her for himself… a legal way, of course. It had to be done legally for the governor sat as judge and he mustn't sully his raiment. She would still have to be given over to death this day. That he had already promised to Ogust. Still, he could have her first and then kill her.

Finding it impossible to think of another thing, Claudesius closed his eyes, dreaming of the child. They suddenly popped back open, filled with dread. What if she *was* a goddess, come to test him out?! It had happened before, at least in his grandfather's day. His father had told him, said the man died a very horrible death for hurting a goddess. This last thought troubled the governor greatly.

He needed some private time to ponder matters. Turning to Ogust, he asked, "Have you been able to search for a better room to rest in tonight? This judicial case will be ever so boring. I assure you, just a few formalities to keep things legal, but may take some time. Do you really wish to waste this beautiful day on such silly matters? After all, the games will begin soon. Taking care of evening's business will allow your full indulgence at more momentous events this night."

Ogust squinted suspiciously, leaning forward and frowning. "I will wait here to see about things myself. A fox offers not to guard an empty henhouse. It's not like *your* kind to suffer the indignities of king's service when excuse offers itself so well to escape such drudgeries. No, I smell 'sweet jam and honey' under your 'stale bread'. I think it best to watch the fox as it dutifully watches the henhouse."

Claudesius waxed apologetic, defending his innocence. "No! No! That is not what I meant at all, not at all. You see, the child had a little accident while coming here. My officer has taken her to be mended. We may be delayed in starting the trial."

Ogust's question was scolding. "So we fixes 'em back up so's to kill 'em? You must have something better for my ears, really..."

Ogust's wit caught Claudesius off guard. The boy was fat and ever so ugly, but his mind was sharp. The governor considered it wise he best remember that. Hesitatingly, he answered, "Ah... well...oh, yes. You see, the girl's father was a loyal engineer in the emperor's army, second assistant to Vitruvius III, himself, made Roman citizen at Vitruvius' request. I felt that if we were forced to judge against the girl, it would be best for her to be treated with the utmost show of fairness in righteous judgment. The emperor would not desire any to question Rome's integrity in such a case as this."

Resting his chin in the palm of his hand while drumming his stubby fingers on his cheek, Ogust thought aloud. "I know this Vitruvius. He does take great liking to some of his officers. Hmmmm... Very well..." Ogust's suspicion was not totally satisfied, but he was at least returned to a more receptive mood.

Claudesius smiled, folding his hands in his lap. "So I can proce..."

Ogust interrupted. "But I think I will remain here until this person arrives. If it pleases us at that time, then Jusslin and I will take our leave. You say you do have better rooms?"

Grinning, Claudesius replied, "Oh, yes! Yes! Any you may choose, anywhere you like, here or or anywhere in this fine city."

A sudden change in the breeze and an aroma of sweet pastries and fresh bread filled the room. Ogust swooned over the smell. His comments started the two men blathering on about good food and drink and other very unimportant matters, as far as Claudesius was concerned. At least he could think now - think how he could satisfy his burning lust and not become tonight's entertainment because of it.

Then it came to him. Why not? Give the girl opportunity to make her confession here and then provide the tools for her atonement. She could then be secreted away, so he could satisfy his passion upon her and later, before the afternoon faded away, invent new accusations to bring against her. The dogs would still be hungry and the crowds willing to witness a just execution of a heretic. It would work!

As a renewed wave of excitement filled his heart, Claudesius motioned to an attendant who, upon hearing the orders, hurried from the room. Strumming his fingers together, the governor relaxed, pondering details of his little plan.

ଛଠ   ଛଠ   ଛଠ

By the time Treston arrived with Ishtar, the throne room was furnished with objects retrieved by the attendant. To one side of the room was placed a small stand with a statue of the emperor in dignified repose, an oil-wicked flame burning at its base. The flickering fire caught Ishtar's eye. Her brow furrowed. Beside the tiny blaze sat a bowl of incense, a little scoop resting near it.

Middle morning was rapidly approaching. The noise from the streets below told the governor that crowds were beginning to arrive. He smiled. There was still time. If things went as planned, he would have several hours to ravish the girl. But as he watched her in the shadows, other disturbing emotions grew in his chest, filling his heart with loathing for this creature. 'No! No!' He fought the demon within, gritting his teeth. 'I shall pleasure myself first and then we will kill her!"

Wrapping his flowing cape around himself, Claudesius stood, signifying the height of justice and how it looks far into the distance searching for truth and honor. Momentarily, he sat, suggesting the weight of responsibility placed upon the office of a judge serving the emperor. Raising an arm with outstretched hand, he commanded, "All give honor to our gracious lord."

Everyone bowed toward the statue of the emperor. Much to his surprise and pleasure, when Claudesius chanced a glance at Ishtar he saw that she, too, had bent forward in a partial bow, her head lowered. He mused in thought, 'She must be coming to her senses, or perhaps my officer has persuaded her to have a change of heart.'

What the governor did not know was that Ishtar viewed the giving of honor to the ruling chief magistrate, even though he be represented with a statue, as an acceptable thing. She saw it as no act of worship to do so. Convincing her to do that would be far more difficult, a fact he was to soon discover.

Treston had no need to wait, though. No sooner was the girl out of earshot of the governor than she let go on him with one vile oath after another. When a guard made some suggestive remark concerning her, she bared her teeth, growling out a curse while threatening him with her fingernails, so disturbing the guard that he backed away, leaving the girl alone. Treston's passions cooled somewhat, too, fearing what those long nails could do to a man being careless while funning with the girl.

After invoking the gods for wisdom and understanding, and burning incense on the flaming altar before the statue, Claudesius called out, "The accused shall step forward."

Immediately, Ishtar moved out of the shadows until she stood at the base of the judgment chair. Then, with bended knee, the girl bowed low in front of the governor, her eyes cast toward the floor.

A gentle breeze caught the light fabric of Ishtar's dress, it shimmering with delightful colors. Ogust and Jusslin stared in amazement, quietly chattering with each other over its beauty. Claudesius did not see the dress as he stared. His eyes searched for any hint of flesh the dress might reveal, and it was generous. The girl's shapely form was not hidden by the fabric, it acting more like a silken shade on a moonlit night.

'On with it, fool! You're wasting the day!' Claudesius chided himself, breaking the trance he was in. 'But she is so beautiful! Another moment, just one...' His heart pleaded. 'Be up at it now, fool! Or all will be lost forever.' The voice in his head cried. 'Forever!'

Blinking away the voices, the governor sat back, placing his arms on those of his chair. Gathering his thoughts, he began, "You have been brought before this court today on the charge of blasphemy – one count of which I am also personally privy to – and on the charge of practicing an unlawful religion. How do you answer to such charges?"

Ishtar lifted her eyes to meet his, Claudesius most disappointed to see no fear in them. The girl stood up and calmly answered, "As to the second charge, I practice a religion that is pleasing to my God. It may be of your choosing to deem it illegal before men, but that is of little importance to me."

An exclamation of disbelief echoed across the chamber. Claudesius raised his hand, quieting those in the room. He then asked Ishtar, "And...?"

"And..." The girl's face hardened in resolve. "as for the charge of blasphemy? I say I am not guilty. The gods you speak of are the inventions of weak men's minds and are thus valueless, impotent non-gods." She pointed. "They do not even have the power to prevent the stink of the river from invading the rooms of the cousin of the god-emperor, nor can they heal the man's loathsome disease, which he cries out day and night for them to remove."

Ogust jumped up from his chair, his face as red as the apple he was angrily waving. "Burn her now! She defames the very gods! She defames *me!* Throw her to the lions!"

The governor ignored Ogust's protest, absorbed he was in what Ishtar had revealed. Filled with wonder, he asked, "Who told you these things?" He was surprised regarding Ogust, something few would know about other than Jusslin or a physician.

Her answer was most disquieting. "There are many things I know and know about. The way I have learned them is not the concern of mortals."

'*Kill her now!*' The voice raged in the governor's head. '*She must die now or she will destroy us!*'

Rage filled Claudesius' heart, chasing away any passion for the girl. Red-faced, he started to stand, shouting angrily, "Do not toy with me, you piece of dirt! I can crush you to pulp or release you! I have that power to do to you as I wish!"

Ishtar's challenge to his authority came on a fiery tongue. "*You'd have no power at all unless my God permitted it!*" She wagged her finger at him. "There was another of your emperor's governors who was told that once, but he didn't listen and learn. Today his bones rot in the dust, and his works are almost forgotten. In the Judgment, how will you stand against the One who rules over heaven and earth?"

Ishtar's rebuke hit Claudesius a severe blow, sweeping away his rage with concern and doubt. He slowly sat down and, head in hand, began pondering the situation. This person standing before him was only a woman-child, having been pampered all her life. She was not wise enough to outsmart him and by no means so stupid she would not realize the great danger such contentions placed her in. He glanced at Treston. Even a seasoned warrior like him would not dare practice this folly in front of the governor. No. There must be something more.

That was it! A talisman! The girl was protected by a talisman or possibly an oath. But the dress! Certainly that must be it, probably bewitched by a sorcerer in a distant land and delivered here by the girl's uncle or his friends. He raised an arm, pointing toward two attendants, thundering a command.

"Remove that creature's garment from her and secure it deep in the wine cellars!"

The two attendants hurried forward, instantly stripping the dress off Ishtar.

A deathly hush fell over the room, and then a collective gasp. Treston's knees buckled, he nearly collapsing to the floor, his heart pounding in such pain that he feared it would burst. He turned his face away, leaning against a ceiling column for support, forcing his eyes closed. It took several deep breaths before he dared open them again.

Ogust's jaw dropped and his eyes bulged. Drooling, he cried, "She is beautiful! She is most beautiful!" Guiltily, his eyes glanced back and forth between Jusslin and Ishtar. Finally, he blubbered again, "She is beautiful!" then staring into Jusslin's angry face, cried, "For a woman...for a woman, she is beautiful!"

Jusslin had enough. He scolded Claudesius, "*Temptress!* You have delivered a temptress to spoil our day! This act cannot be tolerated. We will take our leave this very moment!" Gripping Ogust's arm, he commanded, "Come now, enough of this humiliation! Let us go before my heart breaks."

Still staring at Ishtar, Ogust dumbly nodded, struggling up from his chair and waddling away with Jusslin.

As they left, Jusslin turned, threatening, "*It* better be in today's games if there is wisdom in your heart!"

Claudesius bowed his head in recognition, but didn't really hear what was said. Wisdom was the furthest thing from his mind at the moment. At first he had been taken aback, his heart paining him so he thought death was near, and it might have been except for the little voice in his mind screaming obscenities about the girl. Soon his passion temporarily shoved the voice from his head. He sat for the longest time soaking in unfathomable beauty.

'To bed this woman is cause enough to set the world ablaze with war! To have her for only a night is worth an eternity of damnation!' Round and round these and other thoughts twirled in Claudesius' mind. He could not destroy her this day...another day... another time, maybe... maybe...but not this day. He had to make plans to steal her away for himself unto the end of eternity, and that was not long enough.

'Besides,' Claudesius reasoned, 'she might be a goddess sent to test me. I must find a way to preserve her alive. Yes! Yes!' That was it. He must find a way to keep this goddess from dying. That must be his test.

Mastering heated passion, Claudesius leaned forward and, with a fatherly tone, asked so politely, "I know how difficult it must be for you to suffer such indignity, but truly, it was necessary. Now, my child, the charge of blasphemy against you has been presented before this court. How do you answer such a charge?"

Ishtar did not stand like a woman disgraced, but stood proud and straight, as if clothed in royal attire. She asked accusatively, "Do you really believe my faith is found in a garment made by angels? Look around. Your men and you act like beasts in rut, your prattle only used to prolong Fate's destiny. Tell me, does the air still not stink from rotten fish and has the fat man been cured? I do not blaspheme, for I have not called down evil on any real god, just sallow images created by weak minds."

Claudesius' knuckles whitened as his fingers gripped the chair arms tightly. He mustn't lose control, not now, not yet. He counted to six, breathed a long draught of air and commented, "I have only your best interests at heart. I desire…"

Ishtar cut in, raising her eyes as if in thought. "Let me see, my best interest? What do your prison guards say? Oh yes, I remember… 'giving her the bone'! Is that my 'best interest' that you had in mind?" Her voice filled with contempt. "The rat dung in your prison looked at me with the same passion I see in your eyes, only they were not as polite. They took what they wanted, seeking no justification for their actions!"

The voice in the back of the governor's head cried out desperately, *'Kill it now! Now! Before it destroys us!'* Oh, how much he wanted to…to crush this insolent worm, grinding it under his heel. He would do it now, could do it now. He was judge, his very laws giving him that power. But then his heart sang out in equal desperation. 'Never will you see another like this one. I will not live if you take her from me! Let her live! Find a way! Let her live!'

For the moment, Claudesius' heart won out. He relaxed, seeking the right words that would convince Ishtar to accept his terms. The girl must be persuaded. He began ever so benevolently, "Please, my dear child, as governor, I have a weighty responsibility to balance justice with mercy, and I wish so much to show you mercy."

Claudesius gestured beseechingly, his voice begging, "Please listen, I am only trying to help you. Your actions until now, even though out of line, I can overlook, considering the circumstances of the moment. But you must show more respect… respect for my position and for your country. If you will learn to submit just a little, I may be able to find a way to reunite you and your mother. But you must help me."

He paused, waiting for Ishtar's reply. She said nothing.

Apparently, there was need for more persuasion. Claudesius' voice softened, his words becoming smooth like aged wine. "While it is true that you profess membership in an illegal religion, and while such a thing is *possibly* punishable by death, you have made a case for your defense regarding certain gods, albeit a small one…" he sighed, "but it does give me a place to begin. I may well be able to dismiss some of the charges against you if I receive a tiny bit more cooperation from you."

The thought of her mother's distress, hearing her mother's mournful pleas as the soldiers hauled her daughter away, haunted Ishtar's heart. She did so much want to see her again, if only for a little while. Cautiously, the girl asked, "What must I do?"

'Gently now...' warned his heart. 'Soft and gentle should be your words. We do not want to scare this creature away.' The governor put on his fatherly charm. "Even now the crowds gather to see justice fulfilled. If I were to release you at this time, I could not hold you safe, but by the people's own hands would justice be meted out. No, here, behind these walls should you remain until the righteous ardor of this people be calmed. Then, when it is safe, I can secret you and your family away from here, to lands where your name and misdeeds are not known."

Frowning, Ishtar asked in disgust, "Oh, and what shall be the price for such kindness, a private mistress to warm the secret bed chambers of the governor?"

Pretend shock filled Claudesius' face while his heart raced with desire. He decried Ishtar's accusation. "My child! My child, I am stung by the remark! So little do you understand about me. I cherish my wife and family, seeking whatever is in their best interest. I promise...promise you, my intentions are most honorable. My concern is only for your welfare."

Treston almost choked. He had known the governor for many years. More than one maiden had been tied to his bed and more than one child lost to the harbor when Claudesius' heart took control. But the governor's speech was good. Never was he better than when drawing his prey into his web, and today he was at his best.

Ishtar faltered. The heat of the day, combined with her lack of food and stress of the previous night were weakening her will. She was tired, hungry and very lonely. She missed her mother so. Maybe, just maybe the governor was an honest man. Oh, how much she wanted him to be. She believed there were some good men left in this world of madness. It was possible this man was one. She lowered her head, asking just above a whisper, "My Lord, what must your servant girl do to receive such kindness?"

'So close! So close! Do be careful. We are so close.'

Sweetly, in earnest, Claudesius answered, "My little one, all that must be done is for you to liven the flame that burns before our benevolent leader. By doing this, I can attest to your loyal servitude to the laws of this great land."

Ishtar's face clouded with anger as she pointed, "I have eyes to see. Do not the people cut themselves before the very statues in the city, crying out to the emperor for prayers answered? Full well do you know that is an altar to your most precious of gods!"

Red-faced, Claudesius angrily shouted, "Look! You must do this or you will suffer death in front of the crowds!"

Ishtar stepped back at his outburst.

In solemn apology, the governor pleaded with Ishtar. "I will swear an oath to protect you, even adopting you into my family. You can even worship that God of yours in the privacy of this house. No one will dare bring you harm in this sanctuary."

Ishtar did nothing.

Claudesius stood, motioning toward the statue with uplifted hands. "Look!" He offered in desperation. "Place your hands in mine. I will help you! This way justice will be served and you can tell the others I forced you… that you had no control over what happened."

Ishtar clenched her fists, her arms rigid at her sides. "And what will I tell the God of the living and the dead? Do you really believe anyone can escape his scrutiny?! His eyes are roving about, searching the hearts of men clear to their kidneys."

Claudesius shouted, "He cannot search mine!"

Ishtar spread her feet, extending an arm, pointing. She shook her head accusingly. "He is searching it now, revealing it to children!"

"No!"

"Man of licentiousness!" She countered defiantly, "He shows me your perversions and lusts. Take me now. Ravish my flesh in front of your servants and prove I speak the truth!"

"Liar!" Claudesius screamed. "Your worthless God cannot search me!" He lunged forward, his crushing blow to the side of Ishtar's head spinning her around, and a second one to the face sending her sprawling on the floor. *"Liar! Liar! Liar!"* Claudesius screeched, repeatedly kicking the girl in the ribs and stomach.

'Kill it! Yes! Yes! Kill it now! Kill before it hurts us again! Do it! Do it!' The voice in the back of Claudesius' head had returned, filling his mind with curses and cackling laughter.

Ishtar writhed in agony, her eyes rolled back in her head as she coughed up bloody froth, choking on her vomit. She rolled on her side before passing out.

Treston was aghast. He blurted out, "My Lord!" just as Claudesius was preparing to deliver a killing kick to Ishtar's throat.

"What…?!" Claudesius appeared to be waking from a fog. "What…?" He stumbled back, staring in disbelief at his handiwork. The voice still ranted, chiding him for not killing the girl. But as he continued watching the blood from Ishtar's mouth puddle on the floor, the voice faded away, leaving a heart filled with selfish remorse.

Shaking his head in horror, Claudesius wondered at just how wrong it all was. He always thought himself a reasonable man, even kindly and tolerant. Now this anger that welled up from the innermost recesses of a troubled mind, where had it come from? It was like another person dwelling within his head wanted the girl dead. But why? Why, when the passionate ache in his loins only increased? This was all so peculiar and frightening. On shaky legs, he made his way to the judge's chair and sat.

Treston kneeled down beside Ishtar. He sighed, relieved. She lived. It was so puzzling to him. Why did Claudesius so badly need the girl to offer incense to the emperor? Many a time he watched the governor order one's punishment, even demise, with just a wave of a hand. All he need do was declare this woman guilty of whatever crime he wished and be done with it. He could fun with her through the morning and feed her to the dogs tonight. He could even keep the girl prisoner in his house after passing sentence for as long as he pleased. No one would question him.

And this business with Cephas? That was one of Claudesius' inventions to curry favor with the emperor. He could change it to suit the moment. The governor was an excellent politician, his words smooth like rich wine. No, Treston could find no logic in the governor's actions.

Ishtar groaned, attempting to move. Treston stood up, stepping back into the shadows. He dare not interfere at the moment, not knowing the mood of the governor. Strange, his own blinding passion was fading. The girl was still entrancing in his eyes, but something… something tugged at his soul. What it was, he did not know.

Regaining her senses, Ishtar slowly rolled onto her belly and, pushing with her hands, managed to get on her knees. Sitting back, the girl lifted her head, eyes glaring into the governor's. There was no fear to be found in them, only pain and weariness. At length, with tremendous effort and struggle, Ishtar stood, too tired to speak.

Claudesius pushed away the battle raging between the voices in his heart and mind. Surely this creature must see it his way now. He leaned forward, grinning in triumph, asking, "So, what do you have to say about your *precious God* now? He does not stand beside you providing help. Is he not also a valueless God?"

Ishtar calmed her painful breathing by studying the governor's demeanor. The man was not at ease. Something troubled his thoughts. Was he going mad, or was he already so? Still, *no man* should speak that way about her God, not while she lived, at least. With halting speech, she began, "You stand in front of me, lord of all your kingdom, representing the honor and justice found in *your* divine law? To you and what you represent, I am supposed to kneel?" She shook her head. "I see not a purveyor of righteous law, but an old man usurping law to satisfy personal whims."

Pausing, Ishtar waited for the governor's wrath. When it did not come, she continued. "Unlike your gods, my God puts no man under compulsion nor does he drive someone like a dog. By free will I stand before you, knowing full well my destiny before setting my eyes upon you. Your actions only confirm what I already know."

Claudesius sneered. "So who am I, little girl? Who do you really see?"

Facing him with iron resolve, Ishtar declared, "Then I shall tell you! Confused you are at the war raging in your soul. Also are you afraid and jealous of this little child whom you judge. Afraid, because you wish to see her dead by your own hands but fear your heart will languish forever if you do not take her flesh. Jealous, because this child reflects all the good things you abandoned long ago, selling your soul for momentary glory and fame." She shook her head. "First you will rape this child to satisfy your flesh and then feign *righteous law* to silence her voice. I see a man most to be pitied."

Claudesius went blind with rage, diving from his chair, piling into the girl with his fists, pummeling her face with repeated blows. Instinctively stepping back to avoid the onslaught, Ishtar tripped and fell to the floor.

"*Shit worm!*" the governor screamed as he wildly began kicking the girl, continuing long after she became unconscious.

"My Lord!" Treston did not hear his own voice as he stepped forward, putting a hand on the governor's shoulder. He did not consider that his own life was now in jeopardy, thinking only of the girl. "My Lord! Your plan for the day, my Lord?"

The blow was swift. Treston felt no pain at first, just the warm blood in his mouth. Claudesius stared dumbly, his fist back, ready to strike again. Still enraged over Ishtar's secret knowledge, he cursed, "I should cut out your tongue, bastard! Get out of my way!"

Treston bowed his head, fading back into the shadows, but his swift actions had saved the girl. Claudesius stared down at the bloodied child, seething in anger, but he did not strike her again. "*You shit worm… goddess of the lost… fool! No one shows such disrespect to me and lives. No mercy will you find in this house!*"

A sudden pain gripped the governor's heart. His hands flew to his chest while the man's mind whirled with uncertainty. Was he not the great governor over Ephesus and its many jurisdictional cities, appointed by the emperor, himself? Why should this *creature* trouble him? She had exposed him for who he really was, had always been… a selfish ingrate, luxuriating in his every wanton desire at the expense of any helpless innocent caught in his web. He used his title to dispense justice when he saw fit, or, more often, when it benefited him. These truths the girl had dared to reveal aloud. For that, she deserved death.

Ishtar was now conscious, but was not attempting to get up. She writhed in agony, her cracked ribs making every breath excruciatingly painful. Blood oozed from her mouth, nose and ears, her eyes staring blankly.

Sniggering laughter echoed through Claudesius' head. 'It's dying. Yes, it's nearly dead. Best have it now while it's still warm. You like it warm… much better than dead and cold.'

After shaking his head to drive the voice away, Claudesius stared down at the tortured mess of living flesh sprawled on the floor. Ishtar's appearance repulsed him, but also excited him wildly. Had he been alone with her at that moment, he would have done what the voice suggested. Then he wondered if the girl was really dying. No! It mustn't happen! She was a very important part of coming events.

"Treston!" the governor shouted.

Hurrying forward, Treston answered, bowing. "Here, my Lord." He half expected to hear the governor issue a sentence against him.

Claudesius pointed toward Ishtar, commanding sourly, "Take *it* out of here… Clean *it* up… Fix *it* up. Don't let *it* die lest you die with *it*. When I call, return *it* to my chambers so we can finish this trial."

"Yes… my Lord." Treston bowed again and hurried to get Ishtar.

"Oh… and Treston…" the governor called.

"Yes, my Lord?" Treston turned and bowed again.

Claudesius wagged a finger at him. "And don't *fuck* her!" The words reflected his own burning desire.

"No! No, my Lord." Treston dutifully answered, distressed and puzzled at the governor's orders. True, Claudesius knew Treston's debased reputation. It was one reason the governor retained him in his service – but to this child, now? Well, yes, he could… at one time, maybe… but not now, not anymore. Something in his heart nagged him. Pity? No, he thought not. Respect? How strange an idea, he had never respected anyone, other than possibly his caring wife… possibly. No… No… It must be something else. Still, he wanted to bring no more harm to this child. He ordered two of his guards to take Ishtar away, he quickly following.

Claudesius slammed a fist into his opened hand. "Brat! She will not defy me and win! I will teach her! I will teach her!" Bitter feelings of pride and jealousy were rising in his heart, encouraged by the chiding voice in the back of his head. 'It seeks our throne, it does, it does. Thinks it will become king and rule over us. It must be taught a lesson or it will destroy all that surrounds us, bring our world to nothing, nothing.'

He motioned a servant who soon returned with the lieutenant of his house guard. "My Lord…" The officer bowed.

Waving his hand, Claudesius ordered, "Take some of your men and go to the North Market Street Prison, the place where Cephas and his heretic friends are secured. Give the chief of the jailers this note. He will deliver into your hands what I have requested. Bring it back promptly to the upper jail yard behind the palace."

The officer bowed low, his hand over his heart. "Yes, my Lord. It is already done." He left the chamber, gathering up six of his soldiers before leaving the palace. In a few moments, seven men were hurrying toward Market Street on very important business.

Claudesius rested his elbows on the marble support railing, watching the little troop move away. He smiled, "Little brat! *Stay true to your God now… if you can!*"

⁊ ⁊ ⁊

Midmorning was well passed before the trial resumed. Treston had rushed a doctor to the girl's aid, fearing she was dying. The doctor sutured a deep cut in Ishtar's side and fed her some hot herb tea followed by some chicken broth. Somehow, much to everyone's surprise, the girl not only survived, but also recovered rapidly enough to manage a return to the judicial chambers on her own feet.

Claudesius was again upon the judgment throne, silently observing the child. Ishtar stood quietly, favoring her left side, racked with pain, her eyes fastened on the governor's.

As he studied Ishtar's demeanor, Claudesius' ravenous passion for the girl exploded once more. His palms began to sweat as an ache grew in his groin. He must have the girl! Her cuts and bruises only intensified the man's desire to ravage her. But now the hour was late. In a short time, Ishtar would have to appear in the arena, Cephas' test but a few hours future. The thought of losing the girl to death was too much for him. He must do something to prevent her execution, at least for this day.

"My child…" he began, being so careful to salve over any misimpressions the girl might have earlier had. "My child, my heart aches over this morning's unfortunate events. I accept full responsibility for my actions, you being completely innocent. Let me explain, please. You see, I look upon you like my own daughter. I have one, so beautiful she is, her years but fifteen. She would like you."

He leaned forward, eyes beseeching, voice pleading. "I fear for your safety and want to do everything I can to help you. I acted out of frustration and not anger. My frustration led to my inappropriate actions."

Ishtar said nothing.

Disappointed at the girl's lack of response, but hopeful he could still win her over, Claudesius went on to describe the ordeal of a public execution. "Have you ever been to the arena?" He waited but received no reply. "I thought not. The arena is where criminals, villains, and… and enemies of the state are sent to be put to death, their crimes and punishments put on display for all the people to see. It is done in a way so as to discourage others from following along in the same evil paths of those being brought to justice.

The way the criminal dies must be most gruesome and painful, acting as a deterrent for others."

Ishtar remained calm, silent and calm.

"One of the more torturous ways of death - one that is reserved for crimes such as those you have been charged with - is that of being torn apart by dogs. One does not die quickly when suffering this fate. No! No! It is a long, drawn-out procedure because the punishment is designed to fit the very vile nature of the crime."

"My child, you must understand, these are not ordinary animals, but specially trained to do damage without taking life, maiming and disfiguring their primary purpose. Progressively, one will be released at a time, each dog intended to do specific damage. Slowly, one after another, your extremities will be torn and consumed, you being eaten alive while lying there, writhing in agony. They will devour hands and feet and then groin, thighs and breasts. One or more will eviscerate you, all while the others are busy at their tasks. Yet you will live, screaming for mercy. None will come. Eventually, another dog will be released. You eyes, nose, ears and face will be ripped away, but you will remain alive, living in a silent world with no mouth to cry out for help."

"And finally, after possibly hours of torment, when life is waning, the executioner dog will be released. It will tear out your throat, bringing to a finish what the other dogs started. And then your body and its scattered parts will be gathered up and returned to your family, who will have to decide what to do with you, no one else daring to assist with your remains."

"Think, my child, think of the suffering of your grieving mother as she has to bathe your shattered body for burial. And what about the agony she will have to endure as she watches the dogs eating her only child?" Claudesius reached out with opened arms, palms up. "All this could have been avoided by your willingness to come under the shelter of my humble home and accepting my hospitality."

Ishtar leaned forward, squinting, defiant. She placed her hands on her hips, asking, "So, while you're *tenderly protecting* me here, who will you be sending to tempt my uncle... your scullery maid... or possibly your own daughter?"

Claudesius clenched the arms of his chair, rage growing in his eyes. Who had told this child about Cephas?! Only his trusted officers knew of those plans. He eyed Treston. No, he doubted that Treston would be so bold. The man had lived too long under the governor's rule by understanding the loyalty demanded for survival in this house. Still, he would have a serious talk with the man at a later time.

Then a troubling thought crossed the governor's mind. What if Ishtar truly was a goddess sent to test him out? What if an angel did give her that dress and secret knowledge concerning the governor? Although troubled with growing doubt and fear, he could not help but to push the issue with the girl, he wanting her more by the moment.

"What do you have to say?" Claudesius asked, his frustration growing.

Ishtar stood back, her arms to her side. Not a word did she speak.

The governor angrily chided, "I see you're too stupid to fear for your own death! What do you have to say concerning your uncle's, the man who calls you 'daughter'?"

Ishtar's lips curled as she made rebuke. "You will not lay a hand on that man this day! For should you try, the fiery rage of my God will come down upon you, consigning you and your family to the wiles of that fat man! And your carcass will be cast into the very cesspools used to hide your own perverted handiwork on little children!"

"I will kill you!" Claudesius sprung from his chair. *"Insolent bitch!"* He screamed. His fist went high in the air and froze, chest heaving. Something was not right.

A smile… a serene smile shone on Ishtar's face. She was goading him on. Her eyes spoke to his. 'Kill me and let it all end here…your hopes, your dreams, your ambitions. They will end with me… all end here with me.'

Claudesius almost stumbled as he backed away, shaken. The girl was smart. Should he kill her now, where would it leave matters with Cephas? Cephas must surrender to the governor's demands or all would be for naught. What would Ogust think, seeing his brags come to nothing? Would *he* be entertaining them this eve?

The voice in the back of Claudesius' head cautioned, 'Too late, mustn't kill it now. Not now. Break its will. Make it surrender its faith! You know how to do it. You know who to use. Break it! Break it! Then… then it will surrender to your will and you can have it for yourself.' The voice crooned reassuringly, 'You can save it from the dogs. You know how, have done it before. Then it will be yours forever! Do it! Do it!'

Claudesius continued to listen to the persuasive words echoing in his head. He rubbed his chin in thought. "Umm…" He nodded and smiled. Yes, it would work. He would have success. Turning to his house lieutenant, he asked, "Is everything ready?"

The man bowed. "As you have requested, my Lord."

"Good! At least one of my servants respects me." He eyed Treston. Then, folding his hands piously in a polite manner, Claudesius addressed Ishtar. "You are a strong-willed woman, but not yet tested to fitness. Soon we shall see what you are about… are about."

Pointing toward the statue, Claudesius ordered his house lieutenant to gather it all up and follow along. Then, in a chiding voice, he asked Treston if he was up to obeying orders.

Shaken, Treston bowed. "Yes, my Lord. Whatever is your wish, I shall do."

"Good!" Claudesius grinned. "Take this… this *thing* to the pits. I have a lesson to teach it, and *you* will see to it the carrying of that lesson out. Bring your guards and we shall be on our way."

Behind the palace, near the back of the prison's second level, there had at one time been a series of pits dug for housing animals. Mostly abandon in later years, Treston kept a few large cats to 'help keep the prison tidy' as he would say. Today there were an additional six large beasts recently arrived for the circus, there being no more space at the arena.

'How fortuitous.' Claudesius thought, as he followed along in the little procession. He smiled to think how hungry they must be after such a long journey from the wilds. 'The girl will certainly be impressed when seeing them.'

Treston walked Ishtar up to the edge of one on the pits so that she could personally see the half-starved cats. He stood behind her, his hands firmly gripping the girl's upper arms. Treston was also cautious to keep a steady balance and a wary eye. There had been more than one careless jailer shoved to his death when a prisoner had lunged into a pit.

Ishtar was definitely affected by the sight of hungry animals jumping at her, hearing their voracious growls. Indirect lighting coming from narrow windows high up on the outer wall reflected little beads of sweat glistening on her skin and tiny tremors racing through her body. She turned her face away from the pit only to find herself staring into the governor's grinning face.

"We shall now see what you're really about. You may not fear your own death, though I like to think differently after watching you…but what about?" He looked into the shadows, motioning for others to come forward.

At that instant, a lonely emptiness began growing in the girl's chest, spreading in a flash throughout her entire body. From nowhere, a paralyzing fear reached out to take possession of her soul. It was as if she was being abandoned upon the field of battle, all her companions having run away. She suddenly felt alone with no support. Crying out in her mind to her God brought no relief. Even He had left her. As the terror of the moment grew within her, Ishtar stared wild-eyed at the ghostly shapes approaching from the shadows.

ಏ ಏ ಏ

A painful moan rent the air as Darla fell back against Sirion's chest. The woman cradled Darla close to her breasts, tears welling up in her eyes. "I think our sister is dead." She choked in words barely above a whisper. Filled with despair, she searched for an answer, asking Gabrielle, "Is our little sister dead?"

Exhausted from her own ordeal, Gabrielle attempted an examination to find out Darla's condition. She leaned forward onto her knees, crying out in agonizing pain from sudden leg cramps. Unable to stand or stretch, she tried ignoring the cramps, but with great difficulty. Tears ran down her face as she listened for Darla's vital signs, occasionally crying aloud when a particularly violent spasm raced through her.

At length, Gabrielle lifted her head, unable to open her eyes because of a searing pain, and with panting breath answered, "Our... sister...still...lives. I... I... think... she's... she's gone... into a... coma."

Struggling, Gabrielle pushed herself back. Seeing the anguish in Sirion's eyes, she attempted to explain the situation. "Darla's hemorrghaging on the brain. Lungs are filling with blood."

Darla's lips were turning purple, her face blue. Sirion whimpered as her heart was breaking, "My sister's dying! Can you do nothing to save her?"

Shaking her head, Gabrielle fell forward on her hands, her face only inches from Darla's, tears like rain falling upon her little sister as Gabrielle cried out, dejected, "I have failed! My child is dying and Ishtar stands alone in her evil world." Her lips quivered with remorse. "I have failed! I have ruined it all!" She collapsed on Darla, quietly sobbing in grief.

Sirion softly caressed Darla's face, her tears streaming down onto the woman's satiny black locks. "You cannot die! Do not leave me, my little sister! Do not go, for how will my soul ever be forgiven should you die because of my selfishness? Your demons are not your burden to carry. They are mine... should be mine!"

Sirion was but fourteen when the universe fell into darkness, her coming of age celebration cut short because of the Rebellion. Darla, the youngest of all the children at that time, did not remember those days of uncertainty and terror, but lived them every hour of her life... and Sirion – Darla's next oldest sibling – blamed herself for it all.

Stroking Darla's hair as her tears fell, Sirion waxed poetic, choking out a lament.

> *"Death, Oh sweet death,*
> *How much more pleasant is your bed than mine.*
> *Should I rest in your bosom, I will feel no grief,*
> *I shall enjoy your dark embrace.*
> *Bring to me your peaceful release.*
> *Do not make me wait for the morning light."*

Her sorrow turned to haunting refrains, drifting on the breeze across the camp and filling all hearts with sadness.

"Life is a burden we all must bear,
A grief and a shadow we all must share.
The dead are at peace, in a restful long sleep,
Yet the souls of the living must wail and weep.
The dead are not knowing the pain we endure,
To lose our dear sister so loyal and pure."

"Oh, give us the strength to live through this day,
Or let us retire to the dark, far away.
Our hearts will not heal from your leaving us now.
Oh, sister, my sister, remain with us still.
My sister, my sister, remain with us still."

With chin resting on chest, Sirion groaned defeat, her mournful sobs accompanying Gabrielle's in a sorrowful melody.

~Quiet is the camp when a warrior is mourned in passing~

ଓ ଓ ଓ

Claudesius smiled. The girl was faltering. Only moments before, she faced him with bold insolence. Now she cowered before her governor, trembling with indecision and fear. It was all working out so well! All that was needed was the tipping stone, the one act that would force her to recant all hope and faith. Then he would have her. She could not help but surrender to him.

Ishtar struggled to remain standing, her knees weak and shaky. All courage had vanished from her heart, leaving behind a searing void of trepidation and uncertainty. From deep within Ishtar's soul there grew an overpowering desire to release a screaming breath of desperation, her lungs constricting in preparation. Storm clouds of madness rushed through the girl's mind, chasing away any remaining sanity this world held for her. *It was wrong, all so wrong!*

The governor waved his hand. In moments, three ghostly shapes emerged from the shadows, two guards half dragging someone between them. Stopping in front of Claudesius, they threw their prisoner at his feet. "My Lord!" the man cried, sitting back on his knees and craning his neck to stare up into the governor's eyes. He clasped his hands beseechingly. "Please! My Lord! Mercy! Please!"

Claudesius smiled condescendingly. "Travet, my trusted servant."

Ishtar stared at the man, perhaps in his early forties, groveling in the dirt. He must be a house servant of some kind, but not that of a laborer, his white clothing, now stained and torn, indicating high rank, possibly a director over foodstuffs. He cowered before the governor, occasionally whimpering some incoherent words.

Feigning innocence, Claudesius asked, "Travet, why do you quail before me? Have you not known me to be a fair and just man?"

Travet's eyes darted around nervously at the others and back toward the governor. In a shaky voice, he answered, "Ye… yes, my Lord. You are a most fair and just man… most renowned in all the land."

Claudesius stepped forward, resting his hand on Travet's shoulder and asked, "So, should I make a judgment against someone, it would be fair and honest, correct? Based on true facts and without prejudice?"

Travet nodded assuredly. "Oh yes, my Lord! You are the most noble of all men, fair in all your ways."

"Well…?" Claudesius patted Travet's shoulder. "If that is so, why would a man who is wholly innocent of accusation fear coming before me, quailing upon the ground like a common criminal?"

A shiver swept through Travet. He was being set up to take a fall. Why, he did not know, and the results he was still unsure of. It would matter little what was said in his defense, the governor having already decided the man's fate. His mind began to resign itself to whatever might come, but his heart cried out in desperation, "Have mercy on me, my Lord! *I am an innocent man!* I have done nothing wrong!"

As his face filled with a mock, righteous sadness, Claudesius circled Travet, glancing at Ishtar. 'Good! Good!' He could see growing terror in the girl's face. Stopping at Travet's other side, he again squeezed the man's shoulder, his voice filled with hurt and betrayal. "Your speech is twisted and confusing." With a sly smile, he shot Treston a glance.

Treston tipped his head, recognizing the warning being given. Travet was playing the pigeon in today's game and Treston was being warned just how close he had come to being that fowl instead of Travet. Claudesius was intolerant of imprudent behavior. Treston had seen it before. And when there was a kettle brewing, he was willing to imply imprudence even when there was none to be found. The governor liked Treston, and this day, when he so needed a victim of impropriety, he selected an innocent – that Treston knew – instead of choosing him when he had earlier acted so brashly. That glance was Treston's warning not to act in such a way again.

Claudesius continued, "You claim your innocence, yet you beg for *mercy*." He bent down, staring into Travet's face, scolding, "Only a deceitful man filled with treachery would seek mercy, not one honest in heart and motive. No! No! With a lying tongue and crooked mouth you have preached falsehood, risking the lives of all in my house! I have it on good authority that you intentionally sought the harm of my distinguished guests by spoiling the food served them this very day. Confess your sins to me at this time, my son, so that mercy can be given you."

Travet cried out in desperation, "No! My Lord! No! I gave them our very best there was found to offer. From your own larder, I found the stuffs to provide. They asked for what could not be found in the city, anywhere! I searched and searched. All night, I personally sought out their request and could not find such things anywhere at all."

"*Liar!*" Claudesius screamed.

"No, my Lord!" Travet cried out, sobbing, "I searched the city out…"

"Shut up, you!" the governor shouted in his face. "You attempted to poison my guests, the very magistrate of Caesar and his distinguished councilor! For that, you must be disciplined to the proper degree." He stood back, shaking a finger. "It has been said that a poor cook will blame the pot for a bad meal."

He motioned the guards and, sweeping his hands in broom fashion, ordered them to remove Travet. As they dragged the whimpering man away and toward the cat pit, Claudesius sighed with sweet longing, "I will so miss those ham and clove omelets."

It suddenly clicked in Treston's head. Claudesius had not delivered Ishtar here to feed the girl to the cats. He wanted to put on a convincing show for her, one that might just help adjust her thinking, make the child submissive to his will. What the governor intended to do with her after she had pleasured him, Treston was not sure. Whether it was to the arena to delight the crowds or the secret chambers under the governor's palace where *special guests* were quartered mattered little at the moment. Treston knew it was best he should diligently serve his master's will, or Travet's coming fate might well be his own.

Treston yanked Ishtar around and, with the help of other guards, forced her to the edge of the pit. Pushing her head forward and down, he reached over Ishtar's head, pulling her eyelids back, his nails digging into her flesh until blood oozed from the wounds he made. There the girl stood, helplessly staring into the faces of hungry animals jumping and clawing at her, only feet away.

Ishtar cried out in terror, vomiting as she did. Then all control dissolved. Her bowels surrendered their restraint as her bladder emptied itself on the stone pavement. But she did not fall. The strength of many hands secured her well, carrying the girl's weight, keeping her standing.

A guard assisting Treston laughed, chiding Ishtar, "You ain't seen nothin' yet! Honey, jus' you wait!"

With a grunt, the two men holding Travet shoved him into the animal pit directly under Ishtar's eyes. The man's screams were cut short when he was literally ripped apart in front of her. A mad scramble broke out among the hungry cats, they fighting for pieces of flesh hitting the floor. Crimson liquid squirted up, hitting Ishtar in the face. She screamed. Most gruesome of all, though, was when one of the wild beasts grabbed part of the man's torso and, retreating across the pit, strung Travet's innards along its path.

Ishtar watched on in horror while the animals each settled down to finish their remaining morsel. The crunching and gnawing of bones finished quickly, but to the girl it lasted for an eternity. Finally, after a lifetime of numbing terror, the frenzied tumult below eased until the sounds of raspy tongues licking the stones and an occasional growl were all that was to be heard. Of Travet, nothing remained to tell of his woeful tale other than a few scraps of bloodied cloth and pieces of chewed sandals.

"So's the fate of cooks and fools..." Treston taunted. Clutching the girl by the hair, he jerked her back, throwing her down to the stones. Ishtar sprawled on the pavement, shaking uncontrollably while sobbing in a fit.

"Get up, you!" Claudesius screamed. "You're next on the menu if you fail to offer your proper respect to our lord and king!"

Although her eyes were opened, all Ishtar could see was Travet being torn to pieces by the giant cats, searing forever those ghastly scenes into her brain. Gradually she came to her senses so as to hear the governor's continuing threats. Struggling, she slowly pushed herself up and back until the child sat, rocking back and forth on her knees.

Ishtar's panicked breathing and glassy stare comforted Claudesius. The girl's blood-spattered face and uncontrolled tremors only excited him all the more. His groin ached with an agony he never before experienced. It took all the man's effort to restrain himself from ravishing the girl at this very moment.

'Patience... patience...' a voice called out in his mind. 'Your fun will be better if you wait for her offer. Wait on the girl to surrender to your will.'

Leaning forward with arms outstretched, Claudesius' voice became benevolent and fatherly. "I am so dismayed that such a young thing like you must suffer such travesty as this. Please, if you will now only reach out to me and submit to the generous laws of this land, I can save you from any more of these indignities. Please child, reach out to me. Let me guide you to your rightful destiny."

Rubbing her arms in anxious despair, Ishtar heard only the roar of the beasts and Travet's final screams cycling round and round in her head. The governor needed to repeat his offer twice more before she could comprehend what was being said. Looking toward the source of the words, the girl's eyes gradually focused on Claudesius. As the numbing pain of tormented dreams eased, she began to understand the words' meaning. She was being asked to surrender all that was real to her, all that made life worth living.

"No! I cannot!" She cried. "I cannot! Cannot! No! No! No! I cannot!"

Claudesius' face reddened in anger as he screamed, "Fool! *Damnable, stupid fool!* Do you not fear such a horrid death?!"

Ishtar stared blankly, her lips speaking unuttered words.

"Damn you! Damn you!" Claudesius cursed. "I shall have my way with you if the world should be forced to end!" He turned toward the darkness, pausing in thought, then motioning to others hidden in the shadows, turning back to Ishtar with a wily smile. "To bask in self-sacrifice for such a foolish cause and to risk your own death appears to be an easy matter for you, but what if your actions determine the fate of others? I wonder..."

The cries of a woman fell upon Ishtar's ears. She looked up, searching for the face behind the cries - cries that carried the tone of a familiar voice.

A guard angrily shouted, "Get goin', you, or I'll jab ya again!"

Aghast, Ishtar watched two terrified little boys followed by a very pregnant woman holding a small girl hurrying out of the shadows. The woman came at a waddling run, supporting her naked belly with one hand while clutching her daughter in her other arm. She was stripped to the waist, wearing a torn and bloody garment that was now little more than a rag. It was obvious from the woman's cuts and bruises that she had fared little better after her arrest than had Ishtar.

Catching her breath, Ishtar whimpered, forlorn, "Merna! Oh... oh... Merna!"

Nearing the governor, the guard slammed Merna between her shoulders, sending her sprawling on her belly. The woman's elbows hit the stones with a loud *crack!* she extending them so as not to crush the child she carried. With a painful groan, she sat back, grabbing her belly in agony as she vomited on herself and the child.

The guard shouted at the terrified and confused boys, "Sit down, you brats, or I run ya through! Ya hear!"

"Dilean... Jessie... Hilen, Hilen..." Ishtar was in tears. "Oh, Merna! Merna! I am so... so sorry!"

Claudesius smiled questioningly. "So you know each other? Well, well, what a small world we all live in."

Looking over and into Claudesius' eyes, Ishtar began to comprehend what was on the man's mind. She froze in terror as the full meaning sank in. Then, falling forward on outstretched arms, she rocked her head from side to side, writhing in distress, wailing, "No! No! No! You cannot expect... You cannot... *Can not!*"

Claudesius feigned remorse as he apologized, "I did so much wish for the entire family to make their visit upon you, to help you understand the seriousness of the hour, but, alas, Merna's husband..." He glanced at Merna. "Well, you see this woman, Merna? Her husband had an unfortunate accident this last evening. He was of a rather delicate nature, you know, something he failed to inform the inquisitor about." He looked again at Merna. "Poor fellow, and with such a big, needy family, too." Then he added, with a grin, "And growing bigger every day..."

Turning his attention back to Ishtar, Claudesius crooned wistfully, "It would be such a shame, you know, with everything this family has already suffered, to see any more misfortune befall them today."

Ishtar stared first at Claudesius and then at Merna, saying nothing.

Claudesius replied to her question unuttered, "This family was arrested for being members of an illegal society that is in opposition and a threat to the emperor and this great nation. It is my regrettable duty to pass proper judgment upon these people so that justice is served." He smiled. "Of course, with your help, I might be able to act with added care and leniency, seeing all that your dear friend, Merna, has already suffered."

Tears were now streaming down Ishtar's face as she cried out, pleading, "*Please! Please, my Lord! Cast me to the lions! Kill me! Kill me!*"

Shaking his head, Claudesius calmly answered, "It is not your judgment that is being determined at the moment. Merna has disregarded our laws and shown disrespect to our gracious leader and king. She must answer for her error. But you may be able to decrease the severity of her punishment by assisting me in this matter."

"How!" Ishtar asked. "How can...what can I do?"

'She is yours!' The voice in the governor's head called out. 'Make her worship me and she will become your willing servant.'

He had won... or so he thought. Puffing out his chest in exalted pride, Claudesius answered, "The power is in your hands, my child... has been. Just go to the little statue and show your respect for our gracious leader and chief magistrate, and I will be able to show some mercy to this distraught woman and her needy family."

Ishtar cast her eyes toward the stones, shaking her head and with arms outstretched, cried, "I can not! You know I can not! I can not do such an evil thing to my God and Lord!"

Claudesius was taken aback. Surprised and angry, he shouted, while motioning to the nearby guards, "See to my justice! Take such a little thing and feed it to my pets!"

In less than a breath, a guard had taken hold of Hilen's arm and, whisking her away from Merna, flung the screeching child several feet through the air and over the edge of the animal pit.

Merna struggled up, screaming, "My baby! My baby!" *Crack!* Another guard hit Merna on the side of the head, knocking her down.

The cats made the most terrifying noises as they fought for the tiny morsel. Ishtar clutched her ears, adding her dreadful wails to the tumultuous sounds. "*My God! My God! Why have you forgotten us to these devil beasts who walk like men?! You must help us! Help us! I cannot do this alone!*"

Laughing, Claudesius chided, "Where is your great *Yehowah* now?! Do you think he may be asleep in blissful rest? Maybe he needed to relieve himself? Yes, yes, that's it. He needed to relieve himself." Putting his fisted hands on his hips, he shouted, "*I* am your god! Now listen to me and live! I can give you and all this other rabble life!"

Treston said nothing, but was nearly numb with shock. Never had he seen the governor act in such a violent manner. Yes, he had witnessed murder, deceit, rape and even more disgusting acts come from this man, but never with the abandon being displayed at the moment. '*Devil beasts?*' Ishtar included him in that lot. Was he truly a devil beast-man? The words stung, possibly because they struck chords of truth.

Extending his hand, Claudesius calmly made Ishtar an offer. "Come, my child, just show a little respect to the ruler who can give you strength and life. Come…" He waved his hand toward Merna and the boys. "Come and do your sacred duty, and allow them life."

An inner turmoil tore at Ishtar's heart and soul, she ripping clumps of hair from her head while clawing her face, crying inconsolably. With swollen eyes, the girl pleaded with Claudesius. He said nothing, waiting upon her. Finally, with halted breath, she choked out her reply. "I… I… *I will never surrender my love for my God… not to a demon whore! Never!*"

Shocked and angered, Claudesius fought his feelings, acting as though sad and remorseful. "What a pity. And I thought you were so wise…very disappointing." He studied Merna. "The poor woman is weak. This ordeal has done so much to add to her frail condition already. And look, her baby is due soon. What a shame to lose a life before it sees the world around it. And the boys, to see such loss…both parents in one day."

Ishtar stared at the stones, quietly sobbing.

"*Bitch!*" Claudesius screamed. "It's all *your* fault! You little bitch! *You and that goddamned religion of yours! You've ruined it all! You've ruined it all for me!*" He lifted his arm, motioning the guards.

Two men grabbed Merna and with a grunt, they roughly lifted her to stand and, half dragging her, pulled the whimpering woman toward the pit. At the edge, they stopped, waiting further orders.

Shaking a finger at Ishtar, the governor warned, "You have just one more chance to save your friend and her unborn. Tell me, what will it be?"

Choking back bile from an unruly stomach, Ishtar cried, "*I will not betray my God!*"

Merna stood motionless, mumbling, "Hilen… Hilen..." over and over.

Claudesius nodded toward the guards.

Merna screamed when the two men shoved her into the pit, her cries quickly replaced by the sounds of tearing flesh and crunching bones.

"Mommy…! Mommy…! Mommy…!" Dilean and Jessie cried, tears streaming down their faces. They started to get up and run to her.

"Down you!" A guard gruffly shouted, cuffing one of the boys and grabbing the other. "Now sit!" He shoved them to the stones. "Your time's soon enough. Be patient."

Ishtar wailed Merna's name and pitched forward, almost knocking herself senseless on the pavement. Stunned momentarily, she lay motionless.

Concerned not for the girl's welfare but fearing she might be dead, ruining his hoped-for fun, Claudesius leaned forward to look for signs of life.

Eventually Ishtar stirred, the sound of the cats' feasting pummeling her ears. The sights of blood and gore witnessed at Travet's demise flooded her brain, except this time she was watching Merna and Hilen being ripped apart by the beasts. Slowly her dreaming passed, she awaking to the nightmare of the reality around her.

With her remaining strength, Ishtar pushed herself back on her knees. She hunched forward, resting on her hands, rasping in shallow breaths. There was little expression to be seen in her tortured face and swollen eyes. Like some animal that had been beaten and broken, the girl blankly stared at the paving stones, dumbly nodding her head while bloody froth dripped from her mouth.

Silently relieved to see the girl lived and was strong enough to still sit, Claudesius began to gloat. He could see Ishtar's exhaustion and defeat written on her face. One more little push and she would be his. Then… then…

'Hurry! She is almost ours! Give the creature to us so we can have our fun with it. You have done well.' There were now two voices in the back of the governor's brain calling out to him, but speaking in the way a master does to his servant.

Claudesius smiled, nodding, but his heart was not listening. He was already making new plans. This child was a true contestant. She made his blood heat with passion in a way it had never before been made to do. He would not surrender the girl up to the circus this day, possibly ever. Somehow he was going to whisk her away, she becoming a slave in his house. After all, why should *they* have all the fun? Had he not satisfied *their* desires in the arena so many times before? He wanted this one prize - for once he wanted a prize just for himself…not *the chiding voices in his head.*

Those voices inside Claudesius could not read his mind, but they did feel a change in his emotions, one that disturbed them. 'Be careful, now. We need this prize. You can do with it what you please for now, but it must stand in the crowd today. Do not forget!'

'I will not! This prize is mine! I will not give it up!' Claudesius' anger reddened his face.

A searing pain shot across the governor's eyes. The voices, feeling his defiance, warned him of their power. Always before they had been unobtrusive and merely suggestive, but Ishtar was the key to a far bigger prize. Too much was at stake this day. Already armies in distant realms were gathering, waiting an order to bring the rabble house down. Symeon must surrender his faith this day. His demise would be the linchpin upon which Heaven's War would swing.

Claudesius winced from the pain in his head. He did not understand what was happening, but was aware that other powers were displeased with his attitude. What were the gods doing anyway? Grudgingly, the governor accepted the girl's fate. Still... he had some time to carry out his personal fantasies, but he must hurry in order to satisfy them.

Drawing Ishtar's attention to the boys, Claudesius asked, so concerned, "What a pity. What a pity. Whatever shall become of these two forlorn orphans? To see the death of both parents in the same day and now...and now? What do you say? Their fate rests in your hands. You must decide."

Ishtar stared at Claudesius, saying nothing. She slowly shook her head as tears began anew.

"*Fool!*" Claudesius shouted, infuriated at the girl's resistance. *"Must an entire family come to its end in one day? What are you proving?! Your God does not see you! Fool! Fool!"*

The governor was desperate. What could he do? Ishtar refused all his threats. She would let the boys die before surrendering to Claudesius' wishes. She would... Wait! He rubbed his chin in thought. After studying the two children, he turned his attention back to Ishtar, smiling, forlorn. "Such fair-skinned little children need special attention, someone who understands how to care for them in such a tender hour. I will let them live."

He motioned Treston. "Take these fair-skinned boys to our distinguished guests. They will know how to treat with these little blond-haired fellows."

Ishtar acted before Treston could move. Desperate, she waved her hand for the governor to stop. Gathering up her remaining strength, the girl managed to struggle to her feet with deliberate effort, forcing wobbly legs to move her toward the table on which the statue and incense fire were placed.

Claudesius' body was trembling in orgasmic excitement. He had won! He had won! In only moments, he could whisk the girl away from here to his private sanctum, hidden deep within the bowels of the palace. There was time - a few fleeting hours - for him to enjoy the rewards for such a hard won contest. Then he could decide whether to listen to those troublesome voices or not.

"That's a good girl." He tried to hide the joyful excitement in his voice. "You are acting wisely. Soon this will all be over and everything here will only become like some bad dream. The boys and you can go at your leave. You can see your mother again. All this will soon be over." Claudesius grinned in triumph.

Treston watched closely. Something wasn't right. He caught the glint in Ishtar's eyes. There was a hidden power behind those eyes that sent chills down his spine. Many a battle he had fought and many wild men he had bested in combat, but never had he seen that look of madness - not, at least, from an opponent facing defeat. Still, this was the governor's game. He would not interfere, dared not.

With unsteady steps, Ishtar made her way to the incense table, resting her hands on it, exhausted upon reaching it. Tiny tremors rippled across the girl's naked flesh, making the golden firelight from the incense altar dance on the silver beads of sweat covering her skin. For the longest time she did not move.

Treston watched, wondering if Ishtar had the strength to do what was expected of her. As the time passed, he noticed a strange feeling creeping into his heart. He began to wish, in some way, that she had not surrendered her faith. Somehow, her unwavering strength had moved him in ways never before experienced. And now, while she stood before the god-king statue, he was feeling let down, as if he had also failed, or been failed.

Ishtar's hand slowly moved. Then, to everyone's surprise, her head snapped back, sending her hair floating upon the air. She stood bolt upright, glaring at Claudesius. In a defiant voice that could pierce the heart, she cried out, "If my God rescues us from your hands this day, it is of little consequence! Let it be known to you… man of dust… *I will not bend a knee to any dungy idol and contrivance of man. The Devil be damned and all men with him!*"

With both hands, Ishtar clutched hold of the statue and, swinging it high and wide, swept it down and across the table, splintering wood while scattering burning oil and incense in every direction. Then, with a grunt, she heaved the statue toward the stones, shattering it into a thousand flying shards that sparkled and glittered in the firelight.

The things that happened next arrived in little more than a blur. Treston stepped forward, reaching out to stop Ishtar. Too late! Claudesius lifted his hand in rage and opened his mouth to curse the girl. And Ishtar fell forward, grabbing her head crying out in pain.

"*Fool child!*" Treston took another step toward Ishtar but was suddenly stopped by an invisible wall of chilling cold. Yet it was that step taken that saved his life.

At that moment, the earth began to shake and the sky thundered in anger. Stones and dust fell from the ceiling above them, sending guards and slaves scattering. Then, with a *crack!* and a roar, the palace wall and ceiling behind and above the lions' pit crumbled, cascading tonnes of stones and rubble into the pit. Panicked roars from below rent the air, only to be quickly snuffed out by the smothering dust. Again, the sky shook the palace with its maddening thunders.

Stunned motionless, Claudesius and Treston stared helplessly at the drama unfolding around them. Stormwinds swept through the broken wall while jagged lightning ripped the sky, filling the chamber with blinding flashes of light. The ground continued to shake, tearing giant stones from the ceiling and casting them to the floor. Amidst all this turmoil, Ishtar began to rise.

Treston tried to flee, but his feet refused to move. A dark shadow surrounded him, catching him in its freezing grip. He watched, spellbound, seeing in visions. Or reality? He could not tell, for he heard words spoken as thunders while seeing strange sights, but all through the veil of shadow. It was not the same, though, for Claudesius.

In terror and disbelief, Claudesius watched Ishtar reach out toward him, a black fire growing in her eyes until consuming her in its angry inferno. Her appearance took on the shape of some monster rising from the darkness. His legs trembled as he, not noticing, wet himself in fear. The raging fire-monster approached.

The monster's voice rolled with thunders, hurling pronouncements like lightning bolts crashing in the sky. Claudesius' entire universe, his life and deeds, flashed before his eyes in a heartbeat only to explode into nothingness and be swept away on the words this monster spoke.

From the depths of the abyss, from ages beginning and ending, from beyond the edge of the universe, an angry voice chided him with questions. "Little man! Little man! Tell me, little man, tell me if you can! Where were you when I founded this earth?! Did you, in your mightiness, drive its pedestals down deep for me?! Can you stop the sea when it is agitated or catch an eagle in the sky?!"

The monster lifted a hand, making the air smoke and crackle from its heated energy. "How *dare* you! How *dare* you, you *insolent little speck of dung*, call down evil on *me!* On *me*, the *Maker of all things!*"

Crimson flames grew in the monster's eyes, its indignant rage increasing as it lashed out with venomous rebukes. "Your filthy idols are nothing more than dust beneath my feet! Nothing! Tell me, man of dust and ash, if you have wisdom! Did Pharaoh's gods save him from the torrents when I brushed his military might into the sea?! Tell me!"

Claudesius quailed, raising his hands to cover his face.

"Tell me, *food for maggots!* I brought Dagon down in his own house, smashing his idol to pieces! The Hivites! Hittites! And the Girgashites! Do you know the names of their gods that I, long ago, consumed in my fiery rage?! Tell me, man of dust! If you can, tell me!"

A thunderous crash shook the room, filling the darkness with dozens of blinding static fireballs. The monster stepped closer, reaching out a smoldering hand. "Tell me, little man, one born blind and dumb! How strong was

Goliath's god so that my little child cut him down and carried his head away as spoils?! Tell me, if you have speech! Where is the glory of Assyria, city to the god-king?! Can a person water his camels in Nineveh today?! No! Its gods fled from before my face and… and in my fury, I laid it waste and burned it with fire!"

Claudesius was too terrified to speak or run. He cowered, crying out with tears for mercy.

None was offered, the monster only becoming more enraged. "I do not tolerate my enemies forever! I cut down Belshazzar and his house in one night because he dared to drink wine from my holy cups! These children of mine are worth many cups! And what of your own King Agrippa?! He was haughty, failed to give me glory for gifts given him. My angel, in her rage, struck him with maggots so that he died! Where were all the gods of those people on the day of my glory?! Answer me! Little man of dirt and clay… *ANSWER ME!*"

Flooding rain whipped by hurricane-force winds swept into the chamber, stinging Treston's flesh with a burning, like icy flames. Through half-blinded eyes, he watched, transfixed, seeing Ishtar having taken on the shape of some mythical, fiery beast slowly advancing upon the governor. And Claudesius? Like a man in a drunken stupor, he dumbly stood before the advancing black fire, shaking so that his knees knocked.

Again the storm unleashed its fury with more thunderous outbursts. Immediately following, the monster railed anew, "Who are *you* to set laws and pronouncements against me?! *I* am the *Ruler* of the worlds above and the realms beneath! In my tumult, I burn cities with fire! And in my rage, I drown worlds under the seas! Can you stop me, oh man of nothingness?! Can you stop me from burning your own city with fire?!"

"Look! Because of the insolence of your kind, saying, 'We are gods in men's flesh!' Look! I am bringing your wonderful cities, the jewels of your pride and the home of your birth, I am bringing them to nothing! In smoke and ash, I will bury them forever! And earthling men will forget they existed. Those cities will become a land of astonishment to time indefinite! You, yourself, I shall make to hear of it in your own days! And you will weep but find no comforter."

Claudesius fell down on one knee while lifting up shaking hands, quailing, "Have mercy on me, my Lord! For dumb and stupid a man I am! Have mercy on this fool!"

"*Mercy?!*" roared the monster. "Travet begged for mercy from you!" At that, the smoldering flame burst forth into a raging orange inferno rising high above the cowering governor.

Treston could see his own skin blister, turn black, and then burst into flame. His eyes felt as though they were melting, yet he could still see. The world around him caught fire, dissolving into vaporous mist, then blown away by the violent storm. Ravaged by the ferocity of the tempest, naked to the world, he watched this drama unfold before him.

The monster's raging voice rose in a crescendo, its words howling above the screeching of the wind. From a gaping mouth, fires spat, filling the air with curses and denunciations. Claudesius could feel his very being disintegrating, flesh dissolving off charred bone. But as the fire scourged his soul, he discerned a strange sensation that he was not alone in his body. The presence of hundreds or possibly thousands of beings... if that is what they could be called... the man served host to. And it was to these demons the monster was now addressing its words.

In a howling, the monster screamed, *"Oh, you! Lord of the flies! How will you escape my day of retribution?! Most beautiful of my children you are, but putrid to my nose you have become! Dig for yourself a pit and see if you can hide from my wrath!"*

With an extended hand, it shook a finger in Claudesius' face. *"The Whirlwind! The Destroyer! He is coming in his rage! And he will humiliate you and leave you naked and defiled! My daughters will rape your manhood, cutting off the manliness from your house!"*

The beast then roared wild with laughter, pointing toward itself. *"Look! The maiden standing before you will lift up a great sword and in her vengeance will slaughter your lover, lifting his carcass on a stake in celebration. And you! You will hear of it and weep over your loss."* It reached out a hand, fingers spread. *"Your end will come in one day! My own daughter, the one you despise and call a usurper, by her hand you will perish, in the delight of her laughter!"*

Claudesius cringed in terror, seeking to flee, but his feet would not move. The world spun around him in a dizzying blur and he found no helper, his guards having fled except for Treston, who stood there like a statue, half hidden in mist.

The monster again turned its attention toward the governor, raging on. "Confess to me, if you can! Where is your great power and might?! A tongue?! What has become of a tongue so eager to mock the God of heaven?! Will you humble yourself before my greatness... *or must I destroy you this very hour?!"*

At that moment, the monster's fingers tightened around Claudesius' wrist. A burning pain swept up his arm and through his body, so agonizing he could not scream, but also so purifying, he felt life flow anew throughout his soul. There was a scream, though - thousands of them, one enveloping chorus as the voices in the back of his head cried out collectively in one last, dying gasp.

"It is done!"

Claudesius heard the words, but in a voice nearly forgotten by him. Quickly, his eyes focused upon the face of Ishtar, she holding his arm. Light showers drifted on a summer breeze that echoed the storm's passing. The spatter of water drops falling from the roof onto the cobblestones created a happy melody to the ear. 'Drip… drip… drip all is well, all is well, all is well.'

Treston almost fell when the shadow released its iron grip. He looked up to see the few remaining guards crawling out of hiding places, the rest having fled to the city streets. Eyes filled with wonder and fear searched the lower palace, puzzling over what had really happened. Only Treston had seen the governor's vision, yet even he had not heard what was spoken. Still, any who had witnessed the child speak as if with the thunders of the tempest were filled with trepidation and forever changed regarding the girl and the God she professed. Never did they forget, and many were the ones they told, turning the events of that day into legend and fable.

Ishtar stood facing Claudesius, she again as beautiful as the first moment he had seen her. Gone were the monster's fiery eyes, replaced by the girl's cool, serene stare, almost chilling to the governor's bones. Calmly and gently, she addressed him. "My hour is come. We must leave."

Claudesius stood up, dumbly looking into Ishtar's face. Fumbling in his speech, he said nothing at all.

Ishtar released her grasp and stepped back, warning, "My God can overlook your travesty done this day, but, should you touch only one hair on Cephas' head, your wife and children shall become Ogust's playthings at tonight's festivities and you… you will be burned in the very gown taken from me in your court." She waved her hand, lowering it open-palmed in front of him. "If you will listen to wisdom and truly give ear to my voice, and you do recall with knowledge all that has been yours to see and hear this day, the death of the city you so dearly love will not happen in your lifetime."

A strangling fog, one that had held the governor so long in its grips, was slowly lifting. Claudesius stared into the eyes of a child? Woman? Goddess? He did not know, but he did know that his heart begged for this moment never to end. He desired Ishtar now more than ever, but no longer to satisfy some sordid passion. No! He desired answers… answers to secrets hinted at but not revealed that this child understood. How could she seek death when he needed her insight and wisdom? *Time!* Claudesius needed *time* to sort matters out. And there was precious little remaining unless… unless…

Gazing at Ishtar in fear and amazement, Claudesius sought some way to change time and space. He argued, hands outstretched, "Please! Let us give the coming hour rest. Give me time to find another way to deal with you and your deeds. Give me time to seek the release of your uncle from this curse that I have placed over him. Please! Let us retire from here and we shall decide matters with understanding."

Ishtar's answer stung Claudesius' ears and heart. "No! My hour has come and you cannot stop it. Should the winds of the Great Sea decide to strike the shore with a tempest, can a man brush it aside as nothing? You could better stop the wind than delay the coming hour by one handbreadth."

She then pointed toward the shattered statue and incense stand. "You have a law, and you know well what your law states. Should your own son, in his innocence, fall upon the god-statue and destroy it, he would have to suffer my fate. Besides, the power to reprieve no longer rests in your hands. Look around! See how few of your servants stand with you. The others have already heralded the morning's events to the crowds. Would they not stone even you in their passion to right this great wrong?"

Claudesius persisted to argue his point. "Troubling thoughts cloud my mind with confusion. I cannot judge you until they clear."

Ishtar shook her head. "Gone is the darkness from your heart. You think with a mind freed from its wicked hosts. Better are you the judge now than when you stood silent upon the ramparts of the Tower of Ja-Boccan and swore an oath to Zeus, confessing need for wisdom and understanding."

Stunned speechless, Claudesius dumbly stared in shock and amazement. He was little more than a lad when he stood upon the smoking mountain that overlooked his home city. Ja-Boccan? It was nothing more than a rocky outcropping that cast its shadow into the steaming pit, named by him and his childhood friends when small boys. And his oath to Zeus? Only he knew of it, when first becoming a city concilor, and it was spoken only in his heart. Now the governor was troubled more than ever.

With tears and uncertain speech, Claudesius broke his silence. "Who *are* you? You bind me with deathly cords that I cannot break free of. I am confused and cannot decide right from wrong. I fear you are a god sent here to test me out. How can a man retain hope for life when he seeks the violation and death of a goddess?"

Serenity filled Ishtar's face. Someone else guided her mind while soothing an aching heart so that the atrocities recently heaped upon her were little more than half-forgotten dreams. She softly answered, "I am no goddess. A child of this world, born of dust and clay is all that I am. My mother you have seen and my father I have spoken of. Your attempted violation of my flesh is no more or less damning than what you have done to all so many other maidens."

Claudesius began to quail anew. Ishtar calmed him, reassuring, "This truly was a day of testing, but not yours. The world has changed for me. It no longer holds my spirit bound. Soon I start a new journey. I see its opening door as I speak." She motioned him forward. "Come! The hour is late and you must still cast your judgment against me in the city gate."

The governor refused.

Ishtar touched his hand. "You do not sin at this time. You must exercise your authority given you. It was for this hour that you received it. Now come. I hold you harmless in this matter. I accept responsibility for the price that is to be paid for my insubordination."

Claudesius cast his eyes downward. What could he do? He felt nauseous and his heart ached with regret and loss. There must be something, some loophole, another way. He was good at it, always had been. Ah, but today there was no way. There were too many witnesses to Ishtar's act. She had sealed her fate intentionally. The girl must die in public disgrace. But hadn't he forced such a fate upon her? Was he not even more culpable than she? There was nothing left to be done. Or was there?

Treston came out of his daze when the governor waved, calling his name. He hurried forward. "Yes, my Lord?!"

Claudesius was anxious. "Go to my chamber and tell my wife to deliver into your hands her purple gown, the one with the crest of the governor's house on it. And fetch the servant women with perfumed water and our best oil. And be quick!"

Treston bowed and started to hurry away.

Claudesius ordered him to halt. "And these boys, I place them under your protection. Take them to be with my family until you can return."

"Yes… Yes, my Lord!" Treston saluted, and with another guard assisting, gathered up Merna's sons and departed.

Directing Ishtar and the others to follow, Claudesius addressed the girl. "Whether you are a goddess walking among us is not mine to know, and your choosing death instead of life is not mine to call, but I do have say in other matters. You will live up to your name. You will not pass through these palace gates like some common criminal or lowly slave but as Ishtar, the 'star delivered from heaven', the 'Queen of Heaven', you will journey to your new destiny. That, my child, I *can* do."

ജ ജ ജ

The sound of hurrying steps alerted the camp to trouble. Chisamore jumped from his hiding place among the rocks to block the potential threat, his sword at the ready. It was Periste. She waved him off, rushing past him, her hushed voice sounding alarm.

"They're coming!" Periste cried, casting her voice's power toward the ground in an effort for her desperate words not to carry past the camp. Stopping short of the tiny group gathered around Darla, she excitedly panted, "It's Legion's Gestapo after us! Must be at least a hundred of them!"

Sirion looked up, her pale face stained with tears as she moaned in anguish, "My sister's dying! We can't move her!"

Periste could well see the gravity of the moment, Sirion and Depais holding Darla, while Gabrielle, semiconscious, lay atop the girl, mumbling incoherently. She shook her head, looking down at a sobbing Sirion. "Honey, if we don't git right now, Mother will shed tears for more than one child."

Tzidohn rushed into camp, hunkering down behind some boulders, warning Chisamore to seek protection. Periste watched him duck for cover then shouted to the others with Darla, "They've come for war! They intend to kill us all! We hafta make a run for it. We can't stand against 'em!"

Color was draining from Periste's face as she searched the others for a response. Sirion looked into her frantic eyes and then reached out, taking Gabrielle by the shoulder and gently shaking her, echoing Periste's warning. "Darling, we have to let go. Our girl is dead and we must save ourselves."

Depais got to her feet in an attempt to assist Gabrielle. "C'mon, Honey, we have to go."

Gabrielle struggled to break free of her blind stupor, pushing with her arms to sit, Depais helping as best she could. Sirion wiggled out from behind Darla, resting the woman's head on a blanket. Seeing others assembling near the rocks, she called out for Depais to leave her charge and help with the defense. "It's too late to run now. We need to hold this place the best we can."

Pushing herself up and into a sitting position, Gabrielle told Depais to go, telling her she would be fine. Depais hurried off to help with the defense. But Gabrielle was still too weak to weather the storm by herself. She fumbled and slipped, her arms almost giving way. Shaking her head in dismay, she could do little more than fight off the cobwebs in her mind.

At that instant, Mihai and Planetee dove over the rocks, half dragging EhleenohrKalahnit, who suffered a jillson bolt through her middle thigh. She groaned as she hit the ground, but struggled back onto her feet, sword drawn. Sirion stared at the bloody arrow, its feathers half buried in the back of Ehleenohr's leg, its point sticking two handbreadths out the front. No time to render medical attention, Sirion prepared for the coming combat.

"Get down!" Mihai shouted, as several jillson bolts sliced through the air and ricocheted off rocks or slammed into withered trees.

Periste was motioning Sirion and Depais forward when another bolt swooshed out of the thickets, punching Periste in the upper chest, just to the left of her heart, cracking bones and slicing through tendons before breaking out of her back, smashing the woman's shoulder blade. Knocked off balance and spinning from the force of the blow, Periste pirouetted to her left, a punctured artery splattering Sirion's face with blood as she crashed to the ground.

Everything was moving so fast now. No time to think, just do. Sirion scanned the underbrush beyond the rocks. The thicket was full of movement.

She pulled her sword from its scabbard and took a step toward the rocks. At that instant, her mind picked up a faint disturbance in the harmonics. Another jillson bolt sped toward her...or near her. In less than a heartbeat, she had calculated the arrow's trajectory, sighing relief that it would pass her by. From the corner of her eye, Sirion realized who the intended target was. Gabrielle still sat wrapped up in Darla's legs, the woman unaware of what was going on. The woman screamed out Gabrielle's name as she dove toward the streaking missile.

Sirion heard only a dull explosion in her head when the jillson bolt caught her at midriff just below her sternum, pitching her back and off her feet. She twisted heels over head in crazy cartwheel fashion, drifting as though forever weightless, a deafening silence filling her ears. The woman's eyes watched in amazement as the world spun around her, feeling that time had come to a stop and that she, alone, was moving in the universe. 'So this is how it feels to die.' She pondered. 'Not so bad... not so bad...'

'Crunch!' Sirion crashed hard on her shoulders, crying out in agony as her head hit the hard-packed ground, finally stopping on her side, curled up in a fetal position next to Periste. As quick as may be, she struggled to sit, pain from the shot not affecting her senses yet. Looking down to examine her wound, Sirion saw only the last inch of the bolt's black feathers sticking out of the jagged cut. She could tell that the arrow had missed her spine, but it punched a hole through her stomach, just clearing her diaphragm.

Hiding behind a boulder, Mihai looked back in time to see Sirion take the hit. She cried out her name, watching helpless as the girl struggled to sit. After looking over her injuries, Sirion glanced up at Mihai, who was staring back in dismay. Sirion coughed, spewing hot, frothy crimson from her mouth onto her khaki fatigues. Sirion coughed again, fear of death growing on her face as she realized the danger of drowning in her own blood.

There was nothing else for it, nothing Mihai could do. This would not be the first close companion she had watched die while the heat of battle prevented her giving assistance. "She will do as she does." Mihai cursed, turning her attention back to the matters at hand, hefting her sword for the coming attack. Three more times arrows flew and three more times Mihai deflected them.

Dozens of shapes were emerging from the thickets, advancing for the kill at seeing their opponents had nothing but blades to defend themselves with. A tall, muscular man suddenly appeared in front of the others, shouting orders while pointing at Mihai. "Don't kill her! I want that *bitch-worm* alive... *alive*, I say! Don't hurt her. Finish off the others and give their meat to the dogs, but death to any man touching my prize!"

The advancing horde stopped up short, waiting. No need to risk life and limb against these warriors, some the most renowned in the universe, and those blades - derker blades - a new invention of Erithia's children, light as a feather while holding the power of the sun, with a burning edge sharper than measuring. No, they could wait until their full number was up before charging that line.

While the storm gathered itself to them, Mihai and the others studied the increasing throng. Former lovers and companions, trusted allies in life and intimate associates, that was what these depraved monsters standing before them once were. These servants of the Devil's Keeper, Legion, were become little more than ravenous beasts, like the Stasis Pirates, only more vile and disgusting. There would be no quarter this day. All knew they would die, but they would not go quietly. The ground would run red with the blood of their enemies this day, their own mixing with it as they, too, fell.

These men - for Legion would tolerate no women in his private army - were all the servants of that man. The 'Gestapo Extraordinaire' they called themselves, they taking pride in every repulsive act of violence a person could dispense upon another. These men had fallen into the darkness long ago, having no memories of their former lives in peaceful times. Fear kept them in line - fear of Legion, he willing to deliver even greater malice upon those failing to obey his every whim. Murder and torture were the rewards for their loyalty, the opportunity for each faithful steward to share in others' agony, pain being the only sensual feeling remaining to tell them they still lived.

There the enemy stood, in all their tattooed glory, the Cross of Damien etched on each man's forehead, signifying him to be one of Legion's elite guard, their helms and armor festooned with scalps of heads and pubic hair taken from living victims. Some carried pouches made of tanned breasts or scrotums filled with amulets and totems to protect them from the ever-growing number of gods and demons possessing their world. One officer proudly adorned himself with a necklace of index fingers taken from hapless captives before they were dragged off to die, slaving in some rat-infested prison.

Off to the side, the archer who had been deprived his earlier target stepped into the open to again attempt his prize. The man's mind raced with dreams of future rewards as though already received, for bringing down the Great Lord and Chief Advisor of Erithia, Witch of Secret Evil and Stealer of the Hidden Powers, Gabrielle, a most formidable warriors. Yes, he would be celebrated in the camp tonight, being seated at the great table, with Gabrielle's head skewered on his pike, given any woman he desired… to do with however he pleased. Yes, sweet Carmelit! He would teach her not to spurn him! He could see it all now, a dream come true.

Gabrielle was still struggling to come to her senses, her mind-share with Darla draining. She could hear a commotion around her, but understood little of what it all meant.

The archer raised his crossbow, sighting it in with a smile while squeezing the trigger. "Ah, the moment! Square through the back and into the heart…" His words were no more than spoken when a painful crash erupted in his face, the broken crossbow ripped from his hands. Stunned, he turned to his left at hearing the sounds of horns and shouting. There, at the edge of a distant wood were two men, one who had apparently shot the crossbow from his hands, the other with another weapon raised at him.

Still a bit dazed, the man could see a black dot emerge in his vision. As if chained in time, unable to move, though it seemed such an easy thing to do, the man watched the speeding bolt slowly approach. The arrow began to take on a distinct shape, its four-sided spear points secured to a black shaft, guided along its journey by black eagle's feathers. Ever onward it raced, the man's feet frozen to the ground, he little more than an observer watching the pageantry of theater being played out before him.

Slamming the man between the eyes, the arrow's razor sharp blades tore through bone and brain, splitting the skull as the bloodied point exited the back of the man's head, its force breaking the fellow's neck as he was knocked off his feet and sent crashing to the ground. Within seconds, a dozen more arrows flew, bringing down more archers.

"Send 'em to Hell! After me…!"

Mihai turned her head, wondering what death awaited them on the flank only to see Captain Lonche charging the enemy, dozens of marines and sailors racing from the woods a few steps behind. He waved his pike, shouting, "Bring 'em down! *Bring the bastards down to Hell!"*

Legion's soldiers stared dumbly at this new peril hurrying death upon them, their archers ducking dozens more angry arrows coming from the shadows of the wood. Lonche and his crew only paces away, the enemy braced for the collision of steel, blade upon shield and mace upon helm, when a sudden blinding fireball of plasmatic energy exploded between the two armies, sending people reeling, stumbling and falling.

Before either camp could muster their senses to realize what was happening, a mournful groan rose from the tortured ground, rising into a pitched scream, as the world around them shook and trembled in its agony, sending giant oaks crashing from on high and tossing boulders around as though mere toys.

As suddenly as everything began, it abruptly ended. Both sides regaining their composure, they witnessed in the fading glory of the fireball a comely figure of a woman, the fire's radiant energy drawing itself into the beauteous form. A voice cried out, "Erithia!" and several Pseudes fell to the ground, making signs upon themselves with their hands while calling out to strange gods and demons for protection.

At seeing the anger in the woman's eyes, others bowed a knee in reverent fear to their Queen of Darkness, that is, all save Legion and a few of his bravest lieutenants. He stepped forward, about to utter angry curses against his chief protagonist. Ma-we stopped him up. In a raging voice like that of a she bear confronting her cubs' tormentors, she roared, "How dare you interfere with my purpose while trying to bring ruin to my children! Are we at war at this moment?! This is *my* land! *My* property! *Intruders! Trespassers! I should drive you from life this instant!*"

While the others quailed about him, Legion dare not. He had not ruled among these murdering cutthroats all these years by showing weakness. Better off would he be to become dead this instant, to die a martyr, than to seek solace with the Witch of Damnation. He took a step forward, waving his arm in offense. "Do not try to impress us with stolen parlor tricks, you mother of the birds! How dare you, barren woman, bereft of suckling and youth! How dare you interfere with that which is not yours to meddle in!"

Ma-we's anger flashed white hot, her eyes beaming like two molten suns. She spread her arms wide, screaming, "*In my belly I formed you, a gemstone of gems, your beauty greater than the heavens. Now see the majesty that was shielded from you before the day of your birth. See the God above the heavens and give her glory!*"

The surrounding trees suddenly burst into flaming torches, illuminating a darkening sky. Mountains around shook in torment, crumbling in fright, splitting open, delivering steaming clouds of molten ash and smoke into the heavens. Then, in hissing madness, streaking out of the gathering black clouds, burning missiles of meteors and comets crashed all around, tearing up the world in thunderous riot.

All the people fell to the ground, even Mihai quailing in fright, having never seen Mother in such a foul mood. What she might do was not hers to guess. Legion's men wailed in fear, crying out to their gods to save them from this madness. Some got on their knees, begging for mercy from the Goddess-Maker of Worlds. Darla roused, semiconscious, looking into the raging storm, smiled at the tumult and faded away into dreamless sleep.

Sirion reached out, affectionately touching Periste's placid face with bloodied fingers, weakly calling out to her, "The end of times is not so bad. The ever-world awaits us… Let us sleep until its dawning." Her hand fell limp as the girl drifted into uncaring darkness.

In a voice of greater power than the surrounding thunders, Ma-we cried out to Legion, who remained standing, defiant. "*Legion! Kneel before your Emperor God and worship me! Do this or be forever dead!*"

Legion glanced up to see a burning missile explode from the clouds, crackling and hissing as it hurtled toward him. He dove on his face, landing right at Ma-we's feet, the fireball smashing a giant hole in the ground where he had been standing. Instantly the storm subsided, filling the land with refreshing silence.

Shaken and unhurt, but covered with ash and dust, Legion looked up in a daze into Ma-we's ridiculing eyes. She grinned, laughing derisively, "So! I still *am* your God! You giving me such glory has saved you to live another day."

Ma-we called out to Captain Lonche in a voice gentle but urgent. "Son, if you hurry, my daughters may still live. Quickly, first to Sirion, she is the most damaged, the arrow opening a deep arterial wound. Quickly! Take your troop, for there is no longer any danger here."

Lonche acknowledged Ma-we's command, motioning for the others to assist with the wounded and injured. Sirion had regained consciousness enough to attempt to sit. By now, blood was freely oozing from her mouth and her raspy breathing labored. The woman's head lolled from side to side, her eyes trying to focus on an advancing shadow calling her name.

Kneeling beside her, Lonche quickly realized the gravity of the moment. In seconds the ship's surgeon was tearing away Sirion's blouse while a medic assisted with the instruments. She busied herself with needed battlefield surgery, cutting a wide incision across Sirion's upper belly and, with skilled fingers, probing deep to find the source of the bleeding. When she found the damage, she frantically went to work to halt the rupture. Captain Lonche remained close the entire time, holding Sirion's hand while gently stroking her pallid face and singing to her a sweet healing song.

As Lonche and his team struggled to save Sirion, others were busy assisting the wounded in any way possible. Ma-we looked on, satisfied, confident her children would survive. She looked over to EhleenohrKalahnit, frowning. "Daughter! Get that tended to before you bleed to death!"

Ehleenohr, standing on wobbly legs, stared dumbly over at Ma-we, all the color drained from her face. As her sword fell from shaking hands, two strong arms swooped the woman up as she collapsed. "Got ya', my Lady!" Chisamore held her tight as he carried the woman away, shouting to some of Captain Lonche's crew, "I've got an injured one here! Could use some help!"

By now, medical teams were busy with Darla, Gabrielle and Periste. Captain Lonche shouted, "No one dies today! Hear?! No one!"

In a few minutes a medic ran up to Ma-we, smiling, "All of 'em accounted for, Mother. Snug as bugs in a rug."

Ma-we thanked him and turned to Mihai. "The good captain's ship is nearby. It'll be here in a little bit to take us home."

Mihai slumped, the energy draining from her face. She smiled back, fighting to hold in the tears of relief.

Coughing up dust and grit, Legion staggered to his feet, dusting himself off while attempting to show no fear or awe of Ma-we's display of power he had just witnessed. After regaining his stance, he squinted and angrily rebuked Ma-we. "You have no right to interfere in police activities! These are the people who are in trespass! This territory has been claimed by my people for several millennia without any protest from you. Those…! Those…!" He wagged a finger toward Mihai. "Those *criminals* have destroyed property and murdered good, innocent citizens of this land. My people have only acted to bring these agents of wickedness to justice!"

"Oh stuff it, mouth boy, sissy-girl of your dark master!" Ma-we acidly retorted. "These people came here on my orders. And this is *not* your territory! *Squatter! Thief!*"

Legion cursed, arguing his case. "There, in distant thickets, lie two of your own children, murdered by that witch woman!" He pointed at Gabrielle, who was being assisted onto a stretcher. "And one of your own daughters was struck down by an archer's bolt! She had no weapon to defend herself!"

Before Ma-we could respond, Legion assailed her further. "And that *tramp!*" He frantically waved toward Darla, still being cared for where she lay. "That *tramp* overstepped all the rules of diplomatic agreement, an agreement you swore an oath to long ago. That *thing* took materials from our world and delivered them into the worlds below. *It* has broken all the laws, natural and good."

"Hold your tongue little boy, or I will!" Ma-we's temper was rising. She pointed back toward Darla. "That… that *little tramp* will one day haunt your dreams, stealing away your very sleep! She is my Death Star, Angel of Madness! Her sword will rip apart the heavens! Today you have opened Hell's gates to your own coming destruction. My daughter will drive your armies from the skies, burn your cities to dust and, in her raging anger, shall tear asunder your mightiest warriors!"

She wagged a finger in his face. "Her mercy! Her mercy will equal yours! 'Demon of Darkness' your people will call her, they quailing at the mention of the child's very name!"

"And!" still shaking a finger, "What do you call those evil machines you make and implant in my helpless children in the Lower Realms in order to control them with pain, fear and suffering? Isn't that as *wicked* a deed as any my daughter committed, and for much more sinister purposes?!"

Legion refused to publicly acknowledge Ma-we's prophecies of doom. He answered ruefully to her questions, "You're out of line! We may design our machines here, but if you took the time to search the facts, you would see how empty your accusations are. We use only the elements common to all worlds in their making. We do not wish to use them! *Your* creation leaves us no choice…rebellious bastards, no accounts. We need our machines to control those very creatures that you cast away." He shrugged. "So, we are forced to rule as best we can." then, angrily shaking a finger back in Ma-we's face, accused, "*Your children* have overstepped their rights by forcefully intruding into our business and the way we govern those apish miscreants!"

Ma-we's rebuff was equally accusative. "And I suppose *your* rape and torture of Ishtar, and the forced imprisonment of Cephas and the other innocents is also necessary to keep *my castaways* in control? Listen, you!" She poked a finger at him. "Those machines you used on my child pushed things over the line! You may claim rulership over the lands below for the moment, but *my children* are a free people. If you want to live another day, it will do you well to mind who of those *apish miscreants* you dabble with!"

Legion shrugged, pleading innocence. "Who am I? I can't oversee everything. Things often happen that are beyond my control. I can't be everywhere at once, don't have *palace magic* to move about like you. Besides, as you said, that brattling is a free person. I can't help it if she flirts her charms in front of desperate prison guards."

He snarled. "Bratling got what she deserved! Besides, as your own chatterer once said…" he pointed toward Mihai. " 'Pay back Caesar's things to Caesar.' She lives in Caesar's world and is one of his subjects. You have no part at all in the decisions of that lord, for he is one of my servants. Under law, I can do with my servants as I please."

Ma-we's retort was swift. "You have no hold on that child, for she is *my child* now! You sold her to me by the blood of my daughters here!" She waved a hand back toward the wounded being tended. "And besides, *fool*, her test is passed and *you and your worthless god-king failed…*"

Legion's bewilderment was obvious.

Ma-we sneered, answering his unspoken question. "Loyalty purchased with bribes and threats must be ever watched. Lift the bonds from a slave and see his allegiance fade. Will he not spit upon his former master, once freedom is assured? The child is a free woman now. No longer can your threats or incantations hold her in servitude!"

His nostrils flaring hot with anger, Legion swore oaths and curses, jabbing a finger toward Ma-we. "The *bitch-monkey* dies today! She has broken the laws of her people! And *I…!*" He thumped his chest. "*I* am personally taking charge of her execution!"

Ma-we's face clouded with remorse. She had expected nothing less from this rebel, but her heart hurt in hopes of seeing something more - a tiny spark of humanness still living within the breasts of this man, born of her flesh. She pleaded, "What is there to gain from the girl's torture? You will not win her back…cannot. She is a changed creature and can never return to the darkness. Please! To the extent you show the child mercy, I will give it to you."

"*Mercy!?*" Legion roared, "*Mercy* to that brattling!? *Whore child! I will add seven times to the torments and humiliations she has already received. She will beg for death this day and I shall make it flee from her until she curses Cephas to his face!*"

Flushing red with rage, Ma-we cursed Legion with word and prophecy. *"Fool! You will not succeed! Look and see that my hand is already against you!"*

"Now listen and become afraid! I swear: As I live, like your servant, Sisera, I will sell you into the hands of a woman - a virgin child - who will hunt you down like a wounded she-bear. Your mighty men, in her anger, she will rip apart. Their flesh she will hungrily eat, and their blood she will passionately drink. She will strip your land of inhabitants and burn your glorious city with ruination and fire. Your watchtowers she shall tear down and all your beautiful works she will burn to ashes."

"Then *you*! Yes, *you*, this *monkey child* will tear from your living chest your beating heart, she watching with glee as life fades from your eyes. And your head she will remove from off you, making it into a bowl for excrement and urine. Upon the very gatepost of your resplendent city will my daughter of destruction hang your carcass until your flesh rots from off your bones. And… and my daughter's offspring will write songs of derision concerning you, singing them as they dance upon the mounds of your once mighty fortresses!"

"And Zeus will become a child's…"

Legion began to offer rebuke. Ma-we shouted, *"Shut up, you! Or I will give your tongue to the maggots of the dung heap this very moment! I am not done with you!"*

"The child you cut down today - the child with the name of your sister whom you murdered upon your own bed and then lifted up to that of a goddess – '*Ishtar*' will be the very name you will fear to speak in future days, it being too terrifying a name to behold. That child is the very weapon I will use to destroy you! She learns well… *and what you have forged in the depths of Hell today will become the dragon-slayer of your own flesh tomorrow…*"

"That child will come against you in all her vengeance. Like a maddened, horned beast, she will trample all that is yours. Two more times you will humiliate the girl, but upon her third return, when the King of Kings has been glorified, shall my Sword of Destruction come again, and she will strike down the Usurper King of Memphis and all that is his. And as you did to my children in days before, the bones of your people will be scattered across the Low Plain of Decision, never to see a burial or be given a remembrance."

Those of Legion's guard hearing Ma-we's curses and pronouncements quailed, crying and moaning in fright. The few who had stood fell back to their knees, seeking solace from incantations and beseeching prayers to their gods, but none dared request mercy from their mother. Legion, afraid as he was, ordered them to 'shut up, or be put to death'.

Ma-we pointed again toward Darla. "The flesh of my daughter will become more desirable to your master than that of his *sissy-girl*, he wanting her above all others. In the day your lover requests you deliver that *tramp* into his hand, you will know that the one you murder today has been lifted up to this world. Your sleep will flee from your eyes and you will dread the night. Her destruction will haunt your waking thoughts, but you will find no relief…only the sword of the Whirlwind, who will extinguish your world, leaving it desolate and naked!"

Terrified, but unable to reveal it, Legion screamed, *"The bitch-child dies today!* I will make her a sign for all who follow you!" He then pronounced his curses against Ma-we. "Today I will crush any who follow you, giving them deaths worse than death. Your prophets, puppets of this *whore…"* He pointed at Mihai. "They will feed my cats and light my arenas! Today! Today, before the sun falls behind the mountains, Cephas will bow and worship *me!*"

Ma-we's face reddened with anger. "You'd better pray he does, for should he win in contest over you this day, no man will come to give you any worship. Look! If you lose, I will make your temples the haunts of the horned demons that fly on the darkening nights. No longer will men seek truth from you, nor give honor to you. Zeus shall no longer cause men to cower, but a tale for the suckling and sleepless child will be all that his mightiness will become."

Legion shook his fist in defiance. "Cephas will worship me *today*! I will tear down my own temples if his glory does not escape your hand this day!"

Ma-we raised her hand, shaking a finger in rebuke. *"You will not succeed! You are the most arrogant of fools! My hand will be against you! Already is! See! Your governor is no longer a slave to you!"*

A queer expression filled Legion's face, he not comprehending Ma-we's statement.

Ma-we laughed derisively. "I thought not! You should have secured the barn before chasing my yearlings in the field. Your governor is freed of the machines you have so long used to control him. True, he does not know me, but he does recognize the feeling of being unfettered from evil bondage. Never again will he bow to your wickedness. Look, today, and see the servant spit in his master's face!"

Legion's face went white with rage, he stammering in an attempt to bring his own vile curses to birth. Just as the man was raising his hand to hurl another rebuke, a droning roar echoed over the treetops, warning of an approaching ship. As eyes looked skyward, Captain Lonche's battle-frigate, Zoheret, came into view, it turning to settle down in the forest clearing.

Ma-we motioned to Lonche's crew to gather up the wounded and board them as soon as possible. She then dismissed Legion offhandedly. "You'd better leave now, or I'll have my captain order up his ship's guns." She turned and walked away.

Unleashing a torrent of vile curses that were drowned out by the Zoheret's engines, Legion ranted on at Ma-we as she departed. Finally, after feeling he had shown sufficient bravery, the soldiers were dismissed. "We have more important matters to tend to! Leave these fools to their impudent chattering. Off! To other business!"

In a few minutes, the enemy had melted away into the thickets, taking their dead with them. Mihai settled her sword in its scabbard, her hands still a' tremble at the realization of just how close she and the others had come to their end. She stared at Ma-we, eyes filled with thankful wonder.

Ma-we frowned motherly, shaking her head. "Even my own loyal children forget who I am. Why must you always believe the solution to problems rests only in your hands? Do I not have eyes? Does not the very moth send forth its secret messages to my ears, and does not the eagle tell me when the raven lifts its wings on the hunt?"

She pointed to Darla as the medics carried her up the Zoheret's loading ramp. "Only my youngest remembered to call out to me for help. Because of her, I came. Because of her, I have the bodies of living children to take home with me this day. The child afforded me the time to find your hour's savior." Ma-we smiled. "It was fortuitous that Captain Lonche happened this way so soon."

Mihai bowed her head to the gentle chastisement, resting a hand on Ma-we's shoulder. She looked around for the others. Seeing them all at some distance, she frowned, looking her mother accusatively in the eyes. "You may fool the others, but you have not just happened upon us this hour. Darla may have saved many lives, but… but your hands have been a lot deeper in this mess than you let on. Have it your way. Is not your spirit in all things? And I'm so glad you have listened to the rocks cry out to you in our defense. Thank you for coming, for being here for us in our hour of need."

Mihai fell upon Ma-we's shoulder and began to weep, and being the gentle mother she was, cradled her daughter in her arms, patiently waiting upon Mihai's heart as it released its pent-up emotions. In time, when all other things were finished, she stepped back, softly squeezing Mihai's arms. "Come, my little one. The day has only started and yet there is so much mischief afoot." She winked. "*My* mischief…."

Mihai laughed. "So, the mouse has not escaped the cat. When all hope is lost, when only despair wafts upon the wind, then you just happen along by chance, or by the cry of a desperate, little child. So much would I rather your rescue by accident than to have the navies of all the heavens seeking my deliverance."

She pulled Ma-we close, giving her a tender kiss. Then, as she pondered the hour, frowned, asking, "What of the governor? How did we succeed today? Darla failed in her attempt to help Ishtar finish her test. What happened to turn this day around?"

Ma-we grinned. "My child, how little you understand..." Taking Mihai by the arm, she started for the ship. "Darla did not fail. I caused a deep sleep to come upon the child when her work was finished to keep her life within her."

"You see, I could afford no help to come to Ishtar in her greatest hour which, by the way, will one day be made into song and legend. No, her test needed to match the glory she will eventually attain to. If I had not forced her lone stance, the torments I permitted this day would have been all for naught."

Mihai puzzled over her mother's words.

Ma-we stopped, smiling. "I needed to prove to all my children the mettle of this woman, for what I'm going to request of them concerning her. Oh, had she failed, I would not have held it against her soul, for the test was great…greater than most will ever face. But had she failed, her position of glory would have been forfeit. Now though, now, no one will ever be able to question my wisdom and choice in appointing this child upon the mountains to stand beside the others I have made into gods over my creation."

"Mother!" Mihai groaned, rolling her eyes. "Do you always need to speak in riddles? And what position do you conjure before me as you speak?"

Ma-we gently poked Mihai in the ribs, offering a coy reply. "Riddle? Why do you think I always riddle with you? Oh well, whatever you may think. I… well, all I will say is this: There is a power that is yet to rise in this land, and that girl may one day rival you in glory and majesty. I will twist the minds and bend the hearts of all my children in all my realms. Look, I have fooled them even now into believing what they wish. It serves my purpose, you know..."

Mihai nodded, knowing it useless to probe for answers to Ma-we's puzzles when the mood was upon her. 'Better leave it go to the breeze.' "What of the governor? What has happened to him?"

Ma-we looked toward the ground, contemplating. "Oh, yes, the governor. Um, I had a little chat with the fellow today. Explained to him how I felt about what was going on, suggested a change of attitude." She looked into Mihai's face, her eyes twinkling. "You know, he is really quite a reasonable man when he understands the issues. I think I can depend on him to do us well today."

Ma-we changed the subject. She looked up to see that Captain Lonche had secured the injured aboard the Zoheret and presently he and some of the ship's crew were waiting their arrival. "My dear, the good captain there wishes to rendezvous with his escorts and then offers to take us on another adventure."

She pulled on Mihai's arm, hurrying her along. "There's mischief afoot! And I don't want to miss a moment of it..."

ಬಂ   ಬಂ   ಬಂ

Treston hurried up the stairs to the royal viewing quarters where the governor and his guests were seated. He motioned to Claudesius, worried eyes portending the bad news being delivered. Ogust and Jusslin sat directly behind the governor, lost in mindless merrymaking, wine flowing down their throats in rivers. Claudesius excused himself, no one paying him any attention, meeting Treston as he reached the landing.

Taking a breath and forcing a smile, just in case others were watching, Treston leaned in close, speaking in just above a whisper. "News of Ishtar's revolt against the emperor has traveled swiftly. The jailers and guards are near to rioting. They're so angry that no amount of persuasion or bribery could get them to ease up on the tortures prepared for the girl today. Even my threats of possible repercussions from you would not move them to show pity, some even threatening to burn the palace if the child is given any mercy."

A shocked surprise flashed across Claudesius' face, followed by a worried frown. "What about her? Where is she? Is she safe?"

Treston nodded she was. "For the moment... For one thing, the people want to see the girl publicly executed, holding back the hands of these self-proclaimed executioners. I also have four of my most trusted guards by her side, all having sworn allegiance to the death in carrying out my orders to keep her secure. Still, they will be able to offer protection only to the arena's gates. Why, the dog keepers even refused to speak with me, throwing accusations of disloyalty at me for protecting the girl."

Sighing disappointedly, Claudesius replied, "Let us pray she is a goddess, or at least her god has chosen to protect her. There's nothing I can do now," he motioned behind him, whispering, "...especially with those two goons watching my every move. Ogust is pissed off at me, has been all day, since the gods haven't stopped the stink coming up from the harbor. And then when he found out I didn't include him in the morning's *fun* with the cats? I think he's searching for an excuse to make me trouble. Won't be the first time he's brought the emperor's wrath down on some hapless victim."

With furrowed brow, Treston asked, nervously, "Do you think the gods are angry with us for trying to rescue the girl?"

Claudesius stared at the marble floor. "Possibly, but it's too late now. We have set our sails to the fickle wind and must trust upon it to carry us through." He looked Treston in the face. "Besides, I want to see this to the finish. Tell me, do the gods really rule our lives? Is there one Almighty God? Treston, I know you have a mind. Can you provide me an answer?"

Treston frowned, also looking toward the floor.

Claudesius sighed. "I saw things today that no living man has witnessed.

I saw the face of a majestic being in the eyes of that woman, for it was not by her voice that the knowledge of Heaven and Hell was delivered to me. I will… must… put this God of Ishtar's to the test today. Whatever the cost to me, it will be a small price to have my questions answered."

Looking into the governor's face, Treston agreed. "I did not witness the worlds beyond this one as you have, but the shadow realms of the nether-regions passed my visions this very day. I felt the cold breath of Death and the heated flames of an angry hour. Something… someone… some ancient power arose from fathomless depths to take possession of the moment, sweeping away any and all other gods before it. My Lord, if there is not one god, there is certainly *the* God, the ruler over all other gods. He, I believe, rose in defense of his child this day."

Without thinking, he reached out, grasping the governor's arm. "I will return to the prison hole and see what my strength can accomplish."

Claudesius clasped his hand, smiling. "Good! Good! Thank you. We shall see what this *Yehowah* can do!"

⁝ ⁝ ⁝

The Zoheret and its escort ships skimmed low over an ancient saltwater lake, settling down just north of its brackish, swampy shores. The lake, ringed by snow-covered mountains on a vast high plain, was the last remnant of a once majestic sea torn asunder and lifted ever skyward by the ravages of time, this one lone symbol of its greatness all that remained.

Huge horned beasts made a hasty retreat from their morning frolic when the ships opened their exhaust vent doors, filling the air with a screaming hiss of billowing steam erupting from the super-coolers of whining engines in their rapid shutting down. In a few moments all had quieted and the giant, golden, metallic birds rested peacefully on the ever-changing savannah. In ones and twos, the cautious animals rose from their secure hiding places of spiny trees and thickets and braved the open distance between them and the teasing waters, soon returned to splashing and playing in the marshy green soup.

With a sudden *snap!* followed by the quiet drone of servos, the forward ramp of the Zoheret slowly fell away from the ship's belly, revealing two lone figures riding it down as one would an elevator. No sooner had the ramp's motors stopped than the people were off and about their business, quickly immersed in serious conversation.

Mihai was long troubled about this nearing hour, especially since witnessing Legion's display of obstinate resolve to punish Lowenah through his sick, cruel torture of Ishtar. Now that the hour was upon them, she felt need to seek, again, some form of rescue for the girl. "But I still don't understand,

Mother, why my child has to die this day, especially in the horrid way that despicable man intends to do it."

"*Your* child?" Ma-we cocked her head, raising an eyebrow. "*Your* child? How little you know. Oh well..." Ma-we took hold of Mihai's hand and invited her for a stroll.

ॐ   ॐ   ॐ

(**Author's Note:** *This was a pleasant time in the Middle Realm, a time when the universes were in reconcile, when the aura of all life reflected itself in strange and curious ways. Here was a land where the images of the realms beneath and above mated in orgasmic embrace to bring to birth a world that mimicked all realms, with wildly exotic forms of life oddly different from yet so strangely familiar to the minds and hearts of those who sojourned here. Then there were the laws of this universe - so contrary to all others - a land that paid no heed to rules of nature but made up its own as if by whim.*

When the most ancient of the children braved the foreboding darkness of the mystical portals, they happened upon a world that defied explanation. This world teemed with countless forms of life that tested the logical imagination. Life found no measure nor conformed to any rule. The children soon fell in love with the queerly intoxicating dreaminess of this land.

But there was one discovery about this universe that caused it to become victim to the continuous wars of the Rebellion. One of the strangest of properties in this peculiar place was the way in which it altered matter delivered here from other universes. This was not well understood until after the discovery of the Lower Realms.

A popular EbenCeruboam theory was that the matter making up one universe was sub-atomically different from that of another, based upon the belief that there are many universes, coexisting in clusters, or possibly in a super-cluster, occupying the same physical space with only their different constructs separating one dimension from the other, the theory finally confirmed by Hull and Copeland with the development of SpatialEquanosis Projection, explained in great detail in Copeland's physics thesis, <u>Flying the Albatross Beyond Time's Reign</u>.

Another EbenCeruboam theory stated, in part, that should matter from one universe come in contact with matter from another, a catastrophic reaction would ensue.

In fact, it was the later confirming of this theory that led to the development of plasma kaolinite, used in clearing space debris, and to the mendilevium warheads of the latter rebel wars. This matter/antimatter reaction was first experienced by earthly men when, in the final part of the Third Age, a small piece of debris from a Pseudes warship inadvertently bypassed the Middle Realms and fell into the planet's atmosphere, exploding over a wilderness forest in a place once called 'Siberia'. With this theory confirmed after the discovery of the Lower Realms, the properties of the Middle Realms became invaluable.

So it was that when the Lower Realms were first discovered by Ma-we's children, they could only peer into the Realms Below as if through a looking glass, the sub-atomic differences between the universes making any voyaging from one to the other impossible. Eventually, as though by chance, it was found that by first passing most matter through the Middle Realm, this matter would atomically alter, creating a symbiotic, coexisting relationship in the other universe. Advancing technology eventually permitted people with special suits to personally walk upon the surface of the planets in the Lower Realms.

In time, Chrusion (Asotos) and his scientific cartel developed the process known as 'tibithal fibularinism', the process through which an artificial body - or physical avatar - is melded with, grown into and over the cells of the person, creating a living suit of sorts – a body within a body. Tibithal fibularinism permitted Lowenah's children to experience the Lower Realms in similar fashion to the upper realms. It was by this process that the rebels of later ages were able to cohabit with the women of earth to produce a super race of humans known today as 'Fellers'.

What made all these things possible were the Middle Realms. Everything needed to pass through the Middle Realms to be filtered through its sub-atomic state before entering into the other universe. After the Rebellion began, both sides fought feverishly for control of the strategic portals and locations within that realm. That is why a sojourner to those lands today will discover so many memorials to the thousands of brave and stalwart warriors who fought and died there, defending the Children's Empire and its interests.

The author has not segued from the account, but only succinctly described the lengthy dissertation Ma-we presented to Mihai as they walked along the worn and weathered rocky path that delivered them to their special destination. Other than what has been italicized for the reader's benefit, the gist of the account is thus summed up here. Lowenah does not speak frivolously, but she does enjoy using many words when a few may suffice. 'Better to bore them with knowledge than to quickly fill them with ignorance and misinformation...' was her reply to the author's questions when asking her about this event.)

છ   છ   છ

Ma-we sucked in the invigorating mountain air, smiling. "My children have found this world so peculiar and riddling and yet, as with me, are ever drawn to its intoxicating delights." She reached down, breaking away a stock of green hay, biting it off to just the right length, gripping it with her teeth. Her eyes rolled upward, half closed. "You know, even I forget just how wonderful life is. It has grown past me, taken on a power of its own, you might say. Doesn't need Mother anymore..." She grinned whimsically. "That's how I made it....life, I mean."

Closing her eyes, she returned to her earlier thoughts. "My daughter, Rachel – Darla - reached out to your child by my will. She used what few tools were at her disposal. The money, gown, vision - all the things she did were with my approval, but by her own power, something she knows nothing about, nor would she believe it to be so if I told her. You see, these Middle Realms enhance a person's spirit and mental mindset, that is if a person is in tune with the harmonics of the universe."

She peered into Mihai's eyes. "There are few of my children who are more in tune with the Third Element than my child RachelOchlah." Slowly shaking her head, Ma-we mused, "I do so love that name, but my daughter chooses to use one of her own invention. I don't know why, though I can understand her reasons for doing so."

Ma-we wagged a finger. "You know, Rachel managed to get Ishtar out of that prison for real. Now that's a trick! And then she got her back again - pretty good for a person who doesn't even know her own mind...yet." She grinned. "I'm so proud of her!"

Ma-we stopped, staring from the rise back toward the Zoheret resting peacefully nearly a league away. After a moment of silent meditation, she turned her gaze to the distant hills, pointing. "There, that's our destination. I wanted us to be alone." She took Mihai's hand and started down the ridge in that direction.

After the two had walked in silence for some time, Ma-we stirred, acting as though coming out of a dream. "Child, do you want to know a secret? One I have never revealed to another of my children?"

Mihai stopped, the tone of her mother's voice betraying a rare excitement. "Please! Yes! Ma-we, please tell your little child one of your secrets."

Ma-we peered into the enchanted sky, filled with a rainbow of dancing sheets of mesmerizing hues of gold, green, blue and red that would remind one of the northern lights. For the longest time she said nothing, as if forgetting she had asked a question at all. Finally, as if talking to herself, Ma-we softly offered, "This is where it all began..."

Squeezing Mihai's hand, she stared up and into her eyes through tear-filled orbs. "...the beginning of all mortal life, I mean, right here, in this Middle Realm. *This place* is the *heart* of my universes."

Mihai's mouth fell open, the shock rendering her speechless.

Ma-we grinned. "That's right! *This* place is my secret seat of power, the Land Of Knowledge, the Great Pyramid of Wisdom, the World Beyond Law, the Fountain of Youth, Shangri-La, and every other title your brother has declared my palace on EdenEsonbar to be. Right here, under his very nose, resides everything the fool's been seeking for so many millenniums. That's right! He's been prowling around a long time to discover my secrets and they've been right here all along."

Resting hands on hips, Ma-we scanned the pageantry around her, nodding in satisfaction. "And the fool's too stupid to ever understand it, even if I told him to his face. Stupid fool!" Shaking her head, she added, "Wouldn't know what to do with it if he did believe me. Works on harmonics… the Third Element, you know."

Regaining her senses, Mihai asked, "What is the Third Element of EbenCeruboam? The elusive *elixir of life*?"

Still studying the distant hills, Ma-we answered, "Your kind thinks life here mimics that of the other realms. So wrong! So wrong! Here…" She spread her arms high and wide. "This place is the *jelly* that holds the bread. Everything sticks to this universe, stuck to it in order to survive."

She spun around facing Mihai, her eyes beaming. "Did you believe the Eden Stones were created in my laboratories in the Lower Realms, or possibly in my palace?" She grabbed Mihai's hand. "Come! We must hurry. Even *I* cannot surrender Time to my will."

Despite the brisk walk, Ma-we did not tire of the tale. "This world was my home long before time as you know it began. You see, time only begins… is worth counting… when you have someone to share it with. Before my mortal children, there was no need for time, for clocks, you might say. Oh Silly, yes, Silly, there was time - time to do this and time to have to do that. I didn't invent *time absolute*. But time does not exist unless there is a need to recognize that it does. My children made that happen for me. Oh, well, enough…"

"This is *my* world, the one I chose for me and…" Mihai chanced a glance at the twinkle in her mother's eyes. "This is the world I chose to reside in while I… er… the other universes came into existence. Oh yes, I created this place, or oversaw its creation."

"Mother! Your riddles hurt my ears!" Mihai winced as if in pain.

Ma-we laughed. "I will show you all my secrets. Yes. Yes. One day I will show you everything I have done, maybe even to my child, Rachel. Yes. I will! We will travel to my eternal home, my home beyond the stars, to a world no mortal can imagine." She laughed again. "Yes! Yes! That is why I made you…all of you. Yes!"

Ma-we sighed. "I grew up in knowledge all alone. By myself, I figured out *who* I was and *why* I was. I wasn't lonely, never was. I didn't know what loneliness was. How could I? Then I created life inside me, but it was real, still is. Then I made life grow until I sent it out beyond my living self to warm the dark nothing surrounding me. Oh, to make something independent of yourself and yet so full of symbiotic spirit! It's so wonderful! And then I made…"

Ma-we stopped in mid-sentence, studying her daughter, then, as if jumping across chapters of a story, began anew. "One day I made my children, birthed them, and fell in love with them. I have stayed here with them ever since. One day I will bring them to my real home far from here, unreachable to mortal flesh. They will come to my home and light the rooms with laughter and mirth, and… and…" She frowned. "I will never be lonely again."

As they tripped lightly down some worn granite steps, Ma-we replied to Mihai's earlier question. "The Third Element? What a wonderful thing. You've studied it well. Suffice it to say that what you know of it at the moment is well enough for the good of all. One day, maybe, though you do use it so well, yes, yes, so well, you and my child, Rachel."

Upon coming to a field filled with jepson lilies and crystal-jade butterflies, Ma-we changed the subject. "I do not like death - not of my children - and I do not wish to be alone during the coming moment. Ishtar has served her purpose well and now must shed her flesh this day to begin a new journey that will change all things for all time."

Surprised, Mihai exclaimed in question, "You're bringing her to us now?! In this the hour and time?!"

Shaking her head, Ma-we answered. "No! No! Not today. There will be others of her kind who will walk among us before her feet skip across my palace floor. Still, there is much the child must learn before that day. She will not sleep as many do, but I will be working with the child the many days between now and then. I will give her knowledge beyond knowledge and wisdom extraordinaire. Long will be the years before I accomplish all that is to be done with the child."

Looking into Mihai's eyes, Ma-we added, "Ishtar's personality will belong to her for changing, something that I believe will test the souls of your brothers and sisters. I already feel sorry for some of the old stick-in-the-muds we have among us. She will be quite trying. Spoiled the girl is, foolish and impetuous to the point of being arrogant, the very qualities it will take for her to accomplish her responsibilities."

Mihai was quick to ask, "I know the river ever flows and the rain is master over all save the sun, but as the dam can break the river's stride and the clouds can steal away the sun's power, I know that you abide death's glory only in its purpose served. So, as I have asked and not forgotten, why must Ishtar die such a horrid death at the hands of evil men? And why today? Are a few fleeting years of youthful life not a gallant reward for her loyal actions? Is her training so important that a little time given her to be a woman such a small thing to ask?"

Ma-we's face clouded, her voice filling with remorse, but she spoke beyond Mihai's question. "I mourn Merna's death. Such a waste... But she is not the first to fall victim to the evils of that world. I will reward her with knowledge, wisdom and power. Her shy lack of confidence will one day disappear. See what the woman becomes then. Oh, and for her unborn, there will be many willing surrogates to nurture and birth the child of a king."

She looked away toward the ground, hiding a tear. "I did not want Merna to die, not today or any day, and I do not wish to see Ishtar suffer."

Mihai interrupted, her eyes aglow with passion. "Then why? Why will it have to be so?"

Ma-we took Mihai's hands, kindly scolding, "Remember, it is the slower mouse that escapes the trap. Be patient and learn. True, I have the power to stop the wickedness that will soon swallow up the soul of our child. But it is my power that is being challenged. I have been charged as unfit because they say that I use my power to give gifts and rewards in order to buy the loyalty of my servants. So then, I hold back my hand to prove it isn't true, swearing by an oath what *I say* is true. No sooner are the words out of my mouth than all evil is unleashed against the world of men, creating a land in which terrible things happen to innocent people."

Waving her arms in frustration, Ma-we mourned, "Look at the tortures so many suffer - indescribable, violent! I ask you, do you think a baby driven down upon a stake, its innards skewered through, suffers more than its mother who is forced to watch it slowly die? Yes, they both suffer horribly. But what does your brother foment against me. 'It is the will of God! It is the will of God!' his prophets cry. Then, to my face, they accuse me of cruelty for not rescuing the innocent from the murders they commit."

She shook her head in frustration. "By the use of treachery, these purveyors of evil take the very laws of freedom that I made to protect the minds and hearts of my children... the freedom that allows my children to choose without interference their own roads traveled... and then drive my innocent children upon those sharpened stakes of lies, forcing me to watch, helpless, as my children, in agony, die."

Sadness grew on Ma-we's face. "You must believe me when I tell you that I do not wish Ishtar to die this day or any day...and not as Legion has prepared it to be." She paused, looked away toward the hills, and then again into Mihai's eyes. "Yet, my hands are tied."

She stroked Mihai's arm. "My dear, death comes to all humans. Tell me, does it pain less to hang upon a stake than to be torn apart by a wild boar? Or does a person burning up in a fire hurt less than one torched in the emperor's arena? Or, is a slow cancerous death better than being forced to drink of the hemlock weed? My dearest of my daughters, death through agony is common to earthly men, and Ishtar's death by torture no more painful than what has been blessed upon countless others."

Looking deep into Mihai's eyes and upon seeing such sadness there, Ma-we promised, "For you, for your sake, since you have chosen to become mother to this child, I will soften her blow. Oh yes, her death will come, but I will allow you to force the contest so that your child will pass quickly, like the piercing through of the heart." She smiled. "*Your* hands are not tied!"

Mihai affectionately squeezed Ma-we hands, kissing her softly on the lips. After thanking her, she gave her mother a smothering hug. "Please, my lovely One, I thank you for your gift to me, but remember, please, your loyal daughter. Never have I doubted your love and never have I seen you do one thing out of selfishness or cruelty. I trust that death, no matter how vicious, has no lasting power against the ones you love, and it seems that you have love for everyone."

She paused, a question popping into her mind, stepping back, asking, "How could you offer Legion the gift of mercy when he has already surrendered his soul to the damned, given his spirit to the winds of the universe?"

Ma-we turned away, studying the distant hills. As if addressing an invisible host, she asked, "Has he?" Moments passed. In time, she looked around, peering questioningly into Mihai's face. "Do you know for sure he's gone? Who has whispered the matter into your ear? Can you see into the vast Web of the Minds to secure the answer?" Stepping back and looking down the trail, she offered, "Who is wicked beyond hope? Who is erased from the Book of Records? That, my Dear, I have chosen not to know... There are forces beyond your reach who choose what I wish not to see. Oh yes, I know the results of evil... the severing of soul and mind... but I do not do the severing."

She took Mihai's hand, caressing it so tenderly. "Child of mine, I built a universe upon laws that transcend heart and mind. The Third Element, my sweet child, it is that element that holds all things together...and it also tears asunder. The soul of the universe is *woven* into it, *lives* off it, *exists* because of it."

"Your brother, Chrusion, departed that universe long ago, becoming a life unto himself, a dying ember cast away from the fires of spirit and life. So it is with any who forsake the Third Element. By special mightiness of personal strength and mental fortitude, the person may live many millennia before succumbing to old age and death. But it will come - in ten, twenty, a hundred thousands of years - it will come."

Wiping a tear from her eye, Ma-we added remorsefully, "Your brother is gone. I know that. But of the others… my children… my children… I… I have held… hold… out hope for some of the others."

Looking into the sky, she sighed. "All things are mathematical - equations painted upon the heavens by the brush of indelible certainty. I cannot change one stroke of that brush lest the universes would collapse into lifeless smoke and ash. That brush sweeps its bristles of fate across all my children, all life, comparing their artistry against the eternal pattern of itself. When it concludes the mismatch to be too great, it removes the potential threat of discord from the universes. And in the Day of Readjustment, when Gradian's Clock chimes on the twelves, and all the universes are realigned with the Third Element, then all that is out of harmony with the final equation ceases to exist."

Ma-we shook her head in sadness. "I need not tell my daughter these facts, for has she not witnessed them many, many times during her own existence? How great is the magnitude of species of animals that have reached the limit of cohesive genetic viability that have been swept from life, saving only their harmonically balanced relatives to rebuild a depleted universe? And is that not part of the reason you needed to pass through the depths of the Lower Realms, to bring about a saving of those people?"

Mihai was filled with questions. Ma-we was in no mood to answer them. "Another day, Child, another day. For now, listen and learn."

"My lovely, dear, sweet, innocent child, all things are ruled over by what's mathematical - that cruel, heartless equation based upon a furtive mind's reasoning long before that mind understood her own heart. It is a good thing, though, for as much as that heartless equation seeks only its own logic and reason, it creates a stable environment for freedom, something that a fickle heart would be so willing to steal away to satisfy its own desires."

"You see, guilt and wantonness are measurements made by the heart seeking a balance for its own feelings. The Third Element has grown to understand those feelings, but it refuses to base its judgment upon them. It sees not the feeling but the harmonics. Too far out of harmony and *Poof!* - out of life. It cares not for man or beast. It cares for harmony. It must bring all things back into balance…peace. It is the beast that will destroy all life if that is what it takes to return harmonic balance."

Ma-we again faced the distant hills, lowering her head. "A necessary tool for keeping the clocks of all my universes from falling into chaos becomes the very weapon that may yet destroy all my works of life in those very universes. It is a machine run by machines. Still…when it is gathered to the heart, it becomes a weapon of life instead of death." Looking into Mihai's face, she smiled nodding. "A weapon for *life!* Yes, indeed, when gathered to the heart, an unbeatable one!"

"Let's walk." Ma-we took Mihai's hand. "You see, I have never tested the limit of the Web of the Minds to know how far it will stretch before abandoning its host. For that reason, I don't know how far a wayward child can go before all hope is forfeit."

Mihai looked at her mother in wonder. Here was the Maker of the universes fighting her own inner demons of self-doubt and determined resolve. No, she had made the universes so that the greatest gift given her children could never be stolen from them, but that guarantee came at great cost to her, the wiles of the Fates deciding her own destiny. Forces? What forces was her mother speaking of? Were there others who ruled distant realms beyond the reach of the children and controlled the fate of their world?

Ma-we interrupted Mihai's thoughts. "Legion crossed the line today. There is no longer a returning for him. That I know, now, it being whispered to me across the breeze of time and space. But until I heard that whisper, I found hope - hope that a spark of that Third Element might still remain living in his heart. I see now that it is gone. He is no more…"

With that revelation, Ma-we became silent, eyes cast ever down, hidden from Mihai's own prying orbs. The two traveled on for some time before Ma-we renewed any conversation.

At length they came to a tiny lake, its blue, tepid waters beckoning them to luxuriate in a refreshing splash. Neither accepted. Upon reaching a narrow strip of sandy beach, Ma-we motioned for Mihai to sit. While staring across the glassy, smooth surface of the lake, Ma-we pined, "There is nothing else for it. The hour has come and, should I delay any longer, our daughter will not benefit from our help. I have great need of your service, for my hands are tied, but yours have not the power to do what must be done."

Mihai answered quickly, not waiting to hear further. "Whatever it is that I can do is mine to give to you. Ask! Please! Just ask!"

Ma-we smiled grimly, a serious tone carried on her voice. "You shall think better of your offer tomorrow. I will accept it, along with my apologies. I have no other choice. My strength I shall pour into an unprepared body. You will have but little time to accomplish our purpose and then the shock on your system shall take over, making you believe your death rides upon the day…possibly wishing it be so. It may be several days before you heal."

Mihai closed her eyes. "Your slave girl…"

"Here, take my hands and look into my eyes." Ma-we commanded. Mihai reached out and, sitting up on her knees, took Ma-we hands, she sitting the same way. Ma-we sighed. "Your brother put me under oath long ago. I had no choice. It was the only way I could slow his interference in the Realms Below. I cannot directly intrude in this day's events. Once your spirit leaves us here, I will be unable to return it for many hours without causing you great harm. Helpless, you will have to see the child you love torn and destroyed by the wicked acts of Legion and his infested hordes."

Mihai smiled reassuringly. "No! It is I who am honored by your request. Better would it be for me to perish forever accomplishing your service than to live forever having neglected your smallest request. Tell me what you wish me to do."

Tiny waves rippled across the blue-green waters as Ma-we's harmonic tune increased in its melodious pitch. The women's long strands of hair began to float on the gentle breeze until, like the wings of newborn butterflies, they danced and swayed to the whispering song playing on the air. Soon, all Mihai could hear was her mother's song, it sweeping away all other senses as it, itself, took possession of her very being. In moments, she was withdrawn from her surroundings into a rainbow-filled cacophony of wild colors and heart-numbing music.

When the final, fire-red cosmic gasp passed Mihai's eyes, the woman found herself floating free above the crowded city of Ephesus, quickly drawing close to the arena. Already she could feel her mother's energy overpower her own will. There was no time to waste if she was to effect a coup on her brother this day.

As soon as her feet touched the ground, Mihai was hurrying toward the prison gates. Though physically unable to change matters, she being invisible to all around her, with her mother's mental powers channeled through her, she could *move* the world.

⁣ ⁣ ⁣

Hanna stood aghast at the wild pageantry of chaos enveloping this world of madness. She had arrived early at the arena, dressed as a poor vendor selling sweetroot treats. As hoped, no one paid any attention to an old woman scurrying along with a basket of widow cakes, a pungent bread made from coarse-ground barley flour blended with sweetmint root with a flake of cinnamon and a dab of honey. It was a concoction made by the humblest of people, those of very little means, the reason for the name 'widow cakes'. Surprisingly, the old woman had already been parted from several, she feeling it must be out of pity.

Stealthily making her way to the upper concourse where she was within hearing distance of the governor's station, Hanna had settled down to wait upon coming events. The view was most disquieting for her, though. From here the entire arena was clearly visible. Already there were some pre-event shows going on, mostly local fellows trying to prove themselves, often with violent, bloody consequences. And then there had been the herding along of some of the condemned from the North Market Street Prison, a few of whom she knew. The chanting of the gathering throng convinced Hanna there would be little mercy shown this day.

Then came a raging storm, its arrival so sudden that few escaped the torrent of rain and punishing hail before they had secured shelter. Hanna had been standing under the overhang of an upper portico, being saved from the violent rush of angry wind and water that drenched so many others. As the tempest whipped its fury across the city, a violent quake shook the arena, scattering the terrified crowd back into the cyclonic maelstrom. Pressing her body against an inner wall, the woman watched in confused wonder at the shaking tumult. People stumbled and fell, screaming in fear. Towers swayed and groaned as if in pain. All the while, standards and flags danced like an invisible army was marching them along on parade.

Disgruntled rumbling and quaking had long subsided before Hanna could force herself away from the tiny alcove in the wall. Finally, with determined resolve, she managed to work her way back to the wide portico overlooking the arena floor far below. Hundreds had departed, either desirous of seeing what damage may have occurred elsewhere in the city or, as some had voiced, 'it was not a good day because the gods were in a foul mood.' This did not dampen the festivities for the remaining throng, many of them crowding into the commons, a standing-room-only walled concourse directly across from Hanna.

Blaring of a dozen horns marked the beginning of festivities. This was an extraordinary day, it being declared so by the governor, with special events added, one of which was a breathtaking parade filled with contestants, musicians and decorated wagons filled with all kinds of wild and fearsome beasts. Gladiators, dressed in armor of copper, silver, and iron and plumed with peacock feathers dyed in every hue from gold to purple, marched proudly behind the trumpeters, cymbalists and drummers, closely followed by athletes, gymnasts, and other Olympic-style performers. It was truly a grand sight, the likes of which Hanna had never seen.

Hanna's stare was suddenly torn away from the mesmerizing pageantry when bolted planks securing the western arena gates exploded skyward, quickly followed by dying screams of terrified guards as they were crushed by flying timbers from the ruined gates. Two raging elephants stormed in panic through the shattered opening, bellowing in fright, charging blindly into the marching parade, sending its participants fleeing in terror, overturning wagons, leaving a sea of carnage and death in their wake. Wide-eyed, Hanna stared in disbelief as what looked to her like the belly of Hell disgorged all the beasts of the earth upon the chaotic scene.

Out of the middle of this confused melee raced a caged wagon filled with the most ferocious of giant wild cats. The double team of eight horses was running blind, a troupe of African monkeys jumping and yanking on their manes while screeching in crazy excitement. Paying no heed to the helpless teamster who was frantically pulling on the reins, shouting curses drowned out by the deafening tumult, the nearly insane animals raced headlong into the southern retaining wall supporting the packed commons. A thirty-foot section of the earthquake-weakened wall collapsed in dust and rubble, sending scores of surprised revelers into the roiling cloud-mass below.

The lifting dust cloud revealed a writhing pile of living flesh, both of men and beasts. The kick of dying horses entangled with the flailing, frantic arms and legs of men and boys trying to escape the jumble of splintered wood and jagged masonry. All the while the roar of angry jungle cats, now escaped their iron prison, roused a panic in the hearts of every living being struggling amidst those ruins. Destruction and confusion filled the arena, but what remained hidden behind plastered walls was even more terrifying.

Out of the darkness of hidden terrors and into the bedlam of chaotic nightmares that Hanna beheld raced a flood of living flesh. Hundreds of men and animals fled the darkness with total abandon, the mountain wolf paying no heed to the archer, nor the archer considering the howling hyena. The stampeding was unstoppable. Anyone or anything barring the paths of this insane avalanche was run over or smashed through. There was no thought given to anything other than escape - escape from the bowels of darkness and the evil lurking within.

Though safely perched high above the melee, Hanna could not help but feel a rising panic within her own breast. As if frozen, she stared in heart-stopping wonder, sights so horrid being burned into her brain that it would take weeks before the woman could find a peaceful night's sleep. Still, she had not the power to tear her eyes away from the destruction unfolding before them. And the thought of what lurked deep within those caverns of Hell nearly stole her breath away to the point she felt she might die. The reason for that fear was quickly revealed.

Out of the gaping mouth of that underworld, people still fled. Bloodied and torn, they stumbled into the light. Some collapsed into the dirt, too damaged to ever move again. Others surrendered to the hysterical moment, flinging themselves into the heaving mass of madness surrounding them. A few kept their wits, taking up weapons and preparing a defense…too few to face the coming onslaught.

Hanna watched something fly out of the darkness, rising twenty feet into the sky before plummeting earthward. It looked much like an old torn bundle of rags until it crunched hard, splaying on the ground. A huge dog - or at least what once was a dog weighing better than eight stone lay crumpled in the dirt, its body shattered and crushed. Before her eyes could fully comprehend what they were seeing, another giant beast-dog lay broken beside the first.

Finally, when she thought her heart would burst from anticipation, the raw theater of obscene violence renting itself upon the twisted stage of unreality, there arose such a symphony of discord as to chill even a warrior's heart. Rubbing her eyes in disbelief, Hanna gasped at seeing a mass of hideous shapes emerging from the dark abyss locked in what looked to her like the slow waltz of the damned. Her widow cakes scattered when the basket burst upon hitting the stone floor as Hanna's hands shot to her face in terror, but no sound could escape from screaming lips.

Three giant cave bears burst forth in a tangle with a host of dogs and humans in every stage of destruction, fighting off vicious attacks of a dozen huge, frothing canines locked in a struggle to the death. At least ten cubits from nose to tail, the beasts lashed out against the onslaught of the frenzied fighting dogs. Leashes, harnesses and traces entrapped both living and dead in a macabre web of broken machinery that was once two grand coaches, each pulled by four proud steeds. Several of those horses now lay torn and broken next to what little remained of those shattered wagons.

The combative pageantry gathered in ferocity as it danced further from the darkness, the bears now so enraged that they blindly attacked one another. The dogs mercilessly tore upon neck and flank, locking powerful teeth into flesh until crushing jaws or slashing claws ripped the lifeless animal away - but away was usually not far, the dogs held secure in the jumbled leashes. As the procession cantered first to the left and then to the right, Hanna saw a bloodied corpse emerge from the darkness, a length of rope dragging him by the neck. There would be no dogmaster this day to release any of the governor's judgment upon Ishtar or any trained animals to torture the girl.

As Hanna gathered her wits about her, she became sadly aware that the crowds, instead of being horrified, were shouting, celebrating, and whooping for more blood and gore. Some of the spectators even leaned over the stone retaining wall, pushing escapees from the carnage below back into the melee, laughing and shouting with glee when the hapless victims were snatched away by one of the waiting cats.

Long was the unplanned circus of carnage played out before soldiers from nearby barracks could arrive to take control. Dozens of wild animals had to be killed, many dozens more captured, before the injured could be cared for, the dead removed. All the while, people in the stands were shouting profanities at them for spoiling their fun. Of course, for the victims involved, it was another story. In fact, so much had been destroyed and so many of the day's participants disabled, it was decided not to continue the planned events. Other than for a few acrobats and a couple of bare-knuckled amateur boxing bouts to help entertain the audience while the mess was cleaned up, little other than official judicial matters were to be carried out.

Hanna still trembled long after things had quieted. Taking only time to gather up the basket, leaving the scattered widow cakes, she slowly made her way down past several rows of seating until she stood only two rods from the grand review box, an extended section of the arena that jutted out from the governor's seating area. Whatever the cause or reasons for the day's events, she did not ponder. After all, today was to mark the destiny of a new and fledgling religion. She had come to watch the outcome and pray that greater powers were listening and would intervene.

Meanwhile, Mihai's brain was burning up as her growing headache consumed the last of her vision. The woman had done her best, driven the world mad with the powers given her. In her mind she could see the bears tearing asunder the very animals Legion had planned to destroy Ishtar with. Lifting her arms and crying out another curse against all living flesh, Mihai fell backward, blind, the last thing she remembering was the surge of uncontrolled vomiting as she tumbled into nothingness.

୫ ୫ ୫

"Oh my! Oh my! Oh, what fun! Oh, what fun!" Ogust clapped his hands in excitement and then hugged Jusslin, grinning with pleasure. He nodded his approval, praising Claudesius. "Wonderful! Just so wonderful! I knew you would deliver a fine show for me. But you have even outdone any I have seen in Rome, itself! This must have been very costly, and all done for me!" He grinned wide, revealing rotting teeth. "You are a better man than I was thinking."

Claudesius smiled back, acknowledging Ogust's condescending approval, but his mind was elsewhere. Strange, the circus was once a most enjoyable pastime of his, few things being more pleasurable other, say, than his torture of some disgusting miscreant or the excitement over a frightened maiden's embrace. He shuddered, the thought of such criminality turning his stomach sour.

Today, for the first time in his *sordid* memory, Claudesius could see the suffering and agony of both men and beasts. The wild pageantry of carnage and death sickened him as he watched the lives of the victims play out in his head. The people whose lives were snuffed out so quickly, never to eat another tasty meal, see another sunrise, make love to a beautiful woman, just to never think, breath, or laugh again, and for what? A few minutes of chills and thrills for a heartless gathering of bastards who pushed their own friends and relatives back into the waiting jaws of death for that moment's excitement? He cursed himself under his breath, almost wishing to be the center of attention at tonight's party. But that was not to be.

Earlier, when two eastern tigers had captured a young man, little more than a boy, and torn him asunder at the very base of grand review box, Ogust and Jusslin had both celebrated the governor's 'magnificent presentation', toasting him with 'long life to the house of Claudesius', lifting wine-filled goblets to his good health.

Treston suddenly appeared at the head of the stairs, motioning to the governor. Ogust and Jusslin were so absorbed in the ever-changing show, they paid no attention to either the governor or Treston.

Hiding his anxiety, Claudesius cautiously made his way over, asking of Treston, nervously, "Does the child still live? Does she live unharmed, or has the Devil delivered her up to this?" He lifted a hand, motioning to the tumult still playing itself out in the arena.

Treston nodded Ishtar's safety, wiping bloodied sweat from his brow. He shook his head. "I... I don't know. I don't know..."

He looked the governor in the face, attempting to cover fear showing in his own. "There's something down there." He pointed. "In there, I mean, in that darkness. It felt as if Hell itself rose up to meet the living. I believed I was to die, that all of us would die. My guards could feel it, too. *By the gods, everyone could feel it! Everything went crazy! It just went crazy!*"

Claudesius placed a reassuring hand on Treston's shoulder, encouraging him to remain calm. "Please. Tell me what happened. And don't leave out a thing. You say the girl is safe, even now?"

Treston said it was so, and then attempted his account, his eyes filling with excitement and fear. The governor marveled, thinking about the man speaking to him. Godless, arrogant, heartless, and even worse, that was Treston, but honest and loyal — at least knowing what side his bread was buttered on. He had heard this man curse the gods to their faces on many drunken occasions. It was difficult to believe this was the same person speaking to him now.

"Well... uh, well...." Treston stuttered while collecting his thoughts. He finally began anew. "Well... I had only just returned to my guard, who were successfully managing to keep those wishing harm to Ishtar away. Oh yes, there were vile threats and a few brave souls daring to spit at the girl, but *my* men did their jobs, as promised." Treston was proud of his personal bodyguard, trusting those four soldiers with his life and treating them like brothers.

"No sooner was I arrived than I felt this most unholy chill pass me by, filling my heart with unnatural panic. It was evil, my Lord, like something... or someone... filled with hateful malice, something like I've heard in stories told of demons, or those that are dead but seeking revenge and haunt the shadow-worlds of the living. Anyway, the faces of my men went ghostly white. I imagine mine did, too. But not that girl! No! No! *Not Ishtar!*"

Treston swept his hand across his forehead, wiping away nervous sweat. "I swear I saw the girl's hair stir, like someone was standing close a' talking in her ear, or something. She smiled and closed her eyes and... and..."

"And what?!" Claudesius' voice was filling with excitement. "What?! Tell me man! And what?!"

"And…" Treston shuddered. "And then it looked at me!" He waved his hands anxiously. "I didn't see anything, but I could see where something was, standing there, I mean. Something looked at me and screamed in my head. 'Get!' At that instant Ishtar grabbed my hand and shouted for us to follow her if we wanted to live. Nobody asked her why. We all just ran, she in the lead, pulling on me, and my boys following up real close behind."

Ogust glanced Treston's way, saying nothing. Forcing back his feelings, he motioned toward the shadows. Claudesius quietly shuffled behind Treston to a more private spot.

Treston went on, his hands trembling as he talked. "We were just at the top landing, near the jailer's station, not far from the upper gallery exit, when Ishtar shouted for us to stop. She told us to circle her, holding each other close and then not to move - that is if we wanted to keep alive. We all pressed real tight against her, me staring her square in the eyes, so close I could feel her warm breath on my face. The girl then took hold of my arms and whispered something real strange to the air. And then…and then all Hell broke loose!"

Interrupting, Claudesius anxiously asked, "What happened?! What happened then?"

Tears of nervous release ran down Treston's face. "Some kind of madness swept the chambers like the Kriggerman and his army of the damned was entered among us! A howling that rent the air went up from all the birds and beasts, the people holding their ears from the ferocity of the noise. It was so frightening, my Lord, so frightening I cried. Like a little bratling baby, I cried. I wept like an old hag woman at losing her children, almost wettin' myself. And… and I saw more than one old man keel right over dead from fright. Just over dead, like that!" He snapped his fingers.

"Then the cage doors just broke open, falling right off their hinges. There was something in the air! I felt it - an unholiness that raged those chambers, driving everything and everyone mad. The last thing I saw, for my eyes refused to keep a watch any longer, was when those giant bears came tearing past, piling into the wagons and dogs like they were little sticks of kindling. I just stood there after that, standing there, wailing, my eyes shut so tight, me and my men all a cryin' and wailin'. We were all like little babies."

Treston sighed, lowering his head in shame. "When the danger was passed, it was the girl who had to get us to move. It took some convincing, but finally we took the exit door and hurried up here. I couldn't think of anything else to do but bring Ishtar along with us. Dressed the way she was, nobody bothered to take notice of us."

Claudesius grinned. "Good! Good! You say she's here."

Treston pointed toward the stairs. "She's just outside, with my guards."

Still grinning, Claudesius grasped Treston's upper arm. "Good! Good!

You did well today, my friend, well! Take Ishtar to the alcove the other side of these walls..." He glanced over his shoulder. "away from fat, prying ears. I will be along in a minute or so."

It was an easy matter for Claudesius to escape Ogust's and Jusslin's company, their attention so wrapped up in the ensuing fight between the newly arrived soldiers and the wild, raging animals. He quickly entered the alcove and, after breathing a sigh of relief at seeing Ishtar safe, thanked the guards for their stalwart actions. After requesting they station themselves outside, he approached the girl, Treston standing beside her.

The governor's hands went to Ishtar's, he lifting them up while looking into her face. "Please!" He pleaded. "Tell me truth. Are you a goddess sent here to test us? This, for a certainty, I must know."

Ishtar smiled, her serenity unnerving. She shook her head. "I am a child born of man, my soul being birthed in most ordinary ways. Speak to that woman, my mother. She can tell you of my birth, my conception. Women do remember who father their children. Ask her. Is she not here this day?"

No one replied.

Ishtar shook her head again. "I am no goddess. I am a child of flesh and bone. My home has been this city these many years. Your captain here..." She nodded toward Treston. "knows well the history of my life, he pressing the coin into my father's hand many times while I played as a child inside his booth on a brightly colored carpet."

Shocked, Treston began to recall the many trinkets he purchased for his wife and little daughter from a man wearing a turban with a large feather in it. He spoke aloud, but to himself. "You were the child who made silly faces at me the day I bought that silken scarf for my wife, me putting it on and prancing around in funning."

Ishtar agreed, replying to the governor. "You see? I am a child of your world. This city has been my home until today, but now I must take my leave for another. What I am, my Lord, is a woman-child, spoilt some say. What I am to become remains hidden in mist and shadow. My destiny awaits me; it pants on toward its finish." She gave Claudesius a piercing stare. "And you must now hurry that destiny forward!"

Opening his mouth to make rebuttal, Ishtar raised her hand to the governor, shaking her head. "Your destiny is still uncertain. Do not bring the anger of my God down upon your people at this late hour."

At that, Ishtar lifted her arms back and over her head, pulling her dress up and off. After carefully folding it, she handed it over to a startled and dismayed governor. "Here..." She pressed the garment into Claudesius' hands. "Return this please, to the one it was made for, thanking her for it. Tell her that she is a woman blessed. She will one day again nurse her beloved son, her firstborn so dear to her heart, the child taken away in sickness."

Claudesius was struck speechless, for that child lost was many years ago and in a land strange and foreign to the people of Ephesus. Ishtar smiled, watching the effect her words had on the governor. Touching the dress, she declared, "I am a *free* woman! I will not be indebted to any man or flesh! Naked I came into the world and naked I shall find my leave."

Then, reaching up and touching the governor's cheek, soothing it in the way his mother did when he was but a child, Ishtar cautioned softly, "Remember this day and all you witnessed. Rare does the God over Heaven and Hell treat your kind with such tenderness. You have the soul to be a good man, and my God has cleansed your spirit and flesh of all wickedness. There is no longer any excuse for evil deeds. Do you, man born from woman, have the heart to remain cleansed before the God of all things?" She shrugged. "Your future is yours to choose. You are not destined for good or ill. But this hour is your master. Your duty is upon you. It begs no parley."

At that, Ishtar became silent, speaking no other words in the governor's ears.

Claudesius groaned in sadness, addressing Ishtar. "Should the choice be mine, I would trade places and put myself upon the judgment seat. I am a man ridden with evil guilt - a murdering, vile man, fit for nothing, traitor to my own sworn oath of rulership. Who is there like you, guileless and holy, majestic and sublime in power and glory? May your God have mercy on us…the many, the wicked, callous and cruel. It is I who was born blind and dumb and still remain as such. May your God forgive me… may you forgive me this terrible day I have heaped upon you. A goddess you are to me, but… but…"

A tear rolled down Claudesius' cheek as he lowered his head, choking out his final words. "You have given me no choice, no alternative, no way out. You… you… your God has blocked my path."

₧ ₧ ₧

It was a hurried affair for Claudesius after returning to his viewing stand. Officials were coming and going, constantly seeking directions and updating the governor on the situation. Ogust and Jusslin were absent. No one seemed to know where the mischief-makers might be, and Claudesius didn't bother to search beyond sending an attendant to do a quick look-see. Anyhow, the air smelled better with those two creatures gone, whatever shenanigans they might be up to.

People were running to the governor for the slightest little things. They requested his direction on the most trivial of matters. It was so trying for him to concentrate. After sending one worried and confused officer away, telling him to figure it out himself, he fumed silently, 'Why do they trouble me with such childish matters?!'

His bewilderment turned to thoughtful recognition, and then to shameful sadness. So, *this* was the *great* governor of Ephesus, the man most feared and admired! Well, feared, that was sure. His subjects, officials, officers, everyone knowing him feared him, but not because he was a man deserving of great honor. No! Each man and woman feared for his or her life because he, on the slightest pretense, was willing to cast persons off to the lions as if they were just worthless pieces of rat meat to feed his pets.

Claudesius' belly began to ache while a growing agony consumed his heart. Oh, what an evil man he was! For the first time in his life he wished his birth had never been, he being so wretched and cruel.

Well now Claudesius remembered Decanter's words, taught to him at the base of Vesuvius, his mentor holding forth a mirror to his students. 'Take ye the mirror of truth and look upon its accusations. Will ye become the honest man who seeks its reflection, or will you hide in hideousness because of your betrayal of all good, living things? All men must face the mirror of judgment before they, the gods, will entertain in triumph or anguish. Your oath of fealty to all living flesh that ye take this day before me shall a mirror of judgment be for you against which the gods weigh your soul for all eternity.'

Clenching his fists, Claudesius cursed himself for his betrayal of all good things. His motives in youth were so honorable and pure, yet he allowed the desires for power, wealth, and glory to corrupt any good within him. And now, for the first time in so many sordid lifetimes, when he finally wanted to do the right thing no matter the cost to him, the very God of gods barred his path, forcing him to commit the greatest of all travesties, to murder the most noble and purest of all living flesh while he, the vilest of deformities of mankind, must pretend to be righteous in judgement. Oh, how he hated himself.

And Cephas? His trial had been heralded throughout the entire district. Councils and magistrates were collected here from every major city within twenty leagues of Ephesus. "I will dismiss them!" He cried out to the air. "The destruction here is grand enough to warrant this judgment be delayed for another day!"

No sooner were the words spoken than Claudesius recalled Ishtar's deliberate destruction of the emperor's statue. He cursed aloud again. The entire city was in an uproar. How could the girl escape the people's righteous indignation? Staring into the sky, he called out in anguish, "Why have you brought me to this?! Unfit to live I am, and yet when I seek for once in my life to do right, you condemn me to this evil! Do you hate me so as to allow me life, forcing me to murder the only good thing existing in this damnable world, when all I wish is death! And yet death is too good for this miscreant..."

Turning his face to the empty seats where Ogust and Jusslin had been, Claudesius closed his eyes, forcing a tortured smile. "At least I have sent her away a free woman." Recalling his commands, he nodded satisfaction. 'Don't allow this woman to be bound or fettered. She will not run. Should anyone attempt a coup regarding my orders, run the bastard through!'

Treston had smiled, grasping the hilt of his sword. 'I shall not have to strike twice!' He bowed. 'My Lord…'

Claudesius gripped his arm, shaking his head. 'Do not call me that again, at least not when we are alone. You… you are my friend. My friend, take care of our child. I am trusting you.'

Shortly after Treston departed, another officer hurried in to see the governor, his uniform disheveled and bloodied, grievously announcing, "My Lord! My Lord!" The man bowed low at the waist, lifting his right hand to his head in reverential salute. "I beg you mercy, my Lord, but the execution- er dogs all perished, all save one. I am so sorry, my Lord…"

"What?!" Claudesius exclaimed, his lips curling into a smile. Quickly checking his jubilance, he asked somberly, "You say *dead*?"

An obviously nervous officer confirmed, "Yes, my Lord. There was nothing my men or I could do. By the time we subdued the riot of men and beasts, there was but the animal that brings death to the felon. All the others were scattered, torn asunder upon the field."

Oh, what a day! Claudesius' spirits soared. Maybe this god of Ishtar's was not going to destroy the child today. He would find a way to have her make escape…somehow.

No sooner had those thoughts entered his mind than another officer newly arrived and, overhearing the conversation, quickly offered a solution. "Your Excellency, there was delivered here just a little time ago, so that their wagoned cage remains outside these walls, wild dogs from the north- lands. Hungry they are and wolf-like. Though not trained in the arts of fair execution, they will at least satisfy the judgment of the vengeful crowd."

Claudesius faked a smile. Then patting the shoulders of the two officers and thanking them for jobs well done, ordered them to prepare the dogs. After this he turned to the first officer and asked, "You say the executioner dog remains alive?"

The officer answered affirmatively, "Yes, my Lord, alive and unhurt."

Taking hold of the officer's arm, Claudesius ordered and then warned, "You are to personally bring that beast, leashed, onto the field, keeping an ever watchful eye out for my signal. Should you fail that g… me, it will be better for you to cast your living carcass to the lions, for they will be kinder to you than I!"

"Y.. y.. y.. yes, my Lord!" The officer stuttered, staring into a grim, deter- mined, face. "I will do as you say! The beast will be kept safe at all cost, and I… I will be vigilant, awaiting your signal." He saluted and hurried away.

Stepping to the balcony wall, Claudesius peered out across the arena, studying the crowd milling about. He sadly shook his head. What a proud race and nation they once were, masters of the sciences, the arts, construction and so, so much more. How had they managed in such a short time to degenerate into this living slime of human filth? Here they were - he being the most culpable and vile - murdering one's neighbors, citizens, and fellow man, just so their hearts could race with momentary excitement. And then! And then, when an innocent people comes along professing loyalty to another god, one that says to love your fellow and do good for him, he and his world stand up and accuse them of the greatest of evils and blasphemies.

Then, in all their righteous indignation, they bring these same innocent people to the very blood houses where they practice unspeakable orgies against all living flesh and condemn those innocents to torture and death in the name of justice and honor. How could they not see the obscenity in such reasoning?! How could the ruin of the soul of another divine being – for the gods themselves taught that mankind was brought forth in a divine way – escape the wrath of the gods, their fathers? Would the worlds of future men ever absolve this wicked generation of its wanton guilt?!

Claudesius lowered his head in shame and anguish, turning away from the bloodied field. He needed more time… time to think and ponder… time to beg forgiveness – a new and strange desire recently come over him – time to consider too many things. Finding a secluded seat in the shadows, he sat and drew his fingers through thinning hair. Did it matter anymore? Did it really matter if life or death awaited him? His soul was already damned. He had done it to himself. The face of every man, woman and maiden ever raped, abused, beaten or murdered by him, flashed before closed eyes, condemning him, they standing beyond the River Styx, impatiently awaiting his arrival, the boatman with an outreached bony hand, seeking his fare.

A servant pressed him, asking if his lord "was feeling ill and should he have a doctor summoned". Claudesius – shocked at hearing his own words – thanked the servant for his concern, but declined the offer, asking the man to see he was left alone. It was not fun being governor this day, nor would it ever be again for Claudesius. The pleasure of having unchecked power over his fellow man was now turned sour, bitter upon his stomach. He would willingly surrender his entire kingdom for this one day to pass away into mindless dreams and for him to awake, it having only been a ghastly nightmare. This, though, was no dream, just a dreadful, loathsome reality screaming out its own brand of justice against a much deserving soul.

ဆ   ဆ   ဆ

It was late in the afternoon when the city stadium was finally readied for judicial matters. Claudesius felt ill, telling his court officers to cancel all other legal cases for the day. Only the trial of Symeon was to continue as scheduled.

Claudesius had taken occasion during preparations to get up and observe the progress of workers repairing the arena. Hurried crews had reinforced the damaged commons wall, roping off the section around the point of collapse. Then, burning lamps of perfumed oil were generously distributed along the wall surrounding the field, sending out the sweet smell of juniper and pine to cover the growing stench of blood and gore. This, added to the wagonloads of lime spread about, made the heat of the late day sun more tolerable on the nostrils of the thousands who were now crowding every nook and cranny of the stadium.

The time had come. The governor walked, again, to the balcony. A wild roar of approval rose from the thousands of anxious witnesses, the majority crying out for the death of the heretics. He waved his hand. The hastily replaced gates at the far end of the arena opened as horns, pipes, and cymbals began marshaling music. Then, slowly and steadily, a dozen soldiers dressed in armor and bright red uniforms, calling out cadence, pushed a huge four-wheeled wooden platform onto the field.

As the platform moved ever closer to its station near the governor's balcony, two-dozen archers entered through the small double doors directly below it. Claudesius was much relived to see that these men were from Treston's guard. How his lieutenant had managed to pull off such a coup he did not know, but it was a great relief to see it so. He knew that his friend would protect the girl from the riotous mob.

With a shouted command, the officer over the troop delivering the platform ordered a halt. The men gathered in a line facing the governor, the commander standing in front. All smartly saluted, remaining at attention while other royal soldiers paraded twenty or so shackled men across the field. The crowds went wild, shouting insults while throwing small objects at the bedraggled men, hitting some. One old man fell to the blow of a chunk of broken masonry, a soldier yanking him to his feet and pushing the bleeding fellow forward. At length, the prisoners were driven up to the north arena wall and forced to stand, facing the platform.

Sickness grew again in Claudesius' belly. These were honest, hard-working men who lived in the city, itself. He recognized a few, having seen them labor on the docks or selling stuffs in the marketplace. Their only crime committed? Openly confessing their belief in one supreme God.

Looking away, the governor studied the crowds of his *noble* country-men. He muttered under his breath, "Sewer rats the lot…would stick you in the back as to look at you. And I'm no better than the worst of them. Here we ruin the good to gather the filth. We drink down the vomit while throwing out the good wine." He sadly shook his head, knowing it was by his very hand these atrocities had been heaped upon these innocents. And for what? To make sport of a nuisance people and obtain a pleasing name for himself before one of Caesar's magistrates?

Claudesius nodded toward the soldiers, sending them to their stations on and around the platform. He glanced behind him into the shadows. The viewing stand was filled to overflowing with dignitaries and wealthy guests, but still no sign of Ogust or Jusslin. 'Oh well, the better for it. Maybe they will gift me with a burning for starting without them. Then on with it...'

Turning to the crowds, Claudesius raised his arms in ceremony, beginning the late day's events. He lifted his voice in praise to the gods, the caesars, all the brave men who had come before them, and to generations that would carry the glory of the empire into the unknown future. Oh, how he wanted to puke on his own smooth speech, but no, he could not. For, in his mind, he was developing a plan. Yes, the girl would die. Her god had checked his path. But what of the others? In his mind, Claudesius called out to a strange and unknown deity. 'Just this once, give this fool words to tingle the ears. Just this once...' Signaling to his heralds, the governor began the speech of his life.

"Brothers! My brothers! Our nation! Our nation was built on a set of divine laws of greater value than all the riches of all nations. These laws and principles they embody have made us the greatest kingdom the world has ever known! These very laws have unified people of every tongue, every culture and every ideology, welding them into the largest, strongest, family ever known to mankind. The length, breadth and majesty of this land which we call home is beyond measure. May it last forever!"

The crowd went wild with shouts and applause. Eventually, they quieted. 'Now to bend the road...'

Claudesius raised a fist. "The reason for our success? The reason why we have succeeded where the other great powers of Greece, Babylon, and Egypt all miserably failed is because of the honest and just rule of law that is fairly imparted to all free men. In our nation, all men are offered freedom to think, believe, and act in accordance with the will of the gods! And what do the gods, themselves, prove to us? That freedom subjects all living men to protect and consider the rights of our fellow man. Is there a man among us who disputes those evident truths?!"

The people were silent.

Claudesius shouted, "That being the case then, we, the children of this glorious house, must continue to display this outstanding allegiance to the laws that bind our house together!" then raising a fist, *"Our kingdom forever!"*

The people roared their approval, many standing and, with raised fists, repeating with enthusiasm, *"Our kingdom forever!"*

The governor smiled. 'Fools! Empty-headed fools!'

"We do not judge a man because of his race, home of birth, or even an ideology. Have we not seen the fool before? Yet we have seen tolerance from our greatest of lords. How often has our emperor proved his wisdom by allowing release to the man, though being a fool, or stupid in thought, because our great lord understands that ignorant stupidity was not justification in itself to call down judgment upon such a man. No! Not all children of the gods have been gifted with common sense, yet, are they not also children of the gods? Yes! Do we dare accuse the gods of incompetence because they make stupid men?"

"My fellow children of those very same makers of worlds, we have been given a sacred trust handed to us by those very powers, to care for their creation. Because we have held sacred that trust placed upon us, we have been blessed by those very divine beings. Tell me! Does there exist a more just and fair nation than what the gods have given to you and me?"

Shouts and applause echoed throughout the coliseum.

"We are not the kind of people who will abandon our sacred laws to satisfy any inner selfish desires or perceived offenses. Law! Law! Better is it for the entire world of living things to pass away than for one letter of our holy laws to be abused through greed, hatred, or fear! Are we not the stewards of divine knowledge, given to us through the oracles and priests who serve the gods looking down on us from hidden worlds?!"

Nodding heads shouted agreement…

Raising his hand and pointing skyward, Claudesius exclaimed, "Our fathers levied upon us a great responsibility, warning us so that our nation should last forever! They placed upon us the obligation to be wise and listen, to perceive the motive behind the action, to suffer the fool, to stand mature in a world filled with childishness. We have been placed under obligation to make the punishment fit the crime. And do our laws not also command us to withhold the whip from an innocent son whose father is a thief?"

"Yes! Yes! Should a man be declared guilty, we must still treat that evil-doer's family… if innocent… with the utmost respect offered to any man! Do you! Do you! Do you still stand beside your governor in crying out to the heavens that we…yes we, the children of the gods, now and forever, will live by those divine standards?!"

The crowds were on their feet, wildly shouting and gesticulating, some people throwing kisses while others tossed flower petals toward the governor.

Claudesius smiled and, with a sweeping gesture, bowed to his loyal listeners, all the while feeling a desire to puke. How sour the taste, his words! How phony! It was so clear now. In his mind he could see his world racing headlong into oblivion. The future of the empire was as certain as if it had already happened.

As he stood, a vision suddenly flashed before the governor's eyes. In an instant of time, the man saw his world – no, all the worlds of all living flesh - consumed by cosmic fire, it beginning in Rome and hungrily reaching out until the entire universe was a roaring inferno. Then, to his surprise, he watched a man - a boy from a strange world, yet a child of his own decadent land - rise up from the flames and wrest power from a giant serpent beast that stood above all the earth. And the boy defiantly cried out, *"Law! I will take the law and bring down all mankind! My law! The Law of the living God! It is alive and exerts power even now!"*

At that, the vision passed. Shaken, Claudesius bowed again to regain his composure. He then allowed the crowd time to calm down, all the while pondering his own people. 'So this is the value of speeches with self-righteous bigots. Boost their egos for but the moment and they will follow you beyond the River of the Damned. Declare the evil righteous and these miscreants will bow before them in worship. Speak ill of the innocent and the mobs will stone them to death. Well, today I put the carrot on the stick and shall twist the trail. For once, I shall declare good to the good… and burn this night for such honesty.'

Raising his arms ever upward, the governor called out, "It has been reported there exist among us some certain men of question who preach there is but one true God. Can you believe that?!"

Laughter and mocking arose from many listeners.

"What foolish and ignorant little children they must be!"

Laughter erupted again.

"For men like us, we find it queer and baffling to think anyone could possibly believe such prattle. Only a daylight drunkard or one born without a mind or, possibly, one who has stood too long in the midday sun could find any logic in such folly! Are we so weak of mind that we also must fear that village idiot? Do we not laugh at such silly speech like one does the antics of a little child? What is the harm they have done to our great nation, to us, to our beautiful laws, my brothers?"

The people roared their adulation.

'Gets them every time - a little pat on the head and the tail wags the dog.' Claudesius smiled in disdain. "My brothers! Who among us would beat the child for saying foolish things? Then should we, the people who know for a fact that the *gods* bless our world, should we not be willing to suffer the childish antics of *other* foolish little children? Who do they hurt but themselves? If then, they do not harm those of us with knowledge or the law or our eternal emperor, why can we not suffer their silly speech? After all, is it not a fine thing to have the jester to laugh at while we tarry at our daily chores? My brothers! Would we not lower the beautiful standards of our divine laws if we should declare it a criminal act for being *stupid*?!"

"So then!" The governor raised his right hand, sweeping it outward toward the crowds. "We have gathered in this judicial seat of honor this day those who are perceived as wise, and…" He lifted his left hand, pointing out toward the shackled men standing by the north wall. "We have gathered here also those who are perceived as stupid."

Then searching the faces of the many, he cried, "Our beautiful laws do not allow us the denigration of them to the judging of stupid people, for the gods themselves have destined them to live on this planet so as to be a test for mature men… to test our wisdom and tolerance, so that we may attain the stars, riding upon the great fire ships as they burn across the skies protecting the innocent… and the stupid!"

Now there was a certain Marcus Lucas of Hammond-Tun, a city some leagues north of Ephesus, who stood shackled by the north wall. He cocked an ear and lifted an eyebrow at hearing the judicial speech being presented. He bore the marks of many beatings delivered by this same governor. Something was queer about the man's words. Although unlettered, Marcus could tell something was up. He closed his eyes, listening intently to the unfolding apologies, his heart racing in anticipation.

"So then, my brothers!" Claudesius' voice filled with passion. "We must separate the stupid person from the true criminal. That is what we must decide here this day! Are these same believers in one god and one savior merely stupid… or are they seditionists, acting against our laws and great nation, as some of you have heard rumored? Let us put all rumor aside and judge in truth and knowledge!"

He paused for response. The crowd was silent but, looking into their faces, he saw them pondering, thinking. Never before had he reached this deep into men's hearts. *They were thinking!* He had never before seen anyone quietly thinking within these walls. Oh yes, silently contemplating their coming fate, that was all too common, but to ponder the fate of another? 'Well…' He sighed. Was there a possible future for him and his people? A spark of hope began to burn in his breast.

"We will satisfy law and justice on this eve. If there is treason afoot, we shall weed such evil out, but we will not destroy the whole because one fellow of theirs has chosen to take it upon himself to attempt a ruin of our house. Justice! I say justice will prevail today… and for every day our *grand kingdom* exists!"

The people went wild, their hearts welling up with patriotic pride. Here was their leader! Had not the emperor chosen well when this man was appointed governor over their territories? Justice! Yes, justice would be served. And Governor Claudesius had invited all those present to share in the glory of that decision-making.

Claudesius' voice fell into solemn prose. "In order to find the truth behind these rumors, I have summoned a great leader over these people to stand in front of this judicial seat and testify before all men and gods the truth of all matters. It will not be an easy test for reasons you, yourselves, shall soon see. This court will find the truth and then, by law, decide the fate of the guilty and innocent!"

With that, the governor motioned an attendant. In short order, a door opened beneath the viewing stand. An aged man shackled at his wrists and feet shuffled into the arena, he blinking away the blindness caused by the sudden brightness of day. Surrounding him were smartly dressed prison guards, two of which carried several months' wages worth of newly received silver and gold coins. Following behind them was a middle-aged woman, unshackled, and with but one guard. Distraught she was, dressed in faded merchant wealth, but now with callused working hands and wrinkled brow. She was anxiously wringing her hands while staring at the ground, letting out an occasional sob as tears fell from reddened eyes.

While the tiny procession made its way across the arena and up onto the platform, Claudesius busied himself on some unimportant matters with a local magistrate, he fearing that he, too, would burst into tears should he stare down upon the scene.

The soldiers lifted the aged man's hands, dropping the shackles' chain over a secured hook fastened to an upright pole protruding from the platform's planked floor. The woman, still quietly sobbing, was standing beside the man, a guard's spear keeping her in check. All was ready.

Claudesius excused himself, directing his attention toward the man on the platform. His throat constricted, he forcing his mind to think about duty. Duty? The duty now was to save this man from the fate he, himself, had heaped upon him, and at what cost? It was too much to think about. He shook his head, attempting to clear his thoughts.

"Symeon!" He paused, forcing the nervous anxiety from his voice. "Symeon! Today I put you under oath before all men and gods, to speak truth and honesty in this sacred court. Do you swear, before the glory of our emperor, our people, this nation… before your very own God to speak honestly and truthfully at whatever the cost to the worlds above and below?"

Symeon lifted his head until his eyes met Claudesius'. "Your Excellency! There is but one truth. An honest man need not swear an oath, for God does judge that man for good or bad by what proceeds from his mouth. But for you, to satisfy the needs of this court, I swear an oath of fealty to truth and justice to God and men that what I speak will be honest and accurate. It is an honor to have you judging all matters, for your wisdom is renowned among this people."

Claudesius was taken aback, marveling at the oratory of this unlettered man. 'Should he be permitted, he could convert the world of men to believe that rocks can fly. Pity us all, for our world shall fall to the wiles of these people if this man goes free. But that is what I must do.'

"Tell us then, Cephas of Capernaum, what do you request from your God concerning our great nation?"

Symeon bowed his head in respect before answering. "There exists among us a man, prophet to all the nations, who is by far the greatest and most honored among my people. This man, Paul, speaks to us with the authority of the gods. His words are clear and well-defined. With prayers we are to offer thanks concerning kings and all those who are in high station, in order that we may go on living a calm and quiet life. This command, I and all my brothers hold dear to, as often has been proved to all mankind."

"Tell us!" Claudesius demanded. "Tell us, then, what of the person claiming loyalty to your God who willfully disregards our laws and customs, acting in defiance of our gods and our greatest of all rulers?"

Symeon winced as an ache raced through his head. He knew that in some way his words would affect this day's outcome concerning another person, he believing it to be Ishtar. "So be it!" He muttered under his breath.

"My Lord, it is not our place to stand in opposition to your gods or rulers. We are a peaceful people. Doing an act of aggression in word or action, or supporting a person who carries out such folly would be an act of treason and rebellion against the very God who placed all governments upon this earth to serve in a way that pleases him. For it is spoken of by our Lord, Paul, 'Let every soul be in subjection to the superior authorities, for there is no authority except by the will of God!' We do not condone rebellion in any form!"

A sickness was again growing in Claudesius' belly. He was tightening the noose upon the one creature he would rather die for than continue living. Yet every word, every question, every gesture, was forcing the Fates to bring about that creature's demise. He could not win. Swallowing down bile, he asked, "What then, Cephas - known to others as 'Symeon, the prophet and seer' - you, one of the twelve pillars of your faith, what is an acceptable punishment for someone who wantonly defies the gods and our nation that, you say, your people pray for?"

How well Symeon knew the weight resting upon his shoulders. The lives and future of his people hinged upon the outcome of this trial. Should he falter, all might be lost. Silently, he cried out to his God to give him wisdom. There was a sudden rush of refreshing breath that filled his heart, easing the growing anxiousness. 'Be calm and speak.' A voice whispered in his mind.

Symeon sighed relief, believing the day was not his to fight alone. With respectful boldness, he answered, "My Lord, it has not been granted to common men like myself to pass judgment upon the wicked or the righteous. We trust to our God to set all matters right. It is he who has given to men like yourself the wisdom to lead our world along history's road, choosing the destiny of the men in your charge. For it has been taught to us by our leaders that you are God's minister, an avenger of blood against the wicked and an angel of mercy to the innocent."

"My Lord, I do not choose life or death for any man. My hands do not hold the tiller nor do they unfurl the sails. The river is not mine to set course upon, nor is journey's end mine to choose. You…you, the great magistrate, must choose the fate of all mankind on this earth… and God will choose it beyond."

Clenching his fist in frustration, Claudesius silently cursed Symeon's reply. 'Damn him! Damn him! He binds me with fated chains that I cannot escape. He condemns me to damnation, forcing me to murder the most innocent of beings! A goddess I must destroy to buy his release! Yet, what other choice? For I see his God has bound me to this road. Damn him! Damn him! So now it is come, upon Symeon will arrive a release through declared innocence, me forcing the man to do so. By so doing, I heap the fiery coals of Hell upon my head, for shall I destroy one of the gods.'

Swallowing hard, he asked, shouting out to the ears of his people, "Then tell me, Cephas, lord over this illegal sect, will you hold this nation guilty if it brings to justice one of your own who has practiced such wantonness? Will you permit your God to hold this people responsible for exercising justice against a willful rebel who disregards even your laws?"

Symeon's heart ached, he knowing the sentence being passed. "I am but a man. I cannot speak for God, nor can I excuse the teachings of all men. But, in truth, I can say this: Never have I spoken sedition of any sort, nor have my ears heard one word echoed from the leaders of my people. I do not, cannot support any vile act of rebellion against this nation or its leaders. We have preached, publicly and privately, that all men must remain in subjection to their king and nation and, if at all possible, remain loyal to all the laws, standards, and customs of this land. We will not tolerate a felon!"

Claudesius' reply was instant and cruel, theatrics so practiced that it was now second nature and he hated himself so much for it. He extended an accusing hand. "What of your own *flesh*?! Will you be so bold in your patriotic defense if the person you condemn is of your *own blood*? Tell me, you the great Cephas, if it's your blood, *will you still hold true to your words?!*"

The woman standing near Symeon howled in agony, "Not her! My Lord, not my child! Forgive her foolishness! It is not her fault, but the prattle of this fool that has filled her head with stupid ideas!" Pointing at Symeon, she screamed, "*It is the evil of this man that has corrupted my child, he and his stupid religion! Make him stand in her stead for he rides the winds of evil against her! Make him pay for twisting the mind of an innocent babe!*"

Symeon lowered his gaze, refusing to look at his sister. He asked the governor, "Please, my Lord, what is the charge levied against the child? For I do not know of any foul deed done by the maiden - that is, if the child you speak of is my niece, Ishtar."

"That is the child of whom I speak!" Answered Claudesius, he leaning forward, glaring into Symeon's face, reminding himself, 'Put on the act, you fool! The people must not learn what you are really doing.'

He then declared Ishtar's insubordination. "She is accused of treasonous acts against the gods and men! Against our very emperor she has committed a seditious act!"

"What?!" Symeon blurted out, surprised.

"Yes!" Claudesius shook his fist. "She is accused by many eye witnesses of performing the greatest of atrocities against our lord-king, by willfully smashing, with vile curses, his god-statue and altar upon which it was stationed!"

Symeon could not believe his ears. "There must be a mistake, my Lord. This girl is most law-abiding, she never speaking one word against you or this great nation. She is a loyal child. There must be some mistake!"

"Mistake?!" Claudesius sneered. "Even *I* am witness to this travesty!" He then shrugged, putting on a pious face. "But do not believe me. Let the perpetrator of such heinous crimes speak in her own defense."

At that, he motioned to his attendant. In only moments, the door beneath the viewing stand again opened. Treston, along with four of his most loyal guards, ushered Ishtar onto the field.

A hush fell across the stadium, followed by an audible gasp. The people stood agape at seeing this perfect creature of beauty. Many clasped their chest while others looked away in order to catch their breath as there came the occasional cry, "Let her live! She is a goddess! Let the goddess live!"

Claudesius smiled. Maybe he had won. Maybe this was but a test given him by Ishtar's strange God. At that instant, his hopeful visions were shattered. Someone in the nearby crowd heaved a jagged stone, striking Ishtar across the cheek, the man screaming, *"Traitor! Villain!"*

No sooner were his words exhausted than the man fell backward into the crowd, an arrow piercing his heart. Claudesius glanced first at the archer who was reloading his bow and then at Treston, who was also looking up at him. There would be no more foul deeds attempted against the girl today, other than the most atrocious, and that by his command. He nodded approval to Treston.

The governor shouted to the people, "This is a court of law! Justice will be served up swiftly against anyone failing to show the proper respect concerning it! Another such outburst and I will burn the criminal, his house and household for acting so disrespectfully!"

There were still a few muted cries to release the girl, and a few of more vulgar comments. Claudesius ignored them and went on with business. Ishtar had been taken to within some twelve paces of the platform, well in range of speaking distance of it. She then was faced toward the viewing stand, about an equal distance away.

Motioning the guards to quiet Ishtar's wailing mother, Claudesius leaned forward, peering into the girl's serene face. Oh, how he hated himself. In a voice resolute, pretending offence, he declared, "The charge levied against you is serious and, if true, brings death to the perpetrator! You have been accused of displaying gross disrespect for our chief magistrate and emperor by destroying his effigy in wrath and anger. How do you plead to this charge?"

Ishtar stood defiant. *"I brought to nothing what is mere rock and stone that was shaped in the form of a man! For that, I am willing to die! But let it be known, your leader is no god! I will not bend a knee to a man of flesh and bone!"*

Ear-splitting shouts and cries went up from the people, some covering their ears and crying out to the gods, lest the world be smitten in their anger. *"Throw her to the dogs! Cut out its tongue and burn her with fire!"* Had it not been for the fear of Treston's archers, the coliseum would have exploded into uncontrolled rioting.

Hanna was standing less than four rods from where Ishtar stood, holding her head, mouth agape, not believing what she had heard. Never had any of her people spoken out against the leaders of their world. This was unthinkable! Had the child lost her mind, or had a demon possessed her body and was speaking through a bewitched mouth?

At length, the crowd was silenced.

Claudesius asked Ishtar, concerned, "Does this child speak her own words or have the teachings of your uncle warped your mind toward doing wicked things?"

Ishtar stared at Claudesius, smiling as she had when goading him earlier into killing her. It was a trap! She had set him up, using him to ask a question that would absolve Symeon while condemning her. And now she must answer him, he unable to retract his words.

Ishtar paused a moment, realizing the pain she was about to cause. Her uncle would not know, could not know that what she was about to say was for the preservation of his soul and the souls of all her brotherhood. She must become the evil one, an abomination among her own people if they hoped to survive this hour. There was nothing else for it and she was not afraid to bring it about.

Looking up and into the governor's face, she cried, *"I am a free woman! No man owns my bed or leads me along as a slave. The prattle of my uncle is not my master! I do as I please and live as I wish. You have no say about me! The Tillerman take my soul and all the world be damned to Hell!*"

The crowd went riotously mad, the guards being forced to restrain them.

When it was again quiet, Claudesius asked Symeon, he showing a long face of sadness and offence, "Tell me, please. Be truthful, for you have given your oath. Do you support the actions of this woman? Does your religion permit such outrageous outbursts against not only our leaders but against the very station of womanhood in our land?"

Symeon looked down at Ishtar, confused and dismayed, her eyes searching his, pleading for him to understand, a thing he was unable to do. There was something he could denote about her, as if she were asking him not to hate her, but to be patient and wait before casting judgment upon the child.

Finally, in tears, he called out to the governor, "Please! My Lord! The child must be sick. A fever must be upon her, or a derangement in her mind caused by this excitement. Allow, please, this once, give to me the sentence cast against such deeds done. Let me take responsibility for the girl. Give her to her mother so she may convalesce back to health. She is not acting as the child I know and love."

Ishtar angrily shouted, "*Do not listen to the words of a fool! This man seeks only succor from a woman who curses the day of his birth. He wishes only to pacify his own heart for his silly chatter!*" She waved her fist. "*Release me and I swear, as I live, I shall make a destruction of all your god-men, be they statues or flesh!*"

She ranted on, being drowned out by the uproarious crowd. Seeing them nearly out of control, Treston hurried up behind her, wrapping his hand over the girl's mouth, telling her to be silent. "That's enough! Or do you really wish we all die here today? You can rest assured that your soul will not outlive this hour. That may be your wish, but I would like to keep my skin a while longer. I promised you no harm would come from those people, but it will be hard to do so if we are all rushed upon."

Ishtar stuck out her tongue, smearing Treston's hand with spittle. Reacting in surprise, he released his grip. Ishtar quickly answered, "Your skin is worth little to me, but my God has promised you life if you do his will today. I will not risk you or your men harm. There is nothing left to say. I promise to be silent."

When the people were finally returned to order, Claudesius repeated his question. Symeon said nothing for the longest time, each moment lasting an eternity. When the governor was beginning to think no answer was forthcoming, Symeon broke that silence.

There was no energy left in his voice when he began. Ancient and stoop-shouldered, he appeared a broken man. "Whether this child is guilty before her God, I do not know. He, not I, can judge the heart. We have clear bounds given in our teachings that forbid her actions, actions that I cannot defend. I do not know the child standing before you. She is not the girl I know and love. A fever may be on her brain. She is not herself. Please have mercy on her."

"It is not your place to judge innocence or guilt!" Claudesius huffed. Piously adding, "As for mercy, how well you should know that it is so much part of our law!" Extending an accusing hand, he commanded, "I have put you under oath, Cephas! Leader of this sect of Judaism, a sect you call 'Christian', one of the twelve pillars of this sect, tell me truthfully, do you support this woman in what she has done?! *YES* or *NO?!*"

Symeon lowered his head in grief, tears welling up in his eyes. 'So it has come to this: I must cast the first stone. I must ruin my own flesh and blood.' He then silently cried out to the Heavens for its mercy. Why must he carry the blood of his very own child? A quiet voice in the back of his mind whispered, 'My son, you must go on living even should all flesh around you fall. Do this thing for me and live. I will not forget her, for the child is also my vessel.' He looked at Ishtar, wishing to cry out to her, asking what folly was on her brain. The girl stared off toward the east as if in a dream, seeing something no other human could comprehend. She gave no heed to the moment, serene and calm, as if having already reached some future destiny.

Slowly, Symeon raised his eyes until his met Claudesius'. For but an instant, he witnessed the same grief coming from the governor's eyes as were showing in his own. Without hesitation, he answered. *"NO!"*

Hanna's hands broke into a tremble, dropping her basket at her feet. Covering her mouth to stop a growing need to scream, she hurried to the closest exit, down the many flights of steps and out onto the street, running away in frantic distress. Her feet did not slow until they came to a narrow alley between two buildings some distance from the arena. There she squirreled herself far away, hiding behind some broken crates, curling up into a little ball with her hood pulled down snuggly over her head. Finally, hidden from wondering eyes, she unleashed her sorrow in uncontrolled weeping and lament. There the little creature remained until the late night chill drove sleep from her eyes.

Claudesius paused in momentary consultation with two other officers of the court. When finished, he motioned for Treston to have Ishtar face him. He lifted his voice for all to hear the judicial decision of the court. "Ishtar, daughter of Guillhadden and Naomi, child of this city and subject of this nation! You have been found guilty of insurrection against our chief magistrate and emperor, your traitorous defiance being a rebellion of one, you the sole acting agent. By your own admission, you have declared your guilt while absolving your uncle and those who follow along in his teachings."

Claudesius waved a hand, pointing a finger at Ishtar. "This crime cannot go unpunished! By your own volition, you have proffered to perform more and even greater heinous crimes, thus adding insult to already sordid actions. For past and threatened future acts of treason, you must suffer the penalty of death before the sun sets upon us this day!"

Ishtar looked down, a smile of satisfaction growing on her face. Claudesius felt sick, so sick that he sent an officer forward to read the details of the execution. Sitting down and resting his head in hand, he pondered the preceding hours. Only this morning the man had envisioned a grand feast for his visiting dignitary and other invited guests. Cephas would have been torn asunder by lions and his few surviving followers scattered to the winds, their tales of woe chilling the hearts of any listeners.

Then came into his life the most beautiful creature ever seen, and he stood upon the moment to ravish that creature to satisfy his personal selfish indulgence. Now he sat, broken and confused, wishing Death take him this second. Better to face the fires of Hell or just be dead forever than to carry out this awful crime. He must drop his hand, signaling the release of the dogs. Oh, how he wished for the knife to cut off, eternally, that arm so he this misdeed could not accomplish.

Treston lingered, standing beside Ishtar as the distant doors opened and the caged wagon containing the dogs entered the arena. He waited until the wagon began its turn to face its hinged rear gate toward the accused. The other soldiers were long since scurried away, finding safe perches to watch from before Treston departed. At the last moment, he spoke up. "May your God have mercy on us for the foul deeds we are about to commit." Then taking her arm, Treston pled, "My Lady Divine, please forgive this miscreant for all the insults and injury I have caused you. I do not deserve life because of the many evil deeds my hands have committed. If your God gives me a chance, I will try to compensate for those evils. I don't know how, but I will."

The teamsters were finished backing up the wagon, and the officer holding the executioner dog had climbed aboard the machine's fender. Men, too, stood above the gate ready to pull the release pins. They looked to the viewing stand for the signal. Treston began to leave, stopped, and leaned close to Ishtar's ear. "It will be easier and less painful if you face the beasts like a warrior fending the battle line. Die as though a sword is held in your hand. Imagine it if you can. You can, because you are the greatest of warriors! *You are a free woman!*" He turned away, hiding tears as he hurried toward his soldiers who were holding open the nearby doors.

"My Lord! The time is arrived. The people await your orders." Claudesius looked up wearily into the eyes of his trusted secretary, the man's troubled expression showing concern for his master's welfare. "My Lord, if my Excellency is ill, may I suggest he assign these duties to another of the city's magistrates?"

Claudesius sighed, waving off the man's recommendation. "No, Seulicious, I shall condemn no other man to Hell. The hour comes upon us all when the gods demand we accept our destiny. I must not pass off to another the hemlock I have brewed in my recklessness. The Kriggerman be damned to his darkened worlds, for no coward will he find when he reaches out for my worthless soul!"

Seulicious puzzled, seeking an answer to the governor's black riddle. Claudesius waved him silent. "Another day, my friend, another day... Now come see the world burn. Please, beside me stand this day." The two men slowly made their way to the rail of the viewing stand, Claudesius leaning upon Seulicious' shoulder.

The crowds roared their bloodlust upon seeing their leader and judge. Clutching the rail with both hands, the governor leaned forward to study the people. 'What filth, loathsome rotten filth, the whole lot! Better to burn this world with fire than to let the children of the future know the kind of scum that came before them!'

In his mind, Claudesius formed the words for the speech he most wanted to give. 'What right do you have to live?! What have you done that is worth a breath?! The lion kills because it is hungry, the eagle to feed its young. You! Do you even deserve to be elevated to the glory of those mindless beasts? *Murderers! Murderers!* Men without souls, how will you escape the gates of Hell?! Escape?! Even *Hell* does not want you, your bones not worth the lime to spread on a beggar's field. Death to us all! It is more than we deserve!'

But had it not been by the very teachings of him and his kind that the ignorant and fools of his world gathered themselves to such putrid celebrations, being taught it a noble thing to see one's fellow slaughtered for sport? No, the debauched lives of the people were merely a reflection of the sordid leadership that directed and educated them. They were as much the victims as the girl standing below.

He looked down, disgusted and ashamed, seeing the child awaiting death. How quiet, calm and dignified she appeared, a smile of satisfaction upon her face. Guilt! For the first time in his life, Claudesius was ridden with guilt... guilt for taking an innocent's life... guilt for being the fomenter of this travesty... guilt for being alive. *He* deserved death. How many innocents had he murdered? Numbers were lost to him, faces blurred into the distant past. His cousin was the first...poisoned apple. It was tough – family, you know. After that it became easier until... until it mattered little who or why, just as long as it served his sordid purpose.

Now the man stood upon the parapet of time and space, seeking absolution for one last evil deed, a deed yet uncommitted, but still unstoppable. Fair speech could not undo what the Fates had conspired against him. Ishtar's God was a trickster extraordinaire, playing the worlds of men to music of his own liking.

He had failed; his people had failed. They had forgotten the moral obligation of being divine sparks, beings made from the fires of the heart of a living, caring Creator. So now the Maker of Worlds was going to teach them the folly of such foolishness.

Claudesius lifted his hand, the weight of mountains resisting his efforts. The men at the wagon tensed themselves, pulling fast the ropes that would remove the pins that would release death and judgment upon the nation's offender. High he raised that hand, his stomach churning in convulsive knots. Oh, how he wished to close his eyes and turn away! But he remembered earlier events, how an innocent child was forced to witness torture and destruction. No, he would be a man about it, see the foul deed, watch the ruination of this most wonderful of divine creatures. He would suffer his punishment, murdering this child by his own hand, being witness to his act of wicked cowardice.

The crowd waited with bated breath. Was the governor changing his mind? So long he held his hand high, the people began to think he had become a statue. Then, suddenly, Claudesius' arm fell, its strength as though ruined by the weight of the moment, it dropping to his side limp and broken. His eyes would remain fixed upon the child, refusing to allow their master escape from the horrid manifestations pummeling them from the field below. But the sounds of the raging tempest he did not hear, for within the man's mind, the passionate screams and accusative cries from all his murders rose to condemn him and his race, they refusing to release him until long after the girl's fate was come to a finish.

With a grunt, the men pulled heavy on the pins, releasing the counterweights holding the cage's gate in place. Up it flew, slamming hard against the upper head-beam, violently shaking the machine. Six one-hundred pound wild beasts bolted through the opening, charging the tiny creature standing less than ten paces away.

Ishtar leaned into the coming storm, standing like a soldier facing a fearsome onslaught, but it was all in futility. The first dog jumped toward her face, she fending it off with an arm as she tumbled backward into a heap. And then the other starving canines were upon her.

In that instant of mindless desperation, she stretched out a hand toward a prison guard standing near Symeon, crying out for help. The man's cruel answer was covered by the hungry snarls of the ravenous dogs, but his laughter was not hidden from her eyes. For but an instant, Ishtar watched, the scene frozen forever in her mind. Laughter erupted among the soldiers watching from the platform. Symeon stood silently, his head lowered in grief or shame, and her mother - her mother stunned as if in death.

Ishtar felt a violent tug at her arm and glanced up in time to see a large chunk of bloody meat being chomped down by a hungry mouth full of teeth. Then another violent tug and then another, each beast gulping down whole the first meal it had in days. Through a cloudy mind, the girl recognized these beasts for what they really were, hapless victims starved and beaten until, as an act of survival, they fought each other for one more meal - one more moment satisfied from hunger. At least they had reason…no malice, hatred, or lust…just a need, an instinctive will to live.

She laughed to herself. 'Is it only the reasoning beast who surrenders the fight and wishes for death?'

The animals pulled Ishtar's torn and bloodied body this way and that as the living flesh was ripped from her bones, each one fighting for its share of the evening meal. All this the child saw and heard, but there came no pain nor was there any fear…only peace, a rocking lullaby of peaceful music. A smile grew on pale lips. *She had won!* Today was her victory! *Damn all the worlds of men and gods, for they held no rule over her now!* She cried out in her mind, for her voice had no power, '*I am become the Darkness! Freedom is mine! No one shall ever take it from me!*'

Naomi screamed in grief, cursing Symeon and his God for her daughter's ruination. Symeon stood silent, tears streaming down a haggard face. Claudesius stared down blankly, swallowing his own vomit. He was struggling to hold himself back from jumping from the balcony, wishing to be ripped apart in the feeding frenzy rather than to live another moment. And Treston? He watched through a peephole in the lower door, tensely waiting for the right moment.

With a painful yip, the executioner dog lunged forward, pulling its handler from the wagon and dragging him through the dirt until the heavy leash snapped, broken in two. Driving hard into the pack, it slammed its way through the hungry animals until it stood over Ishtar, staring into the woman's placid face. It howled defiance to the crowd, then, with opened jaws, dove upon the girl's neck, crushing bones and tearing muscle as it violently shook the now lifeless body.

"Drive 'em away or kill 'em!" Treston was diving through the opened door, his soldiers close behind. In only seconds it was over, Treston's bloodied spear running through the last of the defiant beasts. He turned to look upon the handiwork of his demented world, stepping close to examine their damnable act. In growing anger, he stared up into the jeering faces of a threatening crowd, disappointed at his uncalled for intrusion and the girl's quick demise.

As tears streamed down his face, Treston raised a fist, preparing to scream out his curses against this obscene world of *degenerate animals*, when a sudden eerie pall filled the sky, sweeping in a sickly yellowish-red twilight. A stifling silence fell upon the crowds as darkness pressed in upon them. Nothing stirred, the breeze having died with the gloom.

Standing in the dust, dumb struck, there came to Treston's ears distant rumbling the likes of a gathering storm. As this tumultuous agitation grew in power, he realized the noise was rising up from deep within the earth. In seconds, the entire colosseum was a' tremble, the shaking so terrible, it became difficult to stand.

Walls cracked, pillars snapped, buckling, sending marble facades and balconies plunging into the crowded stone bleachers below. People screamed in panic, jumping from the parapets into the arena or clawing at one another to make their escape from certain death. Some men fell to their knees, beseeching their gods' protection.

Reaching out a hand in desperation, Treston clutched onto the arm of a fellow guard, they holding tight, remembering earlier day's events. There soon gathered his entire troop, surrounding Ishtar's lifeless body in hopes of gaining some protection from the wrath of the girl's God.

Then came the sudden explosion of lightnings filling the sky with fiery bolts of crackling, deafening thunders. Fireballs of crimson, gold and blinding white tormented the hysterical crowds, men collapsing and fainting out of fear. Stones were shattered and wood splintered when these divine comets rained down upon the helpless people.

There, above the roofline of the governor's viewing stand, were two life-sized statues, one of the emperor and the other of a goddess holding justice in an upraised arm. Treston watched, amazed, when several fiery bombs blasted away the viewing stand and the statues, sending the pieces crashing into the arena.

As Treston watched a defaced marble head bouncing across the field, there arose such a thundering tempest as to ruin the ears. Above the raging winds, a voice cried out of the thunder - at least some believed there was a voice in that thunder. Treston believed. *"As broken stones shall all your gods become! So is raised a dragonslayer… Sister of the BloodWind!"*

Instantly, before the eyes of five astonished men, a white mist rose from the tortured remains of a holy child and, for but a moment, the mist collected itself into the girl's form, her ghostly eyes turning a warning glance toward each of the spellbound soldiers. Then *poof!* the mist vanished into nothingness. At that, the quaking maelstrom ended, the evening sun peacefully casting its fading light across a terrified and confused crowd staring out upon a ruined world.

What was even more amazing was the fact that when a search was made, it was discovered that no lives were lost. Indeed, if not for the physical destruction done to the colosseum, many would have believed what took place was but a vision from the gods.

A stunned silence hung over the arena, the dusty calm nearly as unnerving as the earlier thrashing of earth and sky. Coming quickly to his senses, Treston ordered his men to remove Ishtar's remains, they hurriedly dragging it past the rubble of the viewing stand and through the twisted door from which the party had entered the killing field.

Surveying the after-scene, Treston was disturbed to see that the ground had soaked up the girl's blood in a most peculiar way, there being virtually no remaining trace of the gruesome contest entered upon only moments before.

As he, too, hurried to catch up with the others, Treston believed he could hear the very ground laughing, calling up to him, "Tomorrow! She is yet to best me on another day, or her heart will be *forever mine!*"

Treston picked up his pace, hair standing up on the back of his neck. 'Enough! Enough witchery for one day... for a lifetime!' The man wished never to see the goblin again, but in his bones a weary dread grew, he feeling the contest was not yet finished.

Claudesius and the others with him had been hurled back by the concussive blast that tore away the statue of the emperor, saving them from an untimely demise. When Treston reached what remained of the viewing stand, the governor was again staring down where Ishtar's bloodied body had lain.

Sensing his captain's presence, Claudesius looked over at him, his face grave and ashen. "My friend, your swift action this day will not be soon forgotten, but there are yet many deeds needed being done before the sun can rest in peace. Will you honor me with those requests?"

Somewhat surprised at the governor's politeness, Treston bowed. "My Lord..."

"Please prepare the child for burial. By your own hands will you do this? I know you will be gentle with her. Do whatever it takes to rebuild her beauty, and order the parlor maids to do her up splendidly with painted lips and braided hair befitting a goddess. When finished, place the child upon the Stone of Artemis in the Great Temple sanctuary. Shroud her in the purple and gold tapestry of the palace." He reached out a hand, clasping Treston's arm. "And... and in the morning sunrise, bring her mother to the shrine to see her child taken to the gods."

Treston bowed again. "It shall be done, my Lord, just as you have requested."

"Good! Good!" Claudesius smiled weakly. "And on the 'morrow, when the winds blow out toward the sea, take the girl to my northern estate near the mountains. Bury her in my family cemetery, in its center, and raise a mound up over her, and place a pillar inscribed upon it. This way all will know this woman was a goddess of flesh, spirit and soul."

"It will be done just as you say, my Lord." Treston stepped back to take his leave, Claudesius waving him to stay.

Turning his attention to Seulicious, the governor gave further orders. "I have not the heart to face the child's mother, Naomi. Please stand in for this coward at the dawning tomorrow. Will you do this for me?"

Surprised, Seulicious stammered, "Y… Ye… Yes… my Lord! I will do this for you, my Excellency."

"And!" Claudesius raised his hand. "You are to seal with my signet ring that Naomi shall receive an officer's stipend in remembrance of her husband's patriotic duties offered to the king for the remainder of her natural life. Then…" His hands began to tremble as he extended a parchment. "Then deliver this to the woman. It is a release from all taxes for as long as she may live. It is the least I can do for the murder of her holy child."

"And…" He chanced a gaze back into the arena before continuing. "and you must speak not a word of this to anyone, but you must see me on the 'morrow, if I still do live and I will arrange with you for all these monies to come from my personal treasure. Is it understood? You must tell no other soul of this!"

Seulicious stammered, "Y… Y… Yes… my Lord! Not a soul!" He chose not to even know the reason, himself. After bowing low and wishing the governor well, he hurried away on his assigned business.

Claudesius looked at a very confused Treston, nodding. "I ask not your silence in this regard for I do believe you truly do know my reasons, and I trust your loyalty in this matter because you are my friend."

Treston confessed, "I do believe I know. My purse is not that fat, for I have not invested well these many years, but my heart wishes it could offer such a rich reward as you generously have. I am truly sorry about this day."

"Wait here another moment." Claudesius requested of Treston, motioning to an officer standing some distance away. Upon that man's arrival, he ordered, "Take those in our custody, the men and women of this strange religion, and deliver each safely to one's home. If a person is from another city, then escort that one there. I want you to give compensation for any damaged done to property or possession as well as returning any confiscated item or fines levied against them. Have the surgeons examine any who may be suffering injury, tending to their needs. Give official parchments of release to each person - man and woman - saving them harmless from any accusation or crime against the people."

Looking with sadness at Symeon, Claudesius added, "Give that man, Cephas, release, escorting him to a place of his choosing outside the district. Give him monies and proper attire for the journey. My captain here…" he pointed toward Treston. "will provide whatever assistance and direction you need. Report back to him when you have finished your duties."

The officer saluted, asking no reason for his orders.

After the man departed, Claudesius asked, "Treston, my friend?"

Treston replied cautiously, he not yet comfortable being addressed as 'friend'. "Yes… yes, my Lord?"

Claudesius frowned, but said nothing concerning the matter. Looking across the ruined scene at the colosseum, he commented, "I don't know if there is but one God or many, but never in the annals of our history has such a display of glory and power been demonstrated by any of our gods. Ishtar's God is most powerful. Who can stand against a Being able to spin sky and earth into doing his will? This God deserves a more studious investigation."

Nodding in thought, he turned back to Treston. "But I will also tell you this, my friend… and please call me so, yourself - that is if the mood strikes you when we're together in private. I would like that so much. My friend, I have learned the answer to one question. What other gods that may exist have no power over us unless we offer it to them. We must open the doors of our minds and invite them into our souls."

"And I believe them for the most part to be cruel and evil, they playing out their own selfish fantasies through our flesh. We are no more than mouse-like toys for their idle amusement. They have no power at all unless we give it to them. My friend, we… you and me… must resist them with our whole mind, heart, and strength, or we will surely lose our destiny to them."

Treston's mind wandered, he thinking about the coming festivities. Curious, he asked. "What about tonight? This very day you promised the magistrate, Ogust, a great banquet. My… friend… er, I see and feel through your eyes and fully understand your sending innocent people away, but there are still the Kriggerman's dues to be paid. We have not yet departed the torrid field. How shall the boy-tyrant be placated when he finds out his toys are gone a'missing?"

Squinting an eye while staring into Treston's with his other, Claudesius smartly answered, "Maybe this is the day we begin to investigate the real power of the gods. Shall we forget so quickly the hero who stood in our midst, defying all gods and men with curses and oaths? To follow her to journey's end beyond the River would be a greater honor than to live another one hundred years."

Looking toward the marble floor, he shook his head. "I will put this God of Ishtar to the test, to see what fate awaits me this day. If I die…" He shrugged. "well, it is only what I deserve, have for so long. This holy child is not the first innocent I have murdered in heart and soul. I ask you not to choose my fate. Arrest me if need be to save yourself. It is the least I can do for someone who has stood my side for these many years."

Treston was about to object, saying he, too, would rather the boatman pay than play the disloyal prince, when Jusslin suddenly appeared on the stairs, his face so serious. Hurrying forward and clasping Claudesius' hand, he grinned sadly. "Ogust is sick, I think from too much wine!"

Nodding reassuringly, he quickly added, "I know you cautioned him. Thank you. But he is a man of strong resolve, and when the mood is on him, he will do as he pleases. It was good wine! Very good wine you delivered to us. It's just that early mornings for him are so tough on his constitution, and he takes to the fermented flower to soothe himself far too soon in the day. He is in a fine mood, I must say, for being sick, you know. You have been such a courteous host, better than any of the others we have happened upon. And... oh, yes! Yours was the best speech I have heard since leaving Rome. It... it made me homesick for the senate and the councils."

Jusslin grinned, remembering, waving a finger. "I am so remiss in my purpose for searching you out... and I'm relieved to see you still well after this terrible storm. I regret to tell you that we must be disrespectful guests. We will not be remaining as lodgers this eve. The fish smell is reported to be far worse than this morning. Ogust would be forever sick should we stay there."

"One of your splendid officers, Qutanius, your retired city constable, has invited us to his humble castle across the river and far from its stink. I'm afraid there will be no time for returning to this most gracious of cities, for when Ogust is feeling better, we must leave for Miletus on emperor's business. We will be pushing the season even now, seeing we desire to arrive there before the winter rains. Thank you again for your kind hospitality. We shall personally tell the senate about your loving generosity and patriotic fervor."

Jusslin turned to hurry away, calling over his shoulder. "We will send for our things on the 'morrow. Sorry, we will not be able to attend any festivities tonight. Do not wait us up!"

Dumbstruck, Claudesius and Treston stared silently at the fleeing figure, both too afraid to speak, fearing themselves only in a dream. The men's minds raced with recollections of the day's events and their implications. In one day...only hours...a woman-child had changed forever the way these two men would look at matters again. Although she no longer walked their world, her spirit haunted their minds and hearts for the remainder of their lives.

Claudesius wondered, asking, "Has there ever been a person willing to sacrifice everything - family, friends, and even death - for love of God and man? Have you ever seen anyone willing to die for a faith, a belief? Should all those believe as this child has, that belief will shake the world to its knees. There is no force in the heavens above, on this earth, or in the worlds below that check such power. Love...*love* my friend, is an *unstoppable force*. Nothing can halt a cause or idea built upon love. It will one day bring to a ruin everything contrived by heartless men and gods."

He turned again to the field of death. "My friend, today we have unleashed the whirlwind. It shall sweep our universe, changing forever the way men view each other. It is a force that is relentless and unstoppable. One can only hope to be caught up with it and carried along by it for, in its tempest, all the world shall be overrun by it!"

*(**Author's note:** Indeed, as fables and stories of this grew among the witnesses of Ishtar's demise, the colosseum itself became a haunted place, filled with accounts of a beautiful witch walking the field on moon-bright nights. Yes, and even superstition arose concerning her. Many a gladiator would seek out the spot of her death, feeling no harm could come to the man standing over it, the child's blood protecting them from death and giving that warrior the victory.*

And of Ogust and Jusslin? Legend has it that on their return trip to Rome, on the anniversary of Ishtar's death, a sudden tempest arose from the depths of the sea, hurtling their ship against the rocks off the Malta coast, sending all hands to the bottom. It is only legend, but it is said the emperor, himself, declared a holiday from work when news of the disaster reached his ears.)

ଌଠ ଌଠ ଌଠ

Section Five

Silent Tombs

The crunch of last season's grass sounded under his feet as the man walked through the flower-filled fields of early summer. It was the kind of grass that did not grow high, but would curl back on itself and stay close to the ground, keeping that shape long after it died back in the fall. In the spring, new shoots replaced the old, but, like the skeleton of an old beast, would remain long after its life had expired.

It was wild grass, like the fields it grew in, fields filled with the careless scatter of plants and flowers. Here and there, small copse of shaking aspen still mourned the loss of last year's greenery, forgetting to see the new colorful growth spreading through the fields around them. To the man walking in this strangely enchanting place, it was peaceful and beautiful, yet sad and lonely. With his eyes set on a distant hillock and his mind pondering past events, his heart lost itself in a world of yester-dreams.

The little hill was over an hour's walk from the west gate of the palace wall. It provided him time to think, time to consider his life and his destiny. He had come here every day since the fleet had departed for the Prisoner Exchange. His heart wondered if he would see Sirion safely come home again. Or would he have to journey here to pay his regards? The sky was clear and the sun towered high overhead. A light breeze filled his senses with the refreshing scents of summer flowers. As he walked, he stooped and picked a handful of the brightly colored ones.

Eventually, the man came to the base of the little hill. Climbing to the top, he arrived at a gate made of what looked like simple wrought iron, but it never needed maintenance, or so he had been told. Passing under the arched leaves that folded in until they almost touched, he came to some stone benches, one on each side of the path. He stopped and, raising his eyes up, scanned the view facing him.

Beyond this hill, the land gradually fell away, allowing a person to see for miles in any direction. At one time, a huge orchard of fruit trees covered the surrounding land, but after the wars of the Rebellion started, it gradually became a vast resting place for Ma-we's children. Row upon row, for mile upon mile, as far as the eye could see, the little mounds reminded the man of the heavy price Ma-we and her children had paid in their attempt to rid this realm of its evil.

He stood in awed silence. It always overwhelmed him when he thought of why this beautiful people who had no reason to die so freely surrendered up their lives. To die for a cause, such as for money or power, he could easily understand. But to sacrifice it for people who didn't appreciate or even care about what was being done for them, and to continue to stand the battle line for all these thousands of years? It was beyond his comprehension. He felt so unworthy to even be in their presence. His heart ached from thinking about his own past failings, knowing he deserved nothing and yet had received so much. Tears came to his eyes and ran down his face.

The children called these fields the 'Resting Place of Quiet Testimony' or the 'Silent Tombs'. Even those who never returned from battle received recognition here by being given a plot and marker to signify their sacrifices. Every name of every loyal child who had perished from the Rebellion was here. It was common to see large numbers of somber people quietly wandering along the many paths, but today it was strangely empty. Only a handful of others were here, some strolling among the graves, their minds deep in thought, others sitting or kneeling next to a grave where someone extra dear lay sleeping.

Several minutes passed before the man, with halting steps, moved toward one of the many stone paths that radiated from the gate. First down one and then another he walked, pausing from time to time, reading a name on a marker. Occasionally he would stop and stare, reading and rereading the words written on some stone or plaque. Then he would take a flower and place it on the grave.

Chisamore…Sirion had said that he helped removed the bodies of Darla's attackers. He fell at Desiah, defending the fleet. It was an ancient battle fought shortly after Ishtar's death.

Avdiel was one of Darla's stretcher-bearers. His fighter disappeared while on patrol and never returned to the convoy. After many days passed without word, Ma-we came here and put up this memorial. Sirion often talked about his laughing green eyes and comforting smile.

Ehleenohr Kalahnit was with Mihai when they hurried into camp, diving behind some rocks while warning the others to get down. Sirion told of her fiery red hair and temper to match. Her leadership abilities were outstanding and did not go unnoticed. By the time of the Great War, she was already a high-ranking officer. Ehleenohr commanded one of the corps that was trapped at Memphis. Few survived. She was not among them.

Tzidohn also died at the second siege of Memphis. Sirion sang many love songs about him. She more often affectionately called him 'big brother' instead of his given name. Whenever they came to his memorial, her eyes would fill with tears and her hands would shake with little tremors. One time she said, 'He was always so gentle and kind.'

Depais, the song maiden, assisted Sirion in supporting Darla while she and Gabrielle helped Ishtar. Later she joined with Darla's company during the first siege of Memphis, and remained with it during the Two Hundred Years War. She died in a futile attempt to retake one of the cities in the Northern Rim. It was her frozen body that Darla refused to leave at the ruined fortress of Mordem.

The man walked along toward a newer section of the Silent Tombs. After the Great War, the slaughter dramatically decreased, but it did not end. If it wasn't a senseless battle, it was some other kind of mischief drummed up by the enemy that would claim another victim. He wondered how many more would enter this place before the wars ended.

He walked on and on until, at the far northwest corner, he came to another trail. It went down a slope into a shallow ravine. A cheerful little brook cut through it, splashing and bubbling along, singing a happy tune, oblivious to the sadness that filled the cut through which it ran. Down there, just where the stream made a sharp bend to the right and dropped over a ledge into a rippling pool, was the man's destination. The stream ran beside the trail until it turned and went over the falls. At that juncture, the trail abruptly stopped, ending at the foot of two earthen mounds.

When Sirion first brought the man to the tombs some years before, this was the spot she hurried to. The mound was recent, with small patches of earth still showing through the grass growing on it. She had come to the end of the trail and stopped, as though fearing to continue. For the longest time, Sirion remained motionless, her shoulders stooped, arms limp, with hands folded together. Finally she turned her face to him, stained from a river of tears that were still flowing, covering her cheeks. 'Periste took the blow for me. I was supposed to take point on that patrol and she ordered me back, leading it herself. So I am here now, a little shadow of nothing, living a life that should have been hers.'

Sirion moved in close and sat down, reaching out and resting her hand on the soft mound. After several moments she began to sing a lament, a lyrical song describing some of the qualities Periste displayed. Her song, like all she sang, was a love song, describing the effect the person's life had on her heart. She sat, legs crossed, eyes closed, her hand on the grave, rocking back and forth in time with the gentle rhythm of the melody. Periste's song was always the most emotional, her loss reaching the deepest into Sirion's soul. Then, when she had finished, she would take some blooms she had picked in the fields near the hillock, and gently place them near the stone marker.

The man stooped and put his remaining flowers near Periste's marker. Slowly he stood back up, his eyes filling with tears. In a soft, gentle voice that was breaking, he choked out some words, while gazing at the grass-covered mound. "I'm sorry she couldn't visit today, but maybe she will come soon. I hope you don't mind that these flowers came from my clumsy hands."

Pausing for a moment in thought, he then continued, "There is no way I can repay you and all the others for the sacrifices you have made. Please, let my 'thank you' suffice for the moment. One day I may find the words or do the deeds that will show my gratitude to all of you…" The tightness in his throat cut off the rest of his speech. In silence, he remained standing, thinking about these wonderful people.

Ten went out to help Ishtar those many years ago. Of them, six now rested here…gone, but still remembered. Only four remained to tell of their valor, or possibly only three. Was Sirion still alive? If so, would she survive to return, to again come to this place of remembrance, to sing her haunting songs of lament?

Finding power to speak again, he added, "Ishtar will be coming soon. You know she won, thanks to you and the others. But you have helped so many win, not just her. You helped a child keep her integrity, and that integrity has altered history. An innocent young woman proved more powerful than all the armies of all the nations that have ever marched to war. Her faith will bring a world to its knees, and changed it forever. You helped a child become a woman, and that woman will soon be here, to help bring a finish to this terrible struggle. You have done so much for us all."

With that, the man started to sing a little lament of his own. He sang it to no one and to everyone. He sang it for those lost. But, most of all, it was to Sirion that his words went out.

"You walked through the mist and the smoke and the fire,
Into the face of destruction you strode.
Your hearts were once filled with such hope and desire,
But you chose a most dangerous road.

You came from a world so happy, so free,
A world filled with joy and rest.
You charged into battle through missiles, through bombs,
Determined to give it your best.

You fought in the fields, the hills and the glades,
Your chariots raced through the sky.
In sorrow you witnessed, experienced and shared,
Your hearts ached over those who did die.

Through planting and harvest, the four seasons round,
Your swords, burnished blades you raised high.
And you moved ever forward 'til you fell to the ground,
In a war that makes generals cry."

The song ended. He silently stood, eyes fixed on Periste's marker. The shadow of early evening filled the draw before the man stirred.

Two more days and Ishtar would be here. How long he had waited, longing for and fearing this day. The world let her down. Could she ever forgive it? In her gravest hour, she was abandoned by the very ones she saved.

Would she ever forgive him for the part he played in her humiliation? Did anyone deserve to be forgiven? 'We acted with incomplete knowledge. We were obeying orders.' How shallow and empty such excuses sounded now. Yet those reasonings still echoed in his heart. Would he ever grow up to accept his personal responsibility for Ishtar's demise?

With head still down, the man turned and retraced his steps from the little ravine. Reaching the crest, he looked back at the setting sun. 'Tomorrow… what a blessing!' There was always a tomorrow - one more chance to make things right. The night would wash away the past and a new day would give birth to the promise of a new start. If enough new days came and went, the child might be able to gain an understanding in her heart…maybe, just maybe. He could only hope and pray that she would one day forgive him and all the others who showed no appreciation for the goddess who walked among them.

Looking back to the east, he spied the gates on the hillock, now miles away. Choosing a more direct path, he started toward them. As he walked, he began to whistle a little tune Sirion once taught him.

Somewhere, light years across space, a woman lying in a cold cell, shivering, beaten and bleeding, dreamed she heard someone singing a lilting little melody. It echoed in her mind and warmed her aching heart. She smiled to herself. 'A few more days…only a few more days.' Then she could rest in the arms of those she loved.

ം   ം   ം

I hope you've enjoyed reading about the struggle of Lowenah and her children in the first book of "The Chronicles of Heaven's War".

Look for their continuing epic saga in "The Chronicles of Heaven's War" to follow in:

Book II: "Phoenix Burns"
Book III: "Blood Moon Rising"
Book VI: "Hell Above the Skies"
Book V: "The Spirits of Lagandow"
Book VI: "The Haunts of Haudenosaunez"

About the author

It is a customary thing to offer a short soliloquy of rhapsodic prose regarding an author of words who has put pen to paper, writing down by a hand not self-made and from a brain not understood, a tale of suspense or intrigue that the reader finds titillating to his or her senses. Credit is then taken by the author for the seemingly random charges of chemical and electrical energy that make those thought processes possible and that have then been woven into a tapestry of verbal music that plays upon the hearts and minds of those who open their eyes to see into the world of the author's mind.

Ava is no such author. "Take the tools you have been given and share your works with the world of men." This is a motto of one who writes from the heart, one wishing to share the emotion felt, to give the reader pause to see beyond the ordinary into a world that may or may not exist in reality, but most certainly does in the heart and soul of any and all who believe there exists something greater than the frail human body. To dream and help others dream of a world beyond their own, to share the life and love of those who might possibly reside there, to help them see that they do not journey upon the secluded path alone... *that* is the goal of this author. ~*Ava Dohn*